kid BEOWULF™

the RISE of EL CID

STORY & ART BY
ALEXIS E. FAJARDO

COLOR BY
JOSE MARI FLORES

PROLOGUE COLOR BY
BRIAN KOLM

Andrews McMeel
PUBLISHING®

para mi abuelita

contents

PROLOGUE...V

part one: pamplona.................................1

part two: La frontera........................73

part three: toledo.............................153

more to explore.................................222

map of spain...224

key terms..225

character glossary............................226

destreza ~ the art of spanish fencing............231

el cantar de mio cid:........................232
origins of the epic poem

the mystery of mithras....................234

boudica the lost princess...............235

fun facts...236

bibliography...237

PROLOGUE

His name was Rodrigo, but they called him "El Cid" for the battles he won on the plain...

He fought amongst Muslim, Christian, and Jew in a war-torn land called Spain.

He came from a town called Burgos, and was born at a very good hour...

He was in Castile's army and rose to a seat of power.

Rodrigo's love was named Ximena, and her beauty eclipsed them all...

Except for their daughters, Doña Elvira and Doña Sol.

With his famed horse, Babieca and his blades Colada and Tizón...

Rodrigo swept through Al-Andalus to win cities for Castile and León.

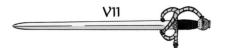

Rodrigo was feared by his enemies but they respected him all the same...

The Moors were impressed by his tactics and called him by another name.

"Al-Sayyid" was the word in Arabic, "lord" or "master" in the English tongue.

In Spanish, simply "El Cid," and it stuck when his tale was sung.

Rodrigo fought for Castile, and his skill won him many new friends...

Among them Martín Antolínez, Pedro the Mute, and Álvar Fáñez.

Rodrigo's army grew. Men joined him from far and wide...

To fight for El Cid Campeador, was a source of great pride!

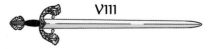

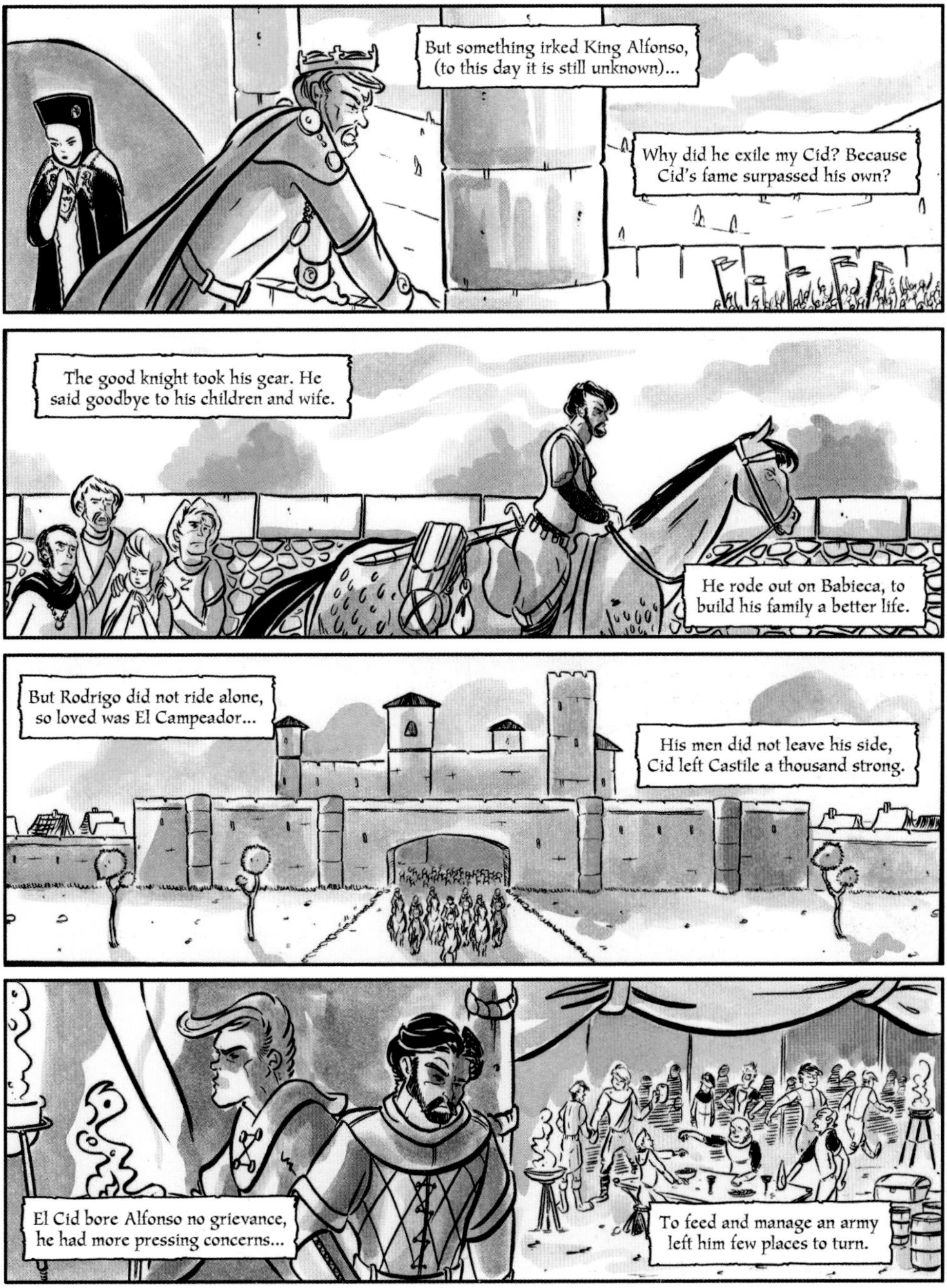
But something irked King Alfonso, (to this day it is still unknown)...
Why did he exile my Cid? Because Cid's fame surpassed his own?
The good knight took his gear. He said goodbye to his children and wife.
He rode out on Babieca, to build his family a better life.
But Rodrigo did not ride alone, so loved was El Campeador...
His men did not leave his side, Cid left Castile a thousand strong.
El Cid bore Alfonso no grievance, he had more pressing concerns...
To feed and manage an army left him few places to turn.

He fought for whoever would take him–
Christian king or Islamic emir.

He became a mercenary–the
Spanish plain was cloaked in fear.

His men tore down from Burgos,
into the land of Al-Andalus,

As Rodrigo claimed victories
so did ease his exile's noose.

El Cid's skills were unmatched,
he fought with cleverness and zeal.

And he always sent his spoils
back to the king of Castile.

My Cid set his sights on Valencia,
a grand city on the eastern shores...

Here he would bring his family,
once taken from the Moors.

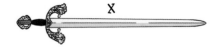

X

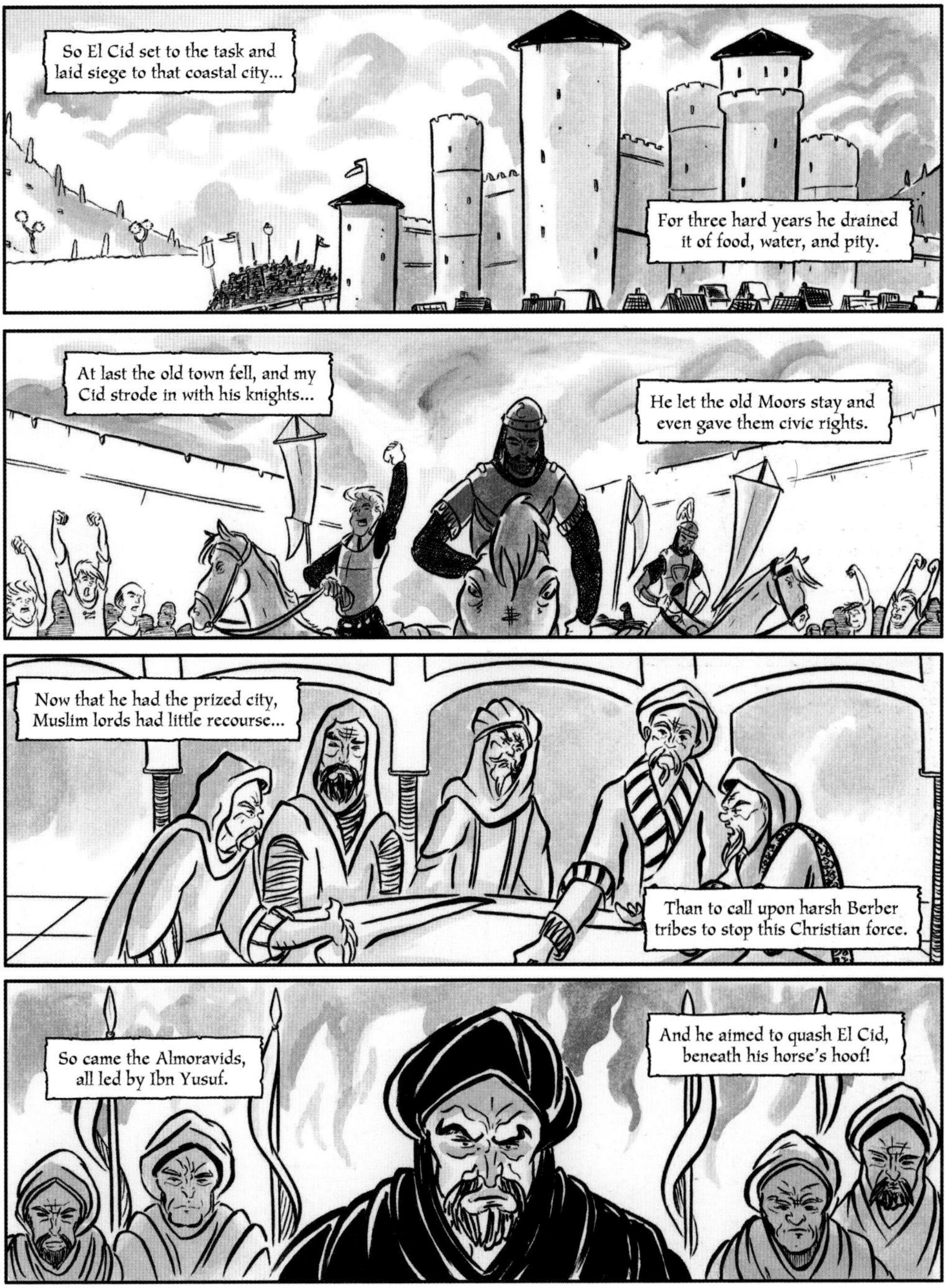
So El Cid set to the task and laid siege to that coastal city...
For three hard years he drained it of food, water, and pity.
At last the old town fell, and my Cid strode in with his knights...
He let the old Moors stay and even gave them civic rights.
Now that he had the prized city, Muslim lords had little recourse...
Than to call upon harsh Berber tribes to stop this Christian force.
So came the Almoravids, all led by Ibn Yusuf.
And he aimed to quash El Cid, beneath his horse's hoof!

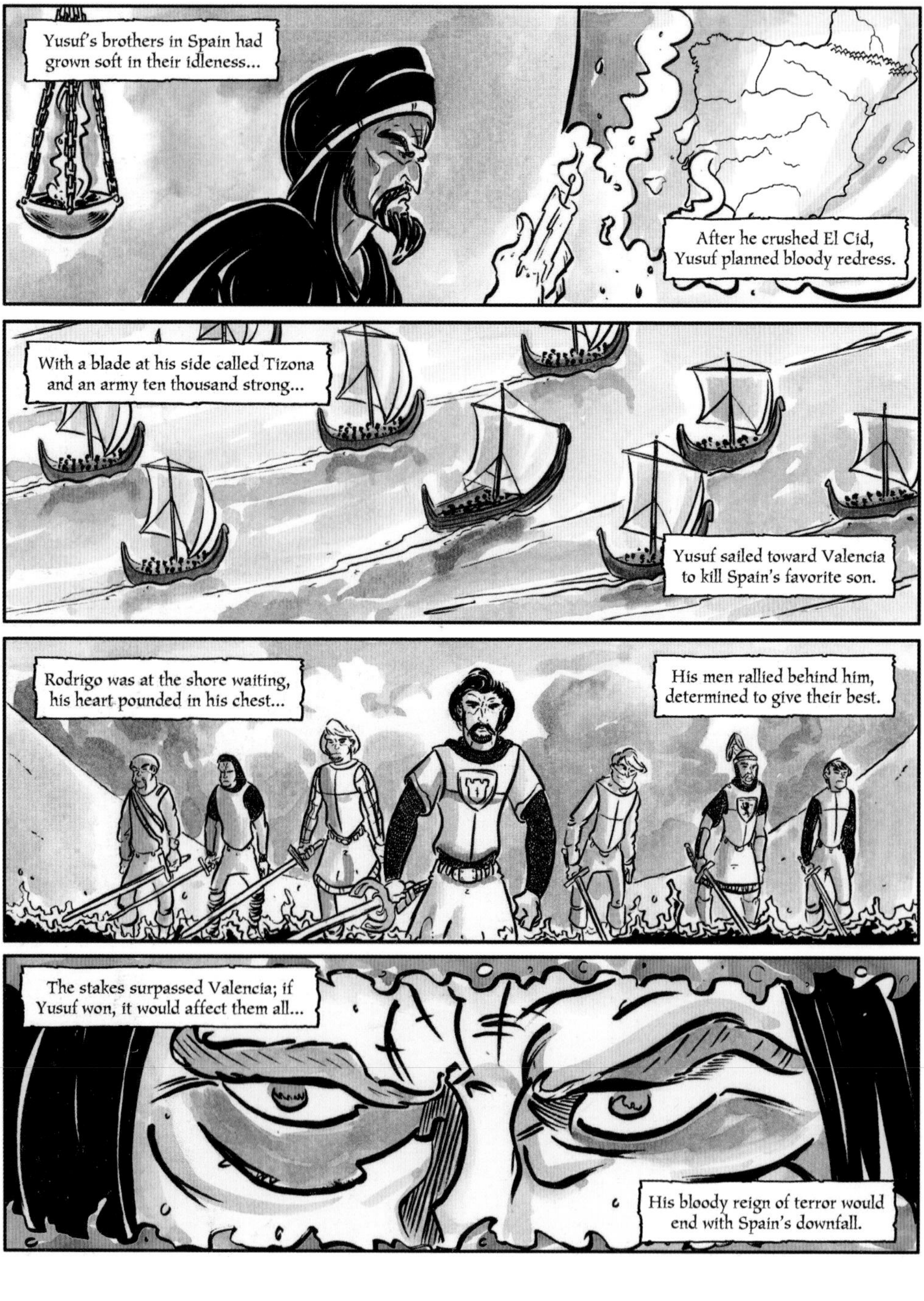
Yusuf's brothers in Spain had grown soft in their idleness...
After he crushed El Cid, Yusuf planned bloody redress.
With a blade at his side called Tizona and an army ten thousand strong...
Yusuf sailed toward Valencia to kill Spain's favorite son.
Rodrigo was at the shore waiting, his heart pounded in his chest...
His men rallied behind him, determined to give their best.
The stakes surpassed Valencia; if Yusuf won, it would affect them all...
His bloody reign of terror would end with Spain's downfall.

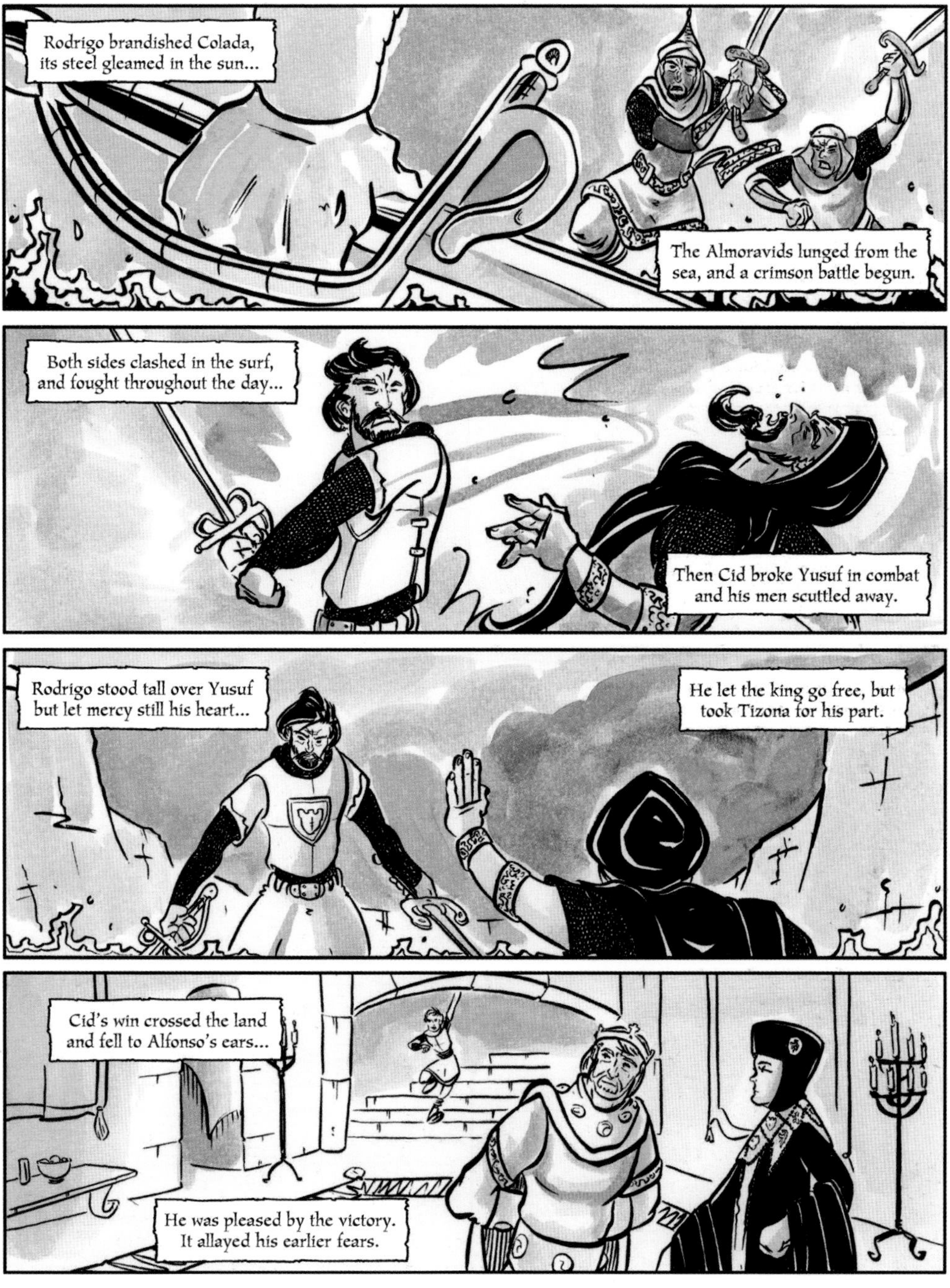
Rodrigo brandished Colada, its steel gleamed in the sun...
The Almoravids lunged from the sea, and a crimson battle begun.
Both sides clashed in the surf, and fought throughout the day...
Then Cid broke Yusuf in combat and his men scuttled away.
Rodrigo stood tall over Yusuf but let mercy still his heart...
He let the king go free, but took Tizona for his part.
Cid's win crossed the land and fell to Alfonso's ears...
He was pleased by the victory. It allayed his earlier fears.

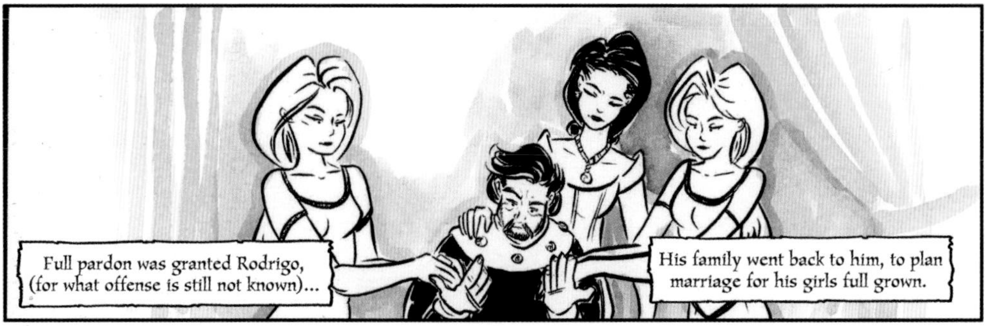
Full pardon was granted Rodrigo, (for what offense is still not known)...
His family went back to him, to plan marriage for his girls full grown.

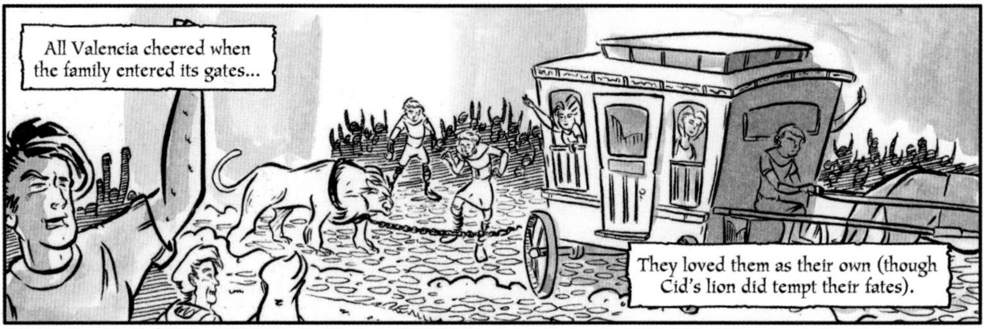
All Valencia cheered when the family entered its gates...
They loved them as their own (though Cid's lion did tempt their fates).

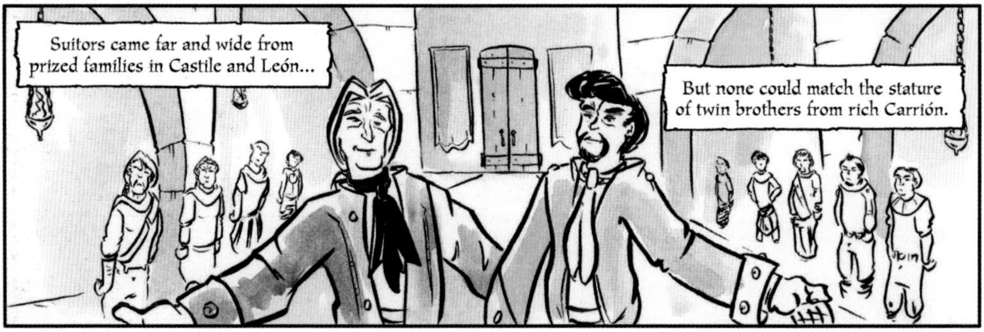
Suitors came far and wide from prized families in Castile and León...
But none could match the stature of twin brothers from rich Carrión.

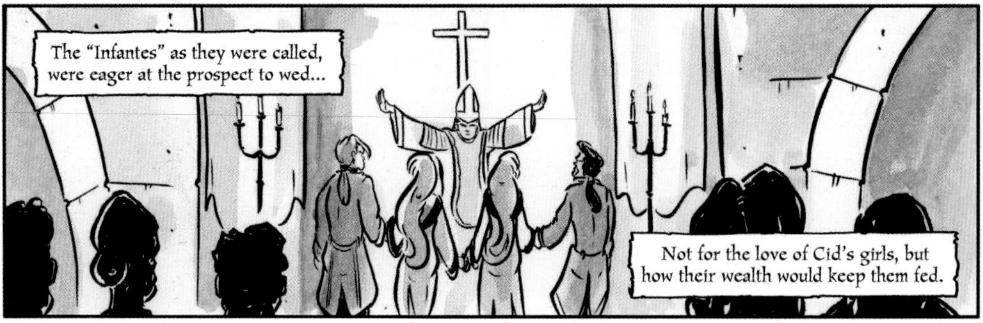
The "Infantes" as they were called, were eager at the prospect to wed...
Not for the love of Cid's girls, but how their wealth would keep them fed.

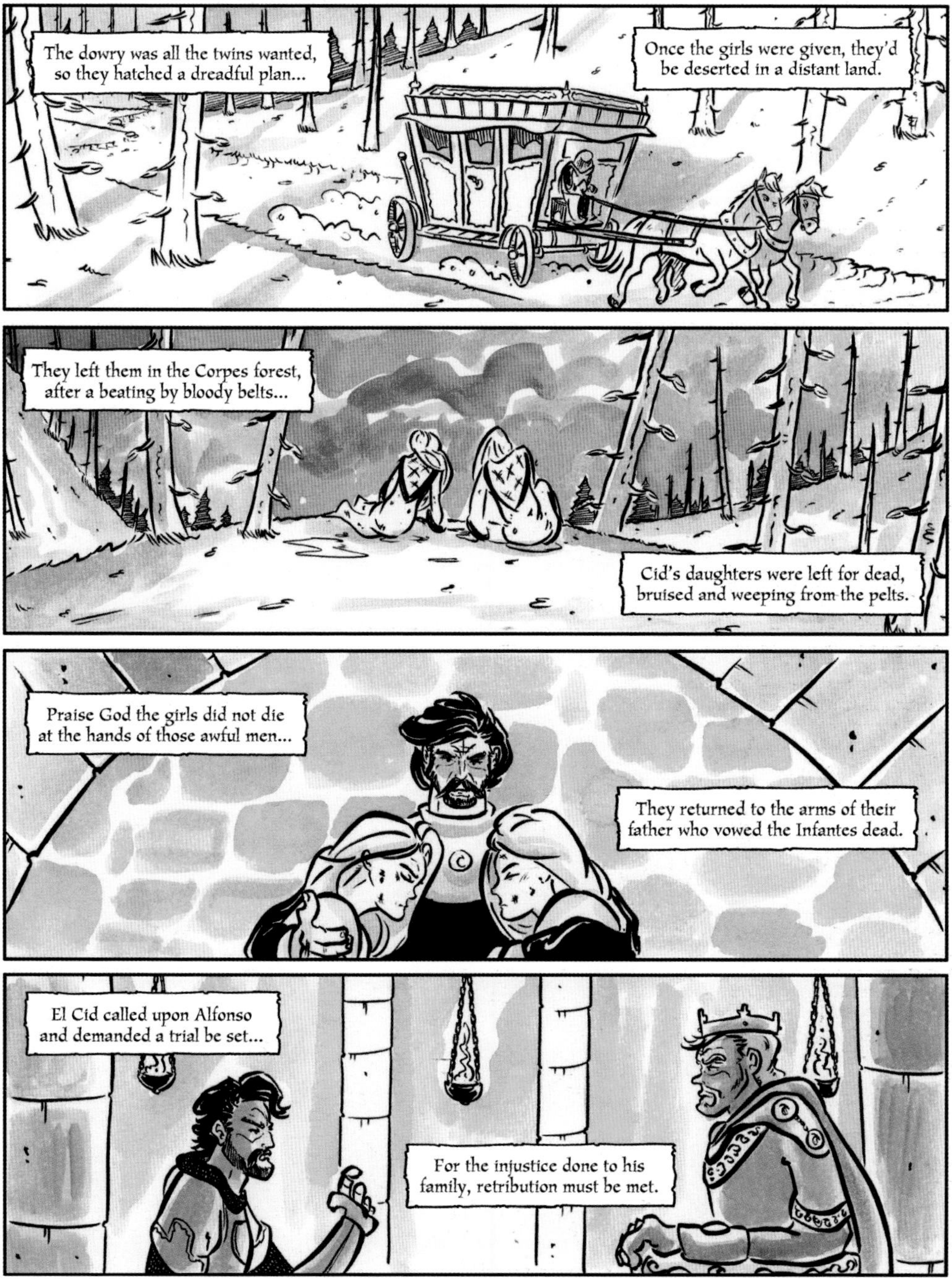

The dowry was all the twins wanted, so they hatched a dreadful plan...
Once the girls were given, they'd be deserted in a distant land.
They left them in the Corpes forest, after a beating by bloody belts...
Cid's daughters were left for dead, bruised and weeping from the pelts.
Praise God the girls did not die at the hands of those awful men...
They returned to the arms of their father who vowed the Infantes dead.
El Cid called upon Alfonso and demanded a trial be set...
For the injustice done to his family, retribution must be met.

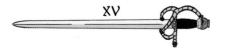

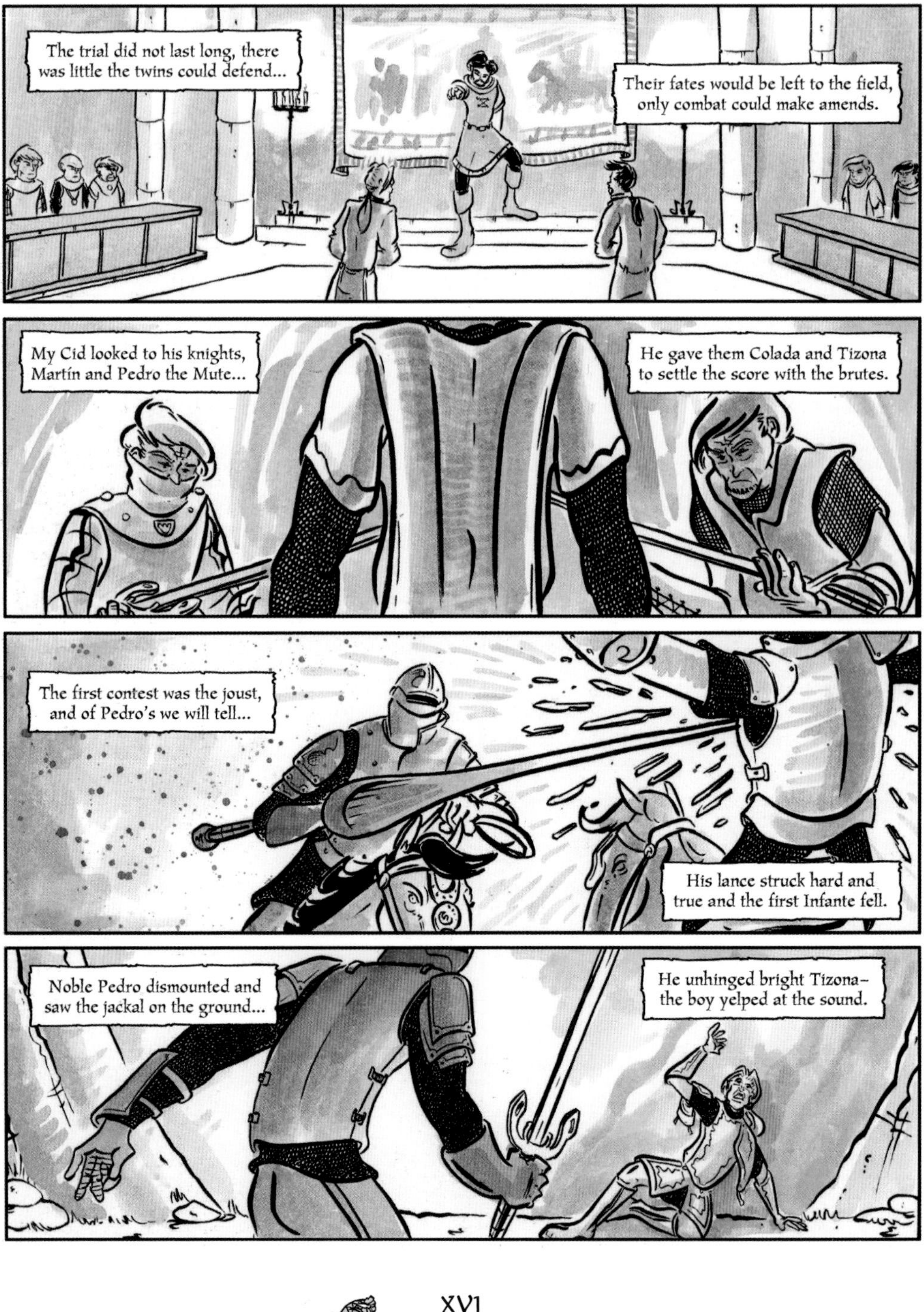
The trial did not last long, there was little the twins could defend...
Their fates would be left to the field, only combat could make amends.
My Cid looked to his knights, Martín and Pedro the Mute...
He gave them Colada and Tizona to settle the score with the brutes.
The first contest was the joust, and of Pedro's we will tell...
His lance struck hard and true and the first Infante fell.
Noble Pedro dismounted and saw the jackal on the ground...
He unhinged bright Tizona– the boy yelped at the sound.

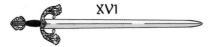

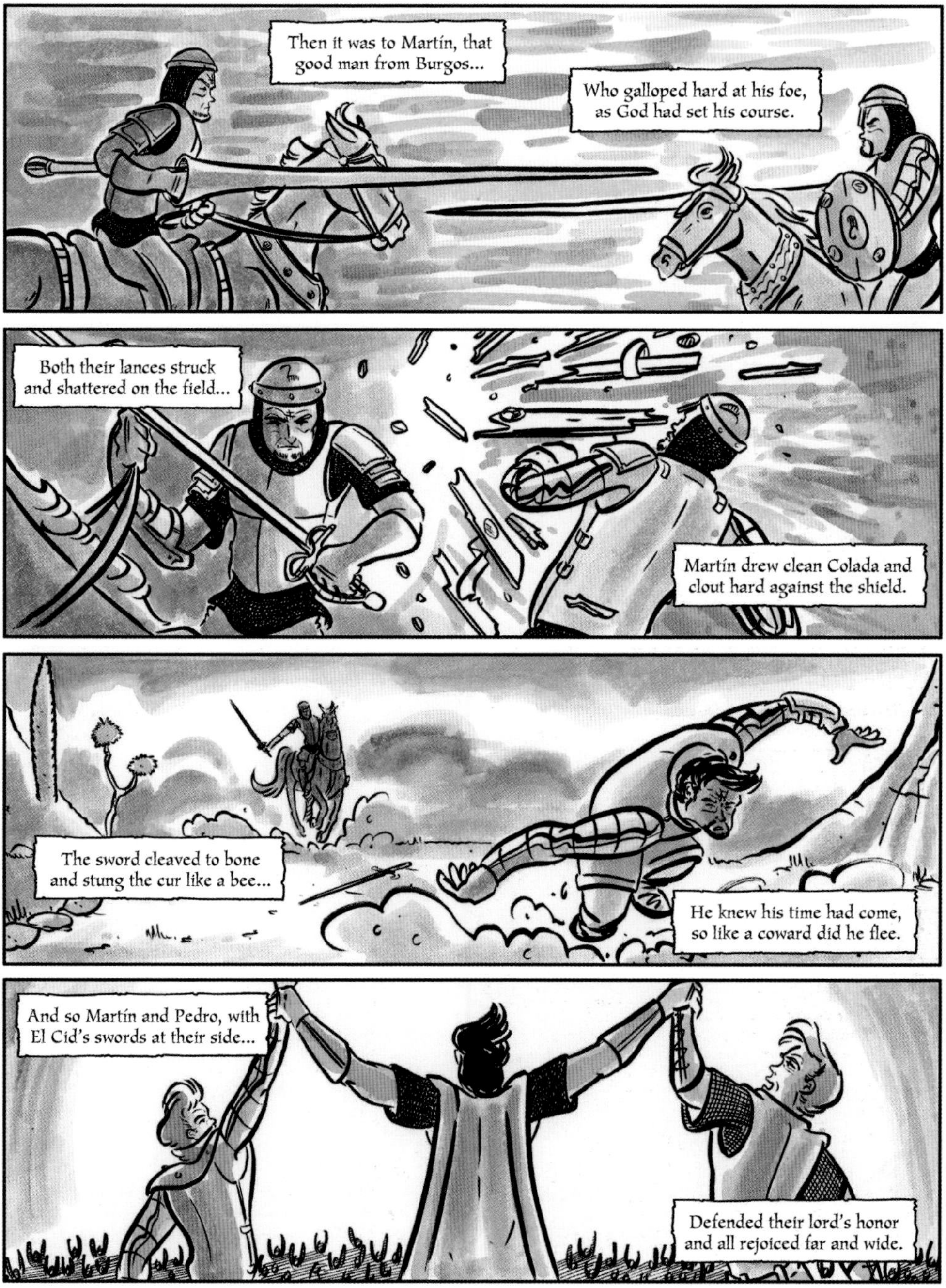
Then it was to Martín, that good man from Burgos...
Who galloped hard at his foe, as God had set his course.
Both their lances struck and shattered on the field...
Martín drew clean Colada and clout hard against the shield.
The sword cleaved to bone and stung the cur like a bee...
He knew his time had come, so like a coward did he flee.
And so Martín and Pedro, with El Cid's swords at their side...
Defended their lord's honor and all rejoiced far and wide.

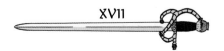

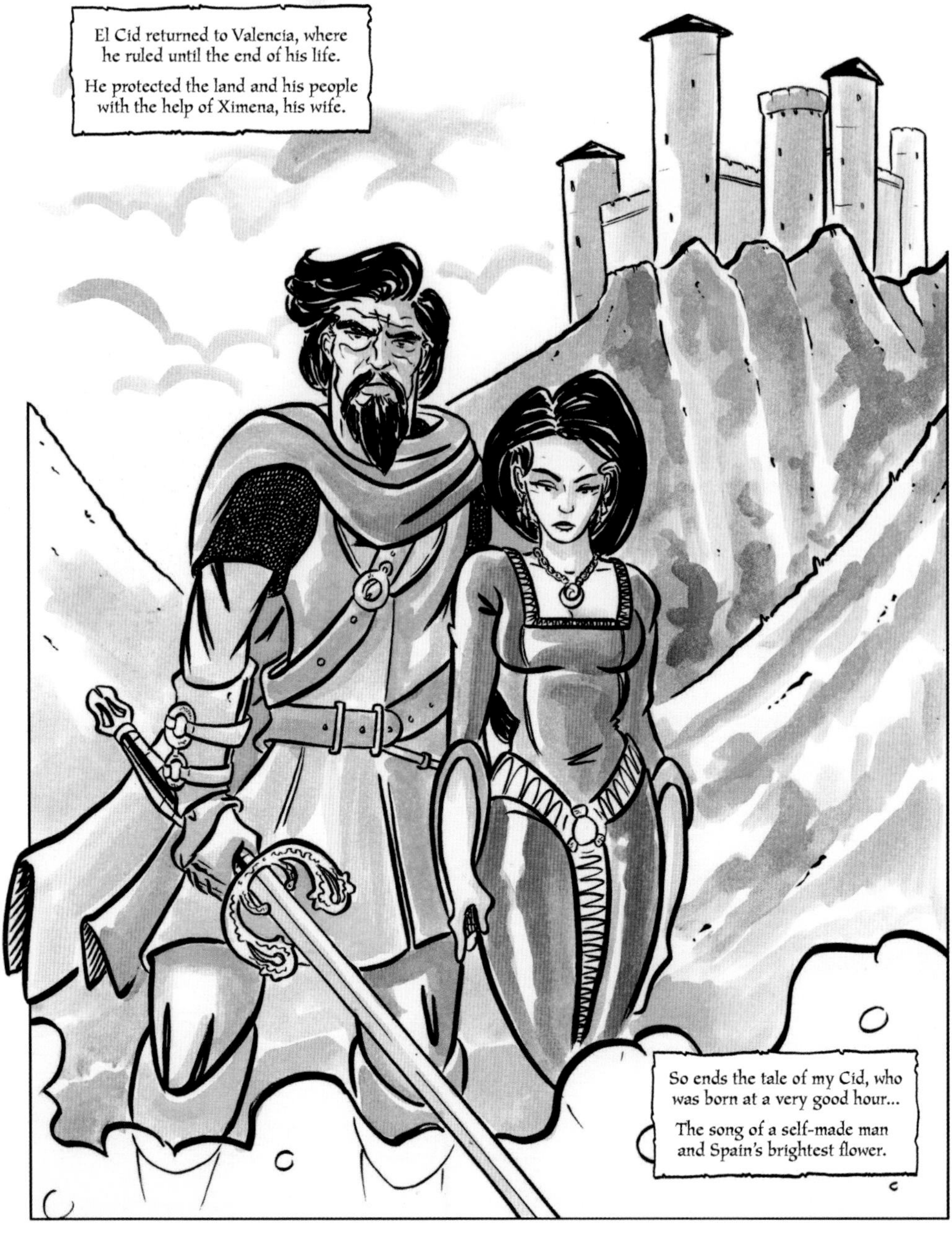
El Cid returned to Valencia, where he ruled until the end of his life.
He protected the land and his people with the help of Ximena, his wife.
So ends the tale of my Cid, who was born at a very good hour...
The song of a self-made man and Spain's brightest flower.

part one

pamplona

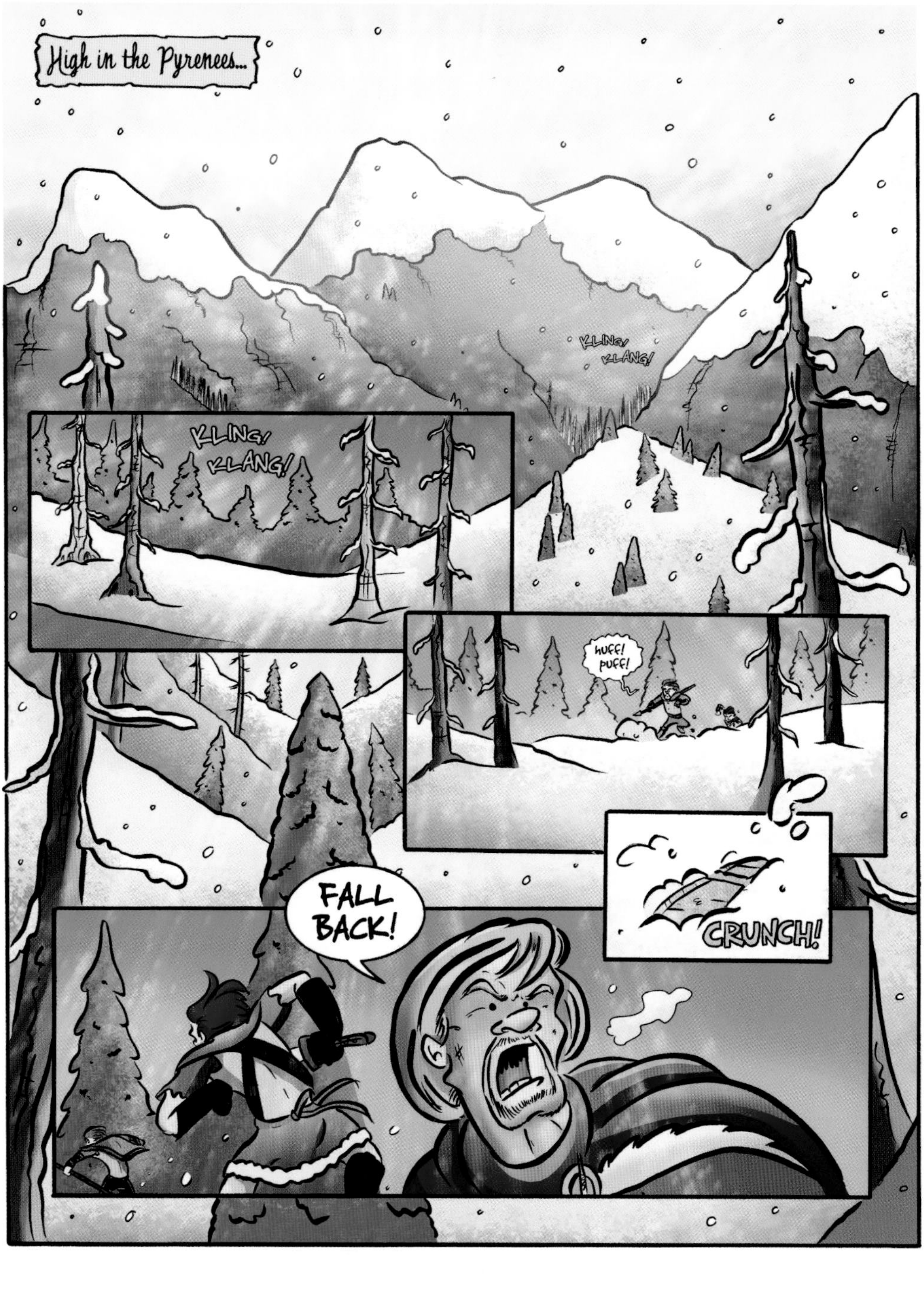
High in the Pyrenees...
KLING! KLANG!
KLING! KLANG!
huff! puff!
CRUNCH!
FALL BACK!

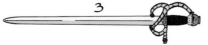

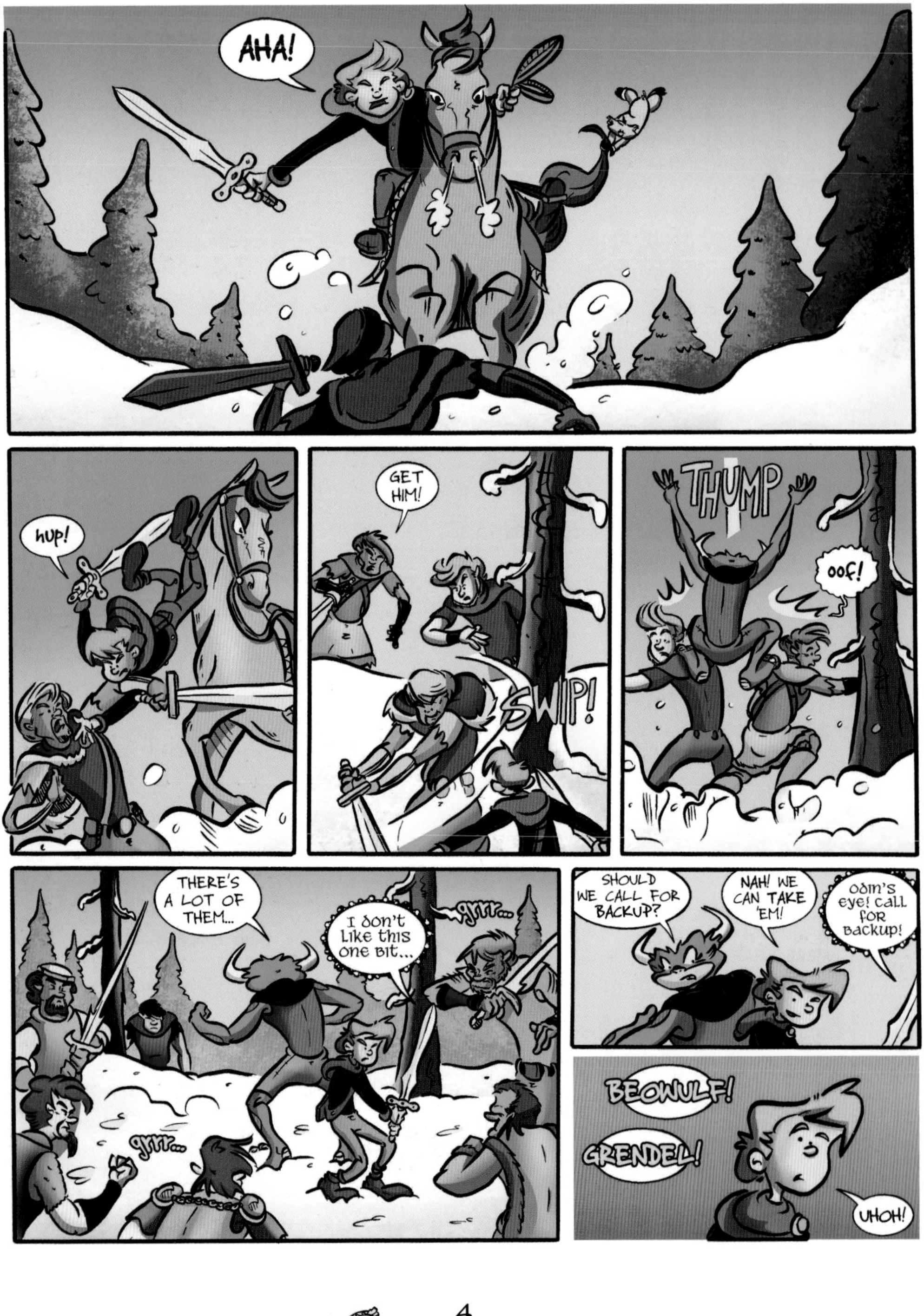
AHA!
hup!
GET HIM!
SWIP!
THUMP
oof!
THERE'S A LOT OF THEM...
I don't like this one bit...
grrr...
grrr...
SHOULD WE CALL FOR BACKUP?
NAH! WE CAN TAKE 'EM!
Odin's eye! Call for backup!
BEOWULF!
GRENDEL!
UHOH!

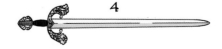

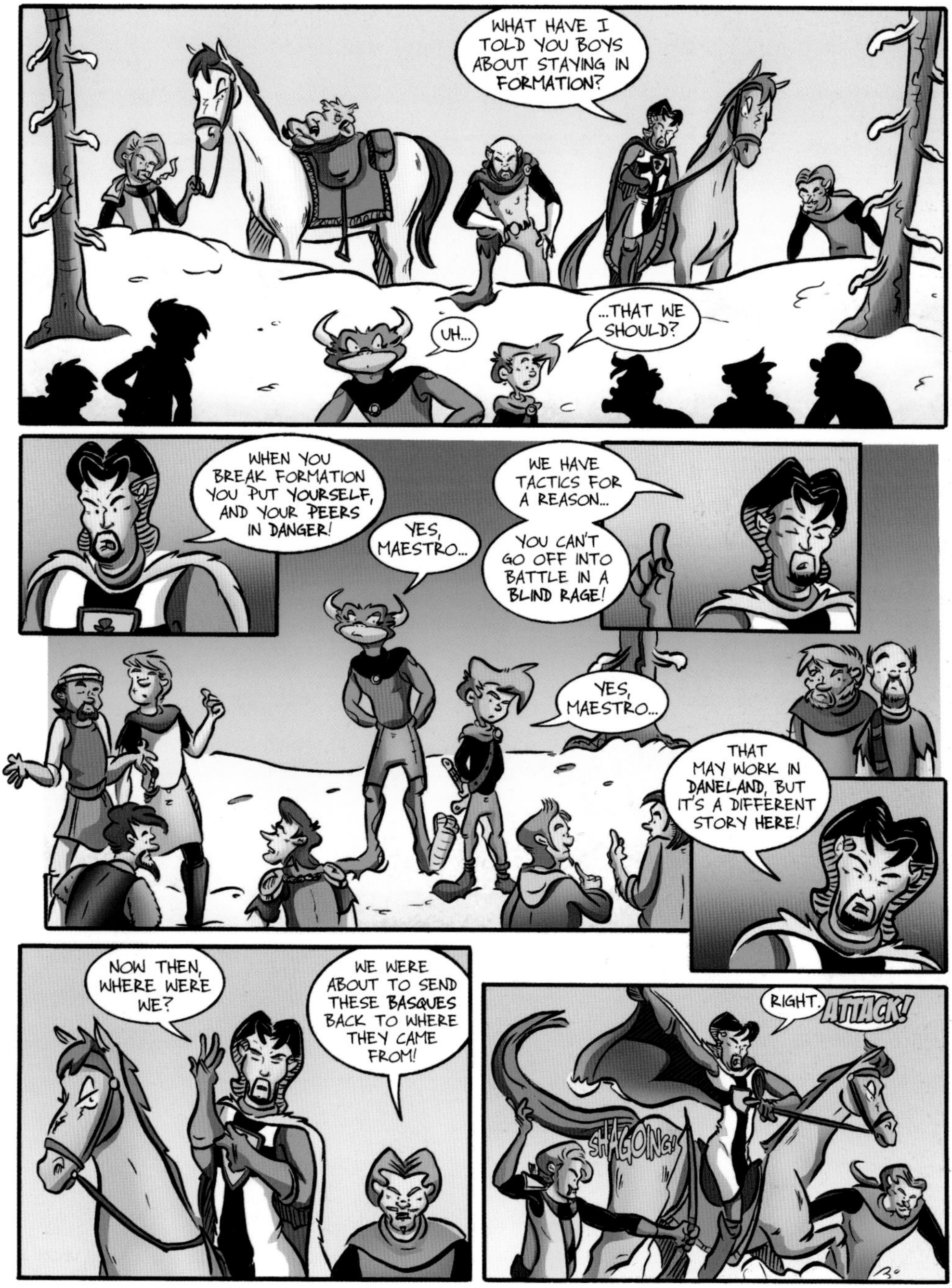
WHAT HAVE I TOLD YOU BOYS ABOUT STAYING IN FORMATION?
UH...
...THAT WE SHOULD?
WHEN YOU BREAK FORMATION YOU PUT YOURSELF, AND YOUR PEERS IN DANGER!
YES, MAESTRO...
WE HAVE TACTICS FOR A REASON...
YOU CAN'T GO OFF INTO BATTLE IN A BLIND RAGE!
YES, MAESTRO...
THAT MAY WORK IN DANELAND, BUT IT'S A DIFFERENT STORY HERE!
NOW THEN, WHERE WERE WE?
WE WERE ABOUT TO SEND THESE BASQUES BACK TO WHERE THEY CAME FROM!
RIGHT.
ATTACK!
SHAGOING!

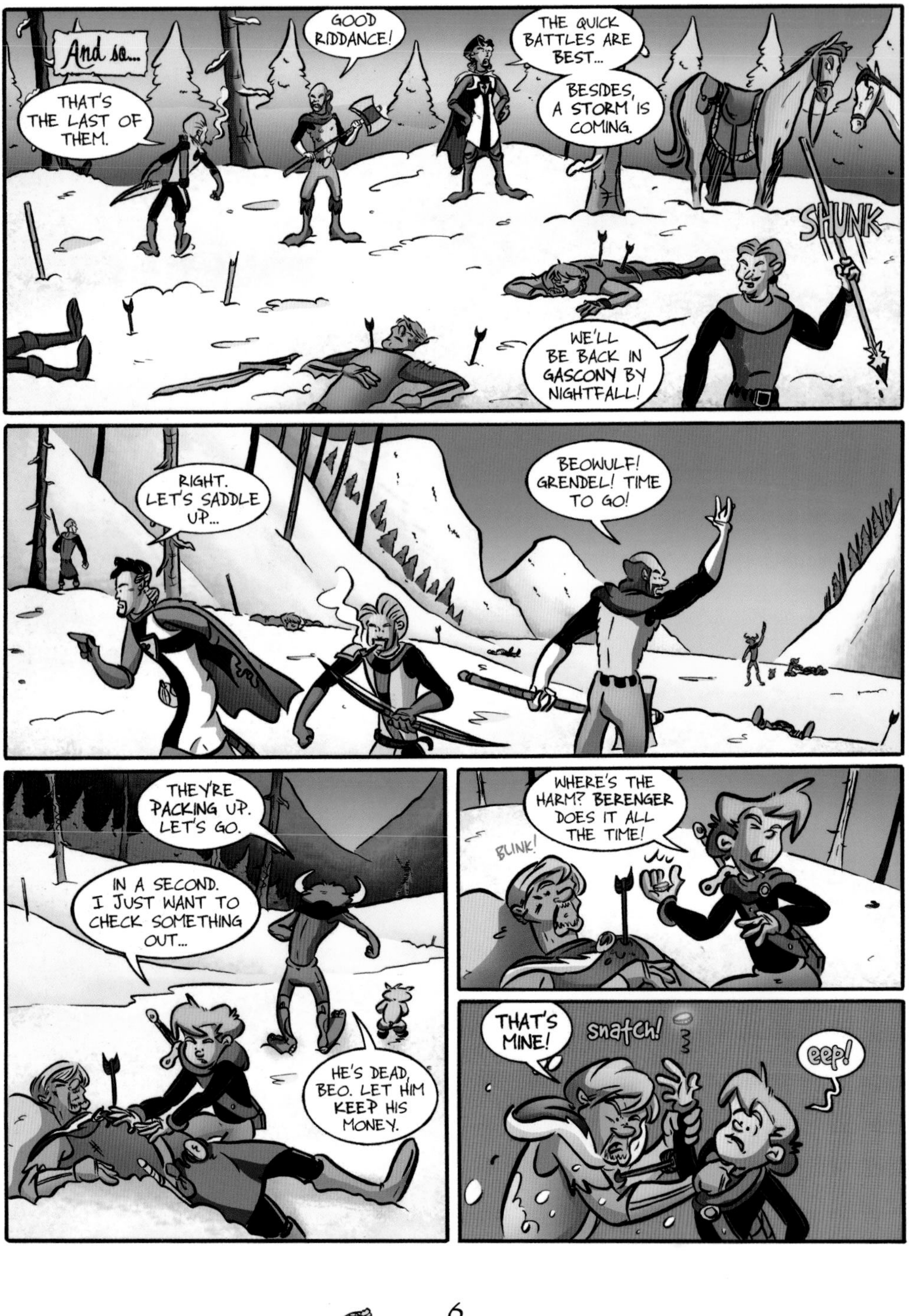
And so...
THAT'S THE LAST OF THEM.
GOOD RIDDANCE!
THE QUICK BATTLES ARE BEST...
BESIDES, A STORM IS COMING.
SHUNK
WE'LL BE BACK IN GASCONY BY NIGHTFALL!
RIGHT. LET'S SADDLE UP...
BEOWULF! GRENDEL! TIME TO GO!
THEY'RE PACKING UP. LET'S GO.
IN A SECOND. I JUST WANT TO CHECK SOMETHING OUT...
HE'S DEAD, BEO. LET HIM KEEP HIS MONEY.
WHERE'S THE HARM? BERENGER DOES IT ALL THE TIME!
BLINK!
THAT'S MINE!
snatch!
eep!

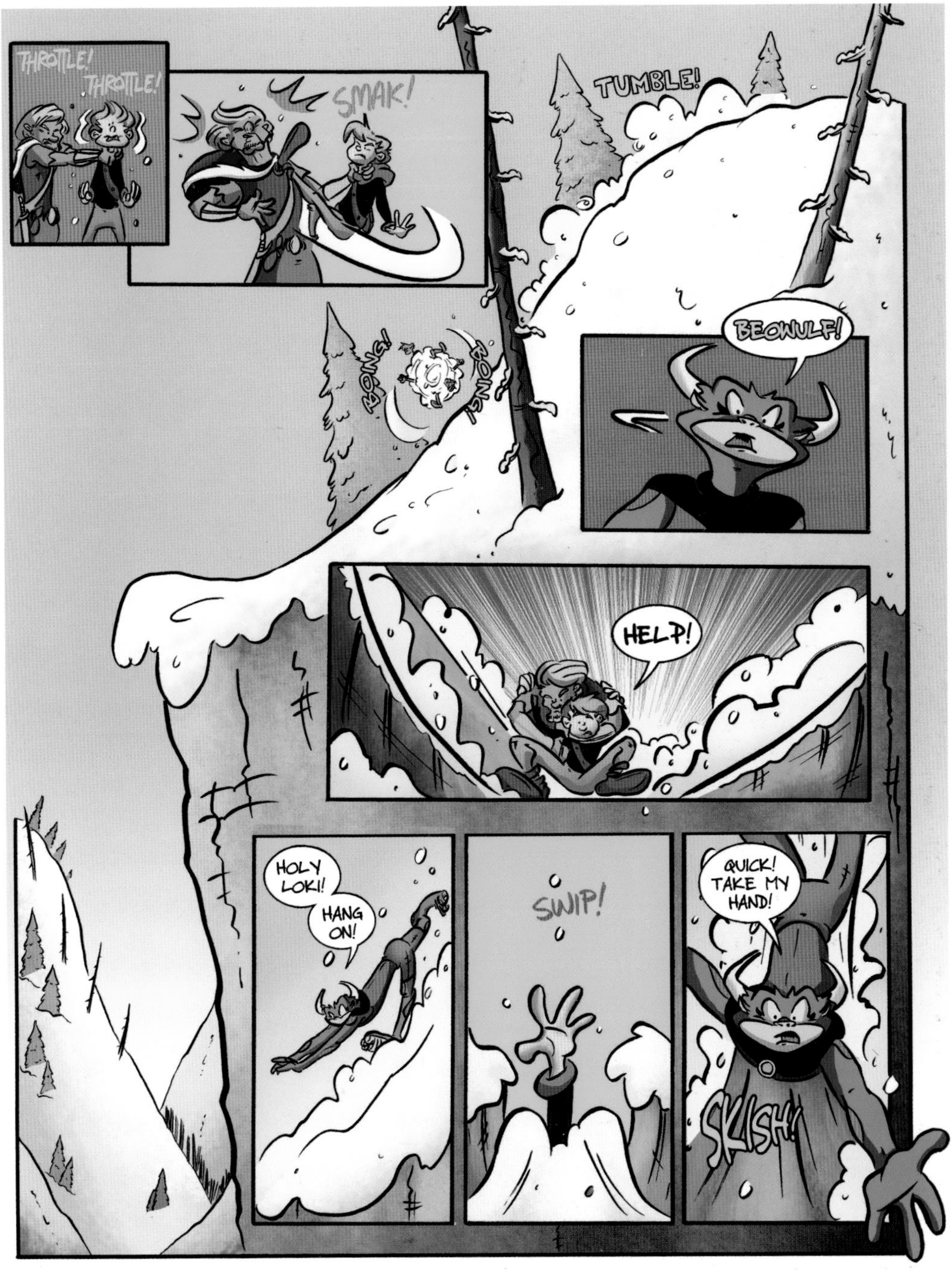
THROTTLE!
THROTTLE!
SMAK!
TUMBLE!
BOING!
BOING!
BEOWULF!
HELP!
HOLY LOKI!
HANG ON!
SWIP!
QUICK! TAKE MY HAND!
SKLISH!

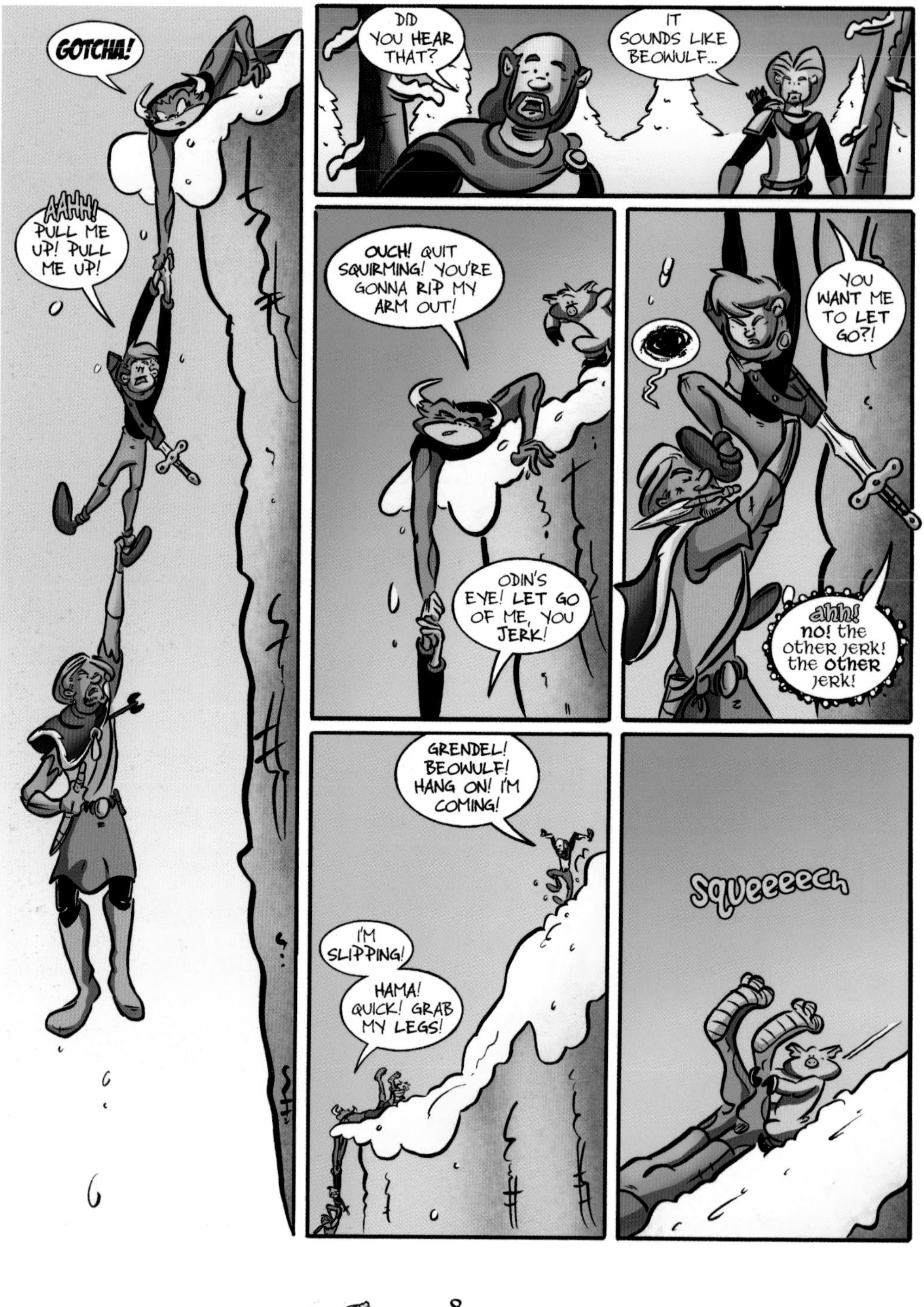
GOTCHA!
AAHH! PULL ME UP! PULL ME UP!
DID YOU HEAR THAT?
IT SOUNDS LIKE BEOWULF...
OUCH! QUIT SQUIRMING! YOU'RE GONNA RIP MY ARM OUT!
ODIN'S EYE! LET GO OF ME, YOU JERK!
YOU WANT ME TO LET GO?!
ahh! no! the other JERK! the other JERK!
GRENDEL! BEOWULF! HANG ON! I'M COMING!
I'M SLIPPING!
HAMA! QUICK! GRAB MY LEGS!
Squeeeech

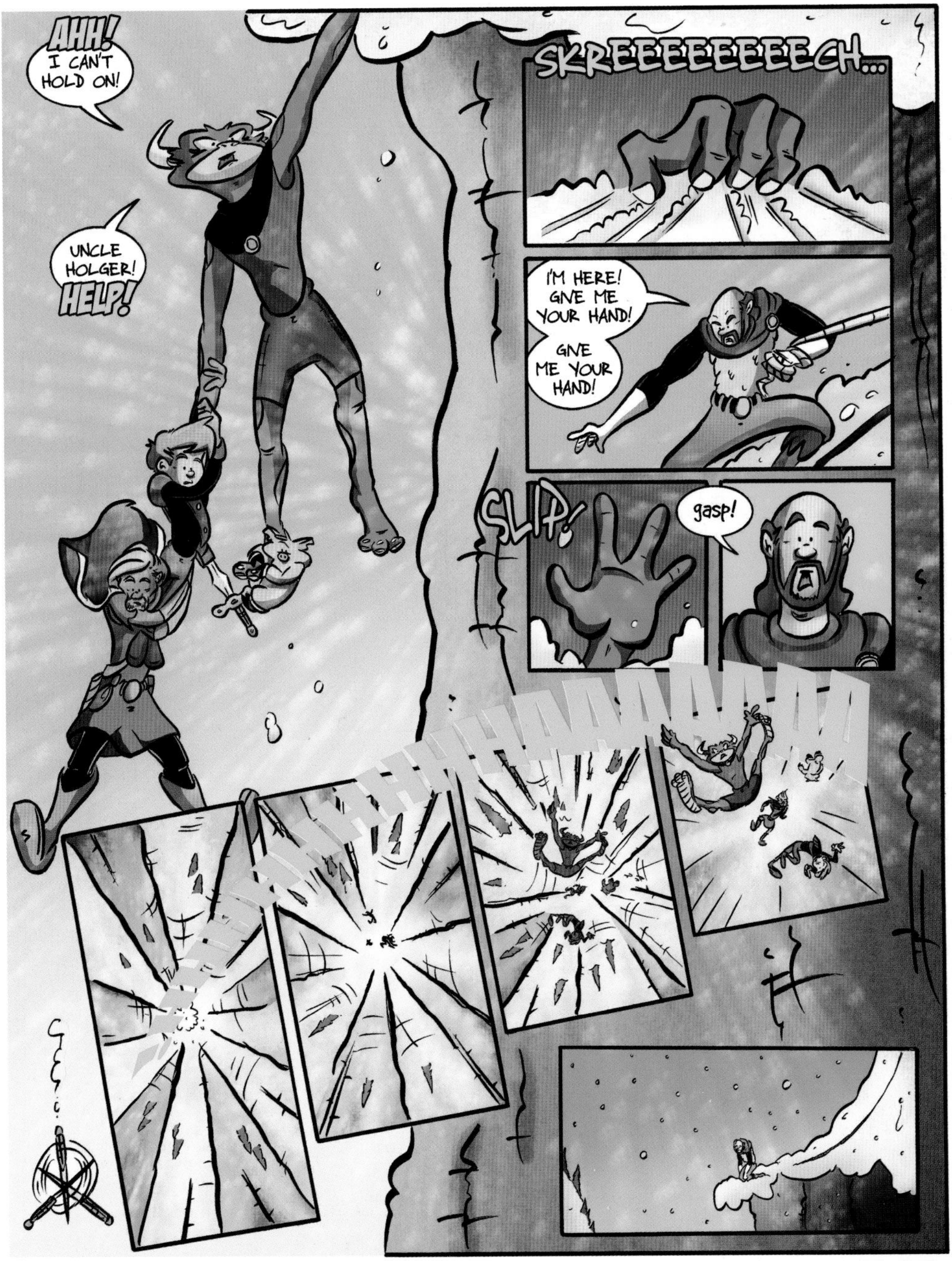
AHH! I CAN'T HOLD ON!
UNCLE HOLGER! HELP!
SKREEEEEEEEECH...
I'M HERE! GIVE ME YOUR HAND!
GIVE ME YOUR HAND!
SLIP!
gasp!

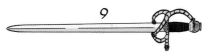

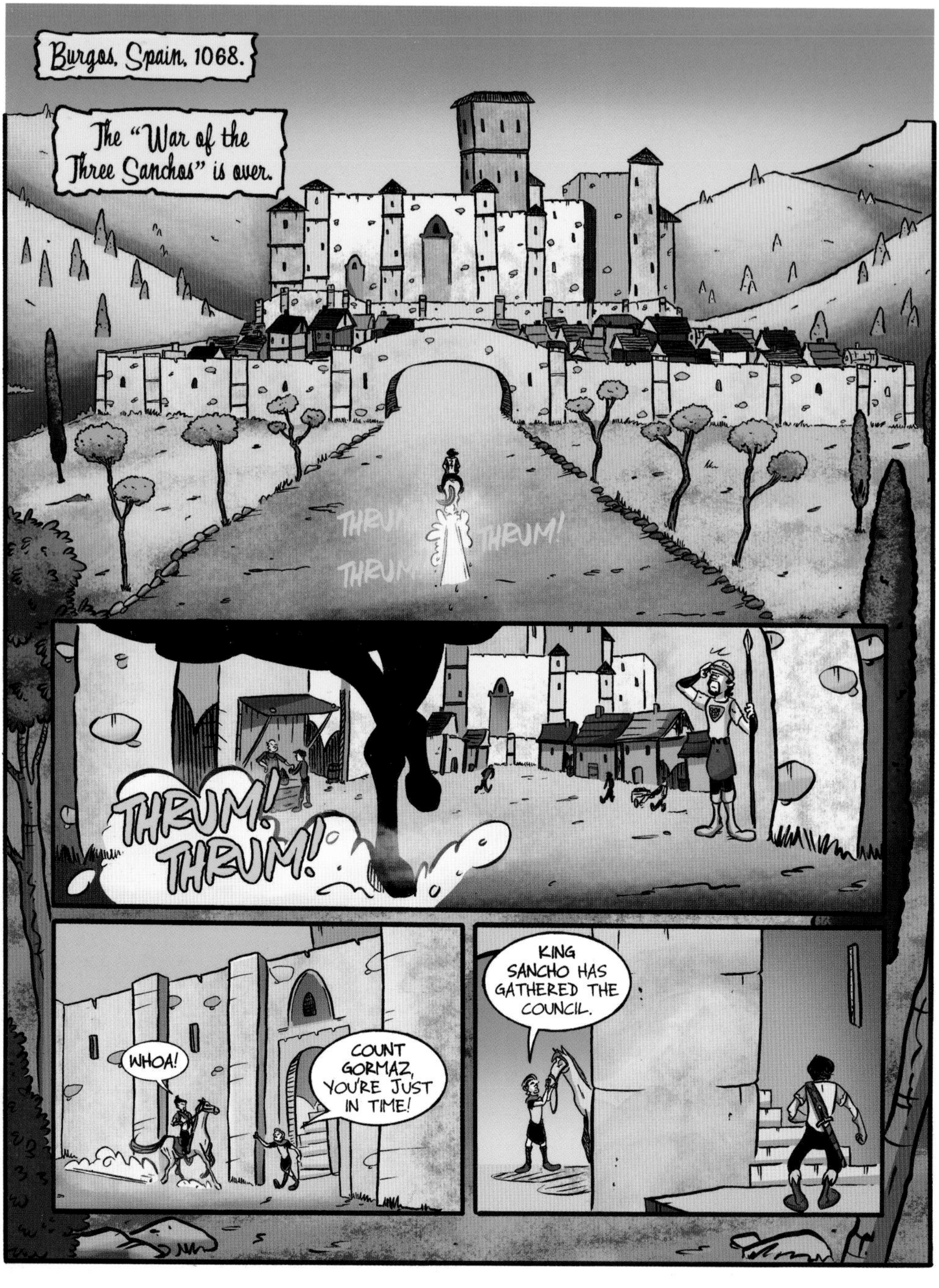
Burgos, Spain, 1068.
The "War of the Three Sanchos" is over.
THRUM! THRUM! THRUM!
THRUM! THRUM!
WHOA!
COUNT GORMAZ, YOU'RE JUST IN TIME!
KING SANCHO HAS GATHERED THE COUNCIL.

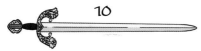

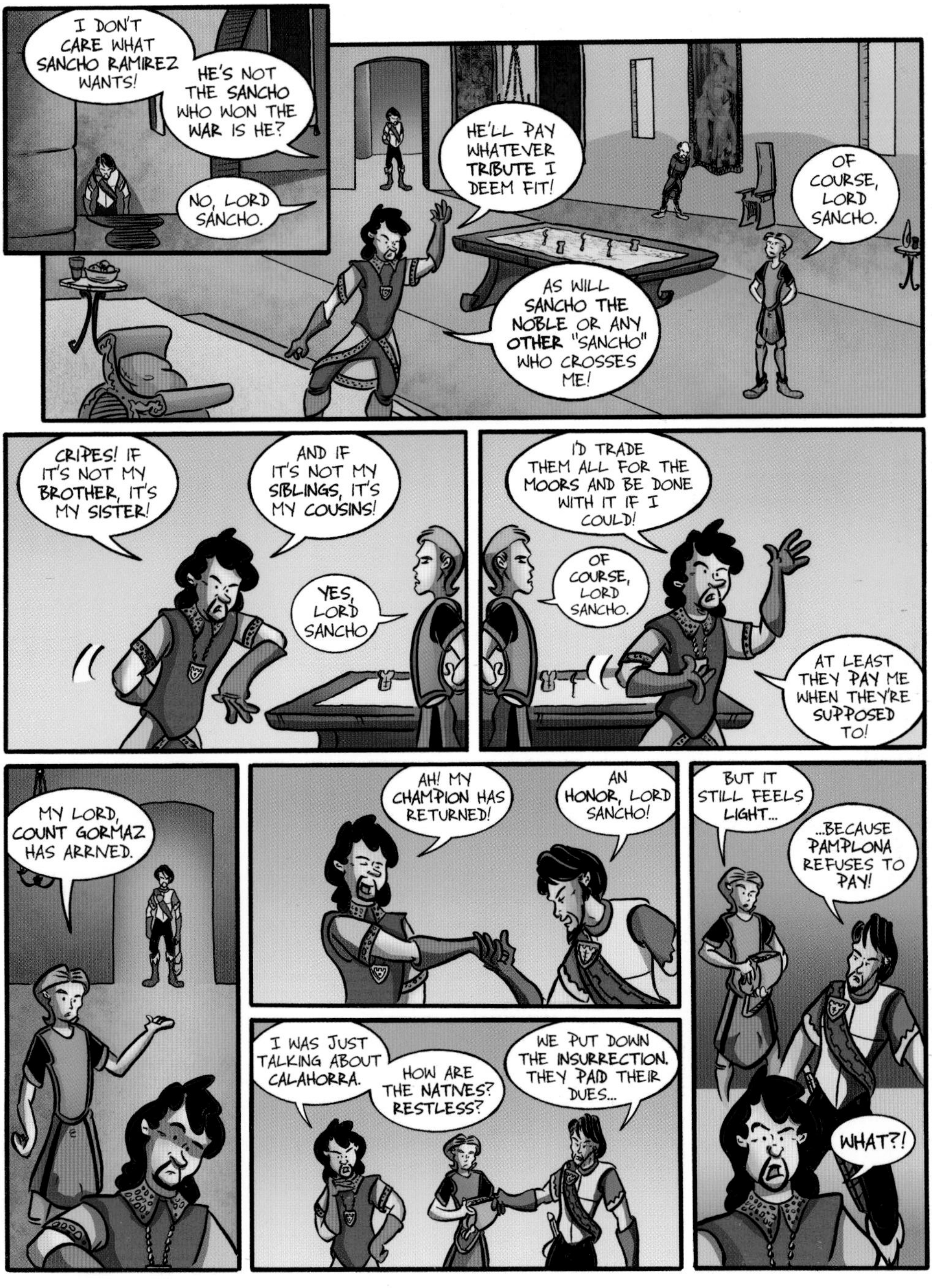
I DON'T CARE WHAT SANCHO RAMIREZ WANTS!
HE'S NOT THE SANCHO WHO WON THE WAR IS HE?
NO, LORD SANCHO.
HE'LL PAY WHATEVER TRIBUTE I DEEM FIT!
OF COURSE, LORD SANCHO.
AS WILL SANCHO THE NOBLE OR ANY OTHER "SANCHO" WHO CROSSES ME!
CRIPES! IF IT'S NOT MY BROTHER, IT'S MY SISTER!
AND IF IT'S NOT MY SIBLINGS, IT'S MY COUSINS!
YES, LORD SANCHO
I'D TRADE THEM ALL FOR THE MOORS AND BE DONE WITH IT IF I COULD!
OF COURSE, LORD SANCHO.
AT LEAST THEY PAY ME WHEN THEY'RE SUPPOSED TO!
MY LORD, COUNT GORMAZ HAS ARRIVED.
AH! MY CHAMPION HAS RETURNED!
AN HONOR, LORD SANCHO!
I WAS JUST TALKING ABOUT CALAHORRA.
HOW ARE THE NATIVES? RESTLESS?
WE PUT DOWN THE INSURRECTION. THEY PAID THEIR DUES...
BUT IT STILL FEELS LIGHT...
...BECAUSE PAMPLONA REFUSES TO PAY!
WHAT?!

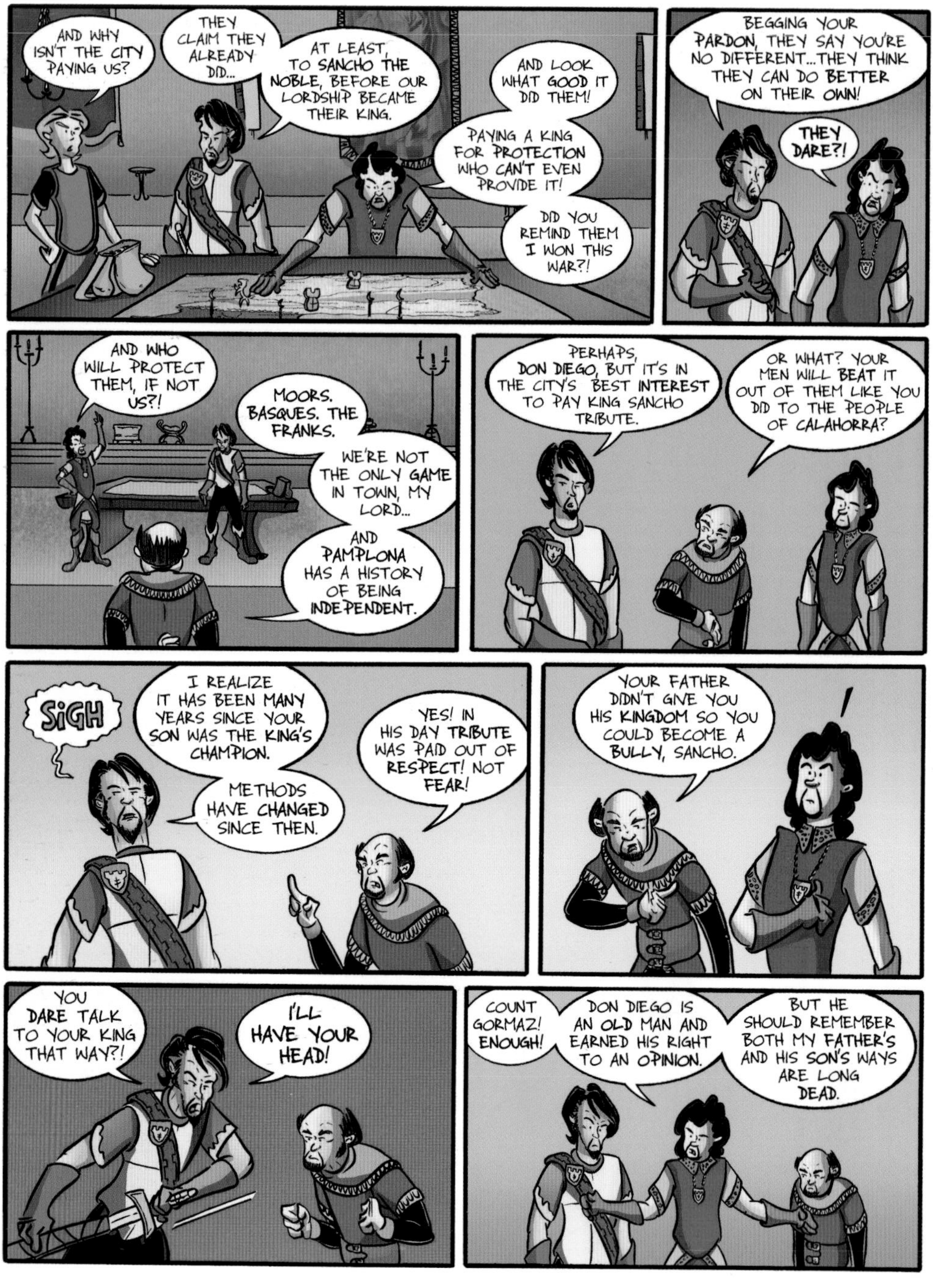
AND WHY ISN'T THE CITY PAYING US?
THEY CLAIM THEY ALREADY DID...
AT LEAST, TO SANCHO THE NOBLE, BEFORE OUR LORDSHIP BECAME THEIR KING.
AND LOOK WHAT GOOD IT DID THEM!
PAYING A KING FOR PROTECTION WHO CAN'T EVEN PROVIDE IT!
DID YOU REMIND THEM I WON THIS WAR?!
BEGGING YOUR PARDON, THEY SAY YOU'RE NO DIFFERENT...THEY THINK THEY CAN DO BETTER ON THEIR OWN!
THEY DARE?!
AND WHO WILL PROTECT THEM, IF NOT US?!
MOORS. BASQUES. THE FRANKS.
WE'RE NOT THE ONLY GAME IN TOWN, MY LORD...
AND PAMPLONA HAS A HISTORY OF BEING INDEPENDENT.
PERHAPS, DON DIEGO, BUT IT'S IN THE CITY'S BEST INTEREST TO PAY KING SANCHO TRIBUTE.
OR WHAT? YOUR MEN WILL BEAT IT OUT OF THEM LIKE YOU DID TO THE PEOPLE OF CALAHORRA?
SIGH
I REALIZE IT HAS BEEN MANY YEARS SINCE YOUR SON WAS THE KING'S CHAMPION.
METHODS HAVE CHANGED SINCE THEN.
YES! IN HIS DAY TRIBUTE WAS PAID OUT OF RESPECT! NOT FEAR!
YOUR FATHER DIDN'T GIVE YOU HIS KINGDOM SO YOU COULD BECOME A BULLY, SANCHO.
!
YOU DARE TALK TO YOUR KING THAT WAY?!
I'LL HAVE YOUR HEAD!
COUNT GORMAZ! ENOUGH!
DON DIEGO IS AN OLD MAN AND EARNED HIS RIGHT TO AN OPINION.
BUT HE SHOULD REMEMBER BOTH MY FATHER'S AND HIS SON'S WAYS ARE LONG DEAD.

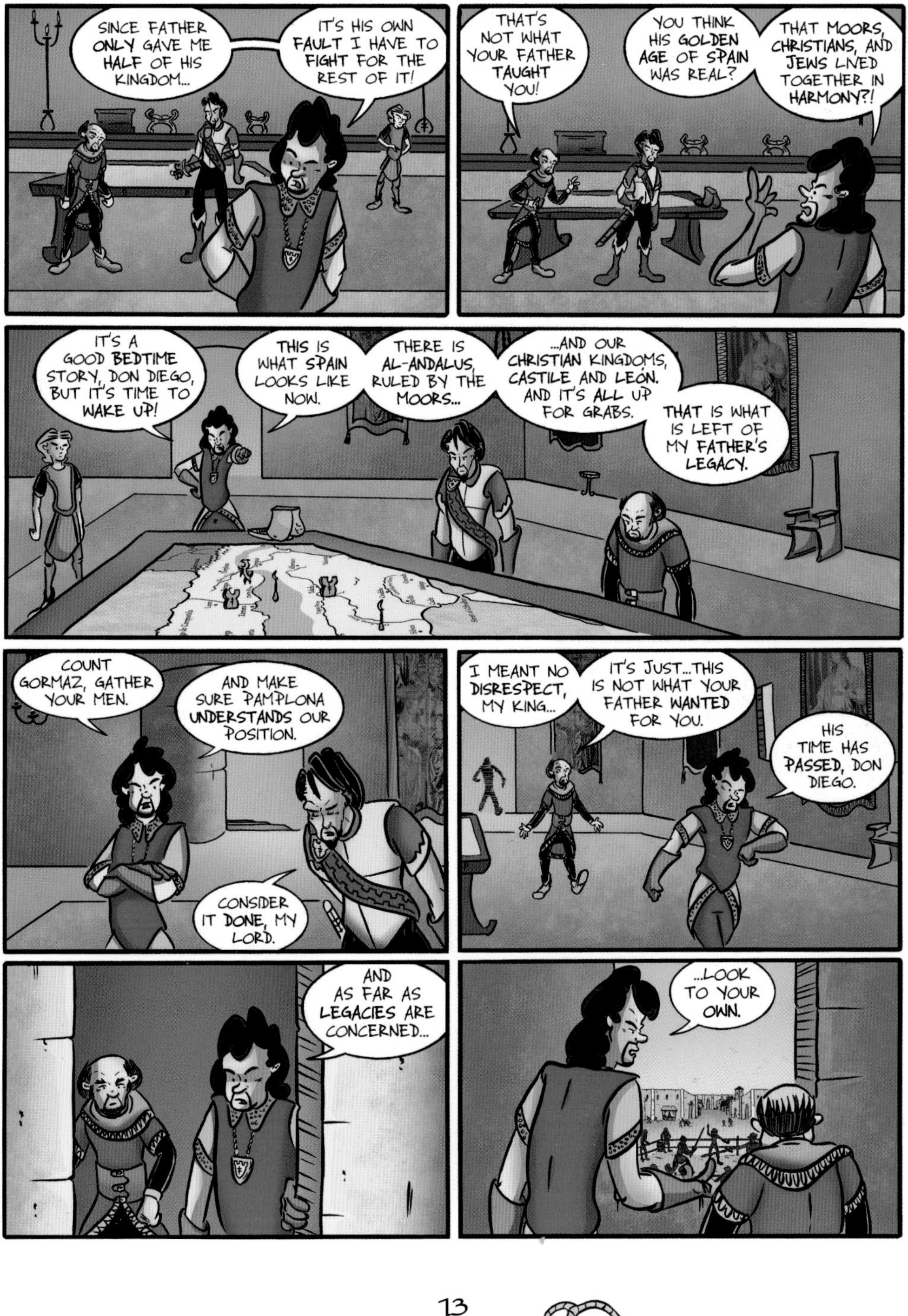
SINCE FATHER ONLY GAVE ME HALF OF HIS KINGDOM...
IT'S HIS OWN FAULT I HAVE TO FIGHT FOR THE REST OF IT!
THAT'S NOT WHAT YOUR FATHER TAUGHT YOU!
YOU THINK HIS GOLDEN AGE OF SPAIN WAS REAL?
THAT MOORS, CHRISTIANS, AND JEWS LIVED TOGETHER IN HARMONY?!
IT'S A GOOD BEDTIME STORY, DON DIEGO, BUT IT'S TIME TO WAKE UP!
THIS IS WHAT SPAIN LOOKS LIKE NOW.
THERE IS AL-ANDALUS, RULED BY THE MOORS...
...AND OUR CHRISTIAN KINGDOMS, CASTILE AND LEÓN. AND IT'S ALL UP FOR GRABS.
THAT IS WHAT IS LEFT OF MY FATHER'S LEGACY.
COUNT GORMAZ, GATHER YOUR MEN.
AND MAKE SURE PAMPLONA UNDERSTANDS OUR POSITION.
CONSIDER IT DONE, MY LORD.
I MEANT NO DISRESPECT, MY KING...
IT'S JUST...THIS IS NOT WHAT YOUR FATHER WANTED FOR YOU.
HIS TIME HAS PASSED, DON DIEGO.
AND AS FAR AS LEGACIES ARE CONCERNED...
...LOOK TO YOUR OWN.

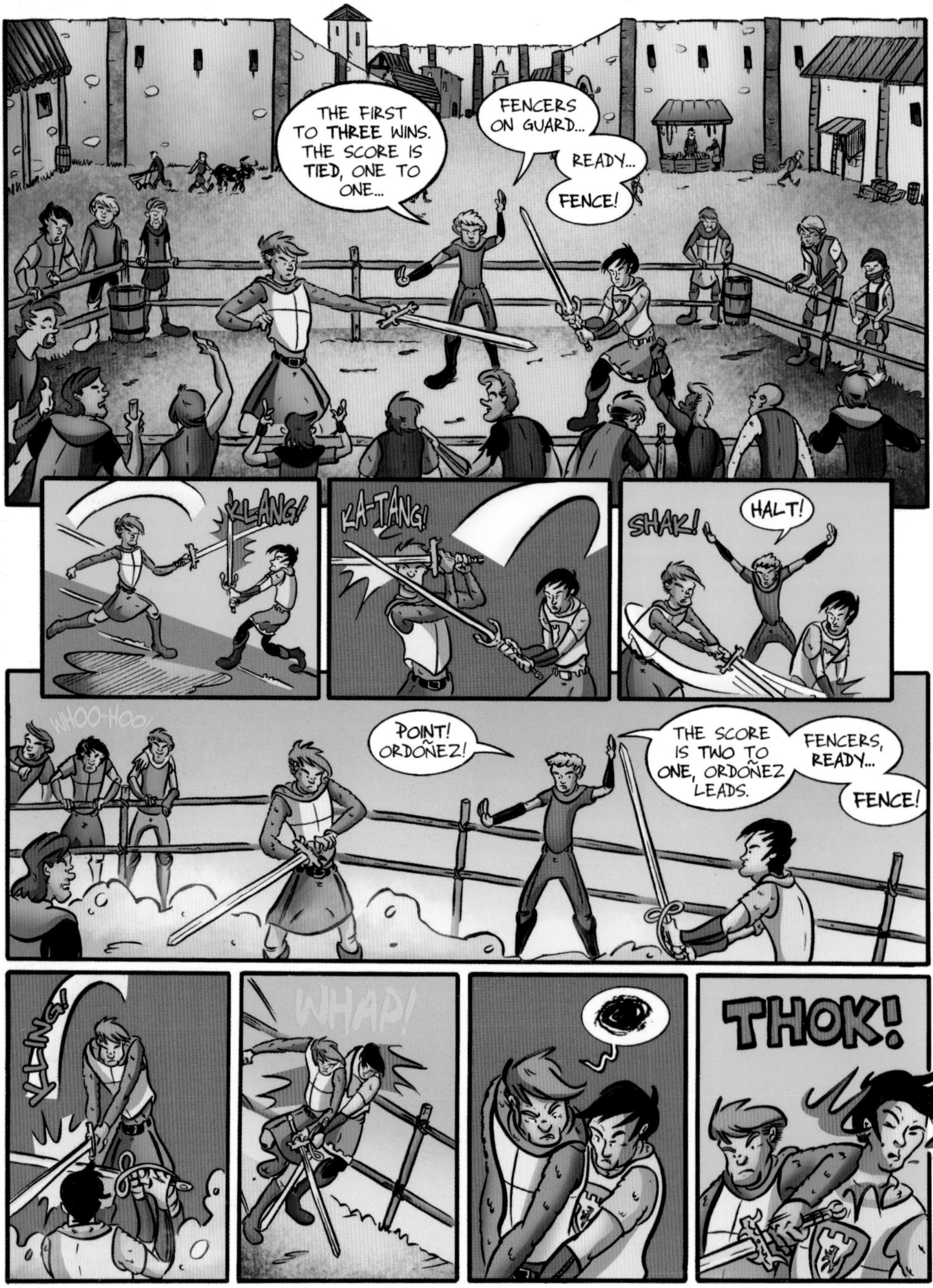
THE FIRST TO THREE WINS. THE SCORE IS TIED, ONE TO ONE...
FENCERS ON GUARD...
READY...
FENCE!
KLANG!
KA-TANG!
SHAK!
HALT!
WHOO-HOO!
POINT! ORDOÑEZ!
THE SCORE IS TWO TO ONE, ORDOÑEZ LEADS.
FENCERS, READY...
FENCE!
KLING!
WHAP!
THOK!

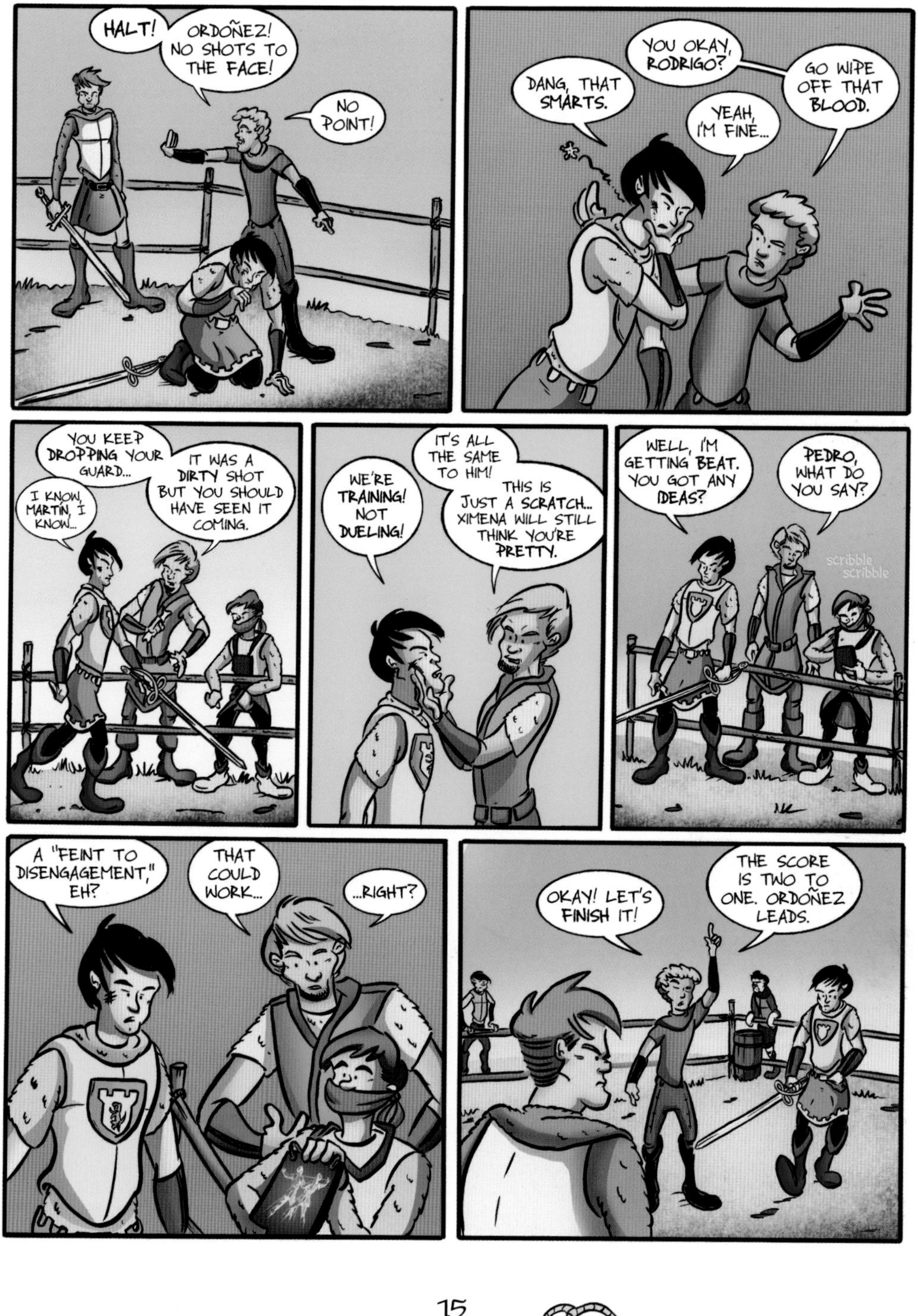
HALT!
ORDOÑEZ! NO SHOTS TO THE FACE!
NO POINT!
DANG, THAT SMARTS.
YOU OKAY, RODRIGO?
YEAH, I'M FINE...
GO WIPE OFF THAT BLOOD.
YOU KEEP DROPPING YOUR GUARD...
I KNOW, MARTIN, I KNOW...
IT WAS A DIRTY SHOT BUT YOU SHOULD HAVE SEEN IT COMING.
WE'RE TRAINING! NOT DUELING!
IT'S ALL THE SAME TO HIM!
THIS IS JUST A SCRATCH... XIMENA WILL STILL THINK YOU'RE PRETTY.
WELL, I'M GETTING BEAT. YOU GOT ANY IDEAS?
PEDRO, WHAT DO YOU SAY?
scribble scribble
A "FEINT TO DISENGAGEMENT," EH?
THAT COULD WORK...
...RIGHT?
OKAY! LET'S FINISH IT!
THE SCORE IS TWO TO ONE. ORDOÑEZ LEADS.

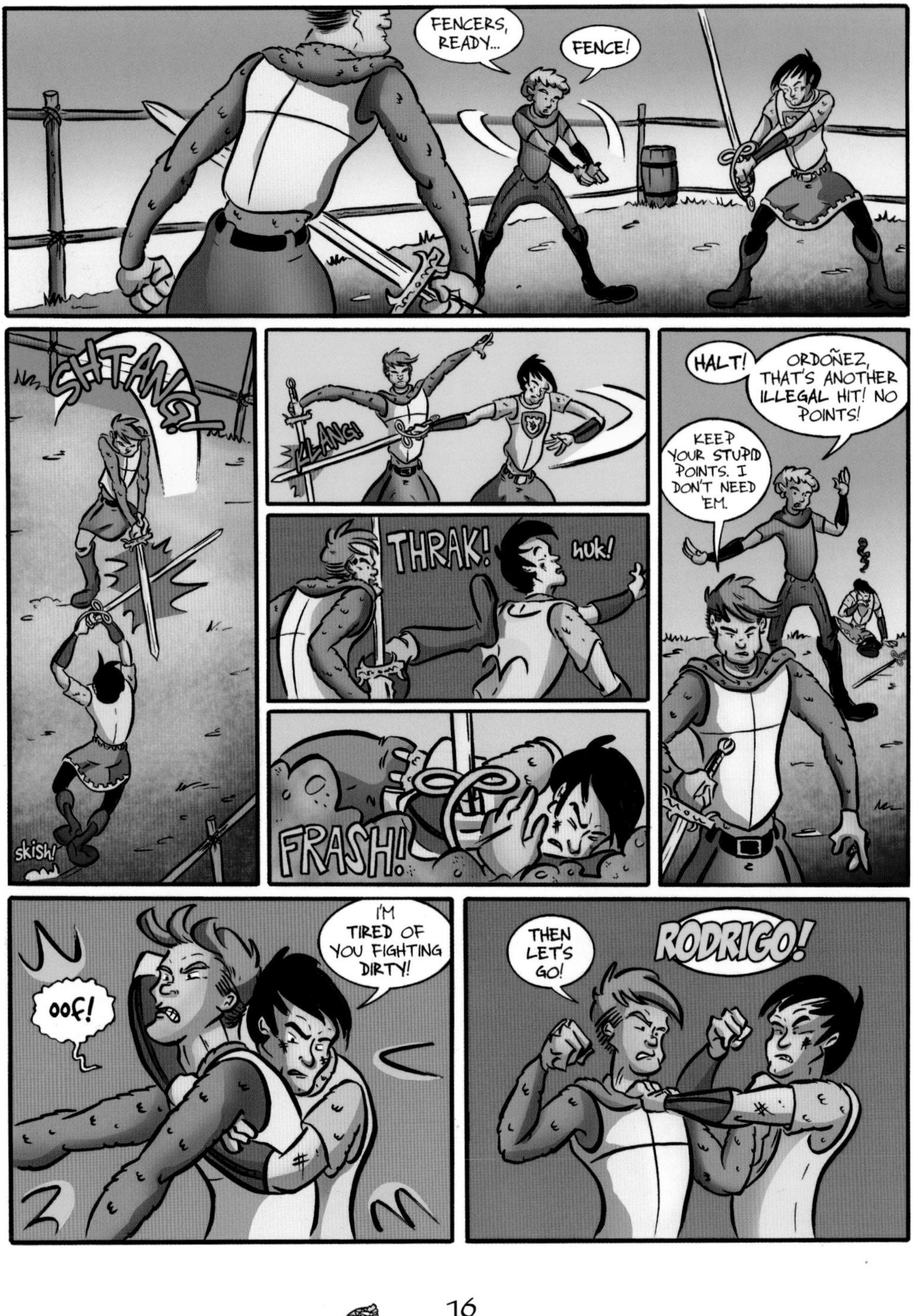
FENCERS, READY...
FENCE!
SHTANG!
skish!
CLANG!
THRAK!
HUK!
FRASH!
HALT!
ORDOÑEZ, THAT'S ANOTHER ILLEGAL HIT! NO POINTS!
KEEP YOUR STUPID POINTS. I DON'T NEED 'EM.
OOF!
I'M TIRED OF YOU FIGHTING DIRTY!
THEN LET'S GO!
RODRIGO!

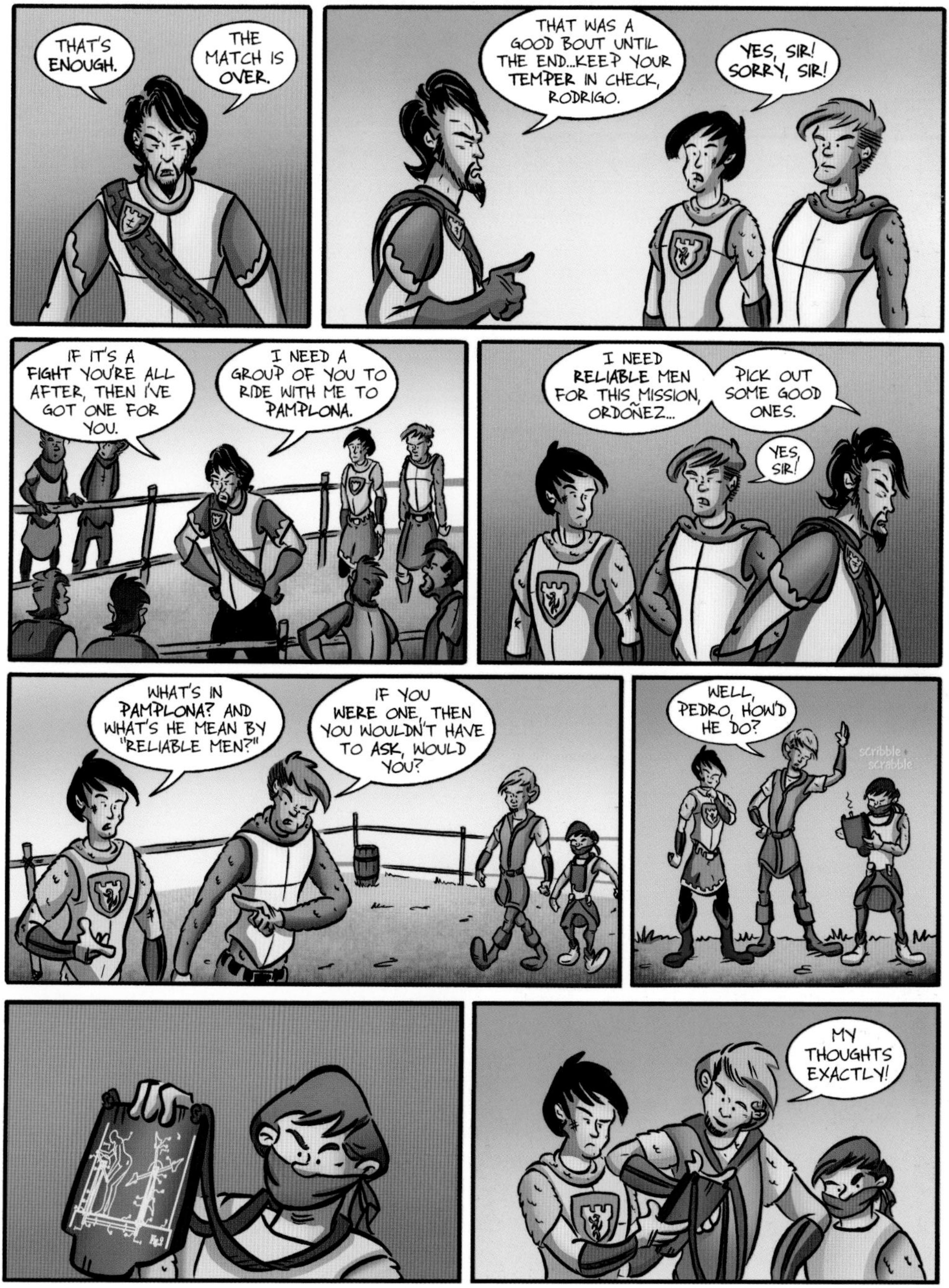
THAT'S ENOUGH.
THE MATCH IS OVER.
THAT WAS A GOOD BOUT UNTIL THE END...KEEP YOUR TEMPER IN CHECK, RODRIGO.
YES, SIR! SORRY, SIR!
IF IT'S A FIGHT YOU'RE ALL AFTER, THEN I'VE GOT ONE FOR YOU.
I NEED A GROUP OF YOU TO RIDE WITH ME TO PAMPLONA.
I NEED RELIABLE MEN FOR THIS MISSION, ORDOÑEZ...
PICK OUT SOME GOOD ONES.
YES, SIR!
WHAT'S IN PAMPLONA? AND WHAT'S HE MEAN BY "RELIABLE MEN?"
IF YOU WERE ONE, THEN YOU WOULDN'T HAVE TO ASK, WOULD YOU?
WELL, PEDRO, HOW'D HE DO?
scribble scribble
MY THOUGHTS EXACTLY!

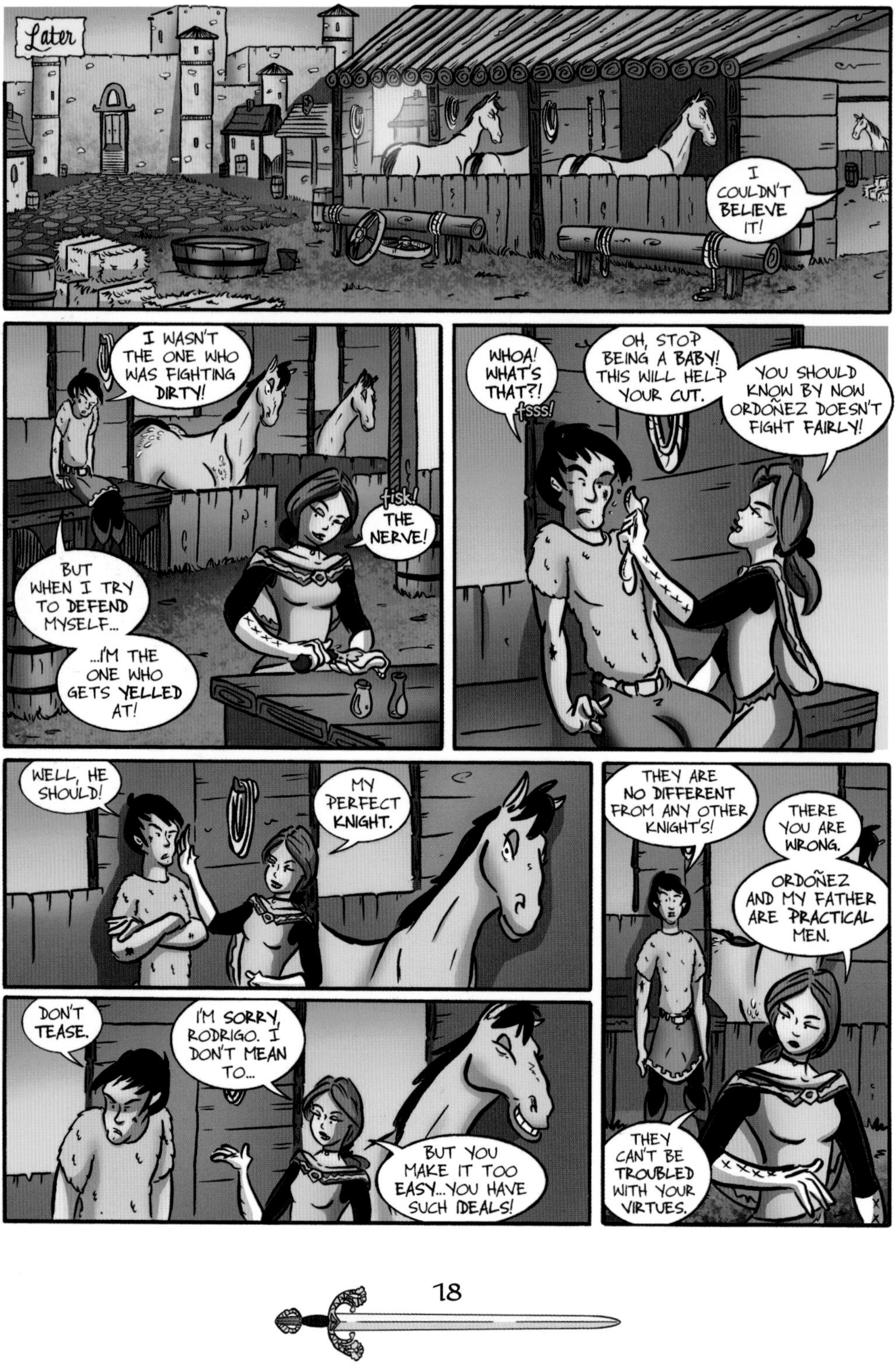
Later
I COULDN'T BELIEVE IT!
I WASN'T THE ONE WHO WAS FIGHTING DIRTY!
BUT WHEN I TRY TO DEFEND MYSELF...
...I'M THE ONE WHO GETS YELLED AT!
tisk!
THE NERVE!
WHOA! WHAT'S THAT?!
tsss!
OH, STOP BEING A BABY! THIS WILL HELP YOUR CUT.
YOU SHOULD KNOW BY NOW ORDOÑEZ DOESN'T FIGHT FAIRLY!
WELL, HE SHOULD!
MY PERFECT KNIGHT.
DON'T TEASE.
I'M SORRY, RODRIGO. I DON'T MEAN TO...
BUT YOU MAKE IT TOO EASY...YOU HAVE SUCH IDEALS!
THEY ARE NO DIFFERENT FROM ANY OTHER KNIGHT'S!
THERE YOU ARE WRONG.
ORDOÑEZ AND MY FATHER ARE PRACTICAL MEN.
THEY CAN'T BE TROUBLED WITH YOUR VIRTUES.

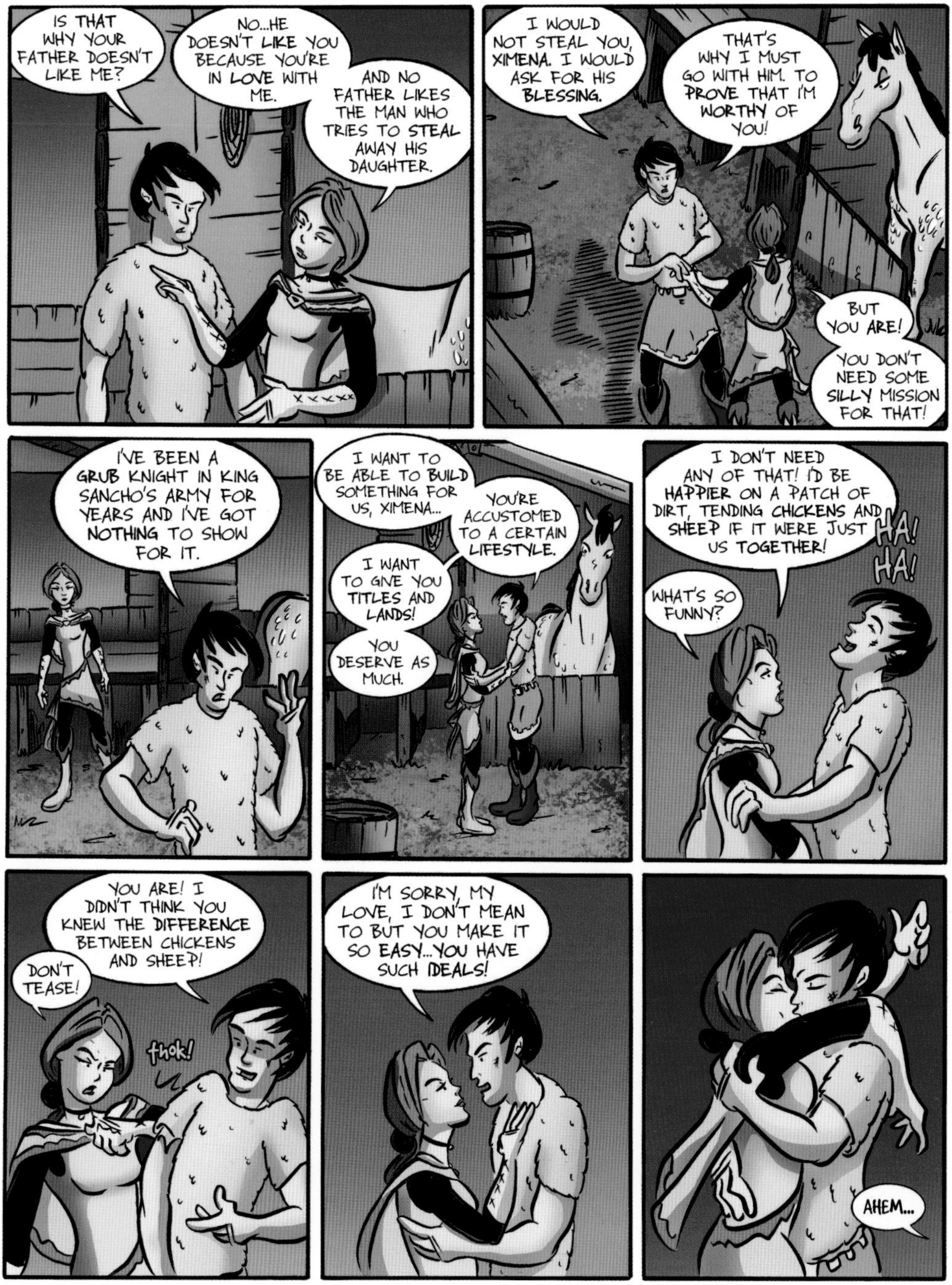
IS THAT WHY YOUR FATHER DOESN'T LIKE ME?
NO...HE DOESN'T LIKE YOU BECAUSE YOU'RE IN LOVE WITH ME.
AND NO FATHER LIKES THE MAN WHO TRIES TO STEAL AWAY HIS DAUGHTER.
I WOULD NOT STEAL YOU, XIMENA. I WOULD ASK FOR HIS BLESSING.
THAT'S WHY I MUST GO WITH HIM. TO PROVE THAT I'M WORTHY OF YOU!
BUT YOU ARE!
YOU DON'T NEED SOME SILLY MISSION FOR THAT!
I'VE BEEN A GRUB KNIGHT IN KING SANCHO'S ARMY FOR YEARS AND I'VE GOT NOTHING TO SHOW FOR IT.
I WANT TO BE ABLE TO BUILD SOMETHING FOR US, XIMENA...
YOU'RE ACCUSTOMED TO A CERTAIN LIFESTYLE.
I WANT TO GIVE YOU TITLES AND LANDS!
YOU DESERVE AS MUCH.
I DON'T NEED ANY OF THAT! I'D BE HAPPIER ON A PATCH OF DIRT, TENDING CHICKENS AND SHEEP IF IT WERE JUST US TOGETHER!
HA! HA!
WHAT'S SO FUNNY?
YOU ARE! I DIDN'T THINK YOU KNEW THE DIFFERENCE BETWEEN CHICKENS AND SHEEP!
DON'T TEASE!
thok!
I'M SORRY, MY LOVE, I DON'T MEAN TO BUT YOU MAKE IT SO EASY...YOU HAVE SUCH IDEALS!
AHEM...

RODRIGO...

...XIMENA...

ABUELO! GOOD TO SEE YOU!

I'LL GO... BUT TAKE MY KERCHIEF... FOR LUCK?

AND REMEMBER WHAT I TOLD YOU.

DON DIEGO, A PLEASURE TO SEE YOU.

AND YOU, MY DEAR.

WELL? DID YOU SPEAK TO KING SANCHO?

YES. AND TO COUNT GORMAZ...

I CONVINCED THEM TO LET YOU GO ALONG TO PAMPLONA.

YAHOO!

THANK YOU, ABUELO!

YES! YES! PUT ME DOWN!

DID YOU HEAR THAT, BABIECA? YOU AND I ARE GOING ON A MISSION!

CRACK!

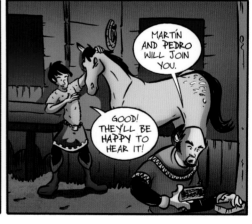

MARTÍN AND PEDRO WILL JOIN YOU.

GOOD! THEY'LL BE HAPPY TO HEAR IT!

FINALLY! A CHANCE TO MAKE OUR MARK!
I SAW THE LIST ORDOÑEZ PUT TOGETHER.
IT'S A ROUGH GROUP OF MEN.
I KNOW THE KIND OF MEN GORMAZ USES, ABUELO.
THEN YOU KNOW WHY I CAN'T SANCTION THIS MISSION!
THERE IS NO HONOR IN WHAT COUNT GORMAZ DOES.
SO IT'S DISHONORABLE FOR ME TO FOLLOW HIM?
THERE WILL BE PLENTY OF OTHER OPPORTUNITIES TO DISTINGUISH YOURSELF.
LIKE ALL THE ONES I'VE HAD SO FAR?
OUR FAMILY HAS FALLEN OUT OF FAVOR WITH SANCHO.
HE DOESN'T CARE THAT FATHER WAS THE KING'S CHAMPION.
AND HE IGNORES THE KNIGHTS YOU'VE TRAINED...
I WAS STUCK HERE DURING THE "WAR OF THE THREE SANCHOS!"
IT WAS A DISHONORABLE WAR TO BEGIN WITH...
IT'S BETTER YOU HAD NO PART IN IT.
YOU SAY THAT ABOUT EVERY WAR!
NO.
SOME WARS ARE WORTH FIGHTING.
YOU'LL KNOW YOU'RE IN ONE WHEN THE CAUSE IS JUST AND THE OUTCOME UNCERTAIN.
FOR A TIME, UNDER KING FERDINAND, THOSE WERE THE WARS YOUR FATHER FOUGHT IN.
BUT THIS IS NOT ONE OF THEM.
I'M SORRY, RODRIGO, BUT THIS IS NOT THE SPAIN YOUR FATHER WANTED FOR YOU.
I KNOW, ABUELO, BUT IT'S THE ONE I'VE BEEN GIVEN.

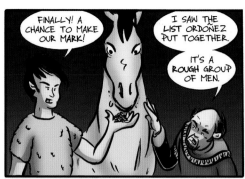

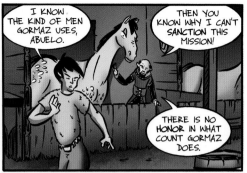

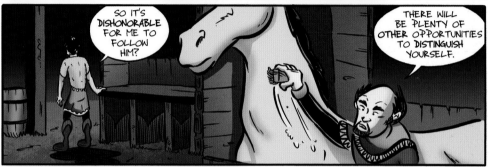

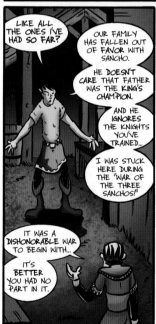

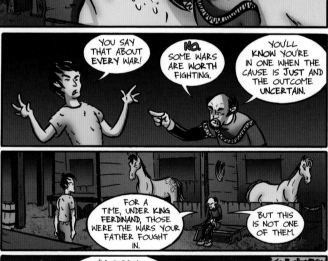

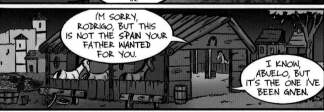

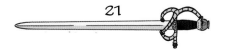

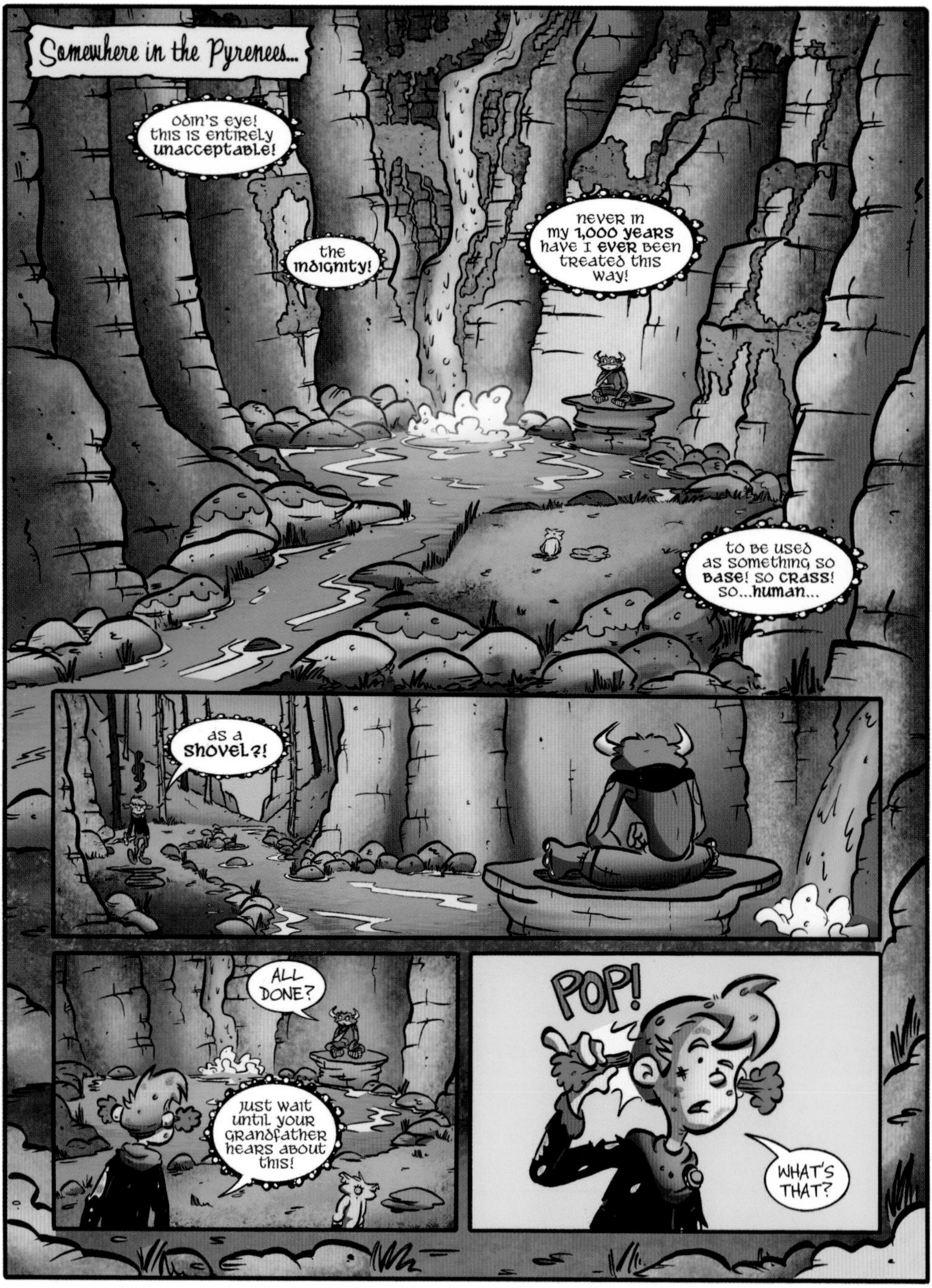
Somewhere in the Pyrenees...
Odin's eye! this is entirely unacceptable!
the indignity!
never in my 1,000 years have I ever been treated this way!
to be used as something so base! so crass! so...human...
as a shovel?!
ALL DONE?
just wait until your grandfather hears about this!
POP!
WHAT'S THAT?

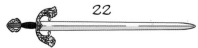

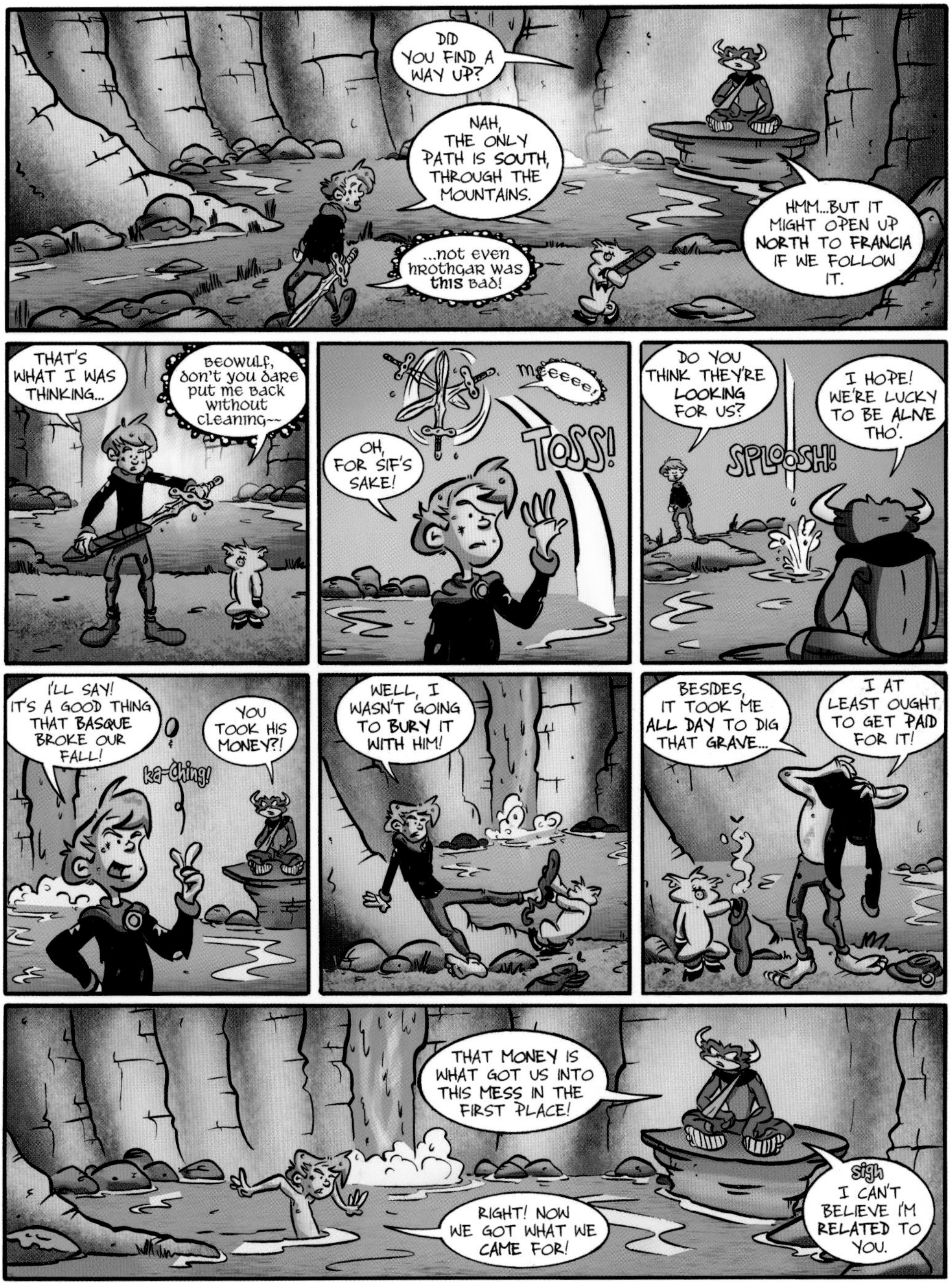
DID YOU FIND A WAY UP?
NAH, THE ONLY PATH IS SOUTH, THROUGH THE MOUNTAINS.
...not even hrothgar was this bad!
HMM...BUT IT MIGHT OPEN UP NORTH TO FRANCIA IF WE FOLLOW IT.
THAT'S WHAT I WAS THINKING...
beowulf, don't you dare put me back without cleaning~~
meeeee!
TOSS!
OH, FOR SIF'S SAKE!
DO YOU THINK THEY'RE LOOKING FOR US?
SPLOOSH!
I HOPE! WE'RE LUCKY TO BE ALIVE THO'.
I'LL SAY! IT'S A GOOD THING THAT BASQUE BROKE OUR FALL!
ka-ching!
YOU TOOK HIS MONEY?!
WELL, I WASN'T GOING TO BURY IT WITH HIM!
BESIDES, IT TOOK ME ALL DAY TO DIG THAT GRAVE...
I AT LEAST OUGHT TO GET PAID FOR IT!
THAT MONEY IS WHAT GOT US INTO THIS MESS IN THE FIRST PLACE!
RIGHT! NOW WE GOT WHAT WE CAME FOR!
sigh I CAN'T BELIEVE I'M RELATED TO YOU.

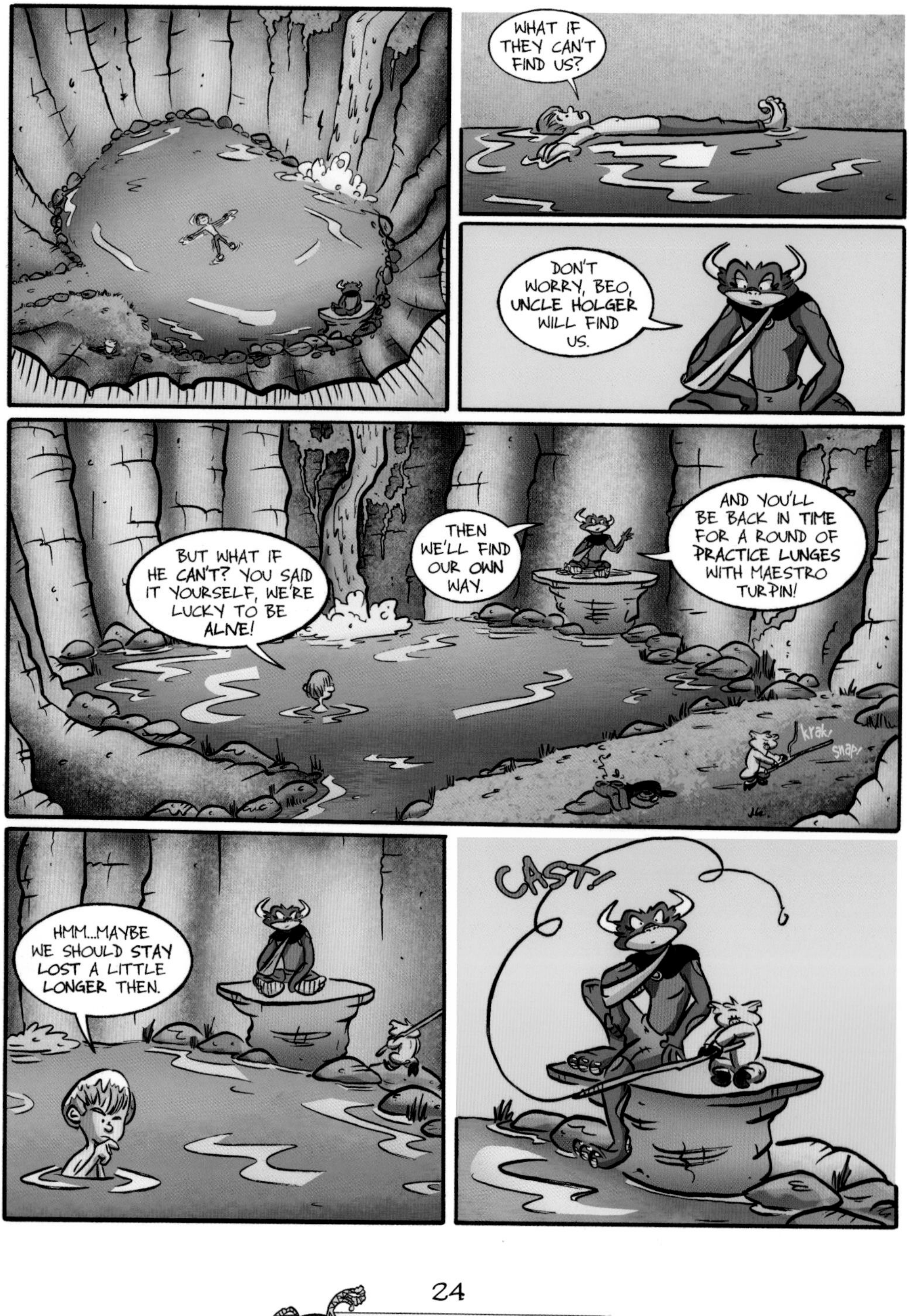
WHAT IF THEY CAN'T FIND US?
DON'T WORRY, BEO, UNCLE HOLGER WILL FIND US.
BUT WHAT IF HE CAN'T? YOU SAID IT YOURSELF, WE'RE LUCKY TO BE ALNE!
THEN WE'LL FIND OUR OWN WAY.
AND YOU'LL BE BACK IN TIME FOR A ROUND OF PRACTICE LUNGES WITH MAESTRO TURPIN!
krak!
snap!
HMM...MAYBE WE SHOULD STAY LOST A LITTLE LONGER THEN.
CAST!

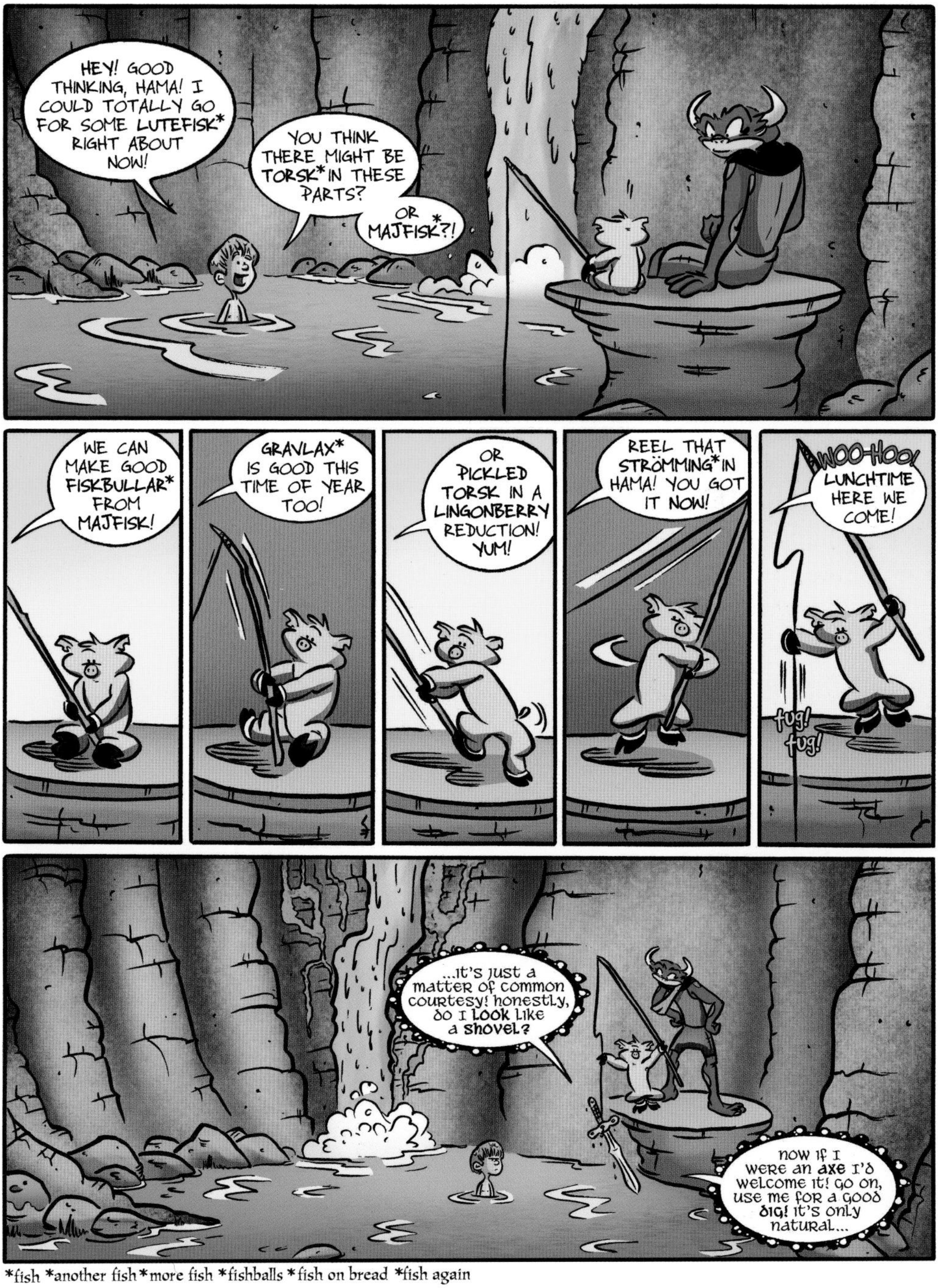
HEY! GOOD THINKING, HAMA! I COULD TOTALLY GO FOR SOME LUTEFISK* RIGHT ABOUT NOW!
YOU THINK THERE MIGHT BE TORSK* IN THESE PARTS?
OR MAJFISK*?!
WE CAN MAKE GOOD FISKBULLAR* FROM MAJFISK!
GRAVLAX* IS GOOD THIS TIME OF YEAR TOO!
OR PICKLED TORSK IN A LINGONBERRY REDUCTION! YUM!
REEL THAT STRÖMMING* IN HAMA! YOU GOT IT NOW!
WOO-HOO!
LUNCHTIME HERE WE COME!
tug! tug!
...it's just a matter of common courtesy! honestly, do I look like a shovel?
now if I were an axe I'd welcome it! go on, use me for a good dig! it's only natural...

*fish *another fish*more fish *fishballs *fish on bread *fish again

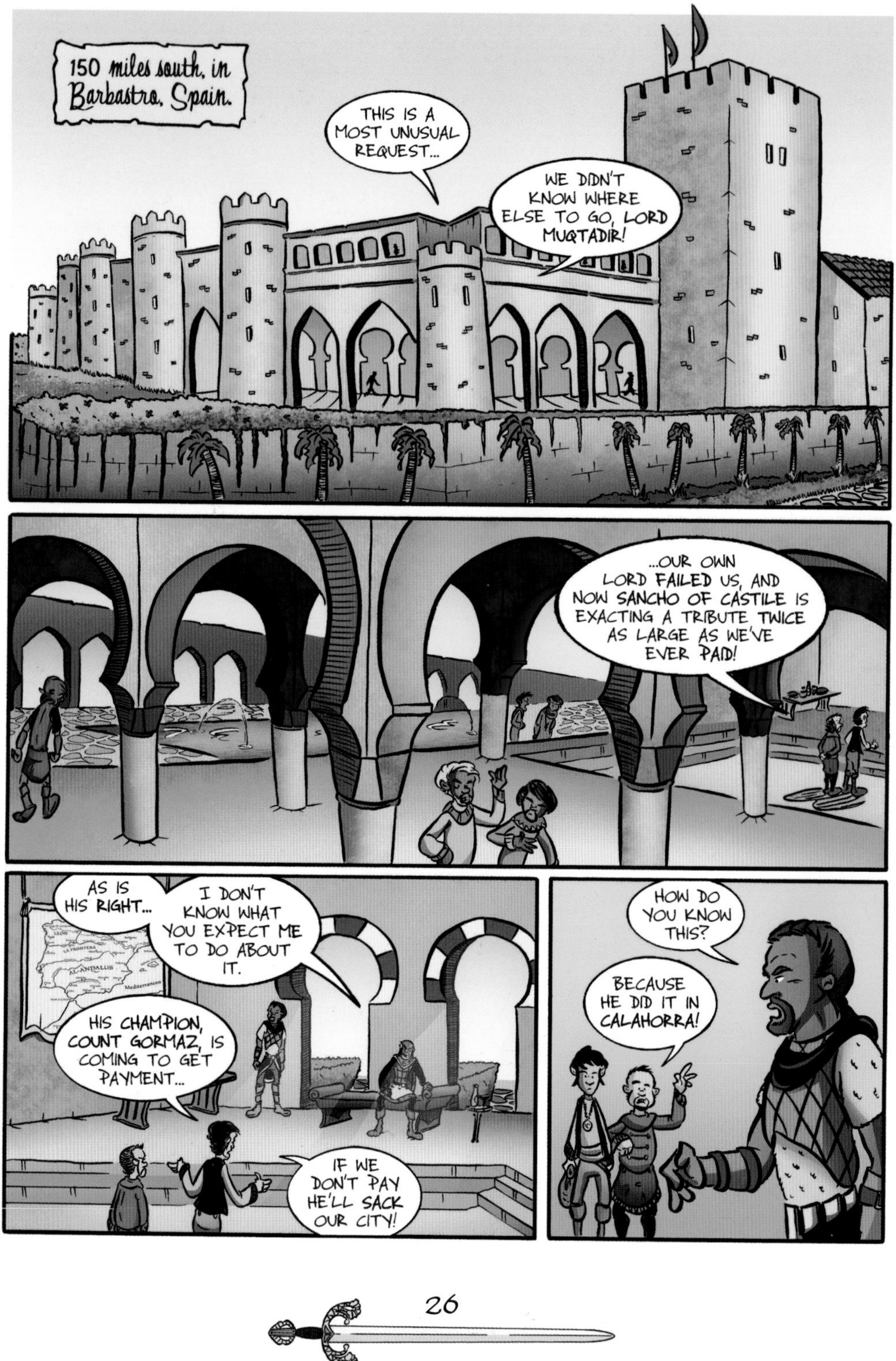
150 miles south, in Barbastro, Spain.
THIS IS A MOST UNUSUAL REQUEST...
WE DIDN'T KNOW WHERE ELSE TO GO, LORD MUQTADIR!
...OUR OWN LORD FAILED US, AND NOW SANCHO OF CASTILE IS EXACTING A TRIBUTE TWICE AS LARGE AS WE'VE EVER PAID!
AS IS HIS RIGHT...
I DON'T KNOW WHAT YOU EXPECT ME TO DO ABOUT IT.
LEON
LA FRONTERA
AL-ANDALUS
Mediterranean
HIS CHAMPION, COUNT GORMAZ, IS COMING TO GET PAYMENT...
IF WE DON'T PAY HE'LL SACK OUR CITY!
HOW DO YOU KNOW THIS?
BECAUSE HE DID IT IN CALAHORRA!

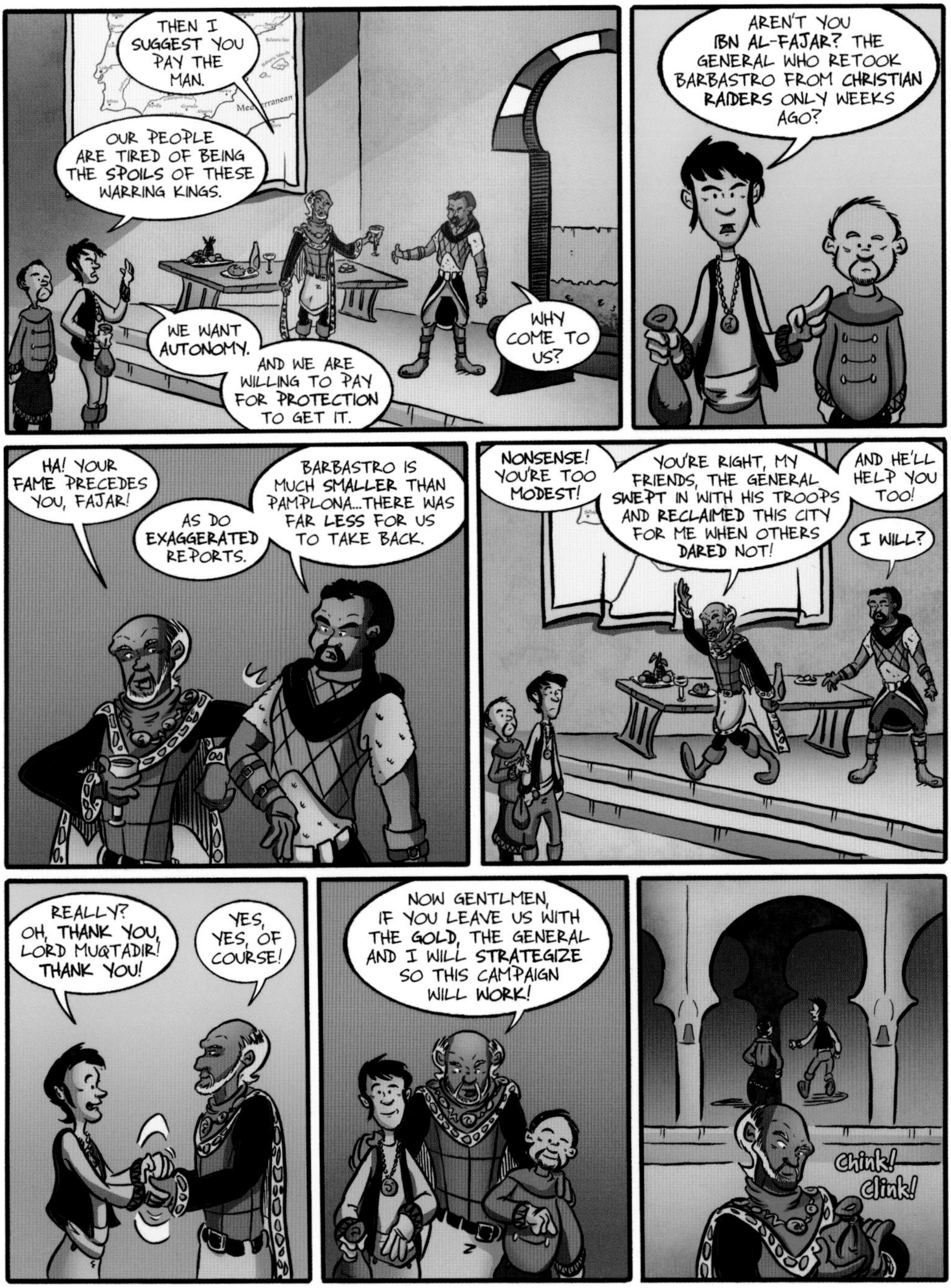
THEN I SUGGEST YOU PAY THE MAN.
OUR PEOPLE ARE TIRED OF BEING THE SPOILS OF THESE WARRING KINGS.
WE WANT AUTONOMY.
AND WE ARE WILLING TO PAY FOR PROTECTION TO GET IT.
WHY COME TO US?
AREN'T YOU IBN AL-FAJAR? THE GENERAL WHO RETOOK BARBASTRO FROM CHRISTIAN RAIDERS ONLY WEEKS AGO?
HA! YOUR FAME PRECEDES YOU, FAJAR!
AS DO EXAGGERATED REPORTS.
BARBASTRO IS MUCH SMALLER THAN PAMPLONA...THERE WAS FAR LESS FOR US TO TAKE BACK.
NONSENSE! YOU'RE TOO MODEST!
YOU'RE RIGHT, MY FRIENDS, THE GENERAL SWEPT IN WITH HIS TROOPS AND RECLAIMED THIS CITY FOR ME WHEN OTHERS DARED NOT!
AND HE'LL HELP YOU TOO!
I WILL?
REALLY? OH, THANK YOU, LORD MUQTADIR! THANK YOU!
YES, YES, OF COURSE!
NOW GENTLMEN, IF YOU LEAVE US WITH THE GOLD, THE GENERAL AND I WILL STRATEGIZE SO THIS CAMPAIGN WILL WORK!
Chink! Clink!

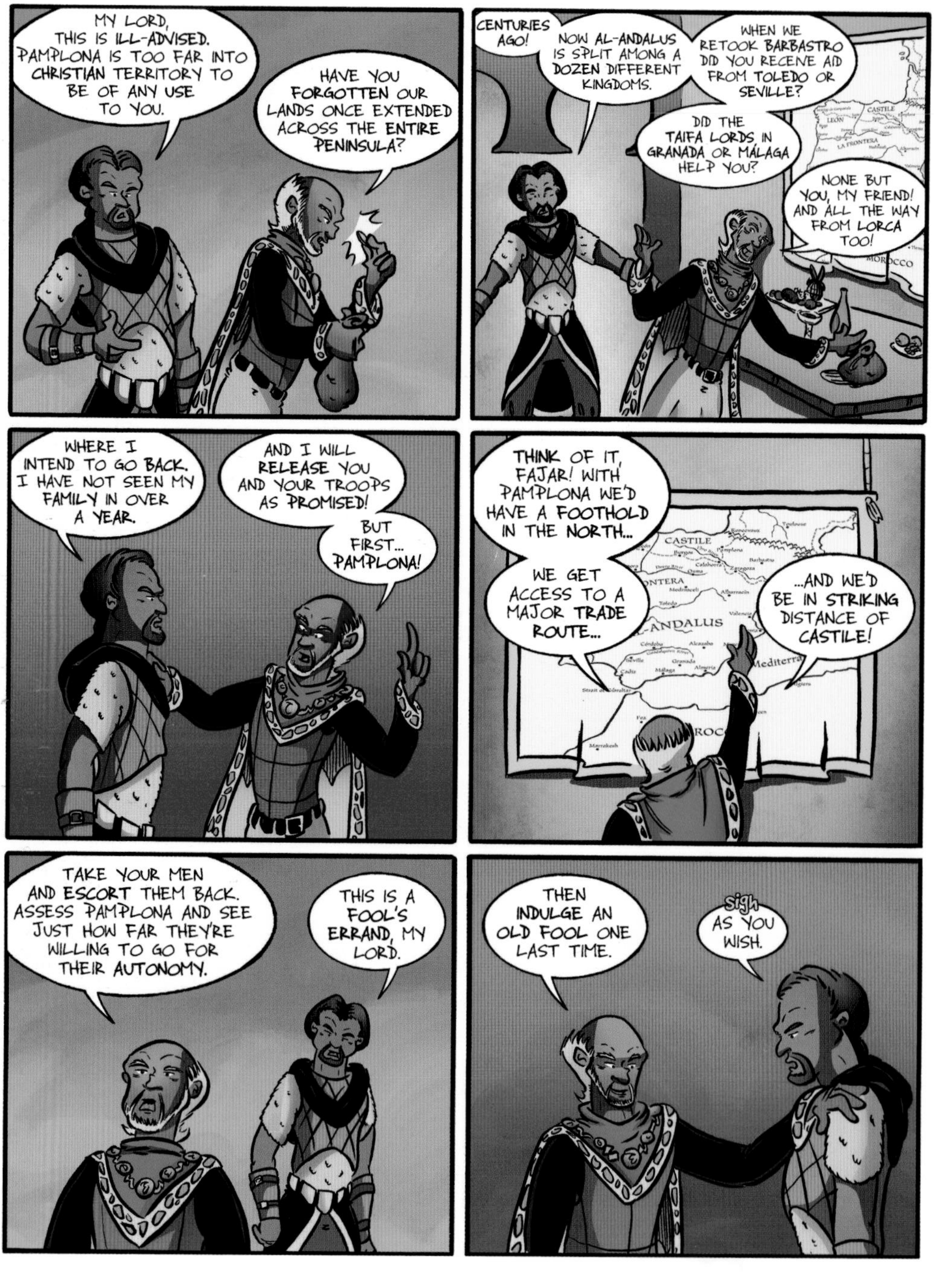
MY LORD, THIS IS ILL-ADVISED. PAMPLONA IS TOO FAR INTO CHRISTIAN TERRITORY TO BE OF ANY USE TO YOU.
HAVE YOU FORGOTTEN OUR LANDS ONCE EXTENDED ACROSS THE ENTIRE PENINSULA?
CENTURIES AGO!
NOW AL-ANDALUS IS SPLIT AMONG A DOZEN DIFFERENT KINGDOMS.
WHEN WE RETOOK BARBASTRO DID YOU RECEIVE AID FROM TOLEDO OR SEVILLE?
DID THE TAIFA LORDS IN GRANADA OR MÁLAGA HELP YOU?
NONE BUT YOU, MY FRIEND! AND ALL THE WAY FROM LORCA TOO!
WHERE I INTEND TO GO BACK. I HAVE NOT SEEN MY FAMILY IN OVER A YEAR.
AND I WILL RELEASE YOU AND YOUR TROOPS AS PROMISED!
BUT FIRST... PAMPLONA!
THINK OF IT, FAJAR! WITH PAMPLONA WE'D HAVE A FOOTHOLD IN THE NORTH...
WE GET ACCESS TO A MAJOR TRADE ROUTE...
...AND WE'D BE IN STRIKING DISTANCE OF CASTILE!
TAKE YOUR MEN AND ESCORT THEM BACK. ASSESS PAMPLONA AND SEE JUST HOW FAR THEY'RE WILLING TO GO FOR THEIR AUTONOMY.
THIS IS A FOOL'S ERRAND, MY LORD.
THEN INDULGE AN OLD FOOL ONE LAST TIME.
sigh
AS YOU WISH.

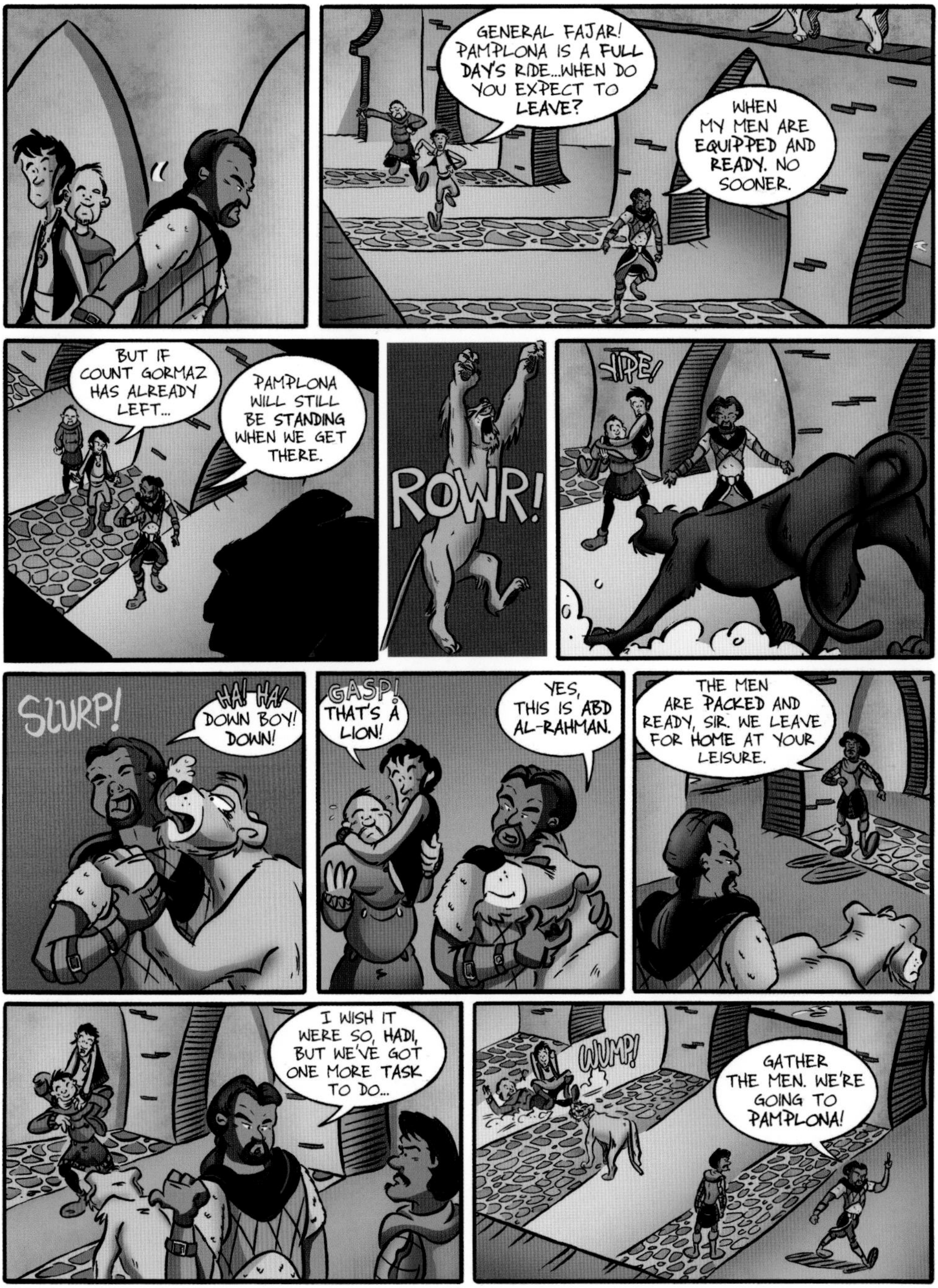
GENERAL FAJAR! PAMPLONA IS A FULL DAY'S RIDE...WHEN DO YOU EXPECT TO LEAVE?
WHEN MY MEN ARE EQUIPPED AND READY. NO SOONER.
BUT IF COUNT GORMAZ HAS ALREADY LEFT...
PAMPLONA WILL STILL BE STANDING WHEN WE GET THERE.
ROWR!
YIPE!
SLURP!
HA! HA! DOWN BOY! DOWN!
GASP! THAT'S A LION!
YES, THIS IS ABD AL-RAHMAN.
THE MEN ARE PACKED AND READY, SIR. WE LEAVE FOR HOME AT YOUR LEISURE.
I WISH IT WERE SO, HADI, BUT WE'VE GOT ONE MORE TASK TO DO...
WUMP!
GATHER THE MEN. WE'RE GOING TO PAMPLONA!

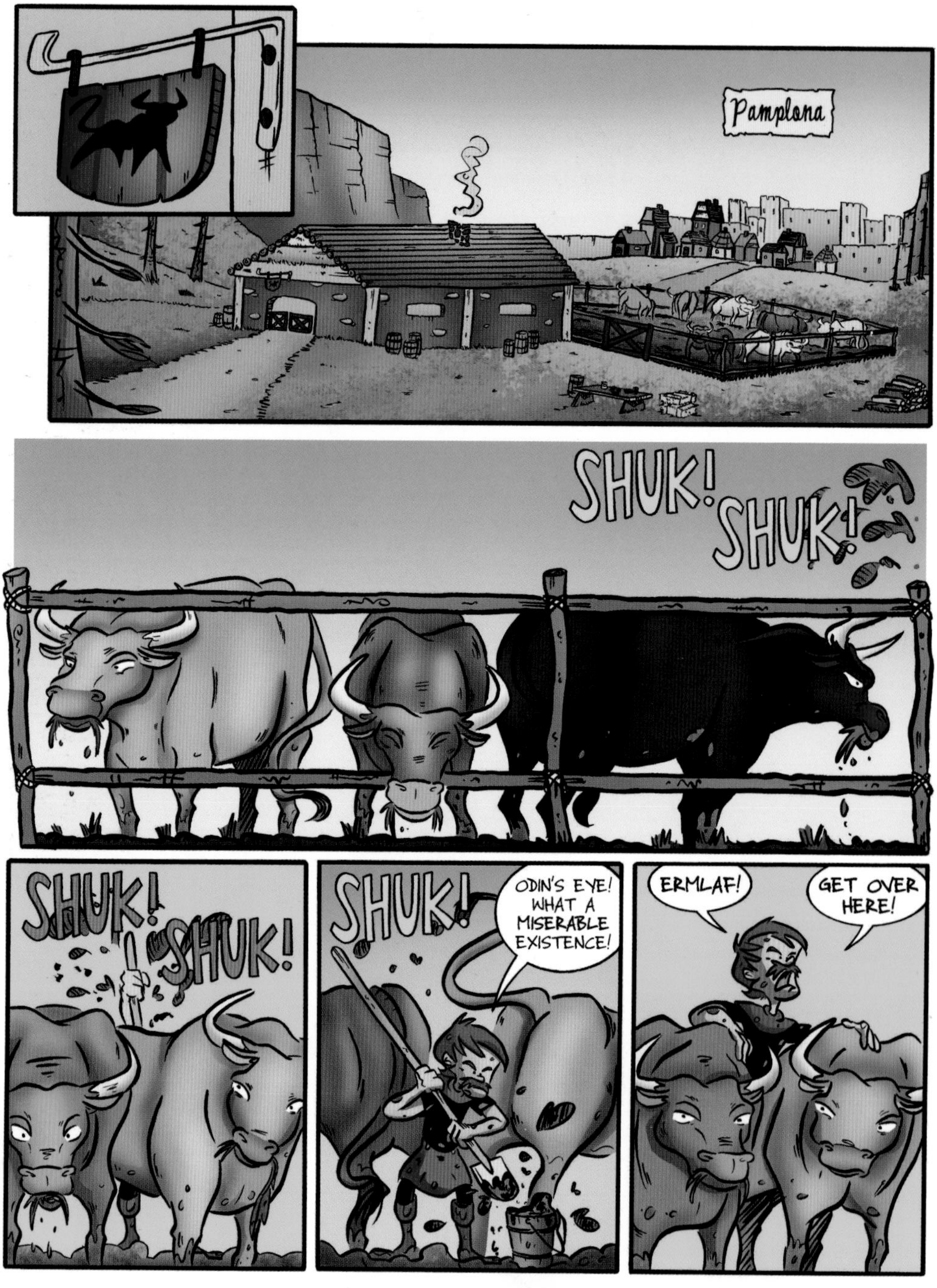
Pamplona
SHUK! SHUK!
SHUK! SHUK!
SHUK!
ODIN'S EYE! WHAT A MISERABLE EXISTENCE!
ERMLAF!
GET OVER HERE!

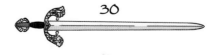

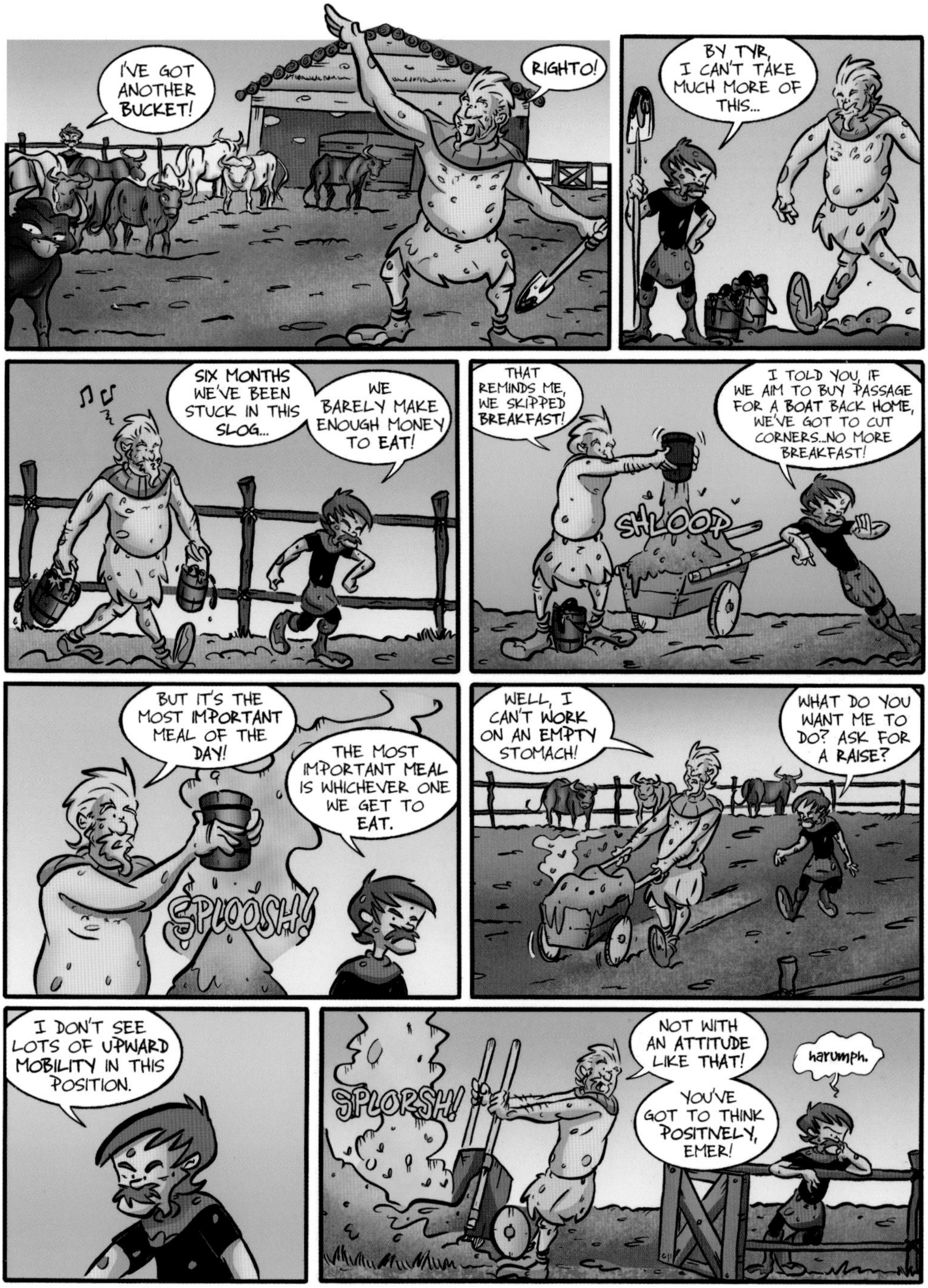
I'VE GOT ANOTHER BUCKET!
RIGHTO!
BY TYR, I CAN'T TAKE MUCH MORE OF THIS...
SIX MONTHS WE'VE BEEN STUCK IN THIS SLOG...
WE BARELY MAKE ENOUGH MONEY TO EAT!
THAT REMINDS ME, WE SKIPPED BREAKFAST!
I TOLD YOU, IF WE AIM TO BUY PASSAGE FOR A BOAT BACK HOME, WE'VE GOT TO CUT CORNERS...NO MORE BREAKFAST!
SHLOOP
BUT IT'S THE MOST IMPORTANT MEAL OF THE DAY!
THE MOST IMPORTANT MEAL IS WHICHEVER ONE WE GET TO EAT.
SPLOOSH!
WELL, I CAN'T WORK ON AN EMPTY STOMACH!
WHAT DO YOU WANT ME TO DO? ASK FOR A RAISE?
I DON'T SEE LOTS OF UPWARD MOBILITY IN THIS POSITION.
SPLORSH!
NOT WITH AN ATTITUDE LIKE THAT!
YOU'VE GOT TO THINK POSITIVELY, EMER!
harumph.

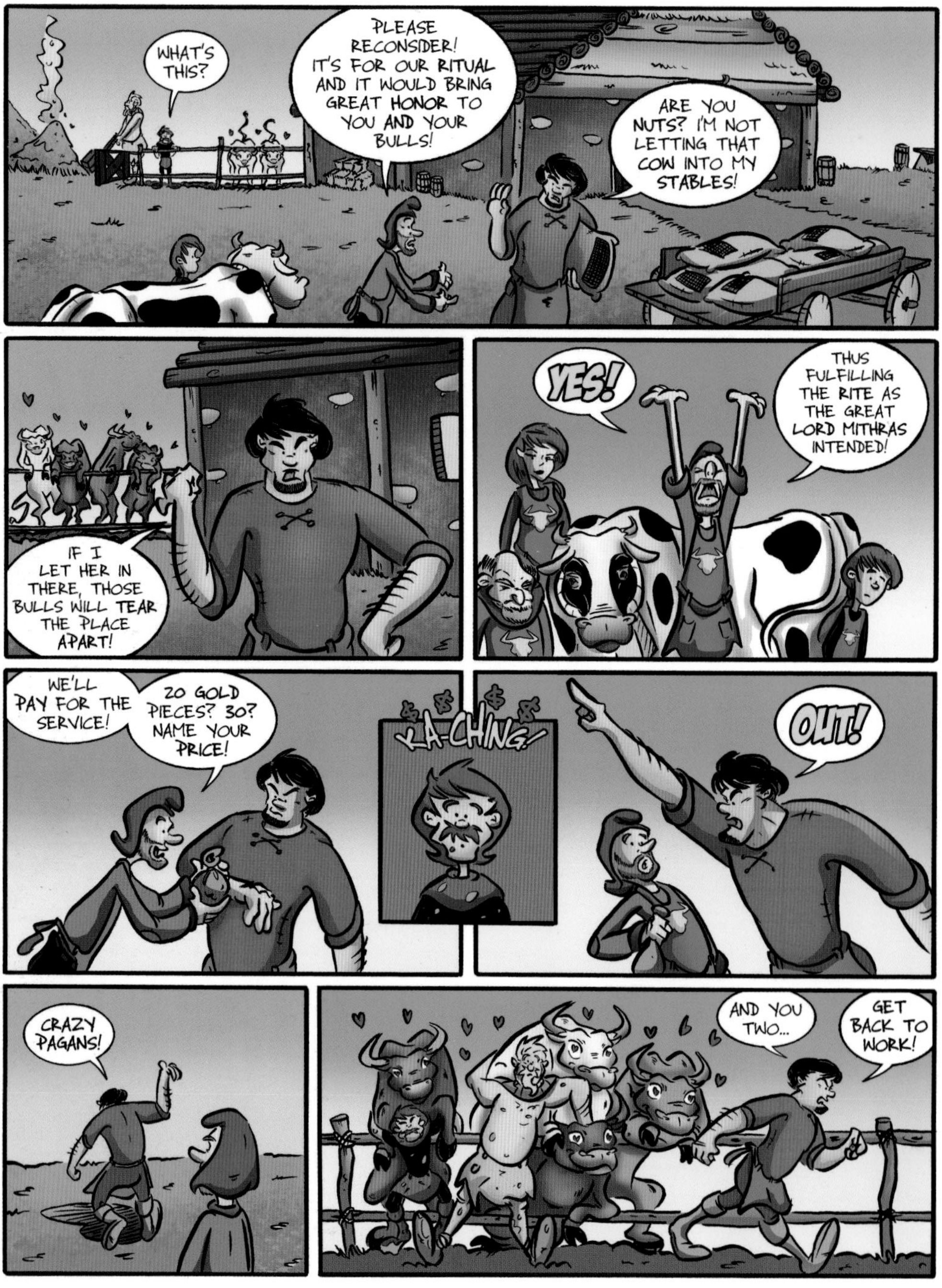
WHAT'S THIS?
PLEASE RECONSIDER! IT'S FOR OUR RITUAL AND IT WOULD BRING GREAT HONOR TO YOU AND YOUR BULLS!
ARE YOU NUTS? I'M NOT LETTING THAT COW INTO MY STABLES!
IF I LET HER IN THERE, THOSE BULLS WILL TEAR THE PLACE APART!
YES!
THUS FULFILLING THE RITE AS THE GREAT LORD MITHRAS INTENDED!
WE'LL PAY FOR THE SERVICE!
20 GOLD PIECES? 30? NAME YOUR PRICE!
KA-CHING!
OUT!
CRAZY PAGANS!
AND YOU TWO...
GET BACK TO WORK!

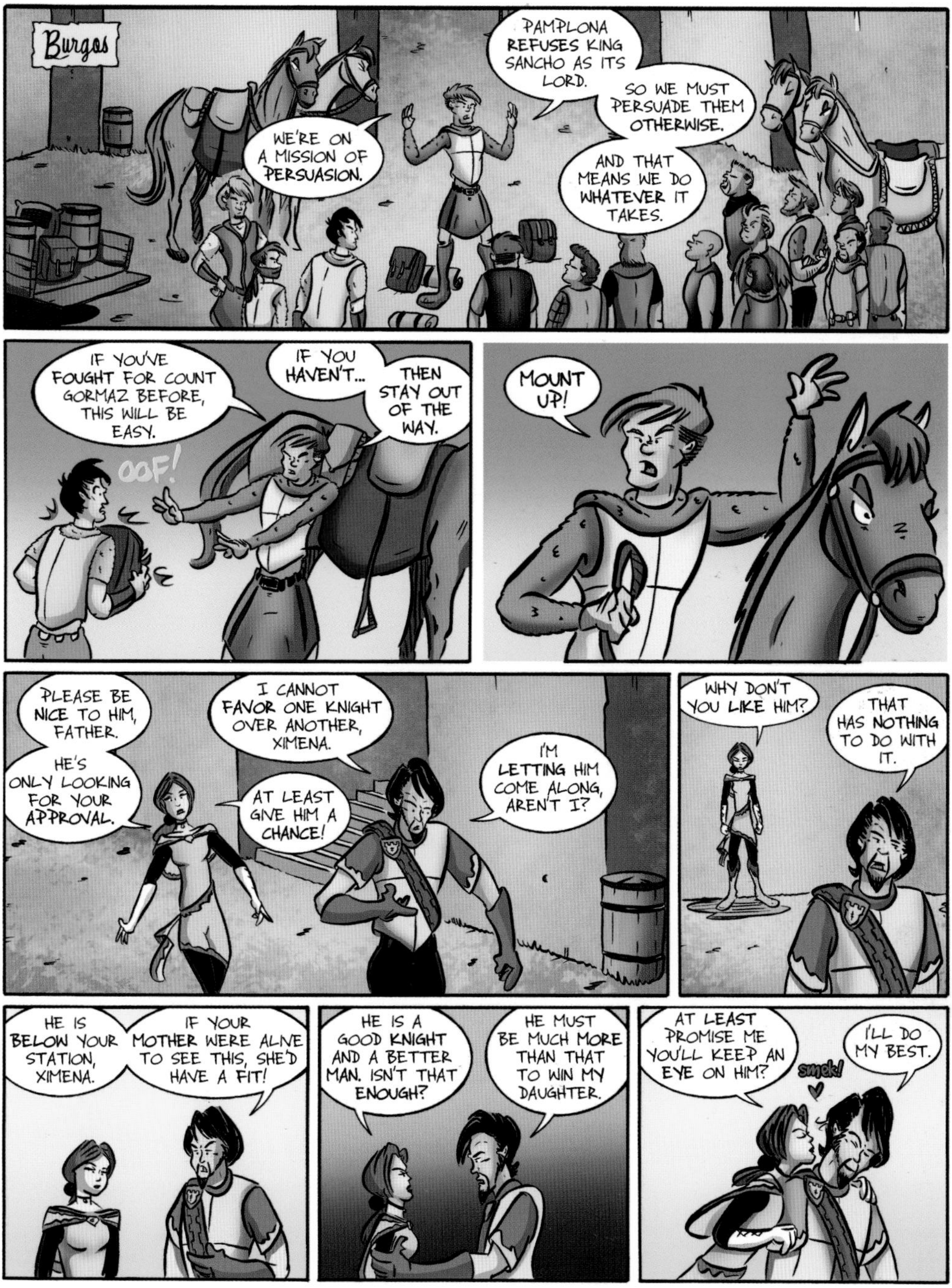
Burgos
WE'RE ON A MISSION OF PERSUASION.
PAMPLONA REFUSES KING SANCHO AS ITS LORD.
SO WE MUST PERSUADE THEM OTHERWISE.
AND THAT MEANS WE DO WHATEVER IT TAKES.
IF YOU'VE FOUGHT FOR COUNT GORMAZ BEFORE, THIS WILL BE EASY.
IF YOU HAVEN'T...
THEN STAY OUT OF THE WAY.
OOF!
MOUNT UP!
PLEASE BE NICE TO HIM, FATHER.
HE'S ONLY LOOKING FOR YOUR APPROVAL.
I CANNOT FAVOR ONE KNIGHT OVER ANOTHER, XIMENA.
AT LEAST GIVE HIM A CHANCE!
I'M LETTING HIM COME ALONG, AREN'T I?
WHY DON'T YOU LIKE HIM?
THAT HAS NOTHING TO DO WITH IT.
HE IS BELOW YOUR STATION, XIMENA.
IF YOUR MOTHER WERE ALIVE TO SEE THIS, SHE'D HAVE A FIT!
HE IS A GOOD KNIGHT AND A BETTER MAN. ISN'T THAT ENOUGH?
HE MUST BE MUCH MORE THAN THAT TO WIN MY DAUGHTER.
AT LEAST PROMISE ME YOU'LL KEEP AN EYE ON HIM?
smek!
I'LL DO MY BEST.

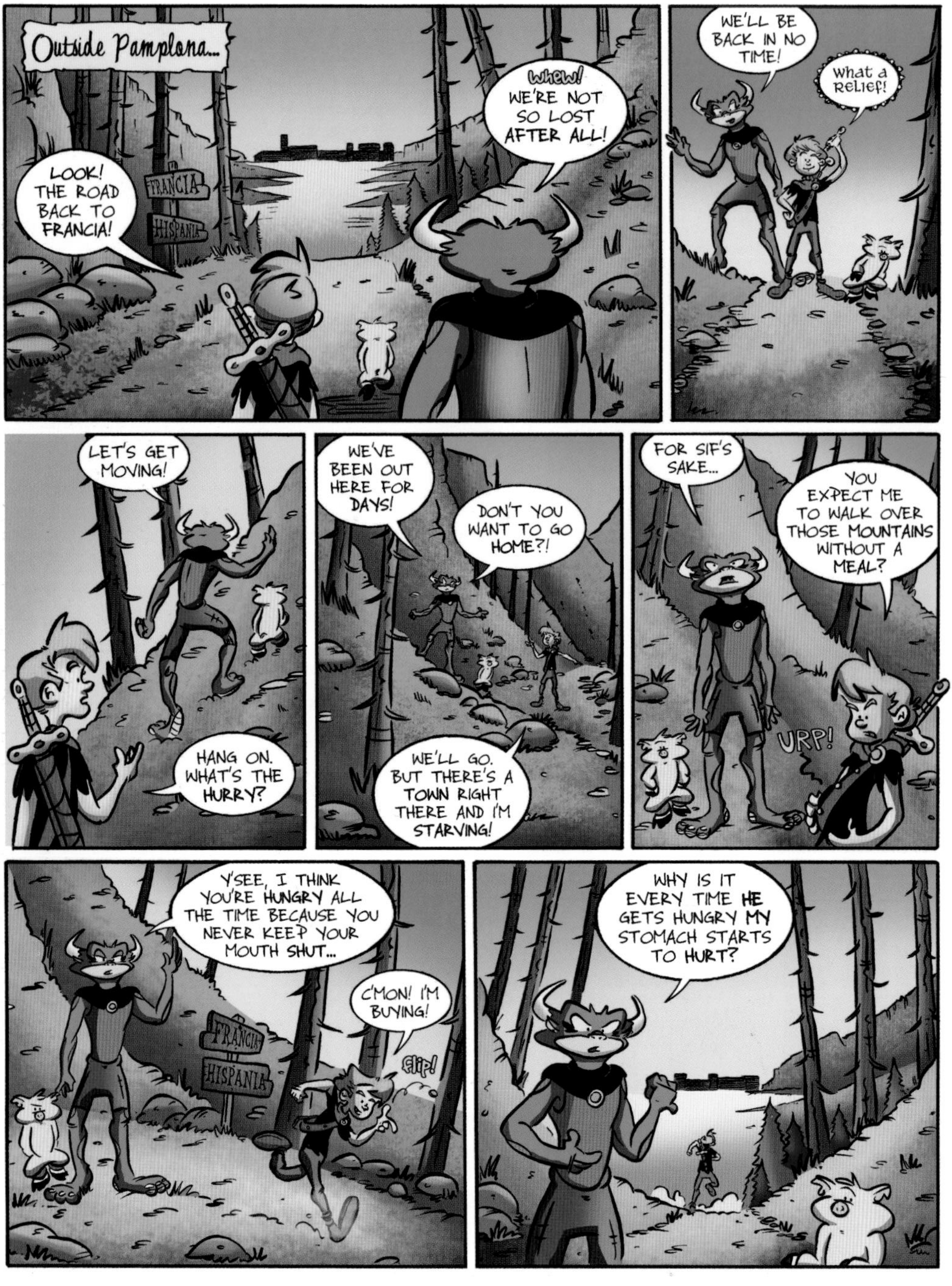
Outside Pamplona...
LOOK! THE ROAD BACK TO FRANCIA!
FRANCIA
HISPANIA
whew! WE'RE NOT SO LOST AFTER ALL!
WE'LL BE BACK IN NO TIME!
What a Relief!
LET'S GET MOVING!
HANG ON. WHAT'S THE HURRY?
WE'VE BEEN OUT HERE FOR DAYS!
DON'T YOU WANT TO GO HOME?!
WE'LL GO. BUT THERE'S A TOWN RIGHT THERE AND I'M STARVING!
FOR SIF'S SAKE...
YOU EXPECT ME TO WALK OVER THOSE MOUNTAINS WITHOUT A MEAL?
URP!
Y'SEE, I THINK YOU'RE HUNGRY ALL THE TIME BECAUSE YOU NEVER KEEP YOUR MOUTH SHUT...
C'MON! I'M BUYING!
FRANCIA
HISPANIA
Flip!
WHY IS IT EVERY TIME HE GETS HUNGRY MY STOMACH STARTS TO HURT?

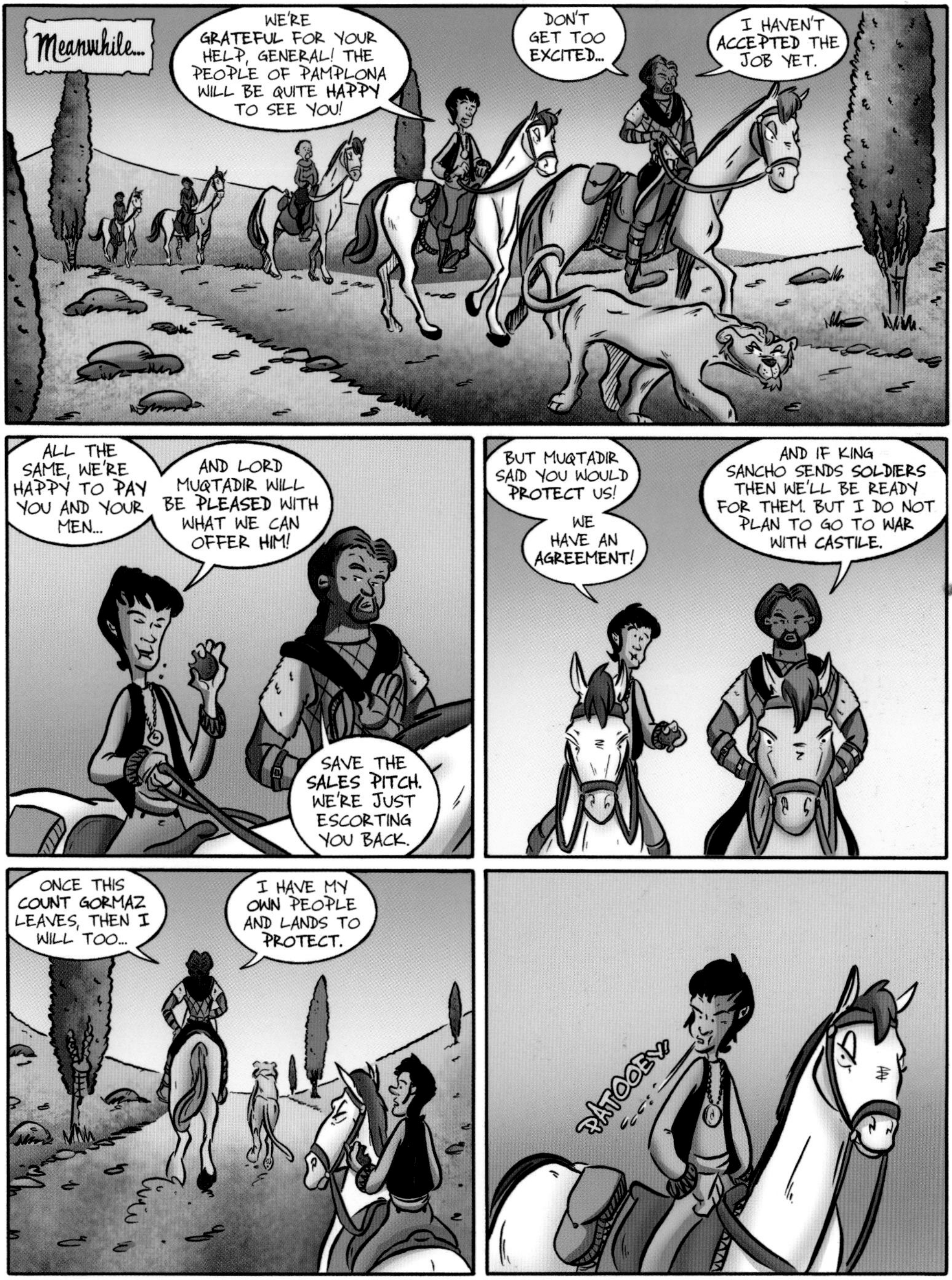
Meanwhile...
WE'RE GRATEFUL FOR YOUR HELP, GENERAL! THE PEOPLE OF PAMPLONA WILL BE QUITE HAPPY TO SEE YOU!
DON'T GET TOO EXCITED...
I HAVEN'T ACCEPTED THE JOB YET.
ALL THE SAME, WE'RE HAPPY TO PAY YOU AND YOUR MEN...
AND LORD MUQTADIR WILL BE PLEASED WITH WHAT WE CAN OFFER HIM!
SAVE THE SALES PITCH. WE'RE JUST ESCORTING YOU BACK.
BUT MUQTADIR SAID YOU WOULD PROTECT US!
WE HAVE AN AGREEMENT!
AND IF KING SANCHO SENDS SOLDIERS THEN WE'LL BE READY FOR THEM. BUT I DO NOT PLAN TO GO TO WAR WITH CASTILE.
ONCE THIS COUNT GORMAZ LEAVES, THEN I WILL TOO...
I HAVE MY OWN PEOPLE AND LANDS TO PROTECT.
PATOOEY!

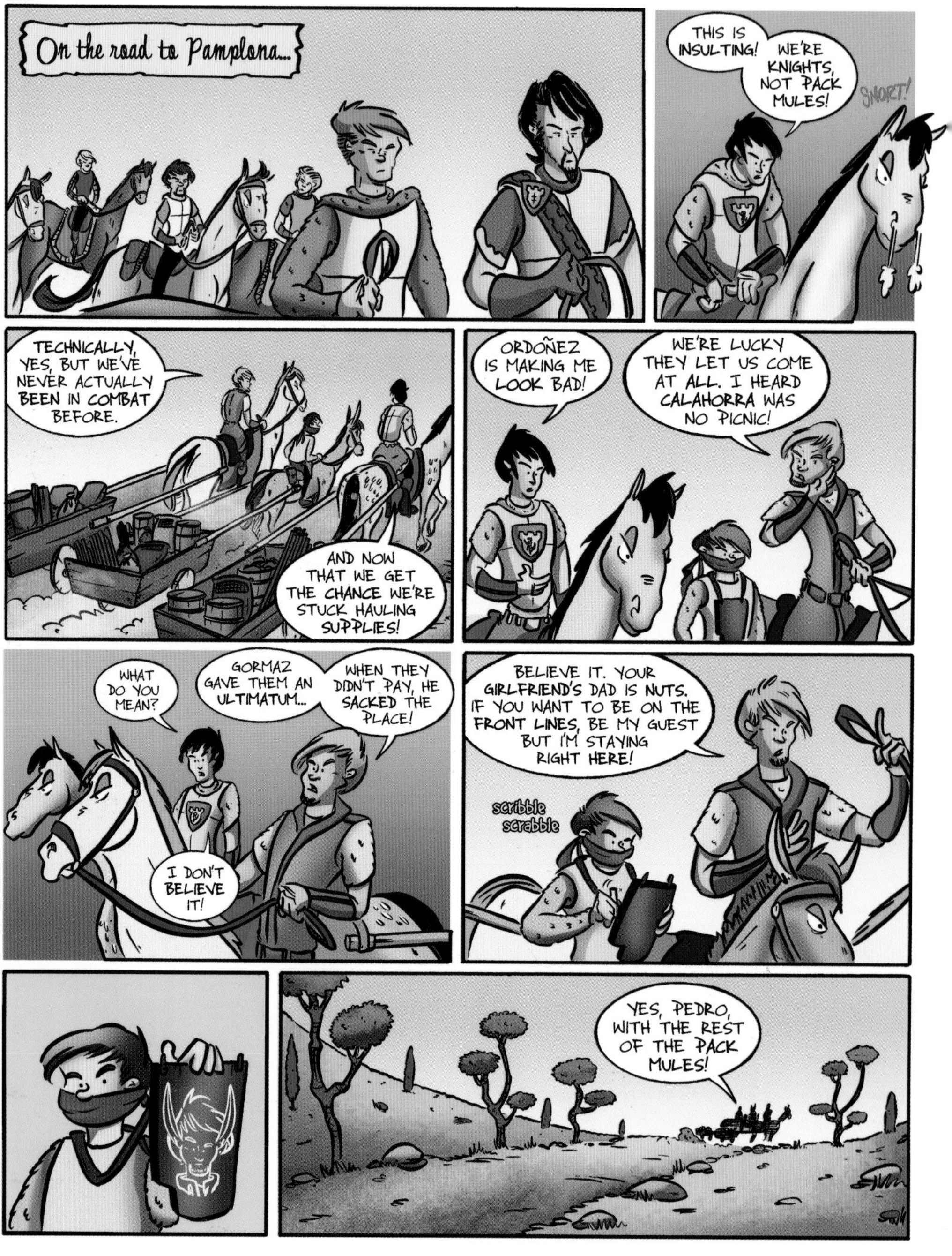
On the road to Pamplona...
THIS IS INSULTING!
WE'RE KNIGHTS, NOT PACK MULES!
SNORT!
TECHNICALLY, YES, BUT WE'VE NEVER ACTUALLY BEEN IN COMBAT BEFORE.
AND NOW THAT WE GET THE CHANCE WE'RE STUCK HAULING SUPPLIES!
ORDOÑEZ IS MAKING ME LOOK BAD!
WE'RE LUCKY THEY LET US COME AT ALL. I HEARD CALAHORRA WAS NO PICNIC!
WHAT DO YOU MEAN?
GORMAZ GAVE THEM AN ULTIMATUM...
WHEN THEY DIDN'T PAY, HE SACKED THE PLACE!
I DON'T BELIEVE IT!
BELIEVE IT. YOUR GIRLFRIEND'S DAD IS NUTS. IF YOU WANT TO BE ON THE FRONT LINES, BE MY GUEST BUT I'M STAYING RIGHT HERE!
scribble scrabble
YES, PEDRO, WITH THE REST OF THE PACK MULES!

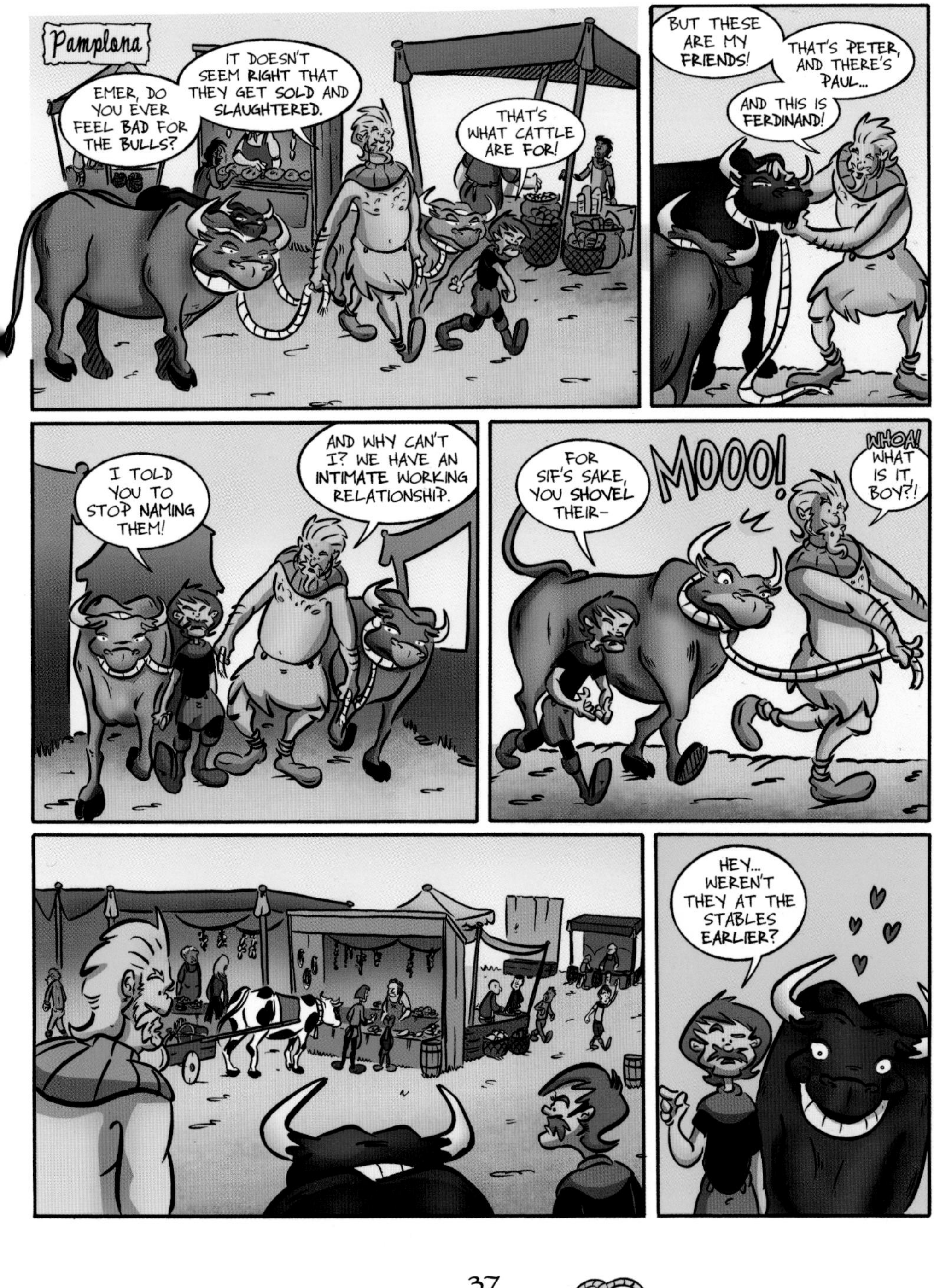
Pamplona
EMER, DO YOU EVER FEEL BAD FOR THE BULLS?
IT DOESN'T SEEM RIGHT THAT THEY GET SOLD AND SLAUGHTERED.
THAT'S WHAT CATTLE ARE FOR!
BUT THESE ARE MY FRIENDS!
THAT'S PETER, AND THERE'S PAUL...
AND THIS IS FERDINAND!
I TOLD YOU TO STOP NAMING THEM!
AND WHY CAN'T I? WE HAVE AN INTIMATE WORKING RELATIONSHIP.
FOR SIF'S SAKE, YOU SHOVEL THEIR-
MOOO!
WHOA! WHAT IS IT, BOY?!
HEY... WEREN'T THEY AT THE STABLES EARLIER?

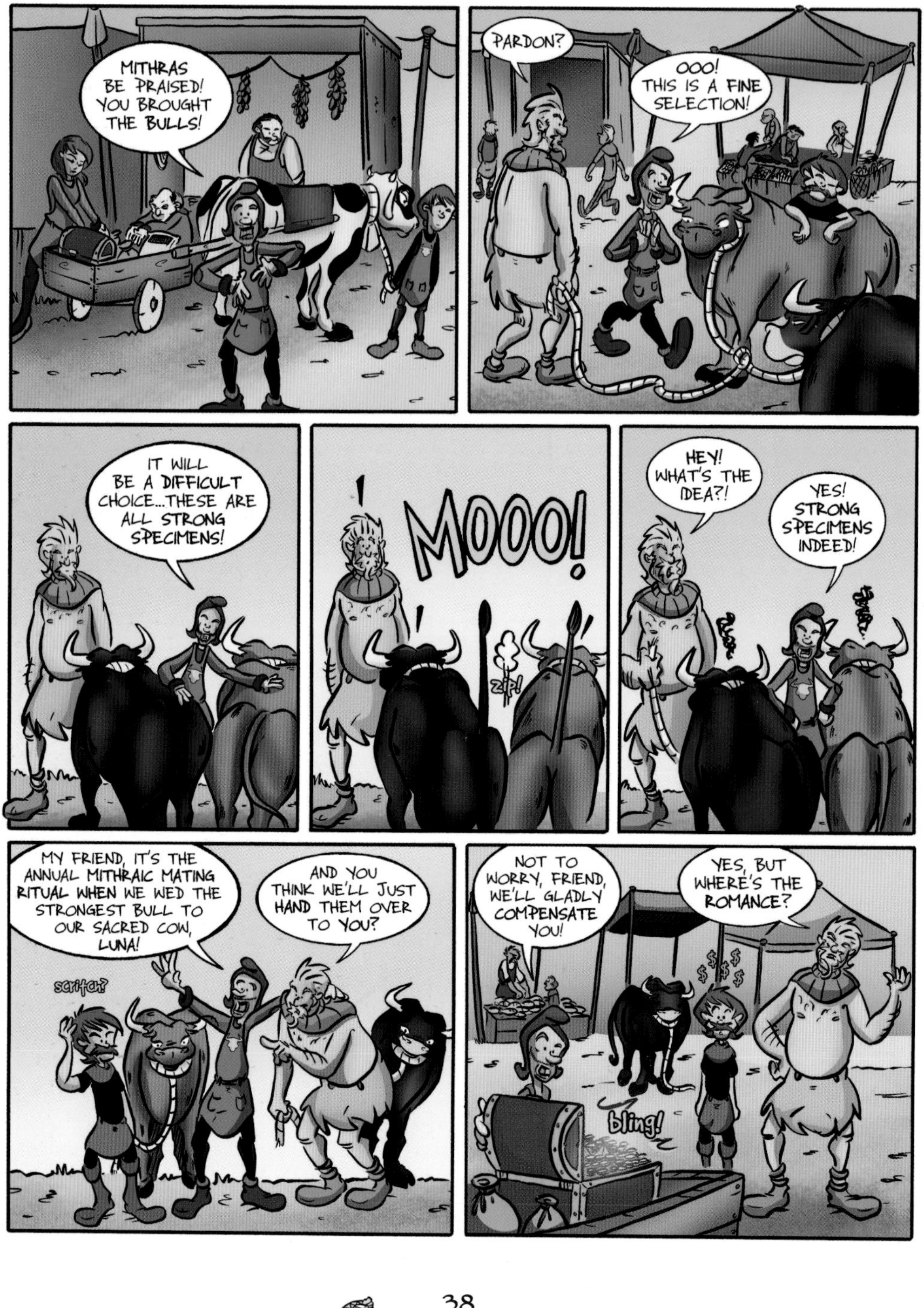
MITHRAS BE PRAISED! YOU BROUGHT THE BULLS!
PARDON?
OOO! THIS IS A FINE SELECTION!
IT WILL BE A DIFFICULT CHOICE...THESE ARE ALL STRONG SPECIMENS!
MOOO!
zip!
HEY! WHAT'S THE IDEA?!
YES! STRONG SPECIMENS INDEED!
MY FRIEND, IT'S THE ANNUAL MITHRAIC MATING RITUAL WHEN WE WED THE STRONGEST BULL TO OUR SACRED COW, LUNA!
AND YOU THINK WE'LL JUST HAND THEM OVER TO YOU?
scritch?
NOT TO WORRY, FRIEND, WE'LL GLADLY COMPENSATE YOU!
YES, BUT WHERE'S THE ROMANCE?
bling!

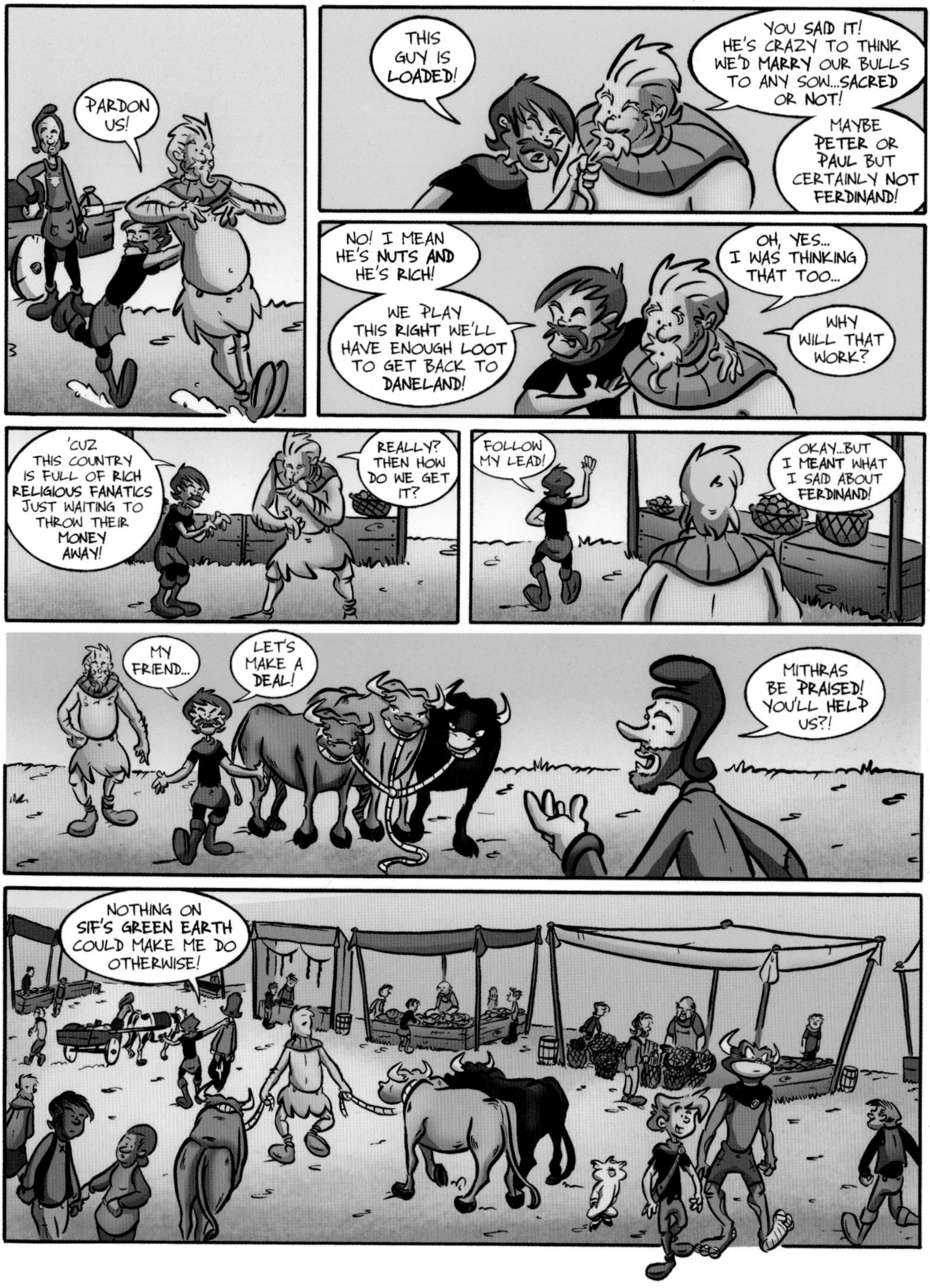
PARDON US!
THIS GUY IS LOADED!
YOU SAID IT! HE'S CRAZY TO THINK WE'D MARRY OUR BULLS TO ANY SOW...SACRED OR NOT!
MAYBE PETER OR PAUL BUT CERTAINLY NOT FERDINAND!
NO! I MEAN HE'S NUTS AND HE'S RICH!
WE PLAY THIS RIGHT WE'LL HAVE ENOUGH LOOT TO GET BACK TO DANELAND!
OH, YES... I WAS THINKING THAT TOO...
WHY WILL THAT WORK?
'CUZ THIS COUNTRY IS FULL OF RICH RELIGIOUS FANATICS JUST WAITING TO THROW THEIR MONEY AWAY!
REALLY? THEN HOW DO WE GET IT?
FOLLOW MY LEAD!
OKAY...BUT I MEANT WHAT I SAID ABOUT FERDINAND!
MY FRIEND...
LET'S MAKE A DEAL!
MITHRAS BE PRAISED! YOU'LL HELP US?!
NOTHING ON SIF'S GREEN EARTH COULD MAKE ME DO OTHERWISE!

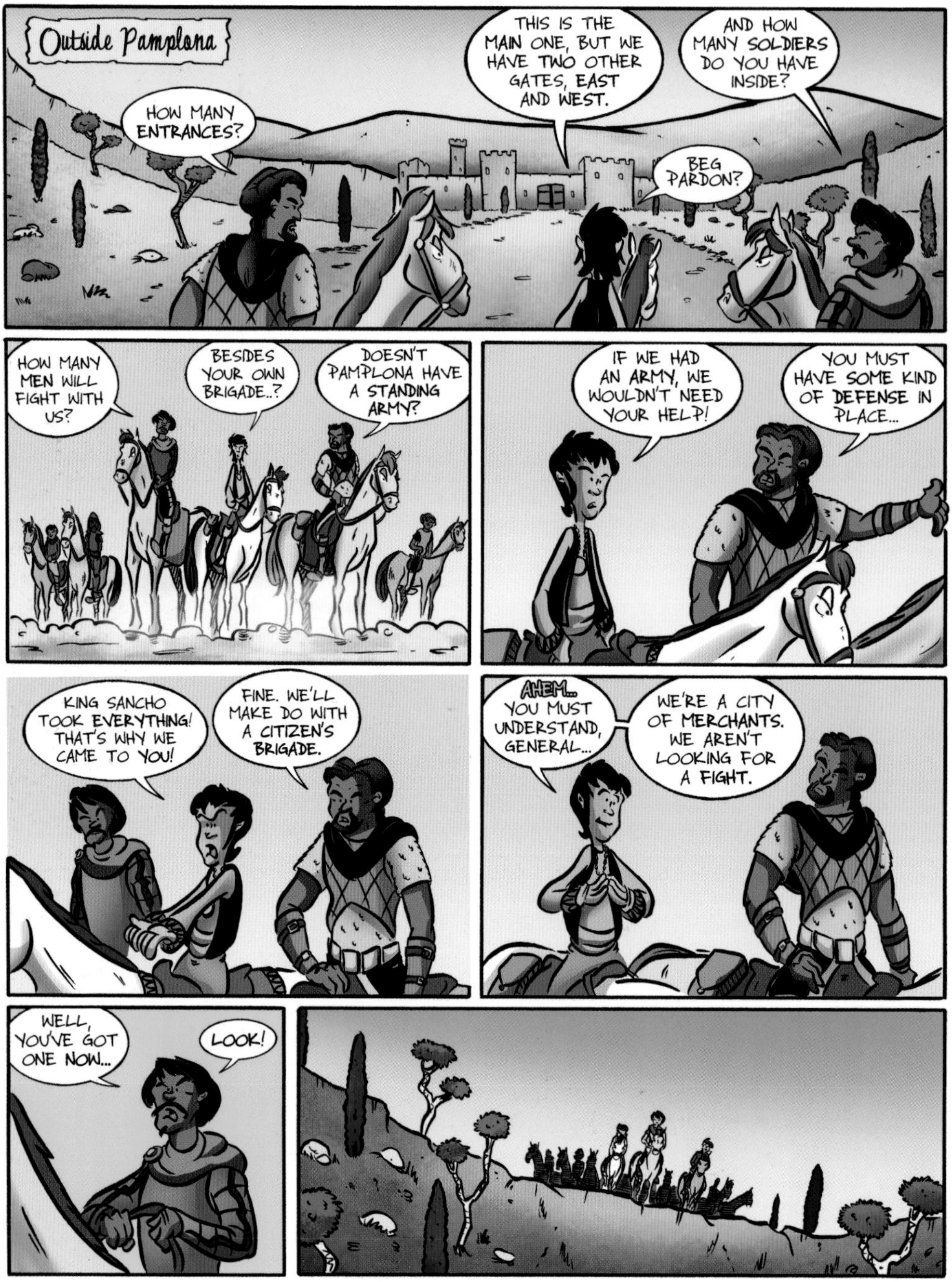
Outside Pamplona
HOW MANY ENTRANCES?
THIS IS THE MAIN ONE, BUT WE HAVE TWO OTHER GATES, EAST AND WEST.
AND HOW MANY SOLDIERS DO YOU HAVE INSIDE?
BEG PARDON?
HOW MANY MEN WILL FIGHT WITH US?
BESIDES YOUR OWN BRIGADE..?
DOESN'T PAMPLONA HAVE A STANDING ARMY?
IF WE HAD AN ARMY, WE WOULDN'T NEED YOUR HELP!
YOU MUST HAVE SOME KIND OF DEFENSE IN PLACE...
KING SANCHO TOOK EVERYTHING! THAT'S WHY WE CAME TO YOU!
FINE. WE'LL MAKE DO WITH A CITIZEN'S BRIGADE.
AHEM... YOU MUST UNDERSTAND, GENERAL...
WE'RE A CITY OF MERCHANTS. WE AREN'T LOOKING FOR A FIGHT.
WELL, YOU'VE GOT ONE NOW...
LOOK!

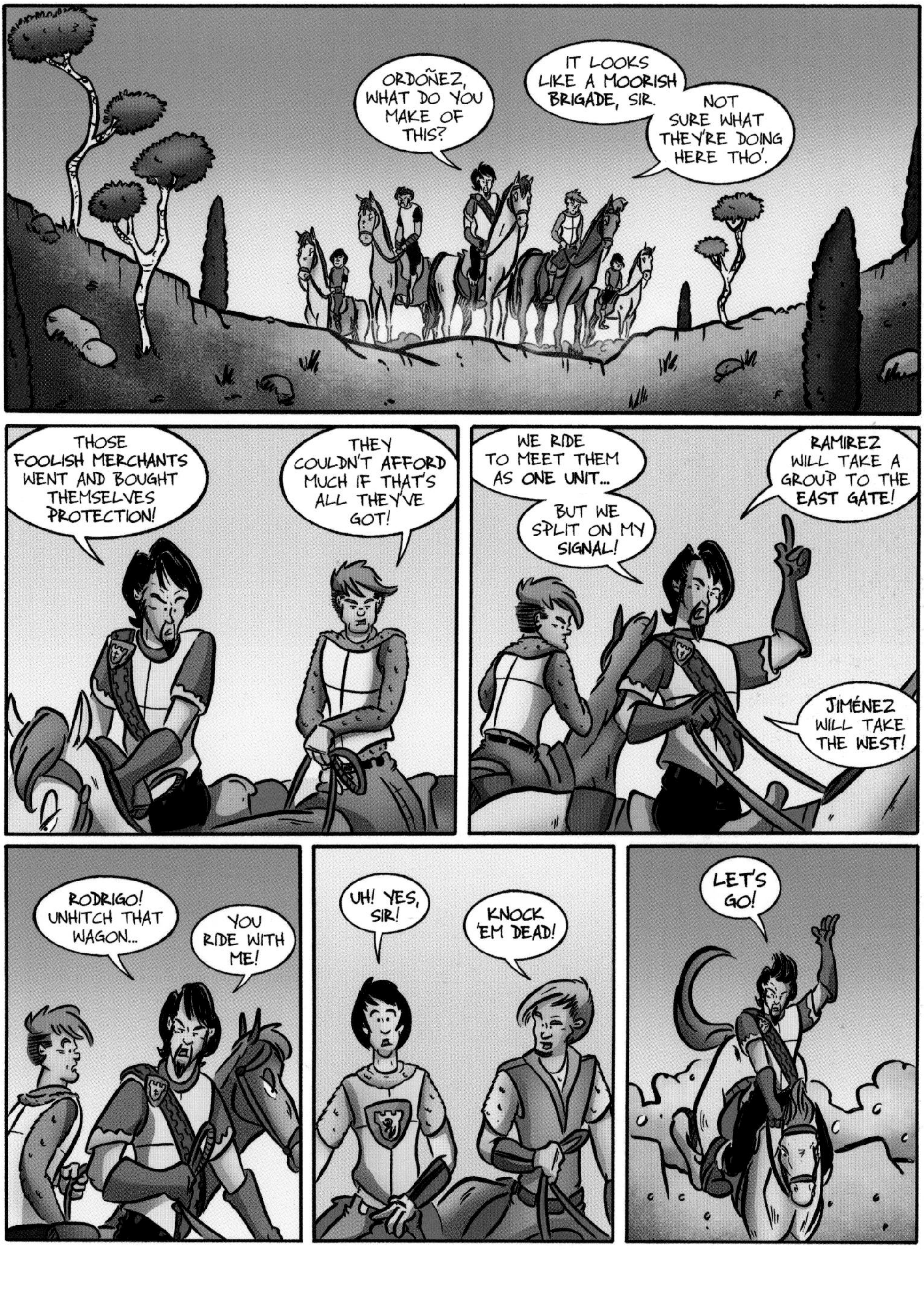
ORDOÑEZ, WHAT DO YOU MAKE OF THIS?
IT LOOKS LIKE A MOORISH BRIGADE, SIR.
NOT SURE WHAT THEY'RE DOING HERE THO'.
THOSE FOOLISH MERCHANTS WENT AND BOUGHT THEMSELVES PROTECTION!
THEY COULDN'T AFFORD MUCH IF THAT'S ALL THEY'VE GOT!
WE RIDE TO MEET THEM AS ONE UNIT...
BUT WE SPLIT ON MY SIGNAL!
RAMIREZ WILL TAKE A GROUP TO THE EAST GATE!
JIMÉNEZ WILL TAKE THE WEST!
RODRIGO! UNHITCH THAT WAGON...
YOU RIDE WITH ME!
UH! YES, SIR!
KNOCK 'EM DEAD!
LET'S GO!

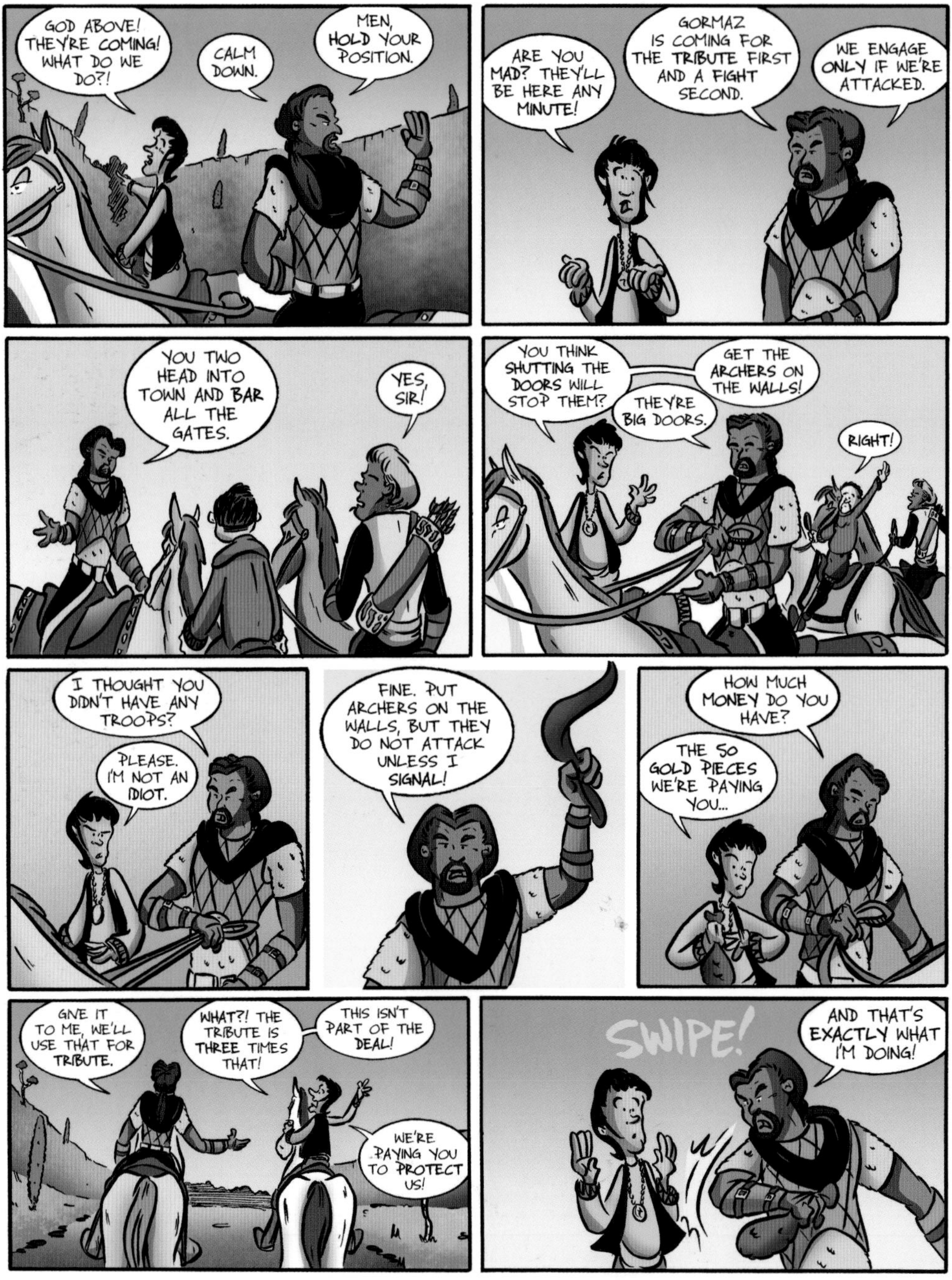
GOD ABOVE! THEY'RE COMING! WHAT DO WE DO?!
CALM DOWN.
MEN, HOLD YOUR POSITION.
ARE YOU MAD? THEY'LL BE HERE ANY MINUTE!
GORMAZ IS COMING FOR THE TRIBUTE FIRST AND A FIGHT SECOND.
WE ENGAGE ONLY IF WE'RE ATTACKED.
YOU TWO HEAD INTO TOWN AND BAR ALL THE GATES.
YES, SIR!
YOU THINK SHUTTING THE DOORS WILL STOP THEM?
THEY'RE BIG DOORS.
GET THE ARCHERS ON THE WALLS!
RIGHT!
I THOUGHT YOU DIDN'T HAVE ANY TROOPS?
PLEASE. I'M NOT AN IDIOT.
FINE. PUT ARCHERS ON THE WALLS, BUT THEY DO NOT ATTACK UNLESS I SIGNAL!
HOW MUCH MONEY DO YOU HAVE?
THE 50 GOLD PIECES WE'RE PAYING YOU...
GIVE IT TO ME, WE'LL USE THAT FOR TRIBUTE.
WHAT?! THE TRIBUTE IS THREE TIMES THAT!
THIS ISN'T PART OF THE DEAL!
WE'RE PAYING YOU TO PROTECT US!
SWIPE!
AND THAT'S EXACTLY WHAT I'M DOING!

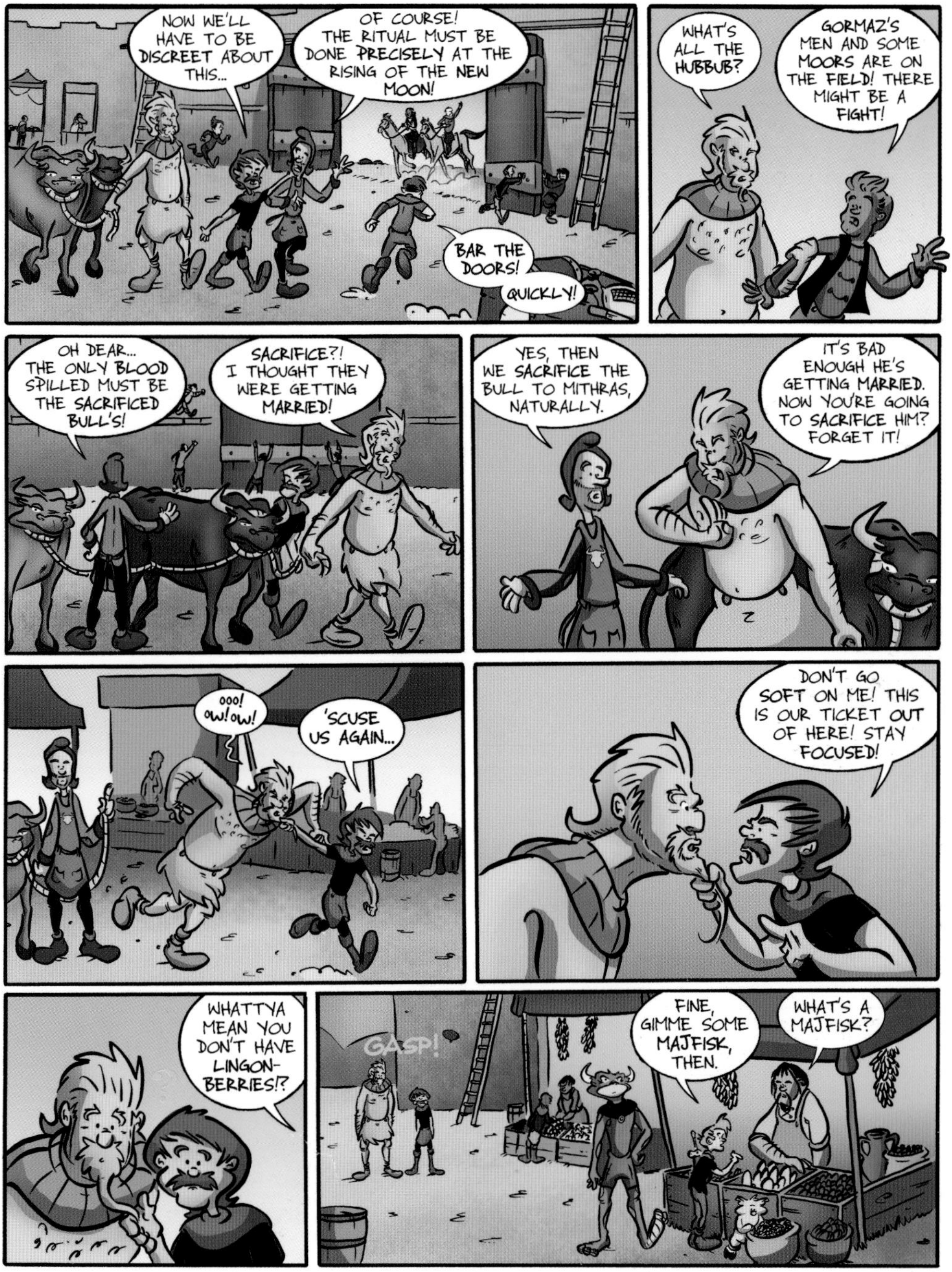
NOW WE'LL HAVE TO BE DISCREET ABOUT THIS...
OF COURSE! THE RITUAL MUST BE DONE PRECISELY AT THE RISING OF THE NEW MOON!
BAR THE DOORS!
QUICKLY!
WHAT'S ALL THE HUBBUB?
GORMAZ'S MEN AND SOME MOORS ARE ON THE FIELD! THERE MIGHT BE A FIGHT!
OH DEAR... THE ONLY BLOOD SPILLED MUST BE THE SACRIFICED BULL'S!
SACRIFICE?! I THOUGHT THEY WERE GETTING MARRIED!
YES, THEN WE SACRIFICE THE BULL TO MITHRAS, NATURALLY.
IT'S BAD ENOUGH HE'S GETTING MARRIED. NOW YOU'RE GOING TO SACRIFICE HIM? FORGET IT!
OOO! OW! OW!
'SCUSE US AGAIN...
DON'T GO SOFT ON ME! THIS IS OUR TICKET OUT OF HERE! STAY FOCUSED!
WHATTYA MEAN YOU DON'T HAVE LINGON-BERRIES!?
GASP!
FINE, GIMME SOME MAJFISK, THEN.
WHAT'S A MAJFISK?

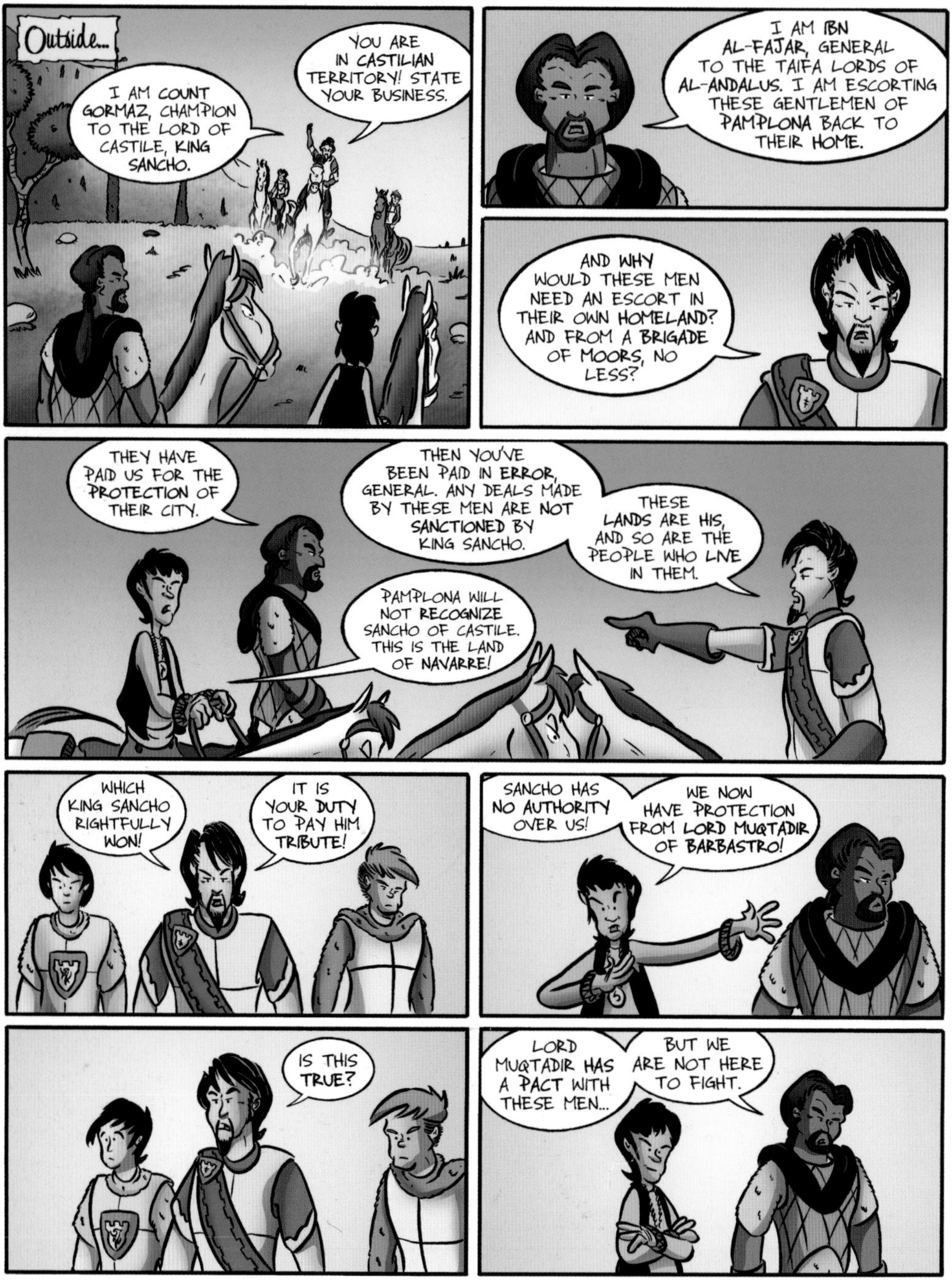
Outside...
YOU ARE IN CASTILIAN TERRITORY! STATE YOUR BUSINESS.
I AM COUNT GORMAZ, CHAMPION TO THE LORD OF CASTILE, KING SANCHO.
I AM IBN AL-FAJAR, GENERAL TO THE TAIFA LORDS OF AL-ANDALUS. I AM ESCORTING THESE GENTLEMEN OF PAMPLONA BACK TO THEIR HOME.
AND WHY WOULD THESE MEN NEED AN ESCORT IN THEIR OWN HOMELAND? AND FROM A BRIGADE OF MOORS, NO LESS?
THEY HAVE PAID US FOR THE PROTECTION OF THEIR CITY.
THEN YOU'VE BEEN PAID IN ERROR, GENERAL. ANY DEALS MADE BY THESE MEN ARE NOT SANCTIONED BY KING SANCHO.
THESE LANDS ARE HIS, AND SO ARE THE PEOPLE WHO LIVE IN THEM.
PAMPLONA WILL NOT RECOGNIZE SANCHO OF CASTILE. THIS IS THE LAND OF NAVARRE!
WHICH KING SANCHO RIGHTFULLY WON!
IT IS YOUR DUTY TO PAY HIM TRIBUTE!
SANCHO HAS NO AUTHORITY OVER US!
WE NOW HAVE PROTECTION FROM LORD MUQTADIR OF BARBASTRO!
IS THIS TRUE?
LORD MUQTADIR HAS A PACT WITH THESE MEN...
BUT WE ARE NOT HERE TO FIGHT.

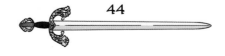

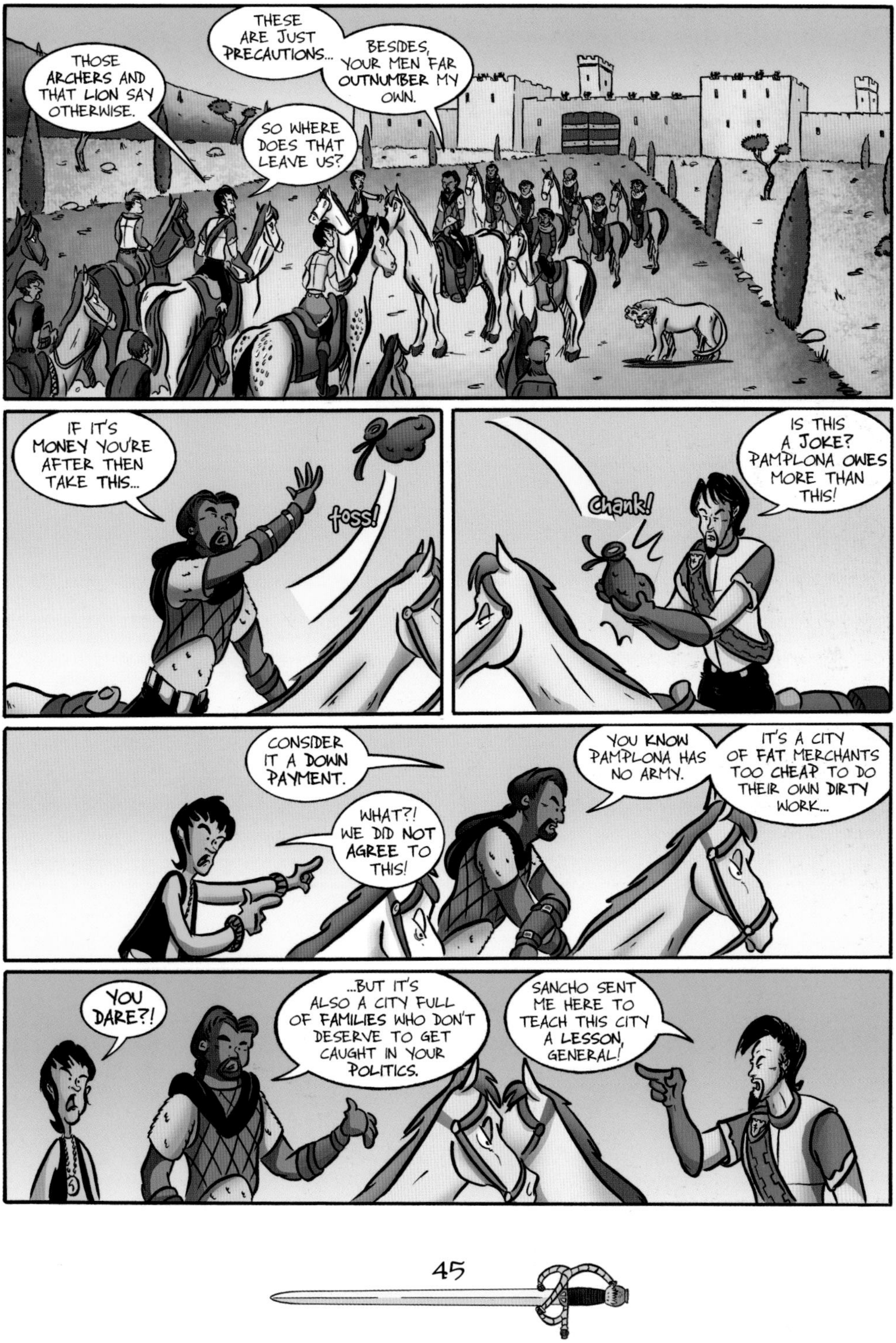
THOSE ARCHERS AND THAT LION SAY OTHERWISE.
THESE ARE JUST PRECAUTIONS...
BESIDES, YOUR MEN FAR OUTNUMBER MY OWN.
SO WHERE DOES THAT LEAVE US?
IF IT'S MONEY YOU'RE AFTER THEN TAKE THIS...
toss!
Chank!
IS THIS A JOKE? PAMPLONA OWES MORE THAN THIS!
CONSIDER IT A DOWN PAYMENT.
WHAT?! WE DID NOT AGREE TO THIS!
YOU KNOW PAMPLONA HAS NO ARMY.
IT'S A CITY OF FAT MERCHANTS TOO CHEAP TO DO THEIR OWN DIRTY WORK...
YOU DARE?!
...BUT IT'S ALSO A CITY FULL OF FAMILIES WHO DON'T DESERVE TO GET CAUGHT IN YOUR POLITICS.
SANCHO SENT ME HERE TO TEACH THIS CITY A LESSON, GENERAL!

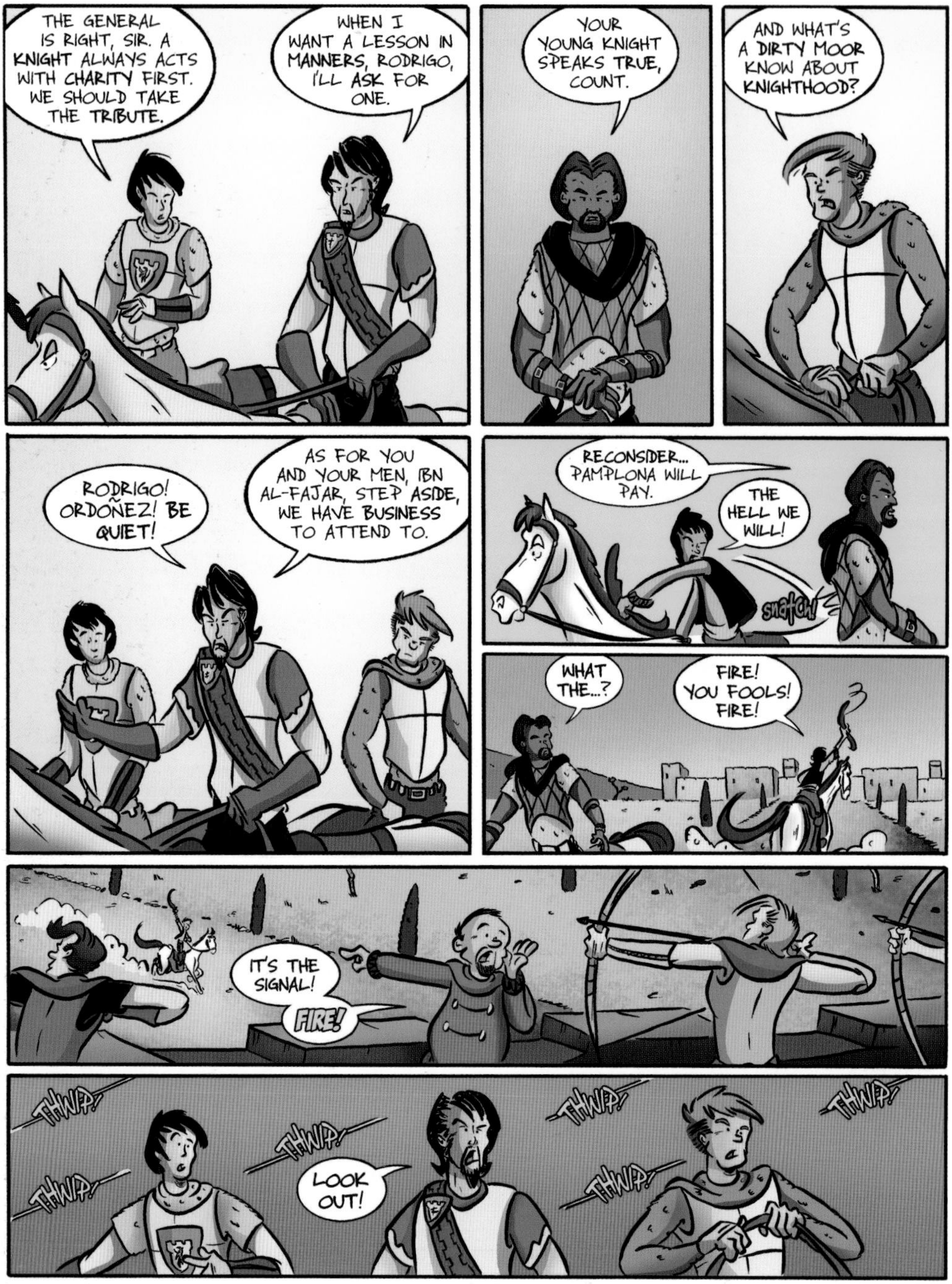
THE GENERAL IS RIGHT, SIR. A KNIGHT ALWAYS ACTS WITH CHARITY FIRST. WE SHOULD TAKE THE TRIBUTE.
WHEN I WANT A LESSON IN MANNERS, RODRIGO, I'LL ASK FOR ONE.
YOUR YOUNG KNIGHT SPEAKS TRUE, COUNT.
AND WHAT'S A DIRTY MOOR KNOW ABOUT KNIGHTHOOD?
RODRIGO! ORDOÑEZ! BE QUIET!
AS FOR YOU AND YOUR MEN, IBN AL-FAJAR, STEP ASIDE, WE HAVE BUSINESS TO ATTEND TO.
RECONSIDER... PAMPLONA WILL PAY.
THE HELL WE WILL!
SNATCH!
WHAT THE...?
FIRE! YOU FOOLS! FIRE!
IT'S THE SIGNAL!
FIRE!
THWIP!
THWIP!
THWIP!
LOOK OUT!
THWIP!
THWIP!
THWIP!

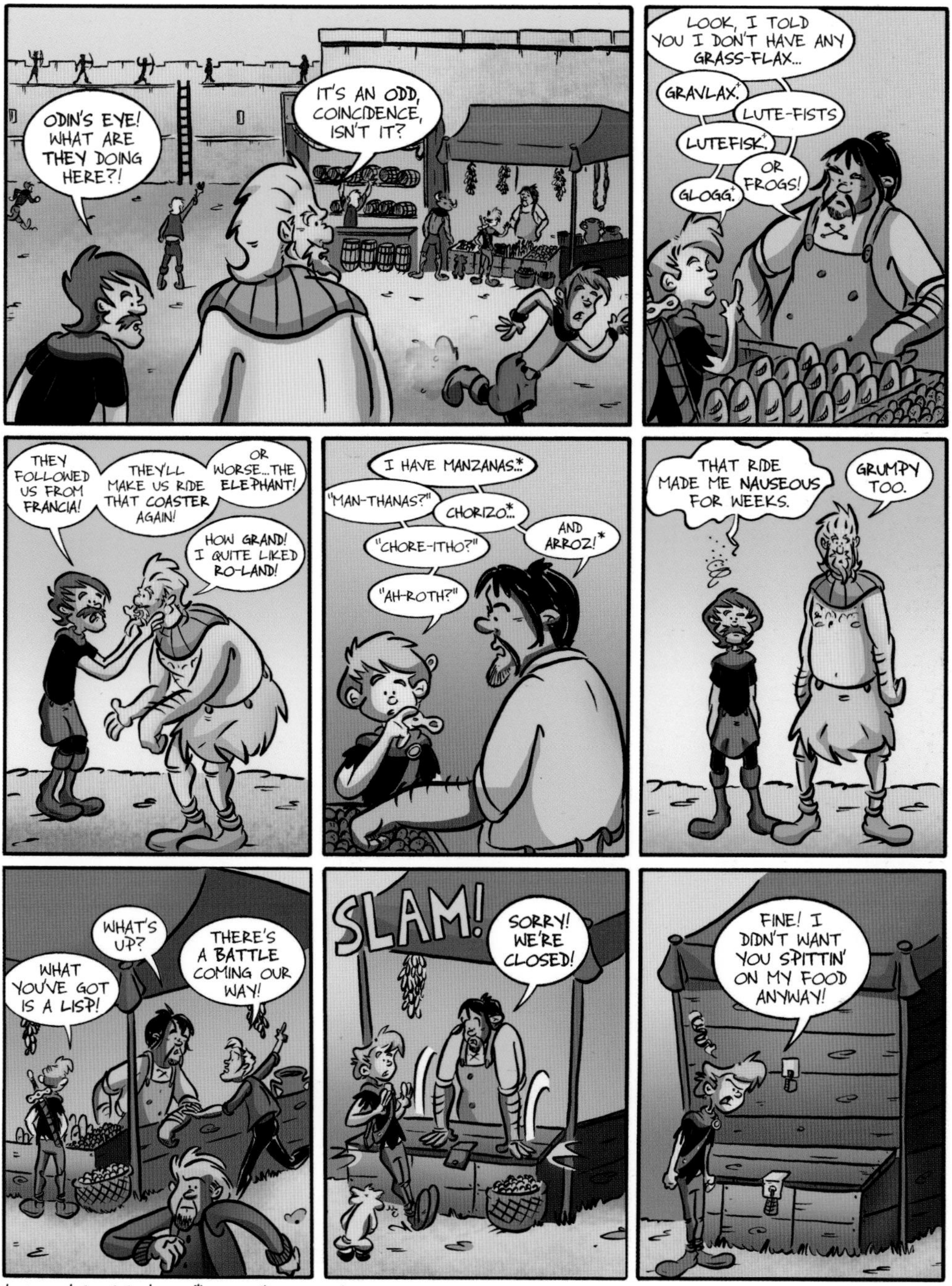
ODIN'S EYE! WHAT ARE THEY DOING HERE?!
IT'S AN ODD, COINCIDENCE, ISN'T IT?
LOOK, I TOLD YOU I DON'T HAVE ANY GRASS-FLAX...
GRAVLAX.+
LUTE-FISTS
LUTEFISK.+
OR FROGS!
GLOGG.+
THEY FOLLOWED US FROM FRANCIA!
THEY'LL MAKE US RIDE THAT COASTER AGAIN!
OR WORSE...THE ELEPHANT!
HOW GRAND! I QUITE LIKED RO-LAND!
I HAVE MANZANAS...*
"MAN-THANAS?"
CHORIZO*...
AND ARROZ!*
"CHORE-ITHO?"
"AH-ROTH?"
THAT RIDE MADE ME NAUSEOUS FOR WEEKS.
GRUMPY TOO.
WHAT'S UP?
WHAT YOU'VE GOT IS A LISP!
THERE'S A BATTLE COMING OUR WAY!
SLAM!
SORRY! WE'RE CLOSED!
FINE! I DIDN'T WANT YOU SPITTIN' ON MY FOOD ANYWAY!

+salmon +whitefish +wine *apples *sausage *rice

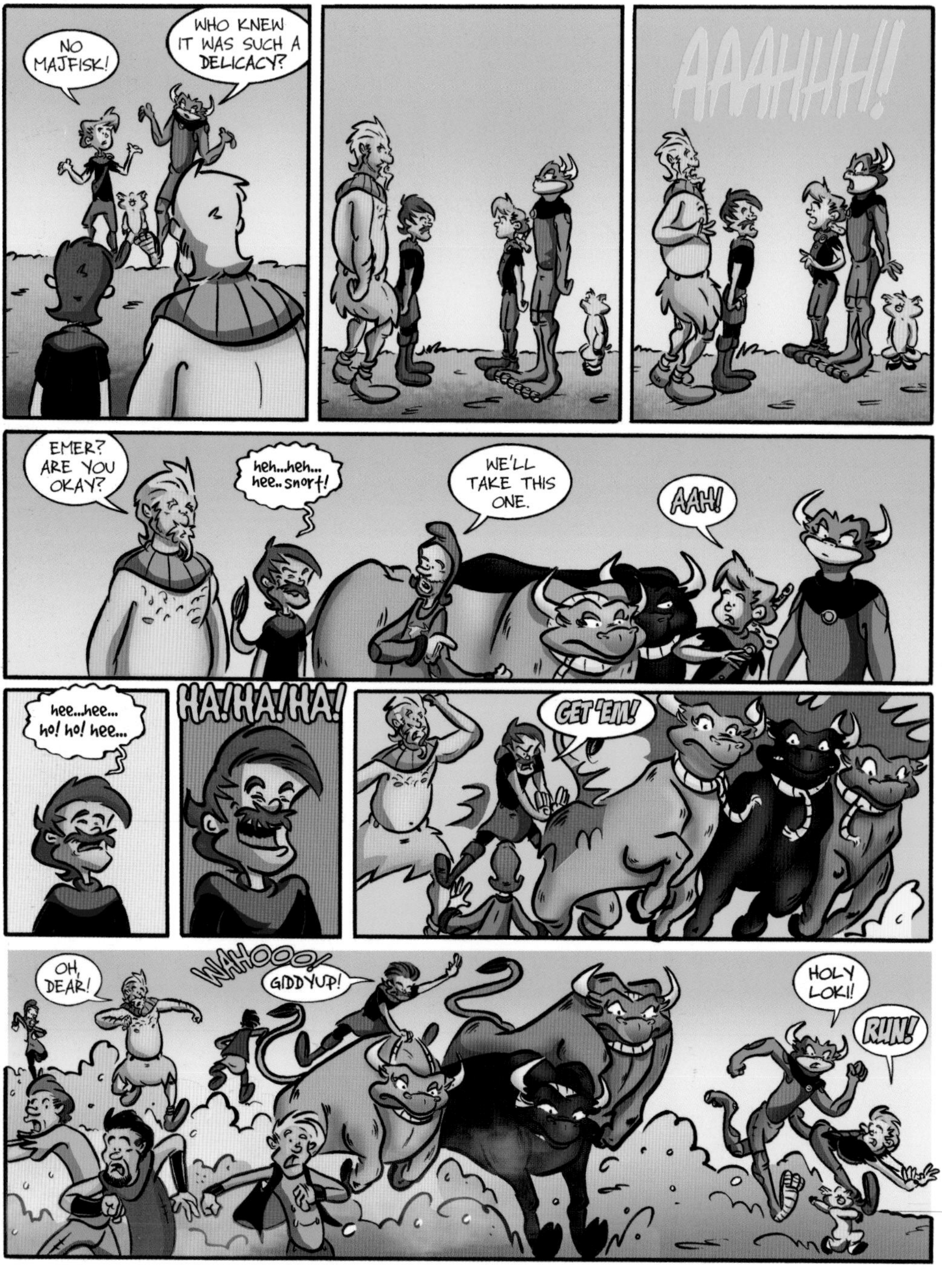
NO MAJFISK!
WHO KNEW IT WAS SUCH A DELICACY?
AAAHHH!
EMER? ARE YOU OKAY?
heh...heh... hee.. snort!
WE'LL TAKE THIS ONE.
AAH!
hee...hee... ho! ho! hee...
HA!HA!HA!
GET 'EM!
OH, DEAR!
WAHOOO!
GIDDYUP!
HOLY LOKI!
RUN!

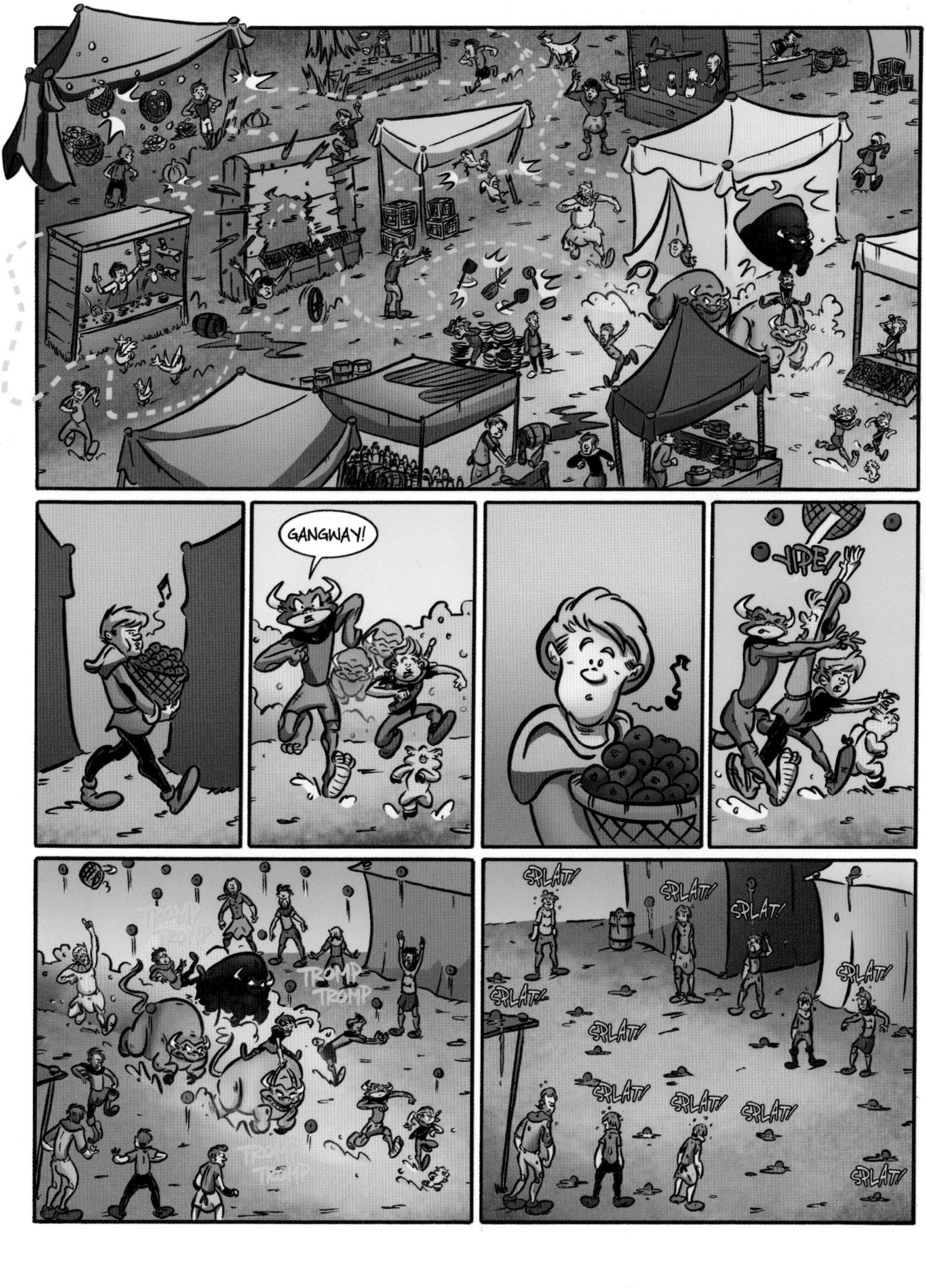
GANGWAY!
YIPE!
TROMP
TROMP
TROMP
TROMP
TROMP
TROMP
SPLAT!
SPLAT!
SPLAT!
SPLAT!
SPLAT!
SPLAT!
SPLAT!
SPLAT!
SPLAT!
SPLAT!

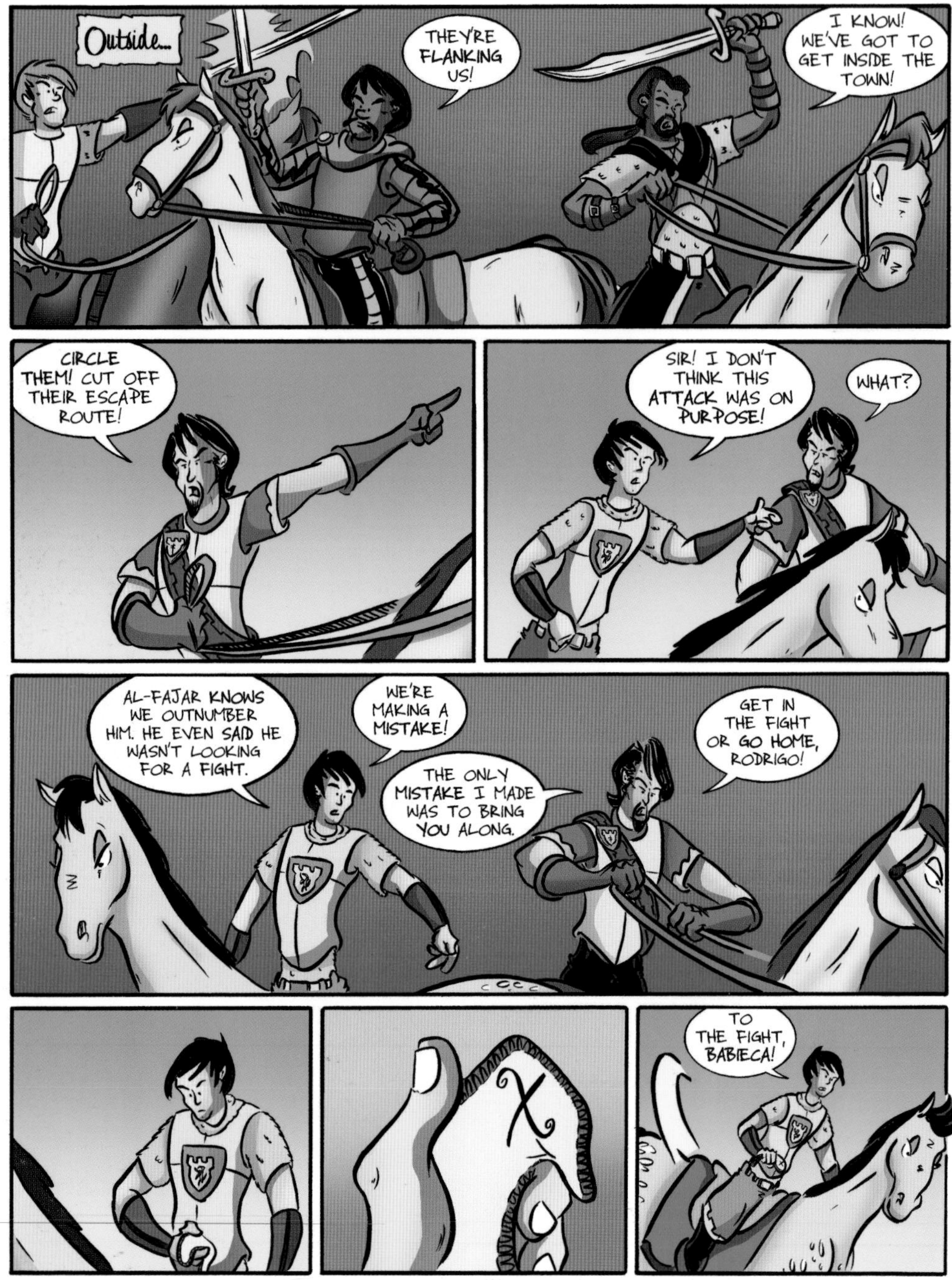
Outside...
THEY'RE FLANKING US!
I KNOW! WE'VE GOT TO GET INSIDE THE TOWN!
CIRCLE THEM! CUT OFF THEIR ESCAPE ROUTE!
SIR! I DON'T THINK THIS ATTACK WAS ON PURPOSE!
WHAT?
AL-FAJAR KNOWS WE OUTNUMBER HIM. HE EVEN SAID HE WASN'T LOOKING FOR A FIGHT.
WE'RE MAKING A MISTAKE!
THE ONLY MISTAKE I MADE WAS TO BRING YOU ALONG.
GET IN THE FIGHT OR GO HOME, RODRIGO!
TO THE FIGHT, BABIECA!

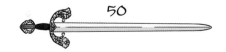

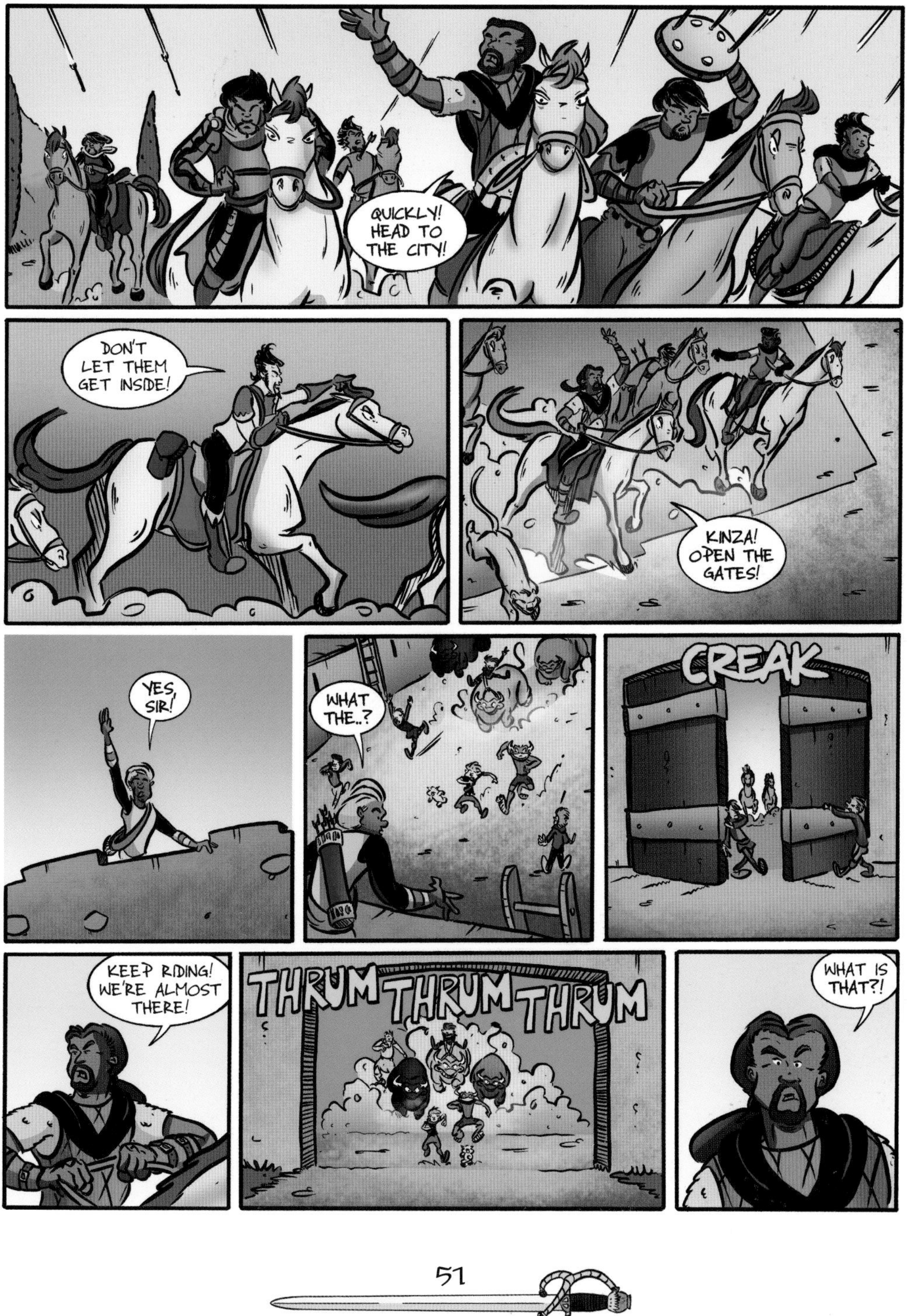
QUICKLY! HEAD TO THE CITY!
DON'T LET THEM GET INSIDE!
KINZA! OPEN THE GATES!
YES, SIR!
WHAT THE..?
CREAK
KEEP RIDING! WE'RE ALMOST THERE!
THRUM THRUM THRUM
WHAT IS THAT?!

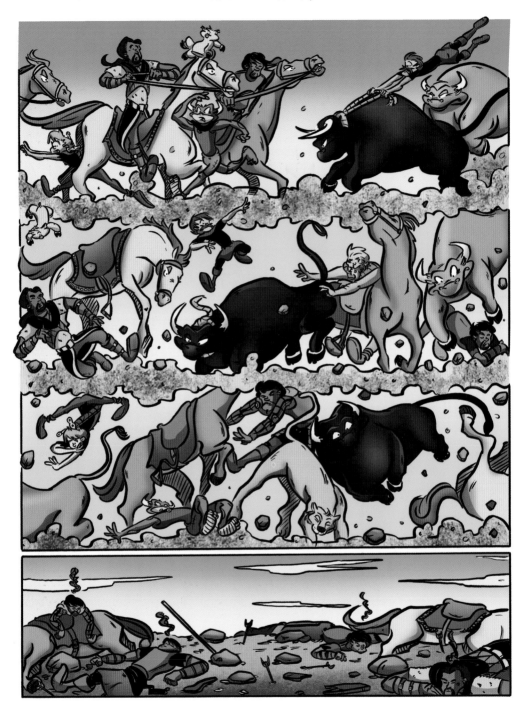

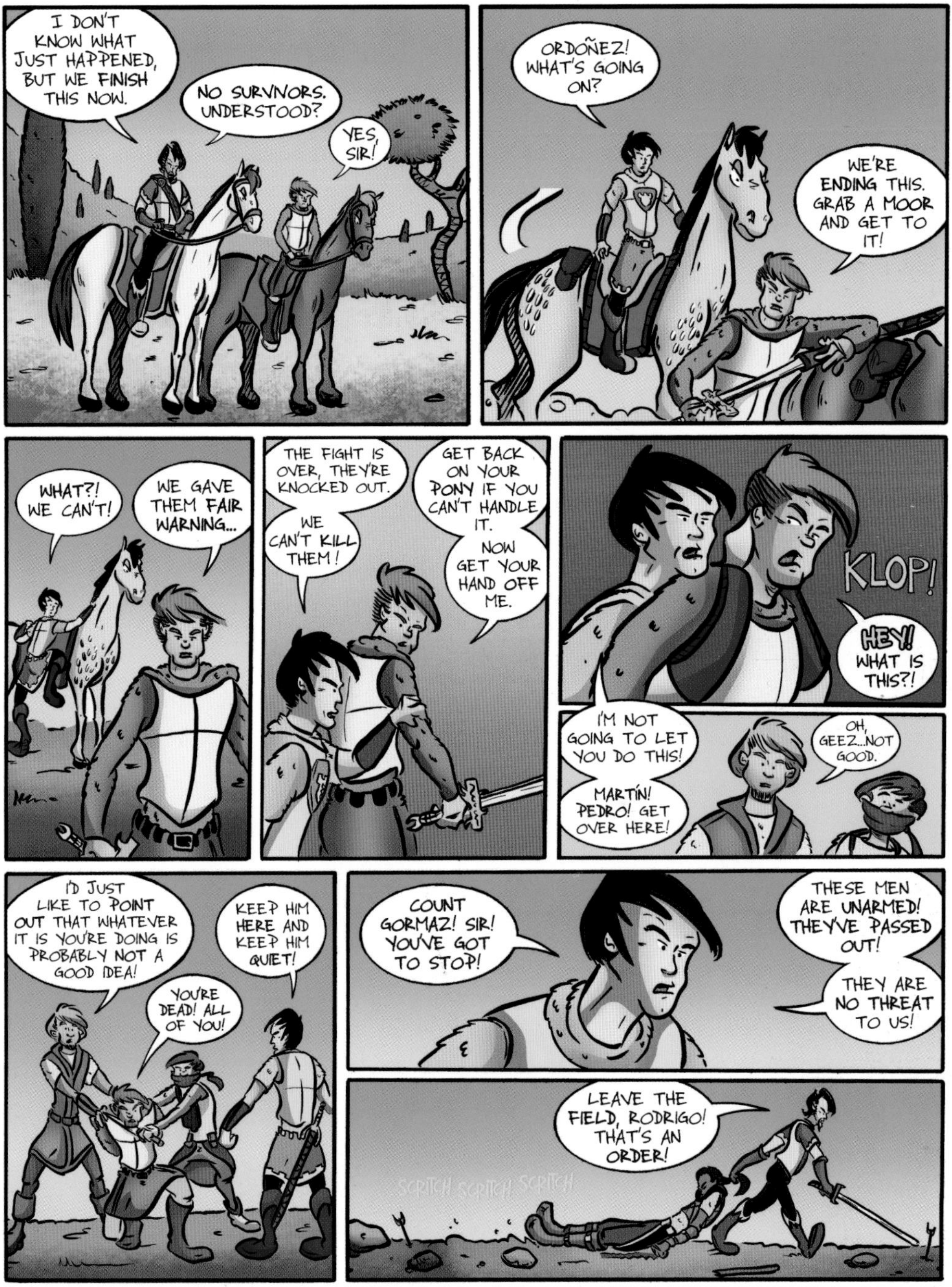
I DON'T KNOW WHAT JUST HAPPENED, BUT WE FINISH THIS NOW.
NO SURVIVORS. UNDERSTOOD?
YES, SIR!
ORDOÑEZ! WHAT'S GOING ON?
WE'RE ENDING THIS. GRAB A MOOR AND GET TO IT!
WHAT?! WE CAN'T!
WE GAVE THEM FAIR WARNING...
THE FIGHT IS OVER, THEY'RE KNOCKED OUT.
WE CAN'T KILL THEM!
GET BACK ON YOUR PONY IF YOU CAN'T HANDLE IT.
NOW GET YOUR HAND OFF ME.
KLOP!
HEY! WHAT IS THIS?!
I'M NOT GOING TO LET YOU DO THIS!
MARTÍN! PEDRO! GET OVER HERE!
OH, GEEZ...NOT GOOD.
I'D JUST LIKE TO POINT OUT THAT WHATEVER IT IS YOU'RE DOING IS PROBABLY NOT A GOOD IDEA!
KEEP HIM HERE AND KEEP HIM QUIET!
YOU'RE DEAD! ALL OF YOU!
COUNT GORMAZ! SIR! YOU'VE GOT TO STOP!
THESE MEN ARE UNARMED! THEY'VE PASSED OUT!
THEY ARE NO THREAT TO US!
LEAVE THE FIELD, RODRIGO! THAT'S AN ORDER!
SCRITCH SCRITCH SCRITCH

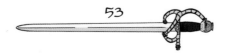

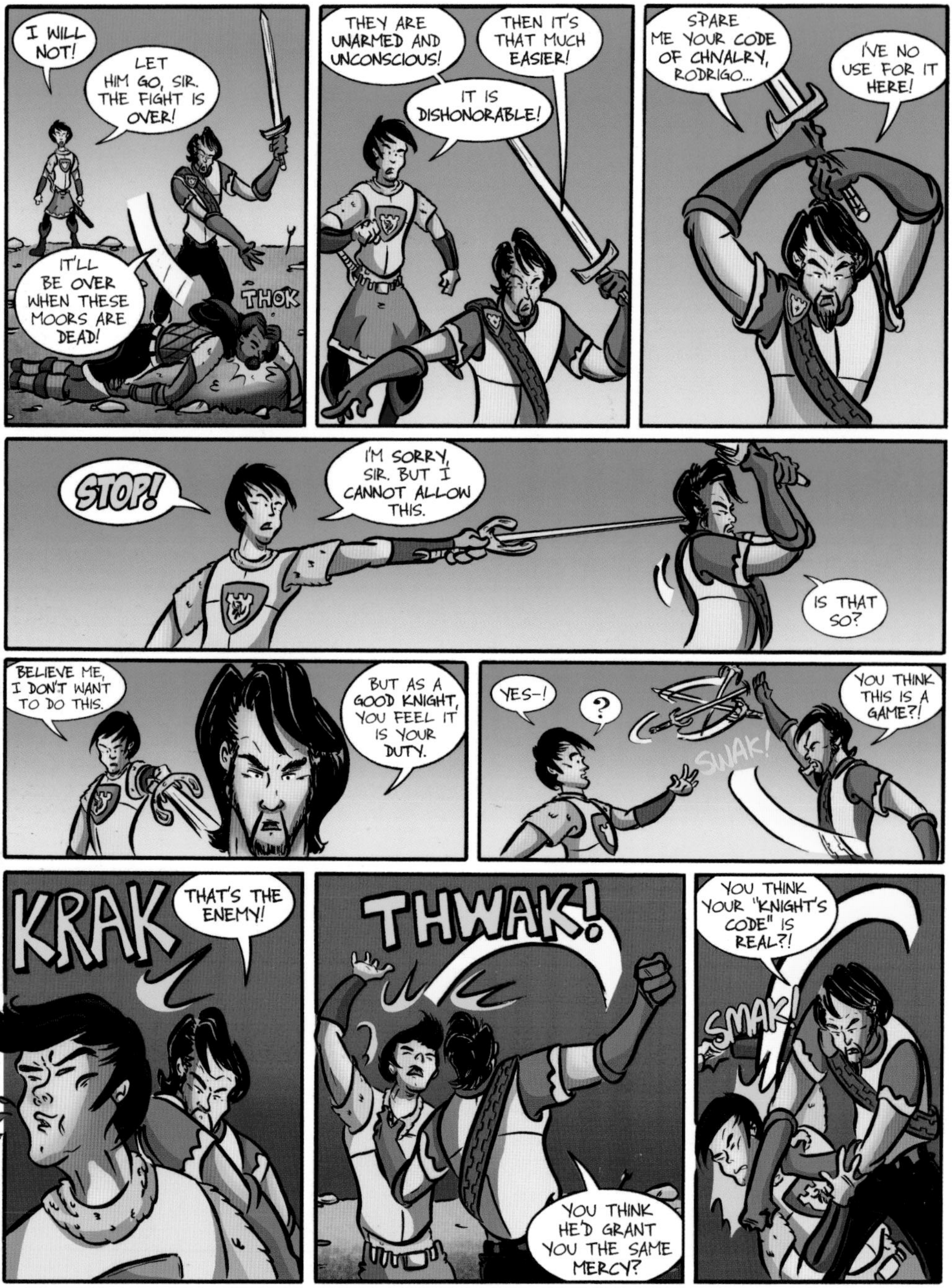
I WILL NOT!
LET HIM GO, SIR. THE FIGHT IS OVER!
IT'LL BE OVER WHEN THESE MOORS ARE DEAD!
THOK
THEY ARE UNARMED AND UNCONSCIOUS!
THEN IT'S THAT MUCH EASIER!
IT IS DISHONORABLE!
SPARE ME YOUR CODE OF CHIVALRY, RODRIGO...
I'VE NO USE FOR IT HERE!
STOP!
I'M SORRY, SIR. BUT I CANNOT ALLOW THIS.
IS THAT SO?
BELIEVE ME, I DON'T WANT TO DO THIS.
BUT AS A GOOD KNIGHT, YOU FEEL IT IS YOUR DUTY.
YES-!
?
SWAK!
YOU THINK THIS IS A GAME?!
KRAK
THAT'S THE ENEMY!
THWAK!
YOU THINK HE'D GRANT YOU THE SAME MERCY?
YOU THINK YOUR "KNIGHT'S CODE" IS REAL?!
SMAK!

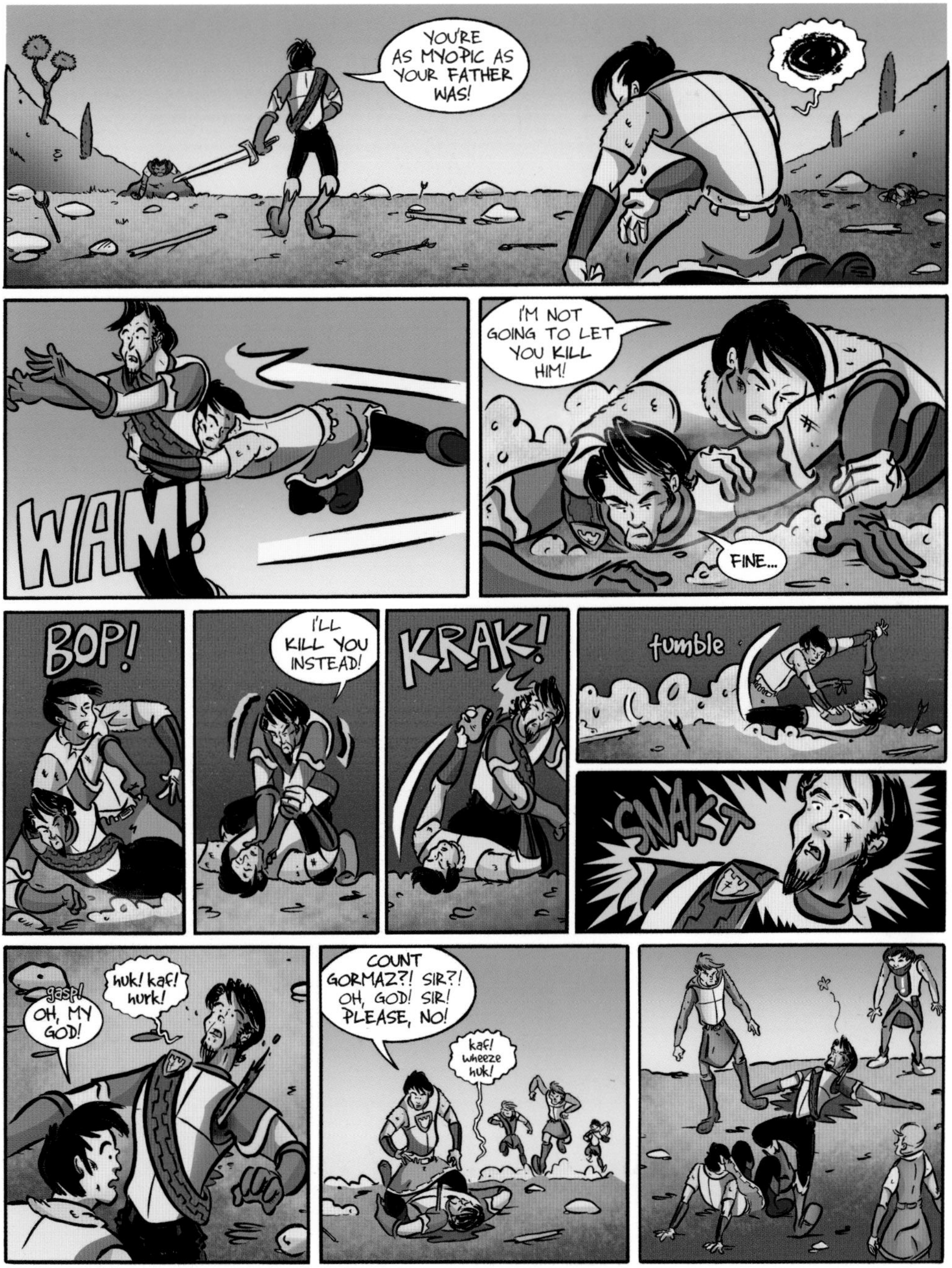
YOU'RE AS MYOPIC AS YOUR FATHER WAS!
WAM!
I'M NOT GOING TO LET YOU KILL HIM!
FINE...
BOP!
I'LL KILL YOU INSTEAD!
KRAK!
tumble
SNAKT
gasp!
OH, MY GOD!
huk! kaf! hurk!
COUNT GORMAZ?! SIR?! OH, GOD! SIR! PLEASE, NO!
kaf! wheeze huk!

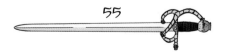

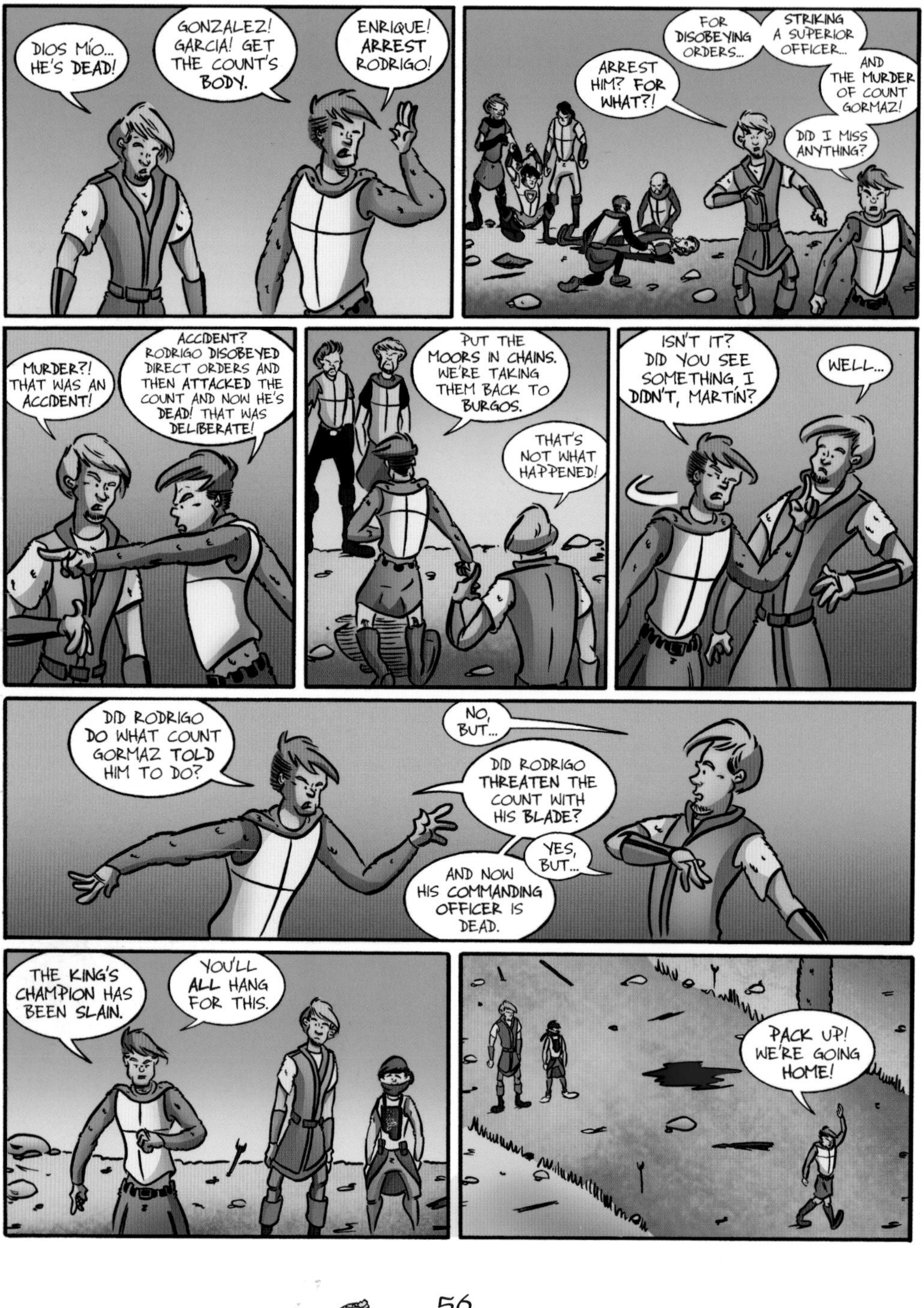
DIOS MÍO... HE'S DEAD!
GONZALEZ! GARCIA! GET THE COUNT'S BODY.
ENRIQUE! ARREST RODRIGO!
ARREST HIM? FOR WHAT?!
FOR DISOBEYING ORDERS...
STRIKING A SUPERIOR OFFICER...
AND THE MURDER OF COUNT GORMAZ!
DID I MISS ANYTHING?
MURDER?! THAT WAS AN ACCIDENT!
ACCIDENT? RODRIGO DISOBEYED DIRECT ORDERS AND THEN ATTACKED THE COUNT AND NOW HE'S DEAD! THAT WAS DELIBERATE!
PUT THE MOORS IN CHAINS. WE'RE TAKING THEM BACK TO BURGOS.
THAT'S NOT WHAT HAPPENED!
ISN'T IT? DID YOU SEE SOMETHING I DIDN'T, MARTÍN?
WELL...
DID RODRIGO DO WHAT COUNT GORMAZ TOLD HIM TO DO?
NO, BUT...
DID RODRIGO THREATEN THE COUNT WITH HIS BLADE?
YES, BUT...
AND NOW HIS COMMANDING OFFICER IS DEAD.
THE KING'S CHAMPION HAS BEEN SLAIN.
YOU'LL ALL HANG FOR THIS.
PACK UP! WE'RE GOING HOME!

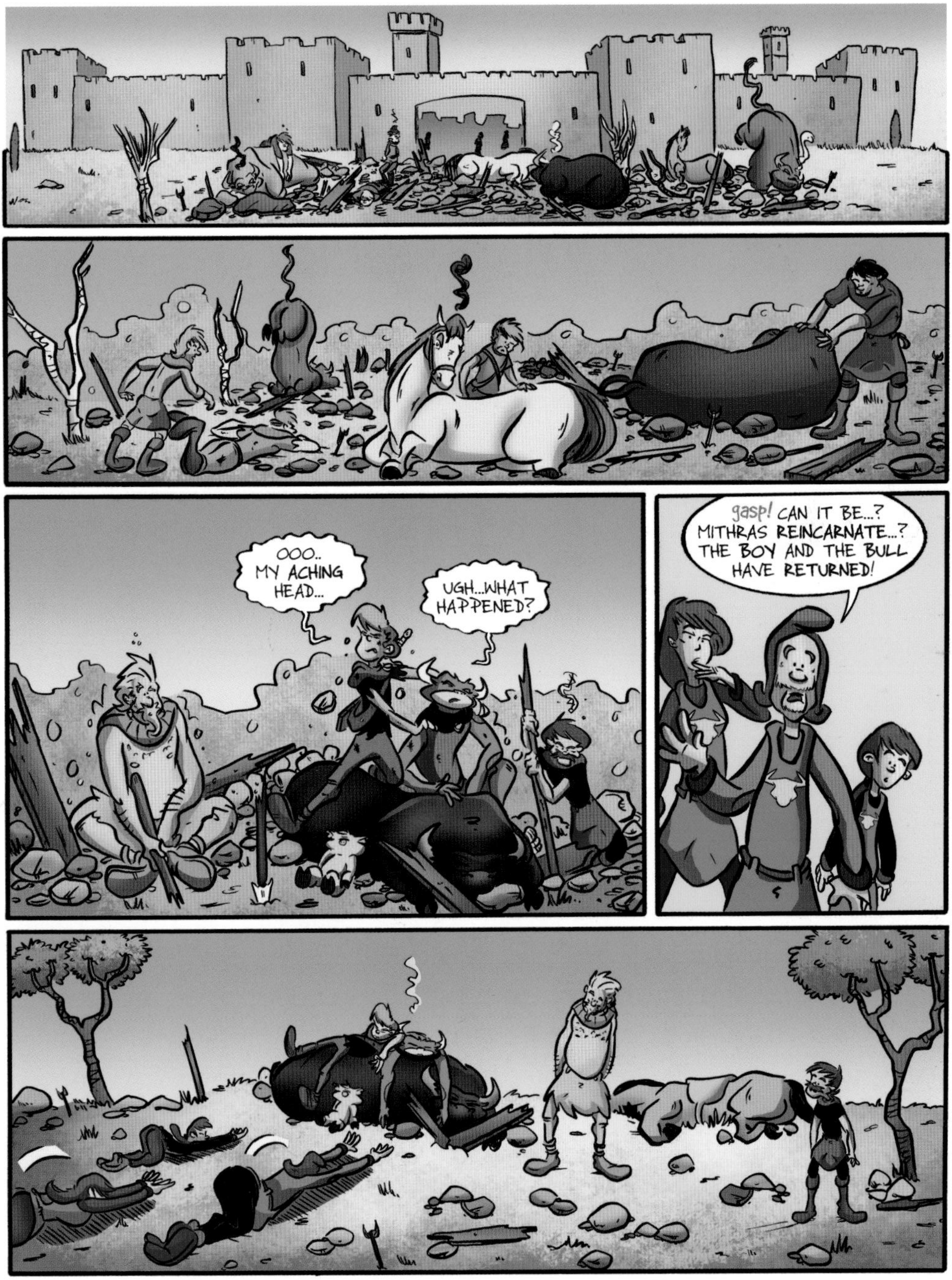
OOO..
MY ACHING HEAD...
UGH...WHAT HAPPENED?
gasp! CAN IT BE...? MITHRAS REINCARNATE...? THE BOY AND THE BULL HAVE RETURNED!

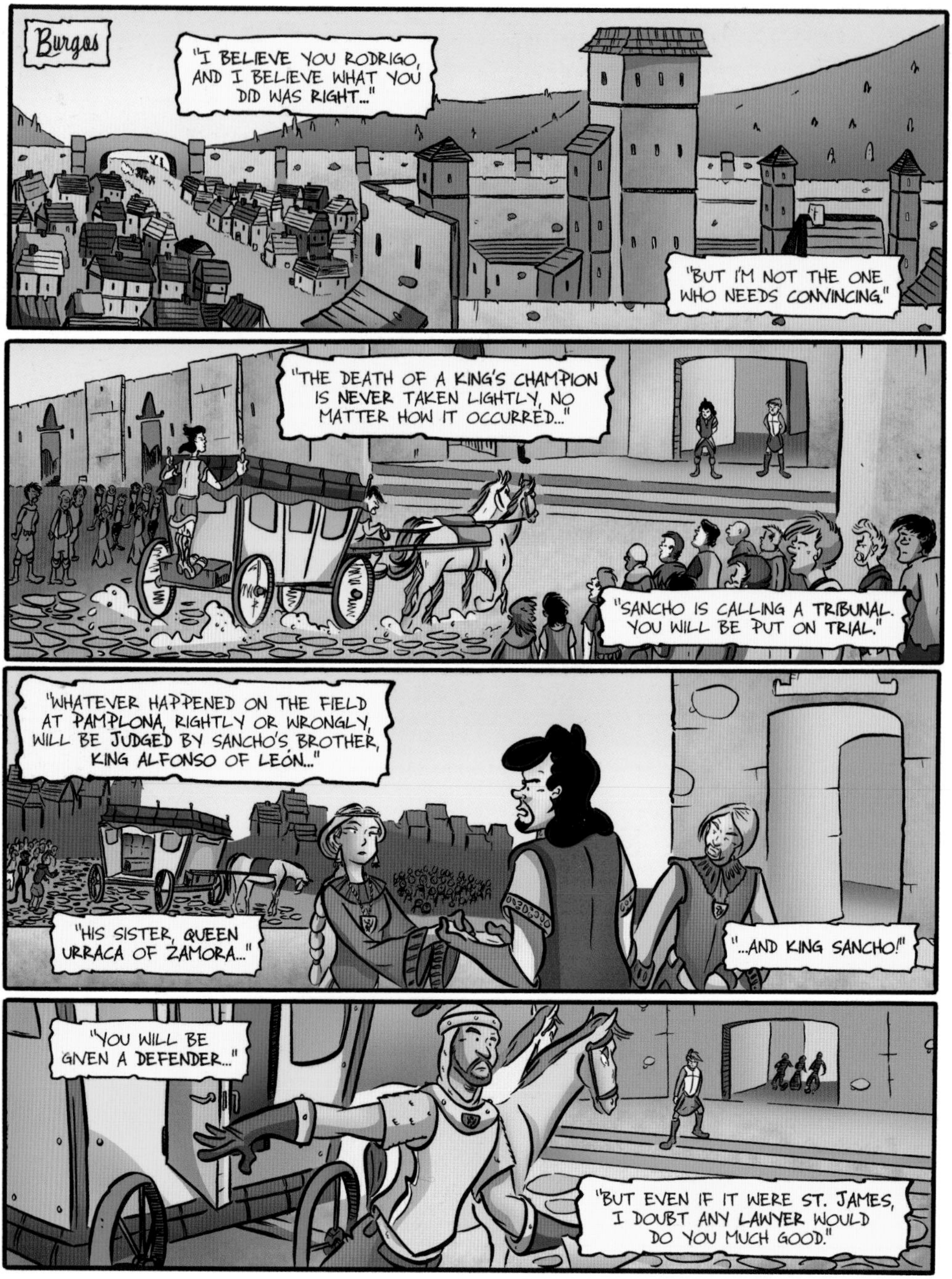
Burgos
"I BELIEVE YOU RODRIGO, AND I BELIEVE WHAT YOU DID WAS RIGHT..."
"BUT I'M NOT THE ONE WHO NEEDS CONVINCING."
"THE DEATH OF A KING'S CHAMPION IS NEVER TAKEN LIGHTLY, NO MATTER HOW IT OCCURRED..."
"SANCHO IS CALLING A TRIBUNAL. YOU WILL BE PUT ON TRIAL."
"WHATEVER HAPPENED ON THE FIELD AT PAMPLONA, RIGHTLY OR WRONGLY, WILL BE JUDGED BY SANCHO'S BROTHER, KING ALFONSO OF LEÓN..."
"HIS SISTER, QUEEN URRACA OF ZAMORA..."
"...AND KING SANCHO!"
"YOU WILL BE GIVEN A DEFENDER..."
"BUT EVEN IF IT WERE ST. JAMES, I DOUBT ANY LAWYER WOULD DO YOU MUCH GOOD."

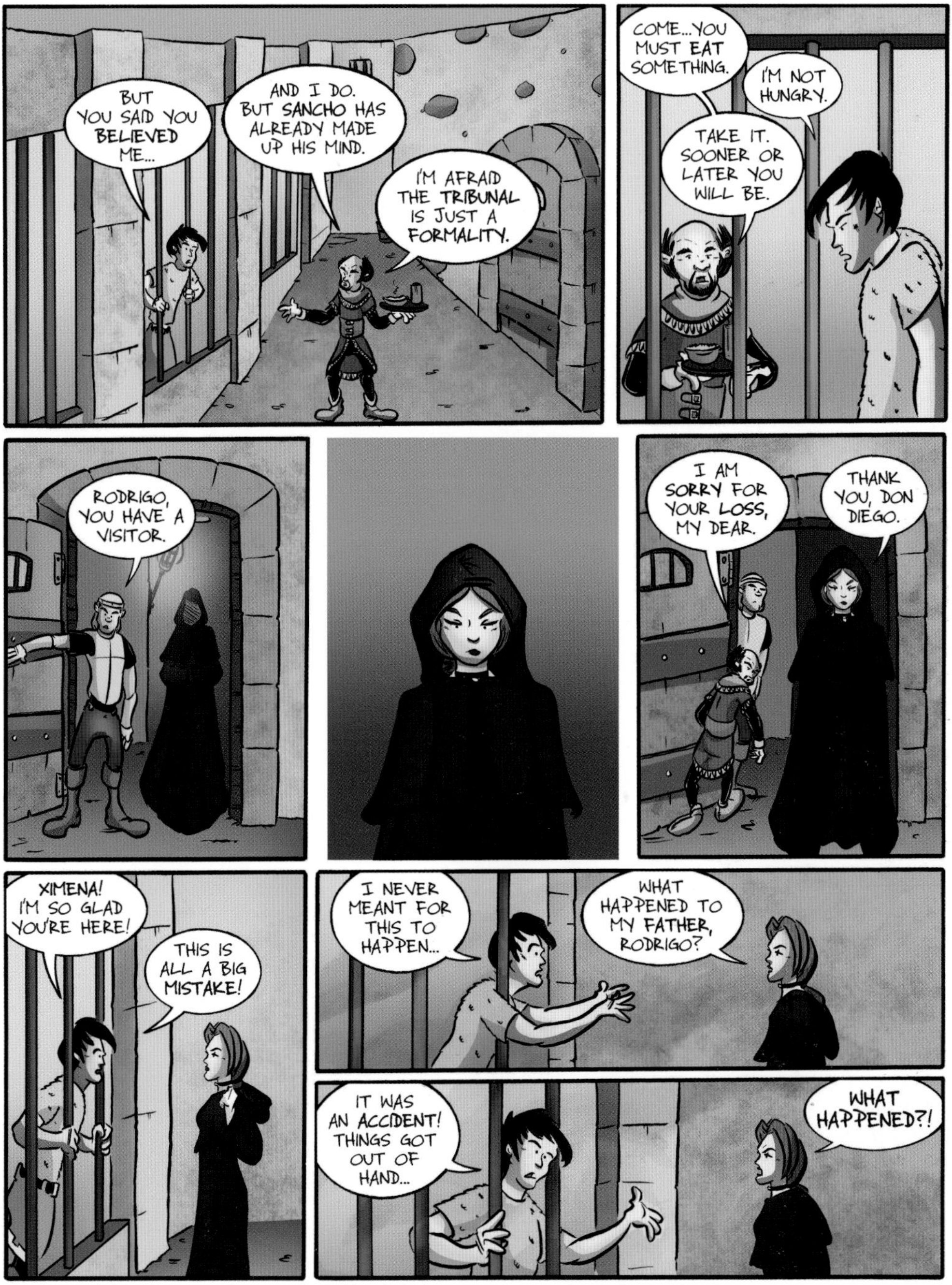
BUT YOU SAID YOU BELIEVED ME...
AND I DO. BUT SANCHO HAS ALREADY MADE UP HIS MIND.
I'M AFRAID THE TRIBUNAL IS JUST A FORMALITY.
COME...YOU MUST EAT SOMETHING.
I'M NOT HUNGRY.
TAKE IT. SOONER OR LATER YOU WILL BE.
RODRIGO, YOU HAVE A VISITOR.
I AM SORRY FOR YOUR LOSS, MY DEAR.
THANK YOU, DON DIEGO.
XIMENA! I'M SO GLAD YOU'RE HERE!
THIS IS ALL A BIG MISTAKE!
I NEVER MEANT FOR THIS TO HAPPEN...
WHAT HAPPENED TO MY FATHER, RODRIGO?
IT WAS AN ACCIDENT! THINGS GOT OUT OF HAND...
WHAT HAPPENED?!

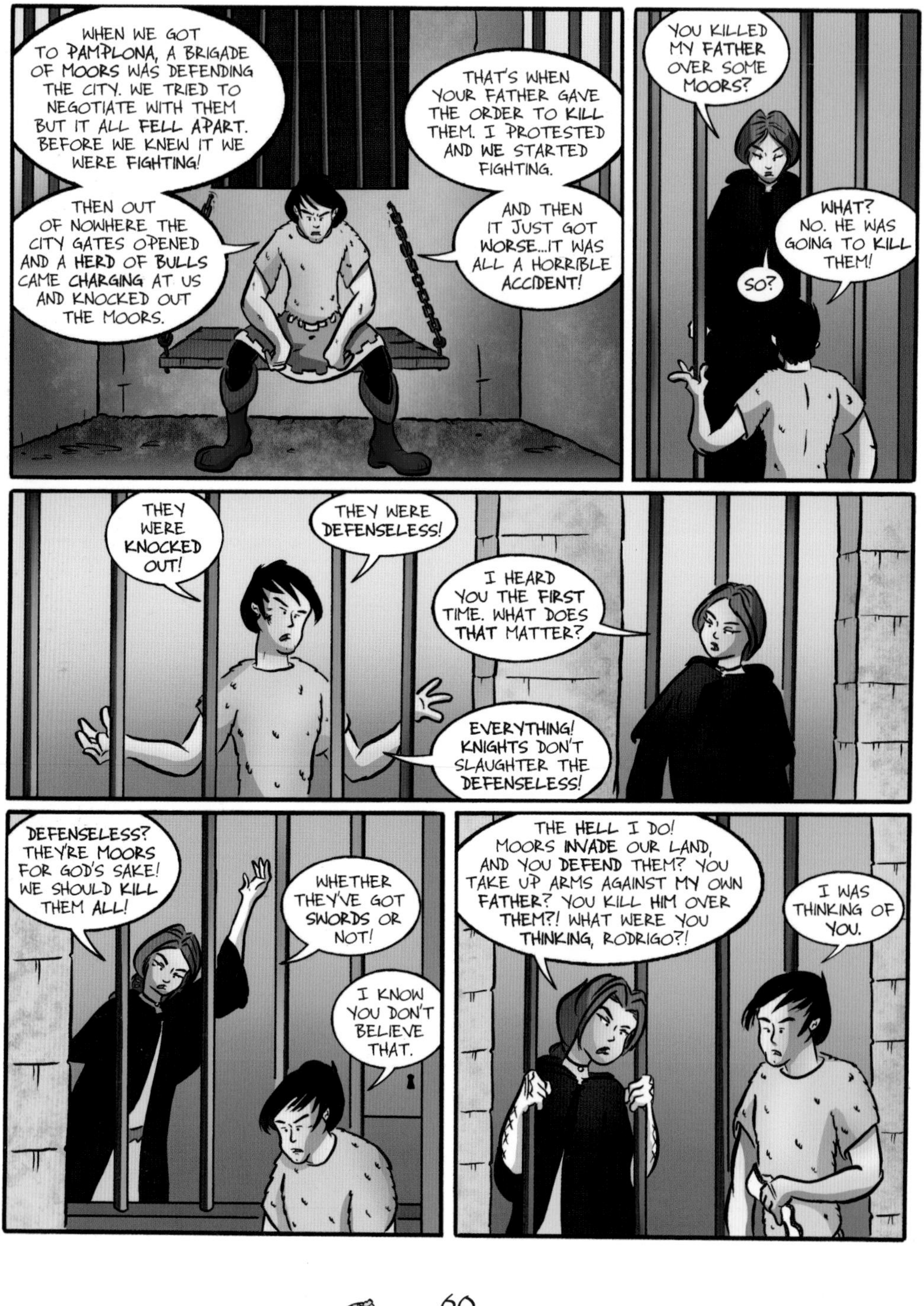
WHEN WE GOT TO PAMPLONA, A BRIGADE OF MOORS WAS DEFENDING THE CITY. WE TRIED TO NEGOTIATE WITH THEM BUT IT ALL FELL APART. BEFORE WE KNEW IT WE WERE FIGHTING!
THAT'S WHEN YOUR FATHER GAVE THE ORDER TO KILL THEM. I PROTESTED AND WE STARTED FIGHTING.
THEN OUT OF NOWHERE THE CITY GATES OPENED AND A HERD OF BULLS CAME CHARGING AT US AND KNOCKED OUT THE MOORS.
AND THEN IT JUST GOT WORSE...IT WAS ALL A HORRIBLE ACCIDENT!
YOU KILLED MY FATHER OVER SOME MOORS?
WHAT? NO. HE WAS GOING TO KILL THEM!
SO?
THEY WERE KNOCKED OUT!
THEY WERE DEFENSELESS!
I HEARD YOU THE FIRST TIME. WHAT DOES THAT MATTER?
EVERYTHING! KNIGHTS DON'T SLAUGHTER THE DEFENSELESS!
DEFENSELESS? THEY'RE MOORS FOR GOD'S SAKE! WE SHOULD KILL THEM ALL!
WHETHER THEY'VE GOT SWORDS OR NOT!
I KNOW YOU DON'T BELIEVE THAT.
THE HELL I DO! MOORS INVADE OUR LAND, AND YOU DEFEND THEM? YOU TAKE UP ARMS AGAINST MY OWN FATHER? YOU KILL HIM OVER THEM?! WHAT WERE YOU THINKING, RODRIGO?!
I WAS THINKING OF YOU.

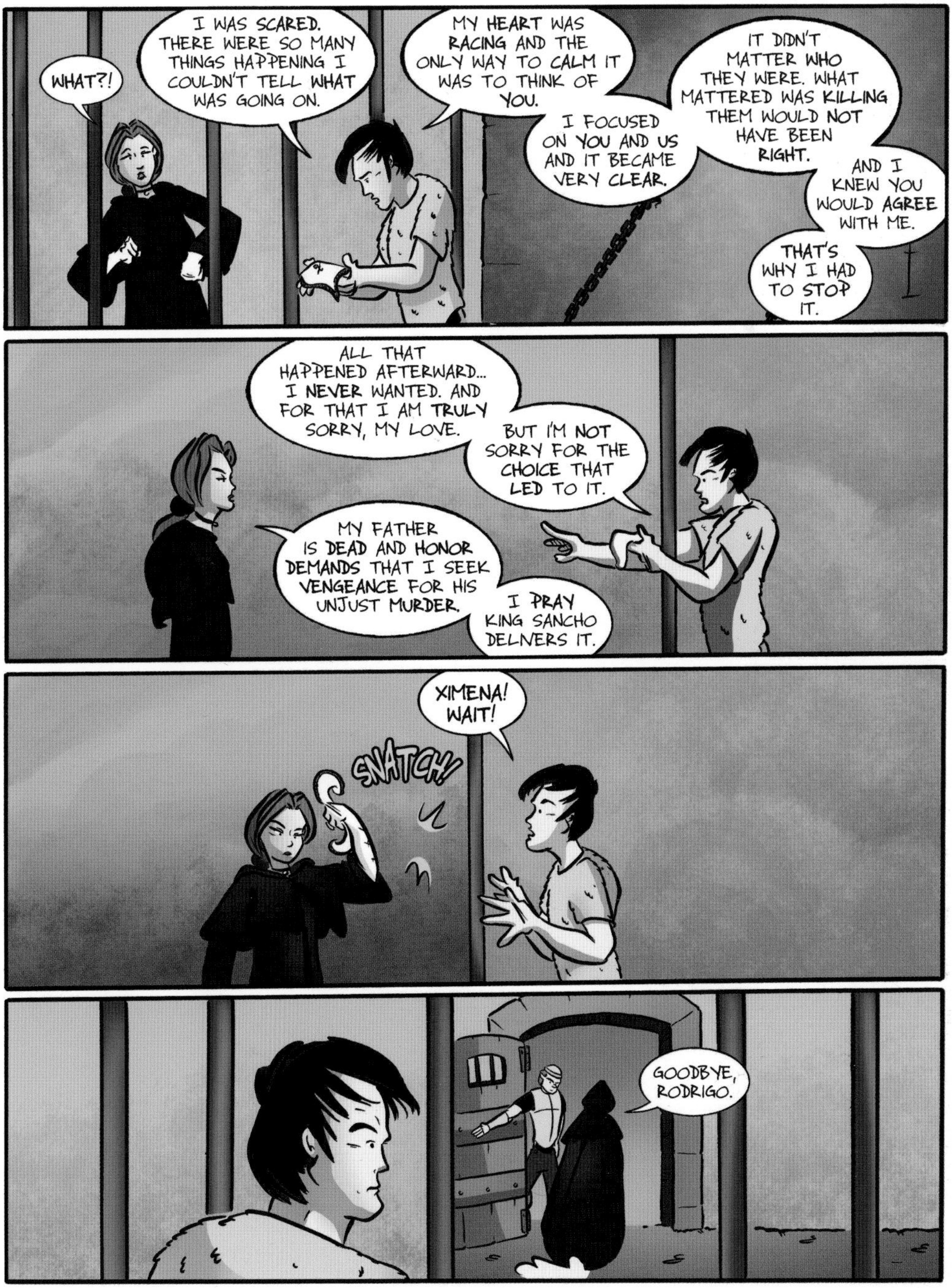
WHAT?!
I WAS SCARED. THERE WERE SO MANY THINGS HAPPENING I COULDN'T TELL WHAT WAS GOING ON.
MY HEART WAS RACING AND THE ONLY WAY TO CALM IT WAS TO THINK OF YOU.
I FOCUSED ON YOU AND US AND IT BECAME VERY CLEAR.
IT DIDN'T MATTER WHO THEY WERE. WHAT MATTERED WAS KILLING THEM WOULD NOT HAVE BEEN RIGHT.
AND I KNEW YOU WOULD AGREE WITH ME.
THAT'S WHY I HAD TO STOP IT.
ALL THAT HAPPENED AFTERWARD... I NEVER WANTED. AND FOR THAT I AM TRULY SORRY, MY LOVE.
BUT I'M NOT SORRY FOR THE CHOICE THAT LED TO IT.
MY FATHER IS DEAD AND HONOR DEMANDS THAT I SEEK VENGEANCE FOR HIS UNJUST MURDER.
I PRAY KING SANCHO DELIVERS IT.
XIMENA! WAIT!
SNATCH!
GOODBYE, RODRIGO.

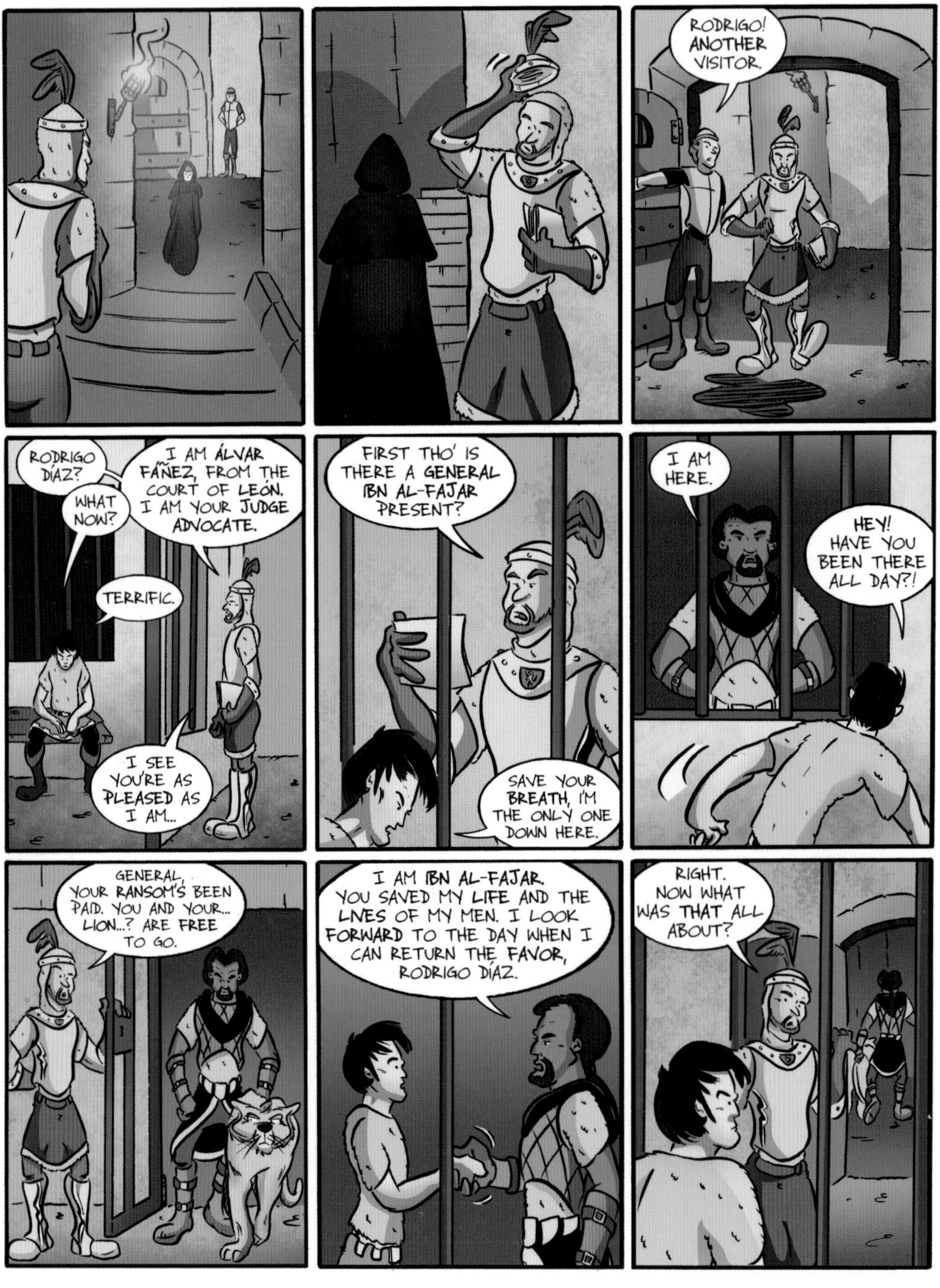
RODRIGO! ANOTHER VISITOR.
RODRIGO DÍAZ?
WHAT NOW?
I AM ÁLVAR FÁÑEZ, FROM THE COURT OF LEÓN. I AM YOUR JUDGE ADVOCATE.
TERRIFIC.
I SEE YOU'RE AS PLEASED AS I AM...
FIRST THO' IS THERE A GENERAL IBN AL-FAJAR PRESENT?
SAVE YOUR BREATH, I'M THE ONLY ONE DOWN HERE.
I AM HERE.
HEY! HAVE YOU BEEN THERE ALL DAY?!
GENERAL, YOUR RANSOM'S BEEN PAID. YOU AND YOUR... LION...? ARE FREE TO GO.
I AM IBN AL-FAJAR. YOU SAVED MY LIFE AND THE LIVES OF MY MEN. I LOOK FORWARD TO THE DAY WHEN I CAN RETURN THE FAVOR, RODRIGO DÍAZ.
RIGHT. NOW WHAT WAS THAT ALL ABOUT?

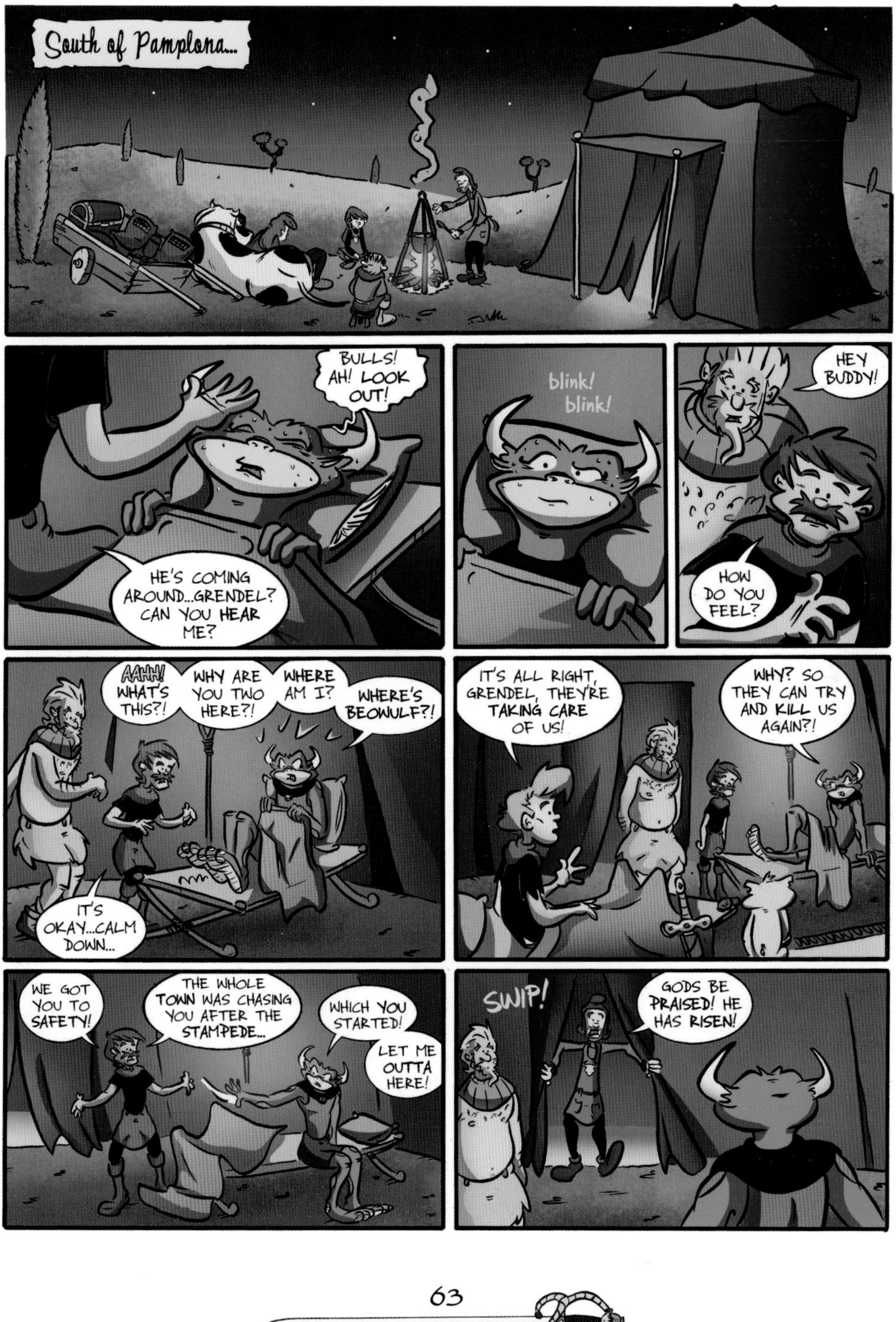
South of Pamplona...
BULLS! AH! LOOK OUT!
HE'S COMING AROUND...GRENDEL? CAN YOU HEAR ME?
blink! blink!
HEY BUDDY!
HOW DO YOU FEEL?
AAHH! WHAT'S THIS?!
WHY ARE YOU TWO HERE?!
WHERE AM I?
WHERE'S BEOWULF?!
IT'S OKAY...CALM DOWN...
IT'S ALL RIGHT, GRENDEL, THEY'RE TAKING CARE OF US!
WHY? SO THEY CAN TRY AND KILL US AGAIN?!
WE GOT YOU TO SAFETY!
THE WHOLE TOWN WAS CHASING YOU AFTER THE STAMPEDE...
WHICH YOU STARTED!
LET ME OUTTA HERE!
SWIP!
GODS BE PRAISED! HE HAS RISEN!

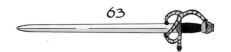

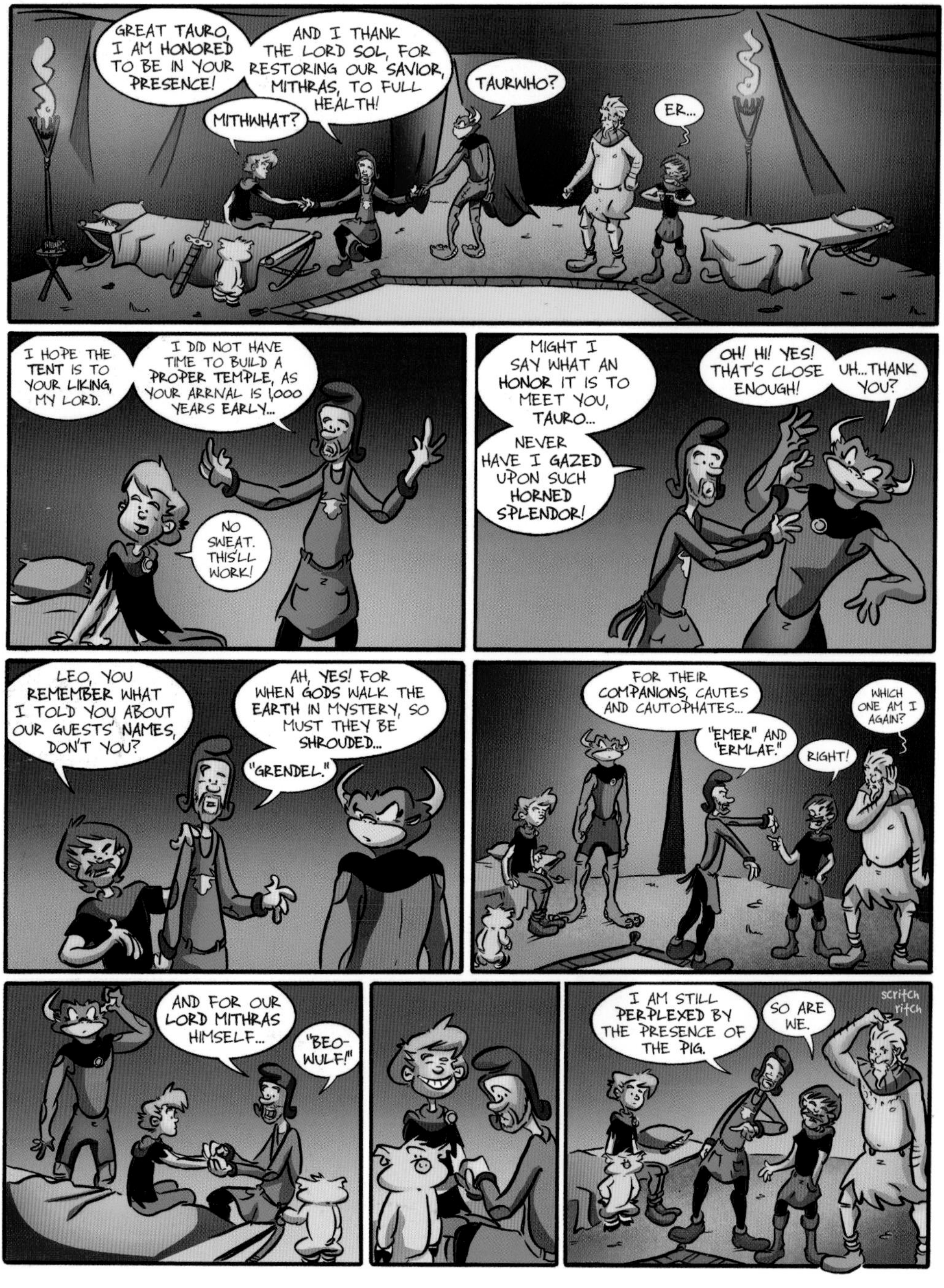
GREAT TAURO, I AM HONORED TO BE IN YOUR PRESENCE!
AND I THANK THE LORD SOL, FOR RESTORING OUR SAVIOR, MITHRAS, TO FULL HEALTH!
MITHWHAT?
TAURWHO?
ER...
I HOPE THE TENT IS TO YOUR LIKING, MY LORD.
I DID NOT HAVE TIME TO BUILD A PROPER TEMPLE, AS YOUR ARRIVAL IS 1,000 YEARS EARLY...
NO SWEAT. THIS'LL WORK!
MIGHT I SAY WHAT AN HONOR IT IS TO MEET YOU, TAURO...
NEVER HAVE I GAZED UPON SUCH HORNED SPLENDOR!
OH! HI! YES! THAT'S CLOSE ENOUGH!
UH...THANK YOU?
LEO, YOU REMEMBER WHAT I TOLD YOU ABOUT OUR GUESTS' NAMES, DON'T YOU?
AH, YES! FOR WHEN GODS WALK THE EARTH IN MYSTERY, SO MUST THEY BE SHROUDED...
"GRENDEL."
FOR THEIR COMPANIONS, CAUTES AND CAUTOPHATES...
"EMER" AND "ERMLAF."
WHICH ONE AM I AGAIN?
RIGHT!
AND FOR OUR LORD MITHRAS HIMSELF...
"BEOWULF!"
I AM STILL PERPLEXED BY THE PRESENCE OF THE PIG.
SO ARE WE.
scritch ritch

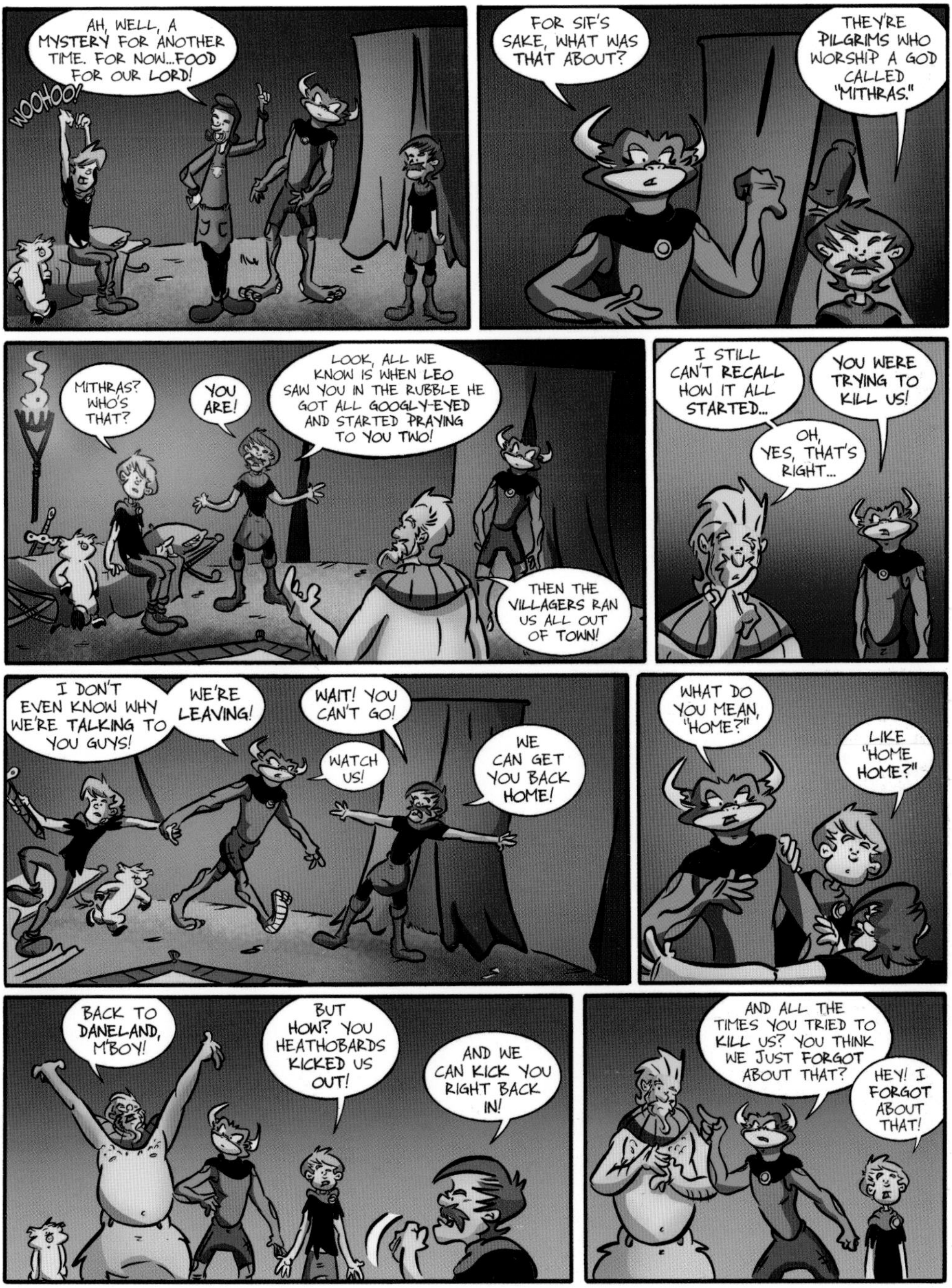
AH, WELL, A MYSTERY FOR ANOTHER TIME. FOR NOW...FOOD FOR OUR LORD!
WOOHOO!
FOR SIF'S SAKE, WHAT WAS THAT ABOUT?
THEY'RE PILGRIMS WHO WORSHIP A GOD CALLED "MITHRAS."
MITHRAS? WHO'S THAT?
YOU ARE!
LOOK, ALL WE KNOW IS WHEN LEO SAW YOU IN THE RUBBLE HE GOT ALL GOOGLY-EYED AND STARTED PRAYING TO YOU TWO!
THEN THE VILLAGERS RAN US ALL OUT OF TOWN!
I STILL CAN'T RECALL HOW IT ALL STARTED...
YOU WERE TRYING TO KILL US!
OH, YES, THAT'S RIGHT...
I DON'T EVEN KNOW WHY WE'RE TALKING TO YOU GUYS!
WE'RE LEAVING!
WAIT! YOU CAN'T GO!
WATCH US!
WE CAN GET YOU BACK HOME!
WHAT DO YOU MEAN, "HOME?"
LIKE "HOME HOME?"
BACK TO DANELAND, M'BOY!
BUT HOW? YOU HEATHOBARDS KICKED US OUT!
AND WE CAN KICK YOU RIGHT BACK IN!
AND ALL THE TIMES YOU TRIED TO KILL US? YOU THINK WE JUST FORGOT ABOUT THAT?
HEY! I FORGOT ABOUT THAT!

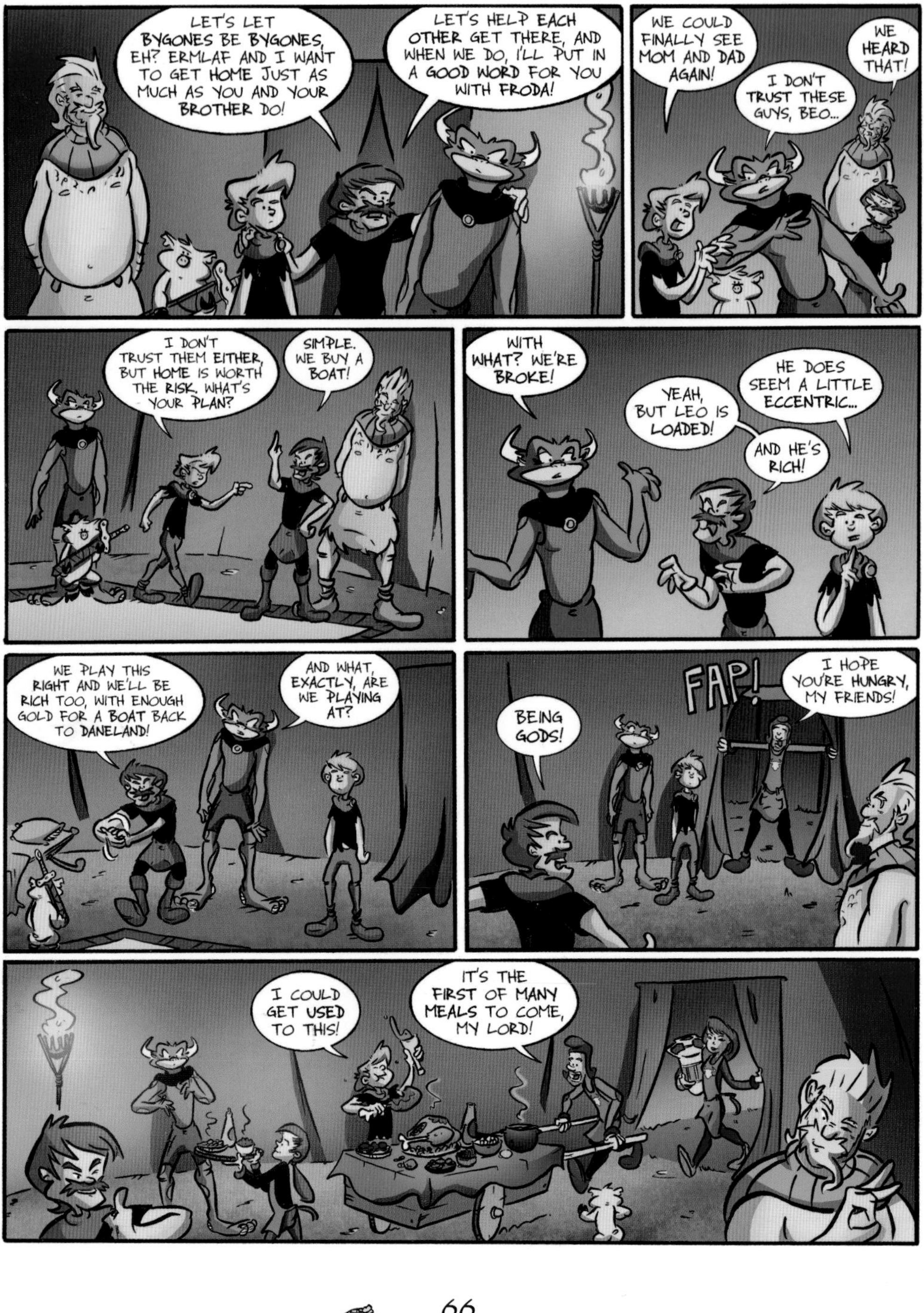
LET'S LET BYGONES BE BYGONES, EH? ERMLAF AND I WANT TO GET HOME JUST AS MUCH AS YOU AND YOUR BROTHER DO!
LET'S HELP EACH OTHER GET THERE, AND WHEN WE DO, I'LL PUT IN A GOOD WORD FOR YOU WITH FRODA!
WE COULD FINALLY SEE MOM AND DAD AGAIN!
I DON'T TRUST THESE GUYS, BEO...
WE HEARD THAT!
I DON'T TRUST THEM EITHER, BUT HOME IS WORTH THE RISK. WHAT'S YOUR PLAN?
SIMPLE. WE BUY A BOAT!
WITH WHAT? WE'RE BROKE!
YEAH, BUT LEO IS LOADED!
HE DOES SEEM A LITTLE ECCENTRIC...
AND HE'S RICH!
WE PLAY THIS RIGHT AND WE'LL BE RICH TOO, WITH ENOUGH GOLD FOR A BOAT BACK TO DANELAND!
AND WHAT, EXACTLY, ARE WE PLAYING AT?
BEING GODS!
FAP!
I HOPE YOU'RE HUNGRY, MY FRIENDS!
I COULD GET USED TO THIS!
IT'S THE FIRST OF MANY MEALS TO COME, MY LORD!

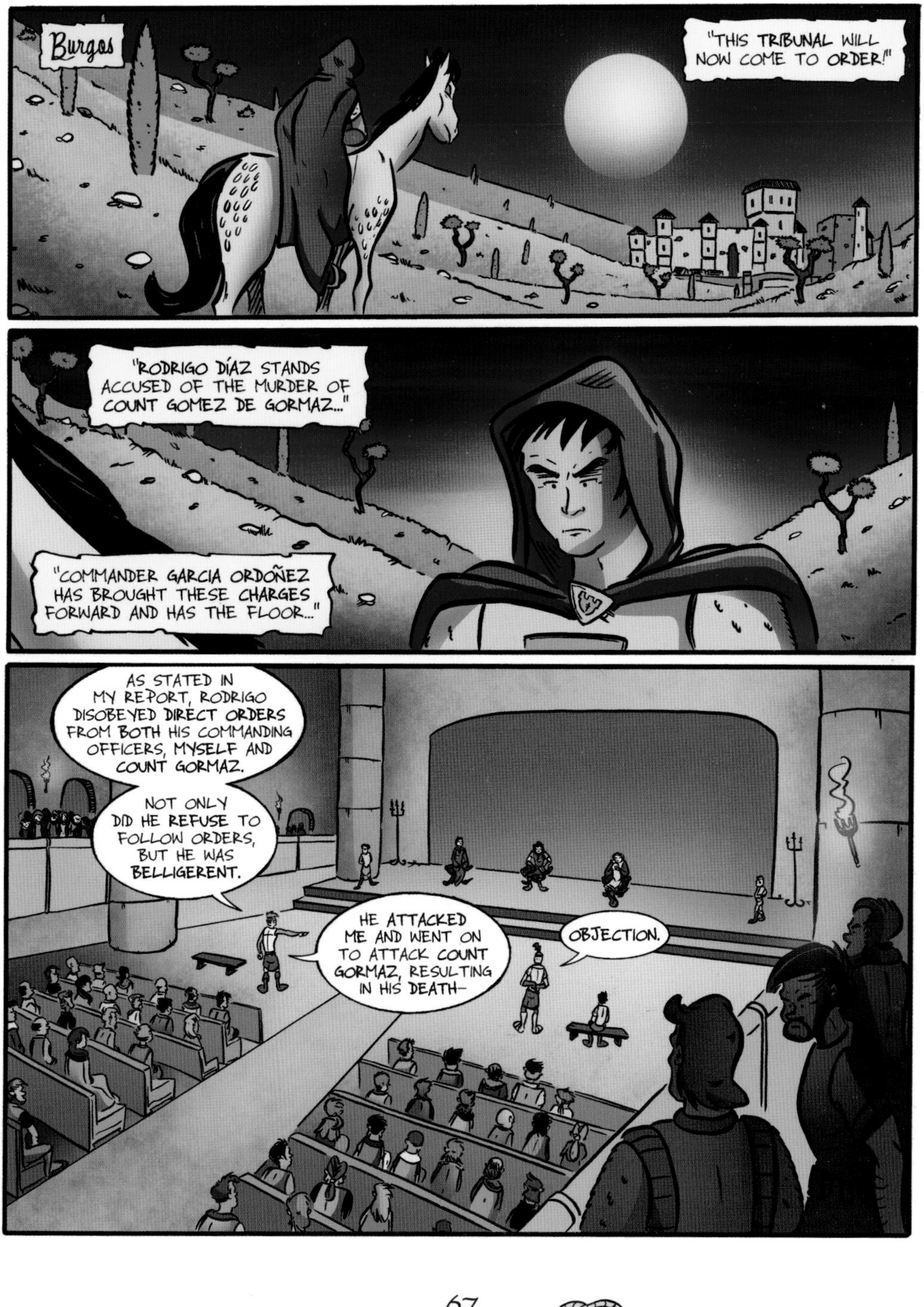
Burgos
"THIS TRIBUNAL WILL NOW COME TO ORDER!"
"RODRIGO DÍAZ STANDS ACCUSED OF THE MURDER OF COUNT GOMEZ DE GORMAZ..."
"COMMANDER GARCIA ORDOÑEZ HAS BROUGHT THESE CHARGES FORWARD AND HAS THE FLOOR..."
AS STATED IN MY REPORT, RODRIGO DISOBEYED DIRECT ORDERS FROM BOTH HIS COMMANDING OFFICERS, MYSELF AND COUNT GORMAZ.
NOT ONLY DID HE REFUSE TO FOLLOW ORDERS, BUT HE WAS BELLIGERENT.
HE ATTACKED ME AND WENT ON TO ATTACK COUNT GORMAZ, RESULTING IN HIS DEATH–
OBJECTION.

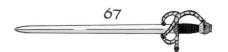

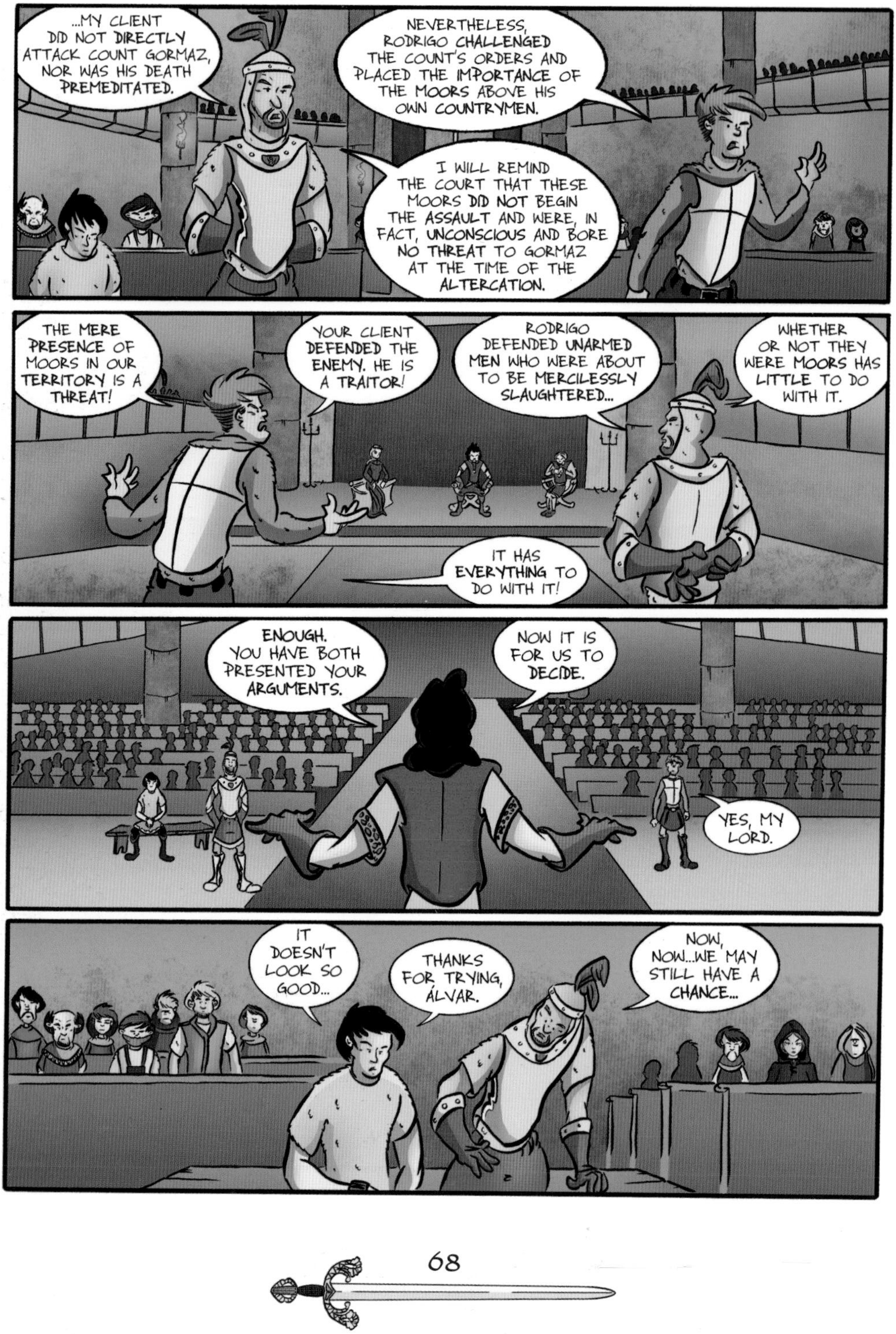
...MY CLIENT DID NOT DIRECTLY ATTACK COUNT GORMAZ, NOR WAS HIS DEATH PREMEDITATED.
NEVERTHELESS, RODRIGO CHALLENGED THE COUNT'S ORDERS AND PLACED THE IMPORTANCE OF THE MOORS ABOVE HIS OWN COUNTRYMEN.
I WILL REMIND THE COURT THAT THESE MOORS DID NOT BEGIN THE ASSAULT AND WERE, IN FACT, UNCONSCIOUS AND BORE NO THREAT TO GORMAZ AT THE TIME OF THE ALTERCATION.
THE MERE PRESENCE OF MOORS IN OUR TERRITORY IS A THREAT!
YOUR CLIENT DEFENDED THE ENEMY. HE IS A TRAITOR!
RODRIGO DEFENDED UNARMED MEN WHO WERE ABOUT TO BE MERCILESSLY SLAUGHTERED...
WHETHER OR NOT THEY WERE MOORS HAS LITTLE TO DO WITH IT.
IT HAS EVERYTHING TO DO WITH IT!
ENOUGH. YOU HAVE BOTH PRESENTED YOUR ARGUMENTS.
NOW IT IS FOR US TO DECIDE.
YES, MY LORD.
IT DOESN'T LOOK SO GOOD...
THANKS FOR TRYING, ÁLVAR.
NOW, NOW...WE MAY STILL HAVE A CHANCE...

THE ACCUSED WILL STAND.
RODRIGO DÍAZ, YOU HAVE BEEN CHARGED OF CONDUCT UNFIT FOR A KNIGHT OF THE CASTILIAN ORDER.
YOU'VE BROKEN THE CHAIN OF COMMAND...
DEFENDED OUR SWORN ENEMIES...
AND ARE COMPLICIT IN THE DEATH OF THE KING'S CHAMPION.
DO YOU HAVE ANYTHING TO SAY IN LIGHT OF THESE CHARGES?
I REGRET THE DEATH OF COUNT GORMAZ BUT NOT THE ACTIONS THAT LED TO IT.
THE DÍAZ FAMILY HAS LONG SERVED THIS COURT, SO IT IS WITH A HEAVY HEART THAT WE DECREE THE FOLLOWING...
RODRIGO, YOU ARE HEREBY STRIPPED OF YOUR KNIGHTHOOD AND CAST OUT OF THE CASTILIAN ORDER.
YOU WILL NO LONGER HAVE ACCESS TO YOUR FAMILY'S LANDS OR TITLES AS YOU HAVE FOREVER TARNISHED THE DÍAZ NAME.
ALL VASSALS OF THE KING ARE FORBIDDEN TO PROVIDE YOU WITH FOOD, LODGING, OR AID ON PENALTY OF DEATH.
RODRIGO DÍAZ IS HENCEFORTH EXILED FROM THE LANDS OF LEÓN, CASTILE, AND ALL TERRITORIES WITHIN THE REALM.
EXILE?!
THE KING'S CHAMPION LIES DEAD AND HIS MURDERER GOES FREE?
RODRIGO SHOULD DIE FOR WHAT HE DID TO MY FATHER!
THIS IS NOT PUNISHMENT!
THIS IS NOT JUSTICE!

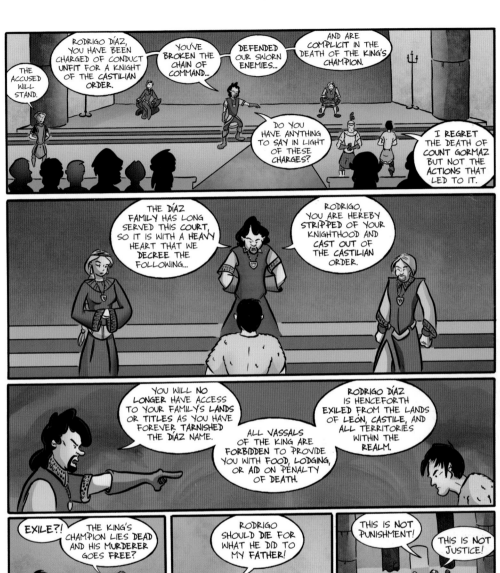

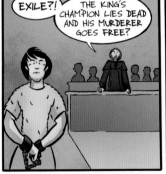

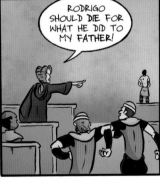

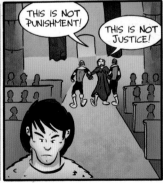

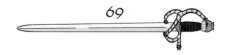

"THIS IS NOT JUSTICE!"

CLIP CLOP CLIP CLOP

WHO'S THERE?!

RELAX, RODRIGO...IT'S JUST US.

YOU NEARLY GAVE ME A HEART ATTACK! WHAT ARE YOU TWO DOING HERE?

WHAT'S IT LOOK LIKE? WE'RE COMING WITH YOU.

ARE YOU CRAZY? GO BACK BEFORE SANCHO FINDS OUT!

OH, HE KNOWS...HE KICKED US OUT!

WHAT?! WHY?!

WE TOLD HIM OFF, WHY ELSE? THO' I THINK PEDRO'S DRAWING IS WHAT REALLY DID US IN...

I CAN'T BELIEVE YOU TWO!

DO YOU THINK THIS IS A GAME? WE'VE GOT NOTHING NOW! NO ONE!

WHAT ARE YOU TALKING ABOUT? WE'VE GOT FRESH AIR! WE'VE GOT FRESH HORSES! AND WE'VE GOT EACH OTHER!

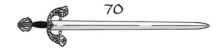

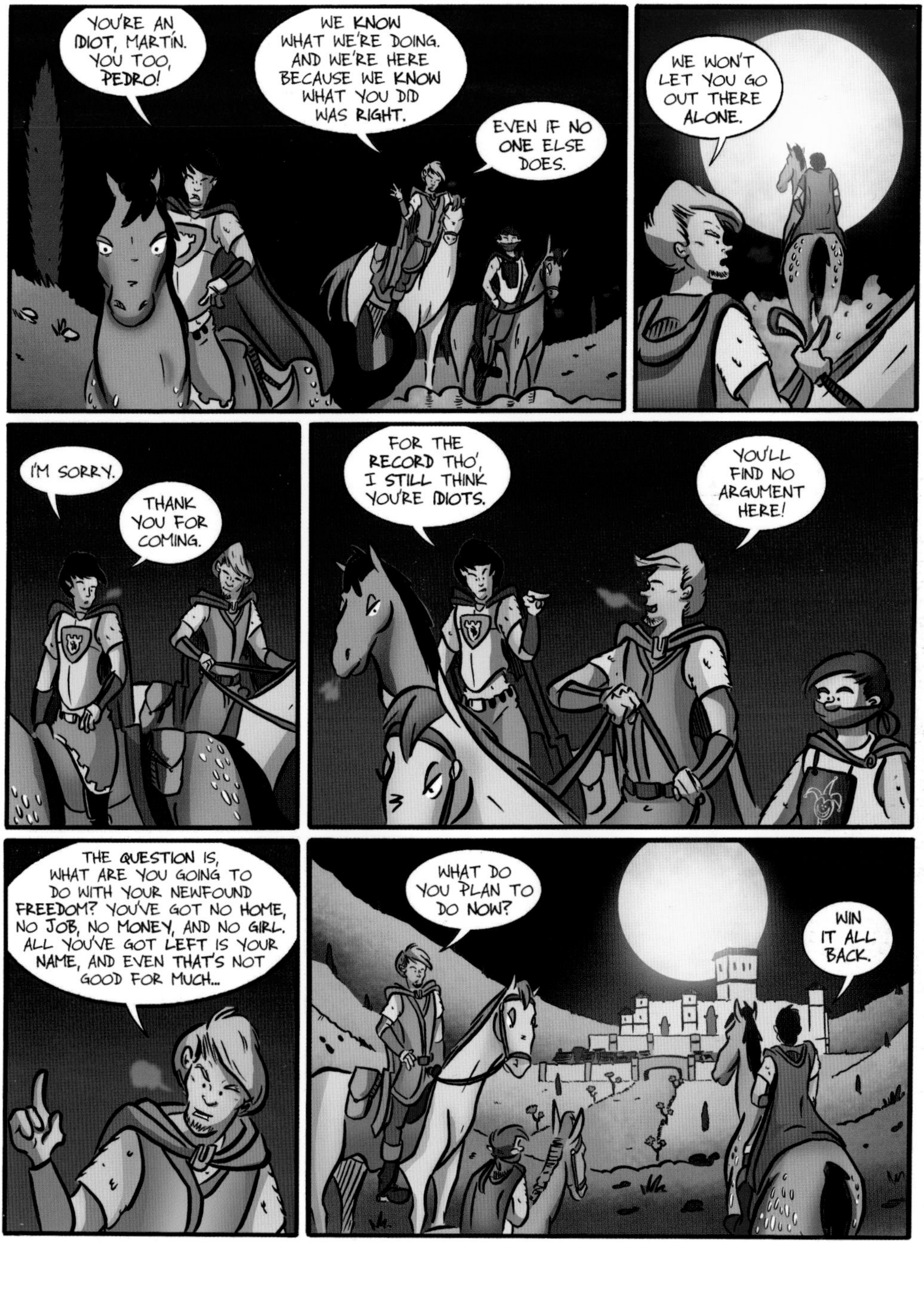
YOU'RE AN IDIOT, MARTÍN. YOU TOO, PEDRO!
WE KNOW WHAT WE'RE DOING. AND WE'RE HERE BECAUSE WE KNOW WHAT YOU DID WAS RIGHT.
EVEN IF NO ONE ELSE DOES.
WE WON'T LET YOU GO OUT THERE ALONE.
I'M SORRY.
THANK YOU FOR COMING.
FOR THE RECORD THO', I STILL THINK YOU'RE IDIOTS.
YOU'LL FIND NO ARGUMENT HERE!
THE QUESTION IS, WHAT ARE YOU GOING TO DO WITH YOUR NEWFOUND FREEDOM? YOU'VE GOT NO HOME, NO JOB, NO MONEY, AND NO GIRL. ALL YOU'VE GOT LEFT IS YOUR NAME, AND EVEN THAT'S NOT GOOD FOR MUCH...
WHAT DO YOU PLAN TO DO NOW?
WIN IT ALL BACK.

part two

La frontera

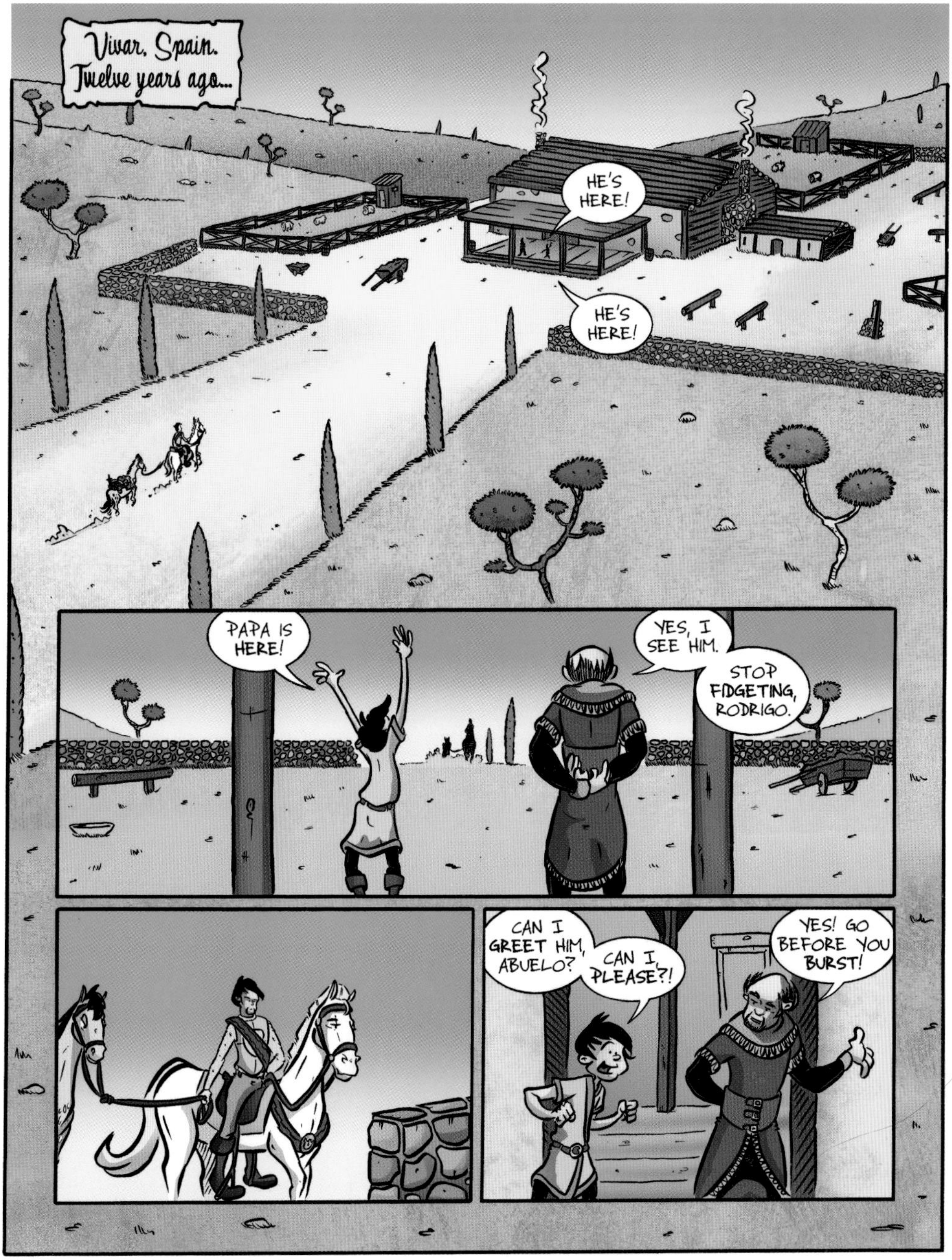
Vivar, Spain. Twelve years ago...
HE'S HERE!
HE'S HERE!
PAPA IS HERE!
YES, I SEE HIM.
STOP FIDGETING, RODRIGO.
CAN I GREET HIM, ABUELO?
CAN I, PLEASE?!
YES! GO BEFORE YOU BURST!

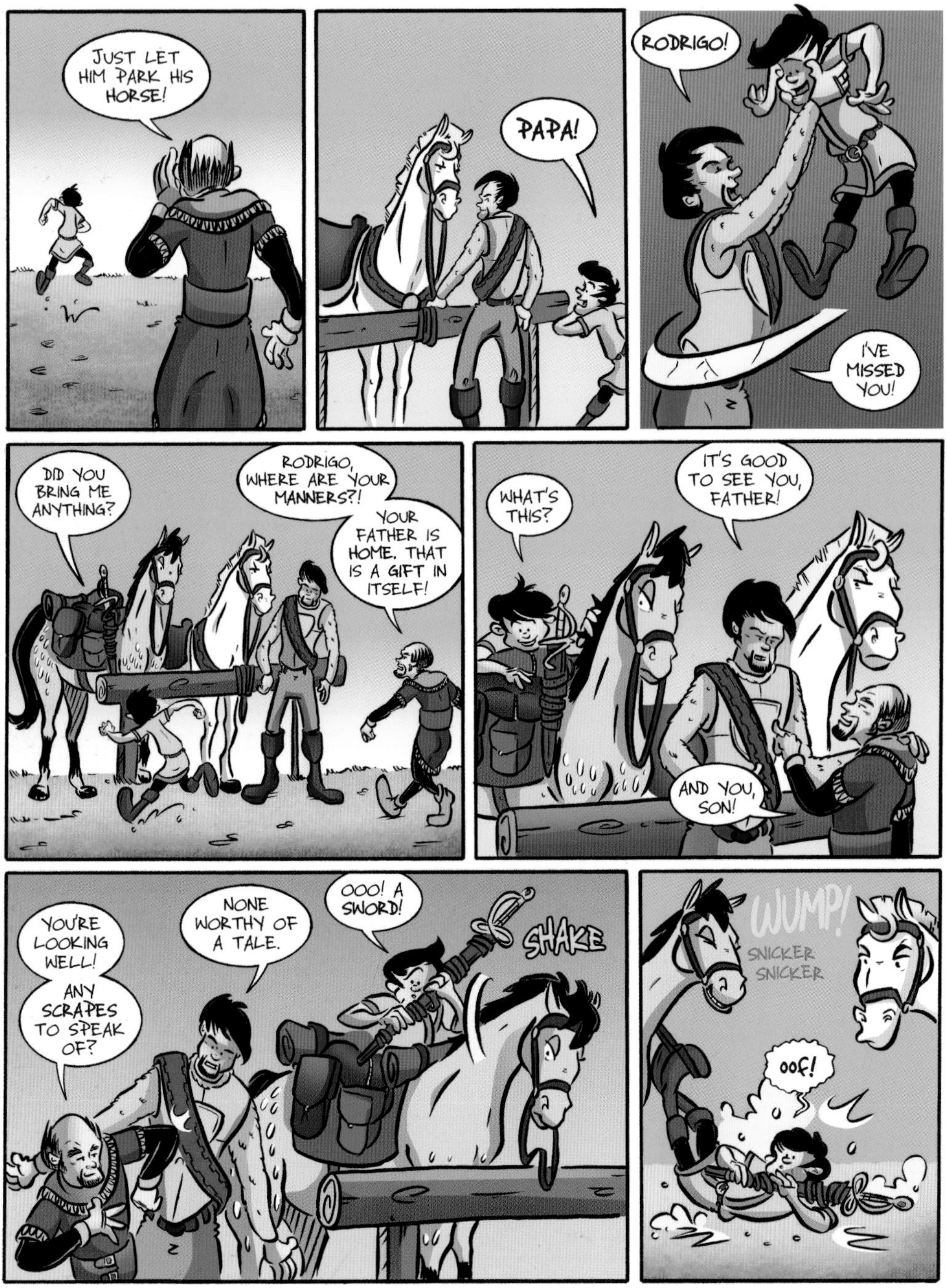
JUST LET HIM PARK HIS HORSE!
PAPA!
RODRIGO!
I'VE MISSED YOU!
DID YOU BRING ME ANYTHING?
RODRIGO, WHERE ARE YOUR MANNERS?!
YOUR FATHER IS HOME. THAT IS A GIFT IN ITSELF!
WHAT'S THIS?
IT'S GOOD TO SEE YOU, FATHER!
AND YOU, SON!
YOU'RE LOOKING WELL!
ANY SCRAPES TO SPEAK OF?
NONE WORTHY OF A TALE.
OOO! A SWORD!
SHAKE
WUMP!
SNICKER SNICKER
OOF!

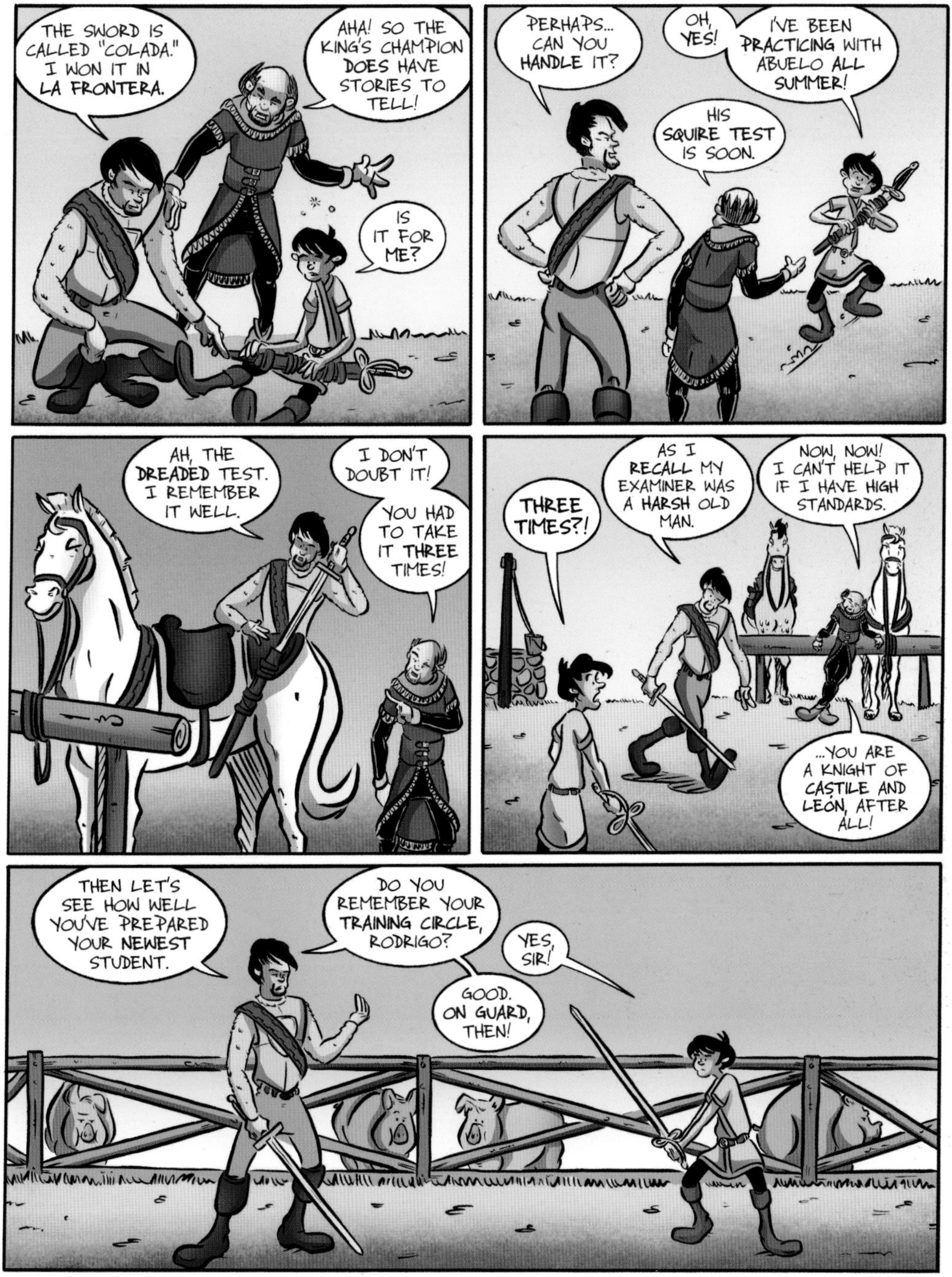
THE SWORD IS CALLED "COLADA." I WON IT IN LA FRONTERA.
AHA! SO THE KING'S CHAMPION DOES HAVE STORIES TO TELL!
IS IT FOR ME?
PERHAPS... CAN YOU HANDLE IT?
OH, YES!
I'VE BEEN PRACTICING WITH ABUELO ALL SUMMER!
HIS SQUIRE TEST IS SOON.
AH, THE DREADED TEST. I REMEMBER IT WELL.
I DON'T DOUBT IT!
YOU HAD TO TAKE IT THREE TIMES!
THREE TIMES?!
AS I RECALL MY EXAMINER WAS A HARSH OLD MAN.
NOW, NOW! I CAN'T HELP IT IF I HAVE HIGH STANDARDS.
...YOU ARE A KNIGHT OF CASTILE AND LEÓN, AFTER ALL!
THEN LET'S SEE HOW WELL YOU'VE PREPARED YOUR NEWEST STUDENT.
DO YOU REMEMBER YOUR TRAINING CIRCLE, RODRIGO?
YES, SIR!
GOOD. ON GUARD, THEN!

WHEN WAS THE BATTLE OF COVADONGA?
IN 718... PELAYO THE GREAT DEFEATED THE MOORS IN ASTURIAS!
ching!
GOOD.
WHO WAS ABD AL-RAHMAN?
kang!
EXILED PRINCE OF DAMASCUS.
HEIR TO THE UMAYYAD DYNASTY AND FOUNDER OF CÓRDOBA.
WHAT YEAR?
ting!
756!
VERY GOOD!
WHO RULES THE KINGDOM OF TOLEDO?
tang!
LORD AL-MAMUN!
AND OF BARBASTRO?
kang!
LORD MUQTADIR!
WHOSE KINGDOM DO YOU SERVE?
GOD FIRST...
tic!
SPAIN, SECOND...
tac!
MY KING, THIRD.
tic!
HOW MUST A KNIGHT ACT?
kang!
WITH PRUDENCE!
kang!
TEMPERANCE!
kang!
AND JUSTICE!
YES... AND...?
AND FORTITUDE!
tang!
MUY BIEN! BUT THERE'S ONE MORE!
THERE IS?

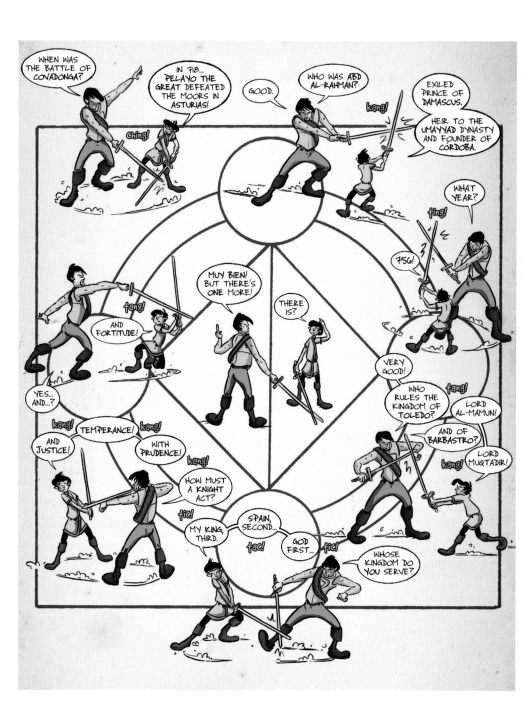

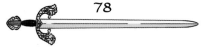

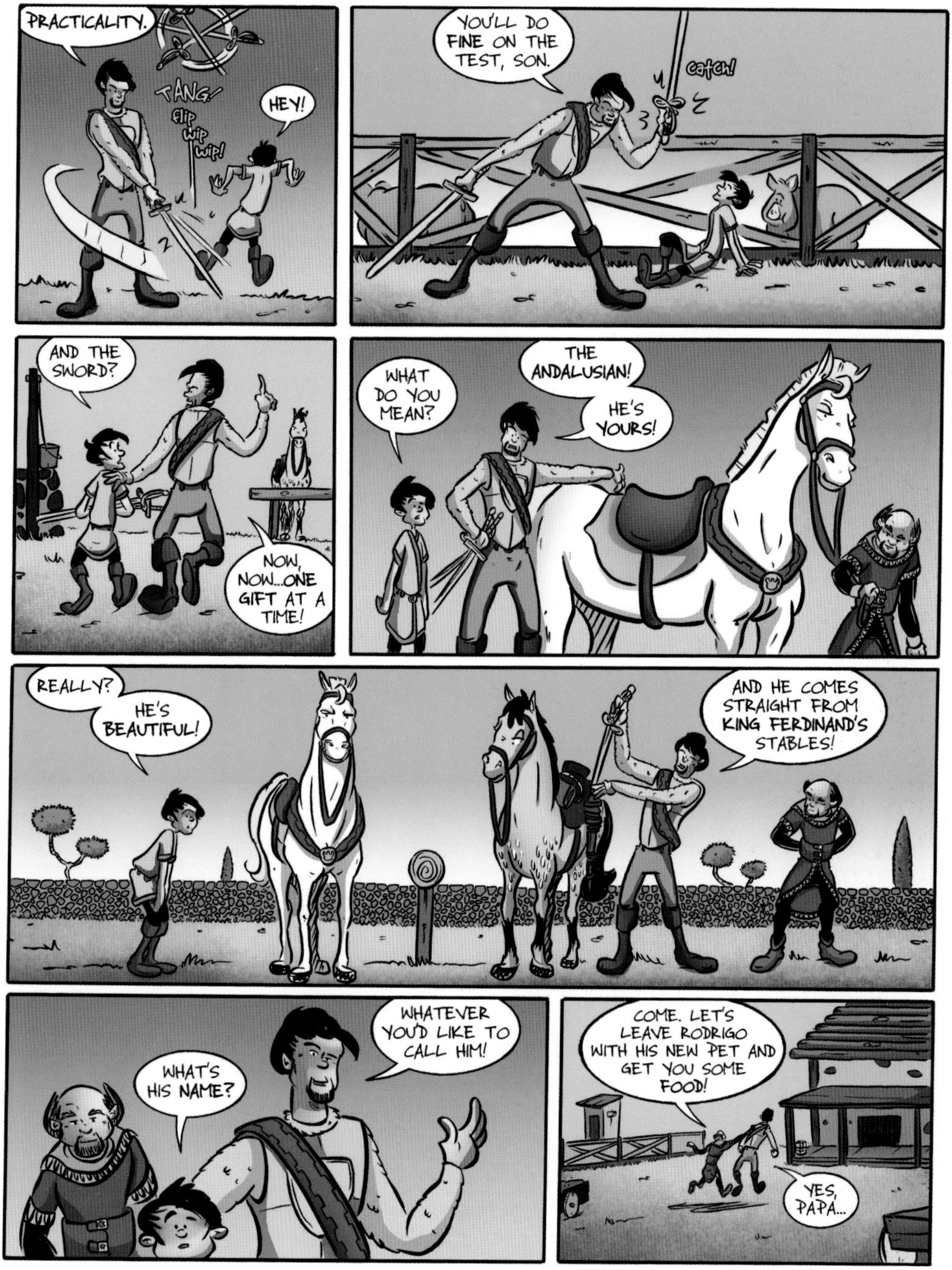
PRACTICALITY.
TANG!
flip
wip
wip!
HEY!
YOU'LL DO FINE ON THE TEST, SON.
catch!
AND THE SWORD?
NOW, NOW...ONE GIFT AT A TIME!
WHAT DO YOU MEAN?
THE ANDALUSIAN!
HE'S YOURS!
REALLY?
HE'S BEAUTIFUL!
AND HE COMES STRAIGHT FROM KING FERDINAND'S STABLES!
WHAT'S HIS NAME?
WHATEVER YOU'D LIKE TO CALL HIM!
COME. LET'S LEAVE RODRIGO WITH HIS NEW PET AND GET YOU SOME FOOD!
YES, PAPA...

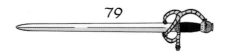

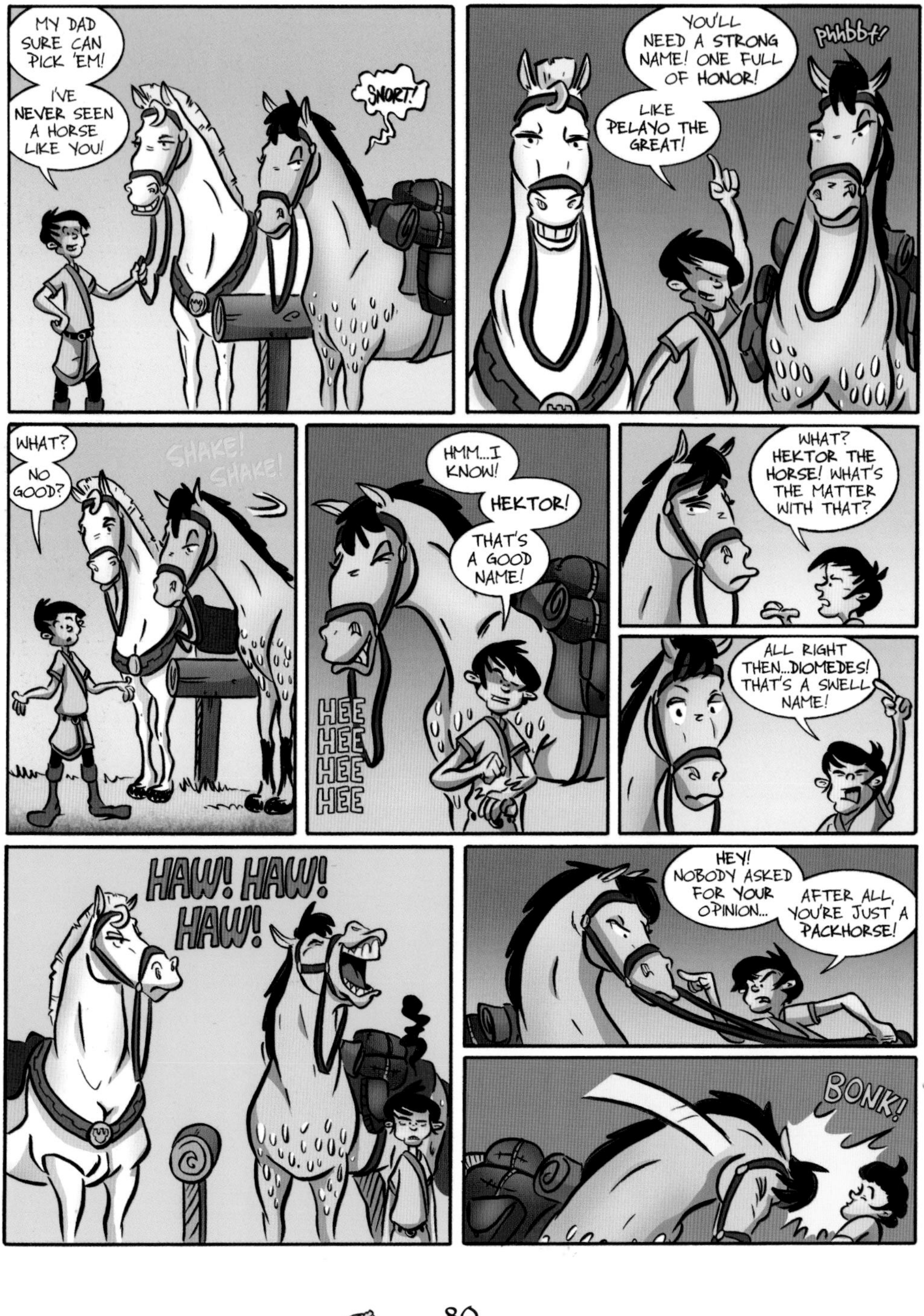
MY DAD SURE CAN PICK 'EM!
I'VE NEVER SEEN A HORSE LIKE YOU!
SNORT!
YOU'LL NEED A STRONG NAME! ONE FULL OF HONOR!
LIKE PELAYO THE GREAT!
phhbbt!
WHAT?
NO GOOD?
SHAKE! SHAKE!
HMM...I KNOW!
HEKTOR!
THAT'S A GOOD NAME!
HEE HEE HEE HEE
WHAT? HEKTOR THE HORSE! WHAT'S THE MATTER WITH THAT?
ALL RIGHT THEN...DIOMEDES! THAT'S A SWELL NAME!
HAW! HAW! HAW!
HEY! NOBODY ASKED FOR YOUR OPINION...
AFTER ALL, YOU'RE JUST A PACKHORSE!
BONK!

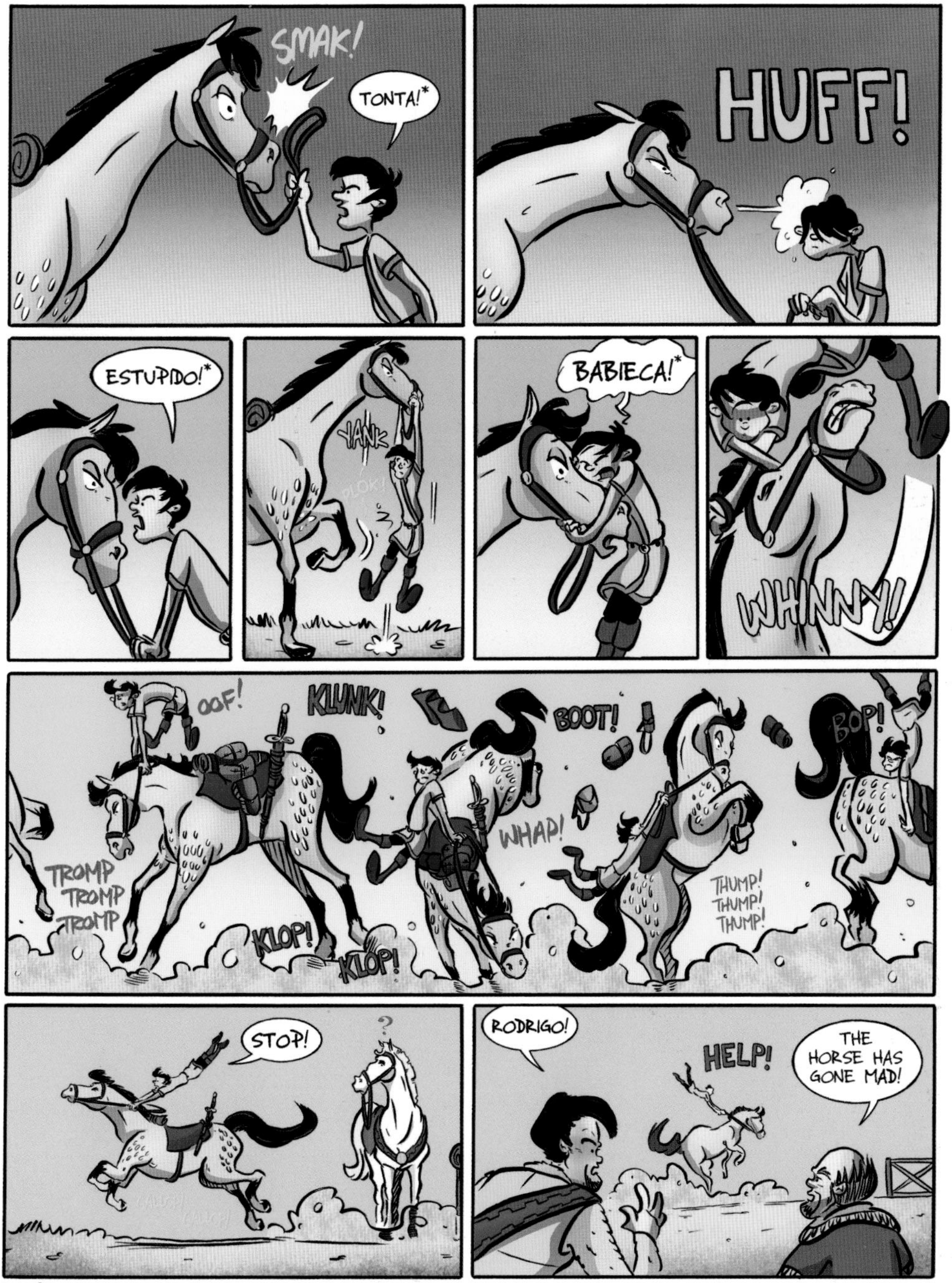
SMAK!
TONTA!*
HUFF!
ESTUPIDO!*
YANK
PLOK!
BABIECA!*
WHINNY!
OOF!
KLUNK!
BOOT!
BOP!
WHAP!
TROMP
TROMP
TROMP
KLOP!
KLOP!
THUMP!
THUMP!
THUMP!
STOP!
?
RODRIGO!
HELP!
THE HORSE HAS GONE MAD!

*Fool! *Stupid! *Dullard!

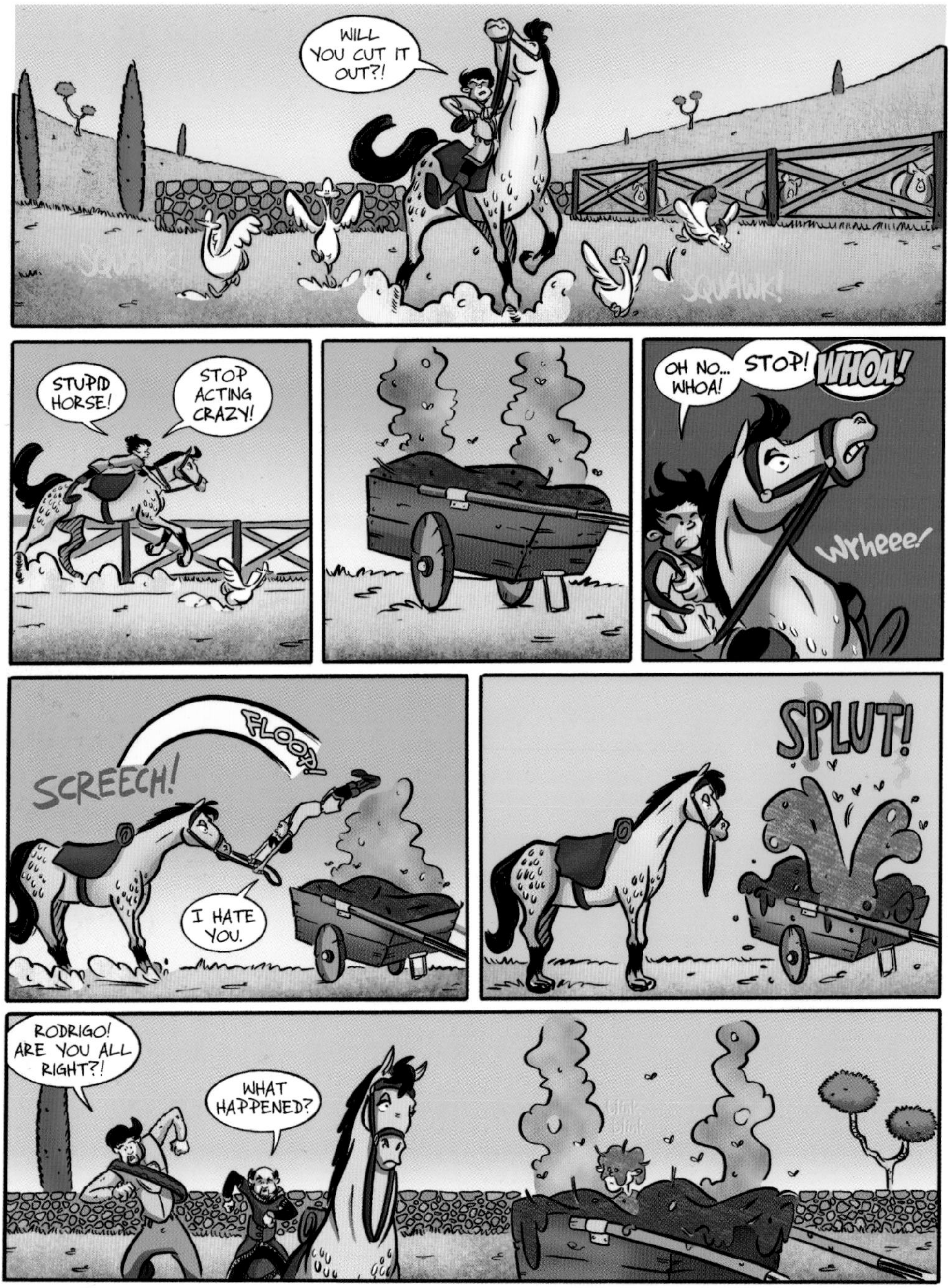
WILL YOU CUT IT OUT?!
SQUAWK
SQUAWK!
STUPID HORSE!
STOP ACTING CRAZY!
OH NO... WHOA!
STOP!
WHOA!
Wrheee!
SCREECH!
FLOOP!
I HATE YOU.
SPLUT!
RODRIGO! ARE YOU ALL RIGHT?!
WHAT HAPPENED?
blink blink

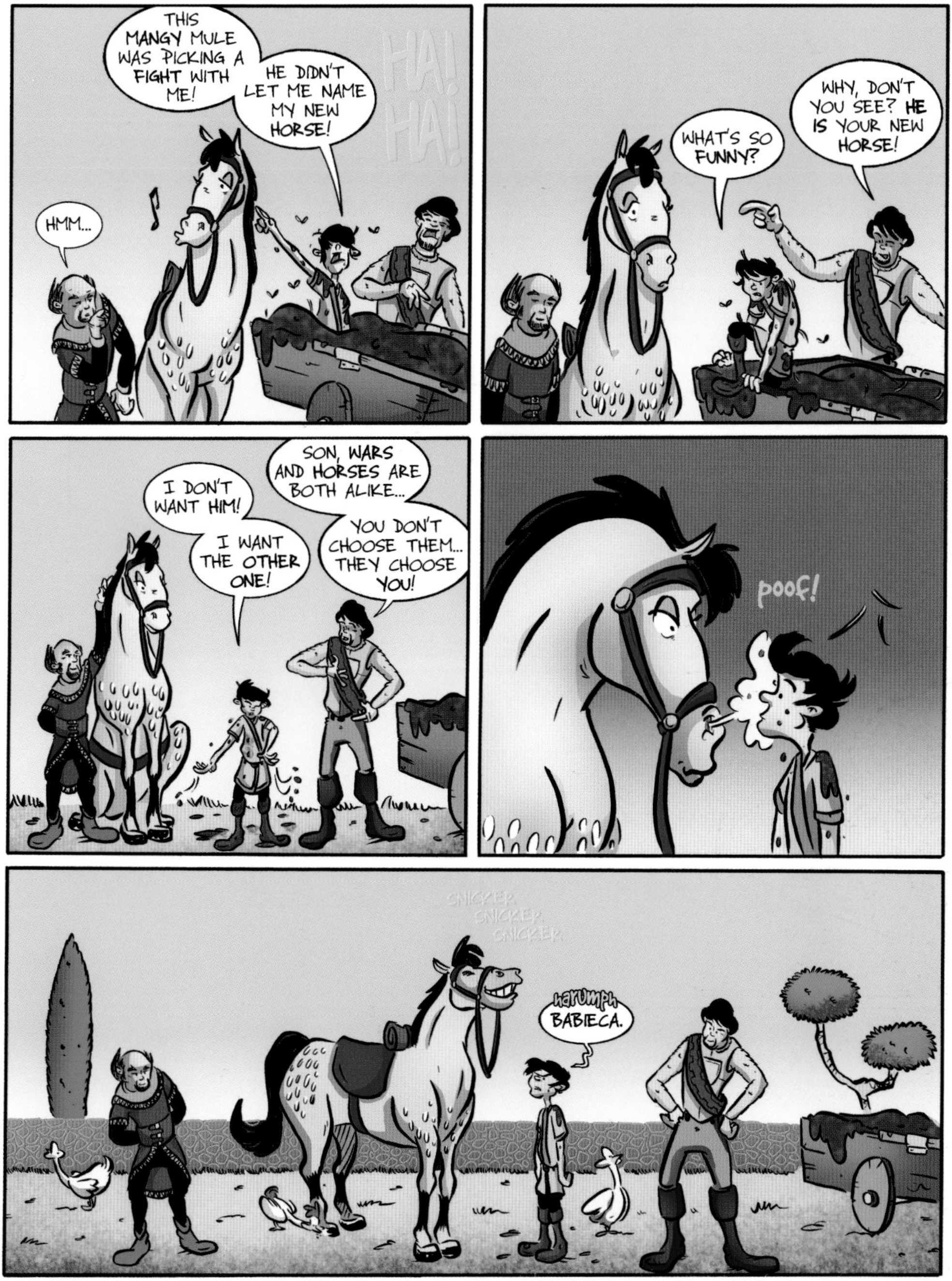
THIS MANGY MULE WAS PICKING A FIGHT WITH ME!
HE DIDN'T LET ME NAME MY NEW HORSE!
HA! HA!
HMM...
WHAT'S SO FUNNY?
WHY, DON'T YOU SEE? HE IS YOUR NEW HORSE!
I DON'T WANT HIM!
I WANT THE OTHER ONE!
SON, WARS AND HORSES ARE BOTH ALIKE...
YOU DON'T CHOOSE THEM... THEY CHOOSE YOU!
poof!
SNICKER SNICKER SNICKER
harumph
BABIECA.

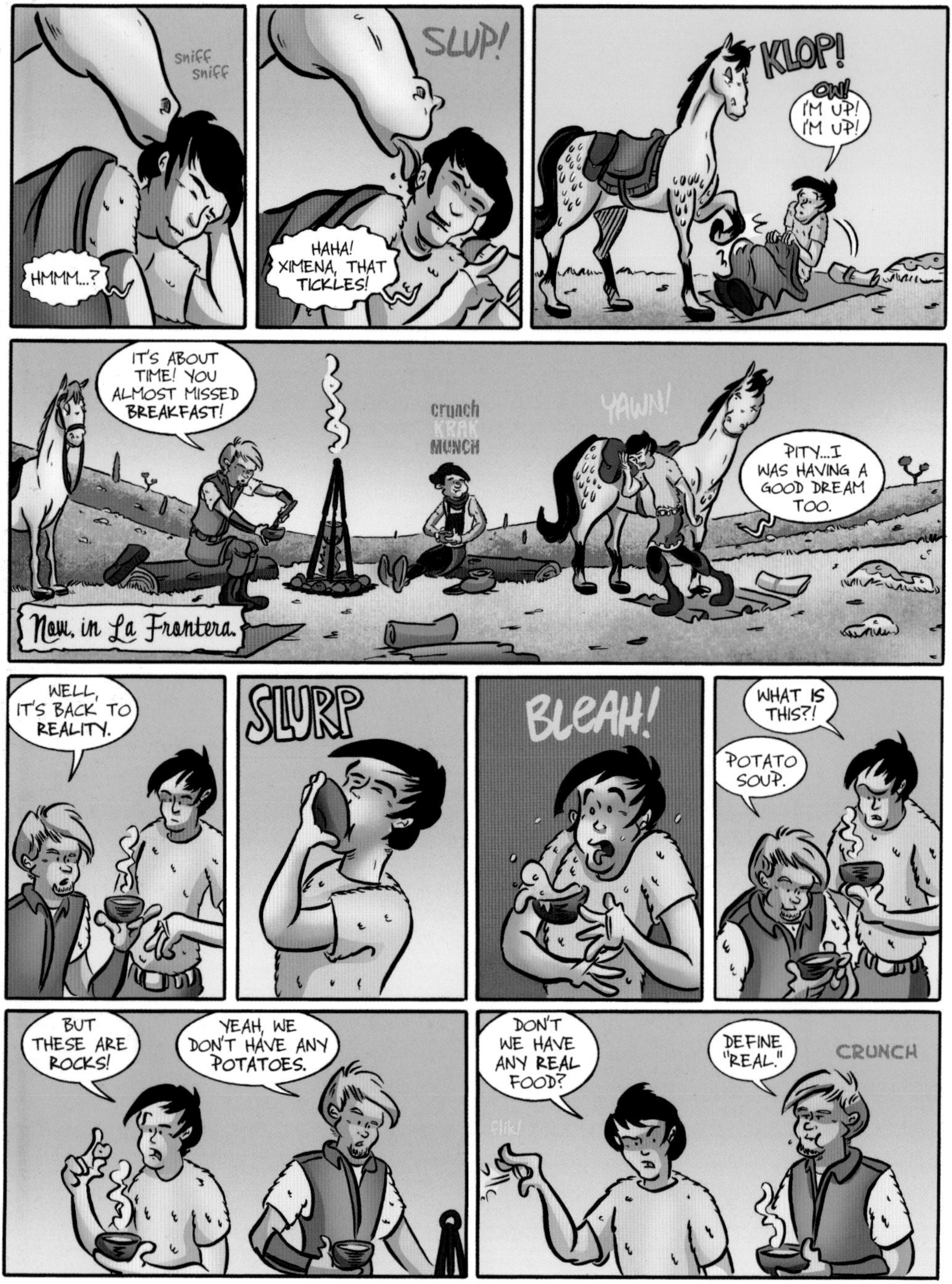
sniff sniff
HMMM...?
SLUP!
HAHA! XIMENA, THAT TICKLES!
KLOP!
OW! I'M UP! I'M UP!
IT'S ABOUT TIME! YOU ALMOST MISSED BREAKFAST!
crunch
KRAK
MUNCH
YAWN!
PITY...I WAS HAVING A GOOD DREAM TOO.
Now, in La Frontera.
WELL, IT'S BACK TO REALITY.
SLURP
BLEAH!
WHAT IS THIS?!
POTATO SOUP.
BUT THESE ARE ROCKS!
YEAH, WE DON'T HAVE ANY POTATOES.
DON'T WE HAVE ANY REAL FOOD?
flik!
DEFINE "REAL."
CRUNCH

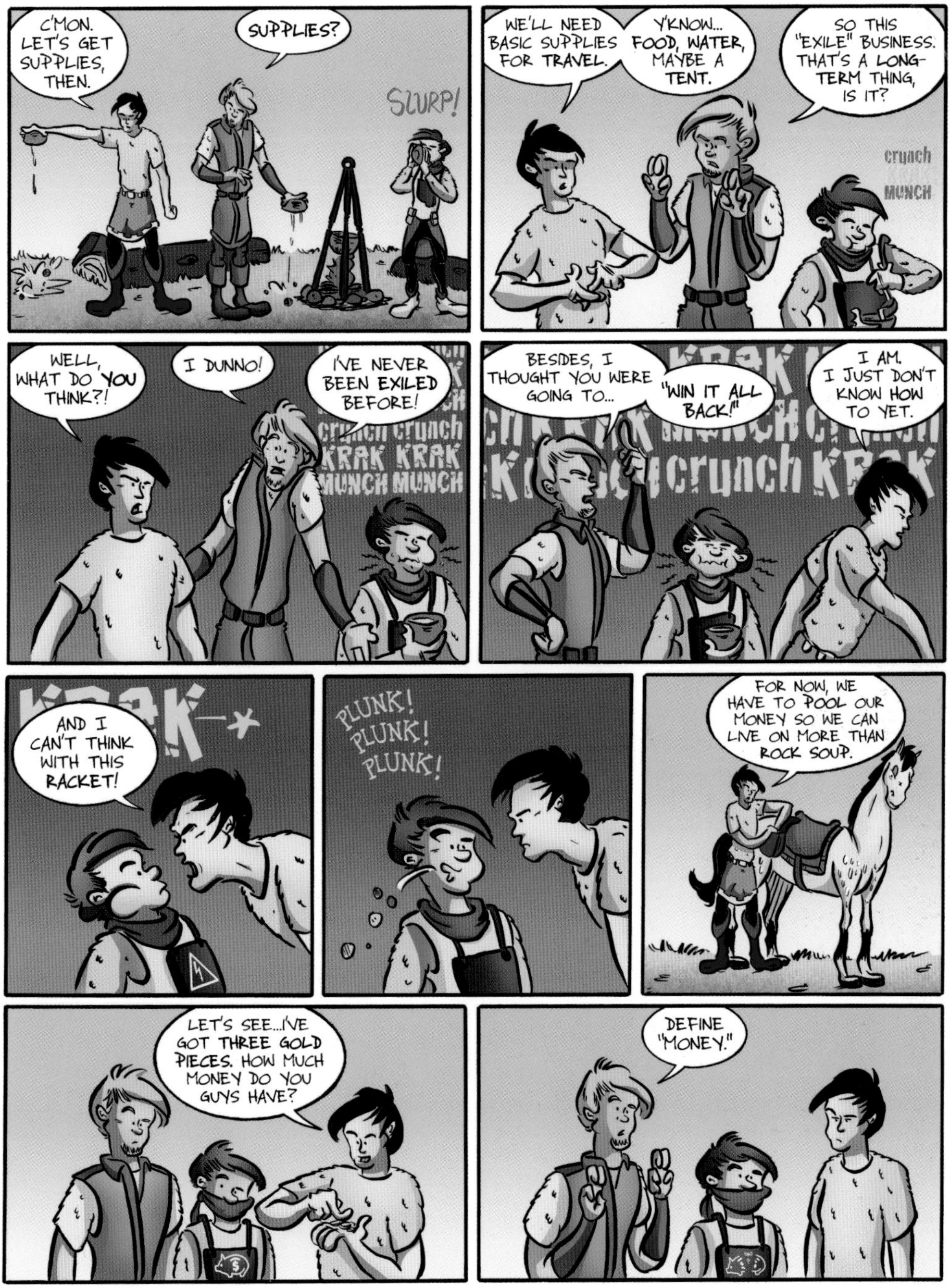
C'MON. LET'S GET SUPPLIES, THEN.
SUPPLIES?
SLURP!
WE'LL NEED BASIC SUPPLIES FOR TRAVEL.
Y'KNOW... FOOD, WATER, MAYBE A TENT.
SO THIS "EXILE" BUSINESS. THAT'S A LONG-TERM THING, IS IT?
crunch KRAK MUNCH
WELL, WHAT DO YOU THINK?!
I DUNNO!
I'VE NEVER BEEN EXILED BEFORE!
crunch crunch KRAK KRAK MUNCH MUNCH
BESIDES, I THOUGHT YOU WERE GOING TO...
"WIN IT ALL BACK!"
I AM. I JUST DON'T KNOW HOW TO YET.
crunch KRAK
AND I CAN'T THINK WITH THIS RACKET!
PLUNK! PLUNK! PLUNK!
FOR NOW, WE HAVE TO POOL OUR MONEY SO WE CAN LIVE ON MORE THAN ROCK SOUP.
LET'S SEE...I'VE GOT THREE GOLD PIECES. HOW MUCH MONEY DO YOU GUYS HAVE?
DEFINE "MONEY."

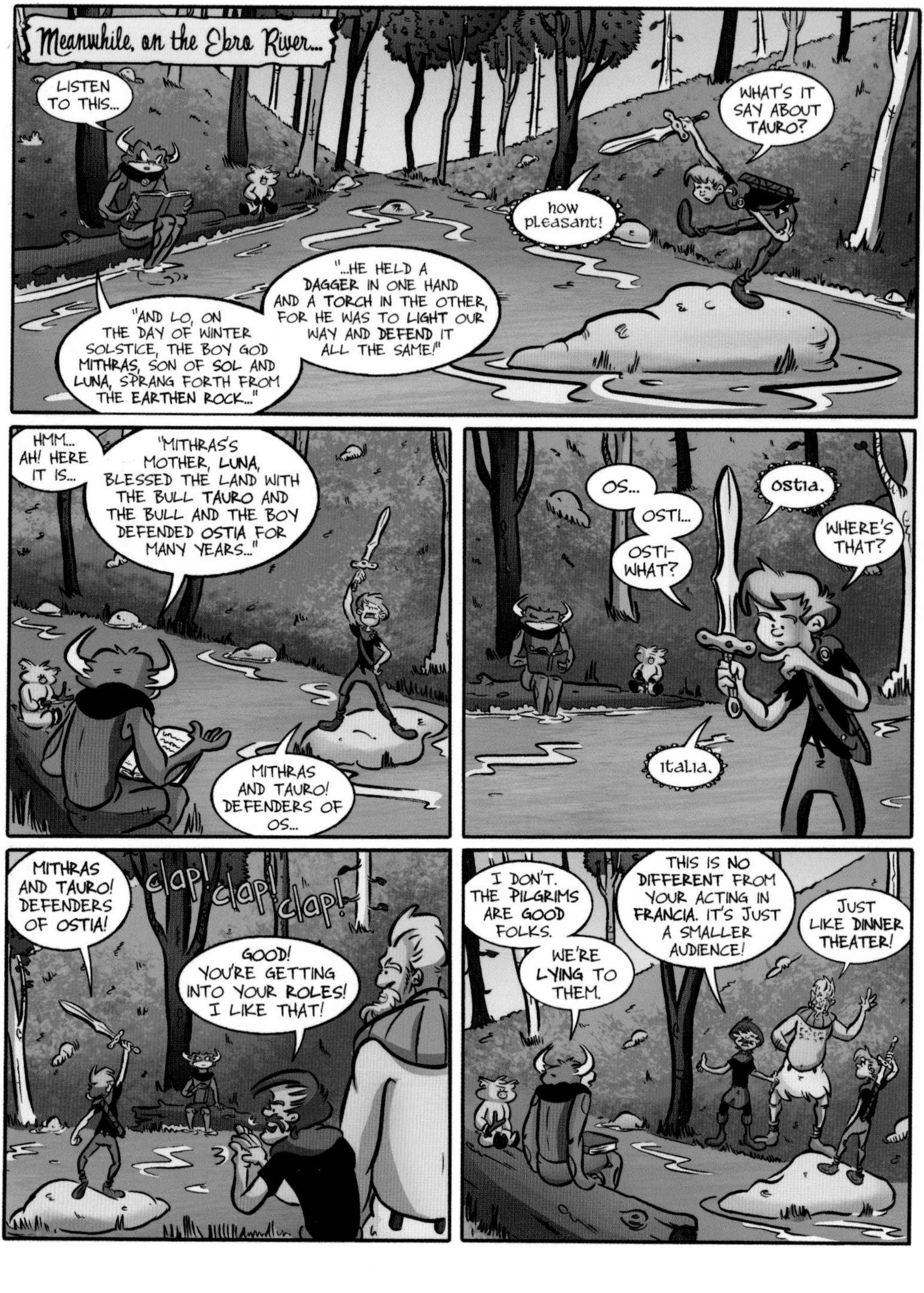
Meanwhile, on the Ebro River...
LISTEN TO THIS...
WHAT'S IT SAY ABOUT TAURO?
how pleasant!
"AND LO, ON THE DAY OF WINTER SOLSTICE, THE BOY GOD MITHRAS, SON OF SOL AND LUNA, SPRANG FORTH FROM THE EARTHEN ROCK..."
"...HE HELD A DAGGER IN ONE HAND AND A TORCH IN THE OTHER, FOR HE WAS TO LIGHT OUR WAY AND DEFEND IT ALL THE SAME!"
HMM... AH! HERE IT IS...
"MITHRAS'S MOTHER, LUNA, BLESSED THE LAND WITH THE BULL TAURO AND THE BULL AND THE BOY DEFENDED OSTIA FOR MANY YEARS..."
MITHRAS AND TAURO! DEFENDERS OF OS...
OS...
OSTI...
OSTI-WHAT?
ostia.
WHERE'S THAT?
italia.
MITHRAS AND TAURO! DEFENDERS OF OSTIA!
clap! clap! clap!
GOOD! YOU'RE GETTING INTO YOUR ROLES! I LIKE THAT!
I DON'T. THE PILGRIMS ARE GOOD FOLKS.
WE'RE LYING TO THEM.
THIS IS NO DIFFERENT FROM YOUR ACTING IN FRANCIA. IT'S JUST A SMALLER AUDIENCE!
JUST LIKE DINNER THEATER!

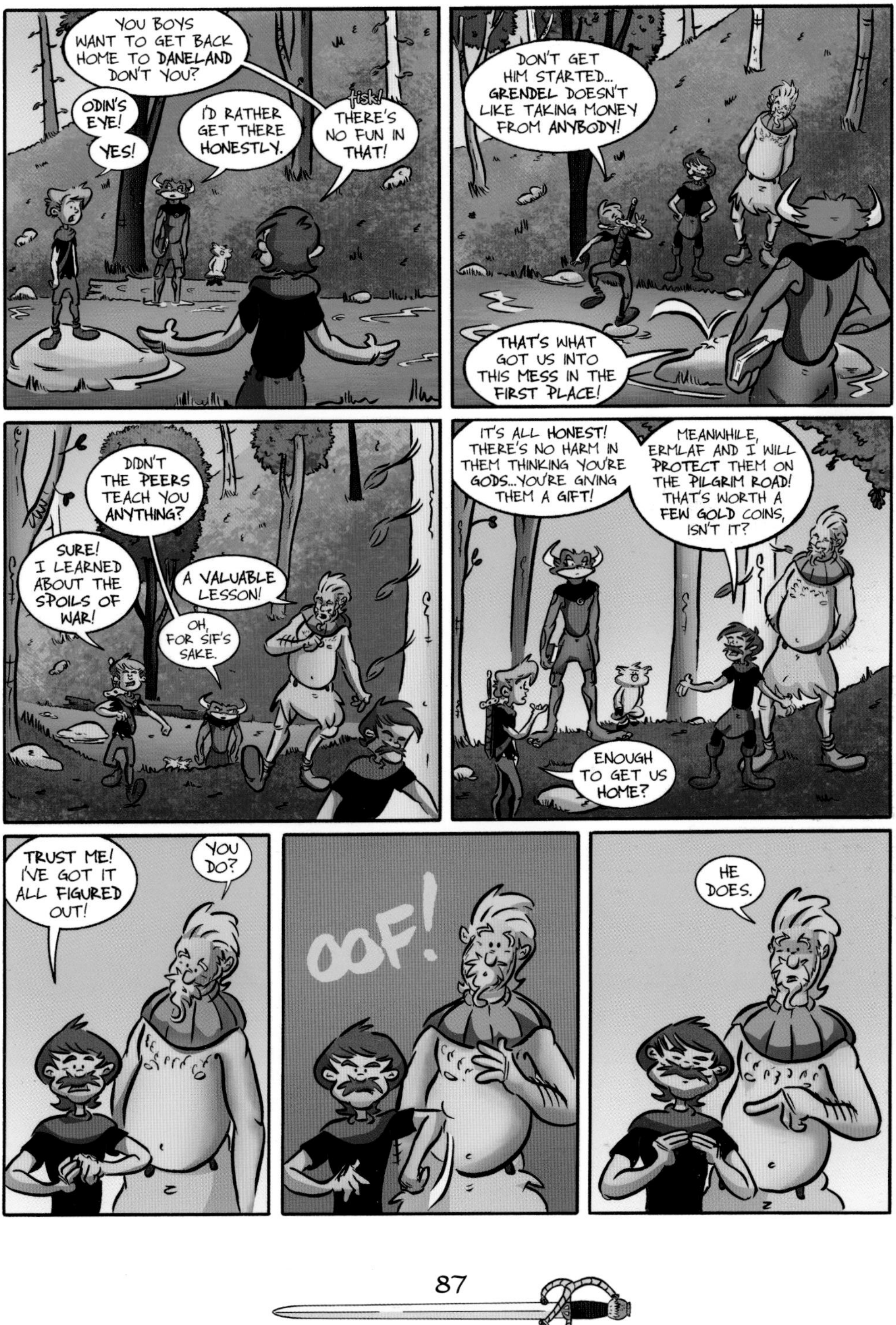
YOU BOYS WANT TO GET BACK HOME TO DANELAND DON'T YOU?
ODIN'S EYE!
YES!
I'D RATHER GET THERE HONESTLY.
fisk!
THERE'S NO FUN IN THAT!
DON'T GET HIM STARTED... GRENDEL DOESN'T LIKE TAKING MONEY FROM ANYBODY!
THAT'S WHAT GOT US INTO THIS MESS IN THE FIRST PLACE!
DIDN'T THE PEERS TEACH YOU ANYTHING?
SURE! I LEARNED ABOUT THE SPOILS OF WAR!
A VALUABLE LESSON!
OH, FOR SIF'S SAKE.
IT'S ALL HONEST! THERE'S NO HARM IN THEM THINKING YOU'RE GODS...YOU'RE GIVING THEM A GIFT!
MEANWHILE, ERMLAF AND I WILL PROTECT THEM ON THE PILGRIM ROAD! THAT'S WORTH A FEW GOLD COINS, ISN'T IT?
ENOUGH TO GET US HOME?
TRUST ME! I'VE GOT IT ALL FIGURED OUT!
YOU DO?
OOF!
HE DOES.

Burgos

AND MAY GOD PROTECT COUNT GORMAZ IN THE NEXT LIFE, AS THE COUNT PROTECTED US IN THIS ONE.

REST IN PEACE.

SHE DOESN'T HAVE ANYONE NOW...

TAKE HER BACK WITH YOU TO ZAMORA. A CHANGE OF SCENERY WILL BE GOOD FOR HER.

YOU'LL NEED A NEW CHAMPION NOW...

THE CHAMPIONS' SASH WILL GO TO ORDOÑEZ. HE IS A GOOD SOLDIER.

UNLIKE RODRIGO?

FEH! I SHOULD HAVE HAD HIM KILLED FOR ALL THE TROUBLE HE'S CAUSED ME! WITH GORMAZ GONE IT WILL BE HARDER TO KEEP THE PROVINCES IN LINE.

ONCE NEWS OF HIS DEATH SPREADS I'M SURE THE TAIFA LORDS WILL PRESS NORTH!

ALL THE MORE REASON, CASTILE AND LEÓN SHOULD UNITE, BROTHER!

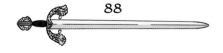

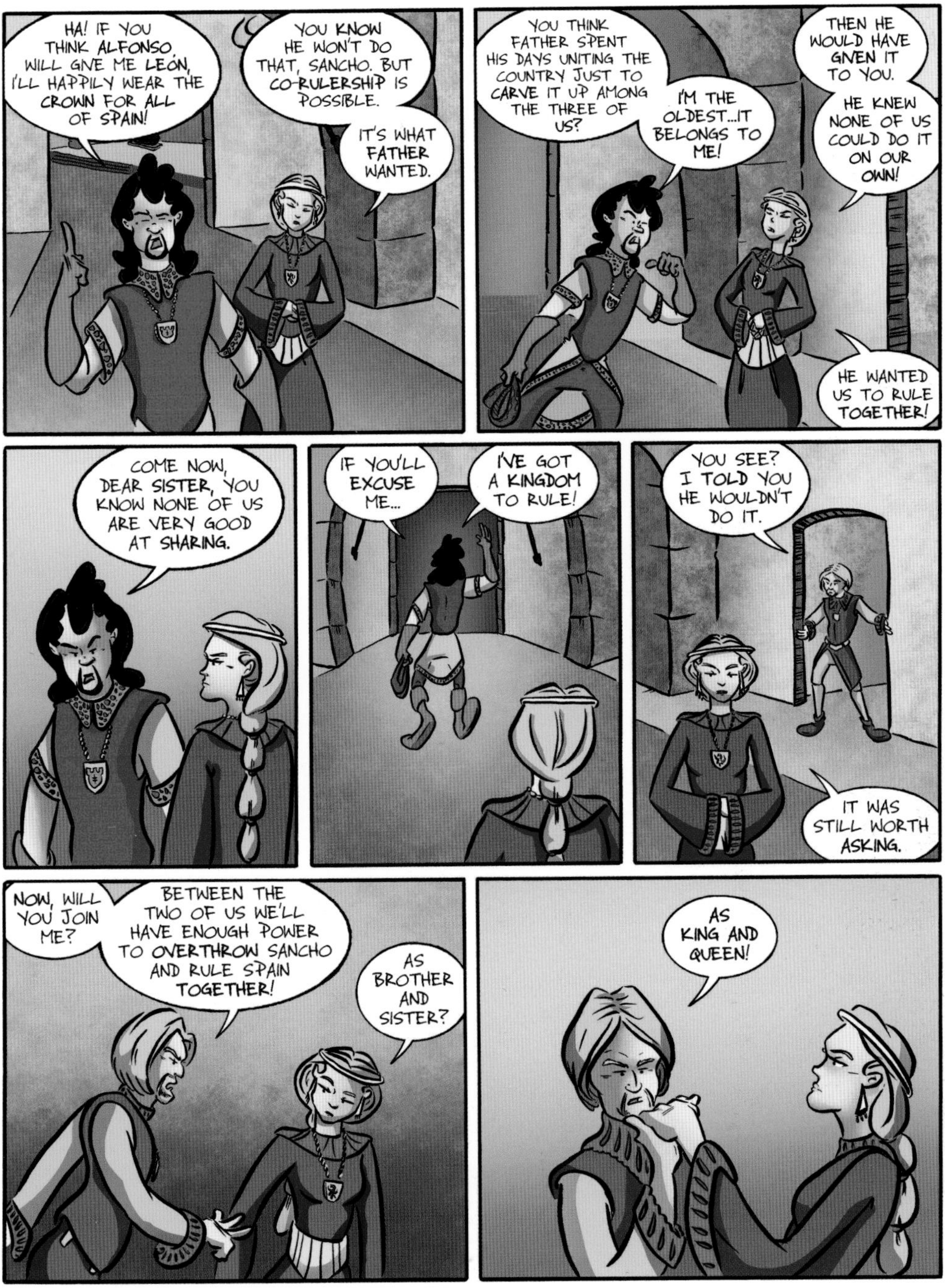
HA! IF YOU THINK ALFONSO WILL GIVE ME LEÓN, I'LL HAPPILY WEAR THE CROWN FOR ALL OF SPAIN!
YOU KNOW HE WON'T DO THAT, SANCHO. BUT CO-RULERSHIP IS POSSIBLE.
IT'S WHAT FATHER WANTED.
YOU THINK FATHER SPENT HIS DAYS UNITING THE COUNTRY JUST TO CARVE IT UP AMONG THE THREE OF US?
I'M THE OLDEST...IT BELONGS TO ME!
THEN HE WOULD HAVE GIVEN IT TO YOU.
HE KNEW NONE OF US COULD DO IT ON OUR OWN!
HE WANTED US TO RULE TOGETHER!
COME NOW, DEAR SISTER, YOU KNOW NONE OF US ARE VERY GOOD AT SHARING.
IF YOU'LL EXCUSE ME...
I'VE GOT A KINGDOM TO RULE!
YOU SEE? I TOLD YOU HE WOULDN'T DO IT.
IT WAS STILL WORTH ASKING.
NOW, WILL YOU JOIN ME?
BETWEEN THE TWO OF US WE'LL HAVE ENOUGH POWER TO OVERTHROW SANCHO AND RULE SPAIN TOGETHER!
AS BROTHER AND SISTER?
AS KING AND QUEEN!

I'M SO SORRY, FATHER. THIS WAS MY FAULT.

IF I HADN'T PUSHED YOU TO TAKE RODRIGO, THEN THIS NEVER WOULD HAVE HAPPENED.

I PUT MY LOVE FOR HIM AHEAD OF YOU, AND I CAN NEVER FORGIVE MYSELF FOR THAT.

KING SANCHO DID A DISSERVICE TO YOU AND OUR NAME.

HE LET RODRIGO LIVE.

AND THOUGH I MAY STILL LOVE HIM, HONOR DEMANDS THAT I AVENGE YOUR DEATH.

AND I WILL DO IT, FATHER. IN THIS LIFE OR THE NEXT...

RODRIGO WILL PAY FOR WHAT HE DID TO OUR FAMILY.

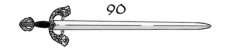

MY LORD... I DON'T KNOW WHAT TO SAY!

I CANNOT MATCH HIM BUT I WILL HONOR ALL THAT HE TAUGHT ME AND DO ALL THAT YOU ASK OF ME.

PROMISE ME YOU WILL BE AS GREAT A CHAMPION AS COUNT GORMAZ, AND THAT WILL BE A GOOD PLACE TO START.

EXCELLENT. NOW GO AND CELEBRATE YOUR SUCCESS!

THANK YOU, MY LORD.

DON DIEGO, IS SOMETHING ON YOUR MIND?

WITH ALL RESPECT, MY KING...

...I DON'T THINK ORDÓÑEZ IS READY TO BE CHAMPION.

I AGREE, BUT MY USUAL ONE IS DEAD...NO THANKS TO YOUR GRANDSON.

SO A NEW CHAMPION IS BORN.

COUNT GORMAZ AND I MAY HAVE HAD OUR DIFFERENCES, BUT AT LEAST HE WAS A SEASONED SOLDIER WHEN HE TOOK UP THE MANTLE!

ORDÓÑEZ IS TOO YOUNG.

HE IS NO OLDER THAN WHEN YOUR OWN SON BECAME CHAMPION.

IS IT REALLY HIS AGE YOU'RE WORRIED ABOUT?

HE IS TOO YOUNG...IN AGE, TEMPERAMENT, AND BATTLE.

THE SAME COULD BE SAID OF RODRIGO...

I AM NOT TALKING ABOUT MY GRANDSON...

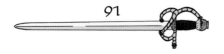

NO. YOU AREN'T. IN FACT YOU'VE SAID LITTLE ABOUT HIM OR HIS FATE.

I'M SURPRISED.

YOU DID WHAT YOU HAD TO, MY LORD.

I AM GRATEFUL EXILE WAS THE EXTENT OF IT.

YES... IT SEEMS THE DÍAZES HAVE OUTLIVED THEIR USEFULNESS.

MY LORD?

COME NOW, YOU DON'T REALLY THINK I CAN KEEP YOU ON AS COUNSEL AFTER I JUST EXILED YOUR GRANDSON!

HOW WOULD I KNOW YOUR OPINIONS WEREN'T COLORED BY REVENGE?

HAVE I EVER GIVEN YOU CAUSE TO QUESTION MY LOYALTY?

MY HONOR?

NONE. BUT THEN AGAIN, A KING'S CHAMPION WAS NEVER SLAIN BY ONE OF HIS OWN MEN. THESE ARE TROUBLING TIMES. I CAN'T RISK THE COMPANY OF MEN I DO NOT FULLY TRUST.

WITH GORMAZ GONE, MY SIBLINGS, THE MOORS, AND GOD KNOWS WHO ELSE WILL BE AFTER CASTILE. I CAN ONLY BE AMONG MY CLOSEST CONFIDANTS.

WHICH I AM!

NO, MY OLD TEACHER, NOT ANYMORE. IT'S TIME YOU WENT BACK TO YOUR RANCH TO RAISE STRONG HORSES FOR MY KNIGHTS.

AND WHAT OF THE KNIGHTS I'VE TRAINED? DO YOU HAVE ANY USE FOR THEM?

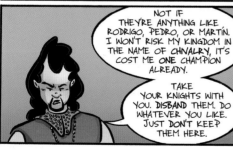

NOT IF THEY'RE ANYTHING LIKE RODRIGO, PEDRO, OR MARTÍN. I WON'T RISK MY KINGDOM IN THE NAME OF CHIVALRY, IT'S COST ME ONE CHAMPION ALREADY.

TAKE YOUR KNIGHTS WITH YOU. DISBAND THEM. DO WHATEVER YOU LIKE. JUST DON'T KEEP THEM HERE.

AS YOU WISH, MY LORD.

THE DÍAZES ARE DONE SERVING YOU.

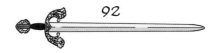

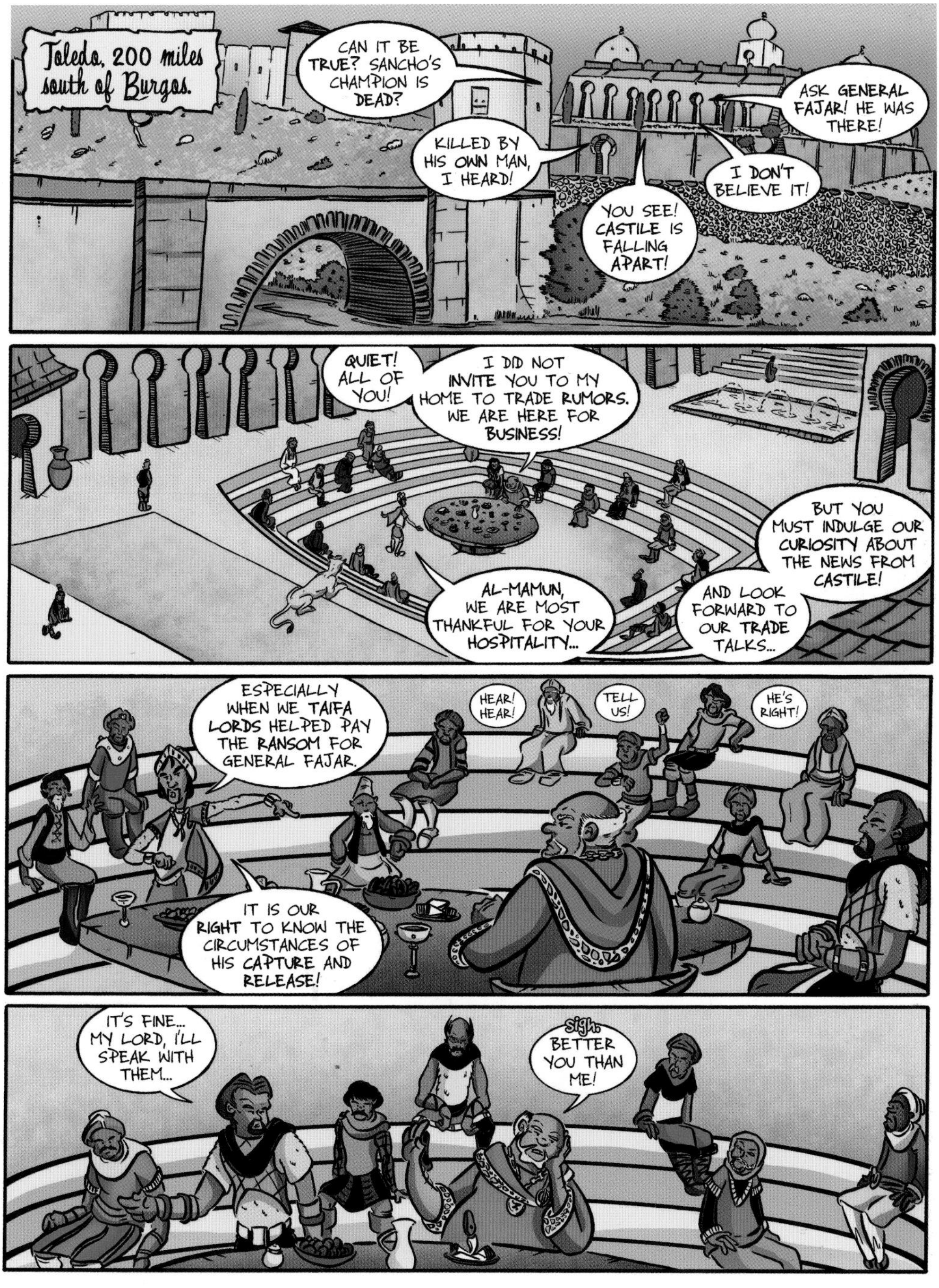
Toledo, 200 miles south of Burgos.
CAN IT BE TRUE? SANCHO'S CHAMPION IS DEAD?
KILLED BY HIS OWN MAN, I HEARD!
ASK GENERAL FAJAR! HE WAS THERE!
I DON'T BELIEVE IT!
YOU SEE! CASTILE IS FALLING APART!
QUIET! ALL OF YOU!
I DID NOT INVITE YOU TO MY HOME TO TRADE RUMORS. WE ARE HERE FOR BUSINESS!
AL-MAMUN, WE ARE MOST THANKFUL FOR YOUR HOSPITALITY...
AND LOOK FORWARD TO OUR TRADE TALKS...
BUT YOU MUST INDULGE OUR CURIOSITY ABOUT THE NEWS FROM CASTILE!
ESPECIALLY WHEN WE TAIFA LORDS HELPED PAY THE RANSOM FOR GENERAL FAJAR.
HEAR! HEAR!
TELL US!
HE'S RIGHT!
IT IS OUR RIGHT TO KNOW THE CIRCUMSTANCES OF HIS CAPTURE AND RELEASE!
IT'S FINE... MY LORD, I'LL SPEAK WITH THEM...
sigh.
BETTER YOU THAN ME!

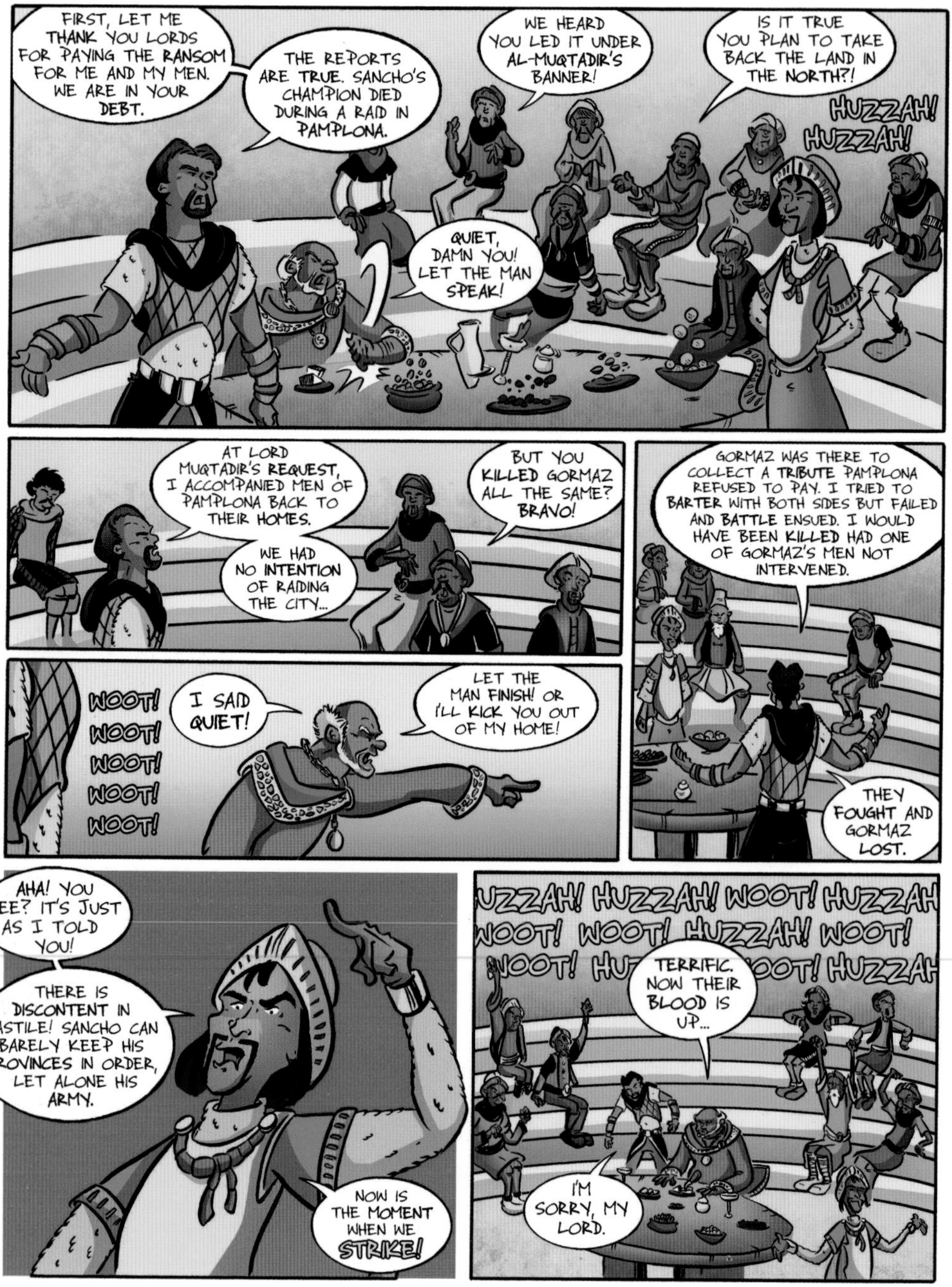

FIRST, LET ME THANK YOU LORDS FOR PAYING THE RANSOM FOR ME AND MY MEN. WE ARE IN YOUR DEBT.
THE REPORTS ARE TRUE. SANCHO'S CHAMPION DIED DURING A RAID IN PAMPLONA.
WE HEARD YOU LED IT UNDER AL-MUQTADIR'S BANNER!
IS IT TRUE YOU PLAN TO TAKE BACK THE LAND IN THE NORTH?!
HUZZAH! HUZZAH!
QUIET, DAMN YOU! LET THE MAN SPEAK!
AT LORD MUQTADIR'S REQUEST, I ACCOMPANIED MEN OF PAMPLONA BACK TO THEIR HOMES.
WE HAD NO INTENTION OF RAIDING THE CITY...
BUT YOU KILLED GORMAZ ALL THE SAME? BRAVO!
WOOT! WOOT! WOOT! WOOT! WOOT!
I SAID QUIET!
LET THE MAN FINISH! OR I'LL KICK YOU OUT OF MY HOME!
GORMAZ WAS THERE TO COLLECT A TRIBUTE PAMPLONA REFUSED TO PAY. I TRIED TO BARTER WITH BOTH SIDES BUT FAILED AND BATTLE ENSUED. I WOULD HAVE BEEN KILLED HAD ONE OF GORMAZ'S MEN NOT INTERVENED.
THEY FOUGHT AND GORMAZ LOST.
AHA! YOU SEE? IT'S JUST AS I TOLD YOU!
THERE IS DISCONTENT IN CASTILE! SANCHO CAN BARELY KEEP HIS PROVINCES IN ORDER, LET ALONE HIS ARMY.
NOW IS THE MOMENT WHEN WE STRIKE!
UZZAH! HUZZAH! WOOT! HUZZAH
WOOT! WOOT! HUZZAH! WOOT!
WOOT! HU OOT! HUZZAH
TERRIFIC. NOW THEIR BLOOD IS UP...
I'M SORRY, MY LORD.

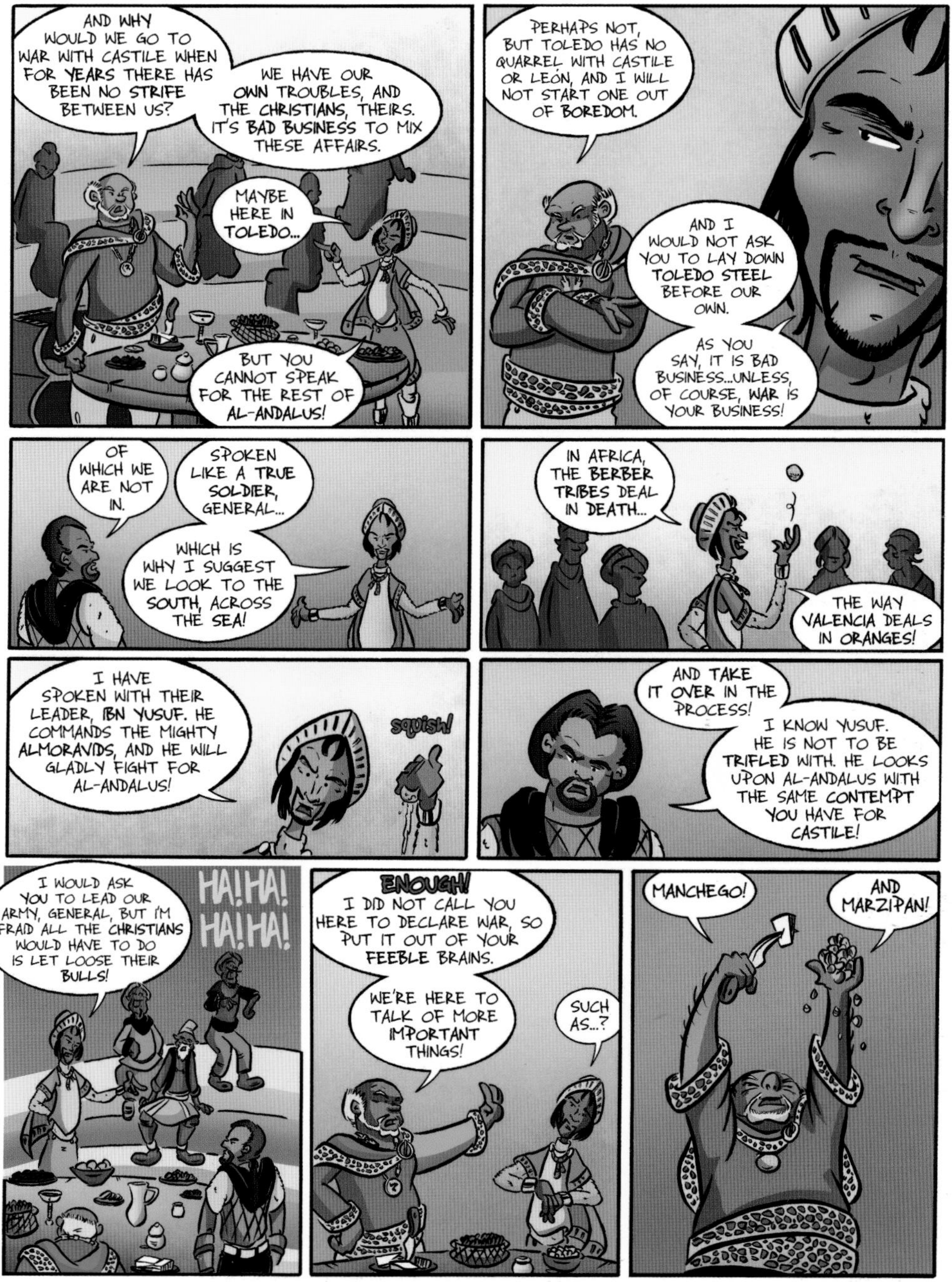
AND WHY WOULD WE GO TO WAR WITH CASTILE WHEN FOR YEARS THERE HAS BEEN NO STRIFE BETWEEN US?
WE HAVE OUR OWN TROUBLES, AND THE CHRISTIANS, THEIRS. IT'S BAD BUSINESS TO MIX THESE AFFAIRS.
MAYBE HERE IN TOLEDO...
BUT YOU CANNOT SPEAK FOR THE REST OF AL-ANDALUS!
PERHAPS NOT, BUT TOLEDO HAS NO QUARREL WITH CASTILE OR LEÓN, AND I WILL NOT START ONE OUT OF BOREDOM.
AND I WOULD NOT ASK YOU TO LAY DOWN TOLEDO STEEL BEFORE OUR OWN.
AS YOU SAY, IT IS BAD BUSINESS...UNLESS, OF COURSE, WAR IS YOUR BUSINESS!
OF WHICH WE ARE NOT IN.
SPOKEN LIKE A TRUE SOLDIER, GENERAL...
WHICH IS WHY I SUGGEST WE LOOK TO THE SOUTH, ACROSS THE SEA!
IN AFRICA, THE BERBER TRIBES DEAL IN DEATH...
THE WAY VALENCIA DEALS IN ORANGES!
I HAVE SPOKEN WITH THEIR LEADER, IBN YUSUF. HE COMMANDS THE MIGHTY ALMORAVIDS, AND HE WILL GLADLY FIGHT FOR AL-ANDALUS!
squish!
AND TAKE IT OVER IN THE PROCESS!
I KNOW YUSUF. HE IS NOT TO BE TRIFLED WITH. HE LOOKS UPON AL-ANDALUS WITH THE SAME CONTEMPT YOU HAVE FOR CASTILE!
I WOULD ASK YOU TO LEAD OUR ARMY, GENERAL, BUT I'M AFRAID ALL THE CHRISTIANS WOULD HAVE TO DO IS LET LOOSE THEIR BULLS!
HA! HA! HA! HA!
ENOUGH! I DID NOT CALL YOU HERE TO DECLARE WAR, SO PUT IT OUT OF YOUR FEEBLE BRAINS.
WE'RE HERE TO TALK OF MORE IMPORTANT THINGS!
SUCH AS...?
MANCHEGO!
AND MARZIPAN!

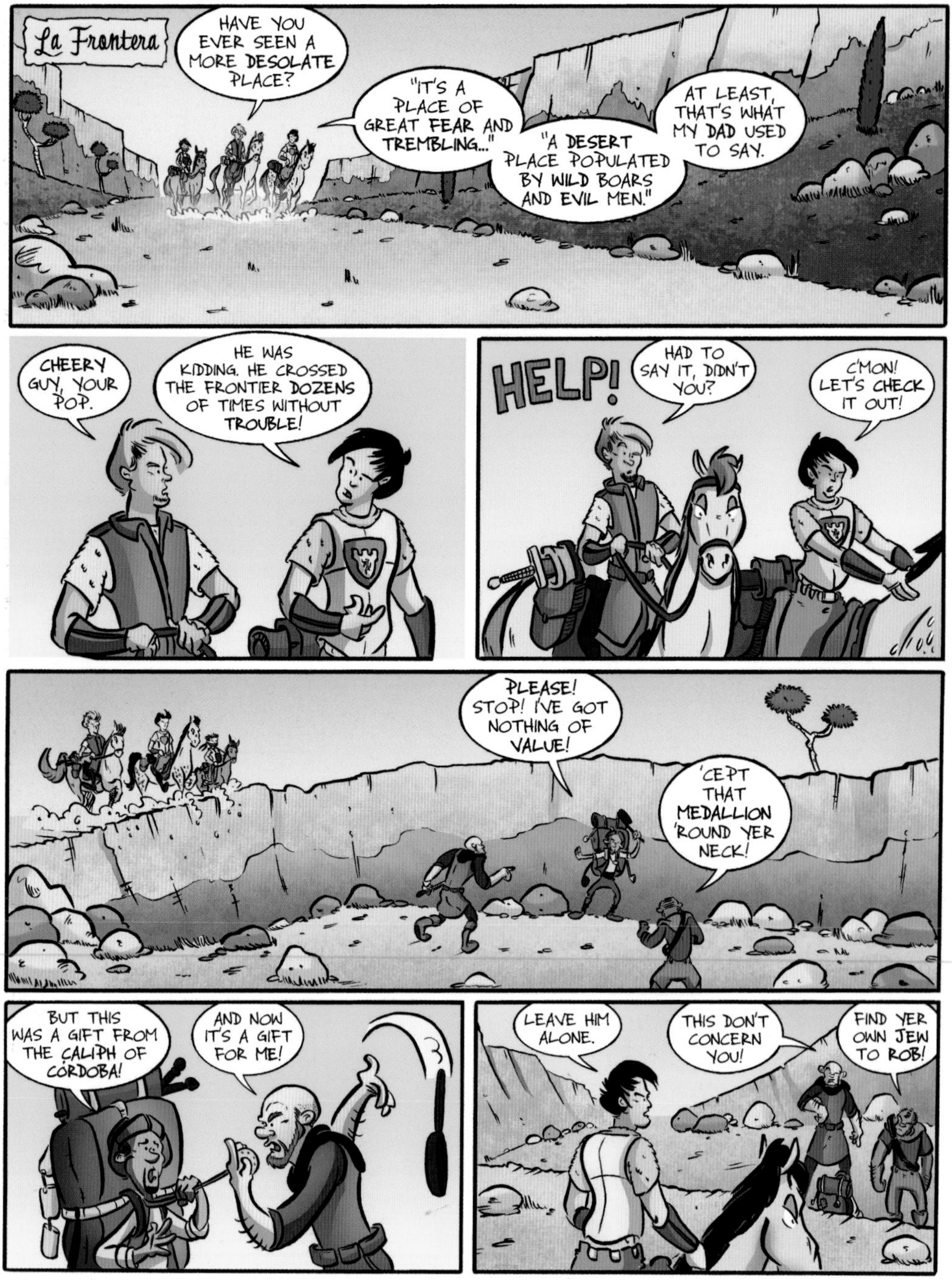
La Frontera
HAVE YOU EVER SEEN A MORE DESOLATE PLACE?
"IT'S A PLACE OF GREAT FEAR AND TREMBLING..."
"A DESERT PLACE POPULATED BY WILD BOARS AND EVIL MEN."
AT LEAST, THAT'S WHAT MY DAD USED TO SAY.
CHEERY GUY, YOUR POP.
HE WAS KIDDING. HE CROSSED THE FRONTIER DOZENS OF TIMES WITHOUT TROUBLE!
HELP!
HAD TO SAY IT, DIDN'T YOU?
C'MON! LET'S CHECK IT OUT!
PLEASE! STOP! I'VE GOT NOTHING OF VALUE!
'CEPT THAT MEDALLION 'ROUND YER NECK!
BUT THIS WAS A GIFT FROM THE CALIPH OF CÓRDOBA!
AND NOW IT'S A GIFT FOR ME!
LEAVE HIM ALONE.
THIS DON'T CONCERN YOU!
FIND YER OWN JEW TO ROB!

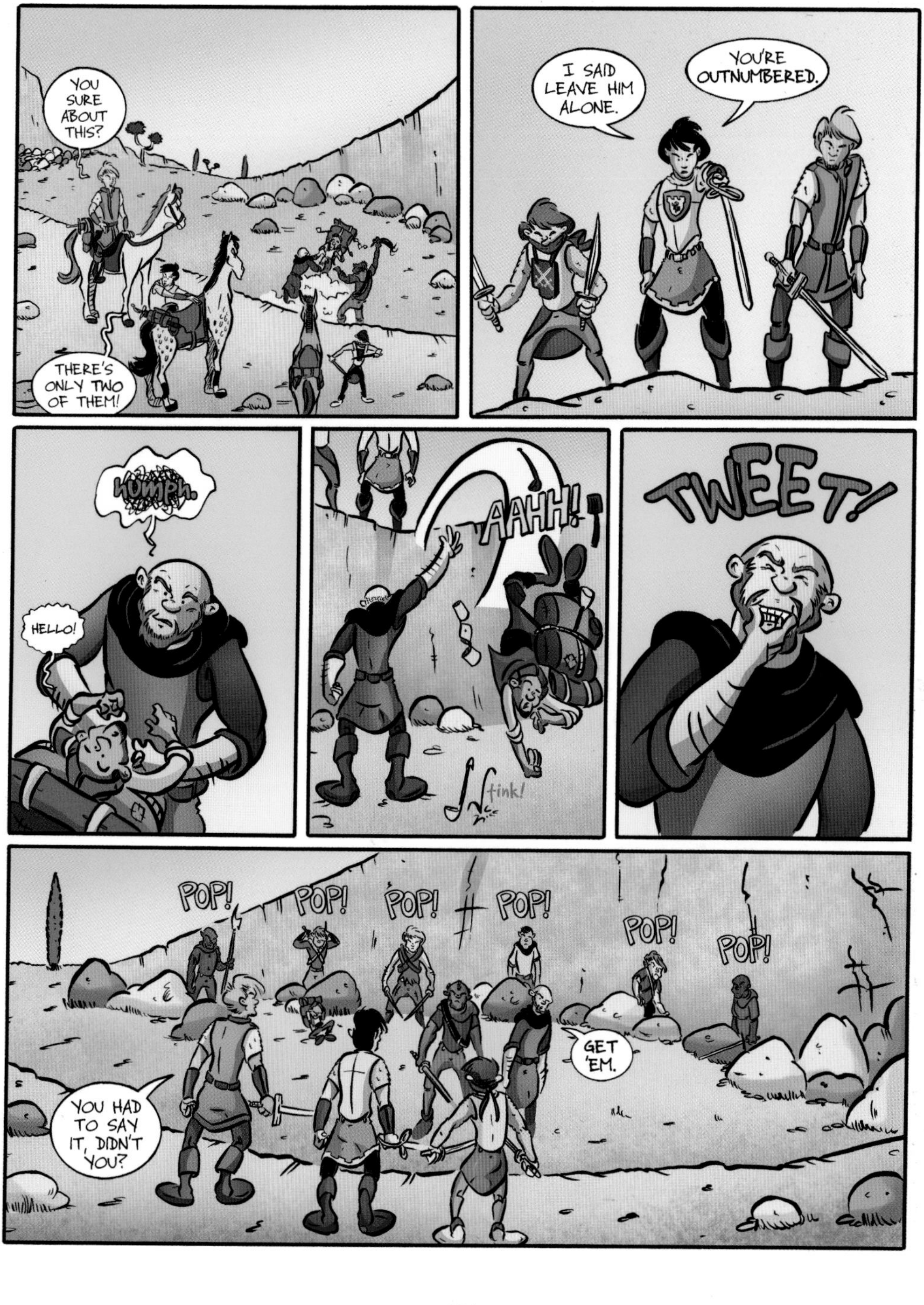
YOU SURE ABOUT THIS?
THERE'S ONLY TWO OF THEM!
I SAID LEAVE HIM ALONE.
YOU'RE OUTNUMBERED.
humph.
HELLO!
AAHH!
fink!
TWEET!
POP!
POP!
POP!
POP!
POP!
POP!
GET 'EM.
YOU HAD TO SAY IT, DIDN'T YOU?

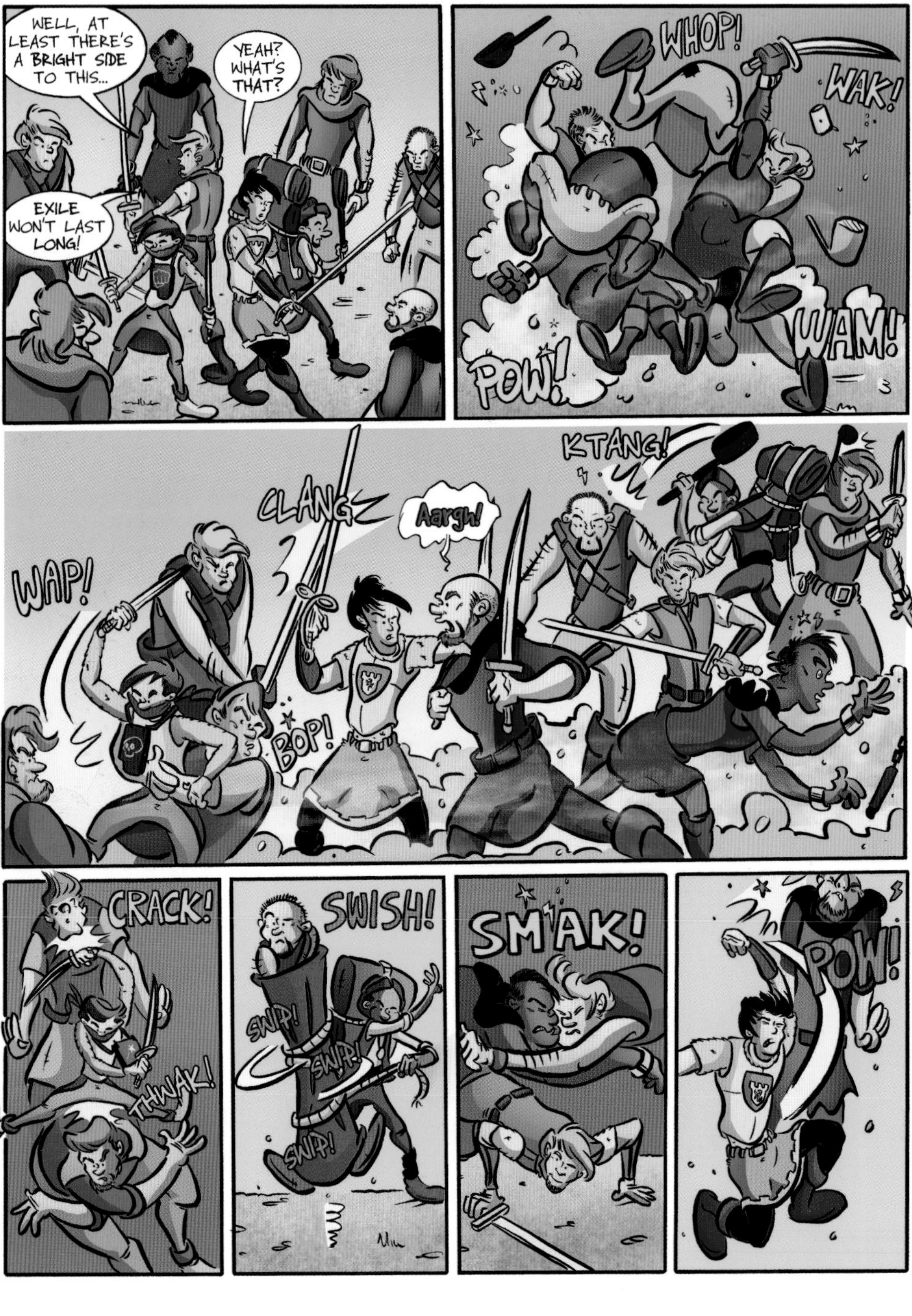
WELL, AT LEAST THERE'S A BRIGHT SIDE TO THIS...
YEAH? WHAT'S THAT?
EXILE WON'T LAST LONG!
WHOP!
WAK!
WAM!
POW!
KTANG!
CLANG
Aargh!
WAP!
BOP!
CRACK!
THWAK!
SWISH!
SWIP!
SWIP!
SWIP!
SMAK!
POW!

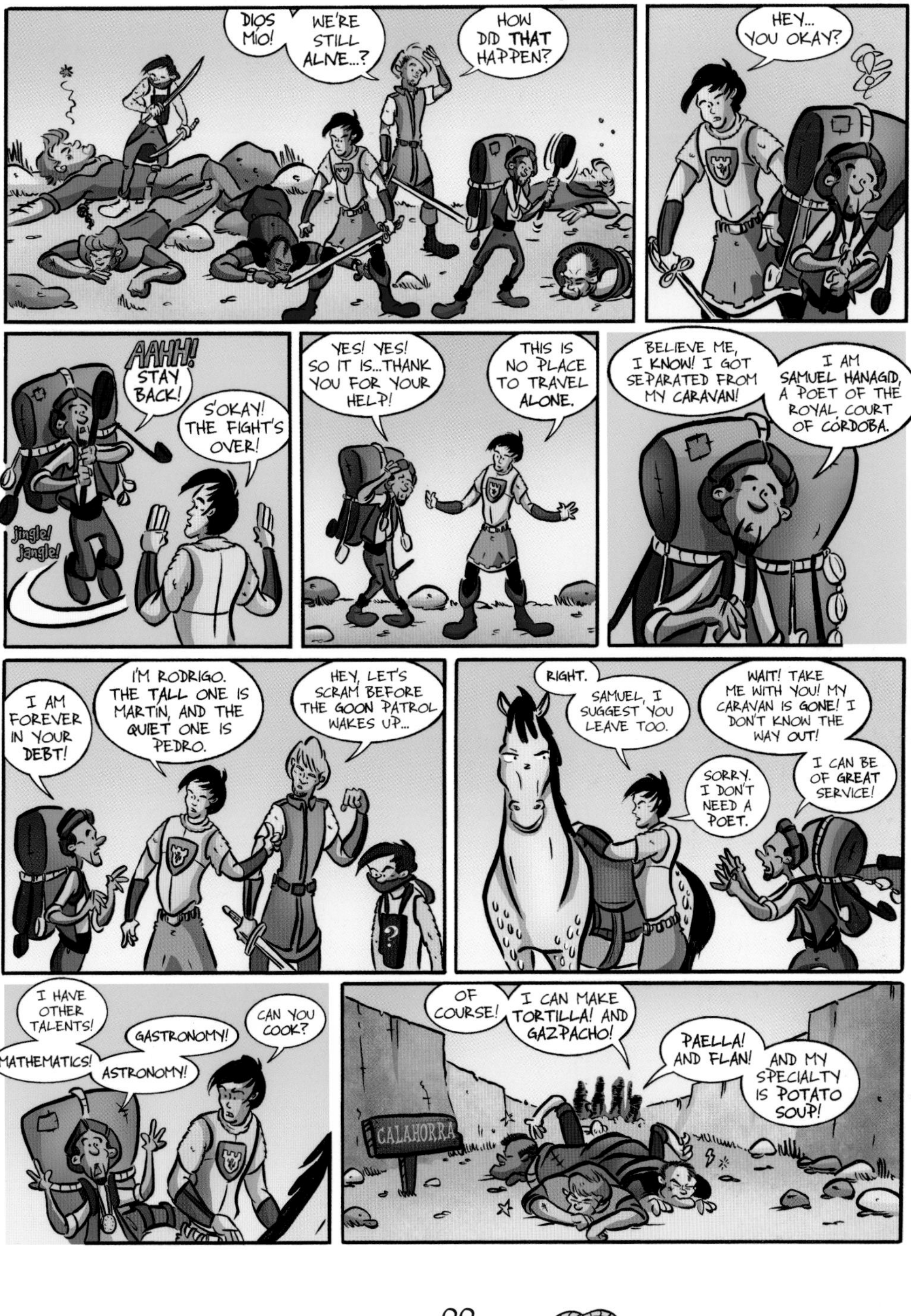
DIOS MÍO!
WE'RE STILL ALIVE...?
HOW DID THAT HAPPEN?
HEY... YOU OKAY?
AAHH! STAY BACK!
S'OKAY! THE FIGHT'S OVER!
jingle! jangle!
YES! YES! SO IT IS...THANK YOU FOR YOUR HELP!
THIS IS NO PLACE TO TRAVEL ALONE.
BELIEVE ME, I KNOW! I GOT SEPARATED FROM MY CARAVAN!
I AM SAMUEL HANAGID, A POET OF THE ROYAL COURT OF CÓRDOBA.
I AM FOREVER IN YOUR DEBT!
I'M RODRIGO. THE TALL ONE IS MARTIN, AND THE QUIET ONE IS PEDRO.
HEY, LET'S SCRAM BEFORE THE GOON PATROL WAKES UP...
RIGHT.
SAMUEL, I SUGGEST YOU LEAVE TOO.
WAIT! TAKE ME WITH YOU! MY CARAVAN IS GONE! I DON'T KNOW THE WAY OUT!
SORRY. I DON'T NEED A POET.
I CAN BE OF GREAT SERVICE!
I HAVE OTHER TALENTS!
MATHEMATICS!
ASTRONOMY!
GASTRONOMY!
CAN YOU COOK?
OF COURSE!
I CAN MAKE TORTILLA! AND GAZPACHO!
CALAHORRA
PAELLA! AND FLAN!
AND MY SPECIALTY IS POTATO SOUP!

Also in La Frontera...

THE MOON GLOWS BRIGHT!

SHE IS HAPPY FOR HER SONS' ARRIVAL!

MMM! THE POTATO SOUP IS GOOD, GEMMA!

THANK YOU! I HOPE MY LORDS ENJOY IT AS WELL!

CHOMP SLURP! MUNCH

IT'S GREAT!

nudge!

VERY SOUPY!

bump!

HA! IF THAT'S MITHRAS AND TAURO, THEN I'M THE QUEEN OF THE GODS!

grunt.

BOUDI! THAT'S BLASPHEMY!

THEY'RE LYING TO YOU!

THEY'RE OUR GUESTS! APOLOGIZE AT ONCE!

YOU BETTER LEAVE WHILE YOU STILL CAN.

OR YOU'LL REGRET IT!

THAT IS NOT AN APOLOGY, YOUNG LADY!

BOUDI! COME BACK HERE!

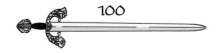

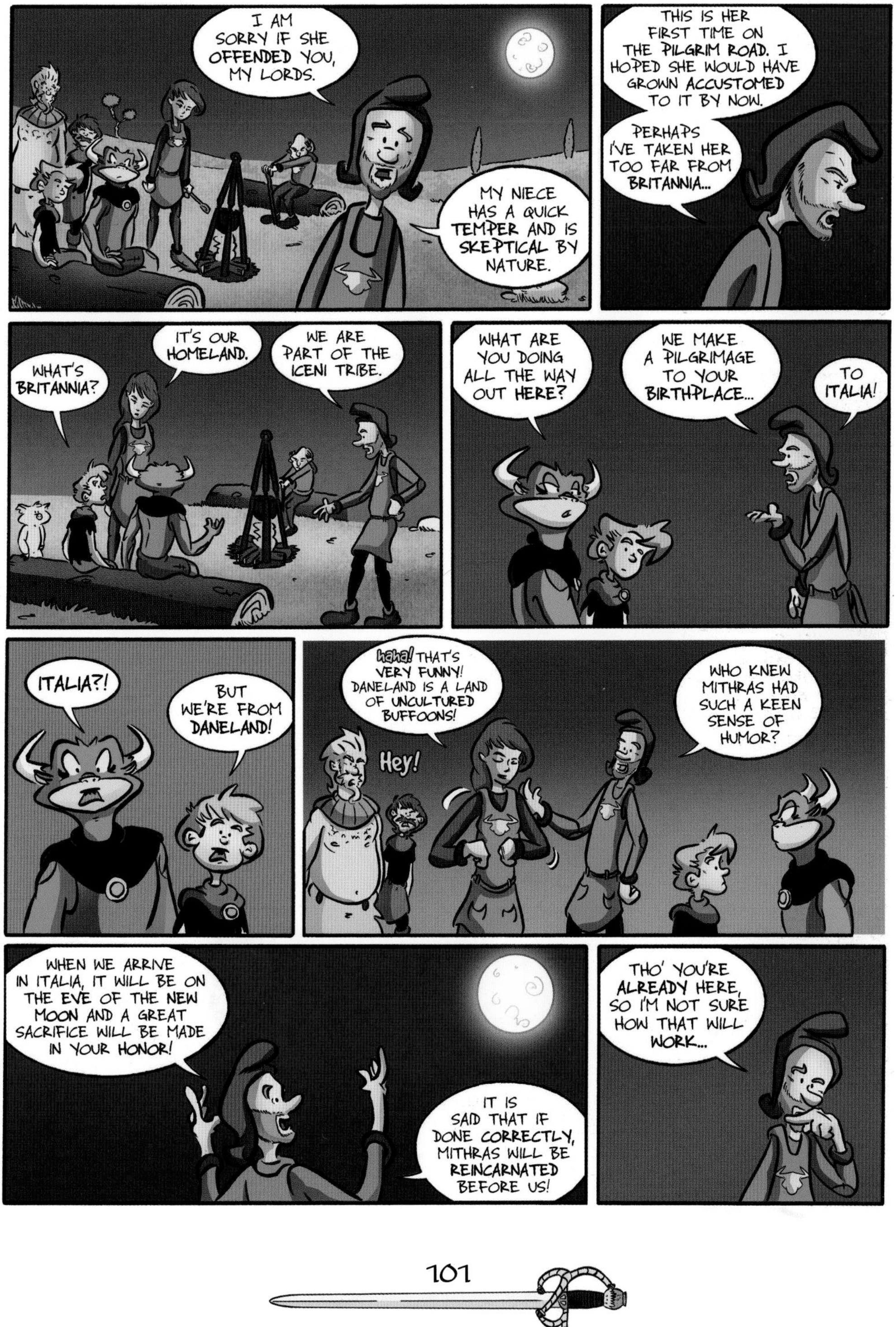
I AM SORRY IF SHE OFFENDED YOU, MY LORDS.
MY NIECE HAS A QUICK TEMPER AND IS SKEPTICAL BY NATURE.
THIS IS HER FIRST TIME ON THE PILGRIM ROAD. I HOPED SHE WOULD HAVE GROWN ACCUSTOMED TO IT BY NOW.
PERHAPS I'VE TAKEN HER TOO FAR FROM BRITANNIA...
WHAT'S BRITANNIA?
IT'S OUR HOMELAND.
WE ARE PART OF THE ICENI TRIBE.
WHAT ARE YOU DOING ALL THE WAY OUT HERE?
WE MAKE A PILGRIMAGE TO YOUR BIRTHPLACE...
TO ITALIA!
ITALIA?!
BUT WE'RE FROM DANELAND!
haha! THAT'S VERY FUNNY! DANELAND IS A LAND OF UNCULTURED BUFFOONS!
Hey!
WHO KNEW MITHRAS HAD SUCH A KEEN SENSE OF HUMOR?
WHEN WE ARRIVE IN ITALIA, IT WILL BE ON THE EVE OF THE NEW MOON AND A GREAT SACRIFICE WILL BE MADE IN YOUR HONOR!
IT IS SAID THAT IF DONE CORRECTLY, MITHRAS WILL BE REINCARNATED BEFORE US!
THO' YOU'RE ALREADY HERE, SO I'M NOT SURE HOW THAT WILL WORK...

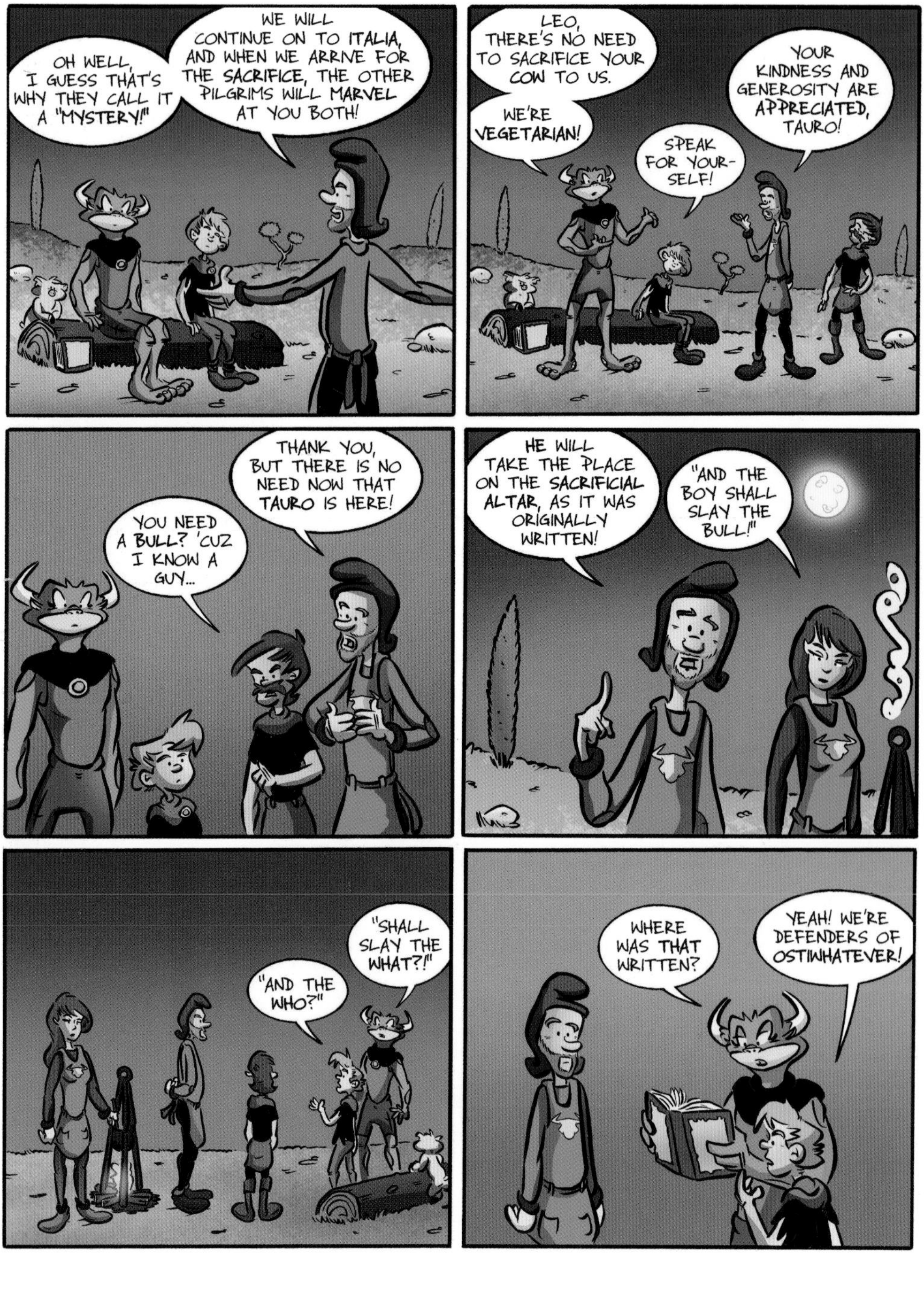
OH WELL, I GUESS THAT'S WHY THEY CALL IT A "MYSTERY!"
WE WILL CONTINUE ON TO ITALIA, AND WHEN WE ARRIVE FOR THE SACRIFICE, THE OTHER PILGRIMS WILL MARVEL AT YOU BOTH!
LEO, THERE'S NO NEED TO SACRIFICE YOUR COW TO US.
WE'RE VEGETARIAN!
SPEAK FOR YOUR-SELF!
YOUR KINDNESS AND GENEROSITY ARE APPRECIATED, TAURO!
THANK YOU, BUT THERE IS NO NEED NOW THAT TAURO IS HERE!
YOU NEED A BULL? 'CUZ I KNOW A GUY...
HE WILL TAKE THE PLACE ON THE SACRIFICIAL ALTAR, AS IT WAS ORIGINALLY WRITTEN!
"AND THE BOY SHALL SLAY THE BULL!"
"SHALL SLAY THE WHAT?!"
"AND THE WHO?"
WHERE WAS THAT WRITTEN?
YEAH! WE'RE DEFENDERS OF OSTIWHATEVER!

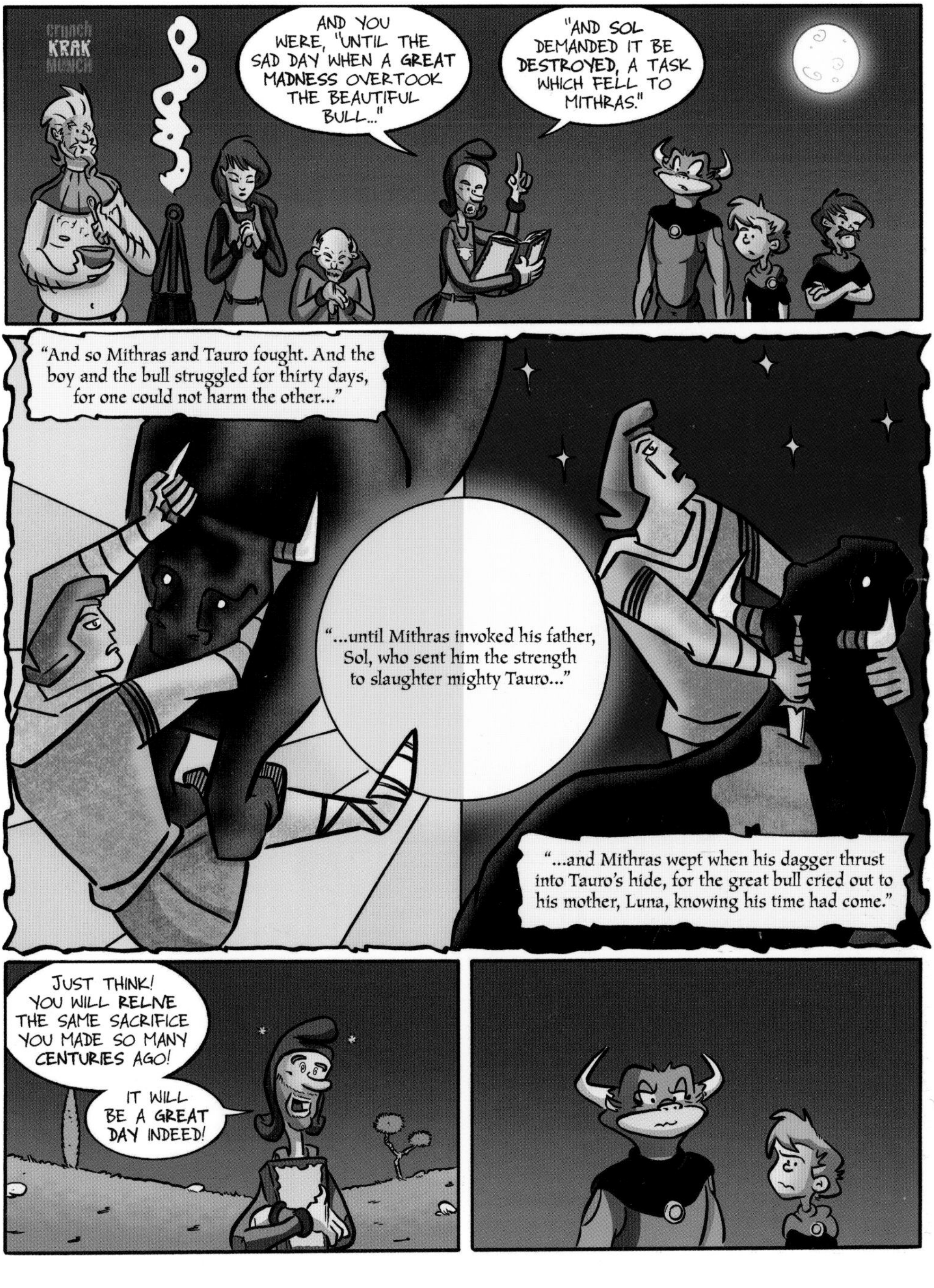
crunch
KRAK
MUNCH
AND YOU WERE, "UNTIL THE SAD DAY WHEN A GREAT MADNESS OVERTOOK THE BEAUTIFUL BULL..."
"AND SOL DEMANDED IT BE DESTROYED, A TASK WHICH FELL TO MITHRAS."
"And so Mithras and Tauro fought. And the boy and the bull struggled for thirty days, for one could not harm the other..."
"...until Mithras invoked his father, Sol, who sent him the strength to slaughter mighty Tauro..."
"...and Mithras wept when his dagger thrust into Tauro's hide, for the great bull cried out to his mother, Luna, knowing his time had come."
JUST THINK! YOU WILL RELIVE THE SAME SACRIFICE YOU MADE SO MANY CENTURIES AGO!
IT WILL BE A GREAT DAY INDEED!

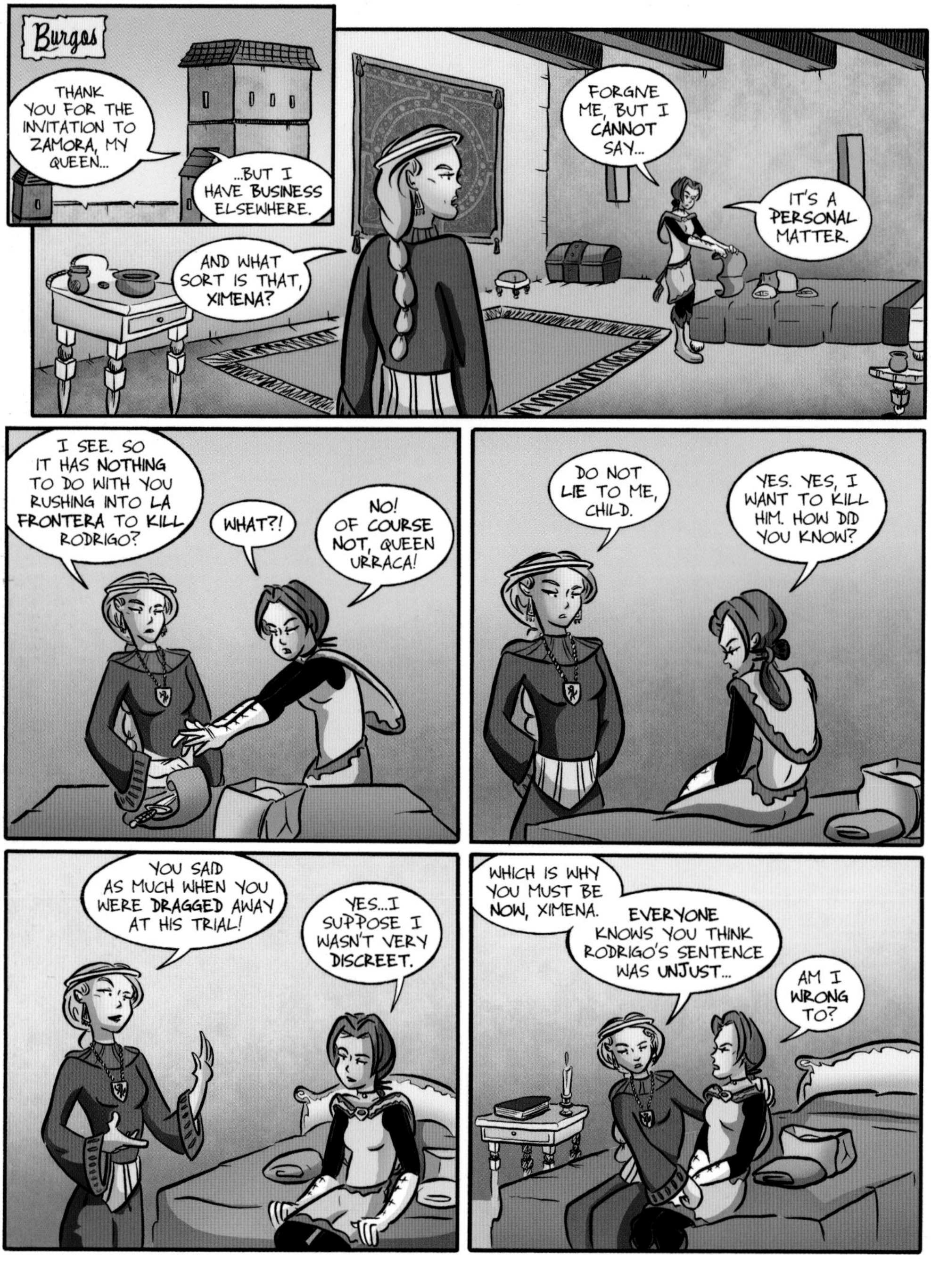
Burgos
THANK YOU FOR THE INVITATION TO ZAMORA, MY QUEEN...
...BUT I HAVE BUSINESS ELSEWHERE.
AND WHAT SORT IS THAT, XIMENA?
FORGIVE ME, BUT I CANNOT SAY...
IT'S A PERSONAL MATTER.
I SEE. SO IT HAS NOTHING TO DO WITH YOU RUSHING INTO LA FRONTERA TO KILL RODRIGO?
WHAT?!
NO! OF COURSE NOT, QUEEN URRACA!
DO NOT LIE TO ME, CHILD.
YES. YES, I WANT TO KILL HIM. HOW DID YOU KNOW?
YOU SAID AS MUCH WHEN YOU WERE DRAGGED AWAY AT HIS TRIAL!
YES...I SUPPOSE I WASN'T VERY DISCREET.
WHICH IS WHY YOU MUST BE NOW, XIMENA.
EVERYONE KNOWS YOU THINK RODRIGO'S SENTENCE WAS UNJUST...
AM I WRONG TO?

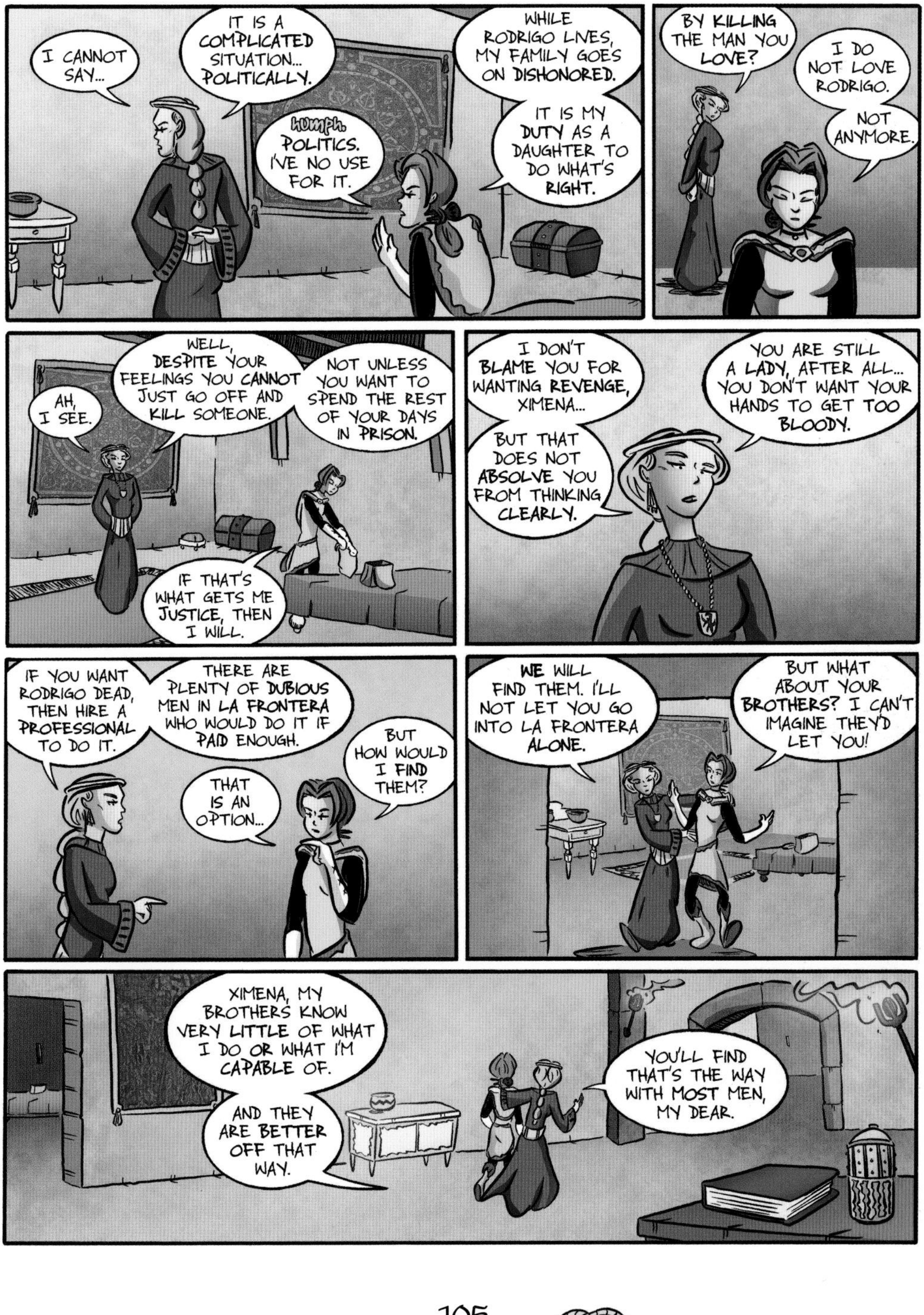
I CANNOT SAY...
IT IS A COMPLICATED SITUATION... POLITICALLY.
humph. POLITICS. I'VE NO USE FOR IT.
WHILE RODRIGO LIVES, MY FAMILY GOES ON DISHONORED.
IT IS MY DUTY AS A DAUGHTER TO DO WHAT'S RIGHT.
BY KILLING THE MAN YOU LOVE?
I DO NOT LOVE RODRIGO.
NOT ANYMORE.
AH, I SEE.
WELL, DESPITE YOUR FEELINGS YOU CANNOT JUST GO OFF AND KILL SOMEONE.
NOT UNLESS YOU WANT TO SPEND THE REST OF YOUR DAYS IN PRISON.
IF THAT'S WHAT GETS ME JUSTICE, THEN I WILL.
I DON'T BLAME YOU FOR WANTING REVENGE, XIMENA...
BUT THAT DOES NOT ABSOLVE YOU FROM THINKING CLEARLY.
YOU ARE STILL A LADY, AFTER ALL... YOU DON'T WANT YOUR HANDS TO GET TOO BLOODY.
IF YOU WANT RODRIGO DEAD, THEN HIRE A PROFESSIONAL TO DO IT.
THERE ARE PLENTY OF DUBIOUS MEN IN LA FRONTERA WHO WOULD DO IT IF PAID ENOUGH.
THAT IS AN OPTION...
BUT HOW WOULD I FIND THEM?
WE WILL FIND THEM. I'LL NOT LET YOU GO INTO LA FRONTERA ALONE.
BUT WHAT ABOUT YOUR BROTHERS? I CAN'T IMAGINE THEY'D LET YOU!
XIMENA, MY BROTHERS KNOW VERY LITTLE OF WHAT I DO OR WHAT I'M CAPABLE OF.
AND THEY ARE BETTER OFF THAT WAY.
YOU'LL FIND THAT'S THE WAY WITH MOST MEN, MY DEAR.

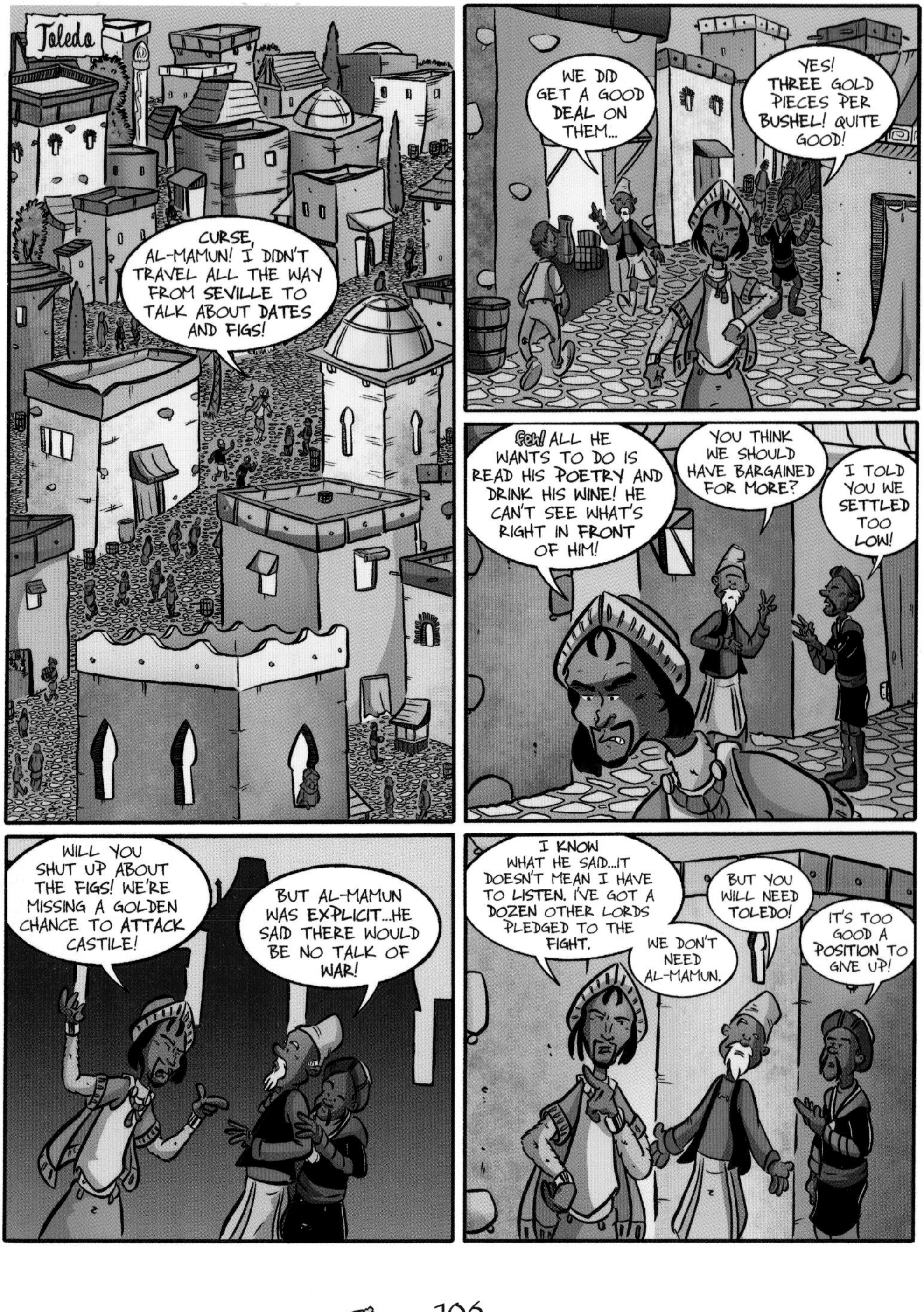
Toledo
CURSE, AL-MAMUN! I DIDN'T TRAVEL ALL THE WAY FROM SEVILLE TO TALK ABOUT DATES AND FIGS!
WE DID GET A GOOD DEAL ON THEM...
YES! THREE GOLD PIECES PER BUSHEL! QUITE GOOD!
Feh! ALL HE WANTS TO DO IS READ HIS POETRY AND DRINK HIS WINE! HE CAN'T SEE WHAT'S RIGHT IN FRONT OF HIM!
YOU THINK WE SHOULD HAVE BARGAINED FOR MORE?
I TOLD YOU WE SETTLED TOO LOW!
WILL YOU SHUT UP ABOUT THE FIGS! WE'RE MISSING A GOLDEN CHANCE TO ATTACK CASTILE!
BUT AL-MAMUN WAS EXPLICIT...HE SAID THERE WOULD BE NO TALK OF WAR!
I KNOW WHAT HE SAID...IT DOESN'T MEAN I HAVE TO LISTEN. I'VE GOT A DOZEN OTHER LORDS PLEDGED TO THE FIGHT.
WE DON'T NEED AL-MAMUN.
BUT YOU WILL NEED TOLEDO!
IT'S TOO GOOD A POSITION TO GIVE UP!

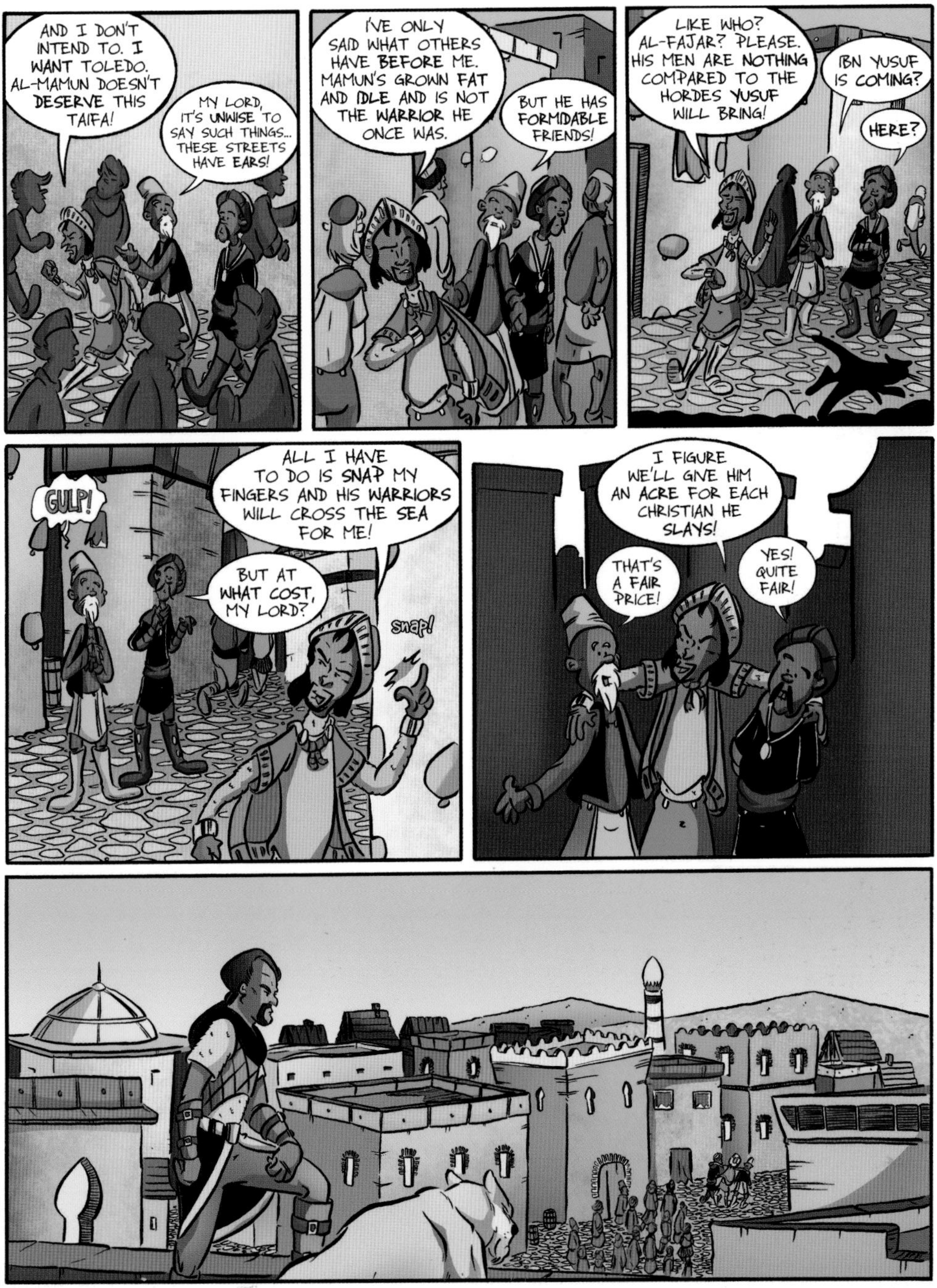
AND I DON'T INTEND TO. I WANT TOLEDO. AL-MAMUN DOESN'T DESERVE THIS TAIFA!
MY LORD, IT'S UNWISE TO SAY SUCH THINGS... THESE STREETS HAVE EARS!
I'VE ONLY SAID WHAT OTHERS HAVE BEFORE ME. MAMUN'S GROWN FAT AND IDLE AND IS NOT THE WARRIOR HE ONCE WAS.
BUT HE HAS FORMIDABLE FRIENDS!
LIKE WHO? AL-FAJAR? PLEASE. HIS MEN ARE NOTHING COMPARED TO THE HORDES YUSUF WILL BRING!
IBN YUSUF IS COMING?
HERE?
GULP!
ALL I HAVE TO DO IS SNAP MY FINGERS AND HIS WARRIORS WILL CROSS THE SEA FOR ME!
BUT AT WHAT COST, MY LORD?
SNAP!
I FIGURE WE'LL GIVE HIM AN ACRE FOR EACH CHRISTIAN HE SLAYS!
THAT'S A FAIR PRICE!
YES! QUITE FAIR!

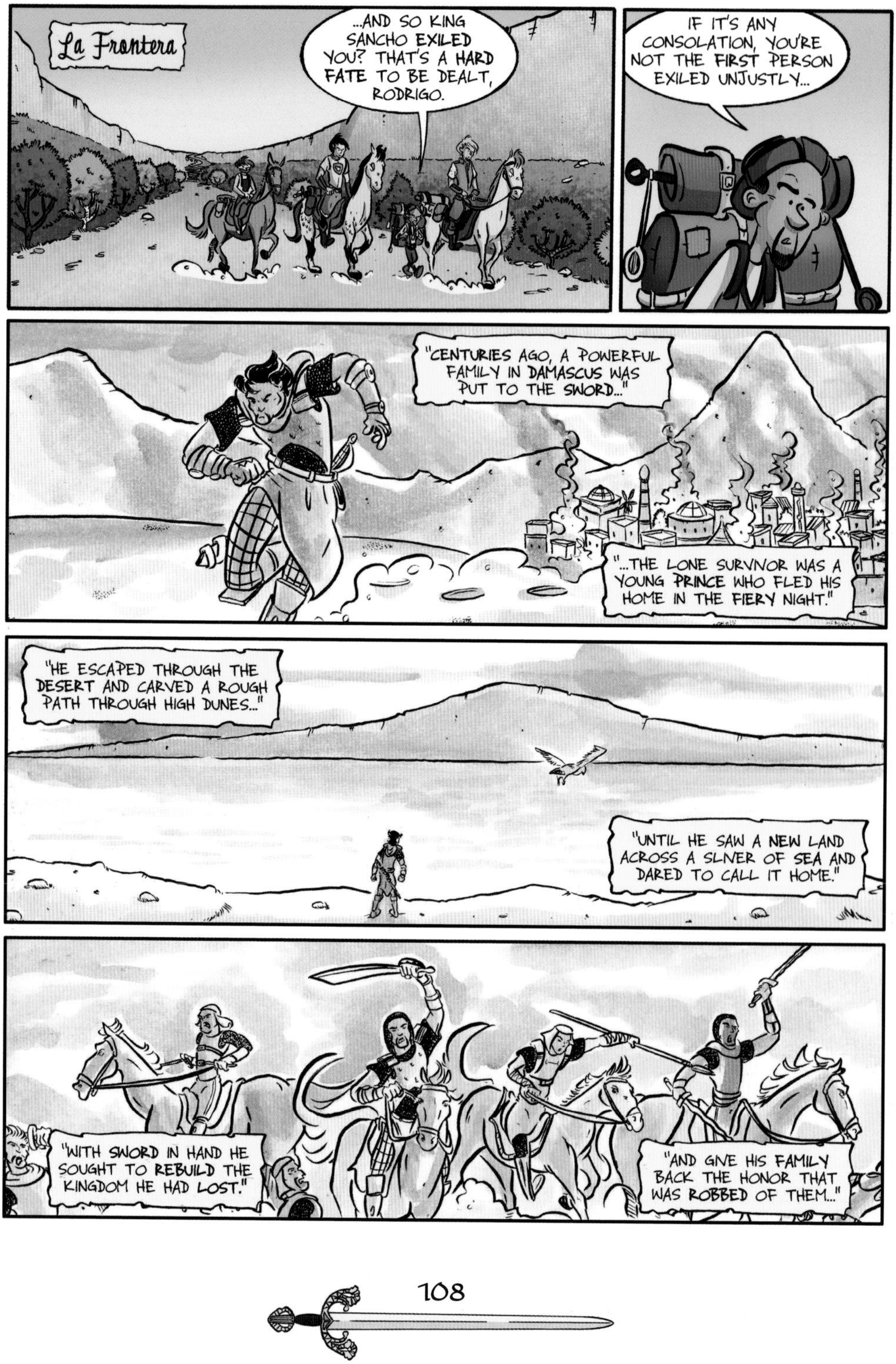
La Frontera
...AND SO KING SANCHO EXILED YOU? THAT'S A HARD FATE TO BE DEALT, RODRIGO.
IF IT'S ANY CONSOLATION, YOU'RE NOT THE FIRST PERSON EXILED UNJUSTLY...
"CENTURIES AGO, A POWERFUL FAMILY IN DAMASCUS WAS PUT TO THE SWORD..."
"...THE LONE SURVIVOR WAS A YOUNG PRINCE WHO FLED HIS HOME IN THE FIERY NIGHT."
"HE ESCAPED THROUGH THE DESERT AND CARVED A ROUGH PATH THROUGH HIGH DUNES..."
"UNTIL HE SAW A NEW LAND ACROSS A SLIVER OF SEA AND DARED TO CALL IT HOME."
"WITH SWORD IN HAND HE SOUGHT TO REBUILD THE KINGDOM HE HAD LOST."
"AND GIVE HIS FAMILY BACK THE HONOR THAT WAS ROBBED OF THEM..."

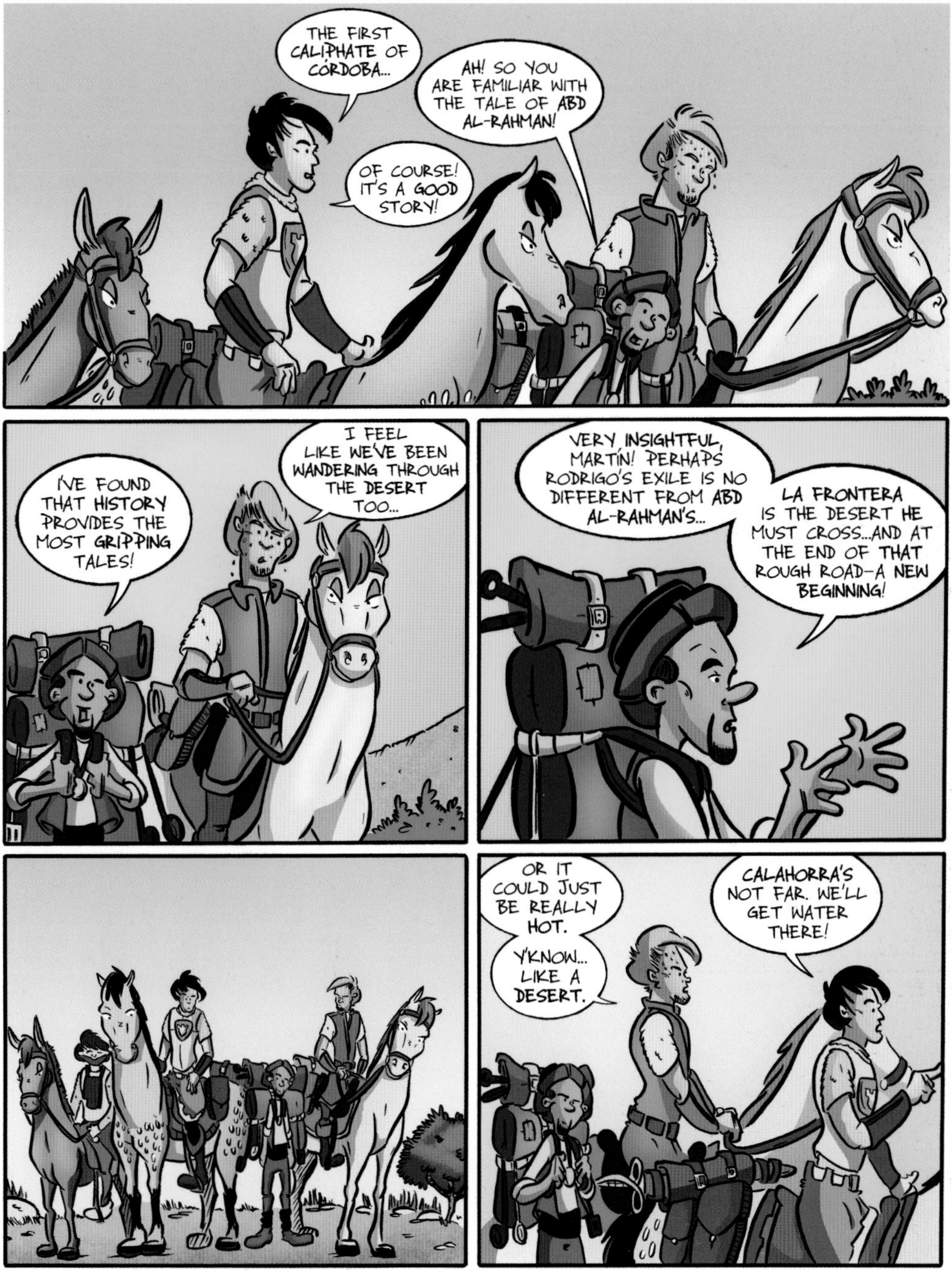
THE FIRST CALIPHATE OF CÓRDOBA...
AH! SO YOU ARE FAMILIAR WITH THE TALE OF ABD AL-RAHMAN!
OF COURSE! IT'S A GOOD STORY!
I FEEL LIKE WE'VE BEEN WANDERING THROUGH THE DESERT TOO...
I'VE FOUND THAT HISTORY PROVIDES THE MOST GRIPPING TALES!
VERY INSIGHTFUL, MARTÍN! PERHAPS RODRIGO'S EXILE IS NO DIFFERENT FROM ABD AL-RAHMAN'S...
LA FRONTERA IS THE DESERT HE MUST CROSS...AND AT THE END OF THAT ROUGH ROAD—A NEW BEGINNING!
OR IT COULD JUST BE REALLY HOT.
Y'KNOW... LIKE A DESERT.
CALAHORRA'S NOT FAR. WE'LL GET WATER THERE!

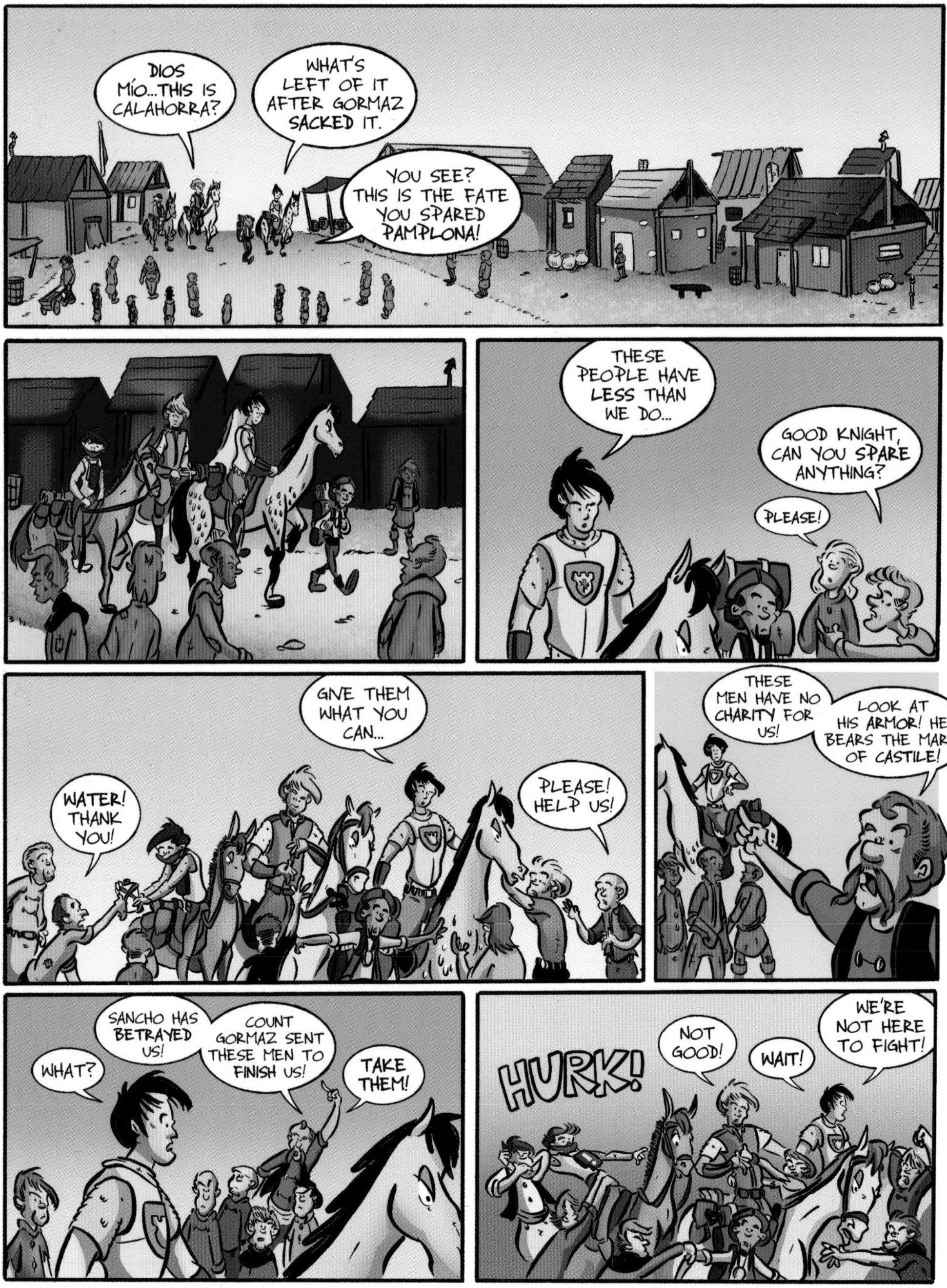
DIOS MÍO...THIS IS CALAHORRA?
WHAT'S LEFT OF IT AFTER GORMAZ SACKED IT.
YOU SEE? THIS IS THE FATE YOU SPARED PAMPLONA!
THESE PEOPLE HAVE LESS THAN WE DO...
GOOD KNIGHT, CAN YOU SPARE ANYTHING?
PLEASE!
GIVE THEM WHAT YOU CAN...
WATER! THANK YOU!
PLEASE! HELP US!
THESE MEN HAVE NO CHARITY FOR US!
LOOK AT HIS ARMOR! HE BEARS THE MARK OF CASTILE!
WHAT?
SANCHO HAS BETRAYED US!
COUNT GORMAZ SENT THESE MEN TO FINISH US!
TAKE THEM!
HURK!
NOT GOOD!
WAIT!
WE'RE NOT HERE TO FIGHT!

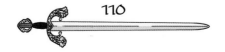

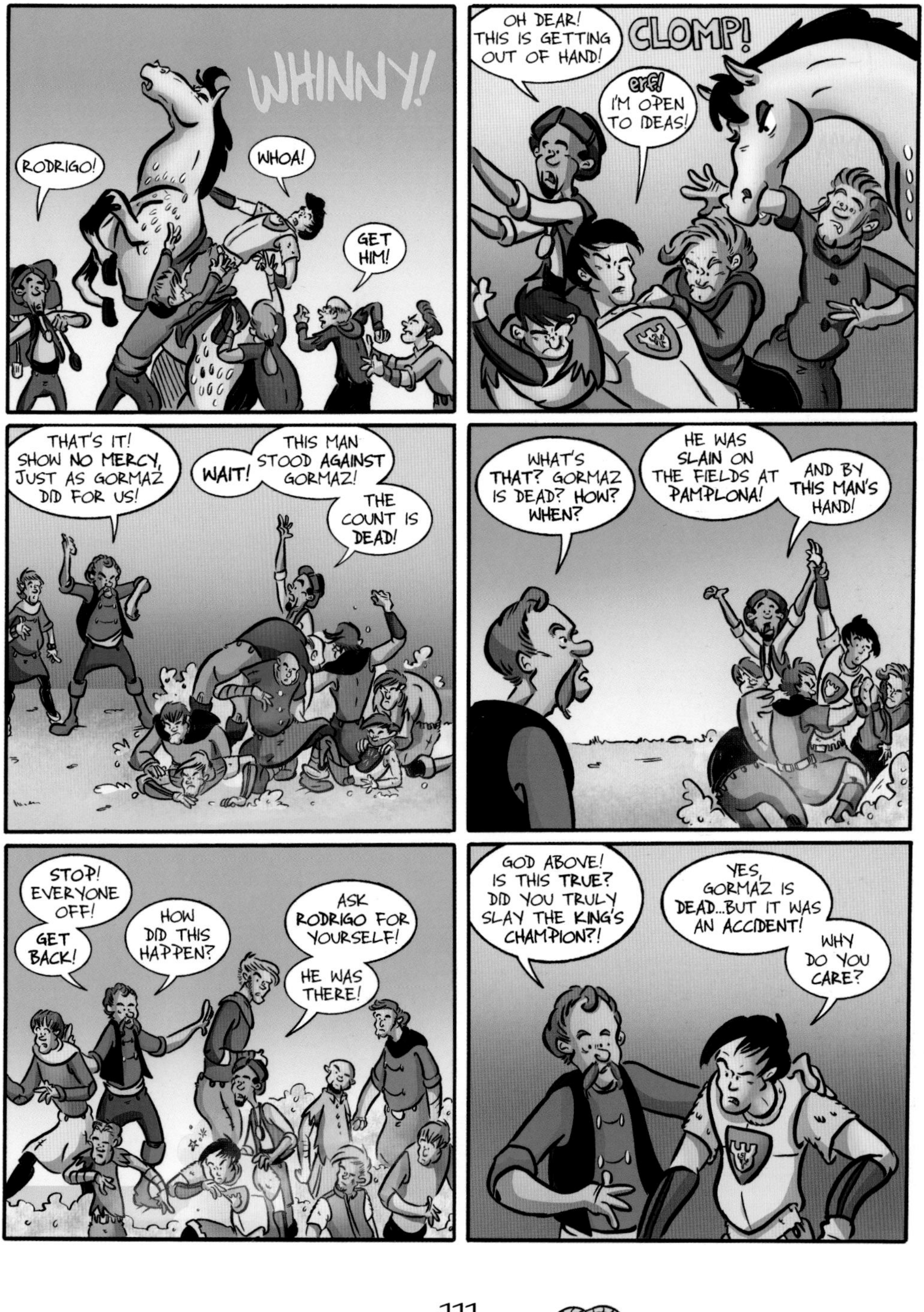
WHINNY!
RODRIGO!
WHOA!
GET HIM!
OH DEAR! THIS IS GETTING OUT OF HAND!
CLOMP!
erf! I'M OPEN TO IDEAS!
THAT'S IT! SHOW NO MERCY, JUST AS GORMAZ DID FOR US!
WAIT!
THIS MAN STOOD AGAINST GORMAZ!
THE COUNT IS DEAD!
WHAT'S THAT? GORMAZ IS DEAD? HOW? WHEN?
HE WAS SLAIN ON THE FIELDS AT PAMPLONA!
AND BY THIS MAN'S HAND!
STOP! EVERYONE OFF!
GET BACK!
HOW DID THIS HAPPEN?
ASK RODRIGO FOR YOURSELF!
HE WAS THERE!
GOD ABOVE! IS THIS TRUE? DID YOU TRULY SLAY THE KING'S CHAMPION?!
YES, GORMAZ IS DEAD...BUT IT WAS AN ACCIDENT!
WHY DO YOU CARE?

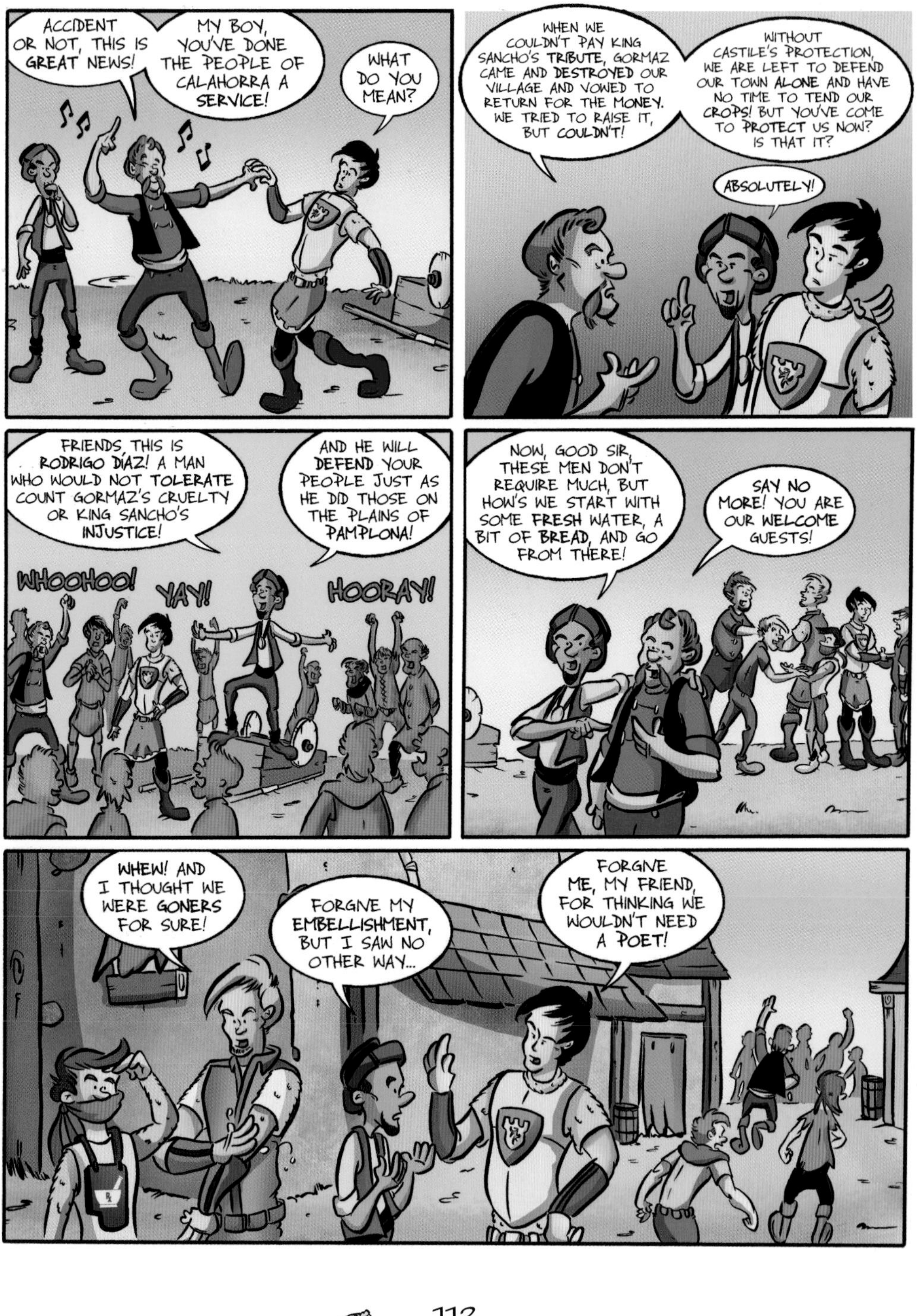
ACCIDENT OR NOT, THIS IS GREAT NEWS!
MY BOY, YOU'VE DONE THE PEOPLE OF CALAHORRA A SERVICE!
WHAT DO YOU MEAN?
WHEN WE COULDN'T PAY KING SANCHO'S TRIBUTE, GORMAZ CAME AND DESTROYED OUR VILLAGE AND VOWED TO RETURN FOR THE MONEY. WE TRIED TO RAISE IT, BUT COULDN'T!
WITHOUT CASTILE'S PROTECTION, WE ARE LEFT TO DEFEND OUR TOWN ALONE AND HAVE NO TIME TO TEND OUR CROPS! BUT YOU'VE COME TO PROTECT US NOW? IS THAT IT?
ABSOLUTELY!
FRIENDS, THIS IS RODRIGO DÍAZ! A MAN WHO WOULD NOT TOLERATE COUNT GORMAZ'S CRUELTY OR KING SANCHO'S INJUSTICE!
AND HE WILL DEFEND YOUR PEOPLE JUST AS HE DID THOSE ON THE PLAINS OF PAMPLONA!
WHOOHOO!
YAY!
HOORAY!
NOW, GOOD SIR, THESE MEN DON'T REQUIRE MUCH, BUT HOW'S WE START WITH SOME FRESH WATER, A BIT OF BREAD, AND GO FROM THERE!
SAY NO MORE! YOU ARE OUR WELCOME GUESTS!
WHEW! AND I THOUGHT WE WERE GONERS FOR SURE!
FORGIVE MY EMBELLISHMENT, BUT I SAW NO OTHER WAY...
FORGIVE ME, MY FRIEND, FOR THINKING WE WOULDN'T NEED A POET!

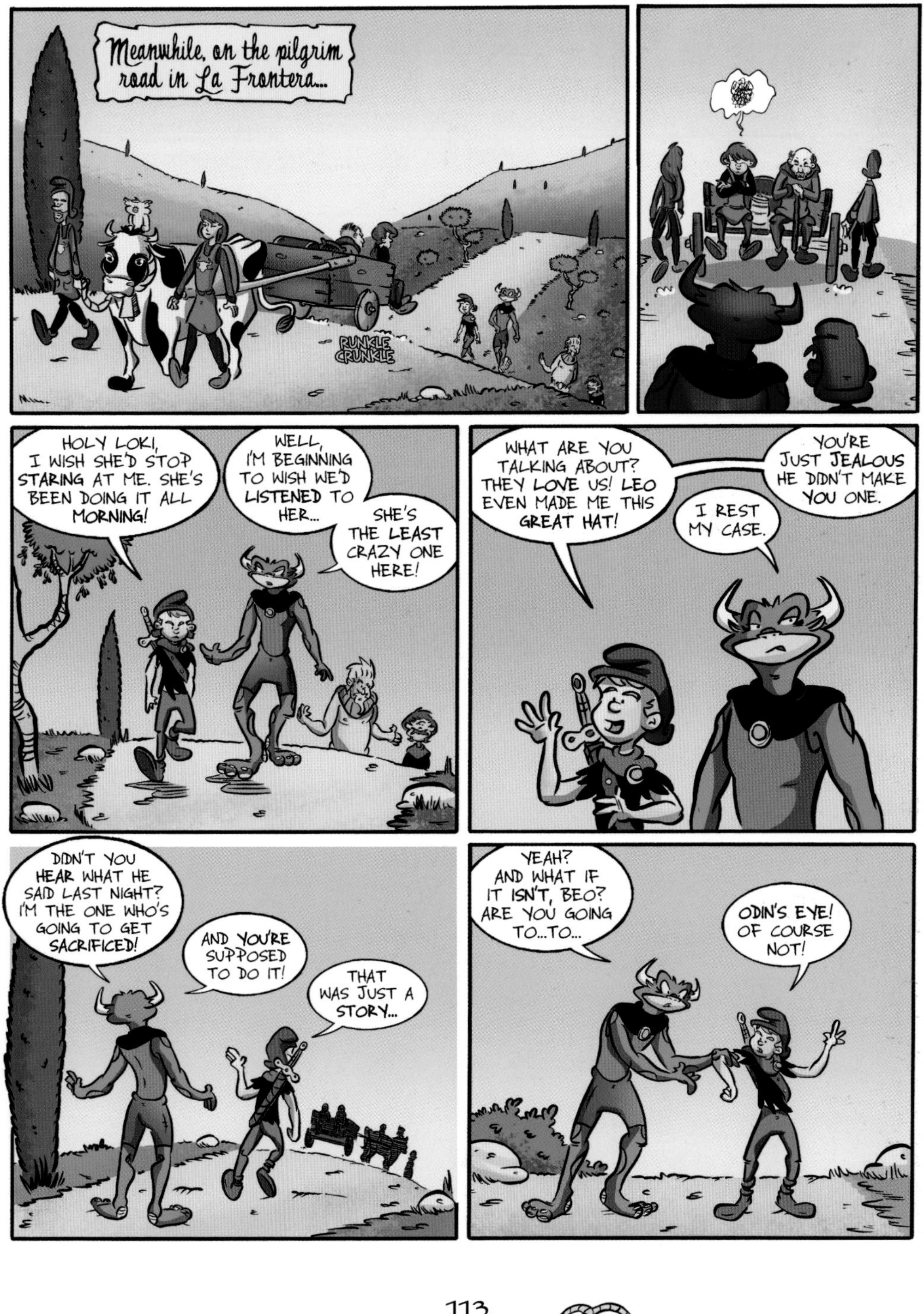
Meanwhile, on the pilgrim road in La Frontera...
RUNKLE CRUNKLE
HOLY LOKI, I WISH SHE'D STOP STARING AT ME. SHE'S BEEN DOING IT ALL MORNING!
WELL, I'M BEGINNING TO WISH WE'D LISTENED TO HER...
SHE'S THE LEAST CRAZY ONE HERE!
WHAT ARE YOU TALKING ABOUT? THEY LOVE US! LEO EVEN MADE ME THIS GREAT HAT!
YOU'RE JUST JEALOUS HE DIDN'T MAKE YOU ONE.
I REST MY CASE.
DIDN'T YOU HEAR WHAT HE SAID LAST NIGHT? I'M THE ONE WHO'S GOING TO GET SACRIFICED!
AND YOU'RE SUPPOSED TO DO IT!
THAT WAS JUST A STORY...
YEAH? AND WHAT IF IT ISN'T, BEO? ARE YOU GOING TO...TO...
ODIN'S EYE! OF COURSE NOT!

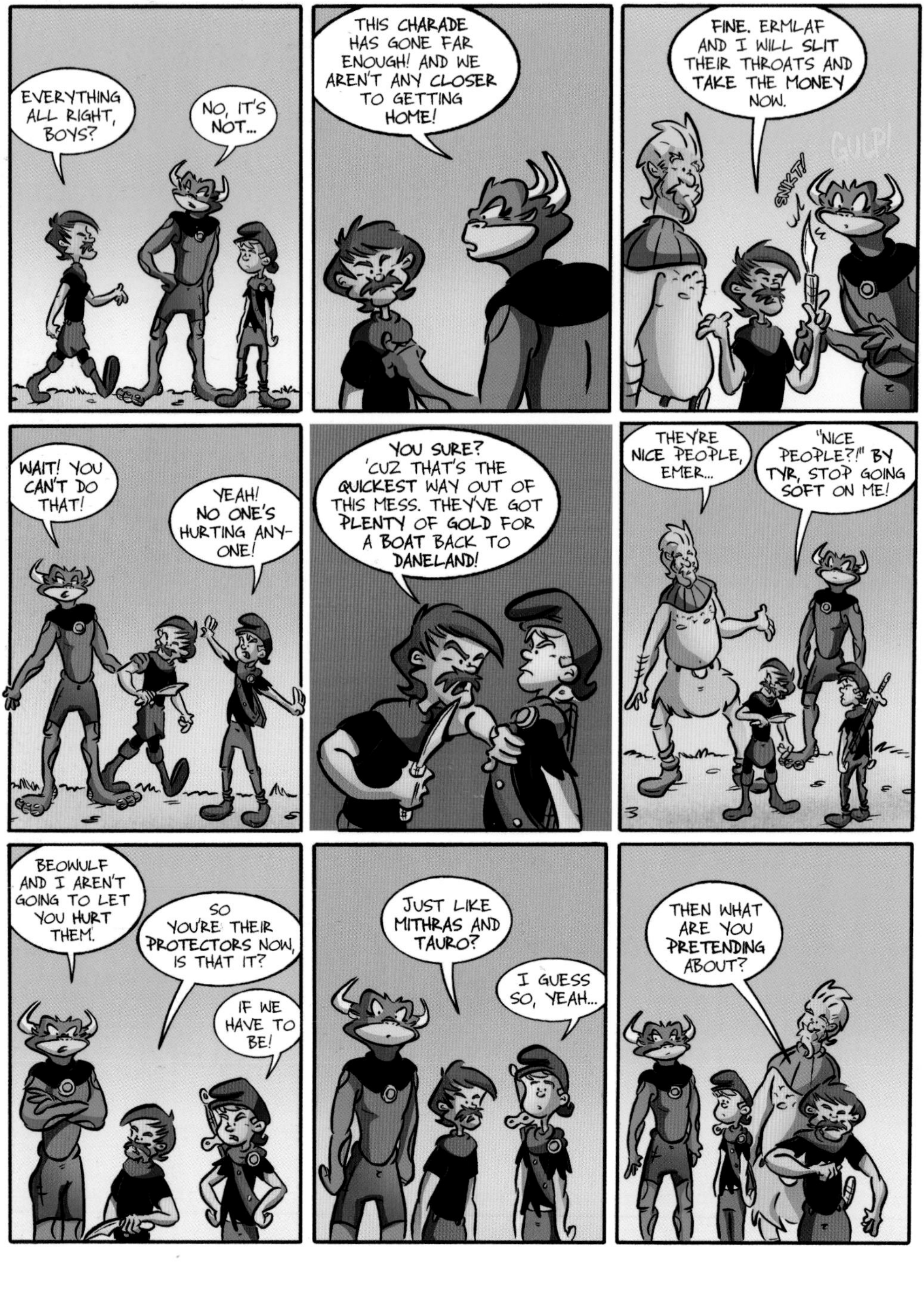
EVERYTHING ALL RIGHT, BOYS?
NO, IT'S NOT...
THIS CHARADE HAS GONE FAR ENOUGH! AND WE AREN'T ANY CLOSER TO GETTING HOME!
FINE. ERMLAF AND I WILL SLIT THEIR THROATS AND TAKE THE MONEY NOW.
SNKT!
GULP!
WAIT! YOU CAN'T DO THAT!
YEAH! NO ONE'S HURTING ANY-ONE!
YOU SURE? 'CUZ THAT'S THE QUICKEST WAY OUT OF THIS MESS. THEY'VE GOT PLENTY OF GOLD FOR A BOAT BACK TO DANELAND!
THEY'RE NICE PEOPLE, EMER...
"NICE PEOPLE?!" BY TYR, STOP GOING SOFT ON ME!
BEOWULF AND I AREN'T GOING TO LET YOU HURT THEM.
SO YOU'RE THEIR PROTECTORS NOW, IS THAT IT?
IF WE HAVE TO BE!
JUST LIKE MITHRAS AND TAURO?
I GUESS SO, YEAH...
THEN WHAT ARE YOU PRETENDING ABOUT?

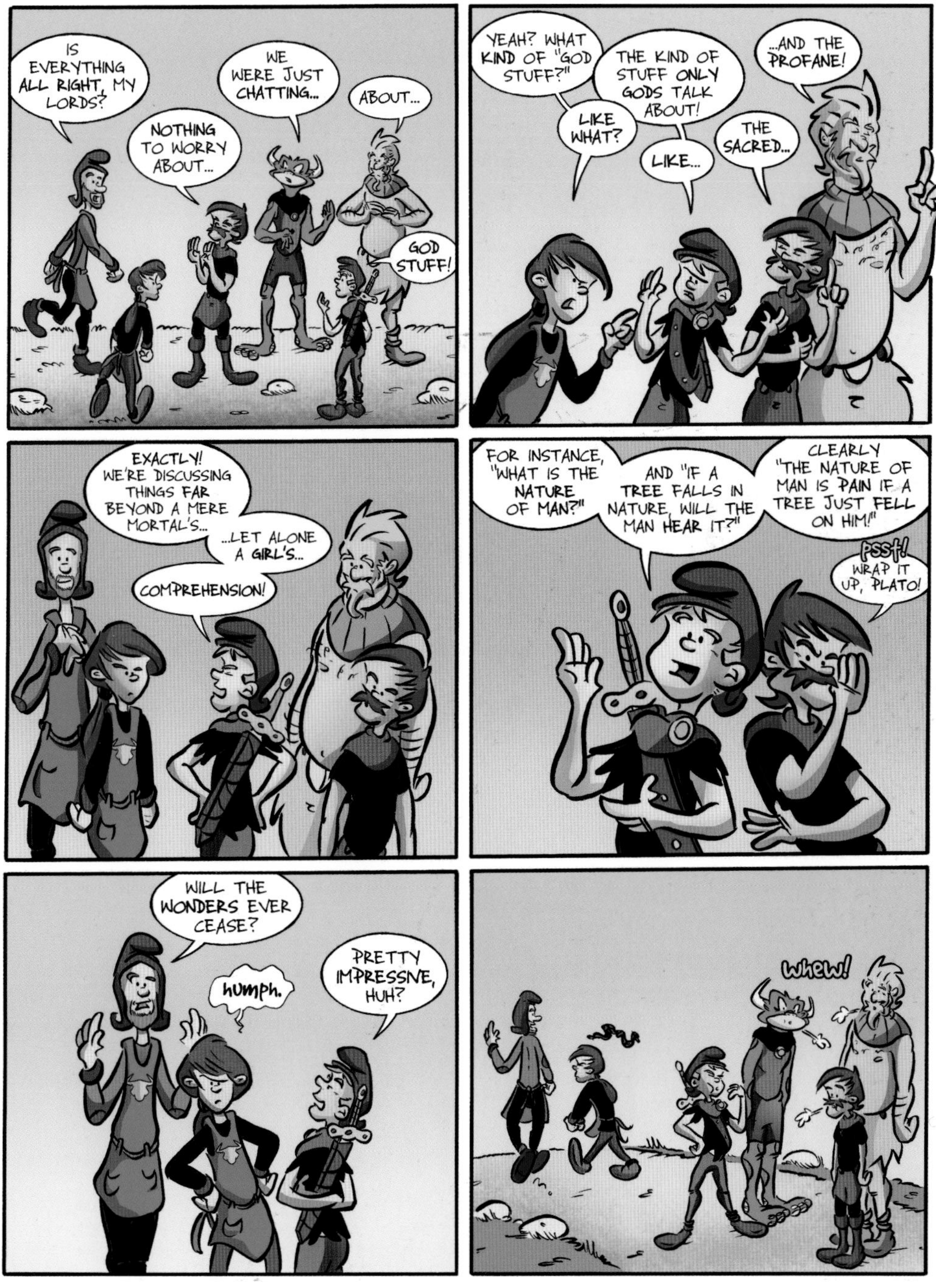
IS EVERYTHING ALL RIGHT, MY LORDS?
NOTHING TO WORRY ABOUT...
WE WERE JUST CHATTING...
ABOUT...
GOD STUFF!
YEAH? WHAT KIND OF "GOD STUFF?"
THE KIND OF STUFF ONLY GODS TALK ABOUT!
...AND THE PROFANE!
LIKE WHAT?
LIKE...
THE SACRED...
EXACTLY! WE'RE DISCUSSING THINGS FAR BEYOND A MERE MORTAL'S...
...LET ALONE A GIRL'S...
COMPREHENSION!
FOR INSTANCE, "WHAT IS THE NATURE OF MAN?"
AND "IF A TREE FALLS IN NATURE, WILL THE MAN HEAR IT?"
CLEARLY "THE NATURE OF MAN IS PAIN IF A TREE JUST FELL ON HIM!"
PSST! WRAP IT UP, PLATO!
WILL THE WONDERS EVER CEASE?
humph.
PRETTY IMPRESSIVE, HUH?
whew!

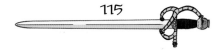

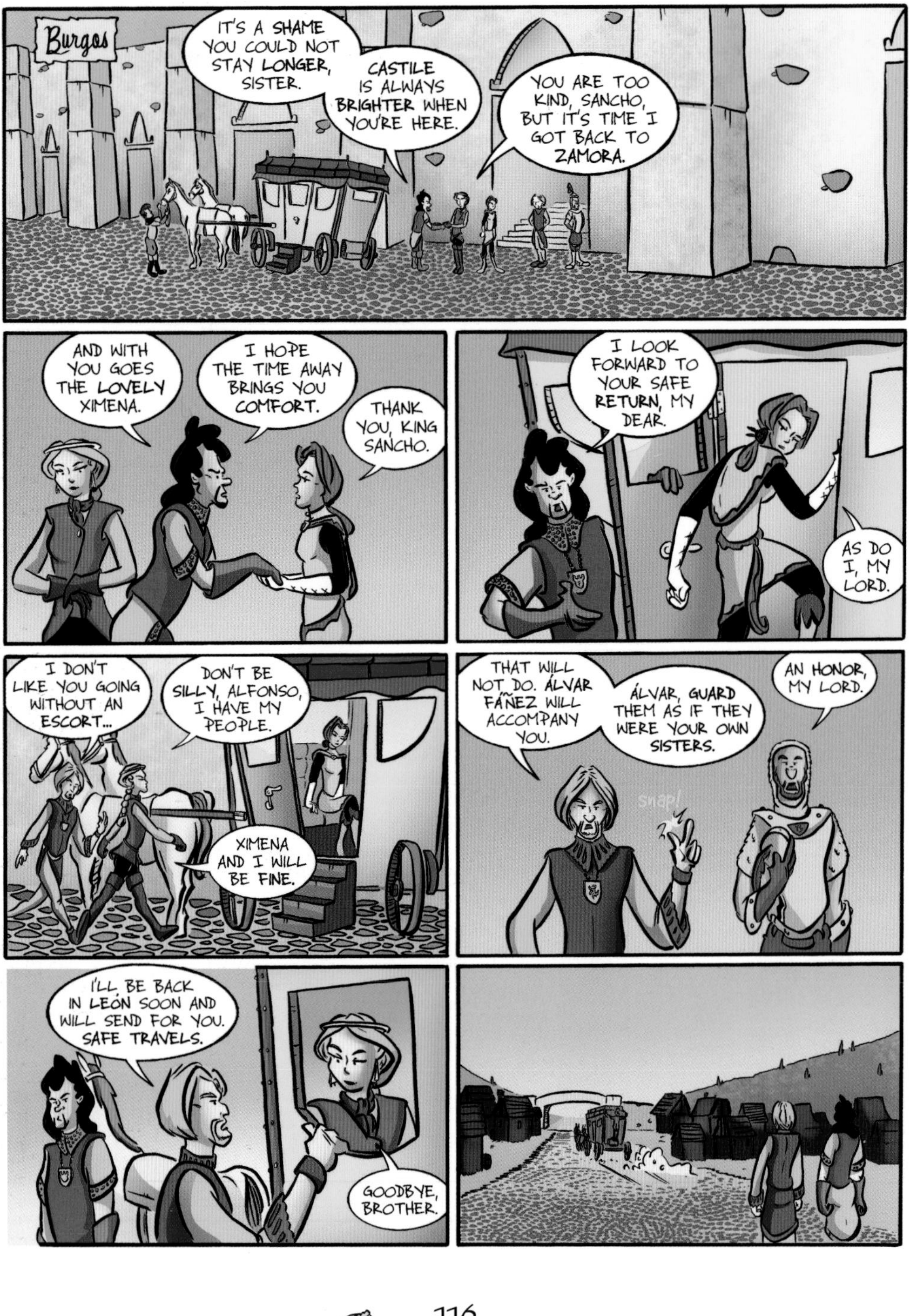
Burgos
IT'S A SHAME YOU COULD NOT STAY LONGER, SISTER.
CASTILE IS ALWAYS BRIGHTER WHEN YOU'RE HERE.
YOU ARE TOO KIND, SANCHO, BUT IT'S TIME I GOT BACK TO ZAMORA.
AND WITH YOU GOES THE LOVELY XIMENA.
I HOPE THE TIME AWAY BRINGS YOU COMFORT.
THANK YOU, KING SANCHO.
I LOOK FORWARD TO YOUR SAFE RETURN, MY DEAR.
AS DO I, MY LORD.
I DON'T LIKE YOU GOING WITHOUT AN ESCORT...
DON'T BE SILLY, ALFONSO, I HAVE MY PEOPLE.
XIMENA AND I WILL BE FINE.
THAT WILL NOT DO. ÁLVAR FÁÑEZ WILL ACCOMPANY YOU.
ÁLVAR, GUARD THEM AS IF THEY WERE YOUR OWN SISTERS.
snap!
AN HONOR, MY LORD.
I'LL BE BACK IN LEÓN SOON AND WILL SEND FOR YOU. SAFE TRAVELS.
GOODBYE, BROTHER.

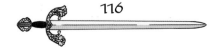

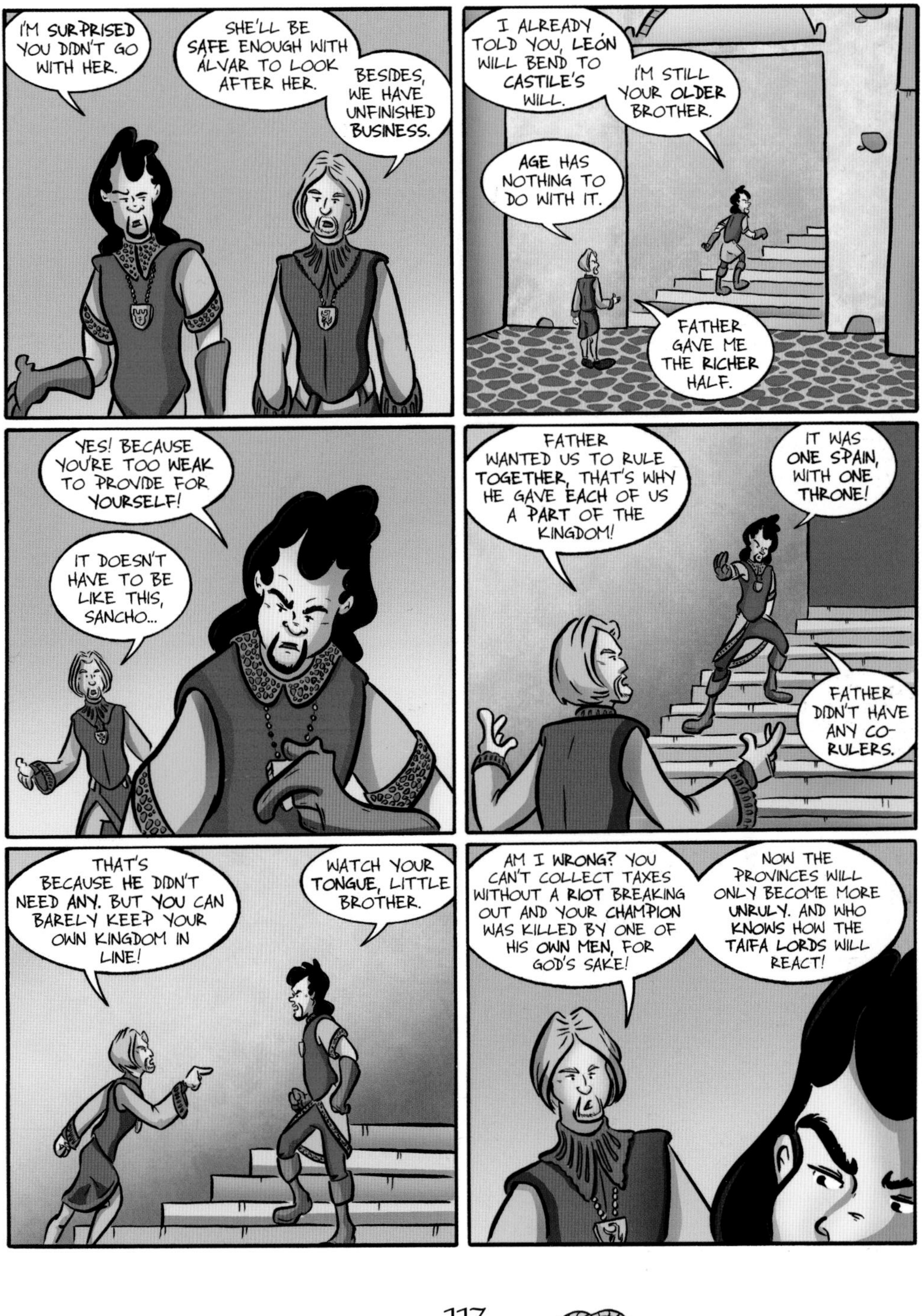
I'M SURPRISED YOU DIDN'T GO WITH HER.
SHE'LL BE SAFE ENOUGH WITH ÁLVAR TO LOOK AFTER HER.
BESIDES, WE HAVE UNFINISHED BUSINESS.
I ALREADY TOLD YOU, LEÓN WILL BEND TO CASTILE'S WILL.
I'M STILL YOUR OLDER BROTHER.
AGE HAS NOTHING TO DO WITH IT.
FATHER GAVE ME THE RICHER HALF.
YES! BECAUSE YOU'RE TOO WEAK TO PROVIDE FOR YOURSELF!
IT DOESN'T HAVE TO BE LIKE THIS, SANCHO...
FATHER WANTED US TO RULE TOGETHER, THAT'S WHY HE GAVE EACH OF US A PART OF THE KINGDOM!
IT WAS ONE SPAIN, WITH ONE THRONE!
FATHER DIDN'T HAVE ANY CO-RULERS.
THAT'S BECAUSE HE DIDN'T NEED ANY. BUT YOU CAN BARELY KEEP YOUR OWN KINGDOM IN LINE!
WATCH YOUR TONGUE, LITTLE BROTHER.
AM I WRONG? YOU CAN'T COLLECT TAXES WITHOUT A RIOT BREAKING OUT AND YOUR CHAMPION WAS KILLED BY ONE OF HIS OWN MEN, FOR GOD'S SAKE!
NOW THE PROVINCES WILL ONLY BECOME MORE UNRULY. AND WHO KNOWS HOW THE TAIFA LORDS WILL REACT!

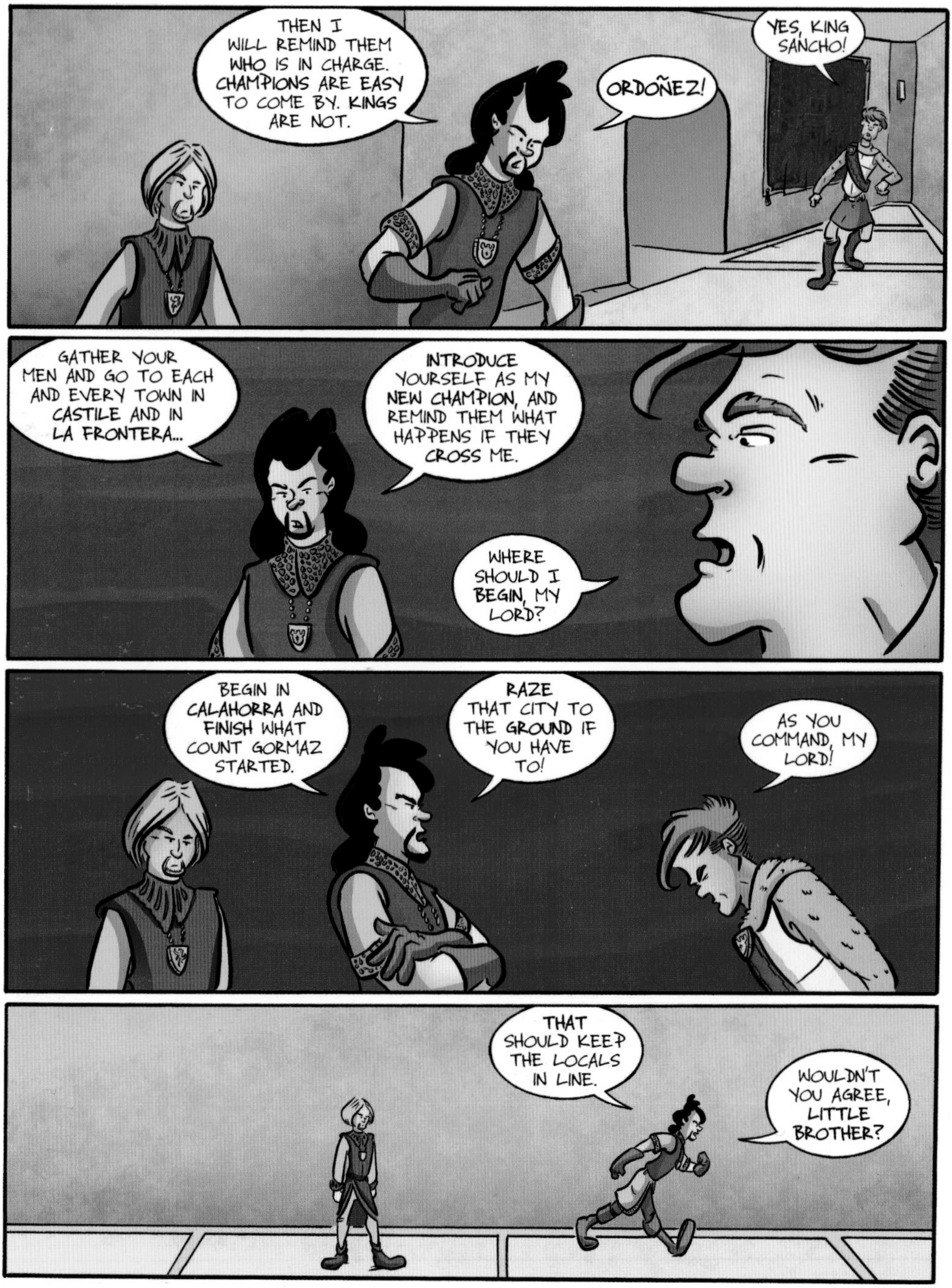
THEN I WILL REMIND THEM WHO IS IN CHARGE. CHAMPIONS ARE EASY TO COME BY. KINGS ARE NOT.
ORDOÑEZ!
YES, KING SANCHO!
GATHER YOUR MEN AND GO TO EACH AND EVERY TOWN IN CASTILE AND IN LA FRONTERA...
INTRODUCE YOURSELF AS MY NEW CHAMPION, AND REMIND THEM WHAT HAPPENS IF THEY CROSS ME.
WHERE SHOULD I BEGIN, MY LORD?
BEGIN IN CALAHORRA AND FINISH WHAT COUNT GORMAZ STARTED.
RAZE THAT CITY TO THE GROUND IF YOU HAVE TO!
AS YOU COMMAND, MY LORD!
THAT SHOULD KEEP THE LOCALS IN LINE.
WOULDN'T YOU AGREE, LITTLE BROTHER?

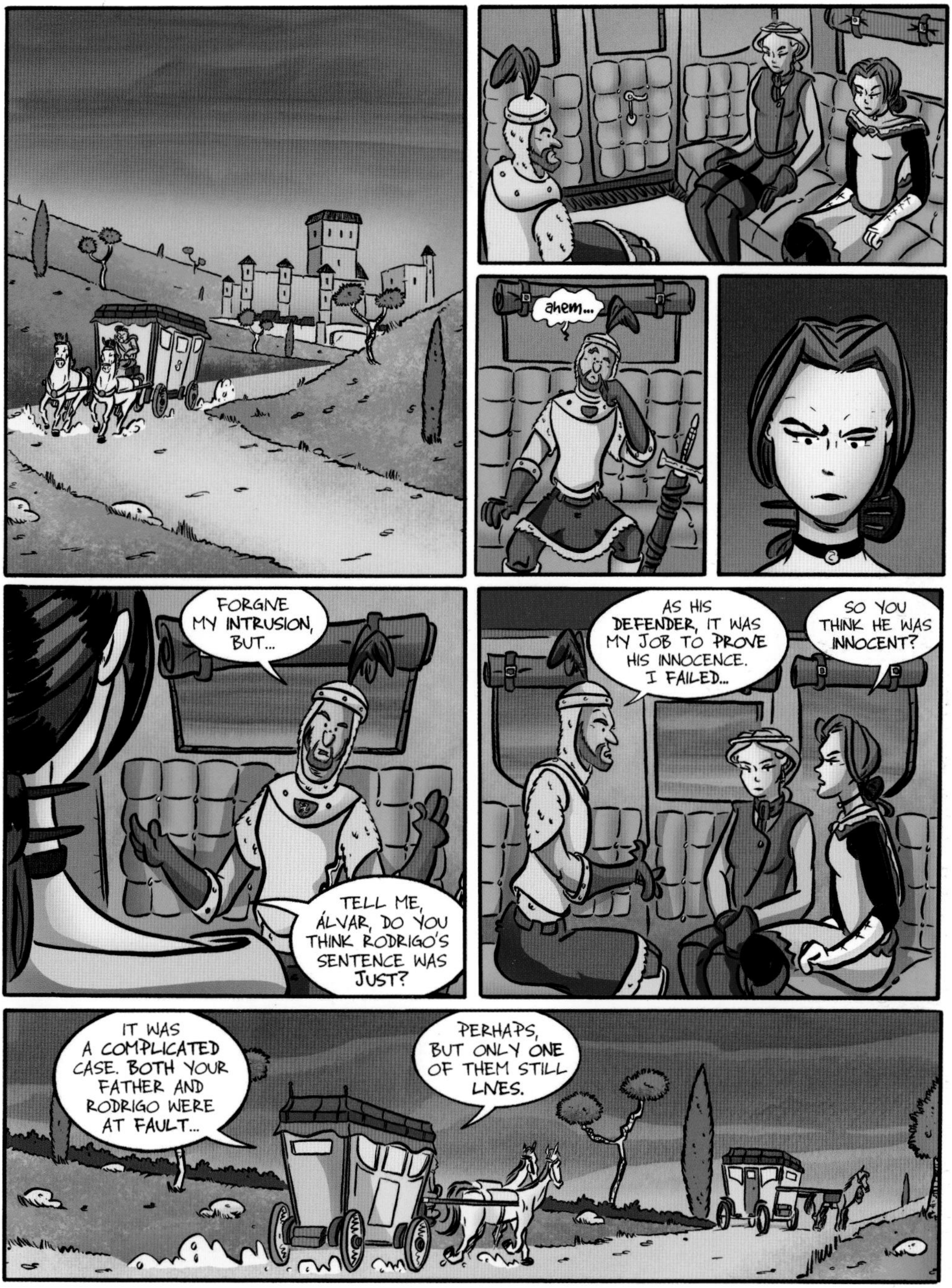
ahem...
FORGIVE MY INTRUSION, BUT...
TELL ME, ÁLVAR, DO YOU THINK RODRIGO'S SENTENCE WAS JUST?
AS HIS DEFENDER, IT WAS MY JOB TO PROVE HIS INNOCENCE. I FAILED...
SO YOU THINK HE WAS INNOCENT?
IT WAS A COMPLICATED CASE. BOTH YOUR FATHER AND RODRIGO WERE AT FAULT...
PERHAPS, BUT ONLY ONE OF THEM STILL LIVES.

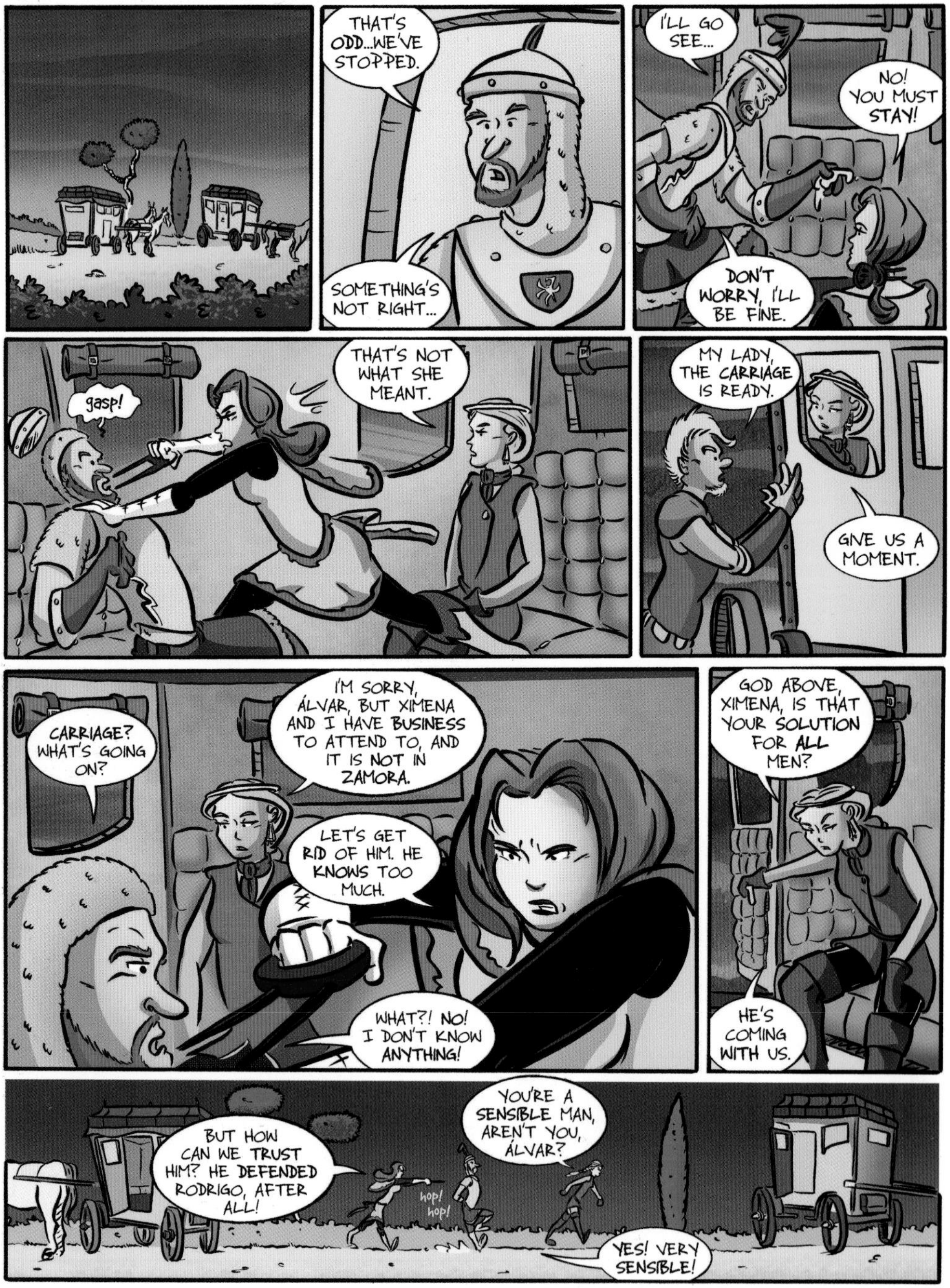
THAT'S ODD...WE'VE STOPPED.
SOMETHING'S NOT RIGHT...
I'LL GO SEE...
NO! YOU MUST STAY!
DON'T WORRY, I'LL BE FINE.
gasp!
THAT'S NOT WHAT SHE MEANT.
MY LADY, THE CARRIAGE IS READY.
GIVE US A MOMENT.
CARRIAGE? WHAT'S GOING ON?
I'M SORRY, ÁLVAR, BUT XIMENA AND I HAVE BUSINESS TO ATTEND TO, AND IT IS NOT IN ZAMORA.
LET'S GET RID OF HIM. HE KNOWS TOO MUCH.
WHAT?! NO! I DON'T KNOW ANYTHING!
GOD ABOVE, XIMENA, IS THAT YOUR SOLUTION FOR ALL MEN?
HE'S COMING WITH US.
BUT HOW CAN WE TRUST HIM? HE DEFENDED RODRIGO, AFTER ALL!
hop! hop!
YOU'RE A SENSIBLE MAN, AREN'T YOU, ÁLVAR?
YES! VERY SENSIBLE!

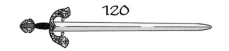

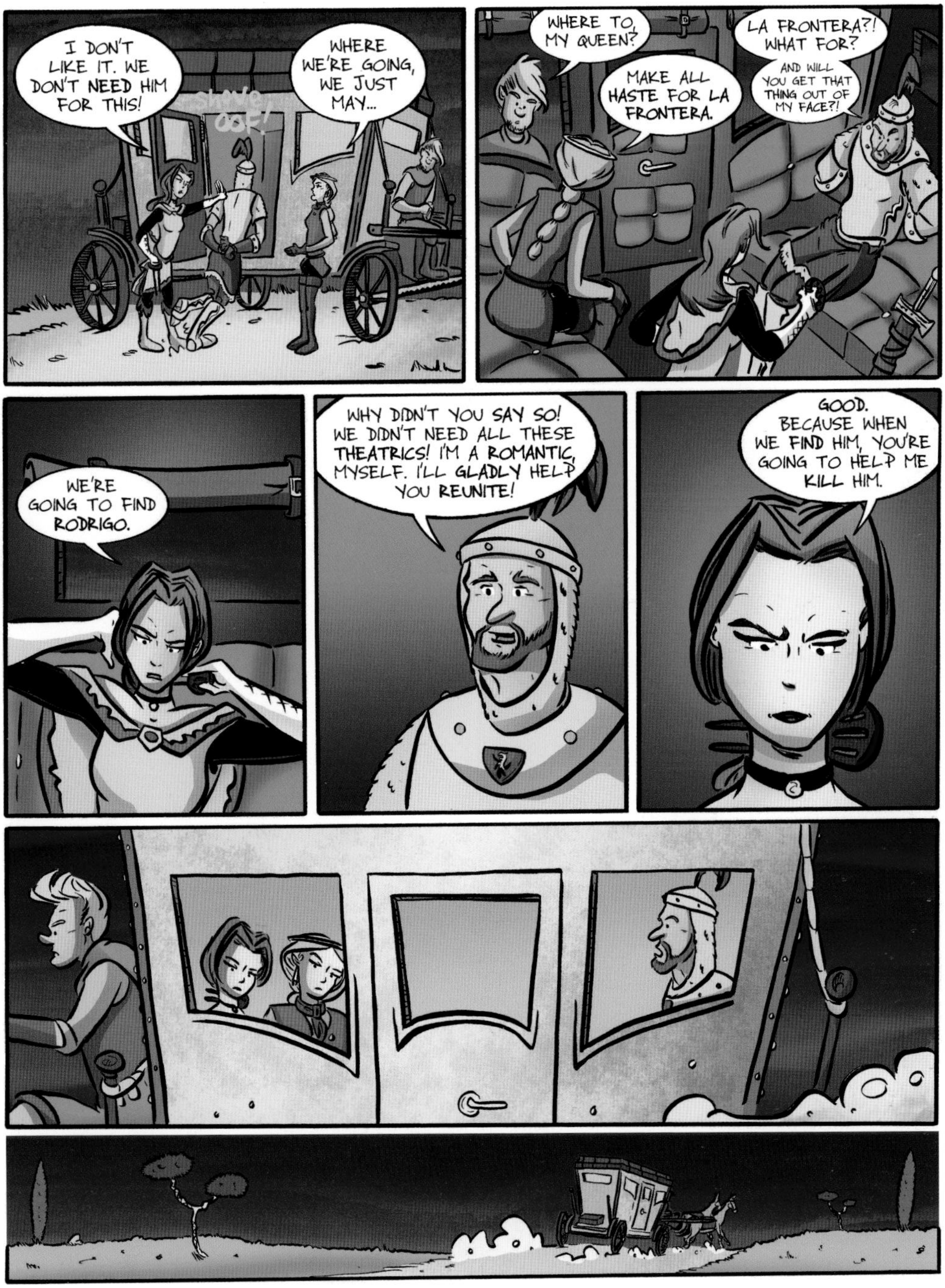
I DON'T LIKE IT. WE DON'T NEED HIM FOR THIS!
SHOVE OOF!
WHERE WE'RE GOING, WE JUST MAY...
WHERE TO, MY QUEEN?
MAKE ALL HASTE FOR LA FRONTERA.
LA FRONTERA?! WHAT FOR?
AND WILL YOU GET THAT THING OUT OF MY FACE?!
WE'RE GOING TO FIND RODRIGO.
WHY DIDN'T YOU SAY SO! WE DIDN'T NEED ALL THESE THEATRICS! I'M A ROMANTIC, MYSELF. I'LL GLADLY HELP YOU REUNITE!
GOOD. BECAUSE WHEN WE FIND HIM, YOU'RE GOING TO HELP ME KILL HIM.

Calahorra

THAT'S A SAD SONG TO WHISTLE FOR ONE SO YOUNG.

IT REMINDS ME OF SOMEONE VERY SPECIAL TO ME.

YOUR HORSE?

?

WE HAVE ROOMS READY FOR YOU AT THE INN. HERE ARE BLANKETS FOR THE HORSES.

THANKS, JOSEP.

ANY NEWS FROM THE OUTSIDE?

YES! THERE ARE RUMORS SWIRLING FROM CASTILE...SANCHO HAS NAMED A NEW CHAMPION!

OH? WHO?

I'LL GIVE YOU THREE GUESSES, AND THE FIRST TWO DON'T COUNT.

I AM HORRIBLE WITH NAMES, BUT I THINK IT'S...

ORDOÑEZ.

THAT'S IT! DO YOU KNOW HIM?

OH, YEAH! THEY GO WAY BACK!

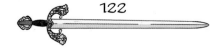

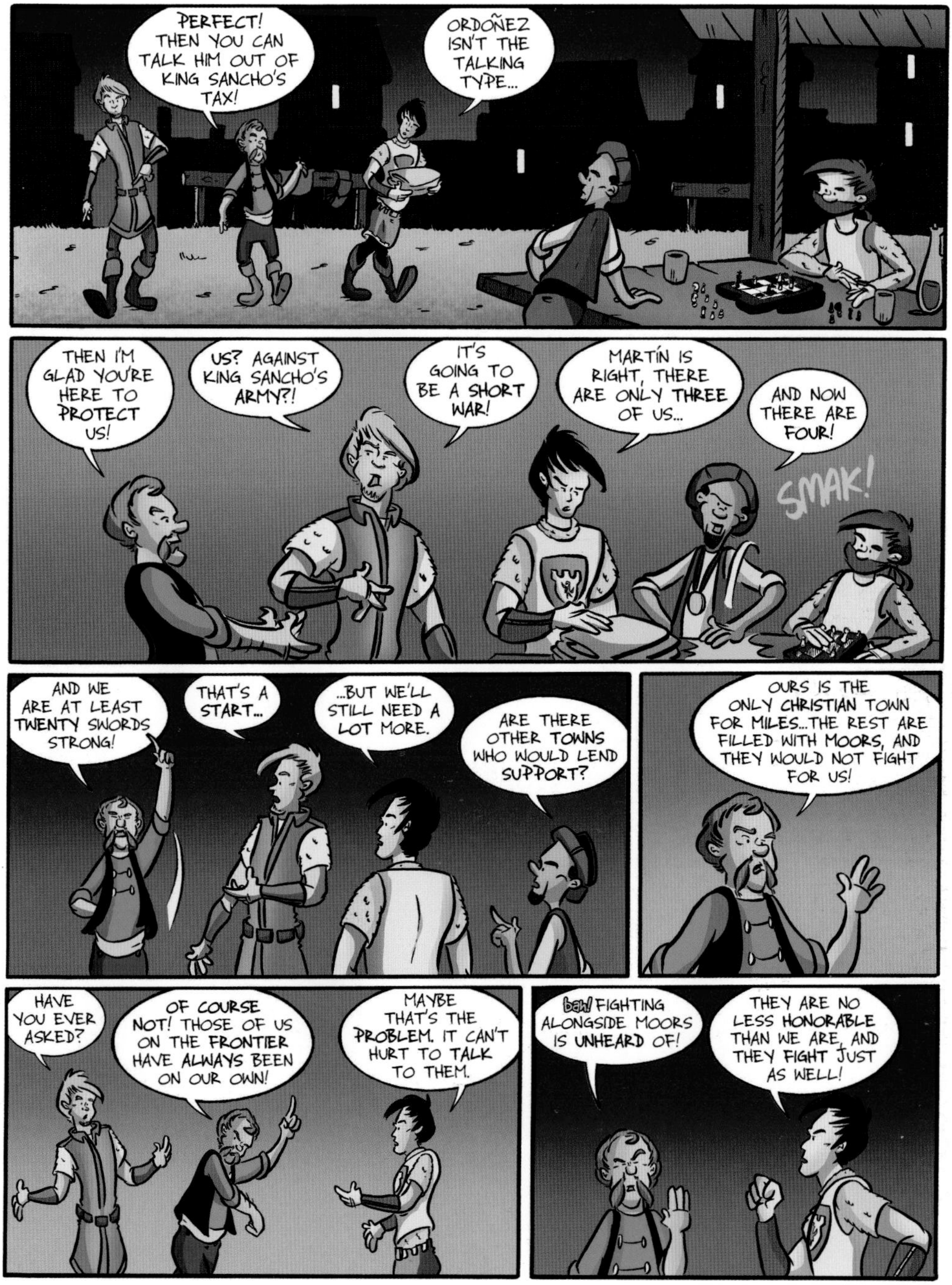
PERFECT! THEN YOU CAN TALK HIM OUT OF KING SANCHO'S TAX!
ORDOÑEZ ISN'T THE TALKING TYPE...
THEN I'M GLAD YOU'RE HERE TO PROTECT US!
US? AGAINST KING SANCHO'S ARMY?!
IT'S GOING TO BE A SHORT WAR!
MARTÍN IS RIGHT, THERE ARE ONLY THREE OF US...
AND NOW THERE ARE FOUR!
SMAK!
AND WE ARE AT LEAST TWENTY SWORDS STRONG!
THAT'S A START...
...BUT WE'LL STILL NEED A LOT MORE.
ARE THERE OTHER TOWNS WHO WOULD LEND SUPPORT?
OURS IS THE ONLY CHRISTIAN TOWN FOR MILES...THE REST ARE FILLED WITH MOORS, AND THEY WOULD NOT FIGHT FOR US!
HAVE YOU EVER ASKED?
OF COURSE NOT! THOSE OF US ON THE FRONTIER HAVE ALWAYS BEEN ON OUR OWN!
MAYBE THAT'S THE PROBLEM. IT CAN'T HURT TO TALK TO THEM.
bah! FIGHTING ALONGSIDE MOORS IS UNHEARD OF!
THEY ARE NO LESS HONORABLE THAN WE ARE, AND THEY FIGHT JUST AS WELL!

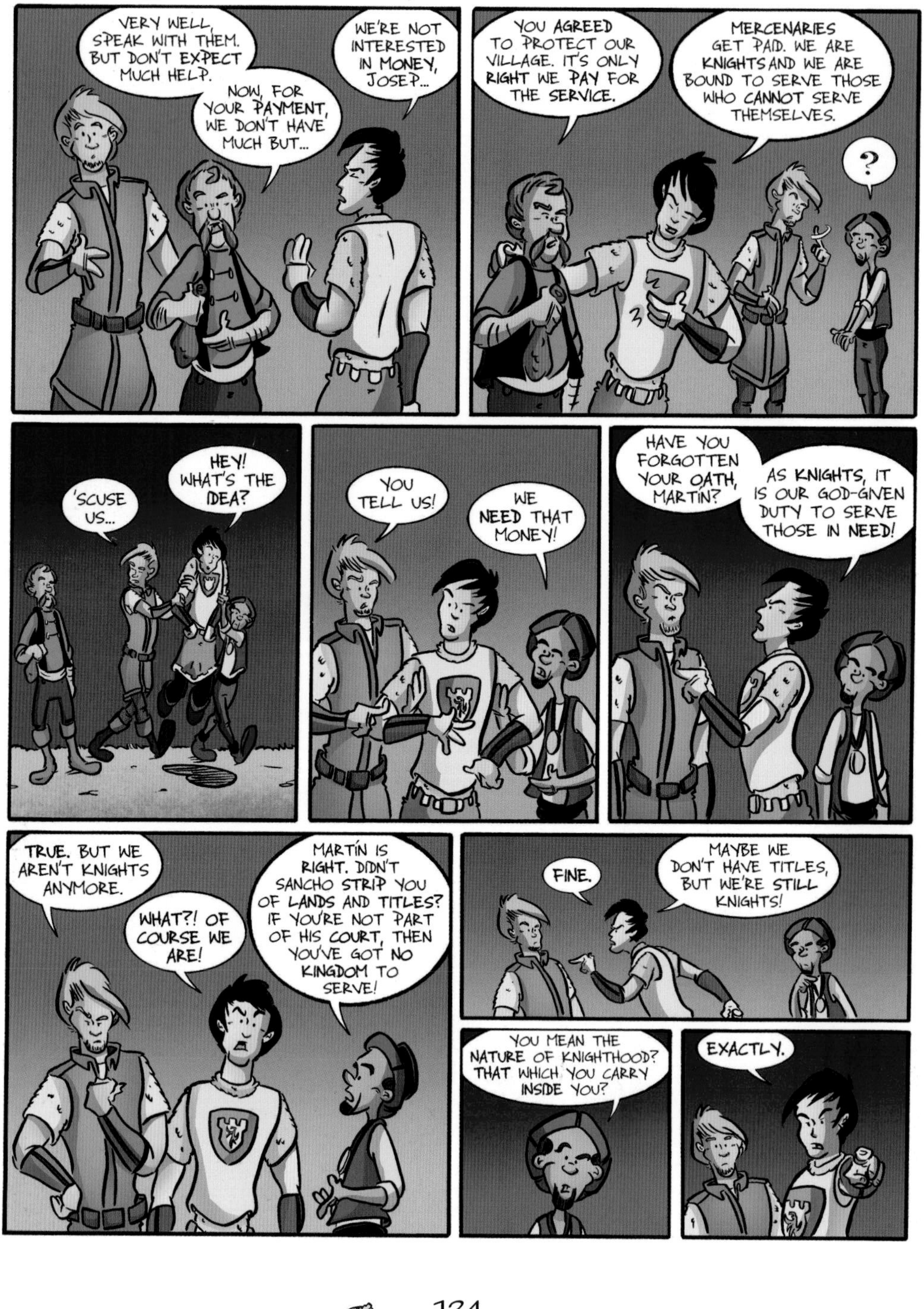
VERY WELL, SPEAK WITH THEM. BUT DON'T EXPECT MUCH HELP.
NOW, FOR YOUR PAYMENT, WE DON'T HAVE MUCH BUT...
WE'RE NOT INTERESTED IN MONEY, JOSEP...
YOU AGREED TO PROTECT OUR VILLAGE. IT'S ONLY RIGHT WE PAY FOR THE SERVICE.
MERCENARIES GET PAID. WE ARE KNIGHTS AND WE ARE BOUND TO SERVE THOSE WHO CANNOT SERVE THEMSELVES.
?
'SCUSE US...
HEY! WHAT'S THE IDEA?
YOU TELL US!
WE NEED THAT MONEY!
HAVE YOU FORGOTTEN YOUR OATH, MARTÍN?
AS KNIGHTS, IT IS OUR GOD-GIVEN DUTY TO SERVE THOSE IN NEED!
TRUE. BUT WE AREN'T KNIGHTS ANYMORE.
WHAT?! OF COURSE WE ARE!
MARTÍN IS RIGHT. DIDN'T SANCHO STRIP YOU OF LANDS AND TITLES? IF YOU'RE NOT PART OF HIS COURT, THEN YOU'VE GOT NO KINGDOM TO SERVE!
FINE.
MAYBE WE DON'T HAVE TITLES, BUT WE'RE STILL KNIGHTS!
YOU MEAN THE NATURE OF KNIGHTHOOD? THAT WHICH YOU CARRY INSIDE YOU?
EXACTLY.

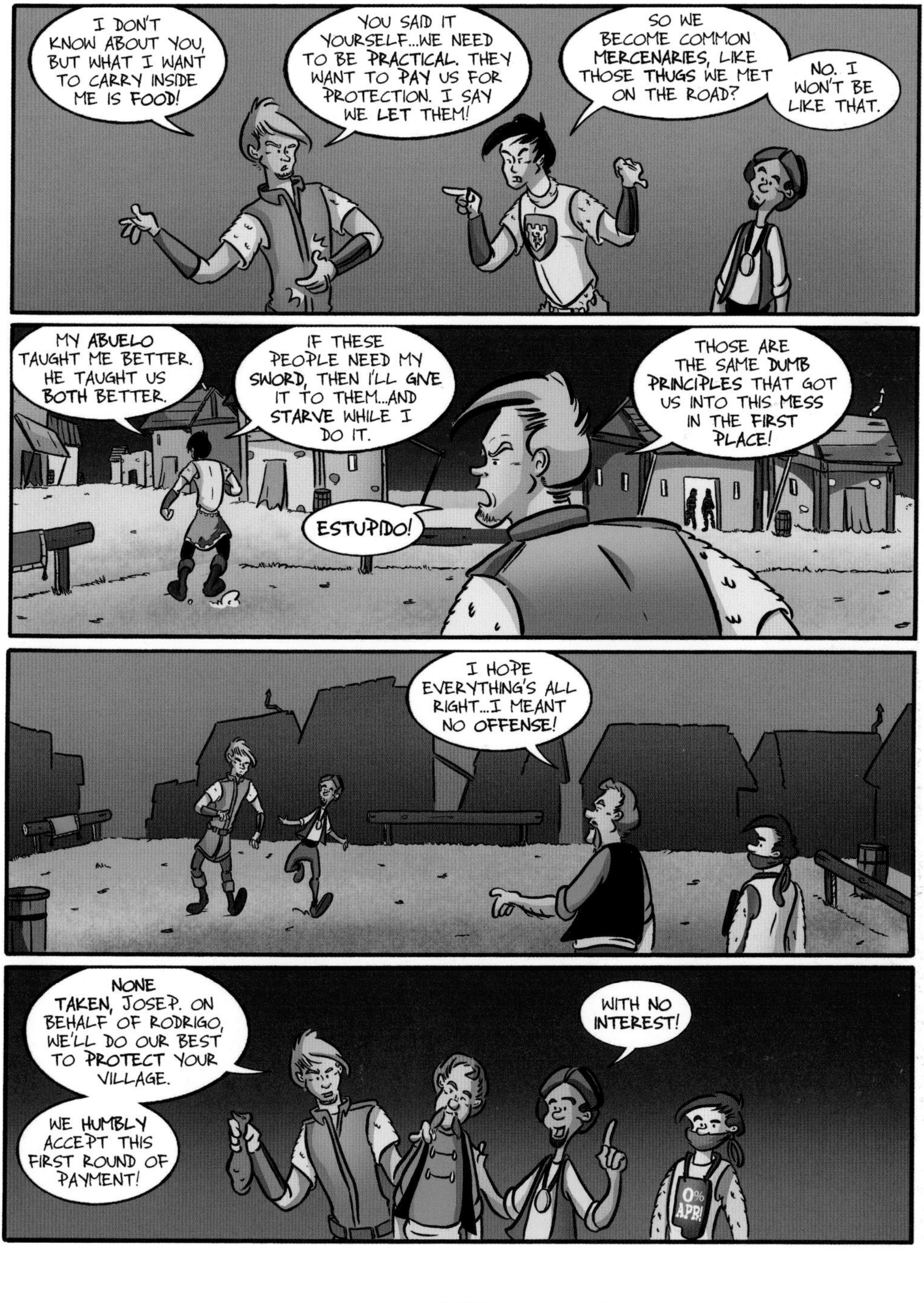
I DON'T KNOW ABOUT YOU, BUT WHAT I WANT TO CARRY INSIDE ME IS FOOD!
YOU SAID IT YOURSELF...WE NEED TO BE PRACTICAL. THEY WANT TO PAY US FOR PROTECTION. I SAY WE LET THEM!
SO WE BECOME COMMON MERCENARIES, LIKE THOSE THUGS WE MET ON THE ROAD?
NO. I WON'T BE LIKE THAT.
MY ABUELO TAUGHT ME BETTER. HE TAUGHT US BOTH BETTER.
IF THESE PEOPLE NEED MY SWORD, THEN I'LL GIVE IT TO THEM...AND STARVE WHILE I DO IT.
THOSE ARE THE SAME DUMB PRINCIPLES THAT GOT US INTO THIS MESS IN THE FIRST PLACE!
ESTUPIDO!
I HOPE EVERYTHING'S ALL RIGHT...I MEANT NO OFFENSE!
NONE TAKEN, JOSEP. ON BEHALF OF RODRIGO, WE'LL DO OUR BEST TO PROTECT YOUR VILLAGE.
WE HUMBLY ACCEPT THIS FIRST ROUND OF PAYMENT!
WITH NO INTEREST!
0% APR!

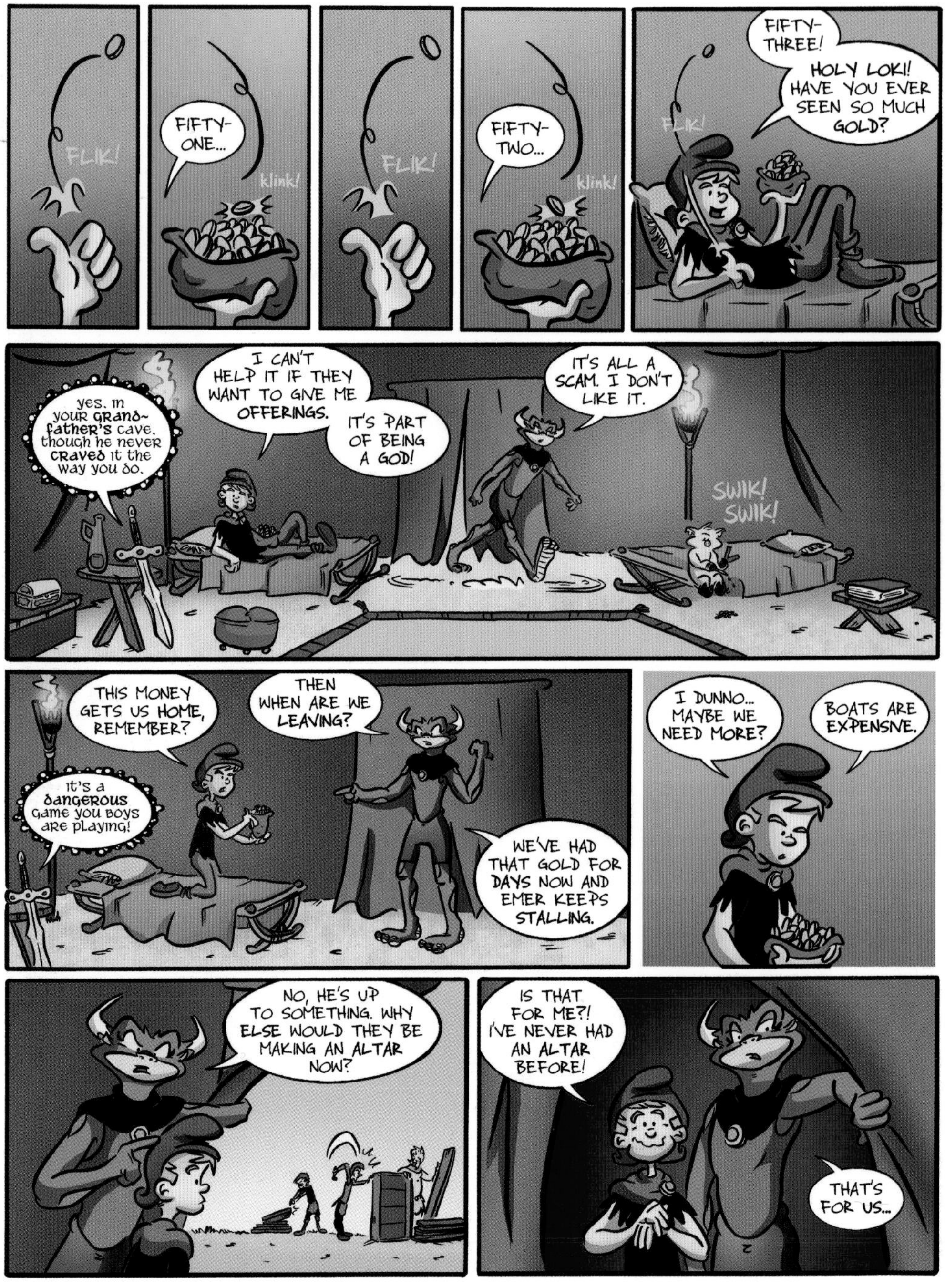
FLIK!
FIFTY-ONE...
klink!
FLIK!
FIFTY-TWO...
klink!
FLIK!
FIFTY-THREE!
HOLY LOKI! HAVE YOU EVER SEEN SO MUCH GOLD?
yes. in your grand-father's cave. though he never craved it the way you do.
I CAN'T HELP IT IF THEY WANT TO GIVE ME OFFERINGS.
IT'S PART OF BEING A GOD!
IT'S ALL A SCAM. I DON'T LIKE IT.
SWIK! SWIK!
THIS MONEY GETS US HOME, REMEMBER?
THEN WHEN ARE WE LEAVING?
it's a dangerous game you boys are playing!
WE'VE HAD THAT GOLD FOR DAYS NOW AND EMER KEEPS STALLING.
I DUNNO... MAYBE WE NEED MORE?
BOATS ARE EXPENSIVE.
NO, HE'S UP TO SOMETHING. WHY ELSE WOULD THEY BE MAKING AN ALTAR NOW?
IS THAT FOR ME?! I'VE NEVER HAD AN ALTAR BEFORE!
THAT'S FOR US...

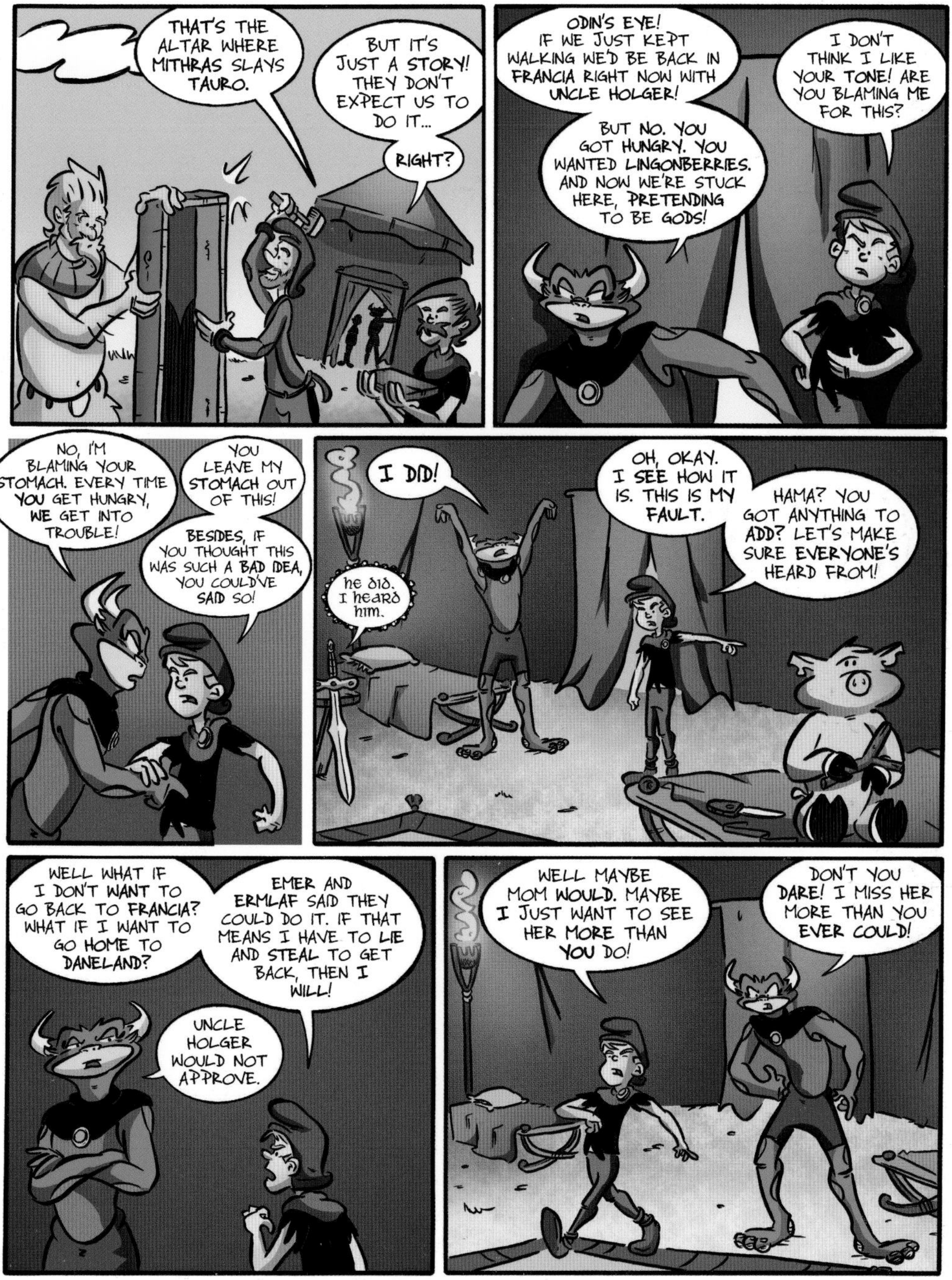
THAT'S THE ALTAR WHERE MITHRAS SLAYS TAURO.
BUT IT'S JUST A STORY! THEY DON'T EXPECT US TO DO IT...
RIGHT?
ODIN'S EYE! IF WE JUST KEPT WALKING WE'D BE BACK IN FRANCIA RIGHT NOW WITH UNCLE HOLGER!
BUT NO. YOU GOT HUNGRY. YOU WANTED LINGONBERRIES. AND NOW WE'RE STUCK HERE, PRETENDING TO BE GODS!
I DON'T THINK I LIKE YOUR TONE! ARE YOU BLAMING ME FOR THIS?
NO, I'M BLAMING YOUR STOMACH. EVERY TIME YOU GET HUNGRY, WE GET INTO TROUBLE!
YOU LEAVE MY STOMACH OUT OF THIS!
BESIDES, IF YOU THOUGHT THIS WAS SUCH A BAD IDEA, YOU COULD'VE SAID SO!
I DID!
he did. I heard him.
OH, OKAY. I SEE HOW IT IS. THIS IS MY FAULT.
HAMA? YOU GOT ANYTHING TO ADD? LET'S MAKE SURE EVERYONE'S HEARD FROM!
WELL WHAT IF I DON'T WANT TO GO BACK TO FRANCIA? WHAT IF I WANT TO GO HOME TO DANELAND?
EMER AND ERMLAF SAID THEY COULD DO IT. IF THAT MEANS I HAVE TO LIE AND STEAL TO GET BACK, THEN I WILL!
UNCLE HOLGER WOULD NOT APPROVE.
WELL MAYBE MOM WOULD. MAYBE I JUST WANT TO SEE HER MORE THAN YOU DO!
DON'T YOU DARE! I MISS HER MORE THAN YOU EVER COULD!

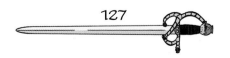

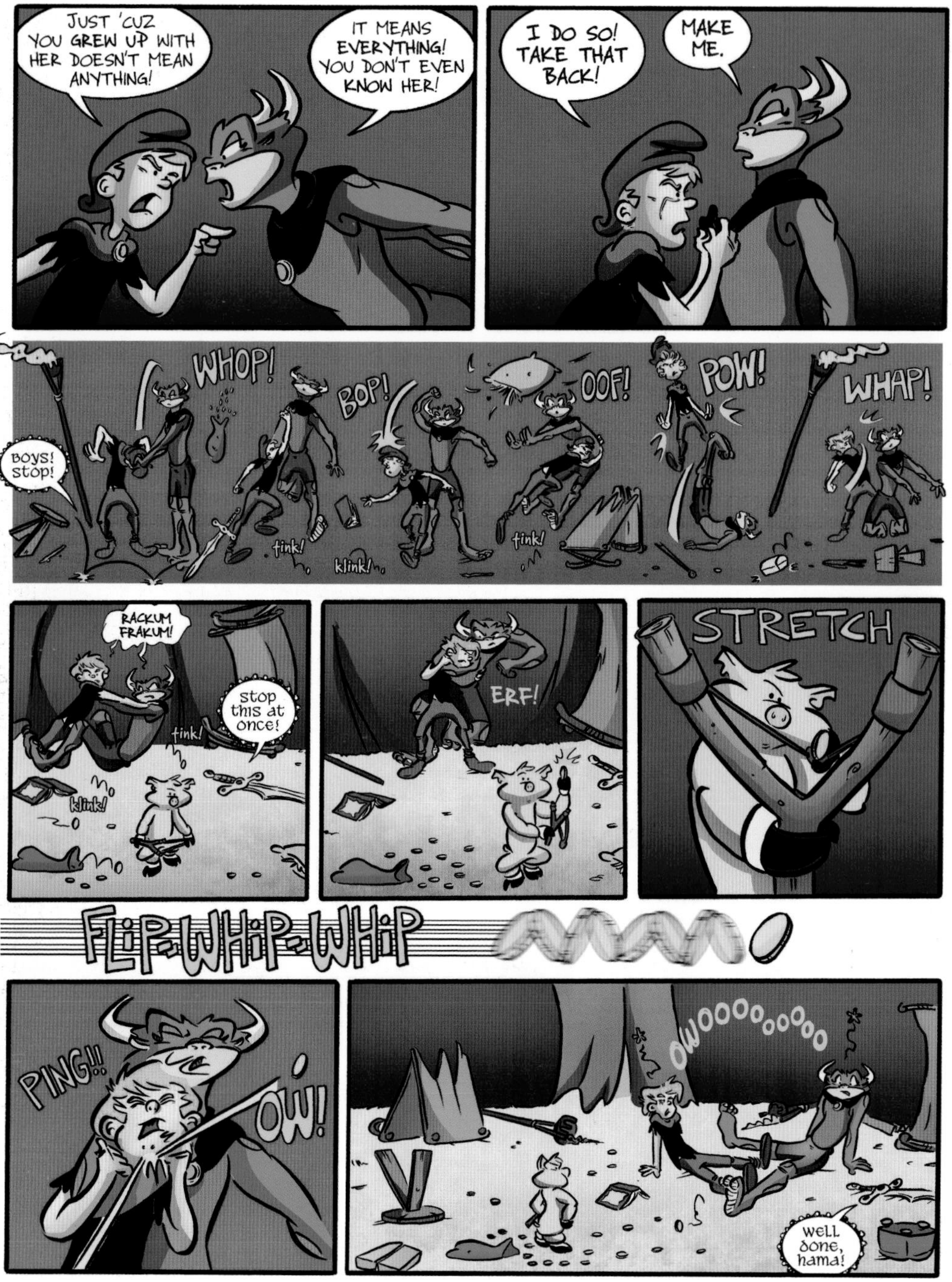
JUST 'CUZ YOU GREW UP WITH HER DOESN'T MEAN ANYTHING!
IT MEANS EVERYTHING! YOU DON'T EVEN KNOW HER!
I DO SO! TAKE THAT BACK!
MAKE ME.
WHOP!
Boys! stop!
BOP!
OOF!
POW!
WHAP!
tink!
klink!
tink!
RACKUM FRAKUM!
stop this at once!
tink!
klink!
ERF!
STRETCH
FLIP-WHIP-WHIP
PING!!
OW!
OWOOOOOOOOO
well done, hama!

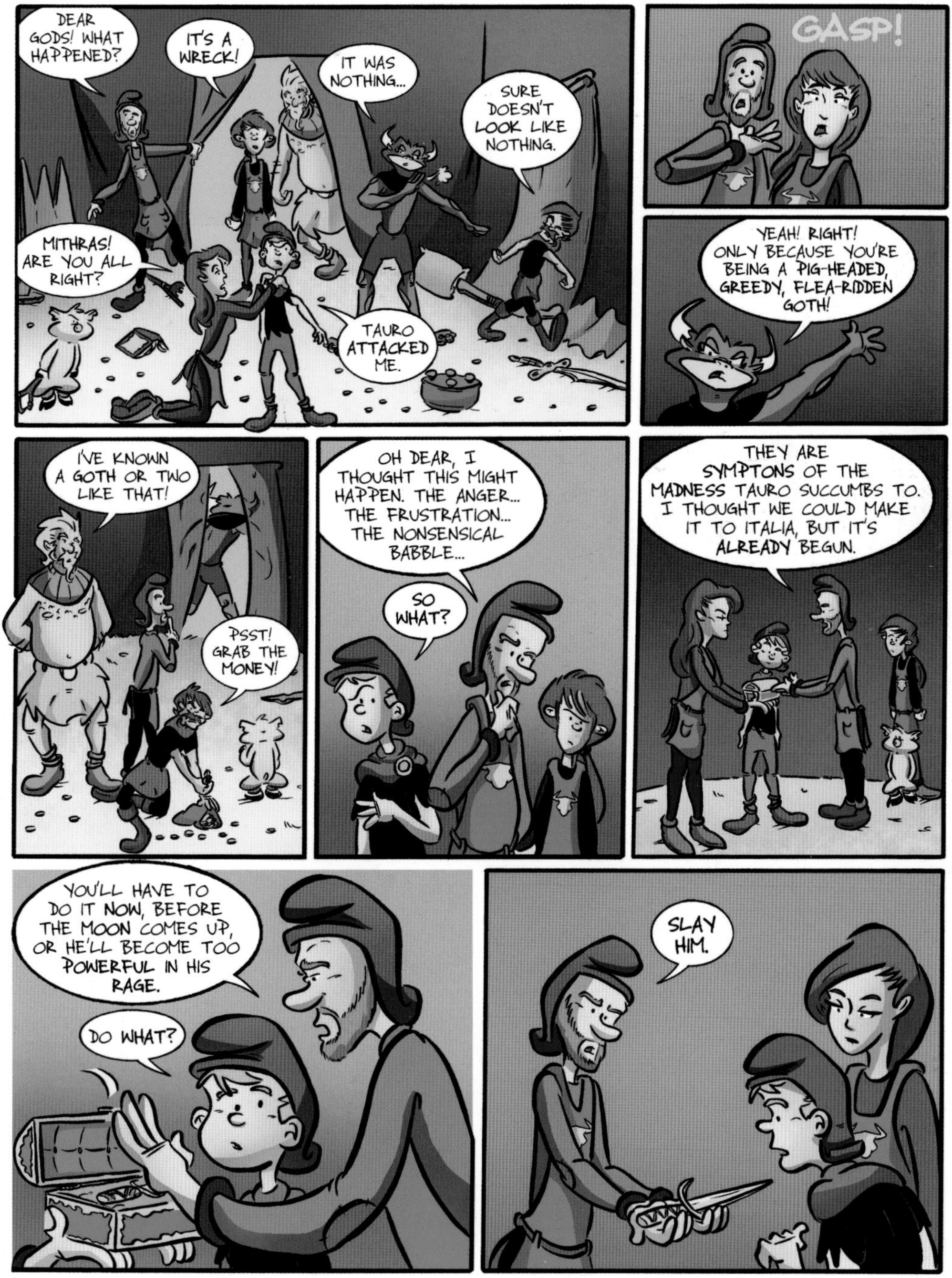
DEAR GODS! WHAT HAPPENED?
IT'S A WRECK!
IT WAS NOTHING...
SURE DOESN'T LOOK LIKE NOTHING.
MITHRAS! ARE YOU ALL RIGHT?
TAURO ATTACKED ME.
GASP!
YEAH! RIGHT! ONLY BECAUSE YOU'RE BEING A PIG-HEADED, GREEDY, FLEA-RIDDEN GOTH!
I'VE KNOWN A GOTH OR TWO LIKE THAT!
PSST! GRAB THE MONEY!
OH DEAR, I THOUGHT THIS MIGHT HAPPEN. THE ANGER... THE FRUSTRATION... THE NONSENSICAL BABBLE...
SO WHAT?
THEY ARE SYMPTONS OF THE MADNESS TAURO SUCCUMBS TO. I THOUGHT WE COULD MAKE IT TO ITALIA, BUT IT'S ALREADY BEGUN.
YOU'LL HAVE TO DO IT NOW, BEFORE THE MOON COMES UP, OR HE'LL BECOME TOO POWERFUL IN HIS RAGE.
DO WHAT?
SLAY HIM.

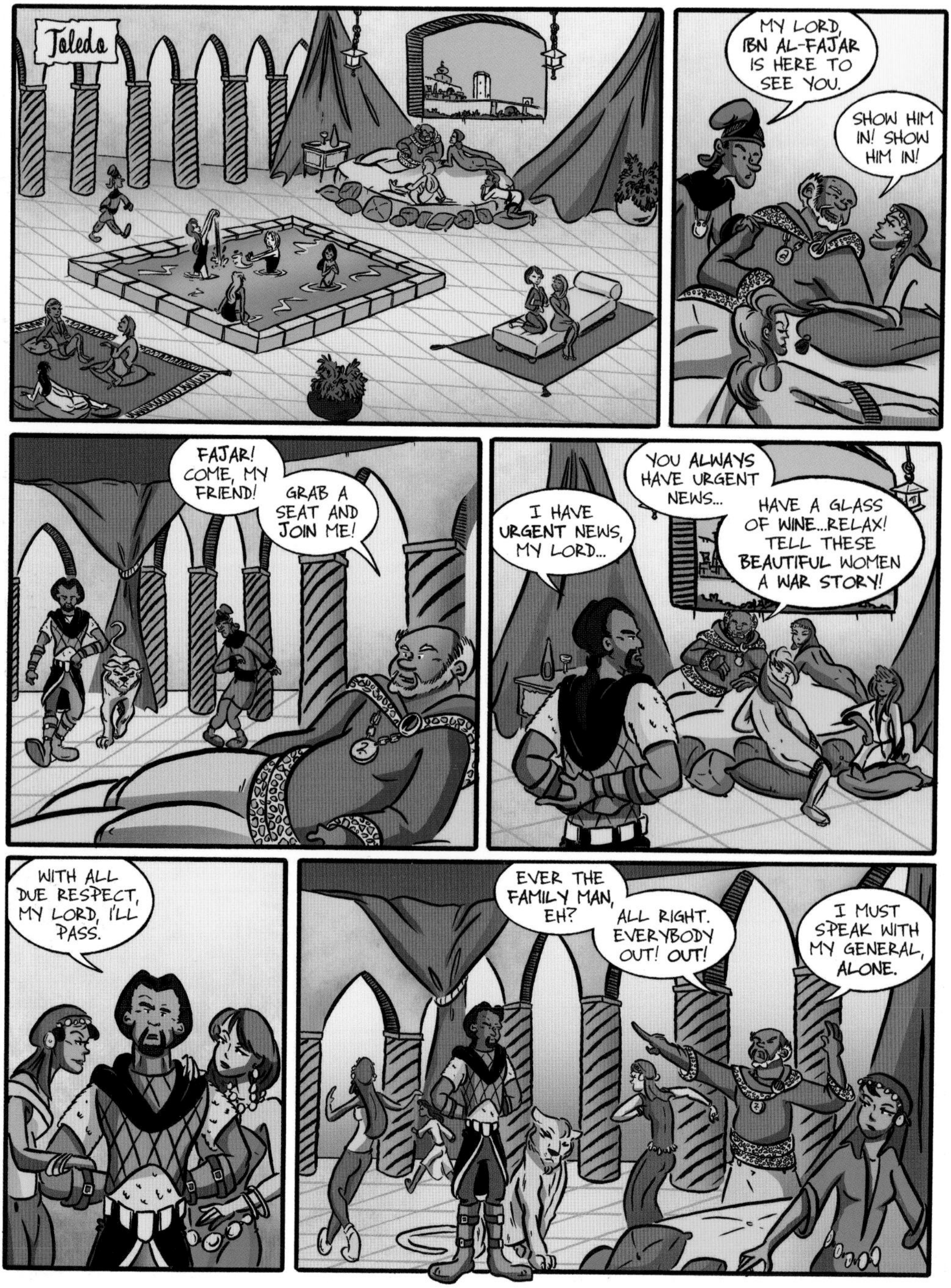
Toledo
MY LORD, IBN AL-FAJAR IS HERE TO SEE YOU.
SHOW HIM IN! SHOW HIM IN!
FAJAR! COME, MY FRIEND!
GRAB A SEAT AND JOIN ME!
I HAVE URGENT NEWS, MY LORD...
YOU ALWAYS HAVE URGENT NEWS...
HAVE A GLASS OF WINE...RELAX! TELL THESE BEAUTIFUL WOMEN A WAR STORY!
WITH ALL DUE RESPECT, MY LORD, I'LL PASS.
EVER THE FAMILY MAN, EH?
ALL RIGHT. EVERYBODY OUT! OUT!
I MUST SPEAK WITH MY GENERAL, ALONE.

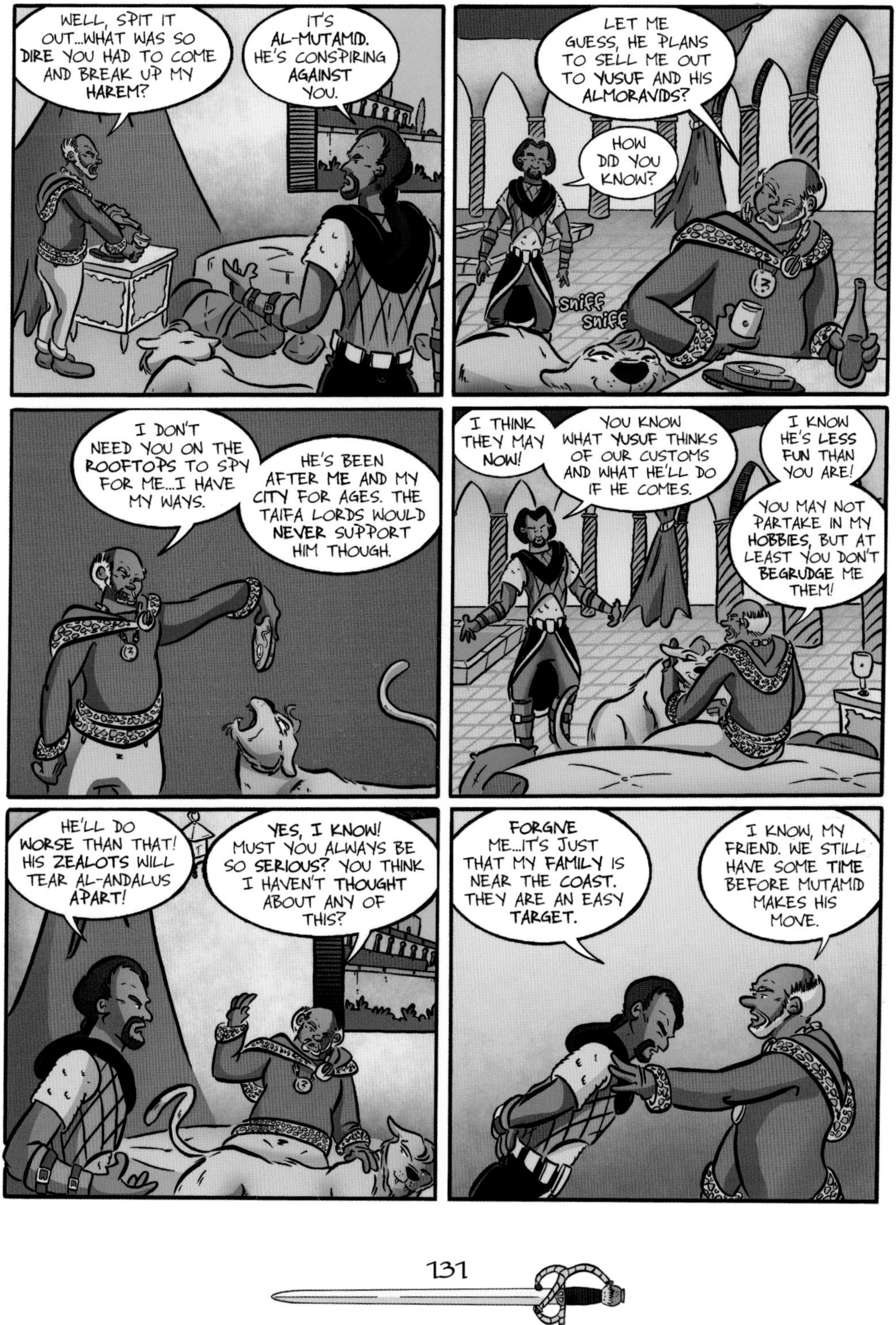
WELL, SPIT IT OUT...WHAT WAS SO DIRE YOU HAD TO COME AND BREAK UP MY HAREM?
IT'S AL-MUTAMID. HE'S CONSPIRING AGAINST YOU.
LET ME GUESS, HE PLANS TO SELL ME OUT TO YUSUF AND HIS ALMORAVIDS?
HOW DID YOU KNOW?
SNIFF SNIFF
I DON'T NEED YOU ON THE ROOFTOPS TO SPY FOR ME...I HAVE MY WAYS.
HE'S BEEN AFTER ME AND MY CITY FOR AGES. THE TAIFA LORDS WOULD NEVER SUPPORT HIM THOUGH.
I THINK THEY MAY NOW!
YOU KNOW WHAT YUSUF THINKS OF OUR CUSTOMS AND WHAT HE'LL DO IF HE COMES.
I KNOW HE'S LESS FUN THAN YOU ARE!
YOU MAY NOT PARTAKE IN MY HOBBIES, BUT AT LEAST YOU DON'T BEGRUDGE ME THEM!
HE'LL DO WORSE THAN THAT! HIS ZEALOTS WILL TEAR AL-ANDALUS APART!
YES, I KNOW! MUST YOU ALWAYS BE SO SERIOUS? YOU THINK I HAVEN'T THOUGHT ABOUT ANY OF THIS?
FORGIVE ME...IT'S JUST THAT MY FAMILY IS NEAR THE COAST. THEY ARE AN EASY TARGET.
I KNOW, MY FRIEND. WE STILL HAVE SOME TIME BEFORE MUTAMID MAKES HIS MOVE.

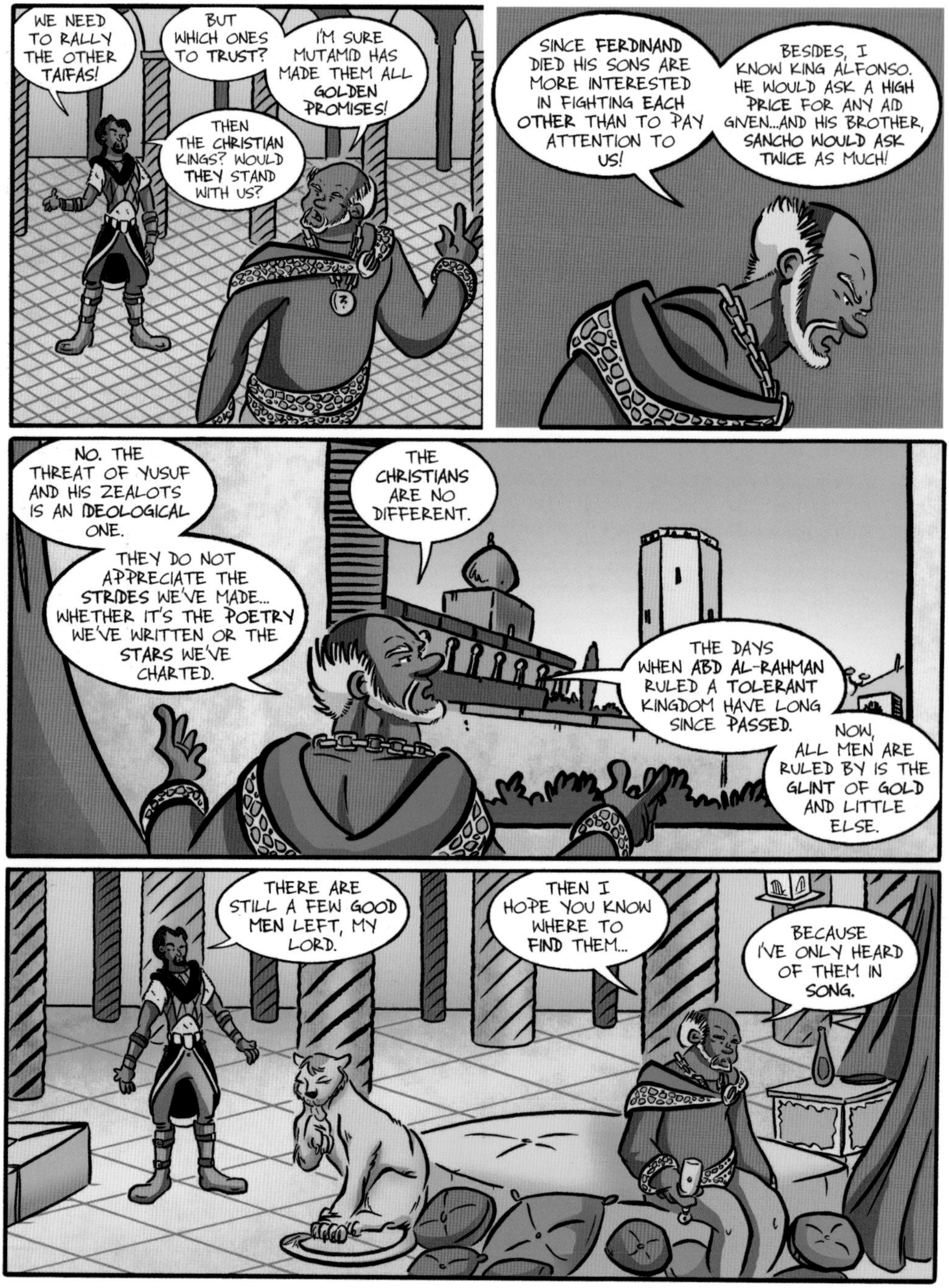
WE NEED TO RALLY THE OTHER TAIFAS!
BUT WHICH ONES TO TRUST?
I'M SURE MUTAMID HAS MADE THEM ALL GOLDEN PROMISES!
THEN THE CHRISTIAN KINGS? WOULD THEY STAND WITH US?
SINCE FERDINAND DIED HIS SONS ARE MORE INTERESTED IN FIGHTING EACH OTHER THAN TO PAY ATTENTION TO US!
BESIDES, I KNOW KING ALFONSO. HE WOULD ASK A HIGH PRICE FOR ANY AID GIVEN...AND HIS BROTHER, SANCHO WOULD ASK TWICE AS MUCH!
NO. THE THREAT OF YUSUF AND HIS ZEALOTS IS AN IDEOLOGICAL ONE.
THEY DO NOT APPRECIATE THE STRIDES WE'VE MADE... WHETHER IT'S THE POETRY WE'VE WRITTEN OR THE STARS WE'VE CHARTED.
THE CHRISTIANS ARE NO DIFFERENT.
THE DAYS WHEN ABD AL-RAHMAN RULED A TOLERANT KINGDOM HAVE LONG SINCE PASSED.
NOW, ALL MEN ARE RULED BY IS THE GLINT OF GOLD AND LITTLE ELSE.
THERE ARE STILL A FEW GOOD MEN LEFT, MY LORD.
THEN I HOPE YOU KNOW WHERE TO FIND THEM...
BECAUSE I'VE ONLY HEARD OF THEM IN SONG.

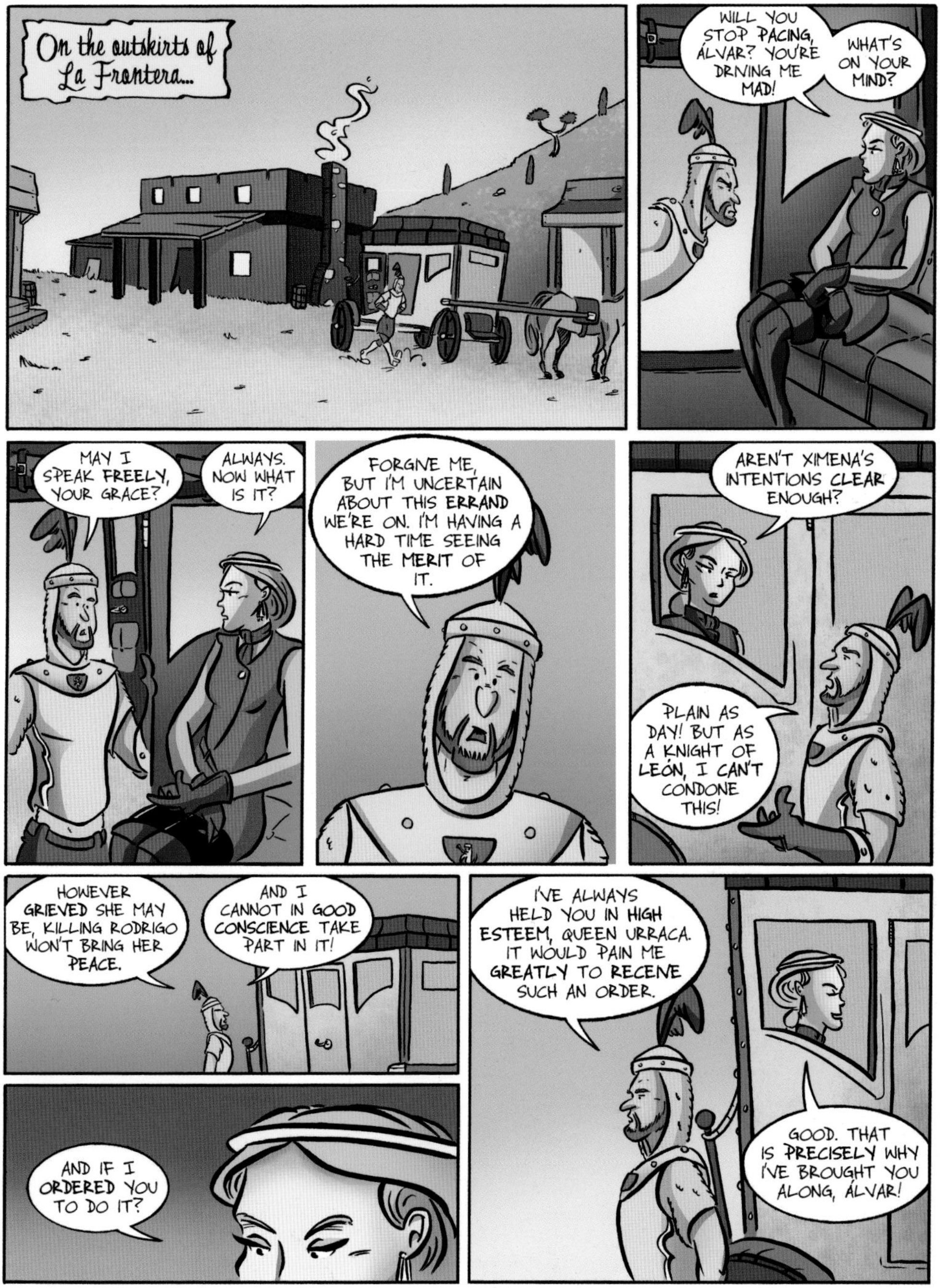
On the outskirts of La Frontera...
WILL YOU STOP PACING, ÁLVAR? YOU'RE DRIVING ME MAD!
WHAT'S ON YOUR MIND?
MAY I SPEAK FREELY, YOUR GRACE?
ALWAYS. NOW WHAT IS IT?
FORGIVE ME, BUT I'M UNCERTAIN ABOUT THIS ERRAND WE'RE ON. I'M HAVING A HARD TIME SEEING THE MERIT OF IT.
AREN'T XIMENA'S INTENTIONS CLEAR ENOUGH?
PLAIN AS DAY! BUT AS A KNIGHT OF LEÓN, I CAN'T CONDONE THIS!
HOWEVER GRIEVED SHE MAY BE, KILLING RODRIGO WON'T BRING HER PEACE.
AND I CANNOT IN GOOD CONSCIENCE TAKE PART IN IT!
AND IF I ORDERED YOU TO DO IT?
I'VE ALWAYS HELD YOU IN HIGH ESTEEM, QUEEN URRACA. IT WOULD PAIN ME GREATLY TO RECEIVE SUCH AN ORDER.
GOOD. THAT IS PRECISELY WHY I'VE BROUGHT YOU ALONG, ÁLVAR!

YOUR GRACE?

YOU'RE RIGHT. KILLING RODRIGO WON'T BRING PEACE OR HONOR BACK TO XIMENA'S FAMILY.

HER FATHER WAS A BRUTE. HE DISHONORED THE GORMAZ NAME LONG BEFORE HE DIED ON THE FIELDS AT PAMPLONA...

XIMENA IS QUITE THE OPPOSITE. SHE AND RODRIGO COULD BE A POWERFUL COUPLE...IF THEIR PRIDE WEREN'T IN THE WAY.

PERHAPS I'M A ROMANTIC LIKE YOU, ÁLVAR. I WANT TO SEE THEM REUNITED. PART OF ME THINKS SHE STILL LOVES HIM.

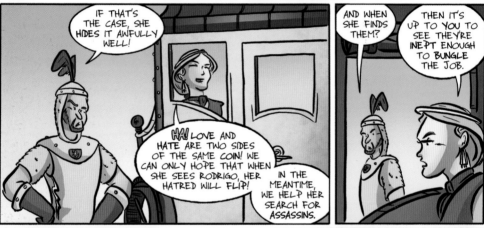

IF THAT'S THE CASE, SHE HIDES IT AWFULLY WELL!

HA! LOVE AND HATE ARE TWO SIDES OF THE SAME COIN! WE CAN ONLY HOPE THAT WHEN SHE SEES RODRIGO, HER HATRED WILL FLIP!

IN THE MEANTIME, WE HELP HER SEARCH FOR ASSASSINS.

AND WHEN SHE FINDS THEM?

THEN IT'S UP TO YOU TO SEE THEY'RE INEPT ENOUGH TO BUNGLE THE JOB.

ANY LUCK?

NONE...

WE'LL HAVE TO PUSH FURTHER INTO LA FRONTERA TO FIND ANY MERCENARIES.

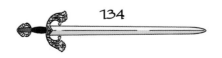

THEN OFF WE GO!

134

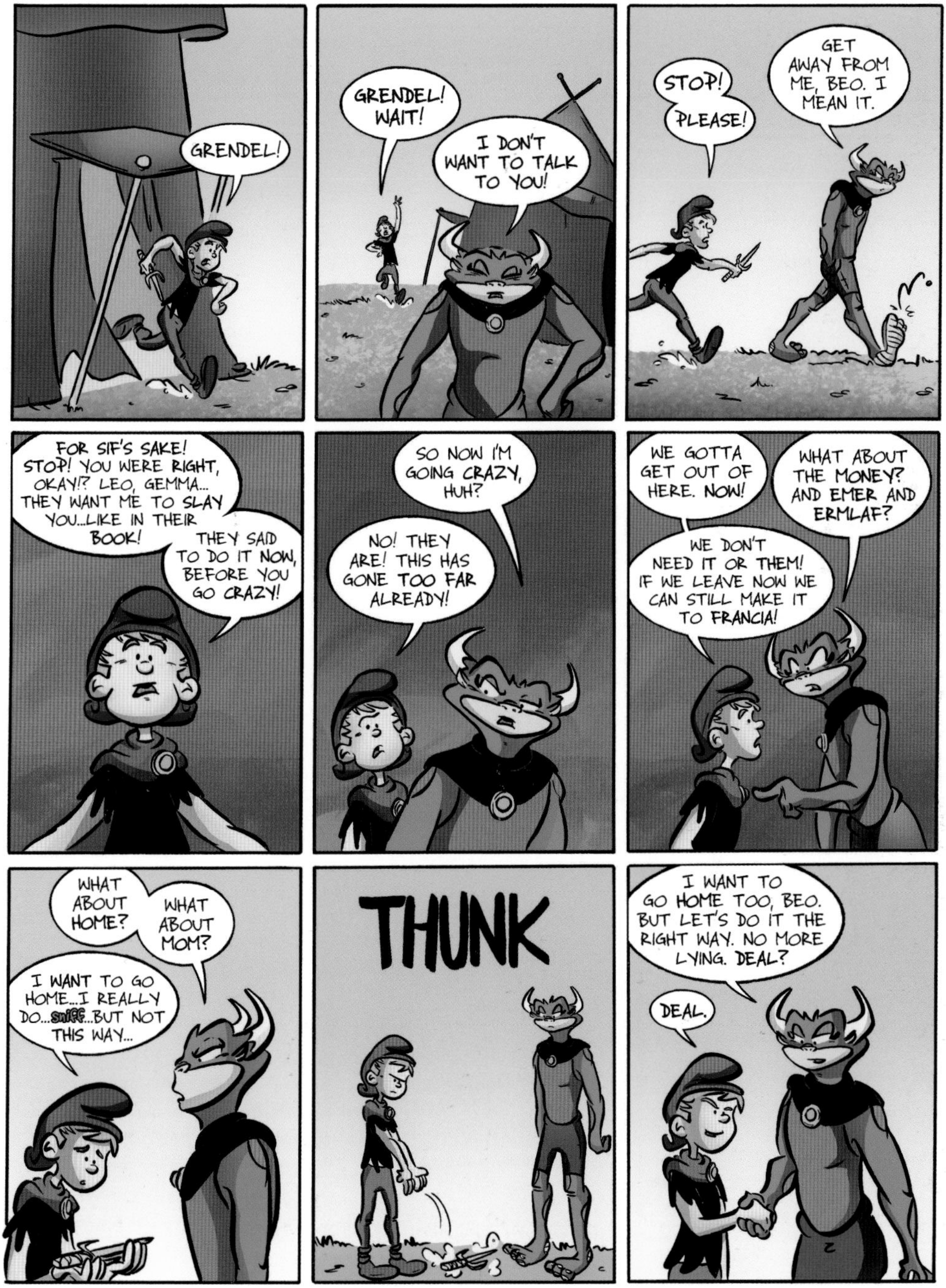
GRENDEL!
GRENDEL! WAIT!
I DON'T WANT TO TALK TO YOU!
STOP!
PLEASE!
GET AWAY FROM ME, BEO. I MEAN IT.
FOR SIF'S SAKE! STOP! YOU WERE RIGHT, OKAY!? LEO, GEMMA... THEY WANT ME TO SLAY YOU...LIKE IN THEIR BOOK!
THEY SAID TO DO IT NOW, BEFORE YOU GO CRAZY!
SO NOW I'M GOING CRAZY, HUH?
NO! THEY ARE! THIS HAS GONE TOO FAR ALREADY!
WE GOTTA GET OUT OF HERE. NOW!
WHAT ABOUT THE MONEY? AND EMER AND ERMLAF?
WE DON'T NEED IT OR THEM! IF WE LEAVE NOW WE CAN STILL MAKE IT TO FRANCIA!
WHAT ABOUT HOME?
WHAT ABOUT MOM?
I WANT TO GO HOME...I REALLY DO...SNIFF...BUT NOT THIS WAY...
THUNK
I WANT TO GO HOME TOO, BEO. BUT LET'S DO IT THE RIGHT WAY. NO MORE LYING. DEAL?
DEAL.

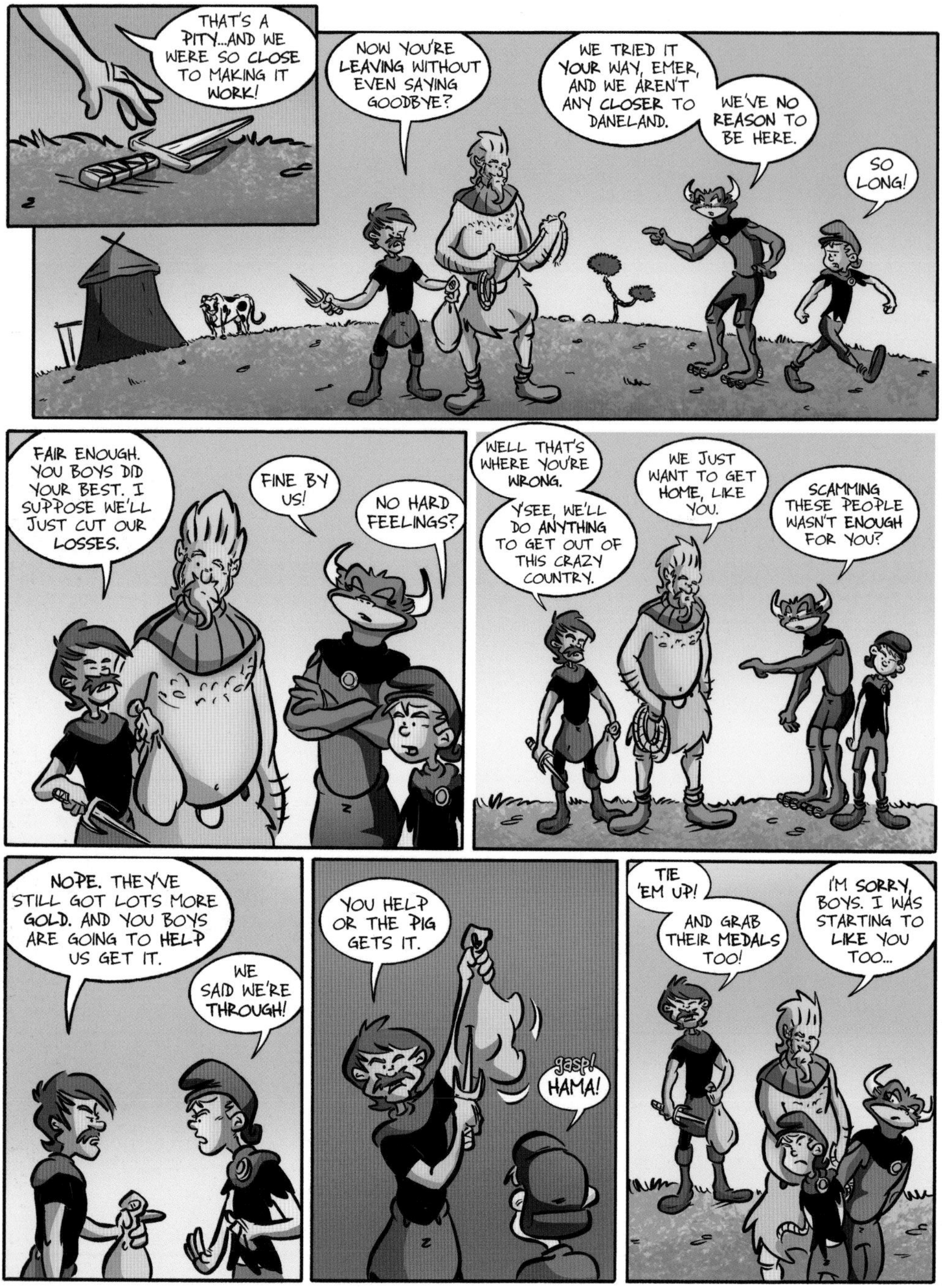
THAT'S A PITY...AND WE WERE SO CLOSE TO MAKING IT WORK!
NOW YOU'RE LEAVING WITHOUT EVEN SAYING GOODBYE?
WE TRIED IT YOUR WAY, EMER, AND WE AREN'T ANY CLOSER TO DANELAND.
WE'VE NO REASON TO BE HERE.
SO LONG!
FAIR ENOUGH. YOU BOYS DID YOUR BEST. I SUPPOSE WE'LL JUST CUT OUR LOSSES.
FINE BY US!
NO HARD FEELINGS?
WELL THAT'S WHERE YOU'RE WRONG.
Y'SEE, WE'LL DO ANYTHING TO GET OUT OF THIS CRAZY COUNTRY.
WE JUST WANT TO GET HOME, LIKE YOU.
SCAMMING THESE PEOPLE WASN'T ENOUGH FOR YOU?
NOPE. THEY'VE STILL GOT LOTS MORE GOLD. AND YOU BOYS ARE GOING TO HELP US GET IT.
WE SAID WE'RE THROUGH!
YOU HELP OR THE PIG GETS IT.
gasp! HAMA!
TIE 'EM UP!
AND GRAB THEIR MEDALS TOO!
I'M SORRY, BOYS. I WAS STARTING TO LIKE YOU TOO...

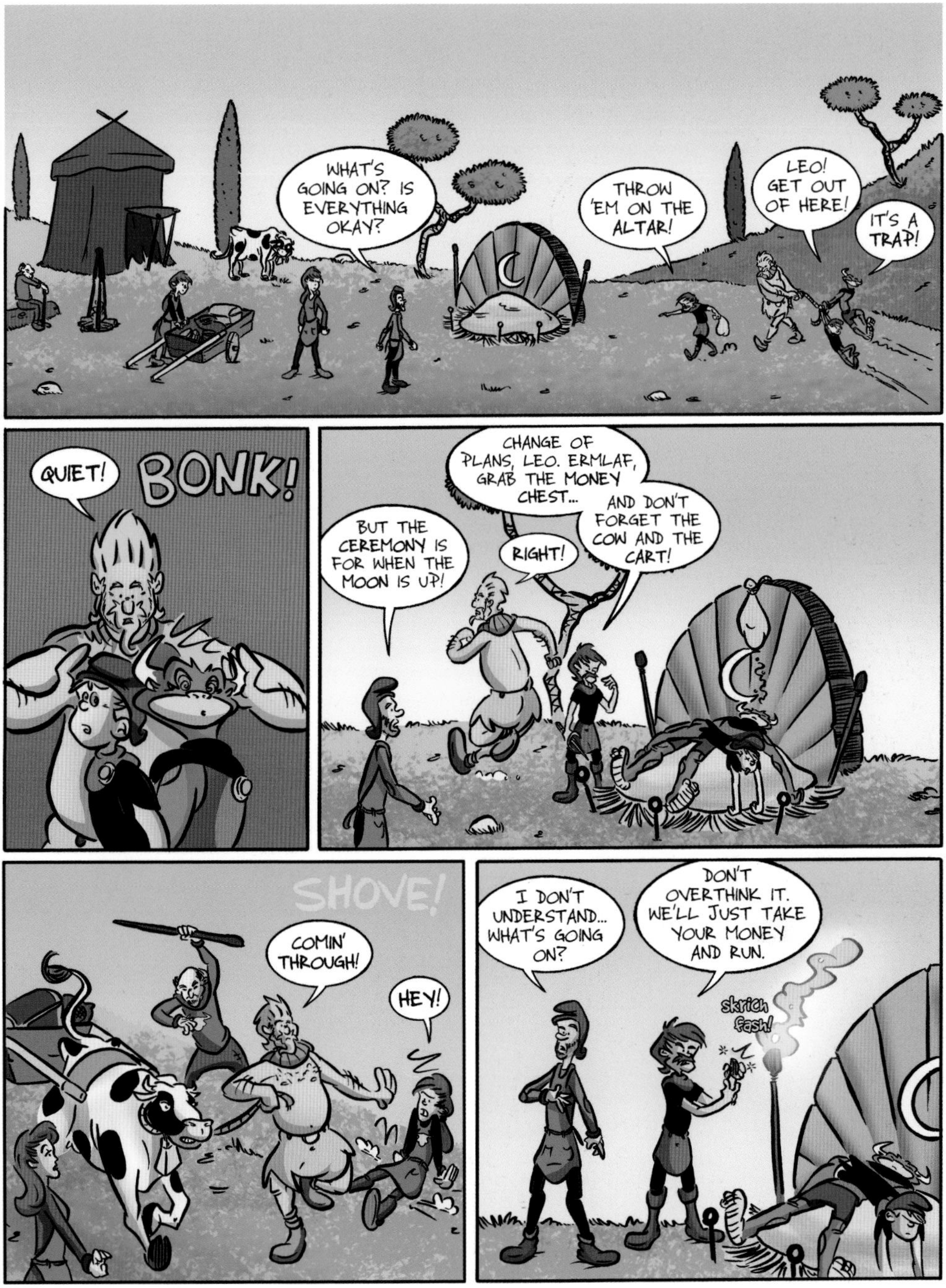
WHAT'S GOING ON? IS EVERYTHING OKAY?
THROW 'EM ON THE ALTAR!
LEO! GET OUT OF HERE!
IT'S A TRAP!
QUIET!
BONK!
CHANGE OF PLANS, LEO. ERMLAF, GRAB THE MONEY CHEST...
AND DON'T FORGET THE COW AND THE CART!
BUT THE CEREMONY IS FOR WHEN THE MOON IS UP!
RIGHT!
SHOVE!
COMIN' THROUGH!
HEY!
I DON'T UNDERSTAND... WHAT'S GOING ON?
DON'T OVERTHINK IT. WE'LL JUST TAKE YOUR MONEY AND RUN.
skrich fash!

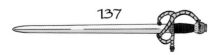

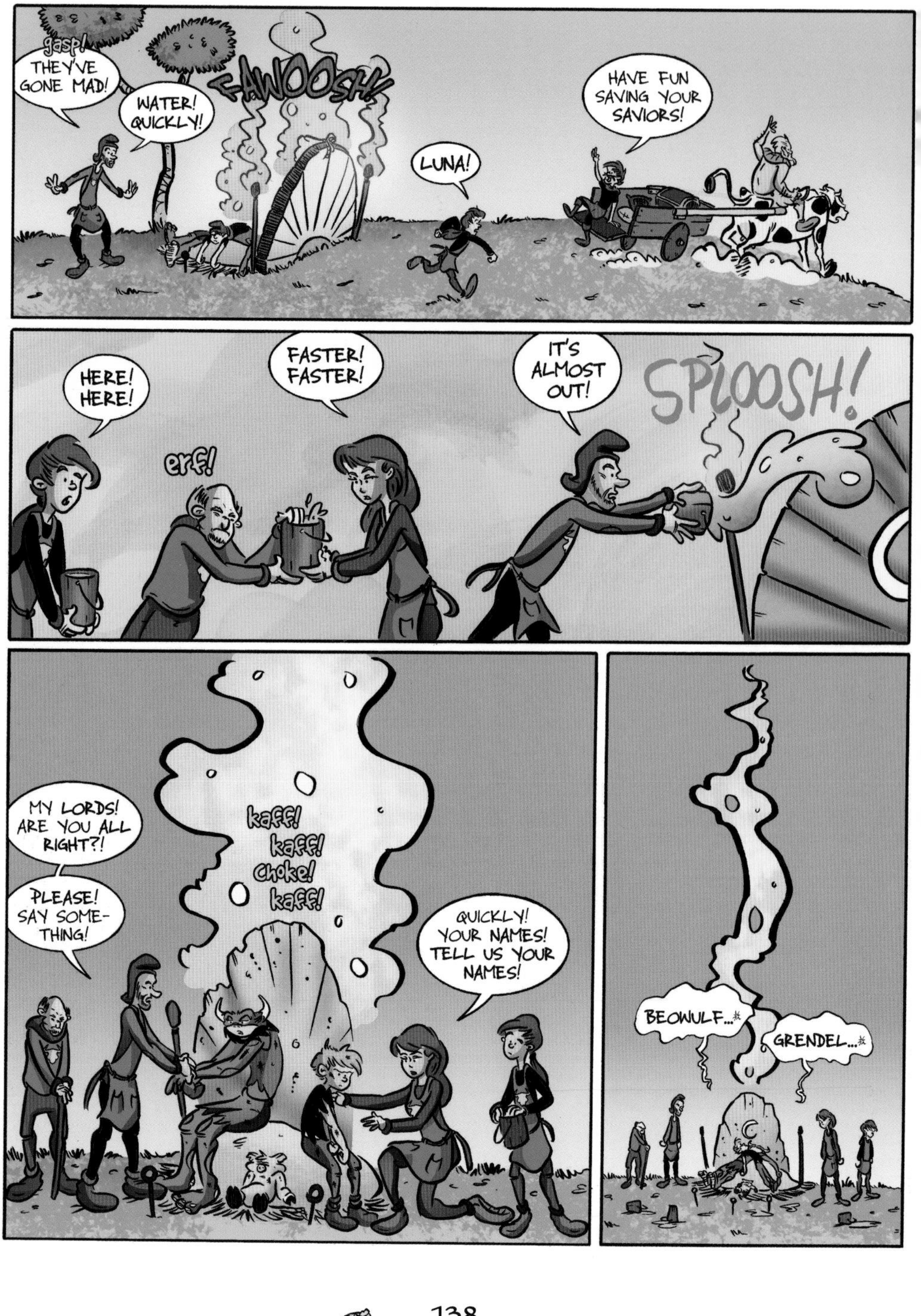
gasp!
THEY'VE GONE MAD!
WATER! QUICKLY!
FAWOOSH!
LUNA!
HAVE FUN SAVING YOUR SAVIORS!
HERE! HERE!
erf!
FASTER! FASTER!
IT'S ALMOST OUT!
SPLOOSH!
MY LORDS! ARE YOU ALL RIGHT?!
PLEASE! SAY SOME-THING!
kaff! kaff! choke! kaff!
QUICKLY! YOUR NAMES! TELL US YOUR NAMES!
BEOWULF...
GRENDEL...

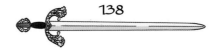

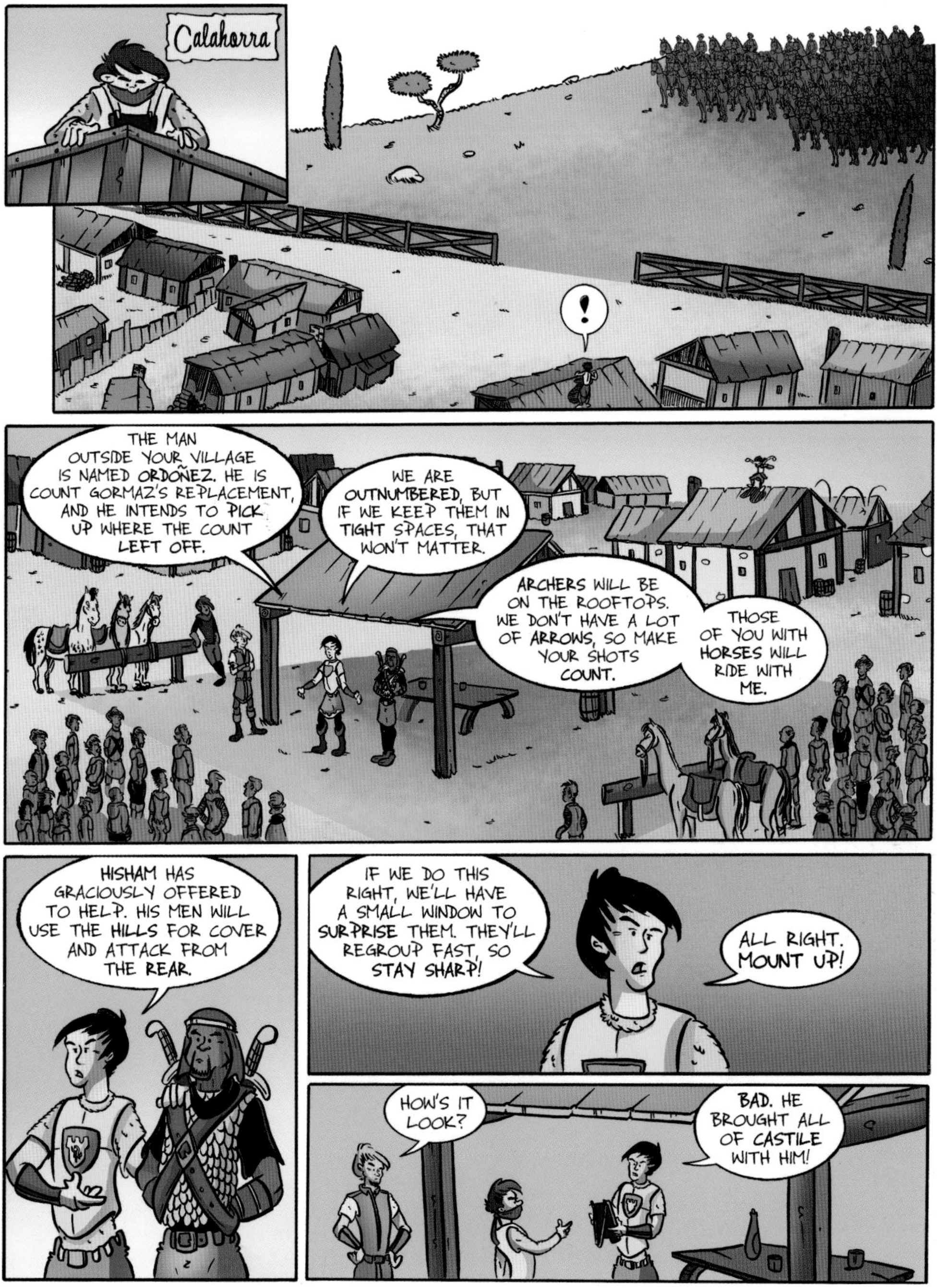
Calahorra
!
THE MAN OUTSIDE YOUR VILLAGE IS NAMED ORDOÑEZ. HE IS COUNT GORMAZ'S REPLACEMENT, AND HE INTENDS TO PICK UP WHERE THE COUNT LEFT OFF.
WE ARE OUTNUMBERED, BUT IF WE KEEP THEM IN TIGHT SPACES, THAT WON'T MATTER.
ARCHERS WILL BE ON THE ROOFTOPS. WE DON'T HAVE A LOT OF ARROWS, SO MAKE YOUR SHOTS COUNT.
THOSE OF YOU WITH HORSES WILL RIDE WITH ME.
HISHAM HAS GRACIOUSLY OFFERED TO HELP. HIS MEN WILL USE THE HILLS FOR COVER AND ATTACK FROM THE REAR.
IF WE DO THIS RIGHT, WE'LL HAVE A SMALL WINDOW TO SURPRISE THEM. THEY'LL REGROUP FAST, SO STAY SHARP!
ALL RIGHT. MOUNT UP!
HOW'S IT LOOK?
BAD. HE BROUGHT ALL OF CASTILE WITH HIM!

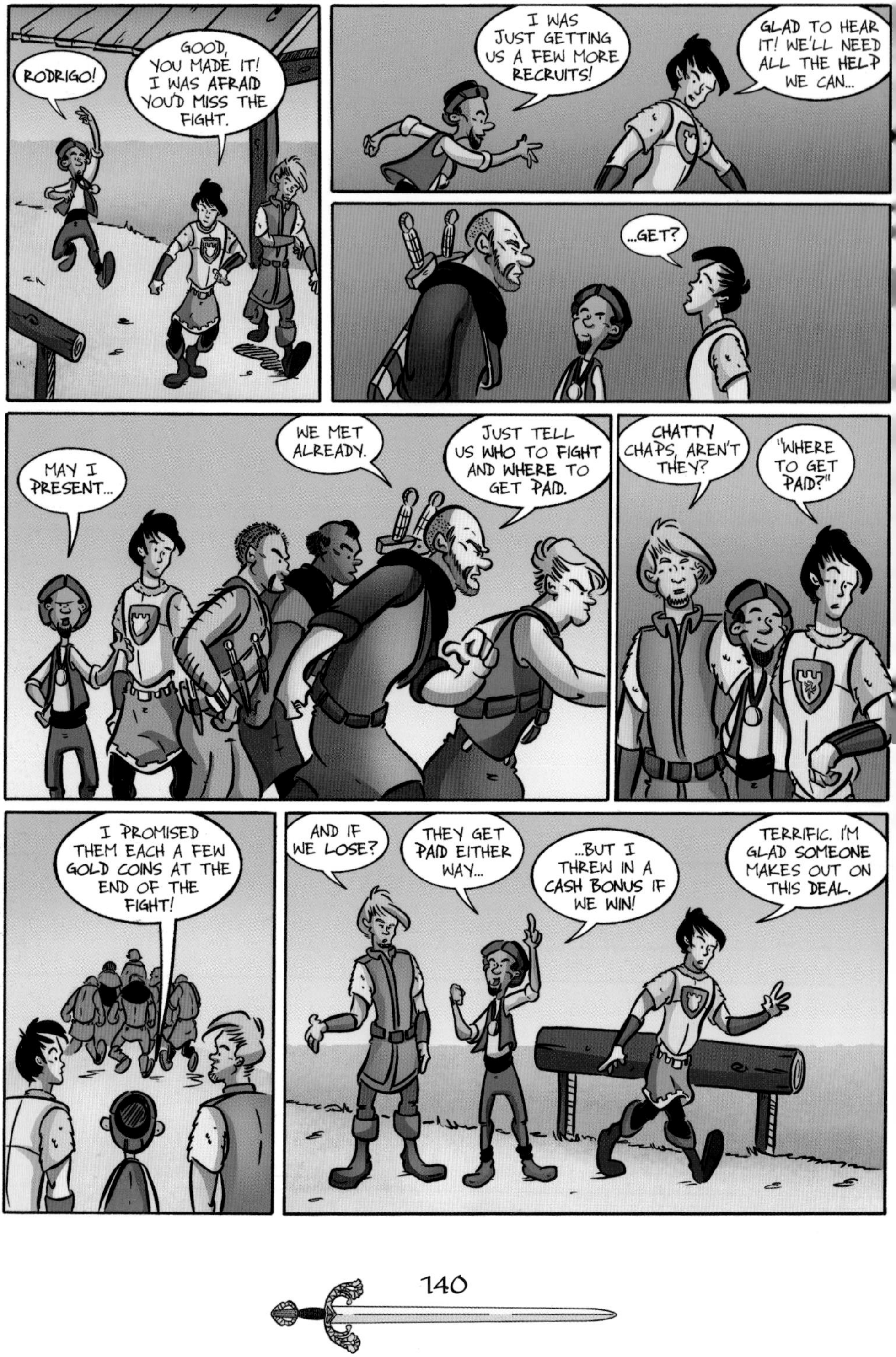
RODRIGO!
GOOD, YOU MADE IT! I WAS AFRAID YOU'D MISS THE FIGHT.
I WAS JUST GETTING US A FEW MORE RECRUITS!
GLAD TO HEAR IT! WE'LL NEED ALL THE HELP WE CAN...
...GET?
MAY I PRESENT...
WE MET ALREADY.
JUST TELL US WHO TO FIGHT AND WHERE TO GET PAID.
CHATTY CHAPS, AREN'T THEY?
"WHERE TO GET PAID?"
I PROMISED THEM EACH A FEW GOLD COINS AT THE END OF THE FIGHT!
AND IF WE LOSE?
THEY GET PAID EITHER WAY...
...BUT I THREW IN A CASH BONUS IF WE WIN!
TERRIFIC. I'M GLAD SOMEONE MAKES OUT ON THIS DEAL.

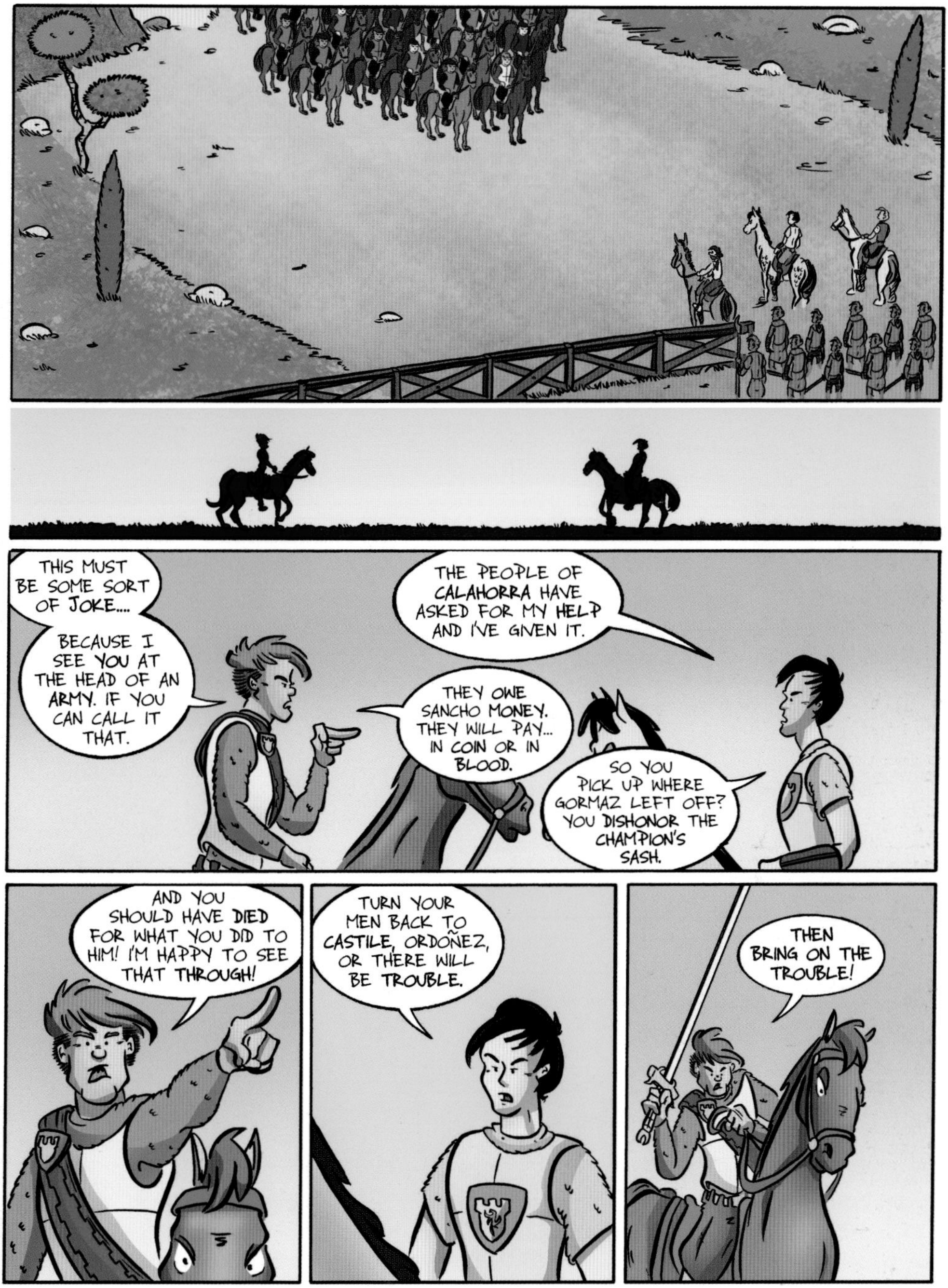
THIS MUST BE SOME SORT OF JOKE....
BECAUSE I SEE YOU AT THE HEAD OF AN ARMY. IF YOU CAN CALL IT THAT.
THE PEOPLE OF CALAHORRA HAVE ASKED FOR MY HELP AND I'VE GIVEN IT.
THEY OWE SANCHO MONEY. THEY WILL PAY... IN COIN OR IN BLOOD.
SO YOU PICK UP WHERE GORMAZ LEFT OFF? YOU DISHONOR THE CHAMPION'S SASH.
AND YOU SHOULD HAVE DIED FOR WHAT YOU DID TO HIM! I'M HAPPY TO SEE THAT THROUGH!
TURN YOUR MEN BACK TO CASTILE, ORDOÑEZ, OR THERE WILL BE TROUBLE.
THEN BRING ON THE TROUBLE!

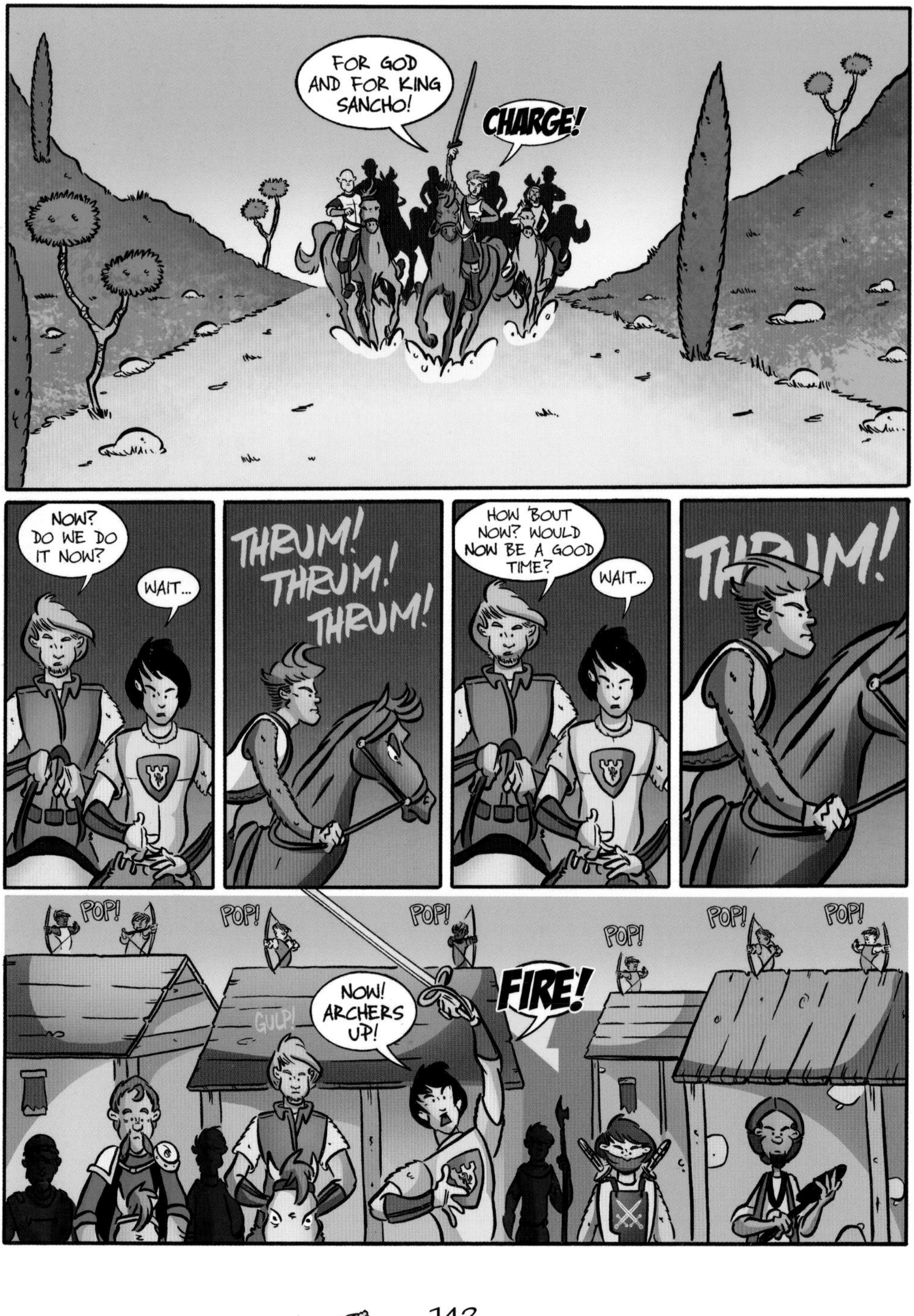
FOR GOD AND FOR KING SANCHO!
CHARGE!
NOW? DO WE DO IT NOW?
WAIT...
THRUM! THRUM! THRUM!
HOW 'BOUT NOW? WOULD NOW BE A GOOD TIME?
WAIT...
THRUM!
POP!
POP!
POP!
POP!
POP!
POP!
GULP!
NOW! ARCHERS UP!
FIRE!

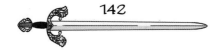

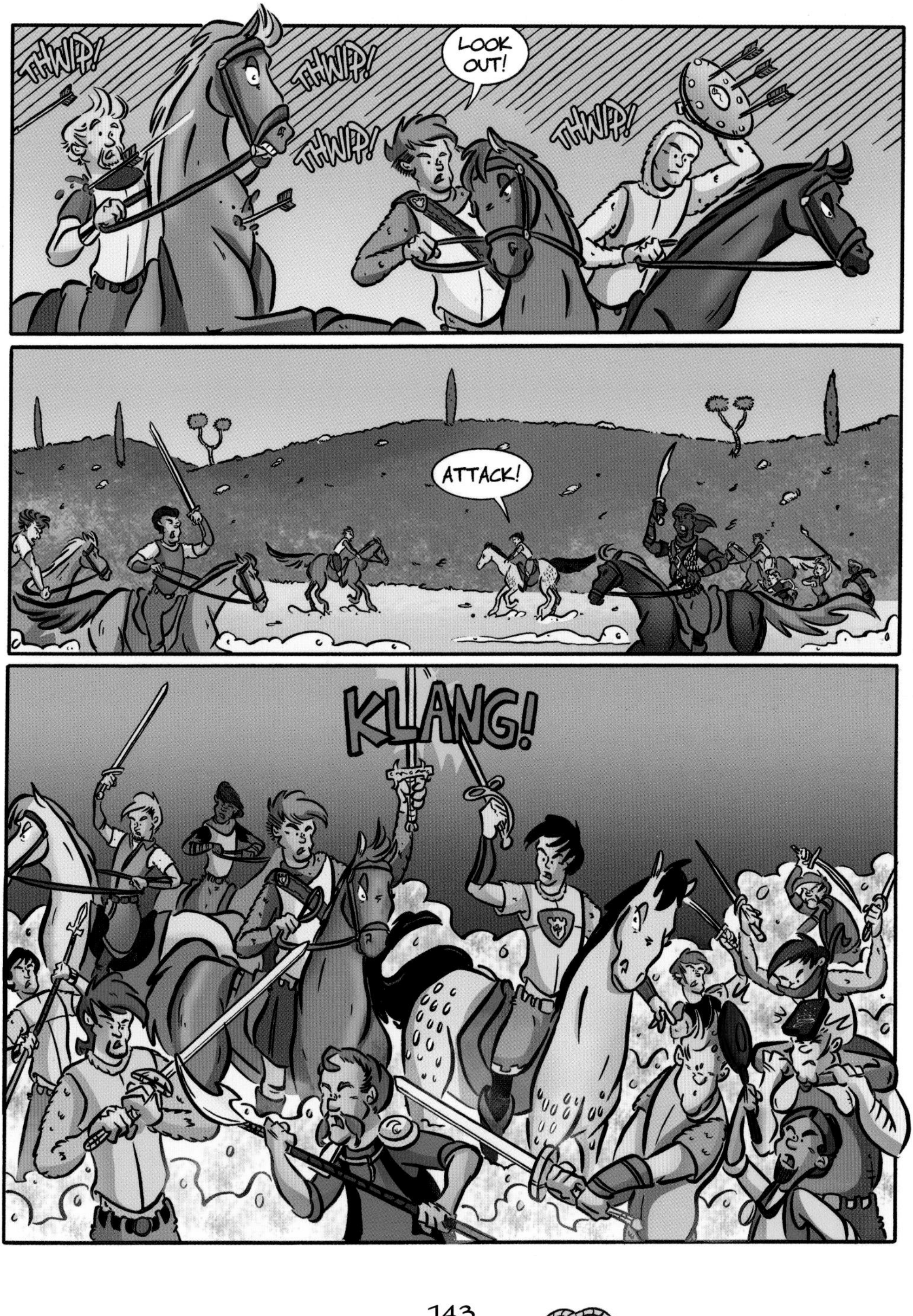
THWIP!
THWIP!
LOOK OUT!
THWIP!
THWIP!
ATTACK!
KLANG!

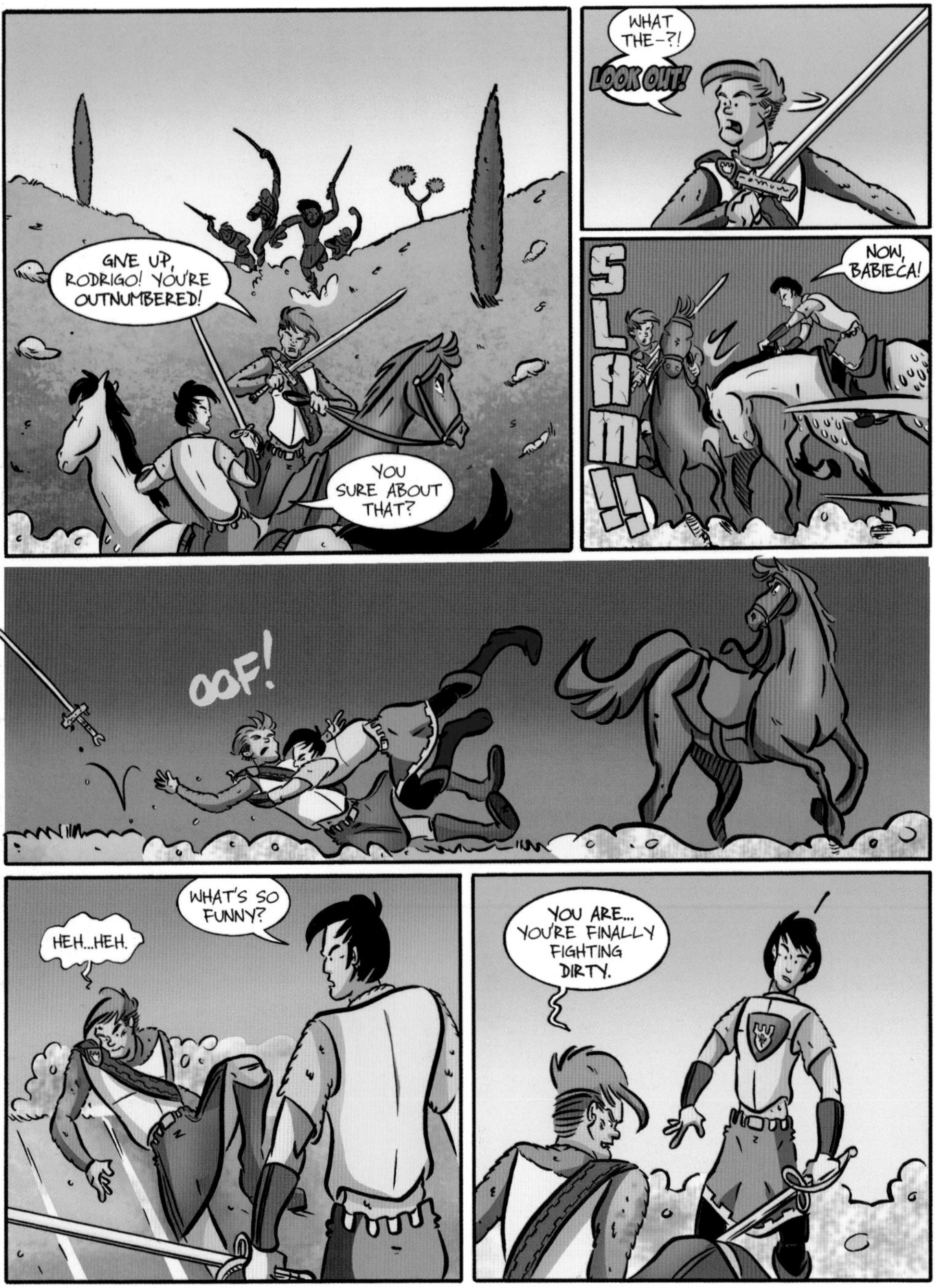
GIVE UP, RODRIGO! YOU'RE OUTNUMBERED!
YOU SURE ABOUT THAT?
WHAT THE–?!
LOOK OUT!
NOW, BABIECA!
SLAM!!
OOF!
HEH...HEH.
WHAT'S SO FUNNY?
YOU ARE... YOU'RE FINALLY FIGHTING DIRTY.

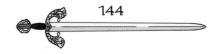

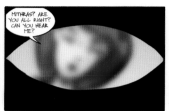

IT'S LIGHT ARE YOU ALL RIGHT? CAN YOU HEAR ME?

MITHRAS? ARE YOU ALL RIGHT? CAN YOU HEAR ME?

MITHRAS?

GOOD! YOU'RE AWAKE!

POOR MITHRAS! SWEET MITHRAS...

FORGIVE US, MY LORD. WE FORGET YOUR FAKE NAMES EASILY...

THOSE ARE OUR REAL NAMES, LEO. I'M GRENDEL AND HE'S BEOWULF.

AHA! I KNEW IT! I TOLD YOU THEY WERE LYING!

BEOWULF... MY NAME IS BEOWULF.

WE'RE NOT MITHRAS OR TAURO. WE NEVER HAVE BEEN.

humph.

IS THIS TRUE, MY LORD?

IT'S TRUE, GEMMA. I'M NOT YOUR LORD...

...I'M JUST A KID, AND GRENDEL IS MY BROTHER.

YOUR BROTHER...?

AND HAMA?

NO RELATION.

grunt.

AND YOUR COMPANIONS THEN? WHO ARE THEY?

EMER AND ERMLAF. THEY'RE HEATHOBARDS FROM DANELAND...OUR HOME.

BUT WHY DID YOU WANT US TO BELIEVE YOU WERE OUR GODS?

WE WANTED TO TRICK YOU INTO GIVING US YOUR GOLD.

WHAT FOR?

A BOAT BACK HOME.

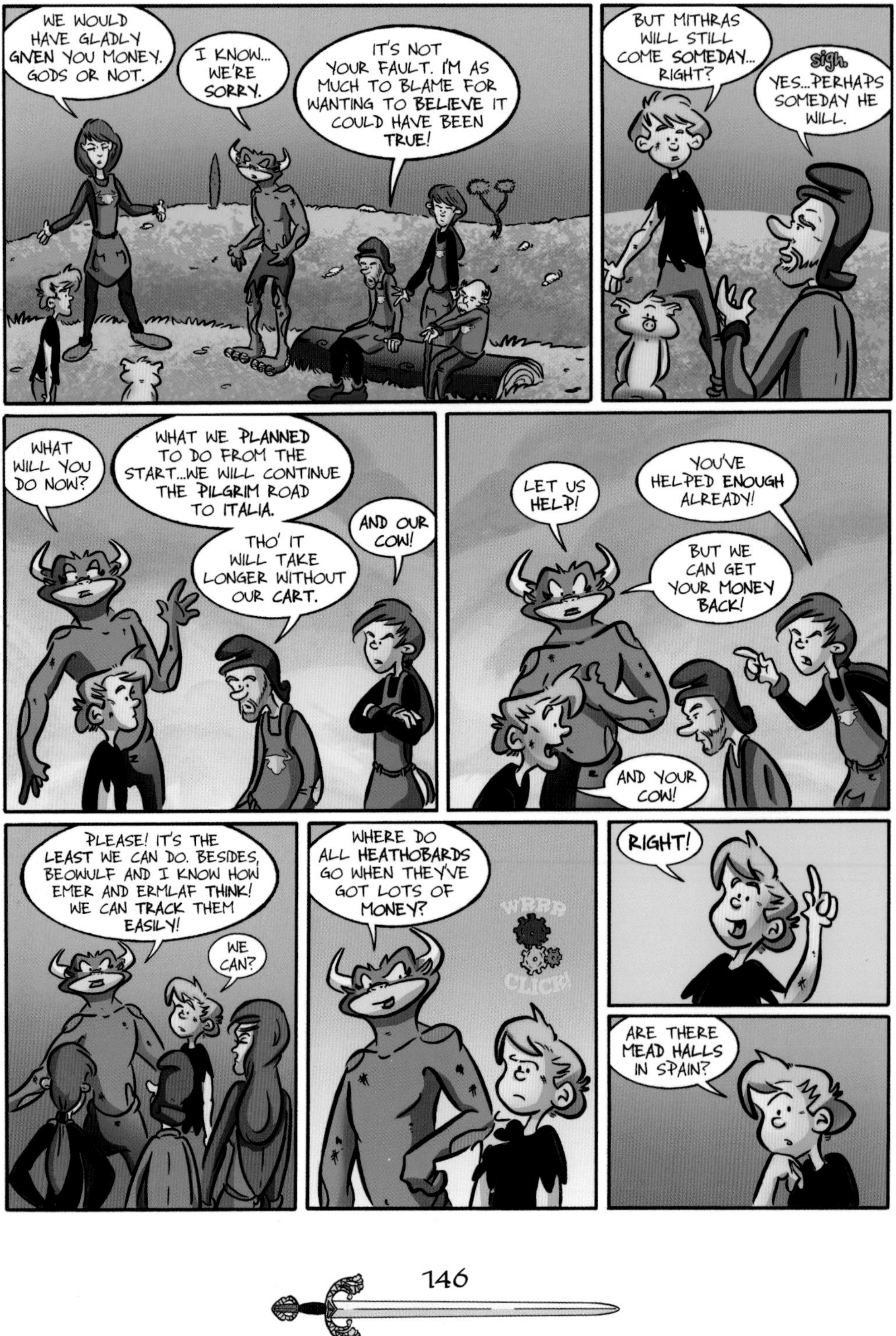
WE WOULD HAVE GLADLY GIVEN YOU MONEY. GODS OR NOT.
I KNOW... WE'RE SORRY.
IT'S NOT YOUR FAULT. I'M AS MUCH TO BLAME FOR WANTING TO BELIEVE IT COULD HAVE BEEN TRUE!
BUT MITHRAS WILL STILL COME SOMEDAY... RIGHT?
sigh.
YES...PERHAPS SOMEDAY HE WILL.
WHAT WILL YOU DO NOW?
WHAT WE PLANNED TO DO FROM THE START...WE WILL CONTINUE THE PILGRIM ROAD TO ITALIA.
THO' IT WILL TAKE LONGER WITHOUT OUR CART.
AND OUR COW!
LET US HELP!
YOU'VE HELPED ENOUGH ALREADY!
BUT WE CAN GET YOUR MONEY BACK!
AND YOUR COW!
PLEASE! IT'S THE LEAST WE CAN DO. BESIDES, BEOWULF AND I KNOW HOW EMER AND ERMLAF THINK! WE CAN TRACK THEM EASILY!
WE CAN?
WHERE DO ALL HEATHOBARDS GO WHEN THEY'VE GOT LOTS OF MONEY?
WRRR
CLICK!
RIGHT!
ARE THERE MEAD HALLS IN SPAIN?

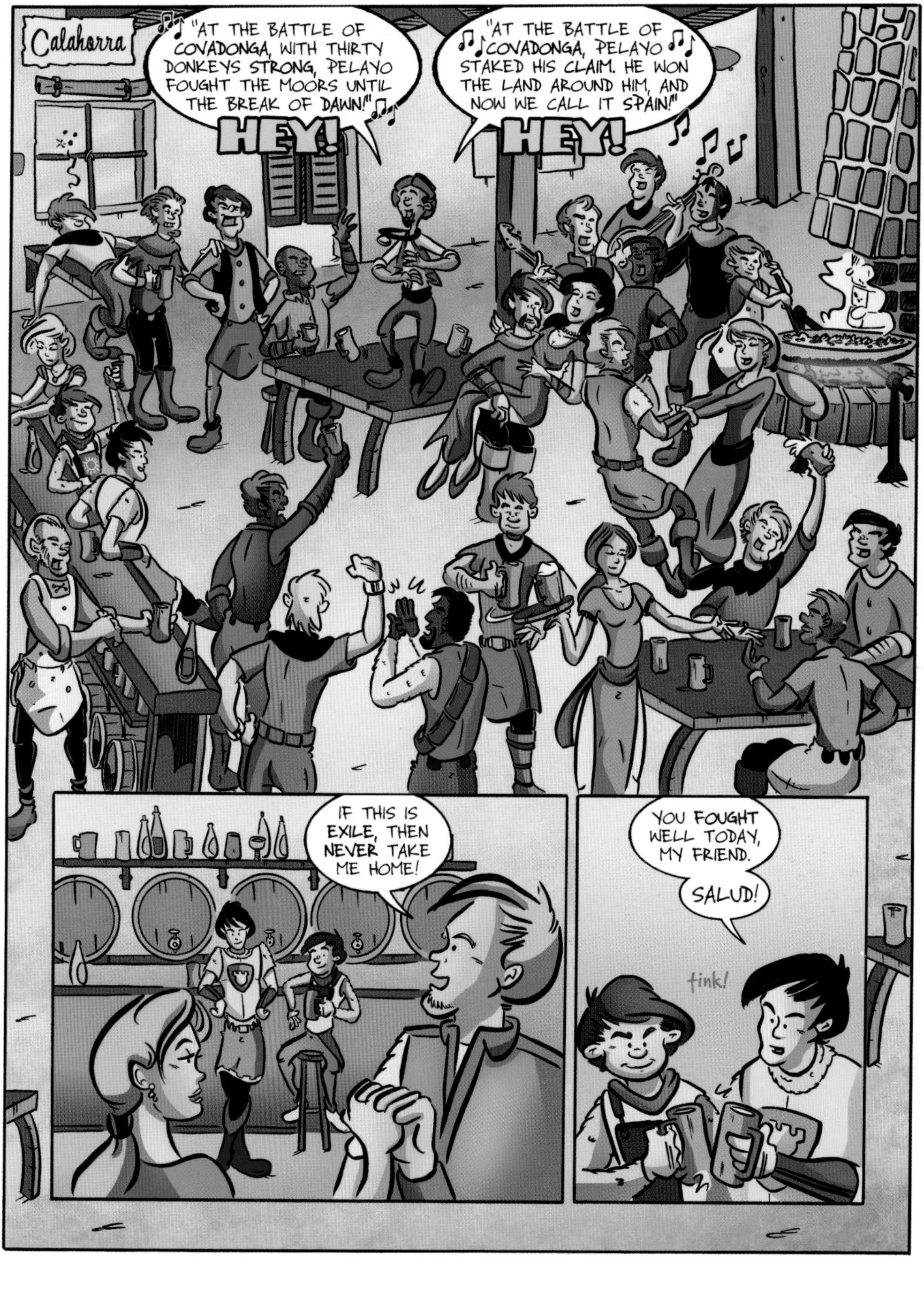
Calahorra
"AT THE BATTLE OF COVADONGA, WITH THIRTY DONKEYS STRONG, PELAYO FOUGHT THE MOORS UNTIL THE BREAK OF DAWN!"
HEY!
"AT THE BATTLE OF COVADONGA, PELAYO STAKED HIS CLAIM. HE WON THE LAND AROUND HIM, AND NOW WE CALL IT SPAIN!"
HEY!
IF THIS IS EXILE, THEN NEVER TAKE ME HOME!
YOU FOUGHT WELL TODAY, MY FRIEND.
SALUD!
tink!

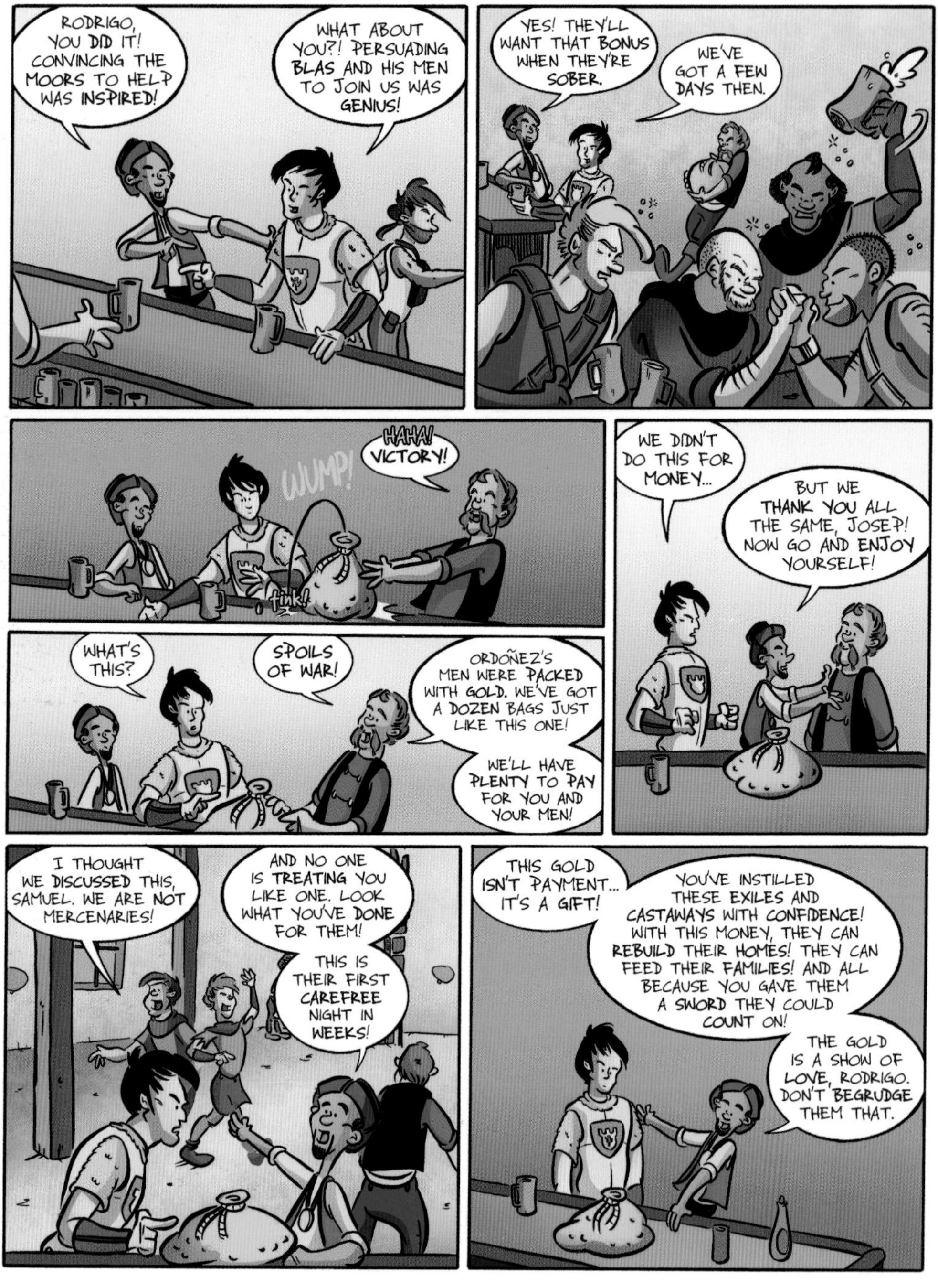
RODRIGO, YOU DID IT! CONVINCING THE MOORS TO HELP WAS INSPIRED!
WHAT ABOUT YOU?! PERSUADING BLAS AND HIS MEN TO JOIN US WAS GENIUS!
YES! THEY'LL WANT THAT BONUS WHEN THEY'RE SOBER.
WE'VE GOT A FEW DAYS THEN.
HAHA! VICTORY!
WUMP!
fink!
WE DIDN'T DO THIS FOR MONEY...
BUT WE THANK YOU ALL THE SAME, JOSEP! NOW GO AND ENJOY YOURSELF!
WHAT'S THIS?
SPOILS OF WAR!
ORDOÑEZ'S MEN WERE PACKED WITH GOLD. WE'VE GOT A DOZEN BAGS JUST LIKE THIS ONE!
WE'LL HAVE PLENTY TO PAY FOR YOU AND YOUR MEN!
I THOUGHT WE DISCUSSED THIS, SAMUEL. WE ARE NOT MERCENARIES!
AND NO ONE IS TREATING YOU LIKE ONE. LOOK WHAT YOU'VE DONE FOR THEM!
THIS IS THEIR FIRST CAREFREE NIGHT IN WEEKS!
THIS GOLD ISN'T PAYMENT... IT'S A GIFT!
YOU'VE INSTILLED THESE EXILES AND CASTAWAYS WITH CONFIDENCE! WITH THIS MONEY, THEY CAN REBUILD THEIR HOMES! THEY CAN FEED THEIR FAMILIES! AND ALL BECAUSE YOU GAVE THEM A SWORD THEY COULD COUNT ON!
THE GOLD IS A SHOW OF LOVE, RODRIGO. DON'T BEGRUDGE THEM THAT.

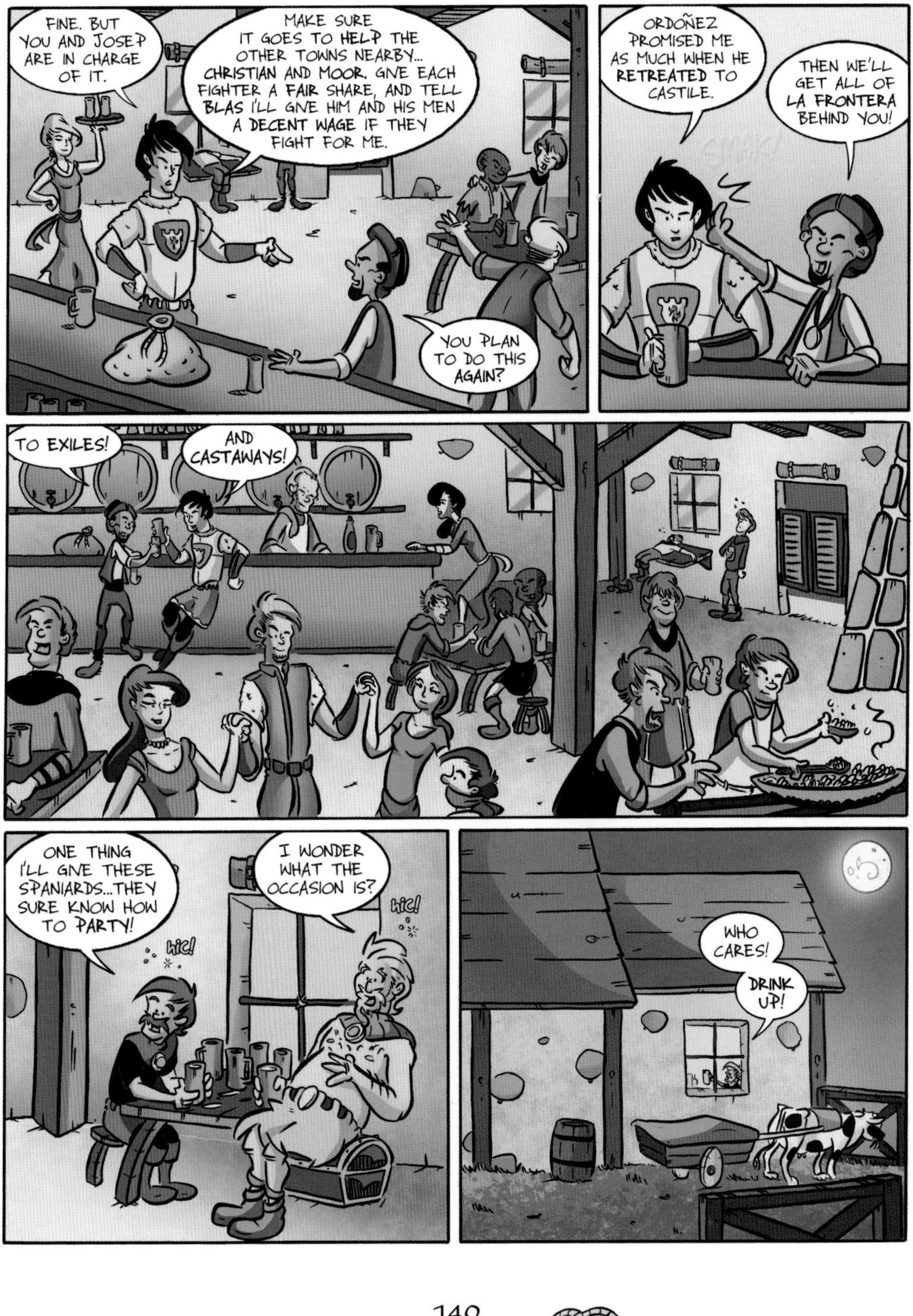
FINE. BUT YOU AND JOSEP ARE IN CHARGE OF IT.
MAKE SURE IT GOES TO HELP THE OTHER TOWNS NEARBY... CHRISTIAN AND MOOR. GIVE EACH FIGHTER A FAIR SHARE, AND TELL BLAS I'LL GIVE HIM AND HIS MEN A DECENT WAGE IF THEY FIGHT FOR ME.
YOU PLAN TO DO THIS AGAIN?
ORDOÑEZ PROMISED ME AS MUCH WHEN HE RETREATED TO CASTILE.
SMAK!
THEN WE'LL GET ALL OF LA FRONTERA BEHIND YOU!
TO EXILES!
AND CASTAWAYS!
ONE THING I'LL GIVE THESE SPANIARDS...THEY SURE KNOW HOW TO PARTY!
hic!
I WONDER WHAT THE OCCASION IS?
hic!
WHO CARES!
DRINK UP!

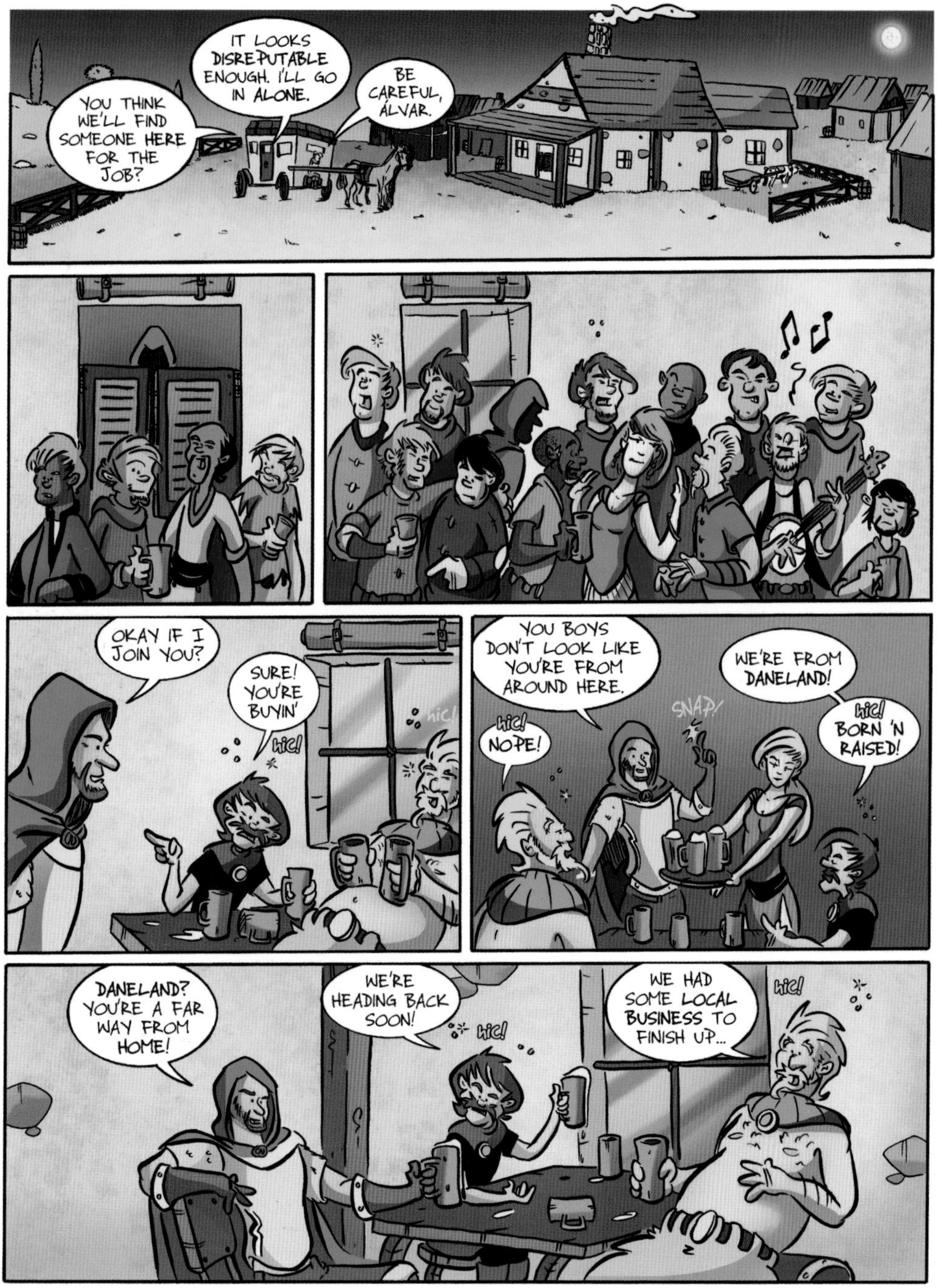
YOU THINK WE'LL FIND SOMEONE HERE FOR THE JOB?
IT LOOKS DISREPUTABLE ENOUGH. I'LL GO IN ALONE.
BE CAREFUL, ÁLVAR.
OKAY IF I JOIN YOU?
SURE! YOU'RE BUYIN'
hic!
hic!
YOU BOYS DON'T LOOK LIKE YOU'RE FROM AROUND HERE.
hic! NOPE!
SNAP!
WE'RE FROM DANELAND!
hic! BORN 'N RAISED!
DANELAND? YOU'RE A FAR WAY FROM HOME!
WE'RE HEADING BACK SOON!
hic!
WE HAD SOME LOCAL BUSINESS TO FINISH UP...
hic!

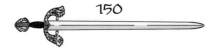

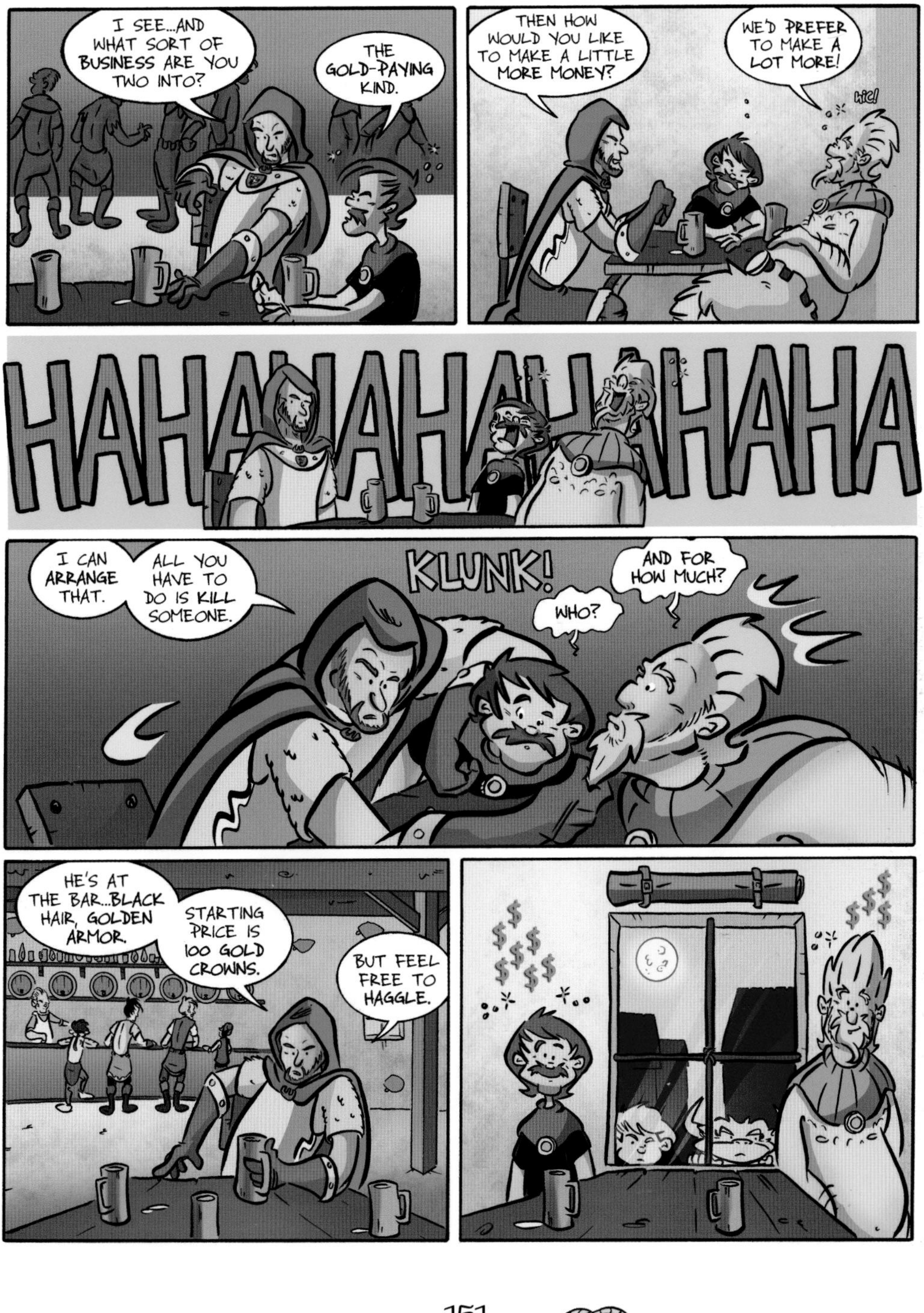
I SEE...AND WHAT SORT OF BUSINESS ARE YOU TWO INTO?
THE GOLD-PAYING KIND.
THEN HOW WOULD YOU LIKE TO MAKE A LITTLE MORE MONEY?
WE'D PREFER TO MAKE A LOT MORE!
hic!
HAHAHAHAHAHAHAHA
I CAN ARRANGE THAT.
ALL YOU HAVE TO DO IS KILL SOMEONE.
KLUNK!
WHO?
AND FOR HOW MUCH?
HE'S AT THE BAR...BLACK HAIR, GOLDEN ARMOR.
STARTING PRICE IS 100 GOLD CROWNS.
BUT FEEL FREE TO HAGGLE.

PART THREE

TOLEDO

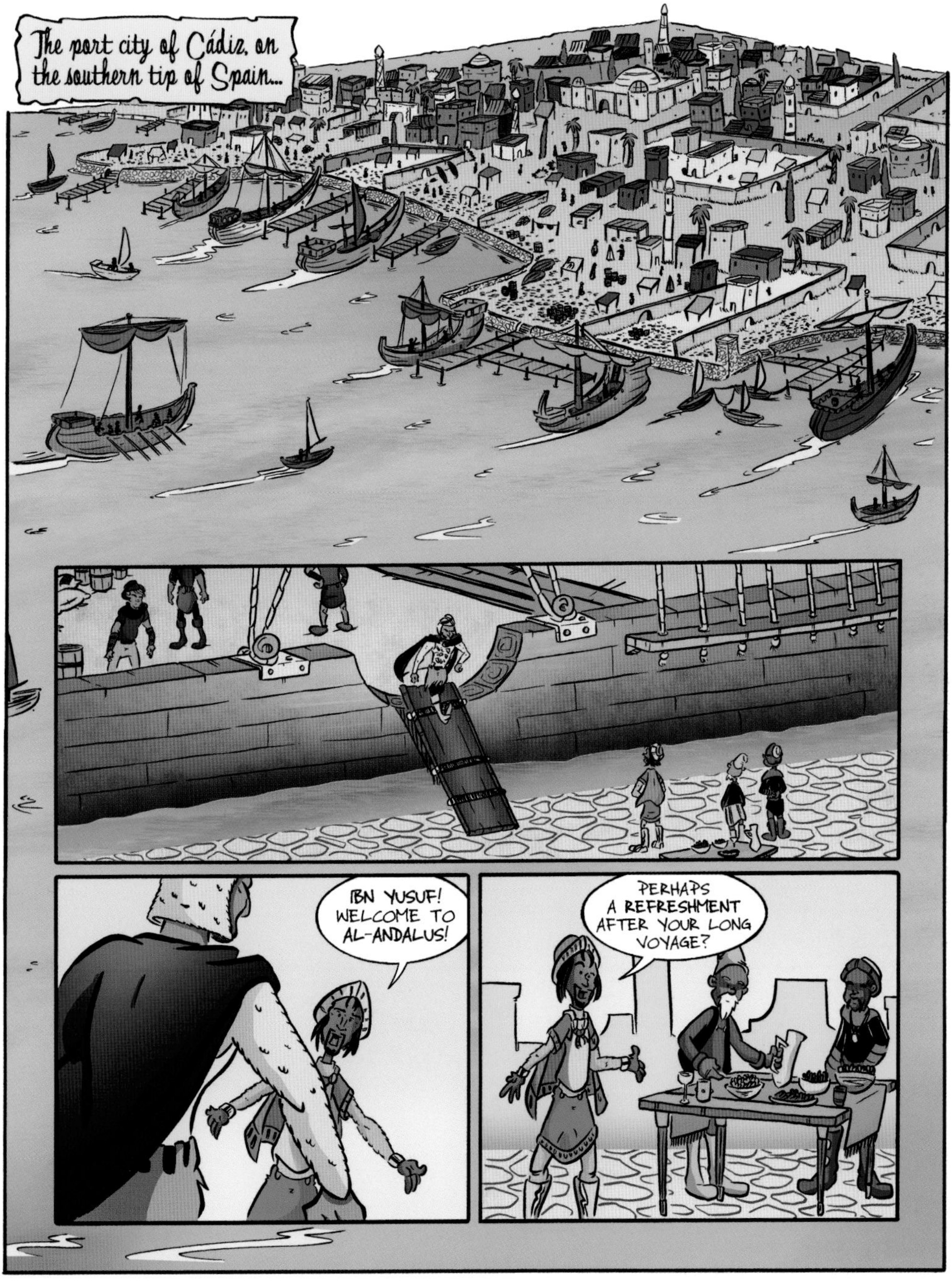
The port city of Cádiz, on the southern tip of Spain...
IBN YUSUF! WELCOME TO AL-ANDALUS!
PERHAPS A REFRESHMENT AFTER YOUR LONG VOYAGE?

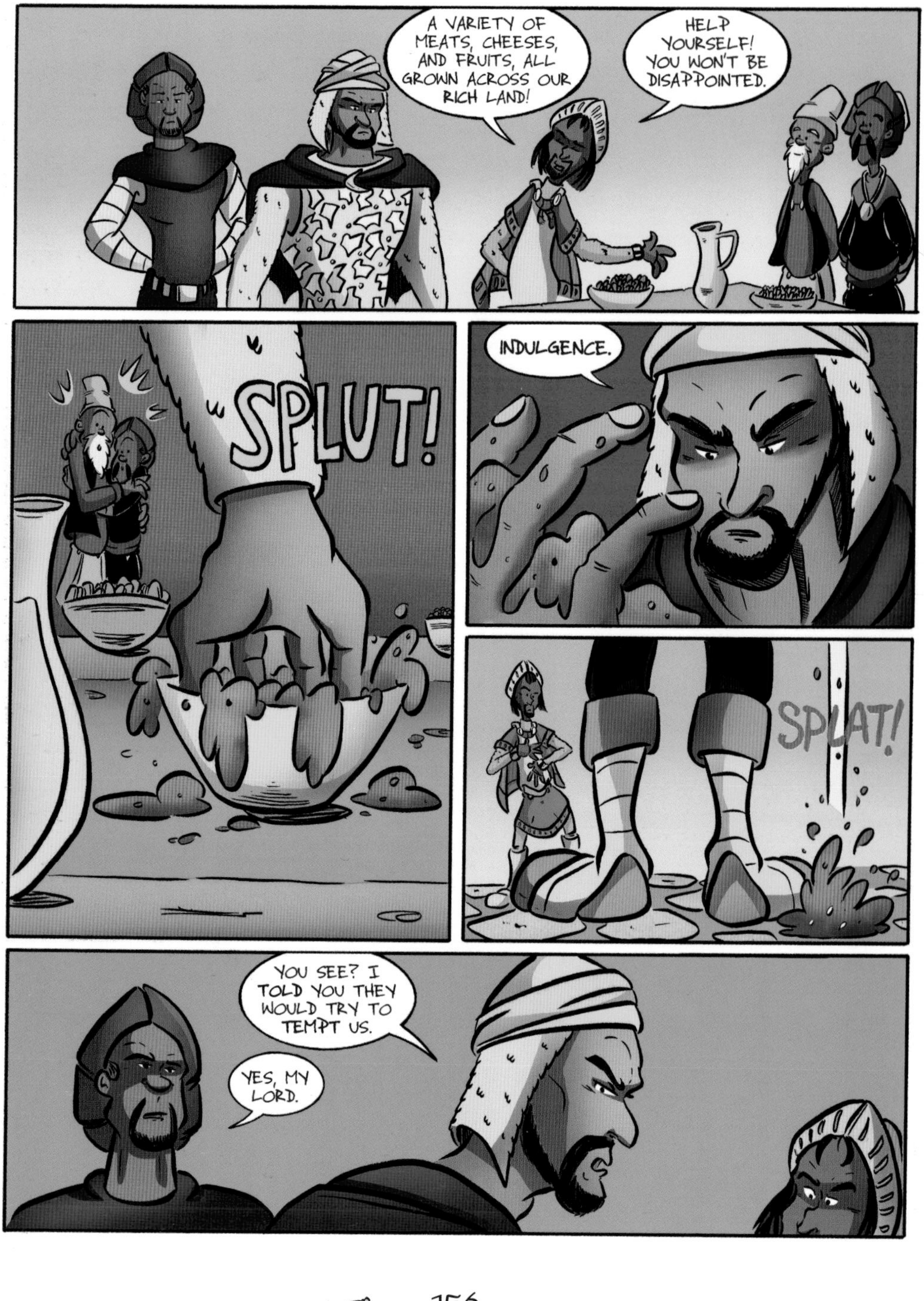
A VARIETY OF MEATS, CHEESES, AND FRUITS, ALL GROWN ACROSS OUR RICH LAND!
HELP YOURSELF! YOU WON'T BE DISAPPOINTED.
SPLUT!
INDULGENCE.
SPLAT!
YOU SEE? I TOLD YOU THEY WOULD TRY TO TEMPT US.
YES, MY LORD.

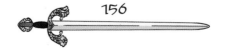

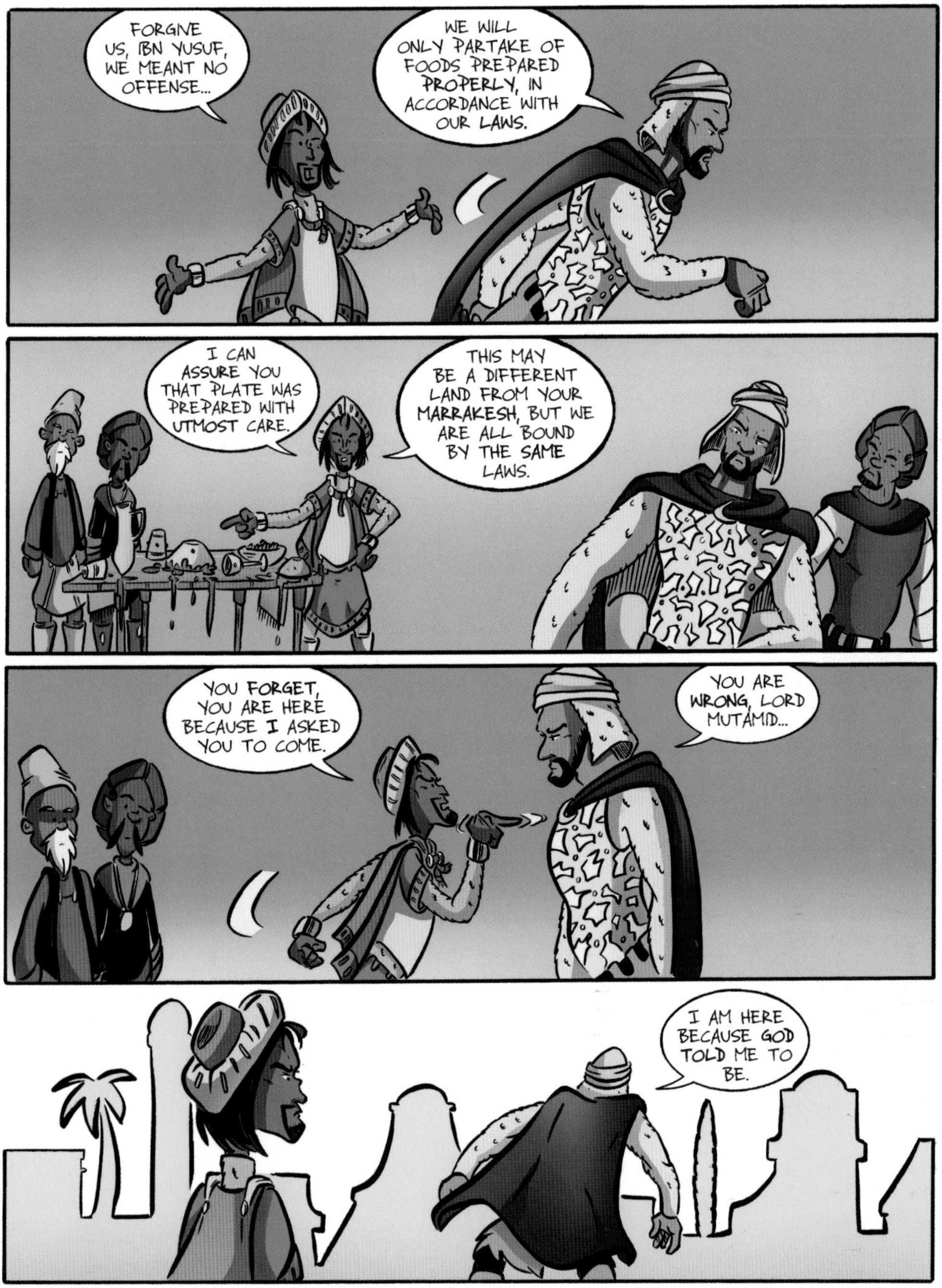
FORGIVE US, IBN YUSUF, WE MEANT NO OFFENSE...
WE WILL ONLY PARTAKE OF FOODS PREPARED PROPERLY, IN ACCORDANCE WITH OUR LAWS.
I CAN ASSURE YOU THAT PLATE WAS PREPARED WITH UTMOST CARE.
THIS MAY BE A DIFFERENT LAND FROM YOUR MARRAKESH, BUT WE ARE ALL BOUND BY THE SAME LAWS.
YOU FORGET, YOU ARE HERE BECAUSE I ASKED YOU TO COME.
YOU ARE WRONG, LORD MUTAMID...
I AM HERE BECAUSE GOD TOLD ME TO BE.

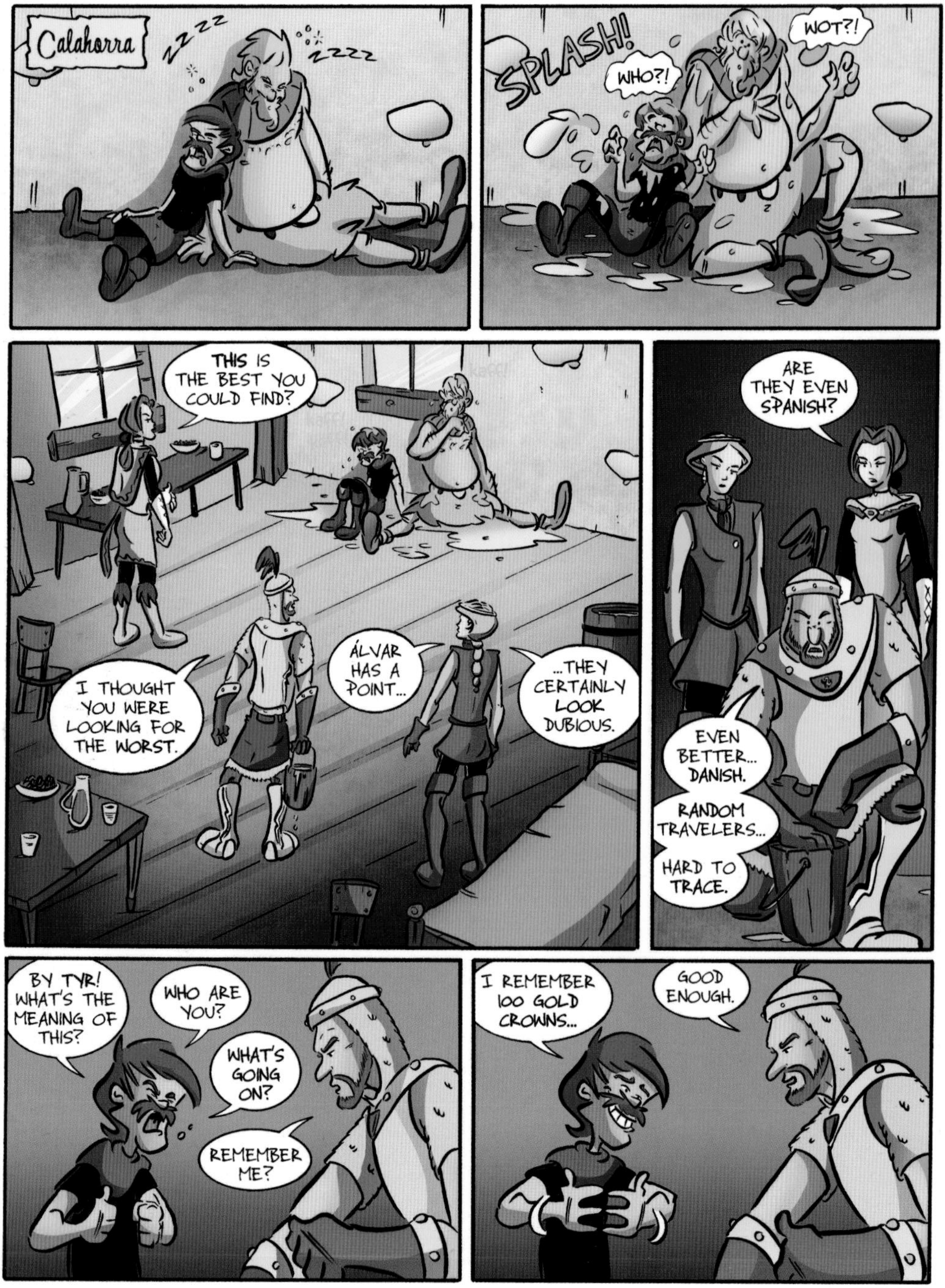
Calahorra
ZZZZ
ZZZZ
SPLASH!
WHO?!
WOT?!
THIS IS THE BEST YOU COULD FIND?
I THOUGHT YOU WERE LOOKING FOR THE WORST.
ÁLVAR HAS A POINT...
...THEY CERTAINLY LOOK DUBIOUS.
ARE THEY EVEN SPANISH?
EVEN BETTER... DANISH.
RANDOM TRAVELERS...
HARD TO TRACE.
BY TYR! WHAT'S THE MEANING OF THIS?
WHO ARE YOU?
WHAT'S GOING ON?
REMEMBER ME?
I REMEMBER 100 GOLD CROWNS...
GOOD ENOUGH.

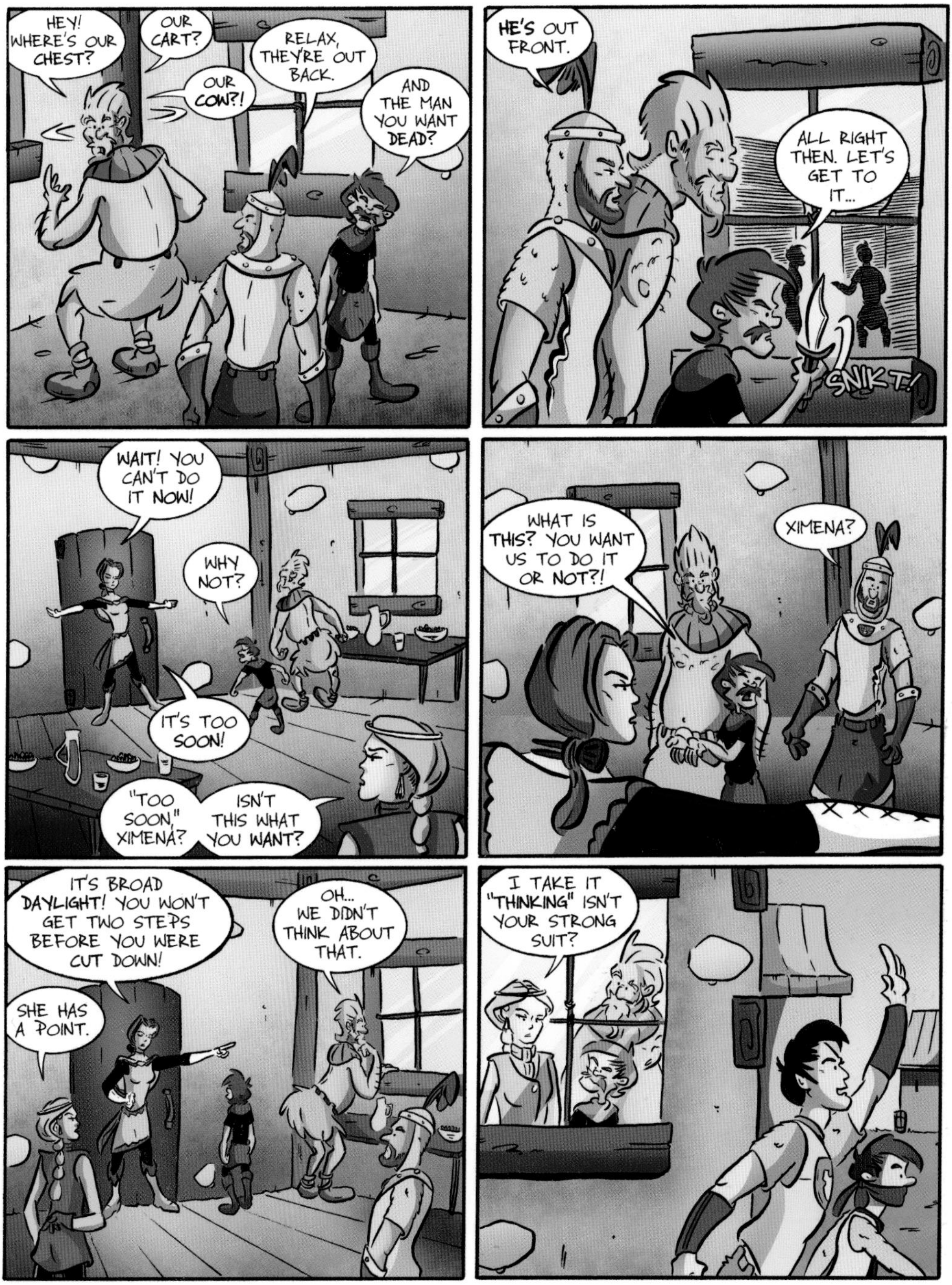
HEY! WHERE'S OUR CHEST?
OUR CART?
OUR COW?!
RELAX, THEY'RE OUT BACK.
AND THE MAN YOU WANT DEAD?
HE'S OUT FRONT.
ALL RIGHT THEN. LET'S GET TO IT...
SNIKT!
WAIT! YOU CAN'T DO IT NOW!
WHY NOT?
IT'S TOO SOON!
"TOO SOON," XIMENA?
ISN'T THIS WHAT YOU WANT?
WHAT IS THIS? YOU WANT US TO DO IT OR NOT?!
XIMENA?
IT'S BROAD DAYLIGHT! YOU WON'T GET TWO STEPS BEFORE YOU WERE CUT DOWN!
SHE HAS A POINT.
OH... WE DIDN'T THINK ABOUT THAT.
I TAKE IT "THINKING" ISN'T YOUR STRONG SUIT?

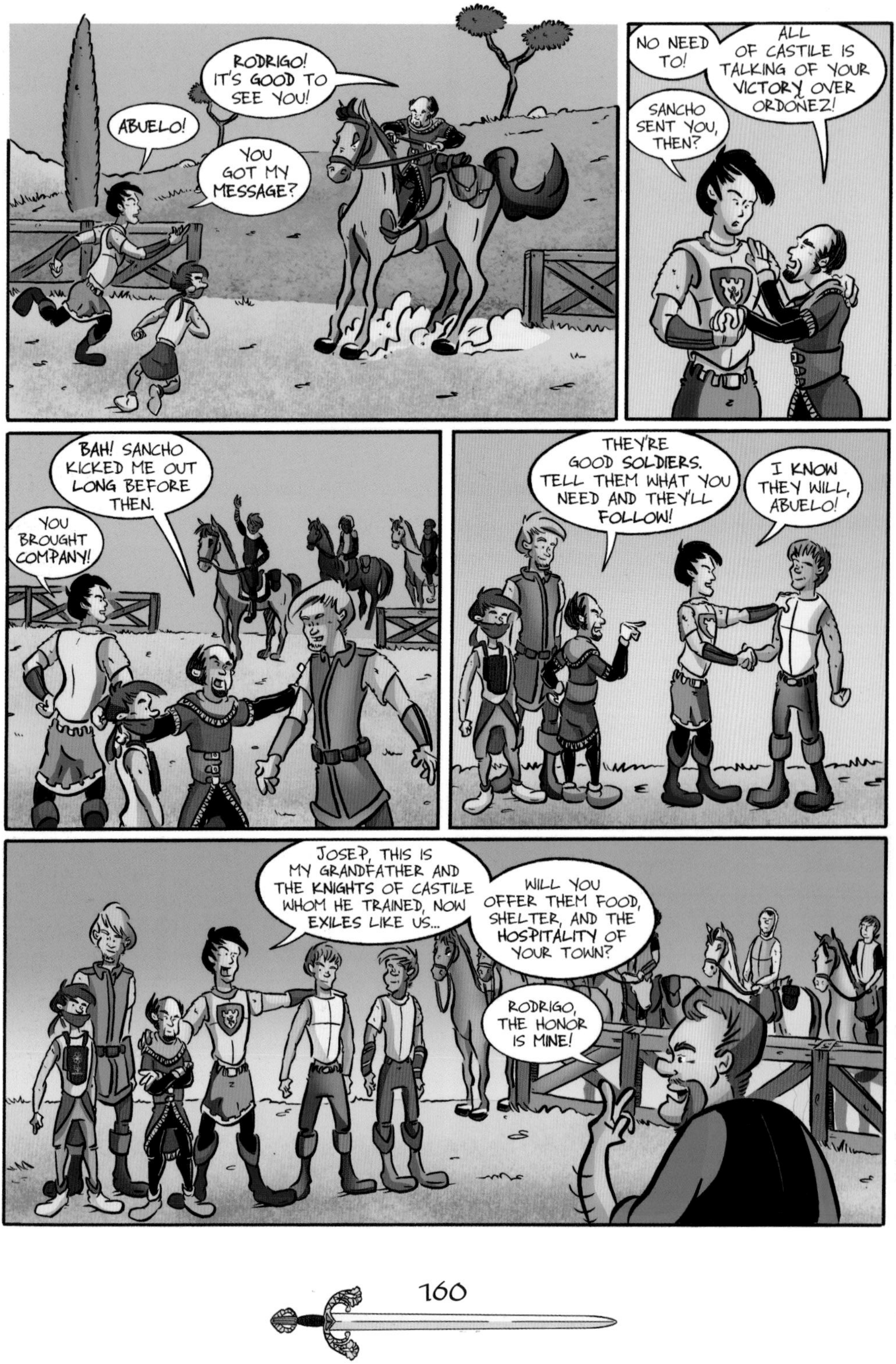
ABUELO!
RODRIGO! IT'S GOOD TO SEE YOU!
YOU GOT MY MESSAGE?
NO NEED TO!
ALL OF CASTILE IS TALKING OF YOUR VICTORY OVER ORDOÑEZ!
SANCHO SENT YOU, THEN?
YOU BROUGHT COMPANY!
BAH! SANCHO KICKED ME OUT LONG BEFORE THEN.
THEY'RE GOOD SOLDIERS. TELL THEM WHAT YOU NEED AND THEY'LL FOLLOW!
I KNOW THEY WILL, ABUELO!
JOSEP, THIS IS MY GRANDFATHER AND THE KNIGHTS OF CASTILE WHOM HE TRAINED, NOW EXILES LIKE US...
WILL YOU OFFER THEM FOOD, SHELTER, AND THE HOSPITALITY OF YOUR TOWN?
RODRIGO, THE HONOR IS MINE!

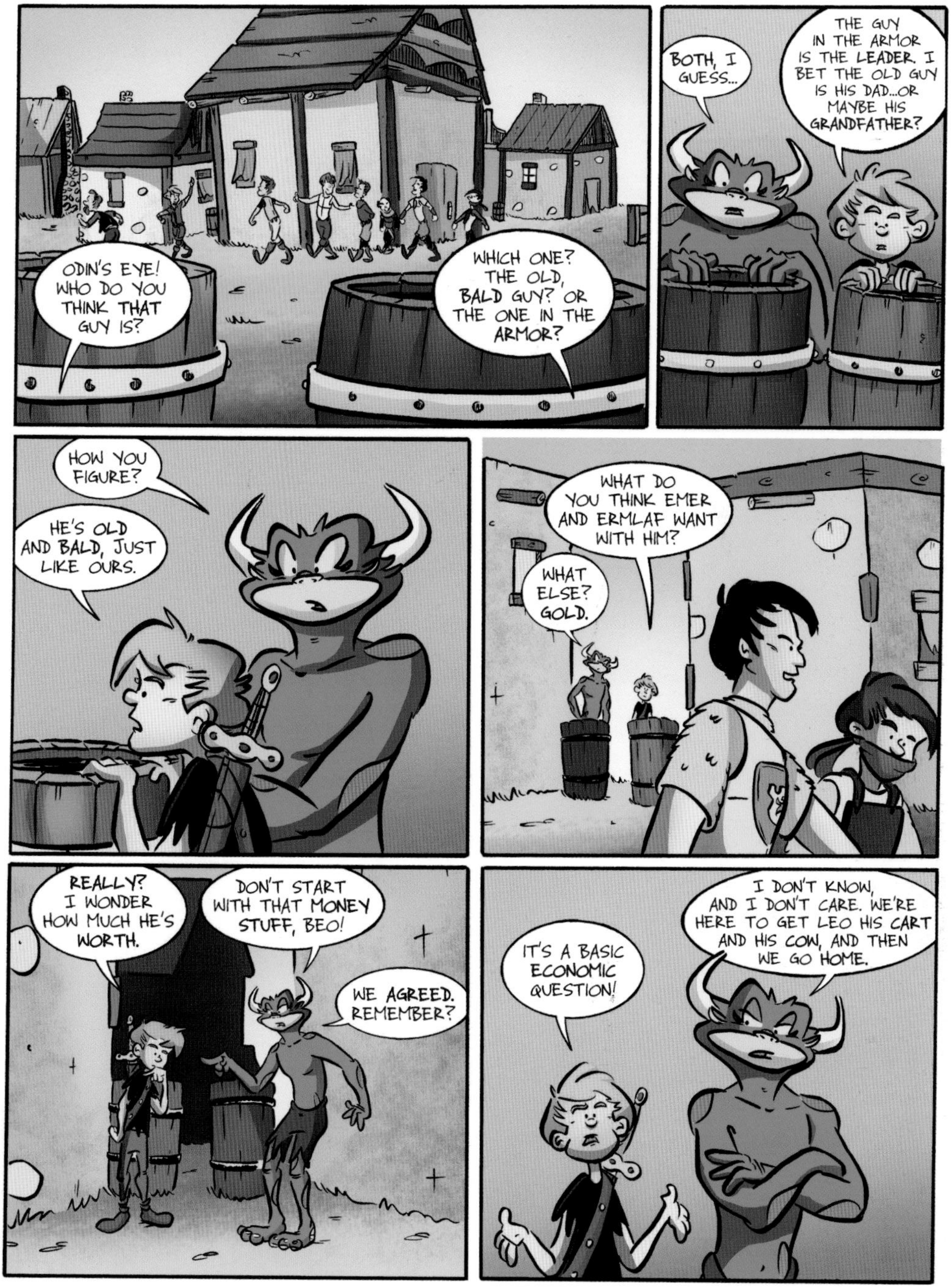
ODIN'S EYE! WHO DO YOU THINK THAT GUY IS?
WHICH ONE? THE OLD, BALD GUY? OR THE ONE IN THE ARMOR?
BOTH, I GUESS...
THE GUY IN THE ARMOR IS THE LEADER. I BET THE OLD GUY IS HIS DAD...OR MAYBE HIS GRANDFATHER?
HOW YOU FIGURE?
HE'S OLD AND BALD, JUST LIKE OURS.
WHAT DO YOU THINK EMER AND ERMLAF WANT WITH HIM?
WHAT ELSE? GOLD.
REALLY? I WONDER HOW MUCH HE'S WORTH.
DON'T START WITH THAT MONEY STUFF, BEO!
WE AGREED. REMEMBER?
IT'S A BASIC ECONOMIC QUESTION!
I DON'T KNOW, AND I DON'T CARE. WE'RE HERE TO GET LEO HIS CART AND HIS COW, AND THEN WE GO HOME.

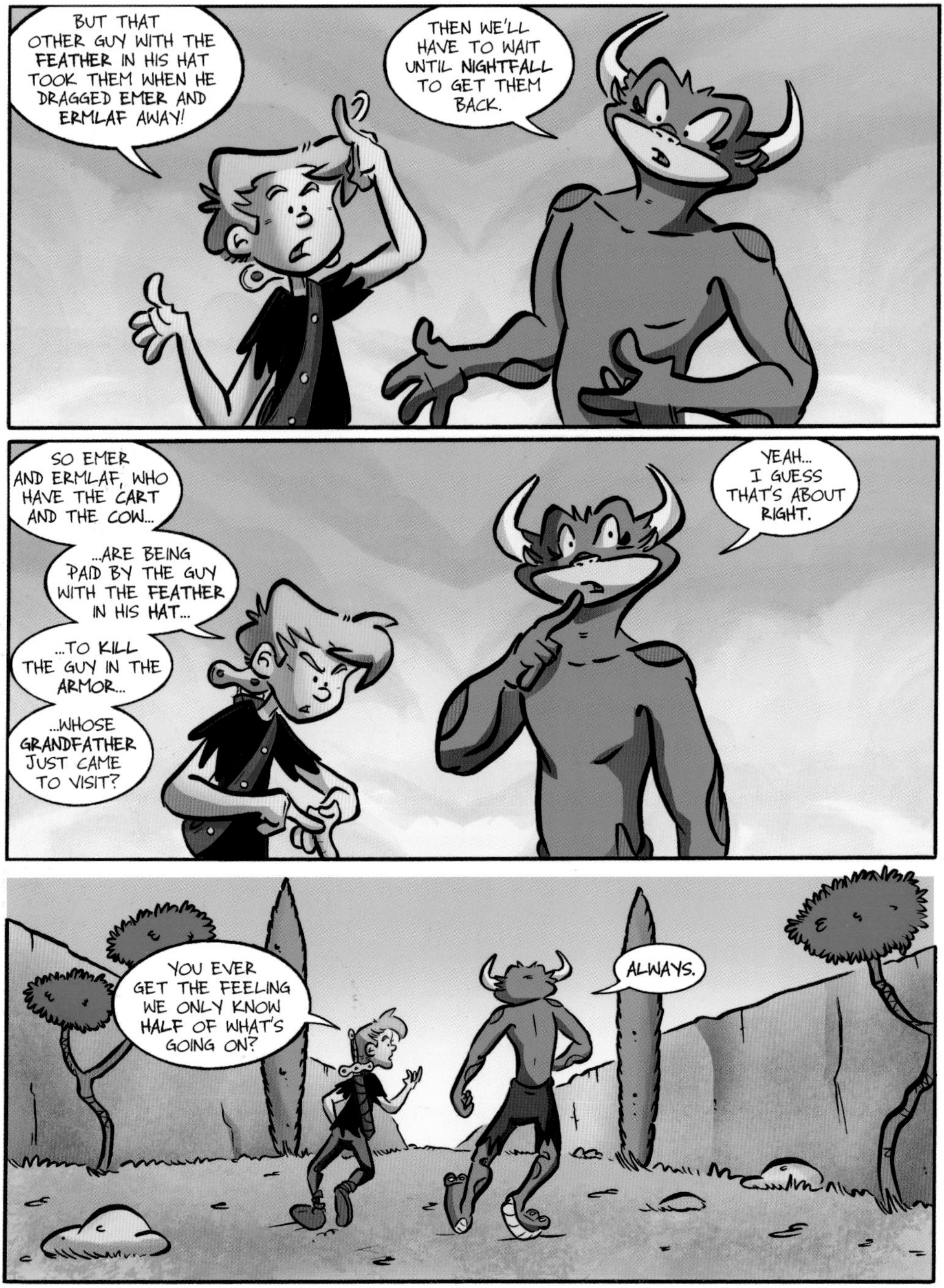
BUT THAT OTHER GUY WITH THE FEATHER IN HIS HAT TOOK THEM WHEN HE DRAGGED EMER AND ERMLAF AWAY!
THEN WE'LL HAVE TO WAIT UNTIL NIGHTFALL TO GET THEM BACK.
SO EMER AND ERMLAF, WHO HAVE THE CART AND THE COW...
...ARE BEING PAID BY THE GUY WITH THE FEATHER IN HIS HAT...
...TO KILL THE GUY IN THE ARMOR...
...WHOSE GRANDFATHER JUST CAME TO VISIT?
YEAH... I GUESS THAT'S ABOUT RIGHT.
YOU EVER GET THE FEELING WE ONLY KNOW HALF OF WHAT'S GOING ON?
ALWAYS.

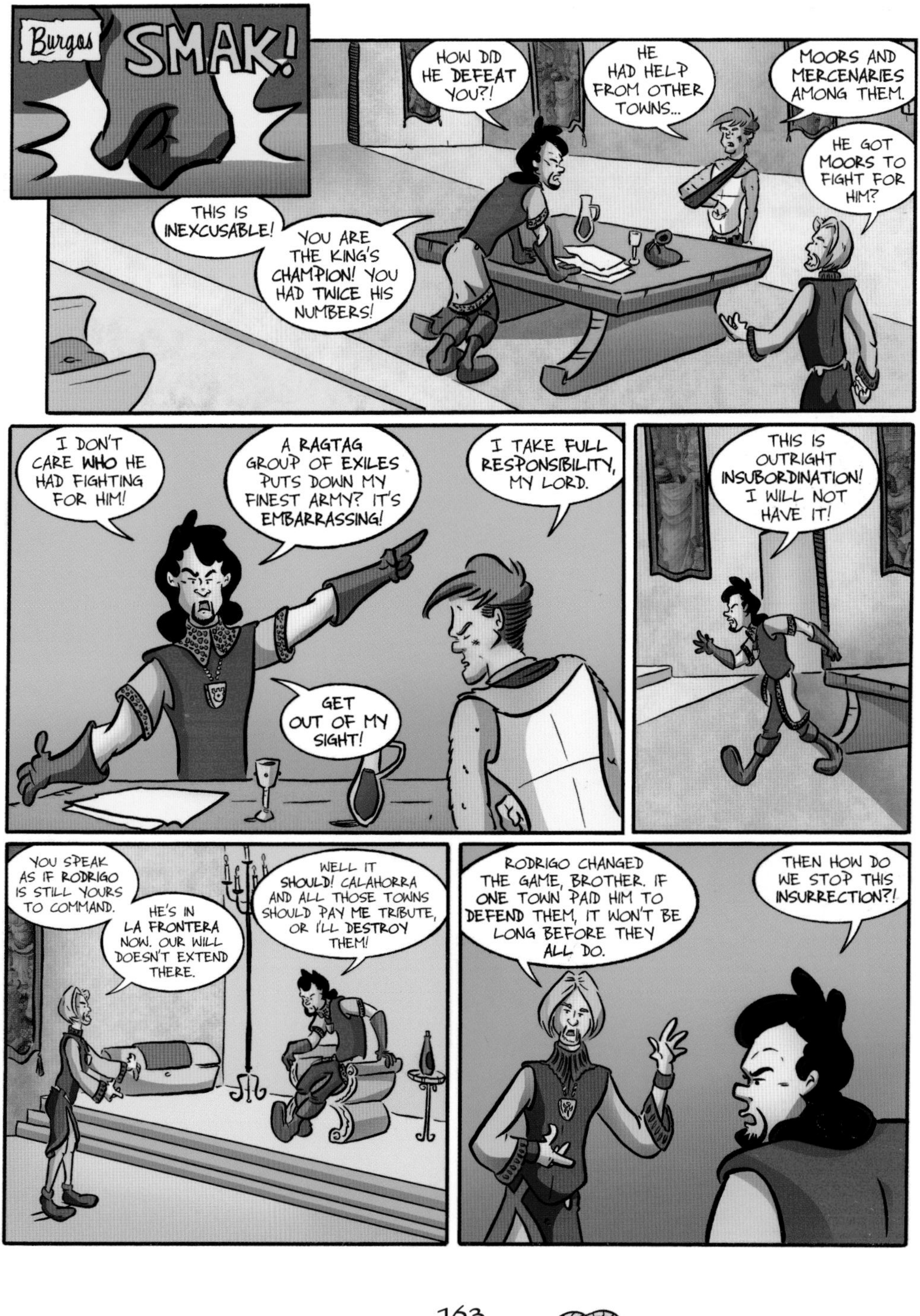
Burgos
SMAK!
HOW DID HE DEFEAT YOU?!
HE HAD HELP FROM OTHER TOWNS...
MOORS AND MERCENARIES AMONG THEM.
HE GOT MOORS TO FIGHT FOR HIM?
THIS IS INEXCUSABLE!
YOU ARE THE KING'S CHAMPION! YOU HAD TWICE HIS NUMBERS!
I DON'T CARE WHO HE HAD FIGHTING FOR HIM!
A RAGTAG GROUP OF EXILES PUTS DOWN MY FINEST ARMY? IT'S EMBARRASSING!
I TAKE FULL RESPONSIBILITY, MY LORD.
GET OUT OF MY SIGHT!
THIS IS OUTRIGHT INSUBORDINATION! I WILL NOT HAVE IT!
YOU SPEAK AS IF RODRIGO IS STILL YOURS TO COMMAND.
HE'S IN LA FRONTERA NOW. OUR WILL DOESN'T EXTEND THERE.
WELL IT SHOULD! CALAHORRA AND ALL THOSE TOWNS SHOULD PAY ME TRIBUTE, OR I'LL DESTROY THEM!
RODRIGO CHANGED THE GAME, BROTHER. IF ONE TOWN PAID HIM TO DEFEND THEM, IT WON'T BE LONG BEFORE THEY ALL DO.
THEN HOW DO WE STOP THIS INSURRECTION?!

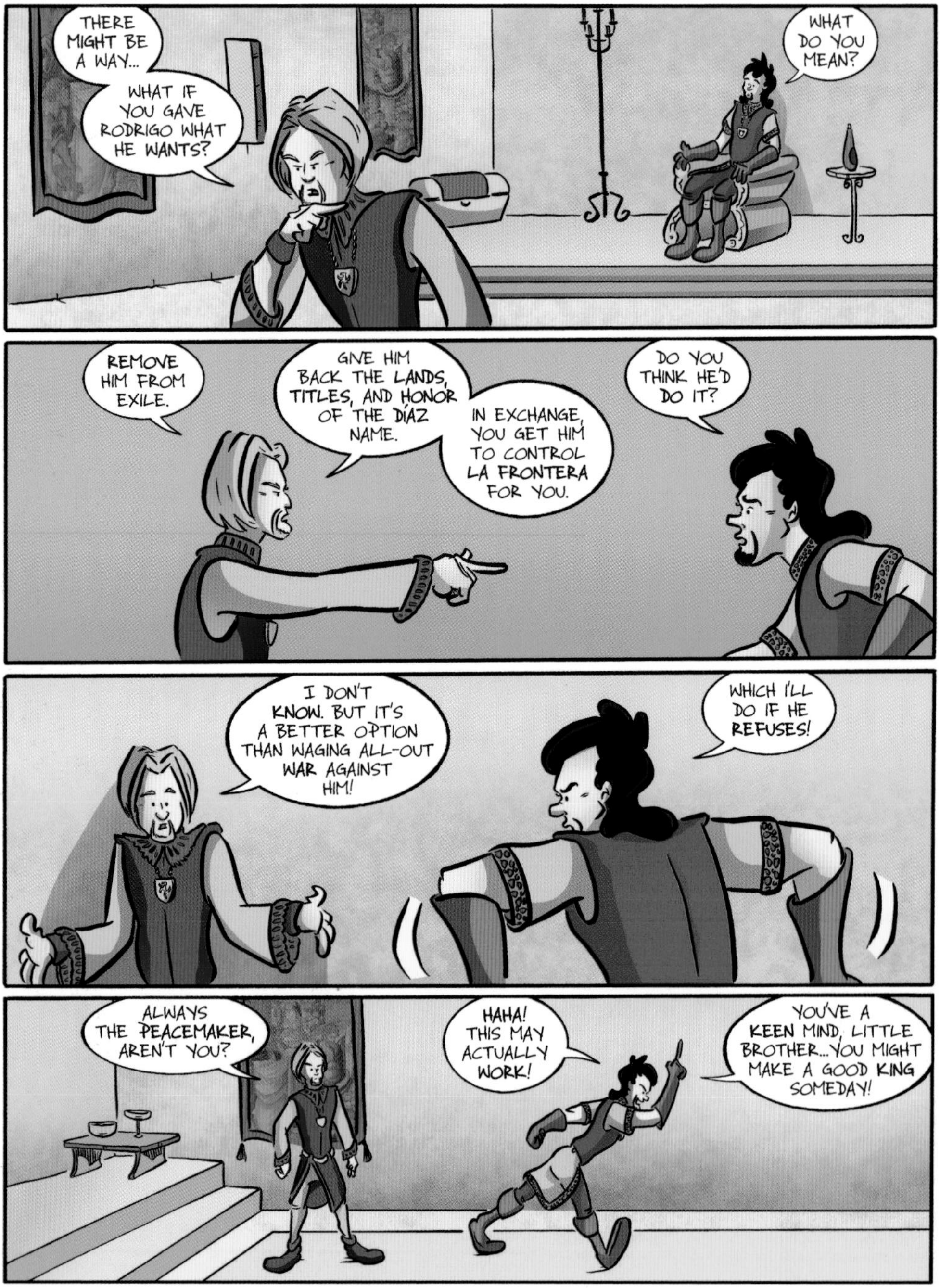
THERE MIGHT BE A WAY...
WHAT IF YOU GAVE RODRIGO WHAT HE WANTS?
WHAT DO YOU MEAN?
REMOVE HIM FROM EXILE.
GIVE HIM BACK THE LANDS, TITLES, AND HONOR OF THE DÍAZ NAME.
IN EXCHANGE, YOU GET HIM TO CONTROL LA FRONTERA FOR YOU.
DO YOU THINK HE'D DO IT?
I DON'T KNOW. BUT IT'S A BETTER OPTION THAN WAGING ALL-OUT WAR AGAINST HIM!
WHICH I'LL DO IF HE REFUSES!
ALWAYS THE PEACEMAKER, AREN'T YOU?
HAHA! THIS MAY ACTUALLY WORK!
YOU'VE A KEEN MIND, LITTLE BROTHER...YOU MIGHT MAKE A GOOD KING SOMEDAY!

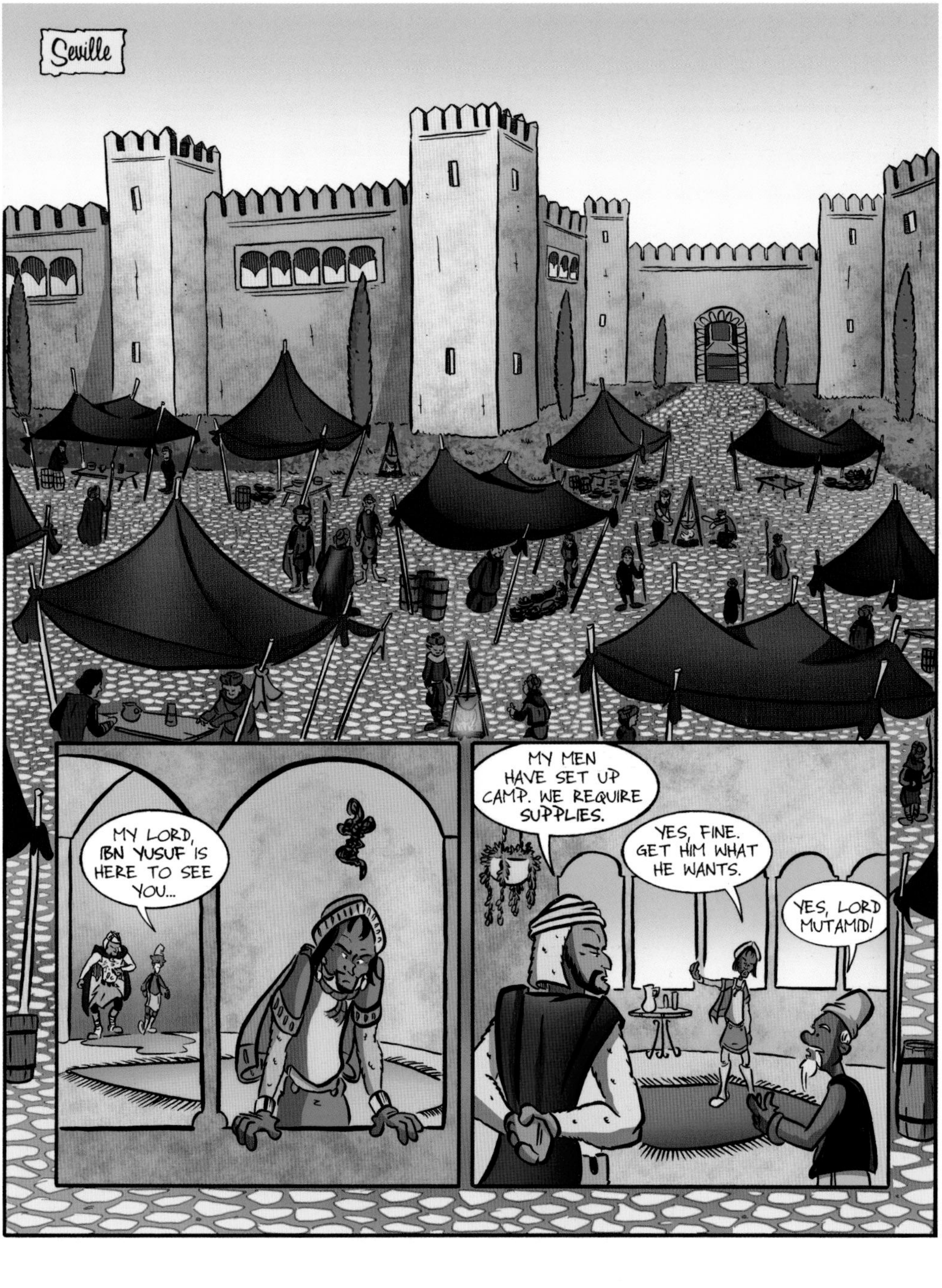
Seville
MY LORD, IBN YUSUF IS HERE TO SEE YOU...
MY MEN HAVE SET UP CAMP. WE REQUIRE SUPPLIES.
YES, FINE. GET HIM WHAT HE WANTS.
YES, LORD MUTAMID!

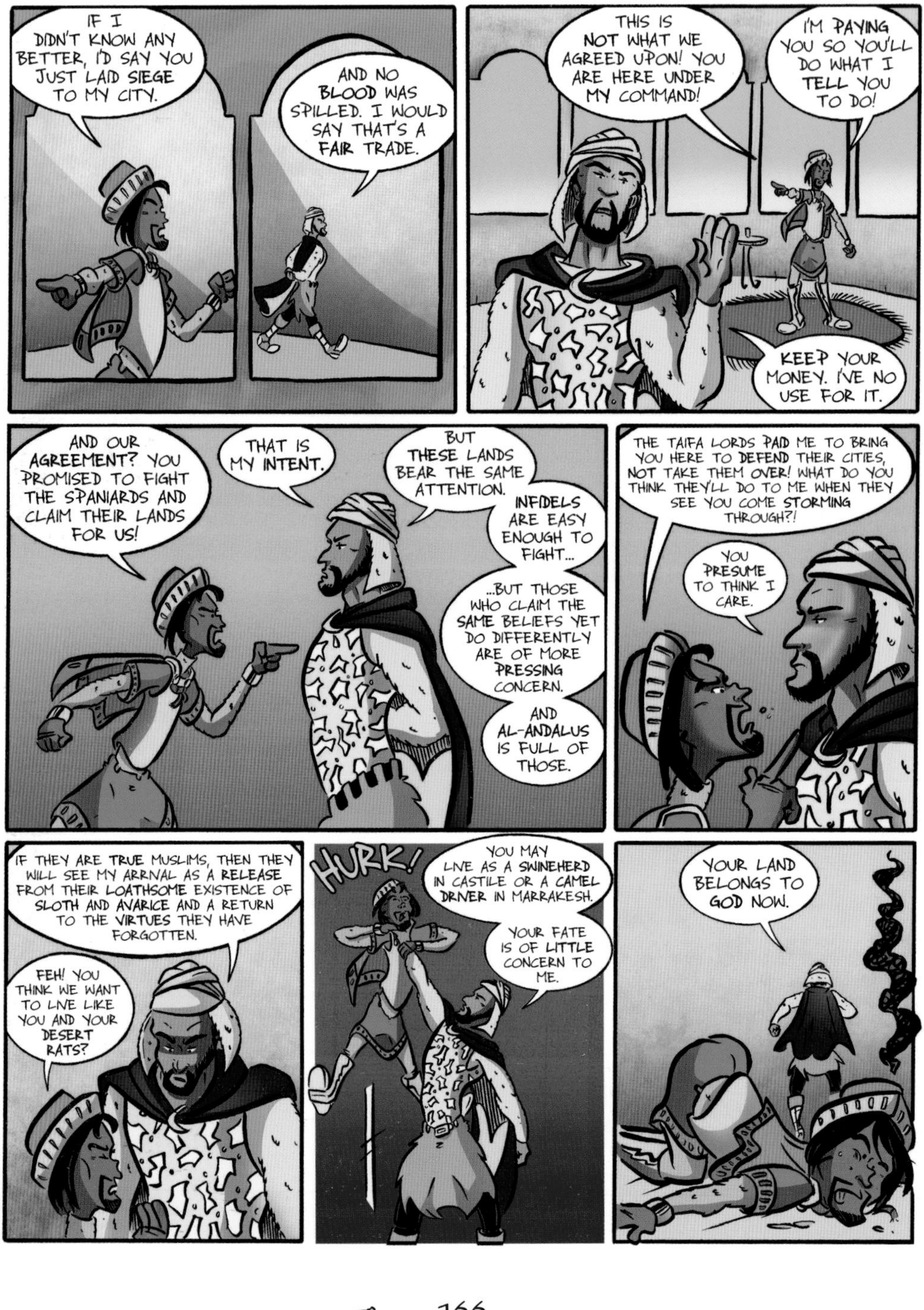
IF I DIDN'T KNOW ANY BETTER, I'D SAY YOU JUST LAID SIEGE TO MY CITY.
AND NO BLOOD WAS SPILLED. I WOULD SAY THAT'S A FAIR TRADE.
THIS IS NOT WHAT WE AGREED UPON! YOU ARE HERE UNDER MY COMMAND!
I'M PAYING YOU SO YOU'LL DO WHAT I TELL YOU TO DO!
KEEP YOUR MONEY. I'VE NO USE FOR IT.
AND OUR AGREEMENT? YOU PROMISED TO FIGHT THE SPANIARDS AND CLAIM THEIR LANDS FOR US!
THAT IS MY INTENT.
BUT THESE LANDS BEAR THE SAME ATTENTION.
INFIDELS ARE EASY ENOUGH TO FIGHT...
...BUT THOSE WHO CLAIM THE SAME BELIEFS YET DO DIFFERENTLY ARE OF MORE PRESSING CONCERN.
AND AL-ANDALUS IS FULL OF THOSE.
THE TAIFA LORDS PAID ME TO BRING YOU HERE TO DEFEND THEIR CITIES, NOT TAKE THEM OVER! WHAT DO YOU THINK THEY'LL DO TO ME WHEN THEY SEE YOU COME STORMING THROUGH?!
YOU PRESUME TO THINK I CARE.
IF THEY ARE TRUE MUSLIMS, THEN THEY WILL SEE MY ARRIVAL AS A RELEASE FROM THEIR LOATHSOME EXISTENCE OF SLOTH AND AVARICE AND A RETURN TO THE VIRTUES THEY HAVE FORGOTTEN.
FEH! YOU THINK WE WANT TO LIVE LIKE YOU AND YOUR DESERT RATS?
HURK!
YOU MAY LIVE AS A SWINEHERD IN CASTILE OR A CAMEL DRIVER IN MARRAKESH.
YOUR FATE IS OF LITTLE CONCERN TO ME.
YOUR LAND BELONGS TO GOD NOW.

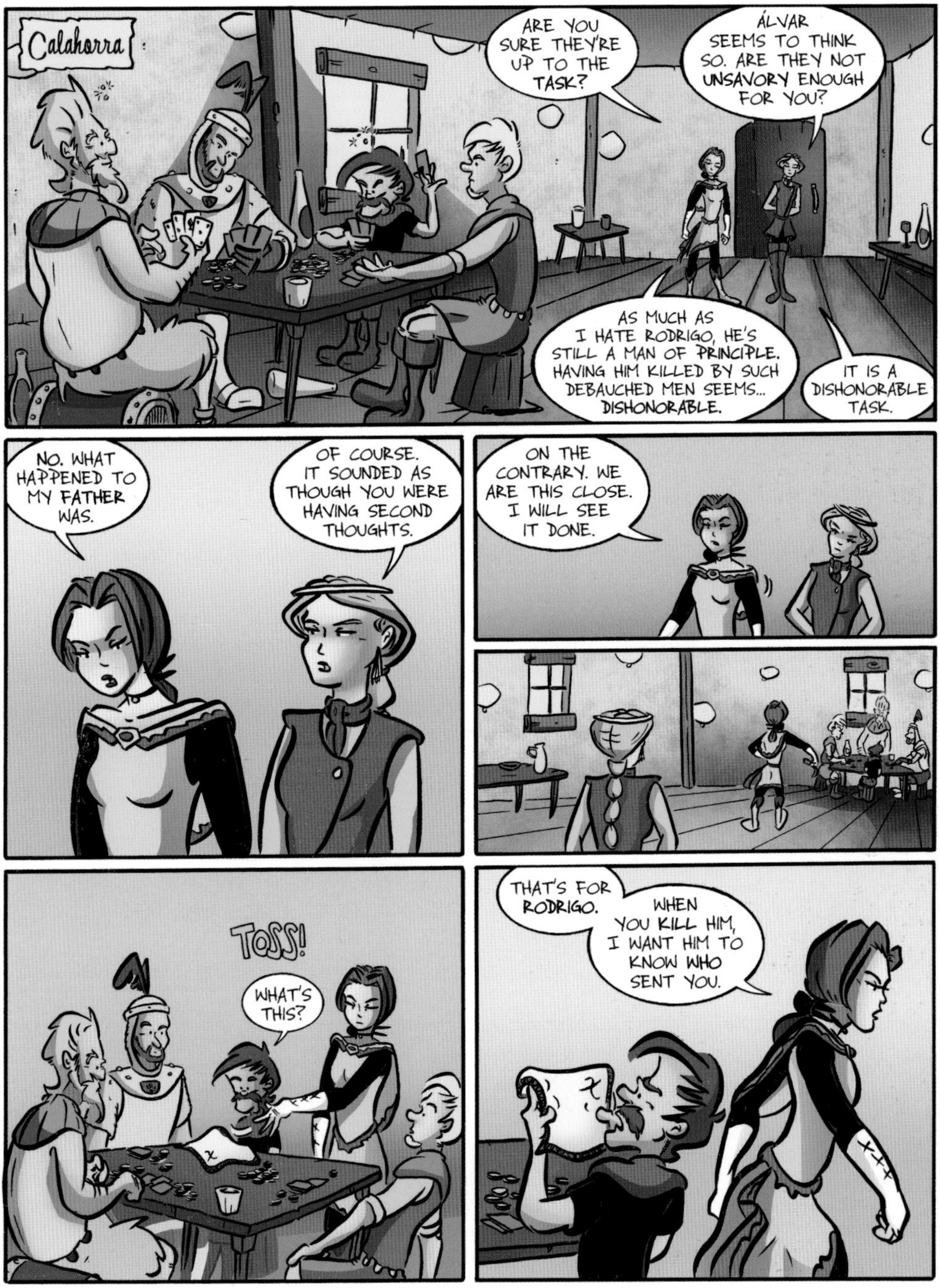
Calahorra
ARE YOU SURE THEY'RE UP TO THE TASK?
ÁLVAR SEEMS TO THINK SO. ARE THEY NOT UNSAVORY ENOUGH FOR YOU?
AS MUCH AS I HATE RODRIGO, HE'S STILL A MAN OF PRINCIPLE. HAVING HIM KILLED BY SUCH DEBAUCHED MEN SEEMS... DISHONORABLE.
IT IS A DISHONORABLE TASK.
NO. WHAT HAPPENED TO MY FATHER WAS.
OF COURSE. IT SOUNDED AS THOUGH YOU WERE HAVING SECOND THOUGHTS.
ON THE CONTRARY. WE ARE THIS CLOSE. I WILL SEE IT DONE.
TOSS!
WHAT'S THIS?
THAT'S FOR RODRIGO.
WHEN YOU KILL HIM, I WANT HIM TO KNOW WHO SENT YOU.

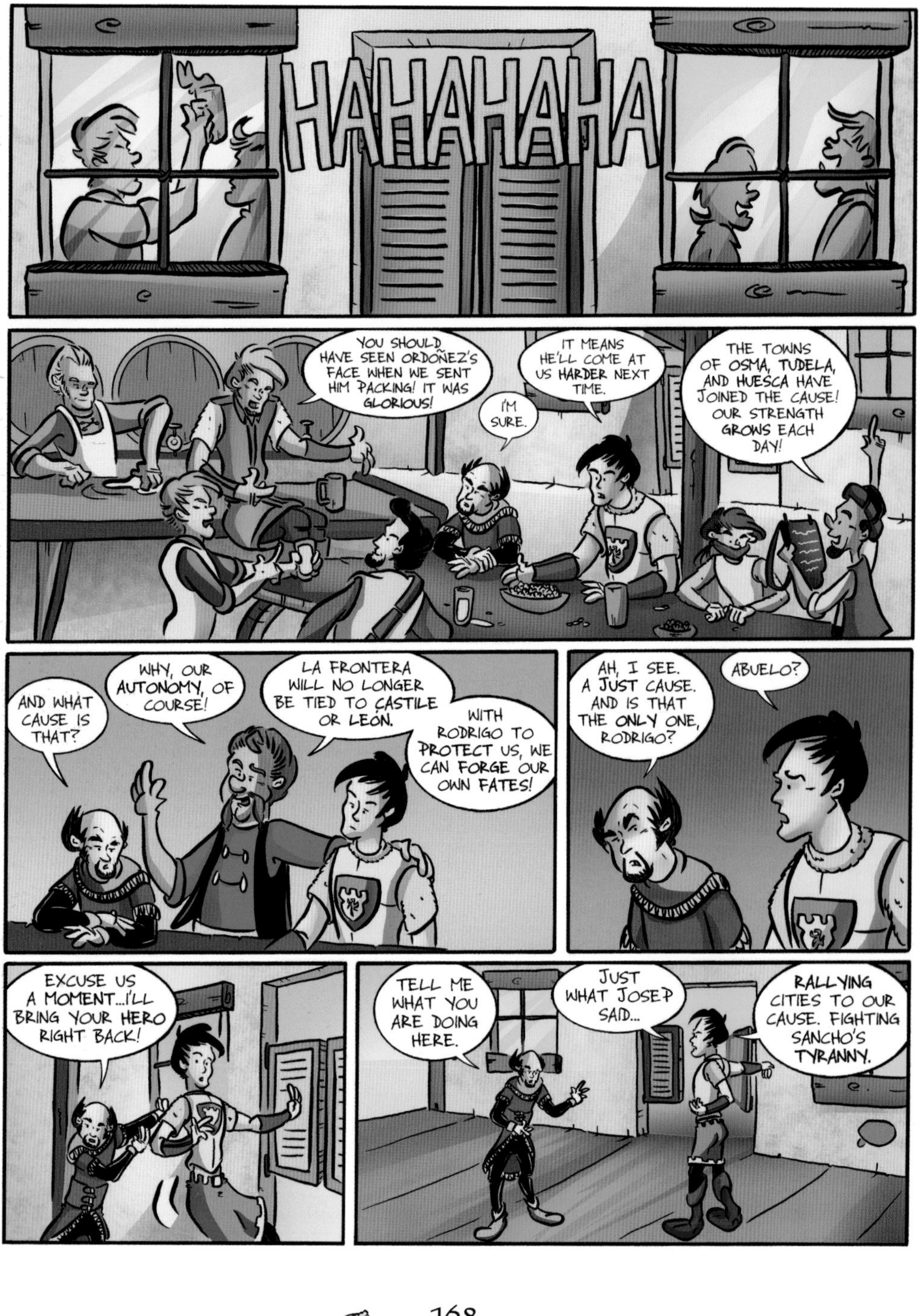
HAHAHAHA
YOU SHOULD HAVE SEEN ORDOÑEZ'S FACE WHEN WE SENT HIM PACKING! IT WAS GLORIOUS!
I'M SURE.
IT MEANS HE'LL COME AT US HARDER NEXT TIME.
THE TOWNS OF OSMA, TUDELA, AND HUESCA HAVE JOINED THE CAUSE! OUR STRENGTH GROWS EACH DAY!
AND WHAT CAUSE IS THAT?
WHY, OUR AUTONOMY, OF COURSE!
LA FRONTERA WILL NO LONGER BE TIED TO CASTILE OR LEÓN.
WITH RODRIGO TO PROTECT US, WE CAN FORGE OUR OWN FATES!
AH, I SEE. A JUST CAUSE. AND IS THAT THE ONLY ONE, RODRIGO?
ABUELO?
EXCUSE US A MOMENT...I'LL BRING YOUR HERO RIGHT BACK!
TELL ME WHAT YOU ARE DOING HERE.
JUST WHAT JOSEP SAID...
RALLYING CITIES TO OUR CAUSE. FIGHTING SANCHO'S TYRANNY.

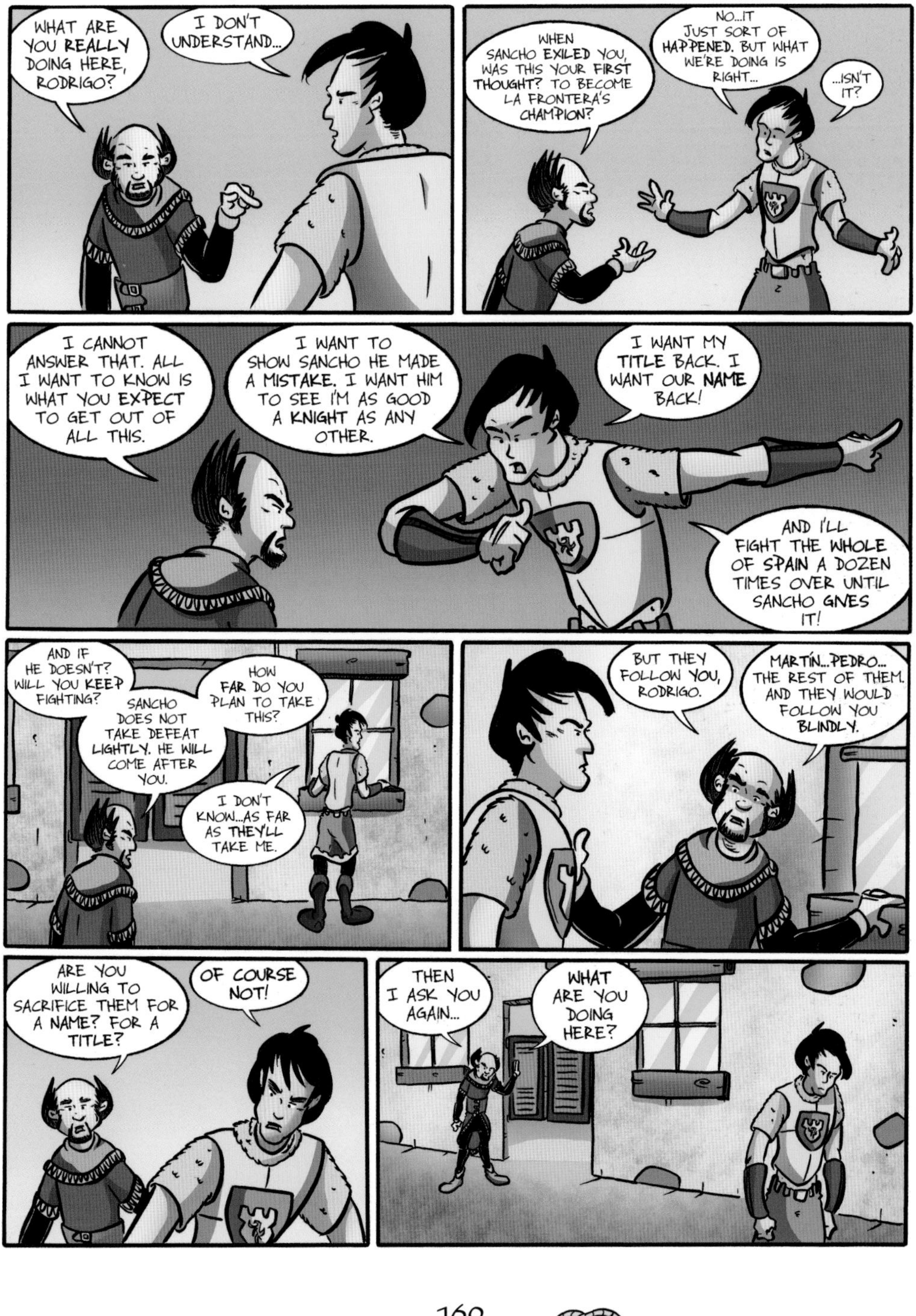
WHAT ARE YOU REALLY DOING HERE, RODRIGO?
I DON'T UNDERSTAND...
WHEN SANCHO EXILED YOU, WAS THIS YOUR FIRST THOUGHT? TO BECOME LA FRONTERA'S CHAMPION?
NO...IT JUST SORT OF HAPPENED. BUT WHAT WE'RE DOING IS RIGHT...
...ISN'T IT?
I CANNOT ANSWER THAT. ALL I WANT TO KNOW IS WHAT YOU EXPECT TO GET OUT OF ALL THIS.
I WANT TO SHOW SANCHO HE MADE A MISTAKE. I WANT HIM TO SEE I'M AS GOOD A KNIGHT AS ANY OTHER.
I WANT MY TITLE BACK. I WANT OUR NAME BACK!
AND I'LL FIGHT THE WHOLE OF SPAIN A DOZEN TIMES OVER UNTIL SANCHO GIVES IT!
AND IF HE DOESN'T? WILL YOU KEEP FIGHTING?
SANCHO DOES NOT TAKE DEFEAT LIGHTLY. HE WILL COME AFTER YOU.
HOW FAR DO YOU PLAN TO TAKE THIS?
I DON'T KNOW...AS FAR AS THEY'LL TAKE ME.
BUT THEY FOLLOW YOU, RODRIGO.
MARTÍN...PEDRO... THE REST OF THEM. AND THEY WOULD FOLLOW YOU BLINDLY.
ARE YOU WILLING TO SACRIFICE THEM FOR A NAME? FOR A TITLE?
OF COURSE NOT!
THEN I ASK YOU AGAIN...
WHAT ARE YOU DOING HERE?

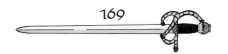

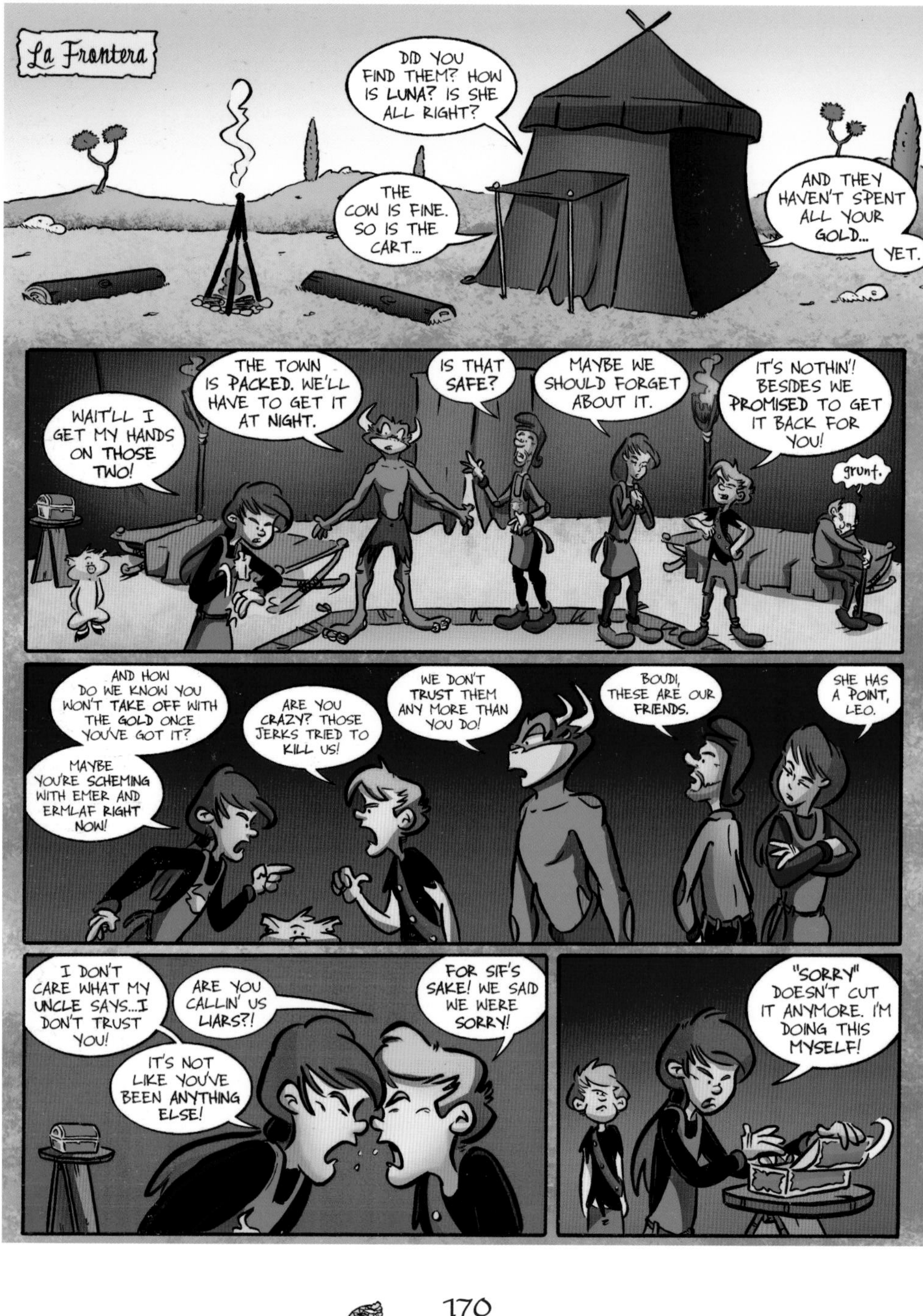
La Frontera
DID YOU FIND THEM? HOW IS LUNA? IS SHE ALL RIGHT?
THE COW IS FINE. SO IS THE CART...
AND THEY HAVEN'T SPENT ALL YOUR GOLD...
YET.
WAIT'LL I GET MY HANDS ON THOSE TWO!
THE TOWN IS PACKED. WE'LL HAVE TO GET IT AT NIGHT.
IS THAT SAFE?
MAYBE WE SHOULD FORGET ABOUT IT.
IT'S NOTHIN'! BESIDES WE PROMISED TO GET IT BACK FOR YOU!
grunt.
AND HOW DO WE KNOW YOU WON'T TAKE OFF WITH THE GOLD ONCE YOU'VE GOT IT?
MAYBE YOU'RE SCHEMING WITH EMER AND ERMLAF RIGHT NOW!
ARE YOU CRAZY? THOSE JERKS TRIED TO KILL US!
WE DON'T TRUST THEM ANY MORE THAN YOU DO!
BOUDI, THESE ARE OUR FRIENDS.
SHE HAS A POINT, LEO.
I DON'T CARE WHAT MY UNCLE SAYS...I DON'T TRUST YOU!
ARE YOU CALLIN' US LIARS?!
FOR SIF'S SAKE! WE SAID WE WERE SORRY!
IT'S NOT LIKE YOU'VE BEEN ANYTHING ELSE!
"SORRY" DOESN'T CUT IT ANYMORE. I'M DOING THIS MYSELF!

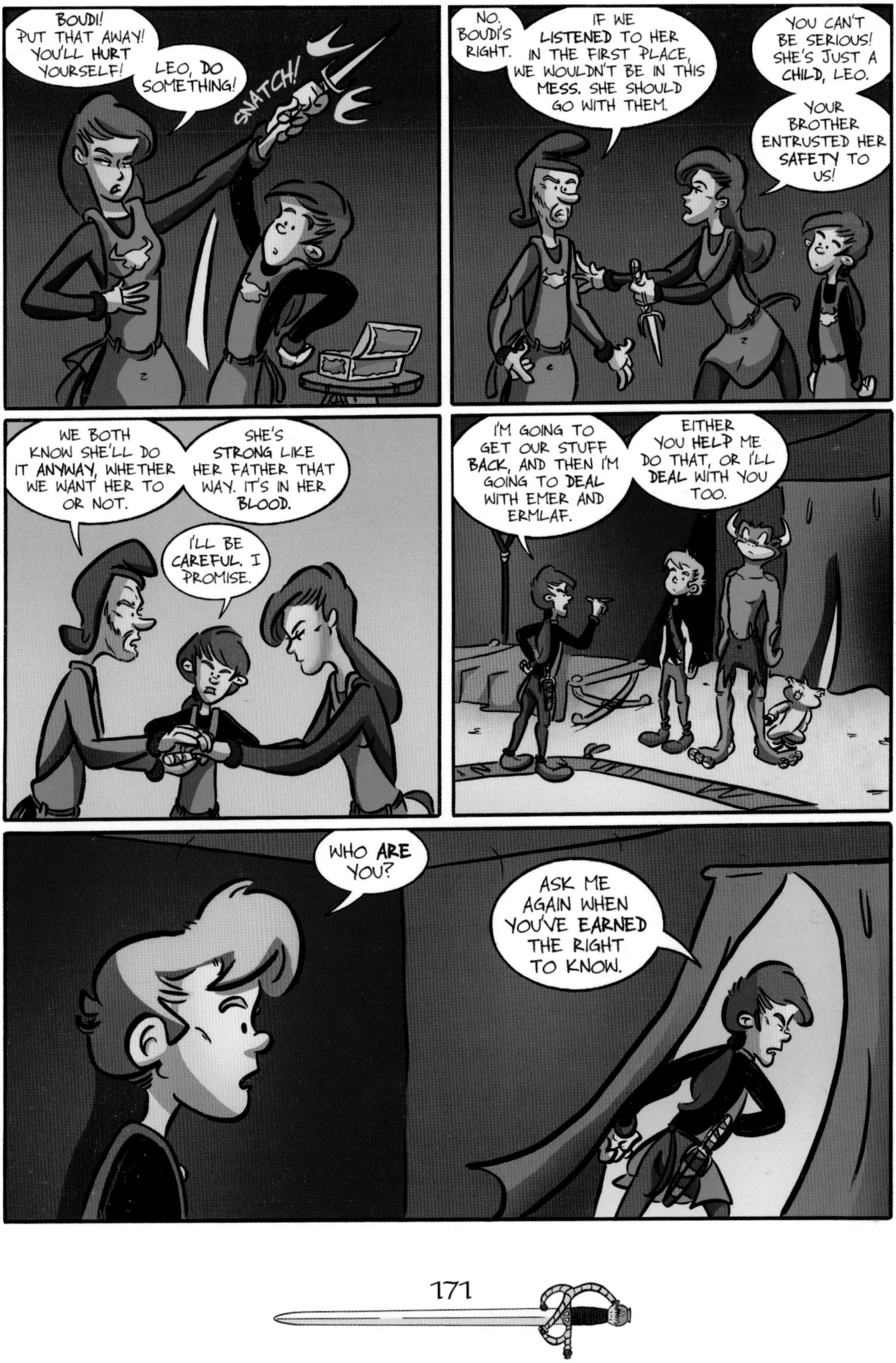
BOUDI! PUT THAT AWAY! YOU'LL HURT YOURSELF!
LEO, DO SOMETHING!
SNATCH!
NO. BOUDI'S RIGHT.
IF WE LISTENED TO HER IN THE FIRST PLACE, WE WOULDN'T BE IN THIS MESS. SHE SHOULD GO WITH THEM.
YOU CAN'T BE SERIOUS! SHE'S JUST A CHILD, LEO.
YOUR BROTHER ENTRUSTED HER SAFETY TO US!
WE BOTH KNOW SHE'LL DO IT ANYWAY, WHETHER WE WANT HER TO OR NOT.
SHE'S STRONG LIKE HER FATHER THAT WAY. IT'S IN HER BLOOD.
I'LL BE CAREFUL. I PROMISE.
I'M GOING TO GET OUR STUFF BACK, AND THEN I'M GOING TO DEAL WITH EMER AND ERMLAF.
EITHER YOU HELP ME DO THAT, OR I'LL DEAL WITH YOU TOO.
WHO ARE YOU?
ASK ME AGAIN WHEN YOU'VE EARNED THE RIGHT TO KNOW.

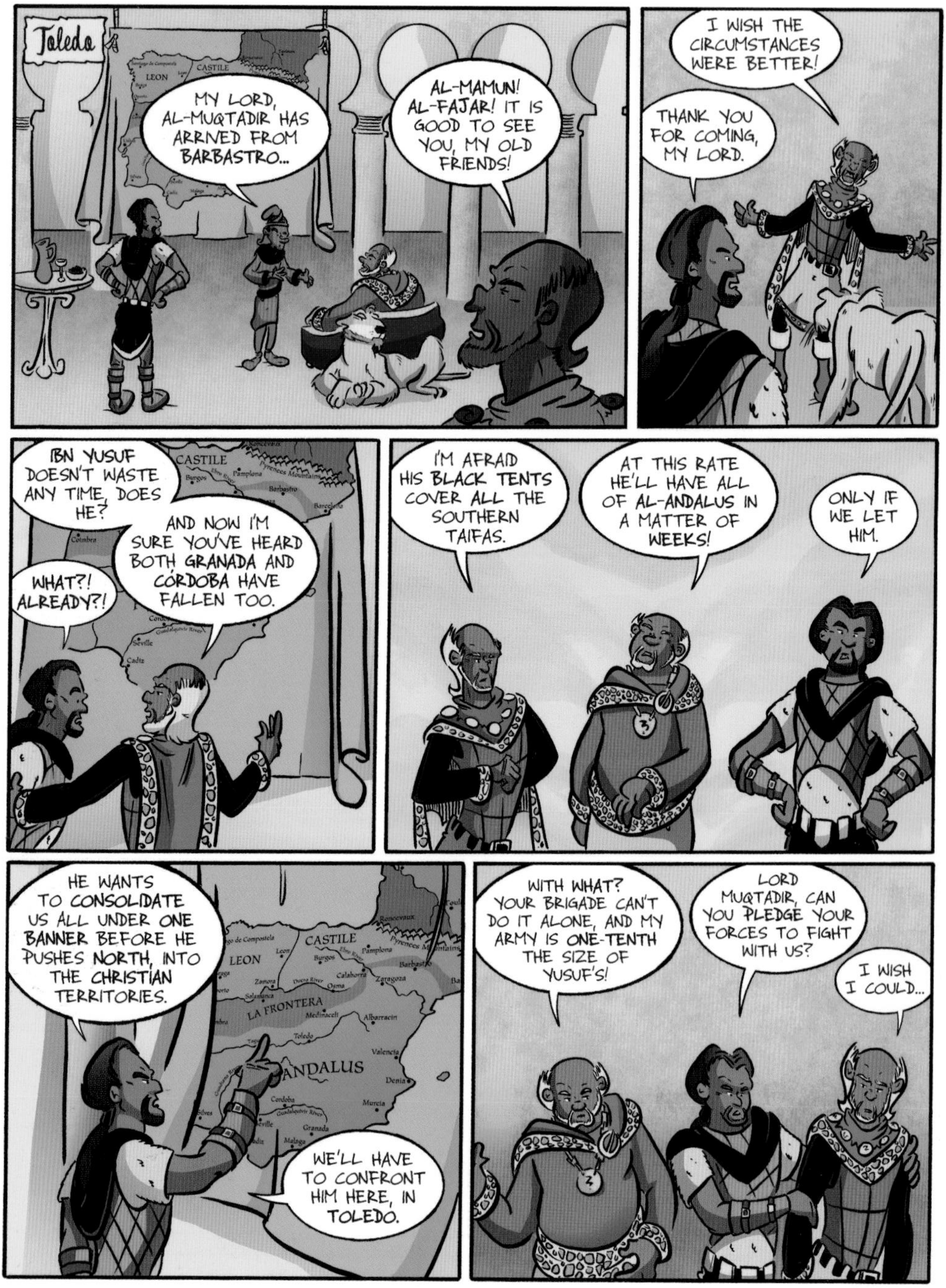
Toledo
MY LORD, AL-MUQTADIR HAS ARRIVED FROM BARBASTRO...
AL-MAMUN! AL-FAJAR! IT IS GOOD TO SEE YOU, MY OLD FRIENDS!
THANK YOU FOR COMING, MY LORD.
I WISH THE CIRCUMSTANCES WERE BETTER!
IBN YUSUF DOESN'T WASTE ANY TIME, DOES HE?
AND NOW I'M SURE YOU'VE HEARD BOTH GRANADA AND CÓRDOBA HAVE FALLEN TOO.
WHAT?! ALREADY?!
I'M AFRAID HIS BLACK TENTS COVER ALL THE SOUTHERN TAIFAS.
AT THIS RATE HE'LL HAVE ALL OF AL-ANDALUS IN A MATTER OF WEEKS!
ONLY IF WE LET HIM.
HE WANTS TO CONSOLIDATE US ALL UNDER ONE BANNER BEFORE HE PUSHES NORTH, INTO THE CHRISTIAN TERRITORIES.
WE'LL HAVE TO CONFRONT HIM HERE, IN TOLEDO.
WITH WHAT? YOUR BRIGADE CAN'T DO IT ALONE, AND MY ARMY IS ONE-TENTH THE SIZE OF YUSUF'S!
LORD MUQTADIR, CAN YOU PLEDGE YOUR FORCES TO FIGHT WITH US?
I WISH I COULD...

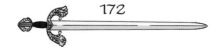

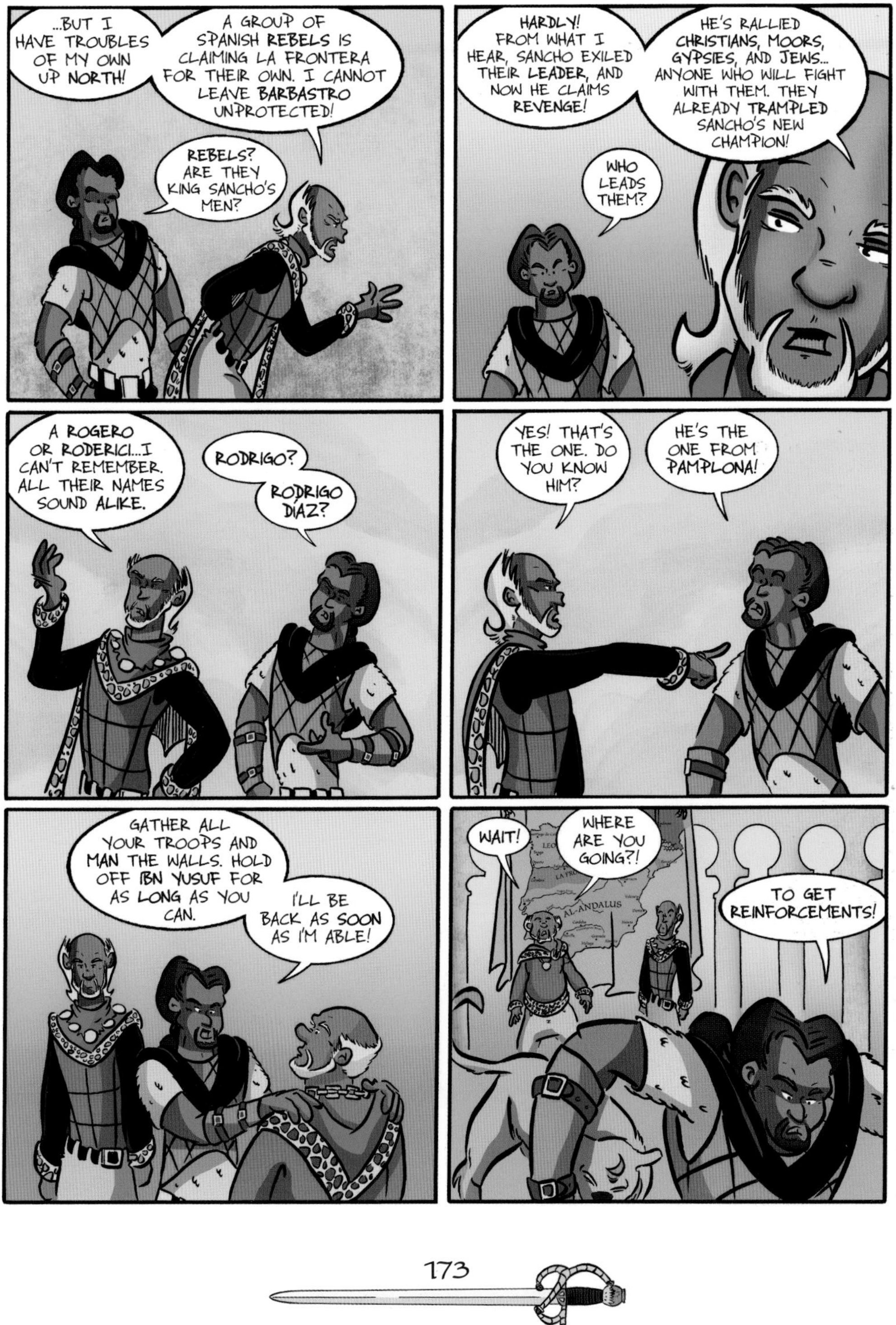
...BUT I HAVE TROUBLES OF MY OWN UP NORTH!
A GROUP OF SPANISH REBELS IS CLAIMING LA FRONTERA FOR THEIR OWN. I CANNOT LEAVE BARBASTRO UNPROTECTED!
REBELS? ARE THEY KING SANCHO'S MEN?
HARDLY! FROM WHAT I HEAR, SANCHO EXILED THEIR LEADER, AND NOW HE CLAIMS REVENGE!
HE'S RALLIED CHRISTIANS, MOORS, GYPSIES, AND JEWS... ANYONE WHO WILL FIGHT WITH THEM. THEY ALREADY TRAMPLED SANCHO'S NEW CHAMPION!
WHO LEADS THEM?
A ROGERO OR RODERICI...I CAN'T REMEMBER. ALL THEIR NAMES SOUND ALIKE.
RODRIGO?
RODRIGO DIAZ?
YES! THAT'S THE ONE. DO YOU KNOW HIM?
HE'S THE ONE FROM PAMPLONA!
GATHER ALL YOUR TROOPS AND MAN THE WALLS. HOLD OFF IBN YUSUF FOR AS LONG AS YOU CAN.
I'LL BE BACK AS SOON AS I'M ABLE!
WAIT!
WHERE ARE YOU GOING?!
AL-ANDALUS
TO GET REINFORCEMENTS!

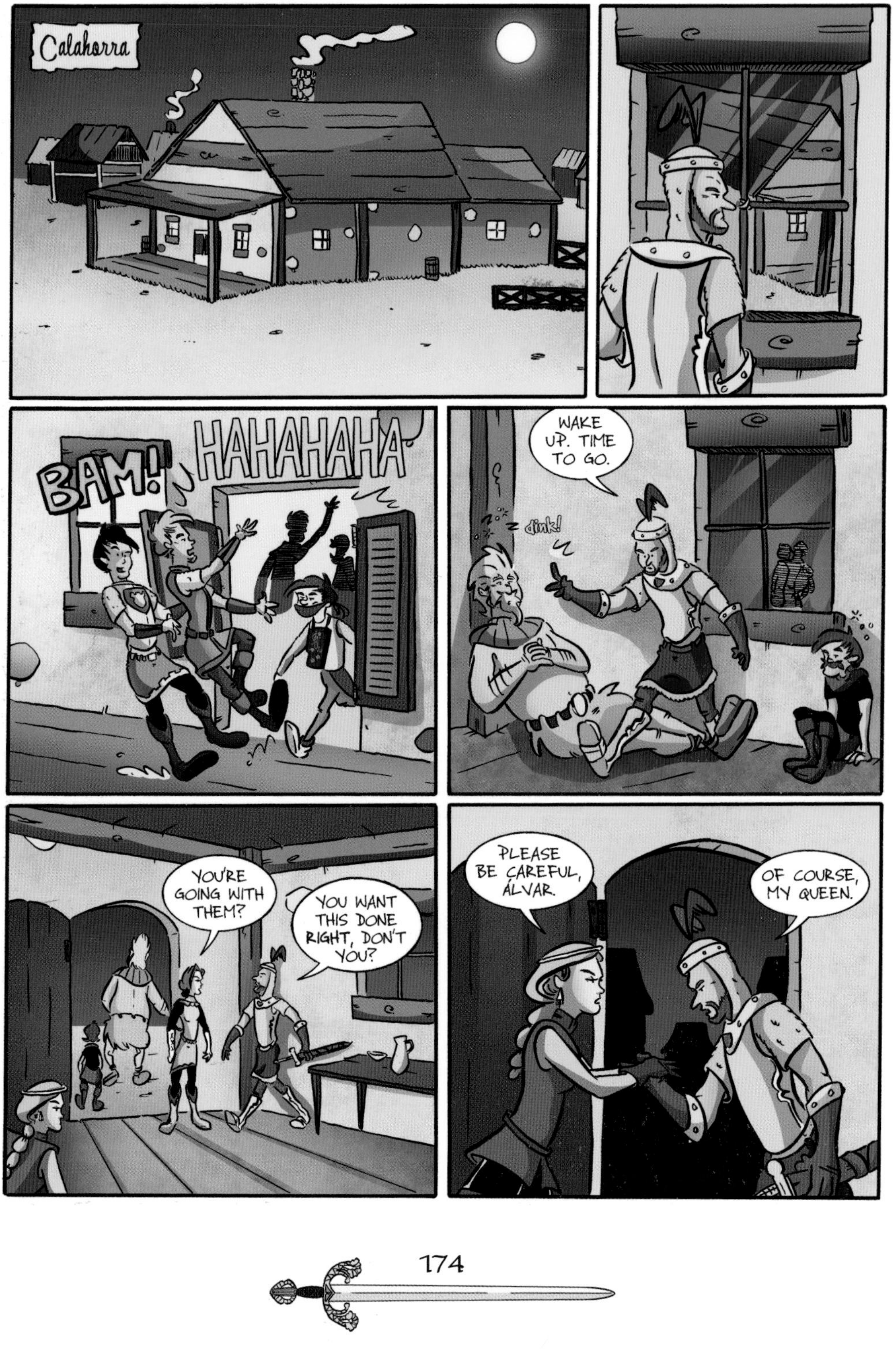
Calahorra
BAM!
HAHAHAHA
WAKE UP. TIME TO GO.
dink!
YOU'RE GOING WITH THEM?
YOU WANT THIS DONE RIGHT, DON'T YOU?
PLEASE BE CAREFUL, ÁLVAR.
OF COURSE, MY QUEEN.

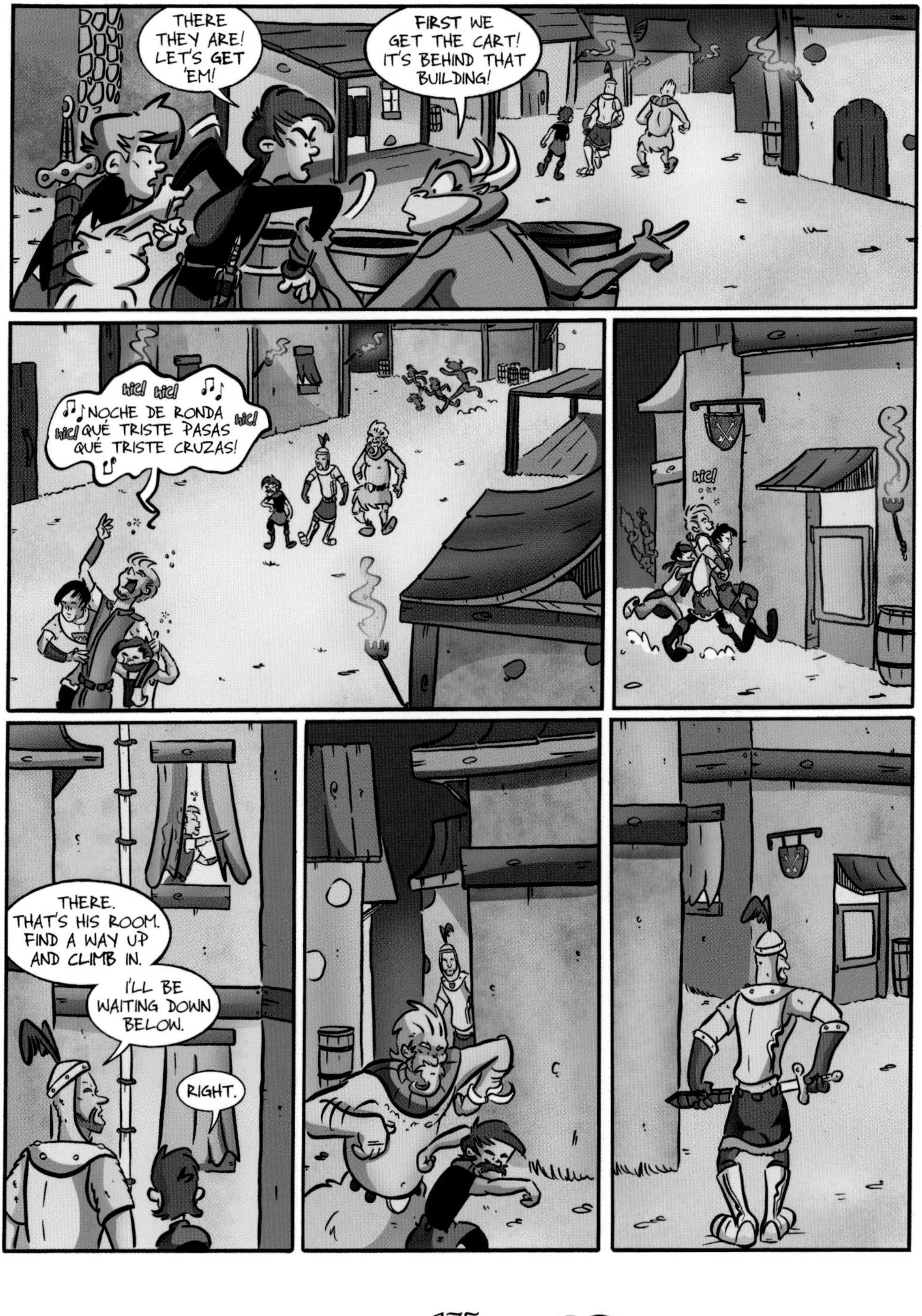
THERE THEY ARE! LET'S GET 'EM!
FIRST WE GET THE CART! IT'S BEHIND THAT BUILDING!
hic! hic!
NOCHE DE RONDA QUÉ TRISTE PASAS QUÉ TRISTE CRUZAS!
hic! hic!
hic!
THERE. THAT'S HIS ROOM. FIND A WAY UP AND CLIMB IN.
I'LL BE WAITING DOWN BELOW.
RIGHT.

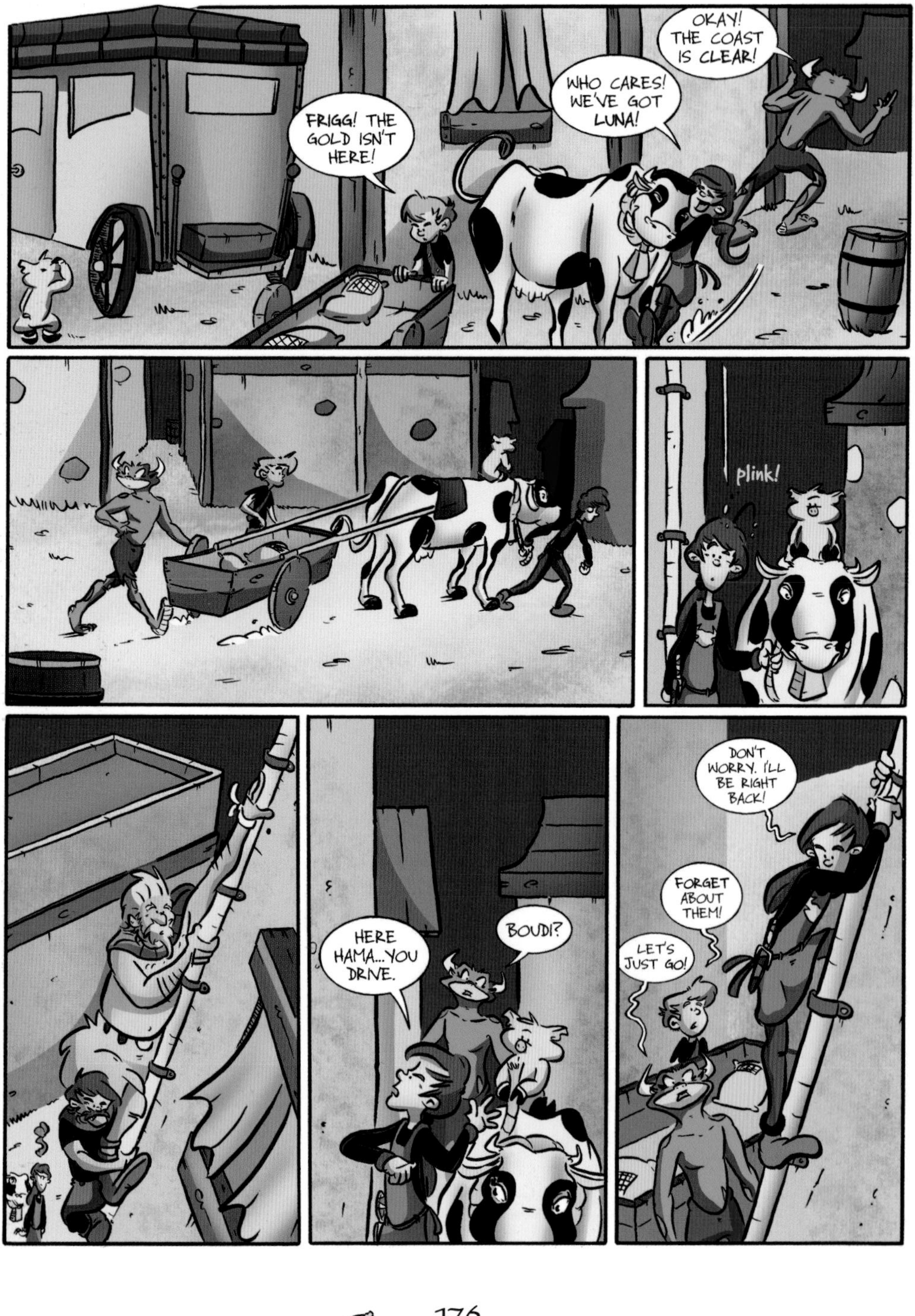
FRIGG! THE GOLD ISN'T HERE!
WHO CARES! WE'VE GOT LUNA!
OKAY! THE COAST IS CLEAR!
plink!
HERE HAMA...YOU DRIVE.
BOUDI?
DON'T WORRY. I'LL BE RIGHT BACK!
FORGET ABOUT THEM!
LET'S JUST GO!

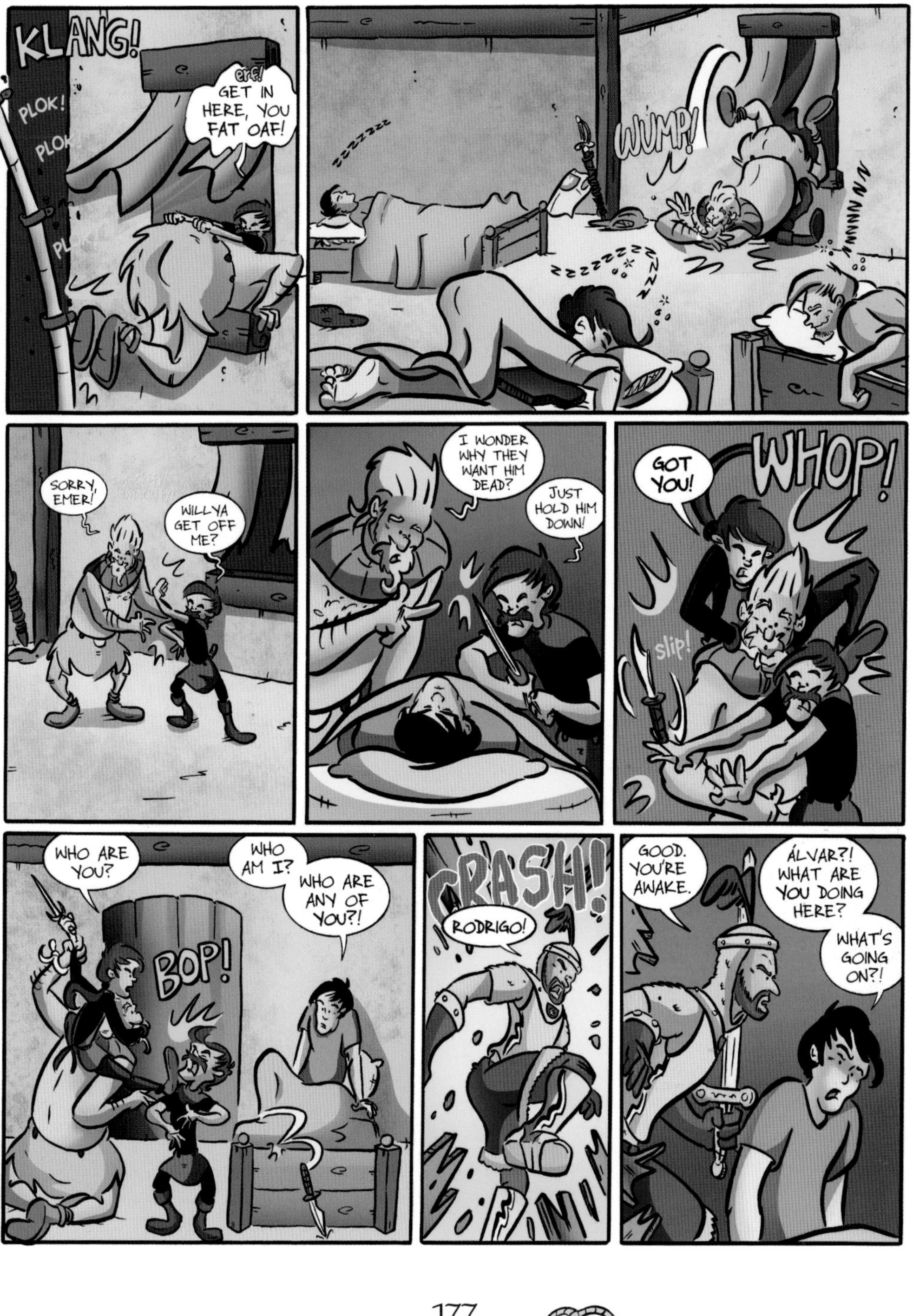
KLANG!
PLOK!
PLOK!
PLOK!
erf! GET IN HERE, YOU FAT OAF!
ZZZZZZZ
WUMP!
ZZZZZZZZ
NNNNNNN
SORRY, EMER!
WILLYA GET OFF ME?
I WONDER WHY THEY WANT HIM DEAD?
JUST HOLD HIM DOWN!
GOT YOU!
WHOP!
slip!
WHO ARE YOU?
WHO AM I?
WHO ARE ANY OF YOU?!
BOP!
CRASH!
RODRIGO!
GOOD. YOU'RE AWAKE.
ÁLVAR?! WHAT ARE YOU DOING HERE?
WHAT'S GOING ON?!

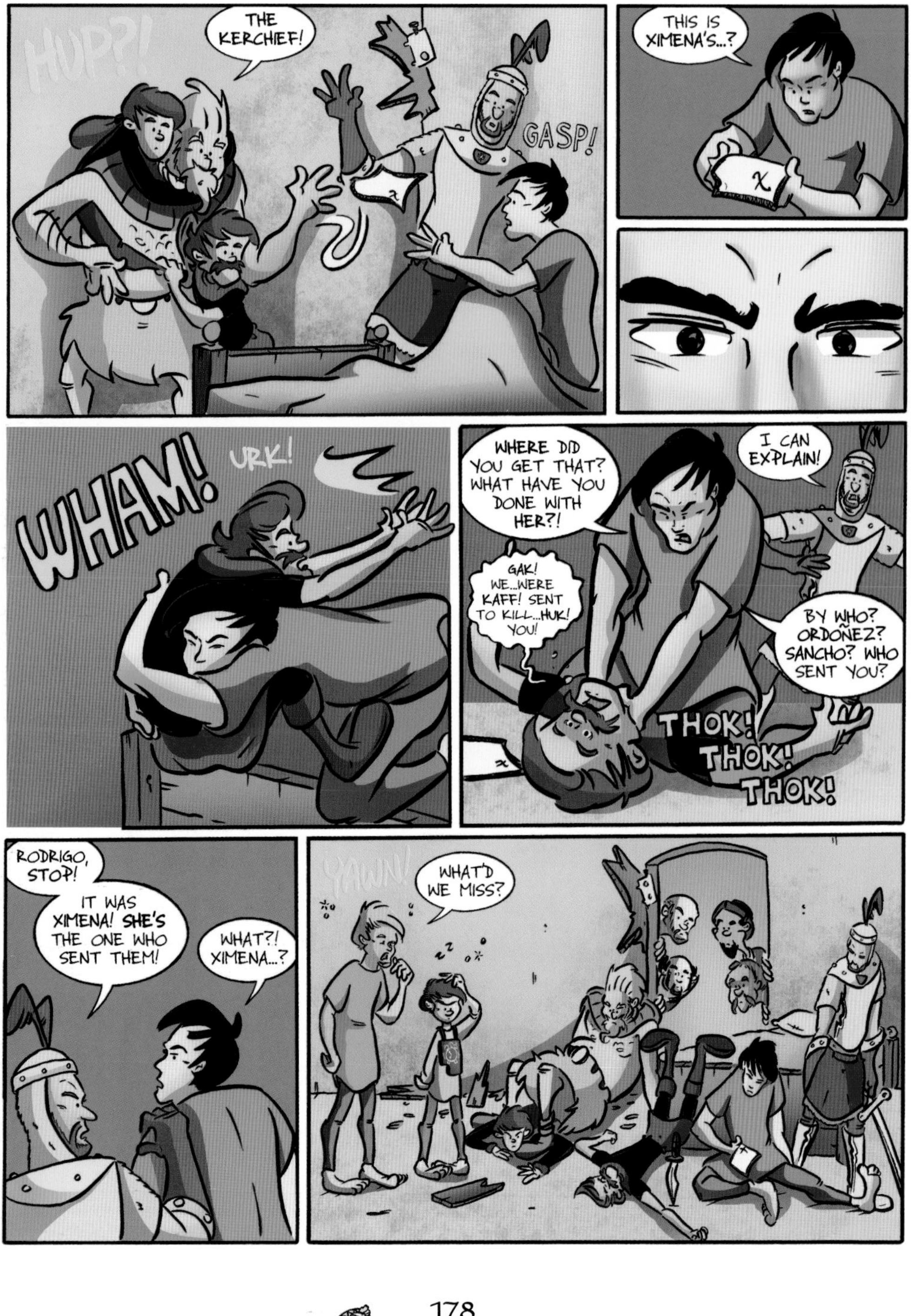
HUP?!
THE KERCHIEF!
GASP!
THIS IS XIMENA'S...?
WHAM!
URK!
WHERE DID YOU GET THAT? WHAT HAVE YOU DONE WITH HER?!
I CAN EXPLAIN!
GAK! WE...WERE KAFF! SENT TO KILL...HUK! YOU!
BY WHO? ORDOÑEZ? SANCHO? WHO SENT YOU?
THOK! THOK! THOK!
RODRIGO, STOP!
IT WAS XIMENA! SHE'S THE ONE WHO SENT THEM!
WHAT?! XIMENA...?
YAWN!
WHAT'D WE MISS?

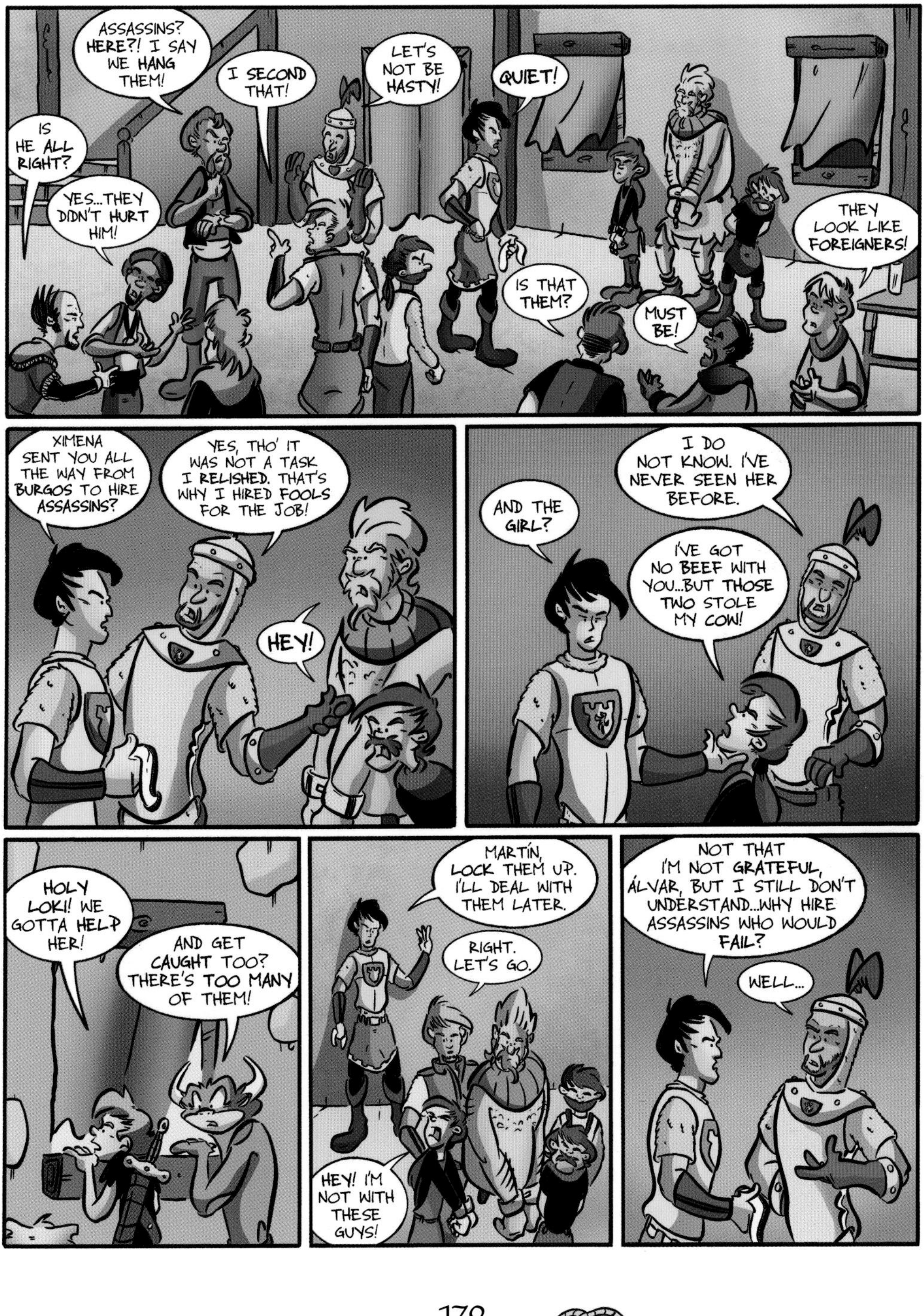
IS HE ALL RIGHT?
YES...THEY DIDN'T HURT HIM!
ASSASSINS? HERE?! I SAY WE HANG THEM!
I SECOND THAT!
LET'S NOT BE HASTY!
QUIET!
IS THAT THEM?
MUST BE!
THEY LOOK LIKE FOREIGNERS!
XIMENA SENT YOU ALL THE WAY FROM BURGOS TO HIRE ASSASSINS?
YES, THO' IT WAS NOT A TASK I RELISHED. THAT'S WHY I HIRED FOOLS FOR THE JOB!
HEY!
AND THE GIRL?
I DO NOT KNOW. I'VE NEVER SEEN HER BEFORE.
I'VE GOT NO BEEF WITH YOU...BUT THOSE TWO STOLE MY COW!
HOLY LOKI! WE GOTTA HELP HER!
AND GET CAUGHT TOO? THERE'S TOO MANY OF THEM!
MARTÍN, LOCK THEM UP. I'LL DEAL WITH THEM LATER.
RIGHT. LET'S GO.
HEY! I'M NOT WITH THESE GUYS!
NOT THAT I'M NOT GRATEFUL, ÁLVAR, BUT I STILL DON'T UNDERSTAND...WHY HIRE ASSASSINS WHO WOULD FAIL?
WELL...

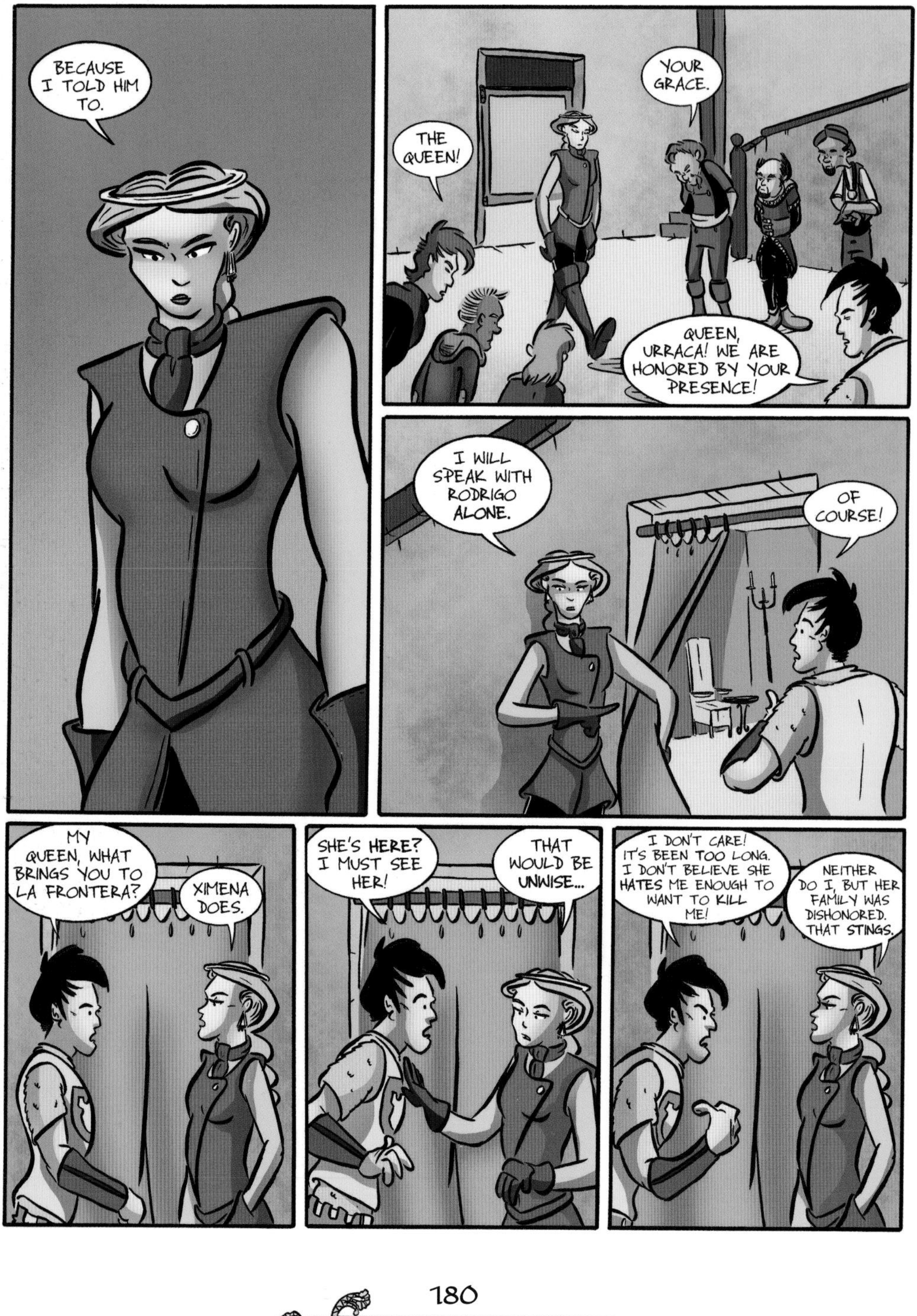
BECAUSE I TOLD HIM TO.
THE QUEEN!
YOUR GRACE.
QUEEN, URRACA! WE ARE HONORED BY YOUR PRESENCE!
I WILL SPEAK WITH RODRIGO ALONE.
OF COURSE!
MY QUEEN, WHAT BRINGS YOU TO LA FRONTERA?
XIMENA DOES.
SHE'S HERE? I MUST SEE HER!
THAT WOULD BE UNWISE...
I DON'T CARE! IT'S BEEN TOO LONG. I DON'T BELIEVE SHE HATES ME ENOUGH TO WANT TO KILL ME!
NEITHER DO I, BUT HER FAMILY WAS DISHONORED. THAT STINGS.

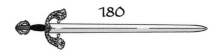

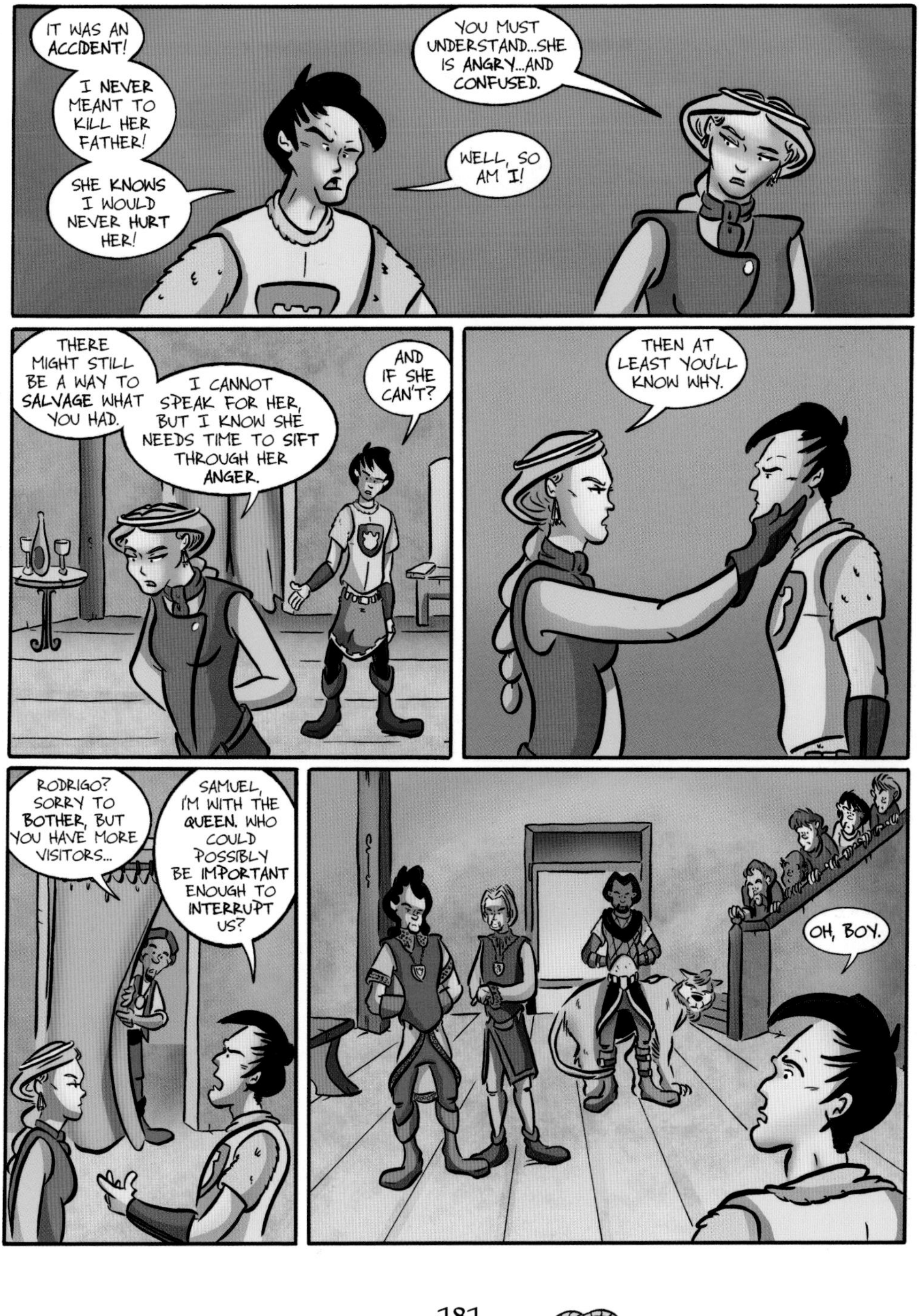
IT WAS AN ACCIDENT!
I NEVER MEANT TO KILL HER FATHER!
SHE KNOWS I WOULD NEVER HURT HER!
YOU MUST UNDERSTAND...SHE IS ANGRY...AND CONFUSED.
WELL, SO AM I!
THERE MIGHT STILL BE A WAY TO SALVAGE WHAT YOU HAD.
I CANNOT SPEAK FOR HER, BUT I KNOW SHE NEEDS TIME TO SIFT THROUGH HER ANGER.
AND IF SHE CAN'T?
THEN AT LEAST YOU'LL KNOW WHY.
RODRIGO? SORRY TO BOTHER, BUT YOU HAVE MORE VISITORS...
SAMUEL, I'M WITH THE QUEEN. WHO COULD POSSIBLY BE IMPORTANT ENOUGH TO INTERRUPT US?
OH, BOY.

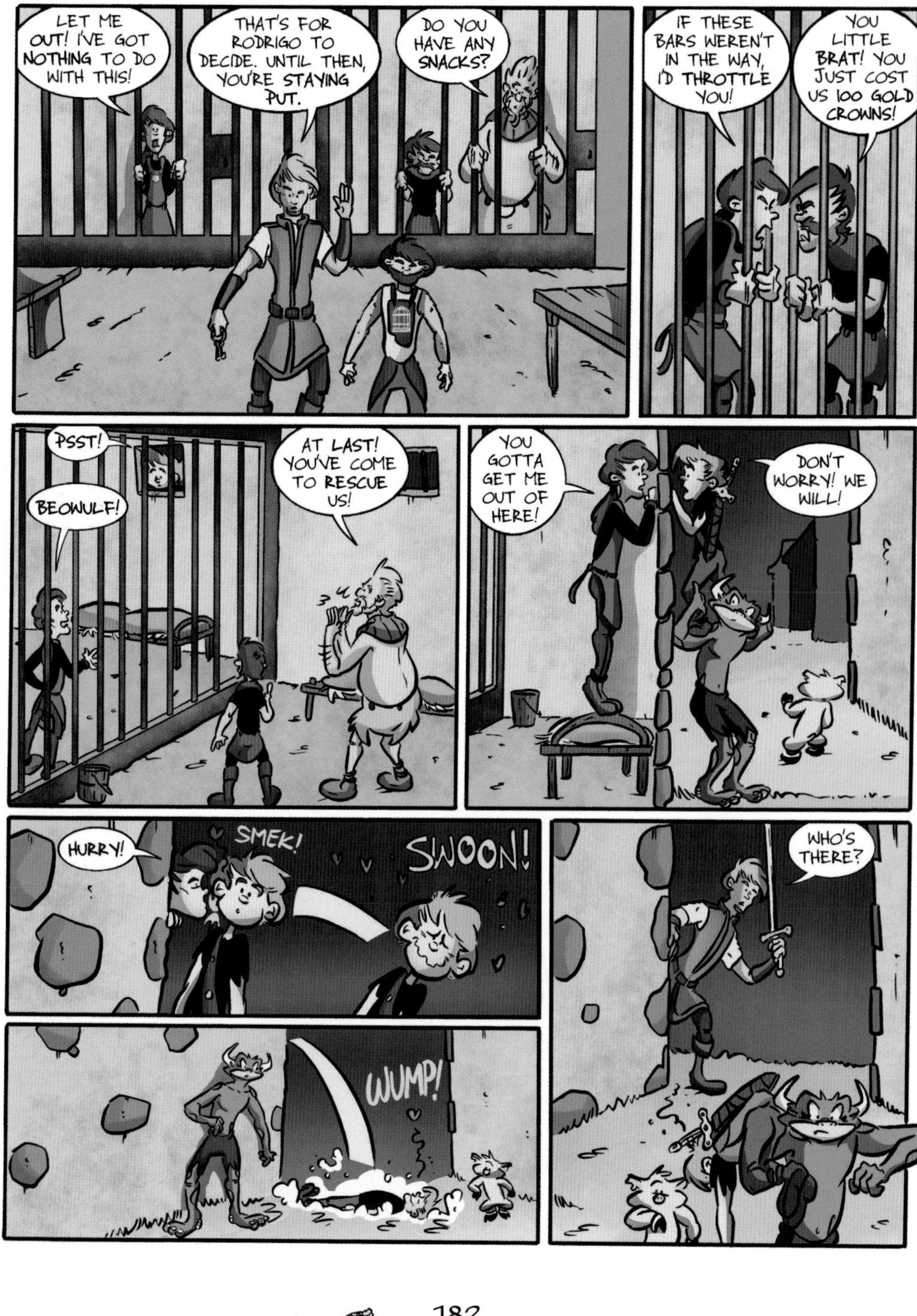
LET ME OUT! I'VE GOT NOTHING TO DO WITH THIS!
THAT'S FOR RODRIGO TO DECIDE. UNTIL THEN, YOU'RE STAYING PUT.
DO YOU HAVE ANY SNACKS?
IF THESE BARS WEREN'T IN THE WAY, I'D THROTTLE YOU!
YOU LITTLE BRAT! YOU JUST COST US 100 GOLD CROWNS!
PSST!
BEOWULF!
AT LAST! YOU'VE COME TO RESCUE US!
YOU GOTTA GET ME OUT OF HERE!
DON'T WORRY! WE WILL!
HURRY!
SMEK!
SWOON!
WHO'S THERE?
WUMP!

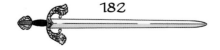

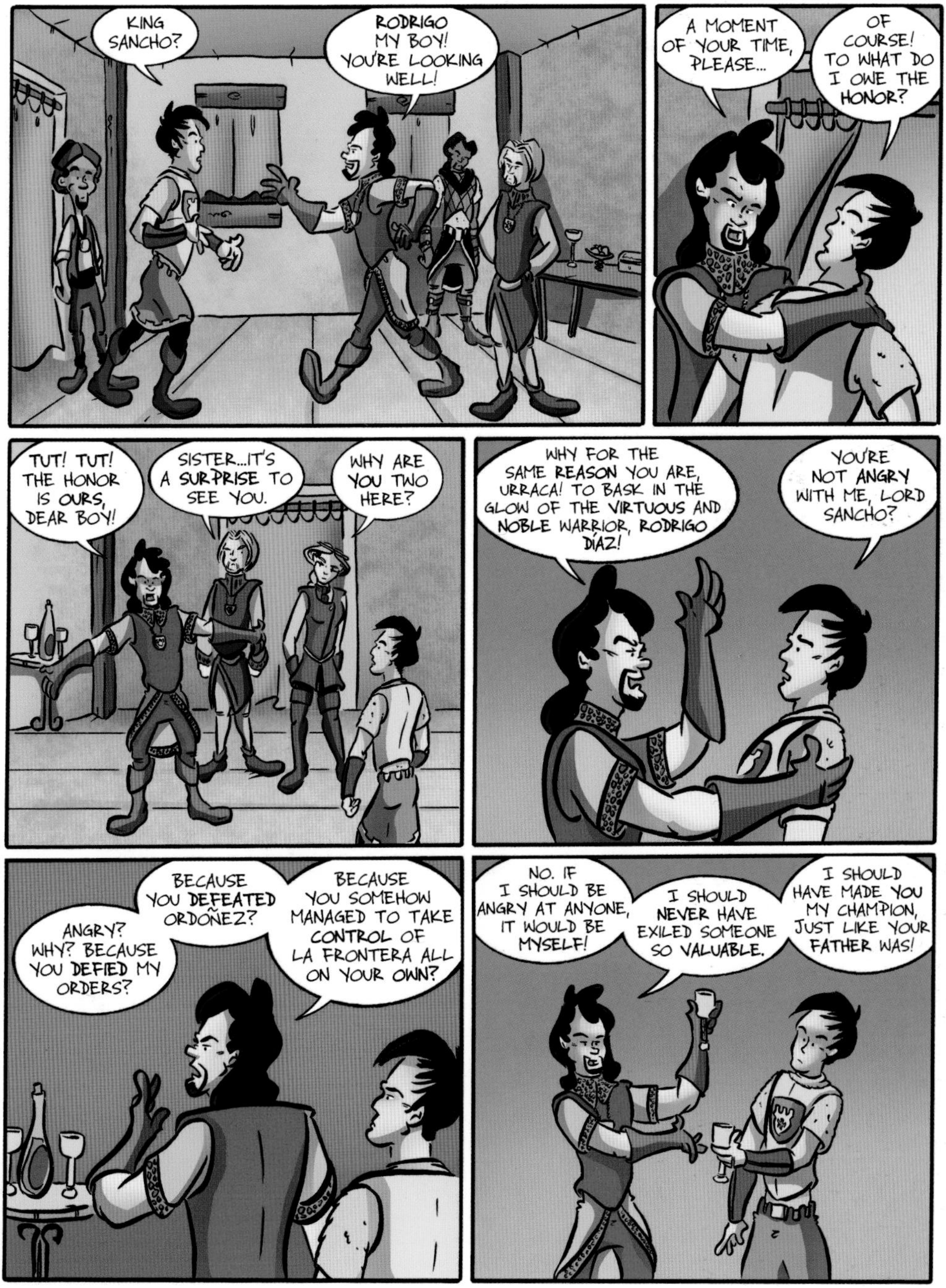
KING SANCHO?
RODRIGO MY BOY! YOU'RE LOOKING WELL!
A MOMENT OF YOUR TIME, PLEASE...
OF COURSE! TO WHAT DO I OWE THE HONOR?
TUT! TUT! THE HONOR IS OURS, DEAR BOY!
SISTER...IT'S A SURPRISE TO SEE YOU.
WHY ARE YOU TWO HERE?
WHY FOR THE SAME REASON YOU ARE, URRACA! TO BASK IN THE GLOW OF THE VIRTUOUS AND NOBLE WARRIOR, RODRIGO DÍAZ!
YOU'RE NOT ANGRY WITH ME, LORD SANCHO?
ANGRY? WHY? BECAUSE YOU DEFIED MY ORDERS?
BECAUSE YOU DEFEATED ORDOÑEZ?
BECAUSE YOU SOMEHOW MANAGED TO TAKE CONTROL OF LA FRONTERA ALL ON YOUR OWN?
NO. IF I SHOULD BE ANGRY AT ANYONE, IT WOULD BE MYSELF!
I SHOULD NEVER HAVE EXILED SOMEONE SO VALUABLE.
I SHOULD HAVE MADE YOU MY CHAMPION, JUST LIKE YOUR FATHER WAS!

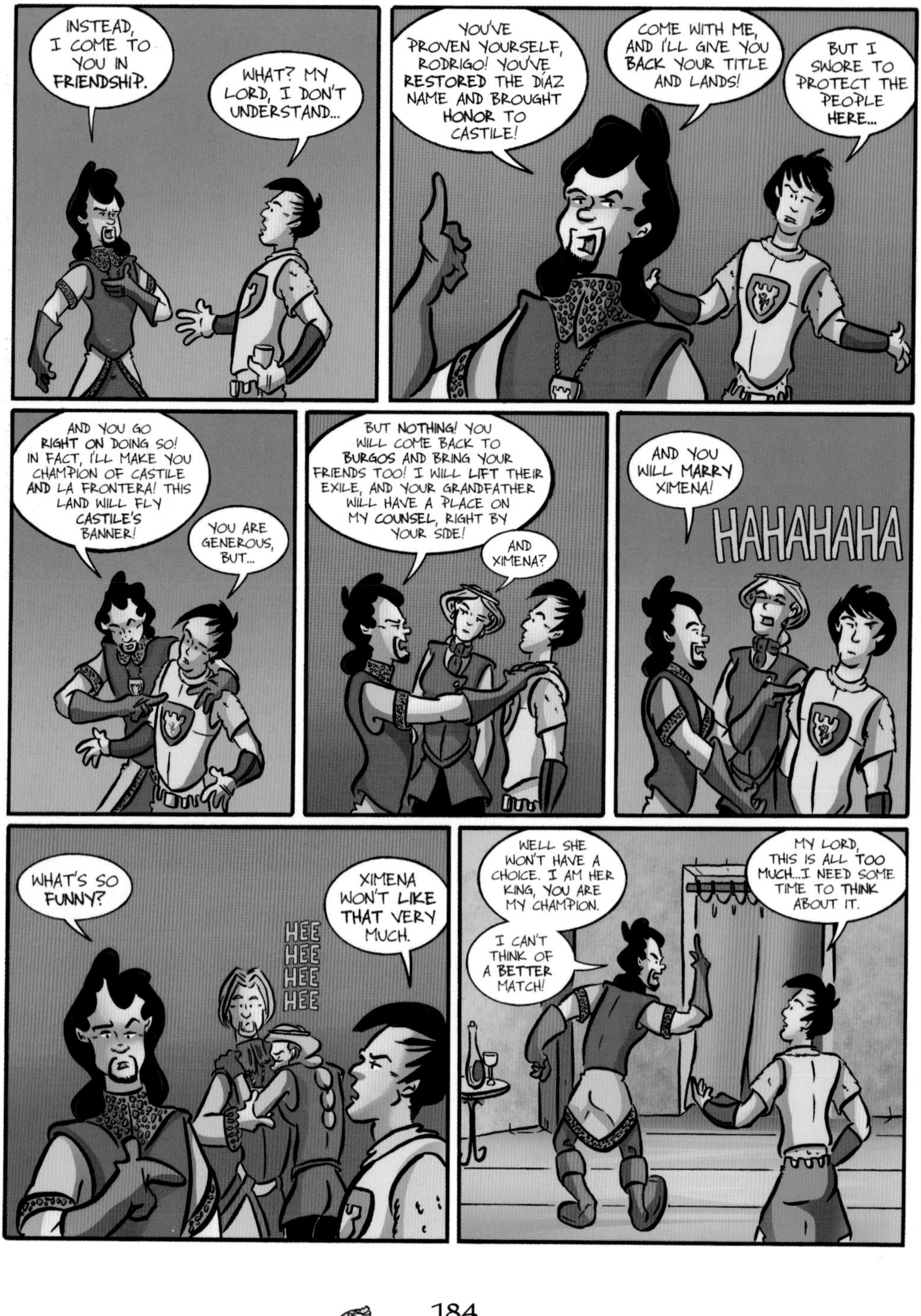

INSTEAD, I COME TO YOU IN FRIENDSHIP.
WHAT? MY LORD, I DON'T UNDERSTAND...
YOU'VE PROVEN YOURSELF, RODRIGO! YOU'VE RESTORED THE DÍAZ NAME AND BROUGHT HONOR TO CASTILE!
COME WITH ME, AND I'LL GIVE YOU BACK YOUR TITLE AND LANDS!
BUT I SWORE TO PROTECT THE PEOPLE HERE...
AND YOU GO RIGHT ON DOING SO! IN FACT, I'LL MAKE YOU CHAMPION OF CASTILE AND LA FRONTERA! THIS LAND WILL FLY CASTILE'S BANNER!
YOU ARE GENEROUS, BUT...
BUT NOTHING! YOU WILL COME BACK TO BURGOS AND BRING YOUR FRIENDS TOO! I WILL LIFT THEIR EXILE, AND YOUR GRANDFATHER WILL HAVE A PLACE ON MY COUNSEL, RIGHT BY YOUR SIDE!
AND XIMENA?
AND YOU WILL MARRY XIMENA!
HAHAHAHA
WHAT'S SO FUNNY?
HEE HEE HEE HEE
XIMENA WON'T LIKE THAT VERY MUCH.
WELL SHE WON'T HAVE A CHOICE. I AM HER KING, YOU ARE MY CHAMPION.
I CAN'T THINK OF A BETTER MATCH!
MY LORD, THIS IS ALL TOO MUCH...I NEED SOME TIME TO THINK ABOUT IT.

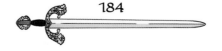

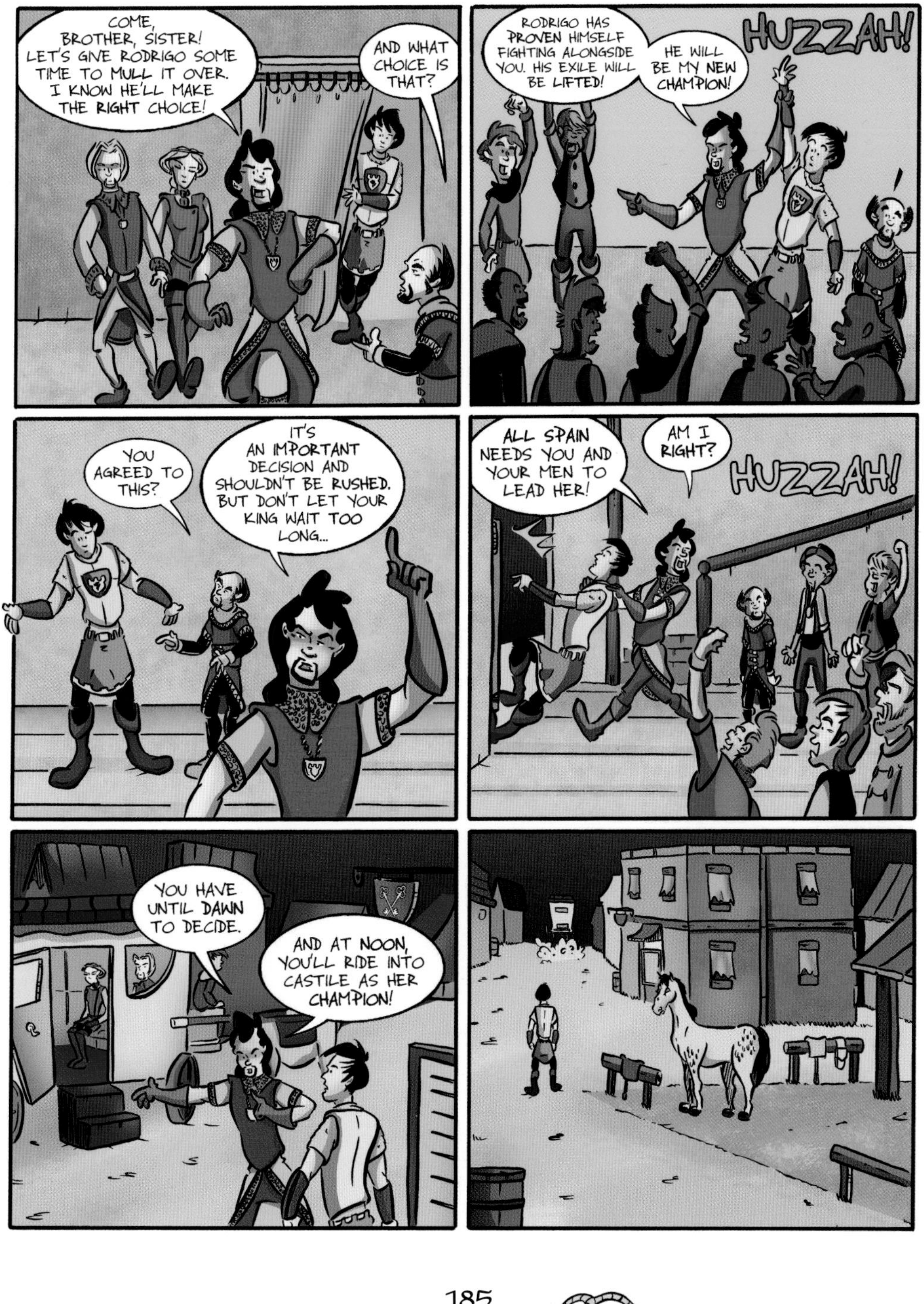
COME, BROTHER, SISTER! LET'S GIVE RODRIGO SOME TIME TO MULL IT OVER. I KNOW HE'LL MAKE THE RIGHT CHOICE!
AND WHAT CHOICE IS THAT?
RODRIGO HAS PROVEN HIMSELF FIGHTING ALONGSIDE YOU. HIS EXILE WILL BE LIFTED!
HE WILL BE MY NEW CHAMPION!
HUZZAH!
YOU AGREED TO THIS?
IT'S AN IMPORTANT DECISION AND SHOULDN'T BE RUSHED. BUT DON'T LET YOUR KING WAIT TOO LONG...
ALL SPAIN NEEDS YOU AND YOUR MEN TO LEAD HER!
AM I RIGHT?
HUZZAH!
YOU HAVE UNTIL DAWN TO DECIDE.
AND AT NOON, YOU'LL RIDE INTO CASTILE AS HER CHAMPION!

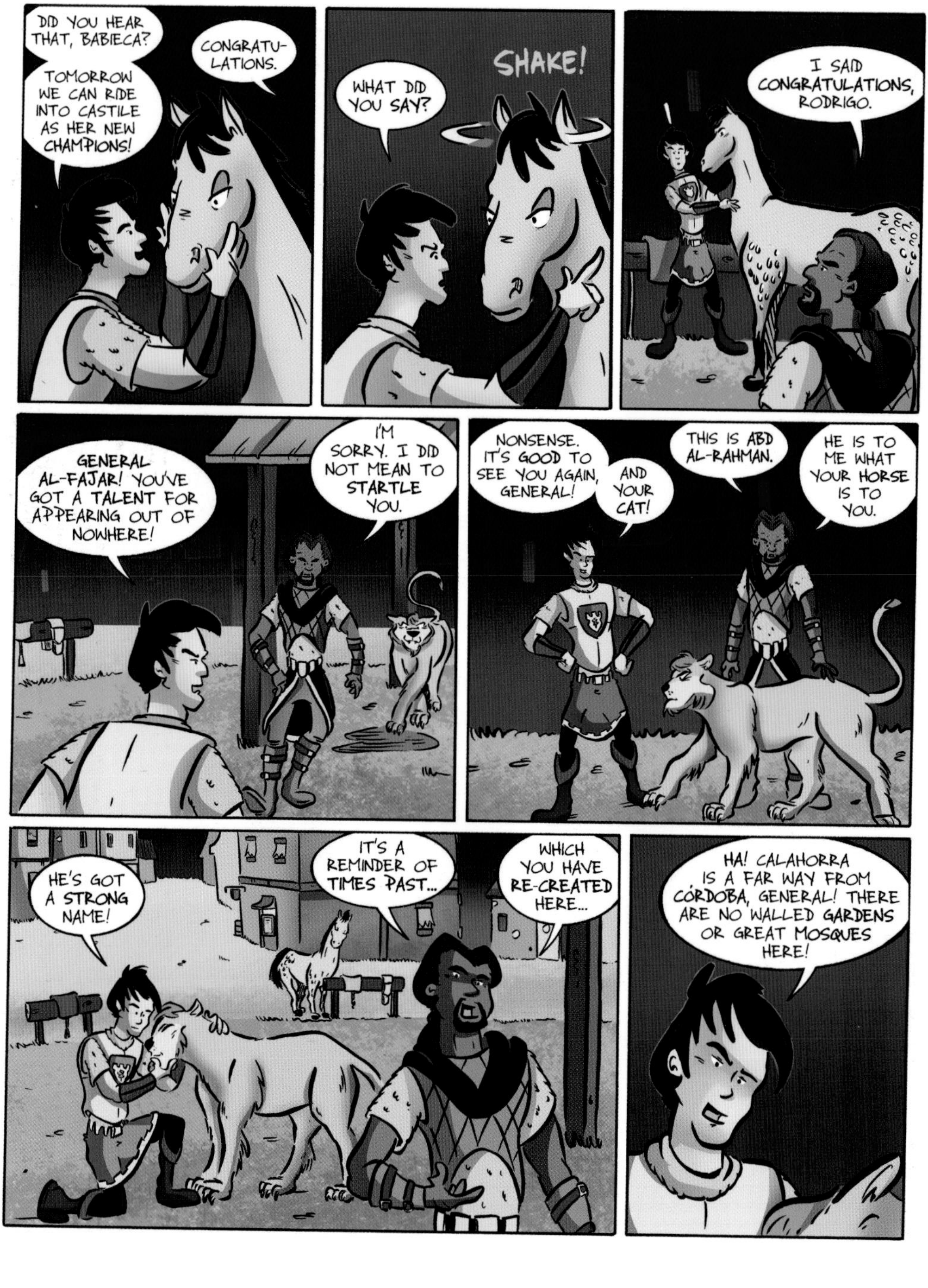
DID YOU HEAR THAT, BABIECA?
TOMORROW WE CAN RIDE INTO CASTILE AS HER NEW CHAMPIONS!
CONGRATU-LATIONS.
WHAT DID YOU SAY?
SHAKE!
I SAID CONGRATULATIONS, RODRIGO.
GENERAL AL-FAJAR! YOU'VE GOT A TALENT FOR APPEARING OUT OF NOWHERE!
I'M SORRY. I DID NOT MEAN TO STARTLE YOU.
NONSENSE. IT'S GOOD TO SEE YOU AGAIN, GENERAL!
AND YOUR CAT!
THIS IS ABD AL-RAHMAN.
HE IS TO ME WHAT YOUR HORSE IS TO YOU.
HE'S GOT A STRONG NAME!
IT'S A REMINDER OF TIMES PAST...
WHICH YOU HAVE RE-CREATED HERE...
HA! CALAHORRA IS A FAR WAY FROM CÓRDOBA, GENERAL! THERE ARE NO WALLED GARDENS OR GREAT MOSQUES HERE!

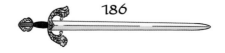

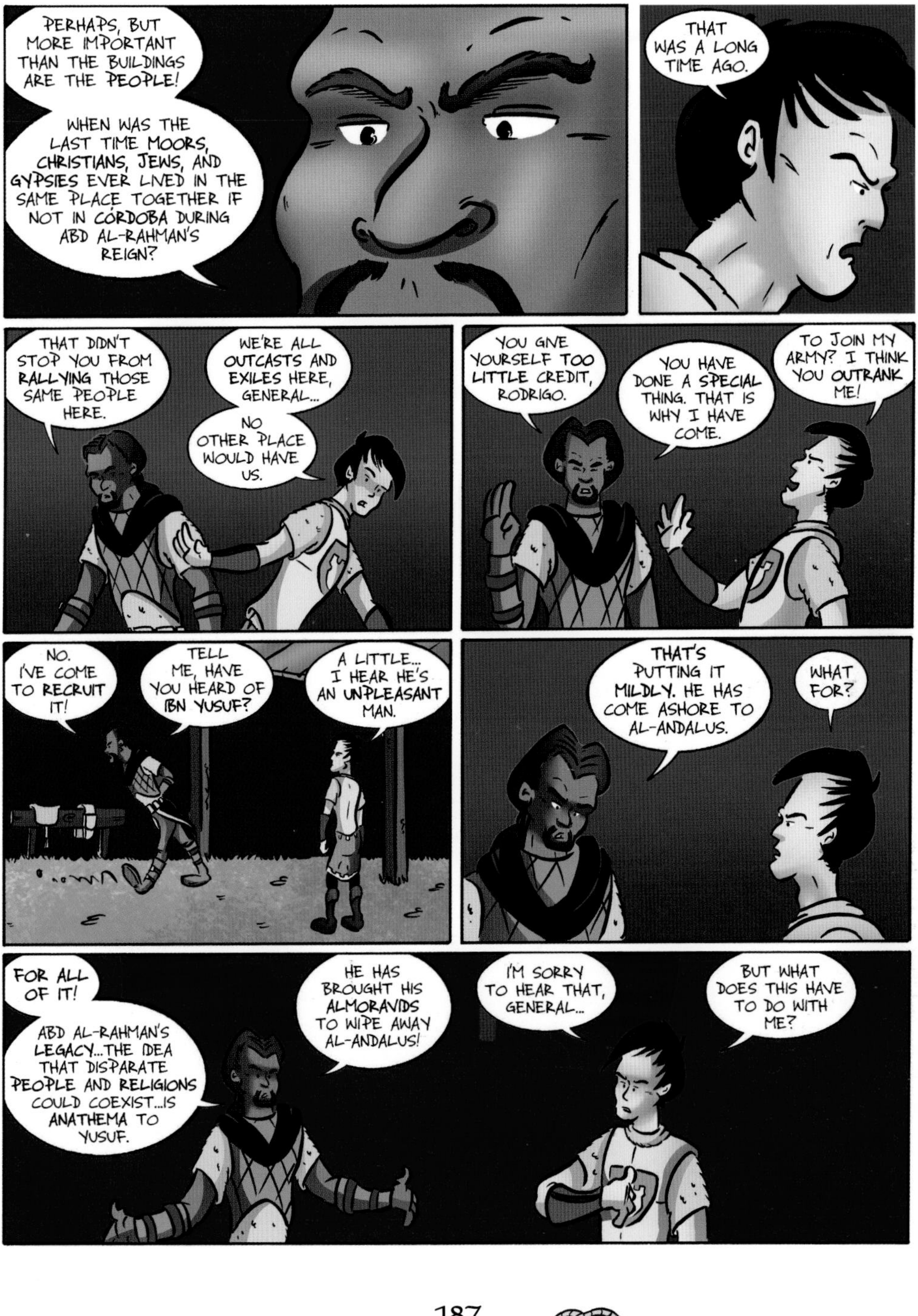
PERHAPS, BUT MORE IMPORTANT THAN THE BUILDINGS ARE THE PEOPLE!
WHEN WAS THE LAST TIME MOORS, CHRISTIANS, JEWS, AND GYPSIES EVER LIVED IN THE SAME PLACE TOGETHER IF NOT IN CÓRDOBA DURING ABD AL-RAHMAN'S REIGN?
THAT WAS A LONG TIME AGO.
THAT DIDN'T STOP YOU FROM RALLYING THOSE SAME PEOPLE HERE.
WE'RE ALL OUTCASTS AND EXILES HERE, GENERAL...
NO OTHER PLACE WOULD HAVE US.
YOU GIVE YOURSELF TOO LITTLE CREDIT, RODRIGO.
YOU HAVE DONE A SPECIAL THING. THAT IS WHY I HAVE COME.
TO JOIN MY ARMY? I THINK YOU OUTRANK ME!
NO. I'VE COME TO RECRUIT IT!
TELL ME, HAVE YOU HEARD OF IBN YUSUF?
A LITTLE... I HEAR HE'S AN UNPLEASANT MAN.
THAT'S PUTTING IT MILDLY. HE HAS COME ASHORE TO AL-ANDALUS.
WHAT FOR?
FOR ALL OF IT!
ABD AL-RAHMAN'S LEGACY...THE IDEA THAT DISPARATE PEOPLE AND RELIGIONS COULD COEXIST...IS ANATHEMA TO YUSUF.
HE HAS BROUGHT HIS ALMORAVIDS TO WIPE AWAY AL-ANDALUS!
I'M SORRY TO HEAR THAT, GENERAL...
BUT WHAT DOES THIS HAVE TO DO WITH ME?

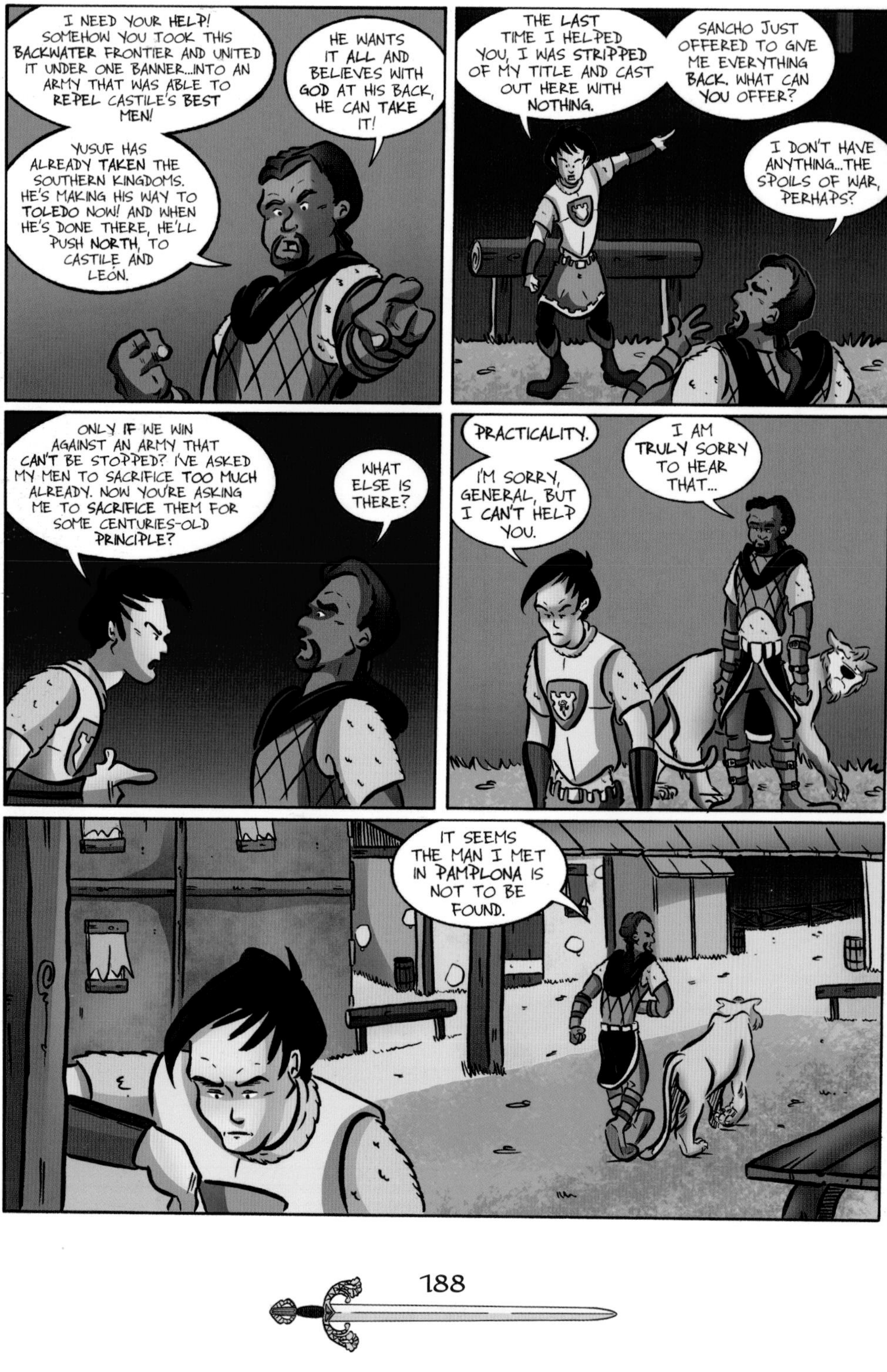
I NEED YOUR HELP! SOMEHOW YOU TOOK THIS BACKWATER FRONTIER AND UNITED IT UNDER ONE BANNER...INTO AN ARMY THAT WAS ABLE TO REPEL CASTILE'S BEST MEN!
YUSUF HAS ALREADY TAKEN THE SOUTHERN KINGDOMS. HE'S MAKING HIS WAY TO TOLEDO NOW! AND WHEN HE'S DONE THERE, HE'LL PUSH NORTH, TO CASTILE AND LEÓN.
HE WANTS IT ALL AND BELIEVES WITH GOD AT HIS BACK, HE CAN TAKE IT!
THE LAST TIME I HELPED YOU, I WAS STRIPPED OF MY TITLE AND CAST OUT HERE WITH NOTHING.
SANCHO JUST OFFERED TO GIVE ME EVERYTHING BACK. WHAT CAN YOU OFFER?
I DON'T HAVE ANYTHING...THE SPOILS OF WAR, PERHAPS?
ONLY IF WE WIN AGAINST AN ARMY THAT CAN'T BE STOPPED? I'VE ASKED MY MEN TO SACRIFICE TOO MUCH ALREADY. NOW YOU'RE ASKING ME TO SACRIFICE THEM FOR SOME CENTURIES-OLD PRINCIPLE?
WHAT ELSE IS THERE?
PRACTICALITY.
I'M SORRY, GENERAL, BUT I CAN'T HELP YOU.
I AM TRULY SORRY TO HEAR THAT...
IT SEEMS THE MAN I MET IN PAMPLONA IS NOT TO BE FOUND.

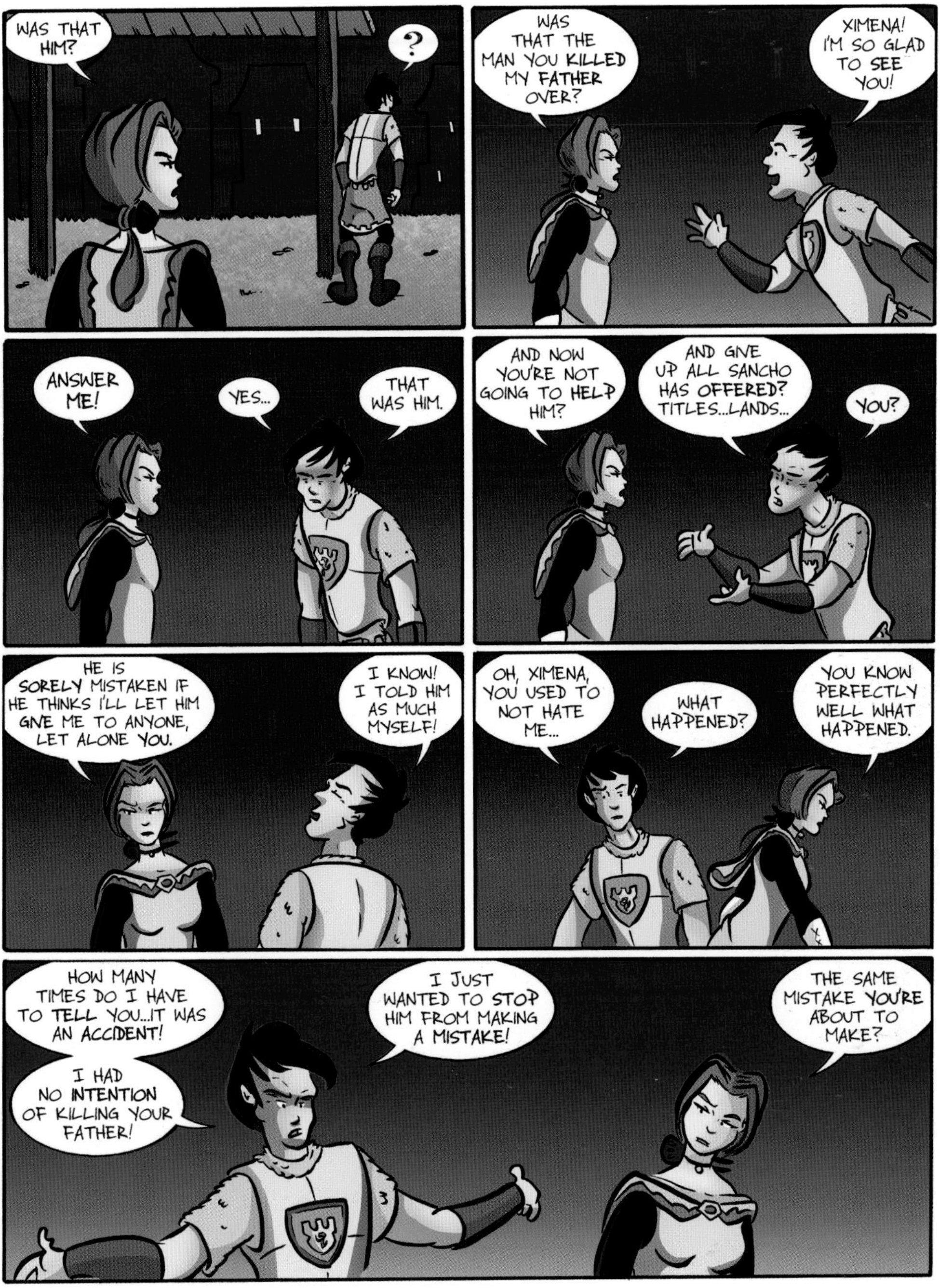
WAS THAT HIM?
?
WAS THAT THE MAN YOU KILLED MY FATHER OVER?
XIMENA! I'M SO GLAD TO SEE YOU!
ANSWER ME!
YES...
THAT WAS HIM.
AND NOW YOU'RE NOT GOING TO HELP HIM?
AND GIVE UP ALL SANCHO HAS OFFERED? TITLES...LANDS...
YOU?
HE IS SORELY MISTAKEN IF HE THINKS I'LL LET HIM GIVE ME TO ANYONE, LET ALONE YOU.
I KNOW! I TOLD HIM AS MUCH MYSELF!
OH, XIMENA, YOU USED TO NOT HATE ME...
WHAT HAPPENED?
YOU KNOW PERFECTLY WELL WHAT HAPPENED.
HOW MANY TIMES DO I HAVE TO TELL YOU...IT WAS AN ACCIDENT!
I HAD NO INTENTION OF KILLING YOUR FATHER!
I JUST WANTED TO STOP HIM FROM MAKING A MISTAKE!
THE SAME MISTAKE YOU'RE ABOUT TO MAKE?

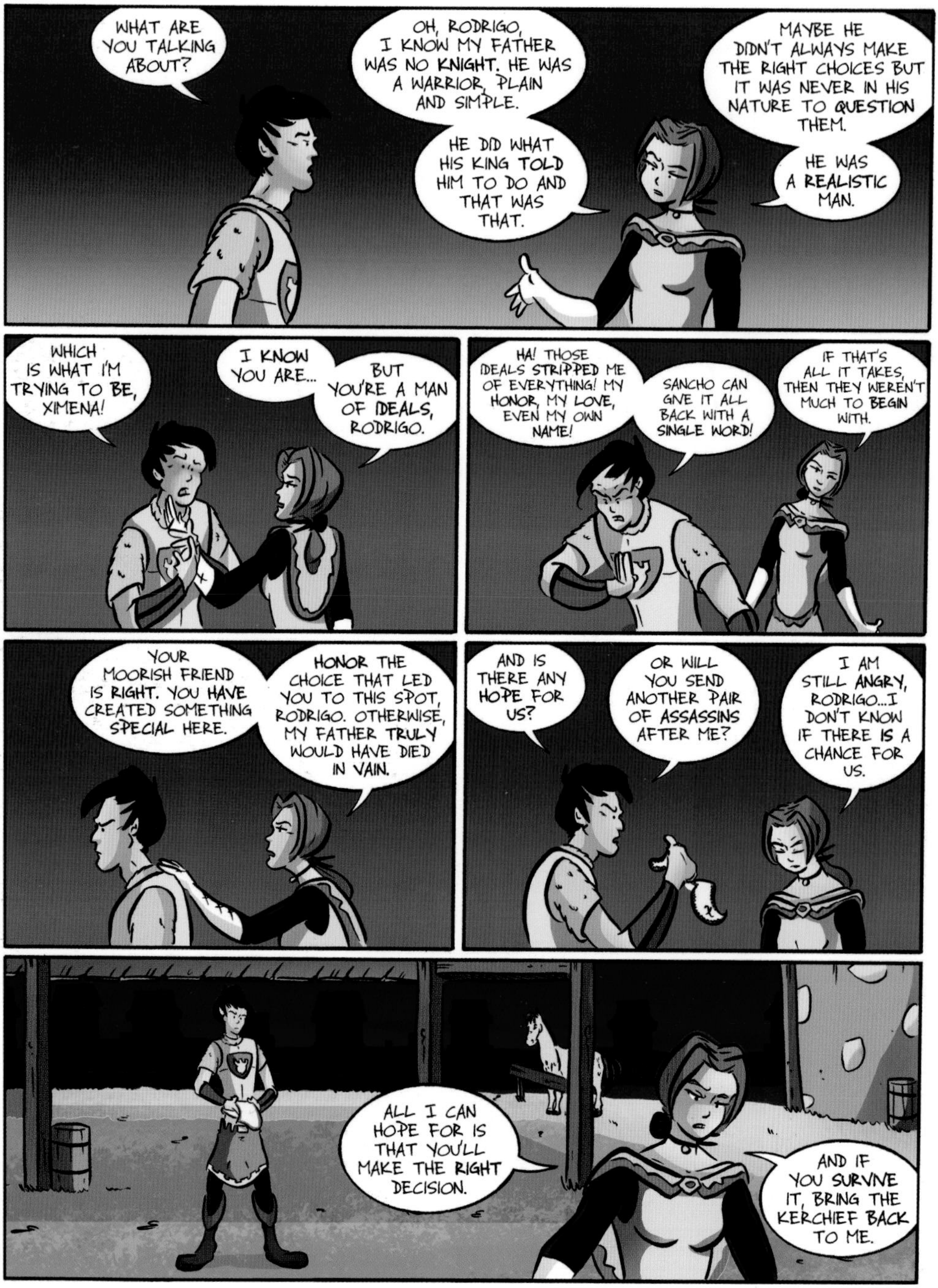
WHAT ARE YOU TALKING ABOUT?
OH, RODRIGO, I KNOW MY FATHER WAS NO KNIGHT. HE WAS A WARRIOR, PLAIN AND SIMPLE.
HE DID WHAT HIS KING TOLD HIM TO DO AND THAT WAS THAT.
MAYBE HE DIDN'T ALWAYS MAKE THE RIGHT CHOICES BUT IT WAS NEVER IN HIS NATURE TO QUESTION THEM.
HE WAS A REALISTIC MAN.
WHICH IS WHAT I'M TRYING TO BE, XIMENA!
I KNOW YOU ARE...
BUT YOU'RE A MAN OF IDEALS, RODRIGO.
HA! THOSE IDEALS STRIPPED ME OF EVERYTHING! MY HONOR, MY LOVE, EVEN MY OWN NAME!
SANCHO CAN GIVE IT ALL BACK WITH A SINGLE WORD!
IF THAT'S ALL IT TAKES, THEN THEY WEREN'T MUCH TO BEGIN WITH.
YOUR MOORISH FRIEND IS RIGHT. YOU HAVE CREATED SOMETHING SPECIAL HERE.
HONOR THE CHOICE THAT LED YOU TO THIS SPOT, RODRIGO. OTHERWISE, MY FATHER TRULY WOULD HAVE DIED IN VAIN.
AND IS THERE ANY HOPE FOR US?
OR WILL YOU SEND ANOTHER PAIR OF ASSASSINS AFTER ME?
I AM STILL ANGRY, RODRIGO...I DON'T KNOW IF THERE IS A CHANCE FOR US.
ALL I CAN HOPE FOR IS THAT YOU'LL MAKE THE RIGHT DECISION.
AND IF YOU SURVIVE IT, BRING THE KERCHIEF BACK TO ME.

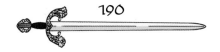

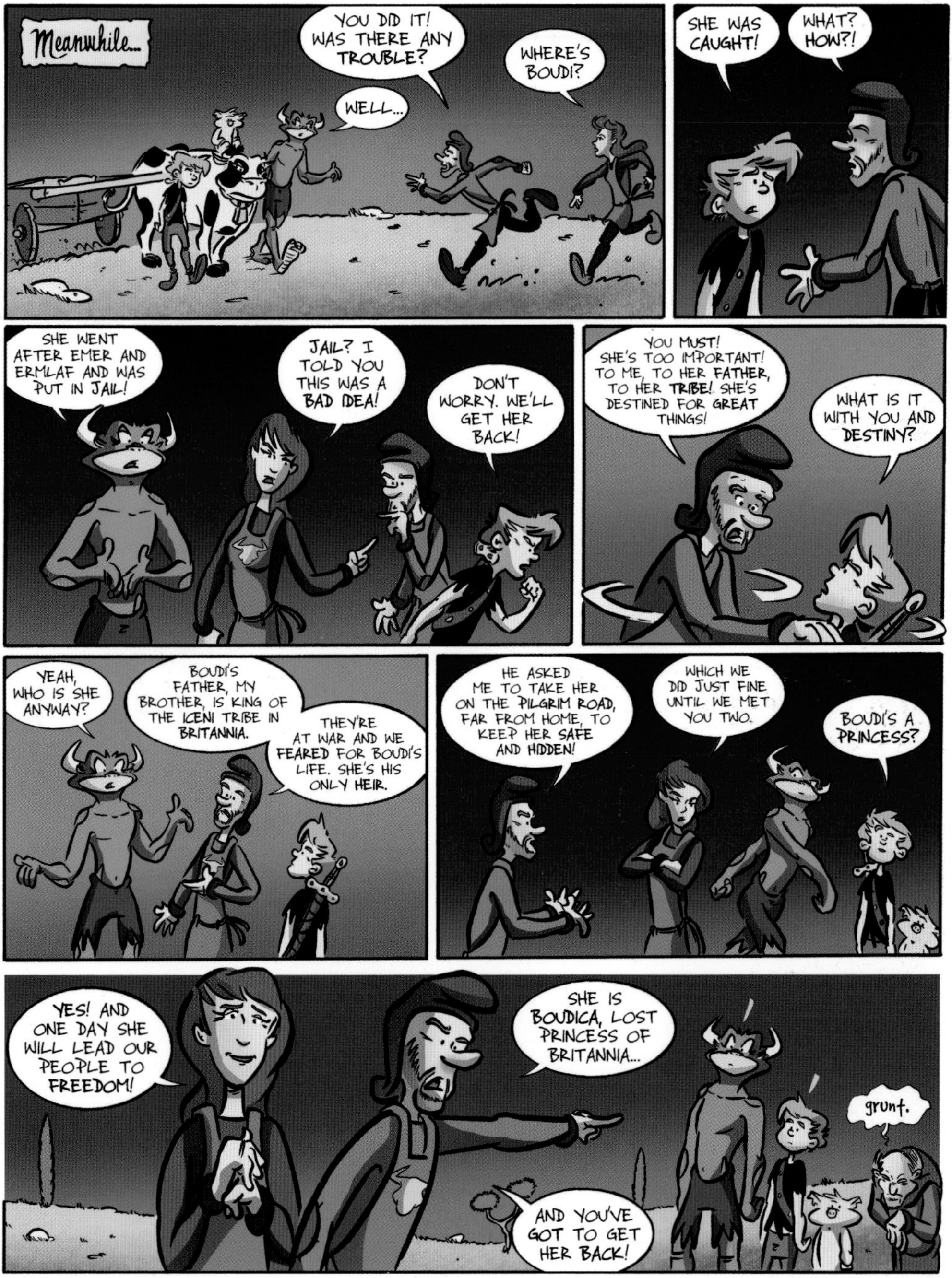
Meanwhile...
YOU DID IT! WAS THERE ANY TROUBLE?
WELL...
WHERE'S BOUDI?
SHE WAS CAUGHT!
WHAT? HOW?!
SHE WENT AFTER EMER AND ERMLAF AND WAS PUT IN JAIL!
JAIL? I TOLD YOU THIS WAS A BAD IDEA!
DON'T WORRY. WE'LL GET HER BACK!
YOU MUST! SHE'S TOO IMPORTANT! TO ME, TO HER FATHER, TO HER TRIBE! SHE'S DESTINED FOR GREAT THINGS!
WHAT IS IT WITH YOU AND DESTINY?
YEAH, WHO IS SHE ANYWAY?
BOUDI'S FATHER, MY BROTHER, IS KING OF THE ICENI TRIBE IN BRITANNIA.
THEY'RE AT WAR AND WE FEARED FOR BOUDI'S LIFE. SHE'S HIS ONLY HEIR.
HE ASKED ME TO TAKE HER ON THE PILGRIM ROAD, FAR FROM HOME, TO KEEP HER SAFE AND HIDDEN!
WHICH WE DID JUST FINE UNTIL WE MET YOU TWO.
BOUDI'S A PRINCESS?
YES! AND ONE DAY SHE WILL LEAD OUR PEOPLE TO FREEDOM!
SHE IS BOUDICA, LOST PRINCESS OF BRITANNIA...
AND YOU'VE GOT TO GET HER BACK!
grunt.

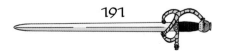

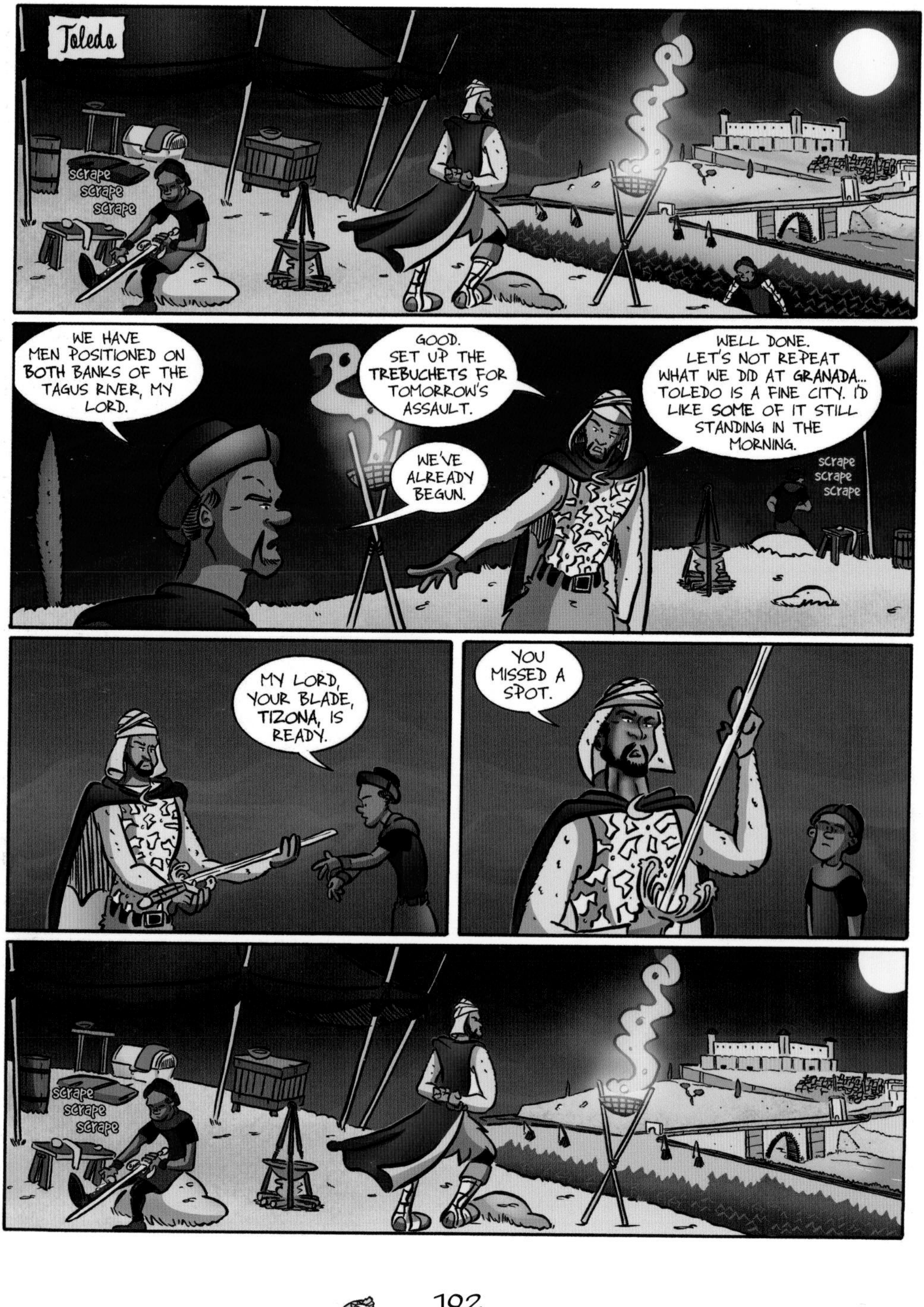
Toledo
scrape
scrape
scrape
WE HAVE MEN POSITIONED ON BOTH BANKS OF THE TAGUS RIVER, MY LORD.
GOOD. SET UP THE TREBUCHETS FOR TOMORROW'S ASSAULT.
WE'VE ALREADY BEGUN.
WELL DONE. LET'S NOT REPEAT WHAT WE DID AT GRANADA... TOLEDO IS A FINE CITY. I'D LIKE SOME OF IT STILL STANDING IN THE MORNING.
scrape
scrape
scrape
MY LORD, YOUR BLADE, TIZONA, IS READY.
YOU MISSED A SPOT.
scrape
scrape
scrape

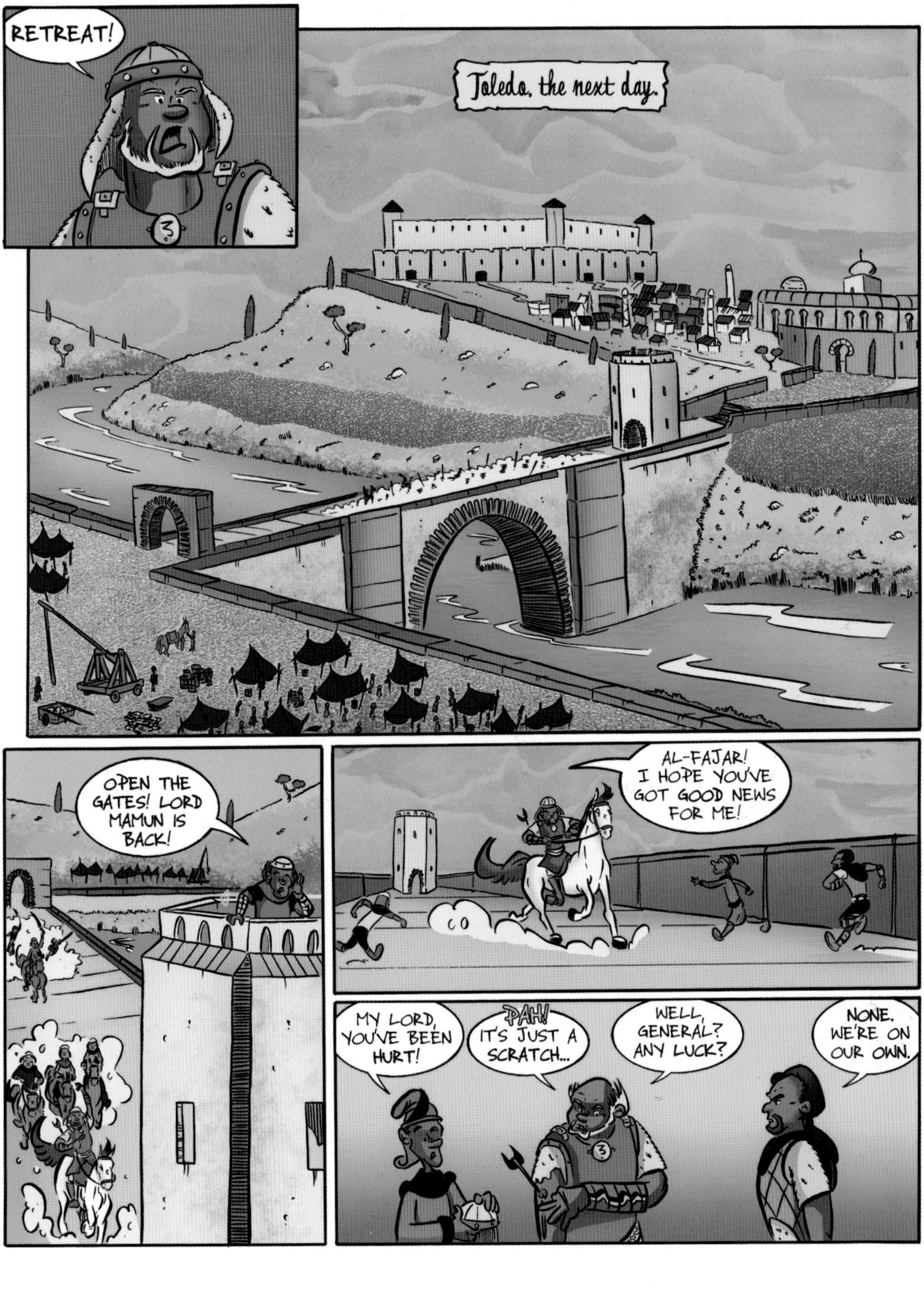
RETREAT!
Toledo, the next day.
OPEN THE GATES! LORD MAMUN IS BACK!
AL-FAJAR! I HOPE YOU'VE GOT GOOD NEWS FOR ME!
MY LORD, YOU'VE BEEN HURT!
PAH! IT'S JUST A SCRATCH...
WELL, GENERAL? ANY LUCK?
NONE. WE'RE ON OUR OWN.

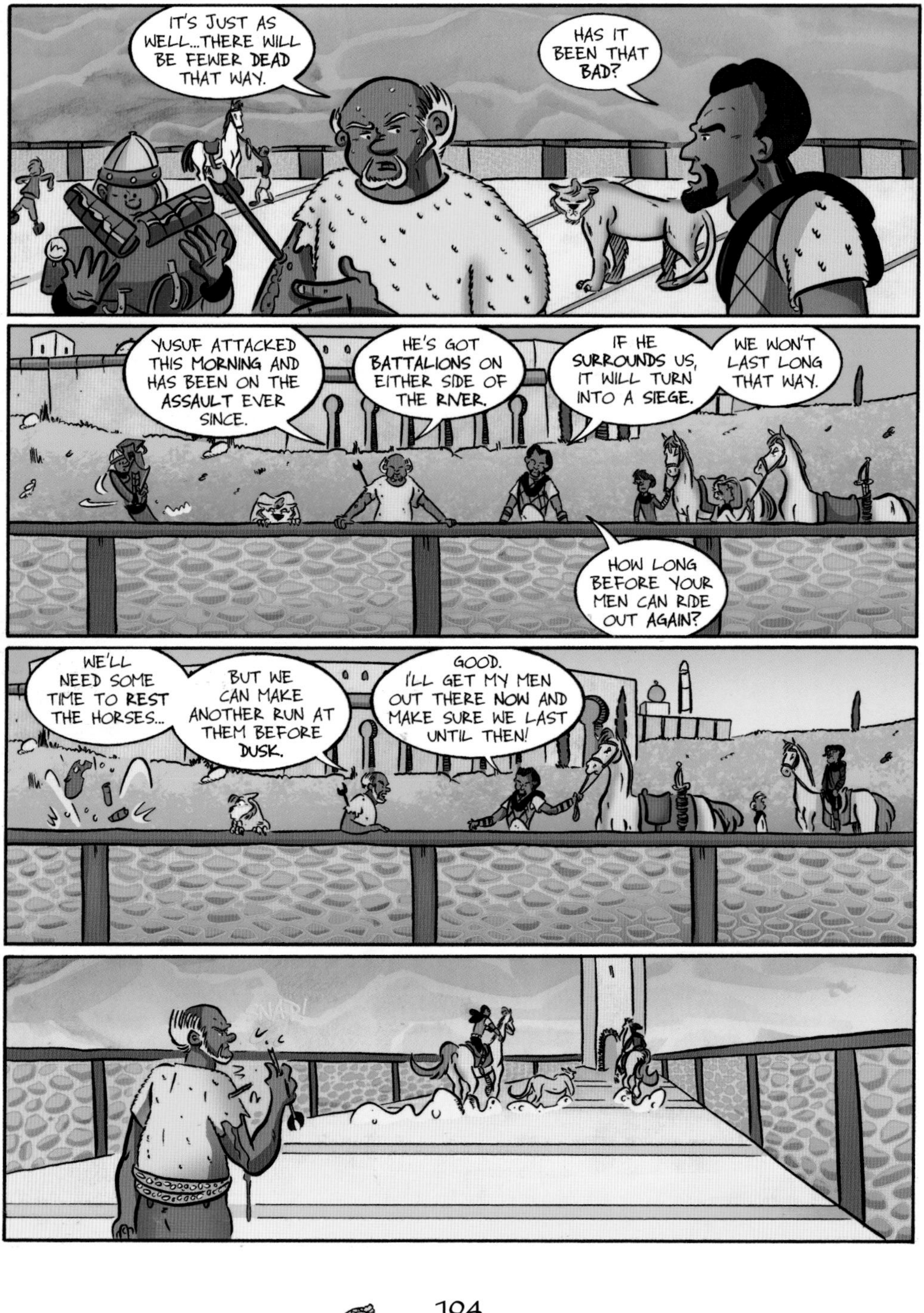
IT'S JUST AS WELL...THERE WILL BE FEWER DEAD THAT WAY.
HAS IT BEEN THAT BAD?
YUSUF ATTACKED THIS MORNING AND HAS BEEN ON THE ASSAULT EVER SINCE.
HE'S GOT BATTALIONS ON EITHER SIDE OF THE RIVER.
IF HE SURROUNDS US, IT WILL TURN INTO A SIEGE.
WE WON'T LAST LONG THAT WAY.
HOW LONG BEFORE YOUR MEN CAN RIDE OUT AGAIN?
WE'LL NEED SOME TIME TO REST THE HORSES...
BUT WE CAN MAKE ANOTHER RUN AT THEM BEFORE DUSK.
GOOD. I'LL GET MY MEN OUT THERE NOW AND MAKE SURE WE LAST UNTIL THEN!
SNAP!

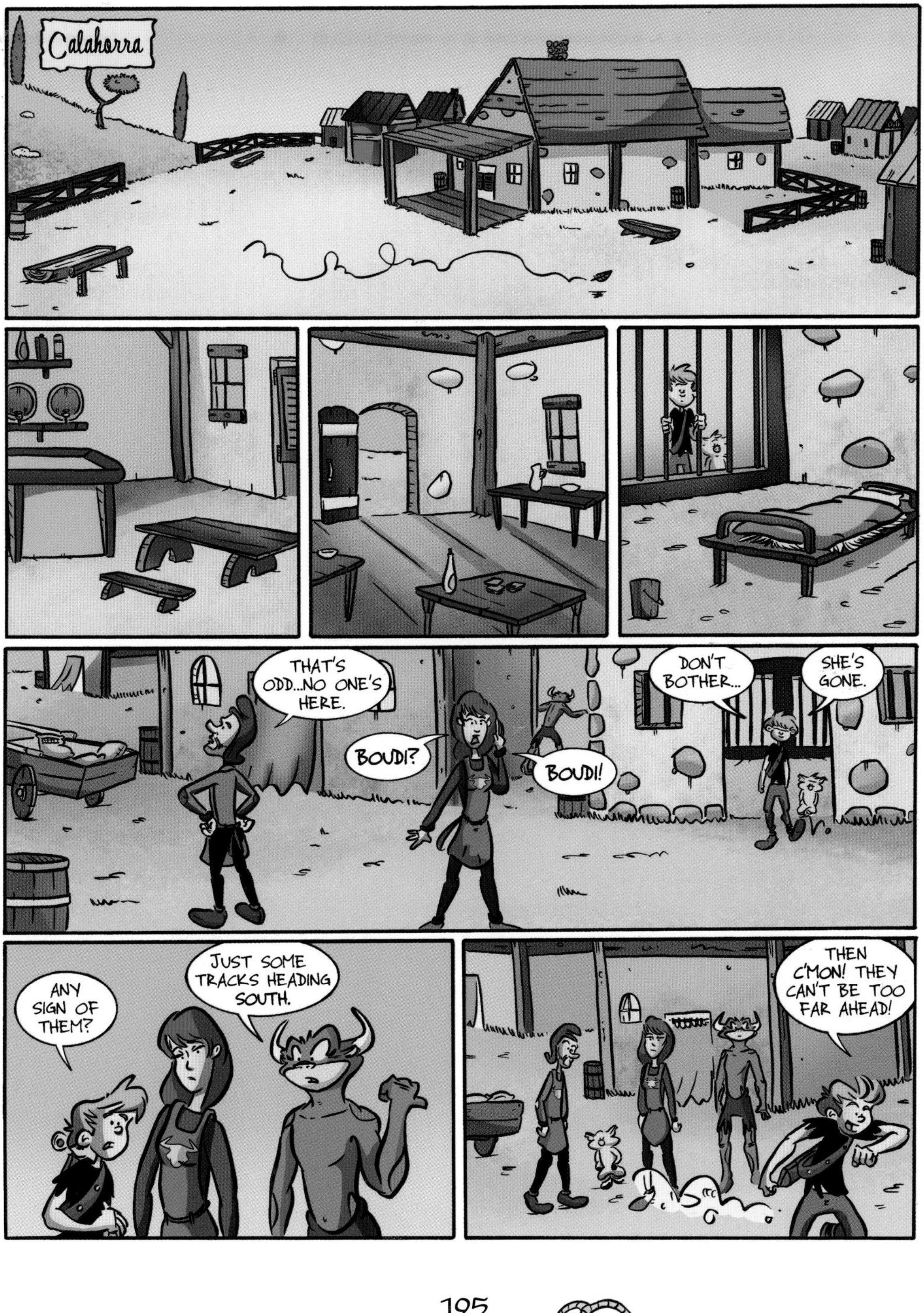
Calahorra
THAT'S ODD...NO ONE'S HERE.
BOUDI?
BOUDI!
DON'T BOTHER...
SHE'S GONE.
ANY SIGN OF THEM?
JUST SOME TRACKS HEADING SOUTH.
THEN C'MON! THEY CAN'T BE TOO FAR AHEAD!

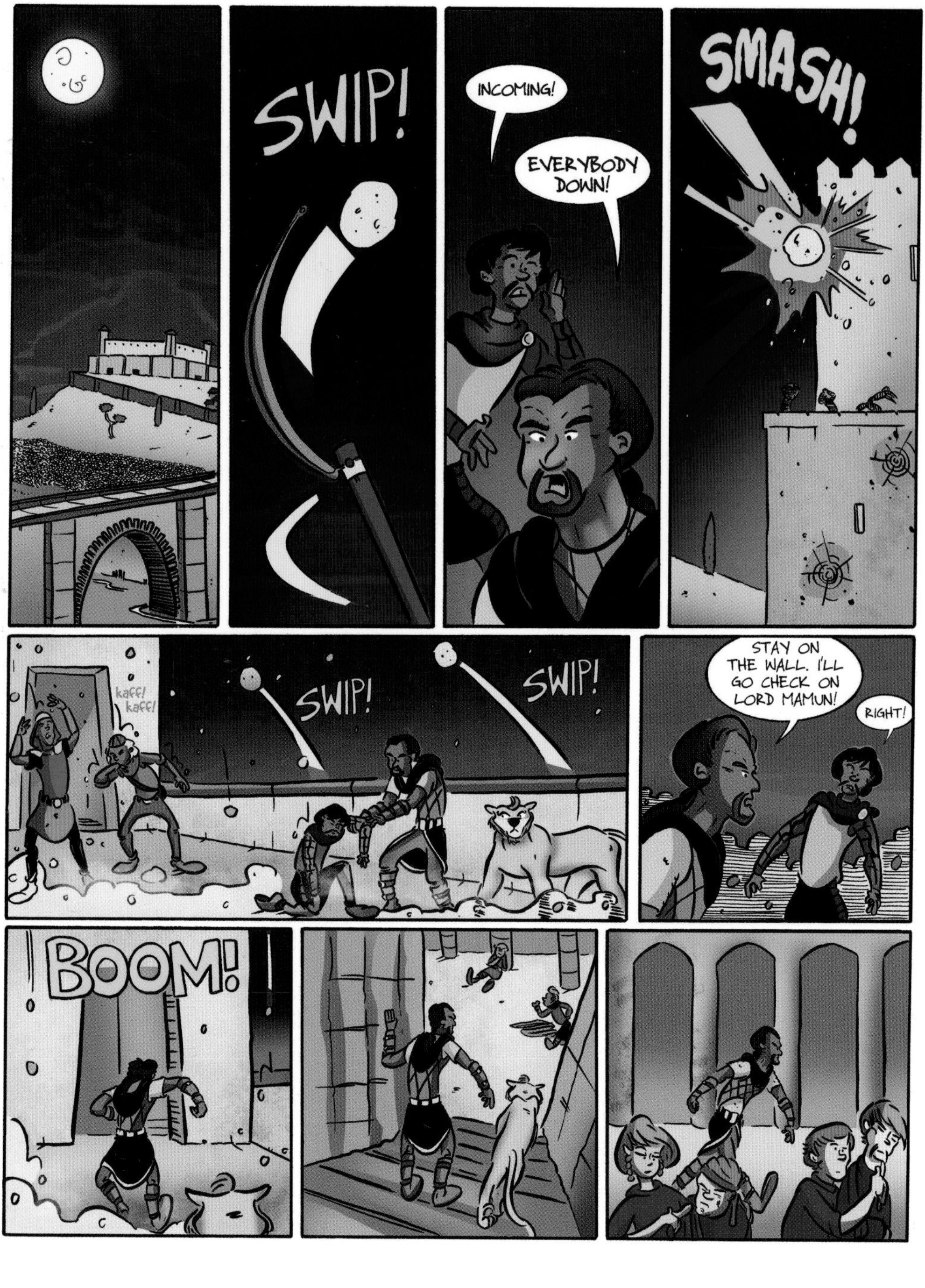
SWIP!
INCOMING!
EVERYBODY DOWN!
SMASH!
kaff! kaff!
SWIP!
SWIP!
STAY ON THE WALL. I'LL GO CHECK ON LORD MAMUN!
RIGHT!
BOOM!

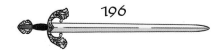

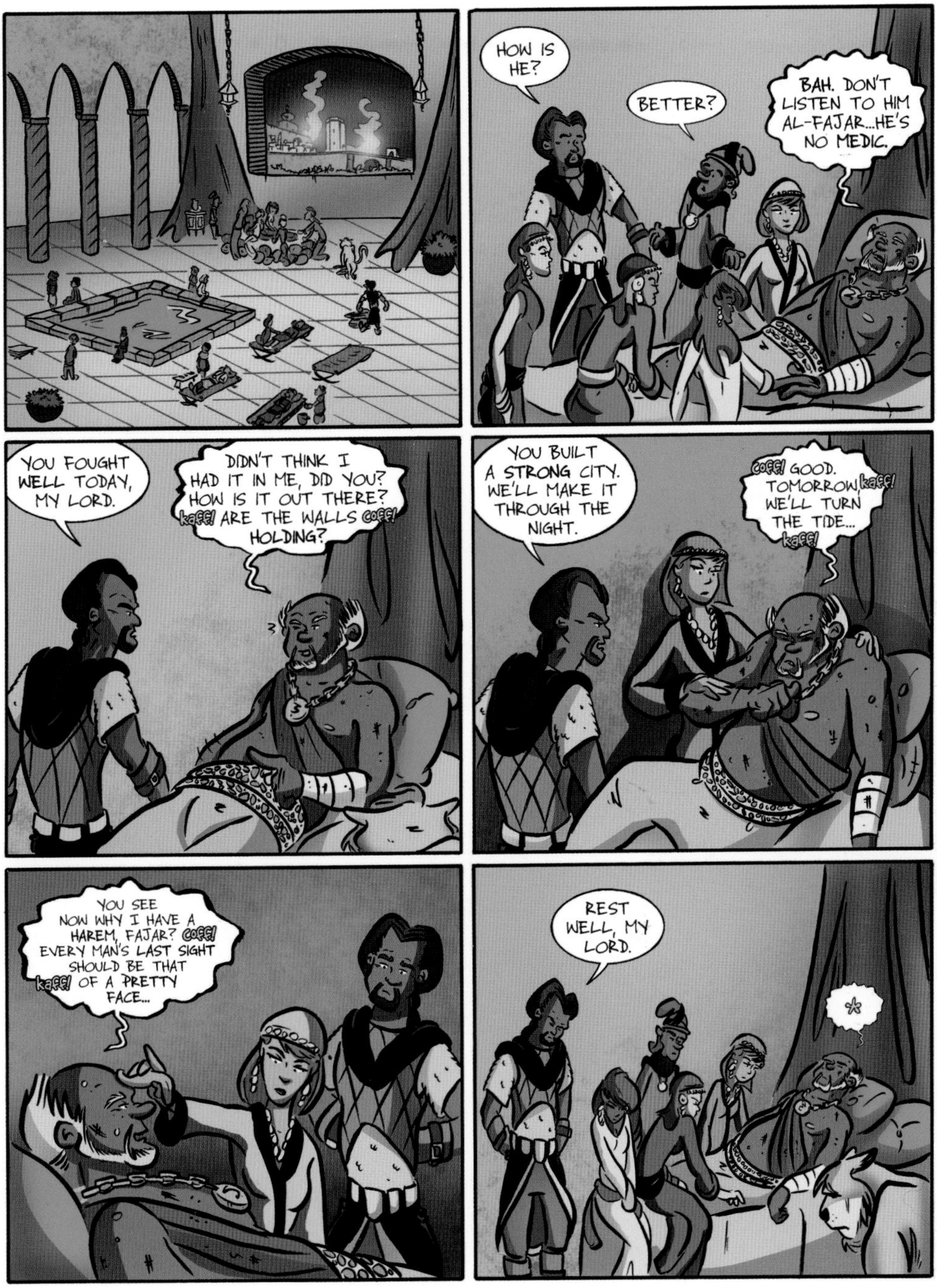
HOW IS HE?
BETTER?
BAH. DON'T LISTEN TO HIM AL-FAJAR...HE'S NO MEDIC.
YOU FOUGHT WELL TODAY, MY LORD.
DIDN'T THINK I HAD IT IN ME, DID YOU? HOW IS IT OUT THERE? KAFF! ARE THE WALLS COFF! HOLDING?
YOU BUILT A STRONG CITY. WE'LL MAKE IT THROUGH THE NIGHT.
COFF! GOOD. TOMORROW, KAFF! WE'LL TURN THE TIDE... KAFF!
YOU SEE NOW WHY I HAVE A HAREM, FAJAR? COFF! EVERY MAN'S LAST SIGHT SHOULD BE THAT KAFF! OF A PRETTY FACE...
REST WELL, MY LORD.
*

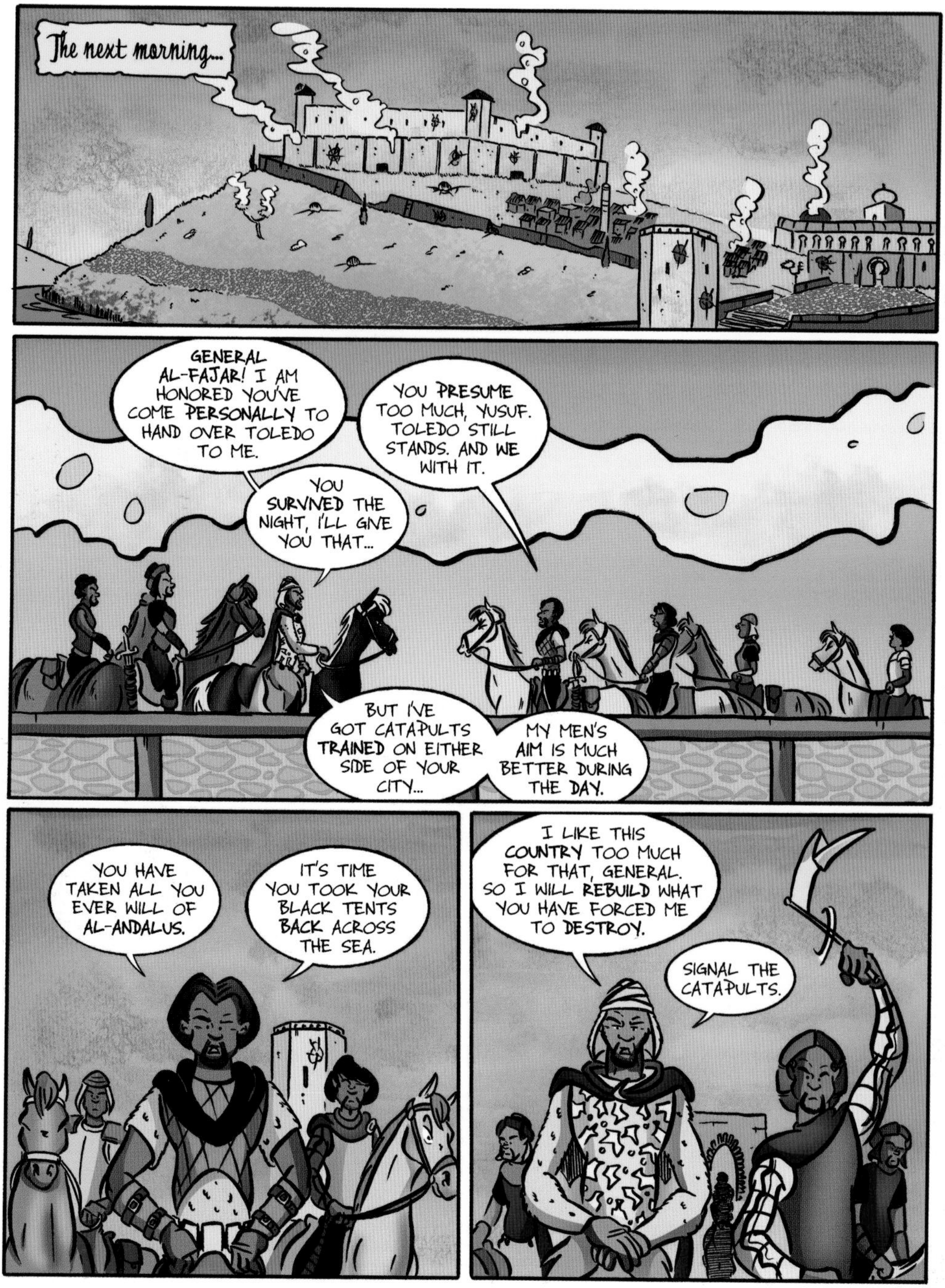
The next morning...
GENERAL AL-FAJAR! I AM HONORED YOU'VE COME PERSONALLY TO HAND OVER TOLEDO TO ME.
YOU SURVIVED THE NIGHT, I'LL GIVE YOU THAT...
YOU PRESUME TOO MUCH, YUSUF. TOLEDO STILL STANDS. AND WE WITH IT.
BUT I'VE GOT CATAPULTS TRAINED ON EITHER SIDE OF YOUR CITY...
MY MEN'S AIM IS MUCH BETTER DURING THE DAY.
YOU HAVE TAKEN ALL YOU EVER WILL OF AL-ANDALUS.
IT'S TIME YOU TOOK YOUR BLACK TENTS BACK ACROSS THE SEA.
I LIKE THIS COUNTRY TOO MUCH FOR THAT, GENERAL. SO I WILL REBUILD WHAT YOU HAVE FORCED ME TO DESTROY.
SIGNAL THE CATAPULTS.

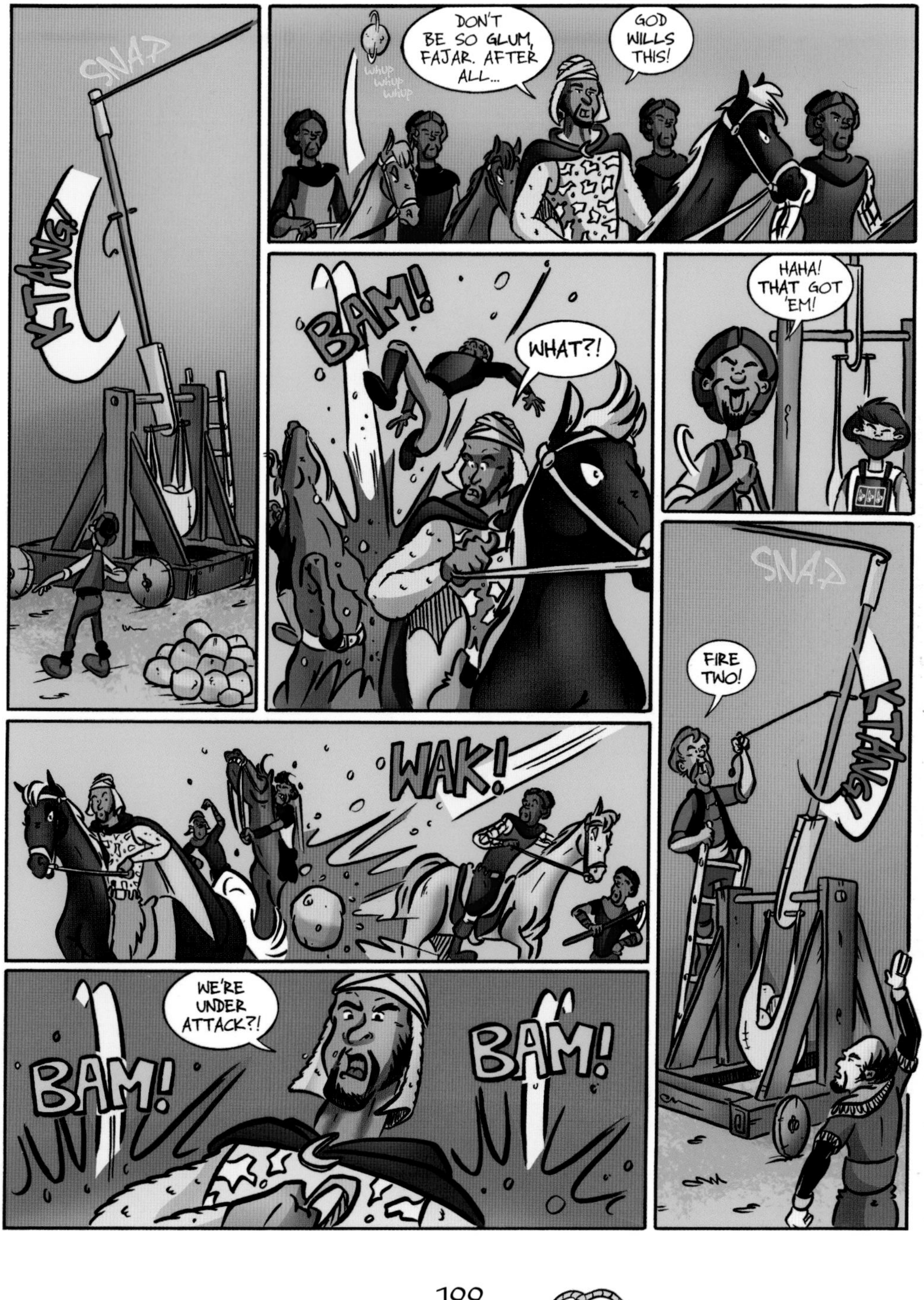
SNAP
KTANG!
whup whup whup
DON'T BE SO GLUM, FAJAR. AFTER ALL...
GOD WILLS THIS!
BAM!
WHAT?!
HAHA! THAT GOT 'EM!
SNAP
FIRE TWO!
KTANG!
WAK!
WE'RE UNDER ATTACK?!
BAM!
BAM!

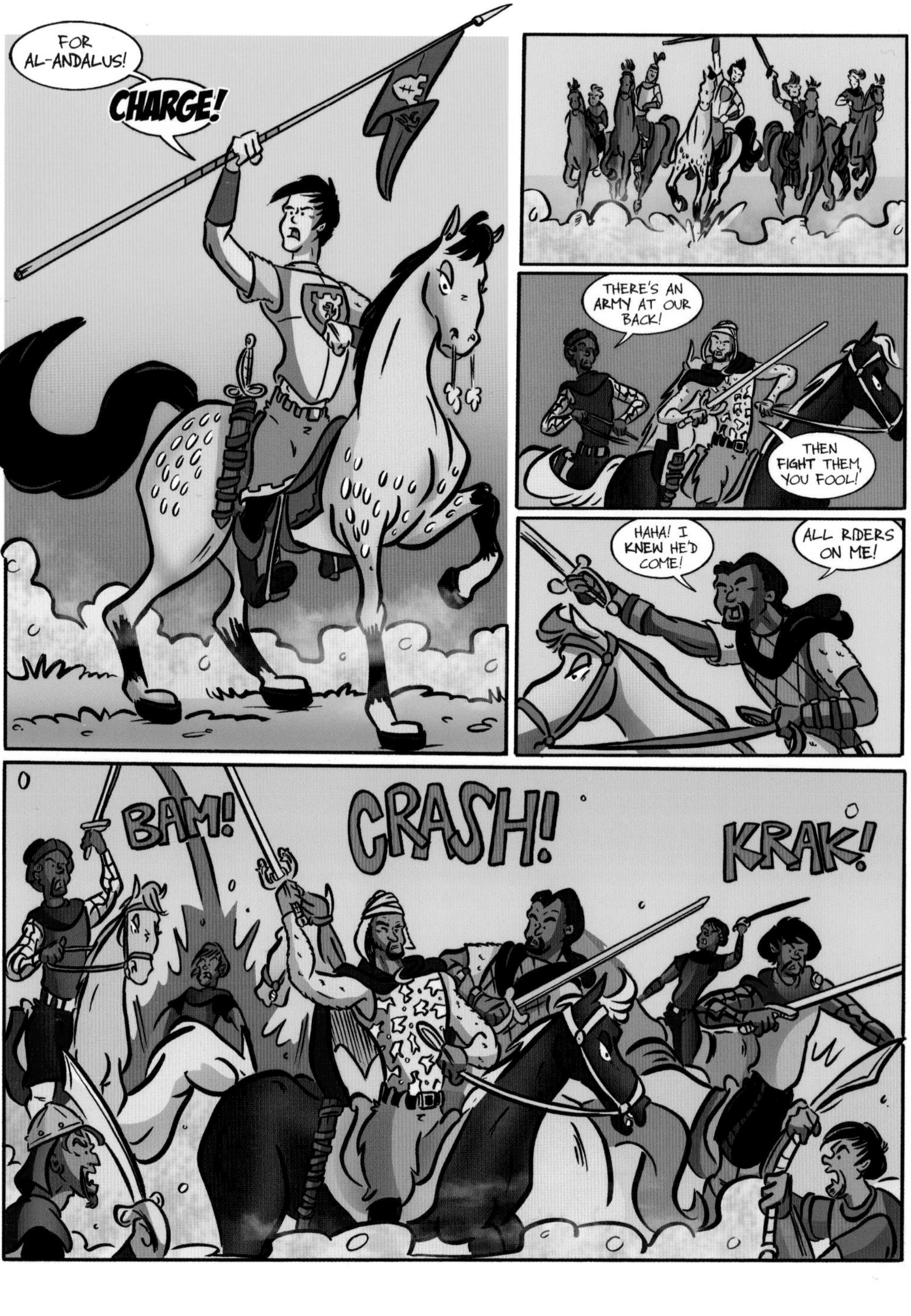
FOR AL-ANDALUS!
CHARGE!
THERE'S AN ARMY AT OUR BACK!
THEN FIGHT THEM, YOU FOOL!
HAHA! I KNEW HE'D COME!
ALL RIDERS ON ME!
BAM!
CRASH!
KRAK!

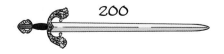

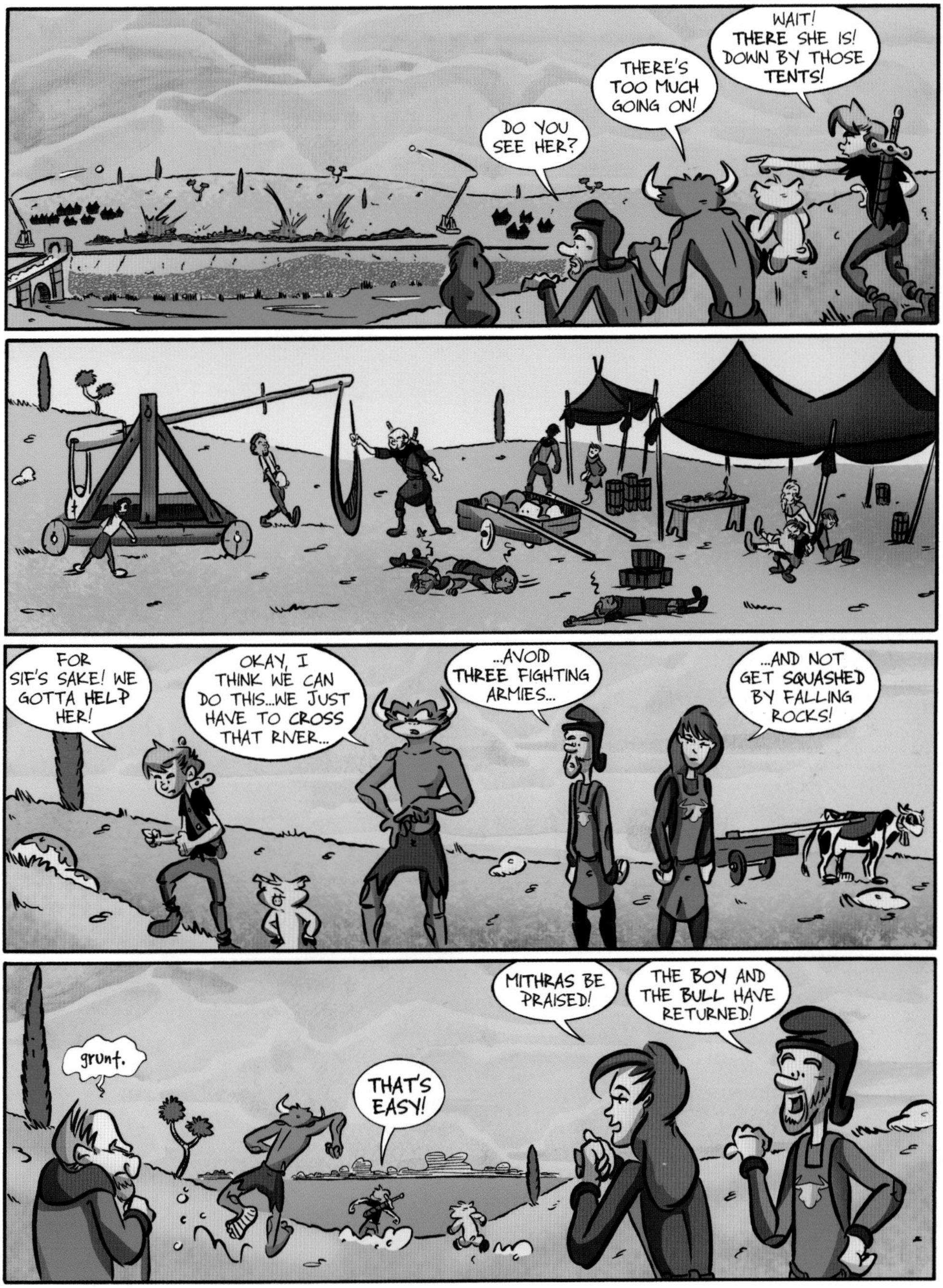
DO YOU SEE HER?
THERE'S TOO MUCH GOING ON!
WAIT! THERE SHE IS! DOWN BY THOSE TENTS!
FOR SIF'S SAKE! WE GOTTA HELP HER!
OKAY, I THINK WE CAN DO THIS...WE JUST HAVE TO CROSS THAT RIVER...
...AVOID THREE FIGHTING ARMIES...
...AND NOT GET SQUASHED BY FALLING ROCKS!
grunt.
THAT'S EASY!
MITHRAS BE PRAISED!
THE BOY AND THE BULL HAVE RETURNED!

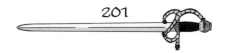

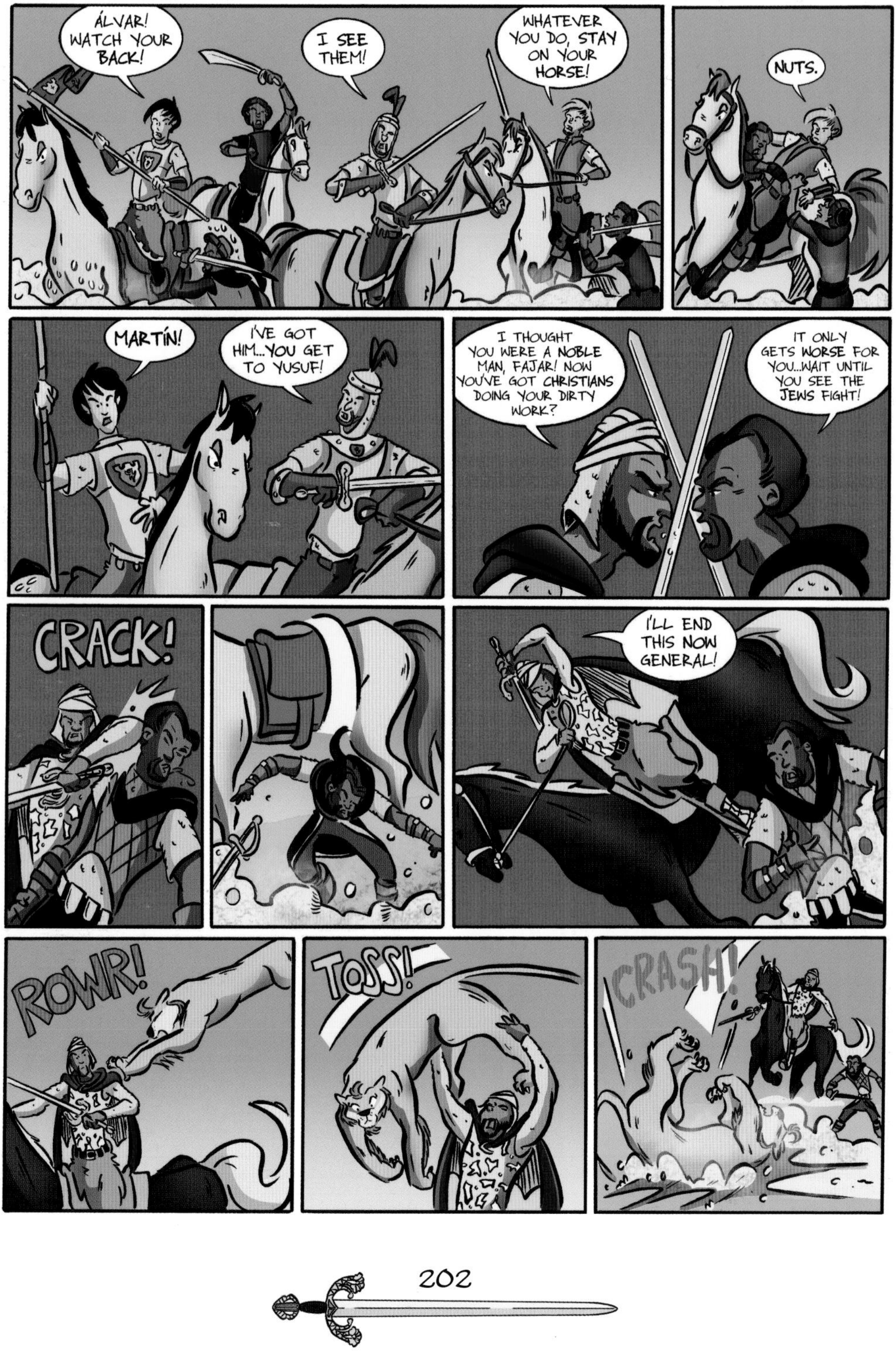
ÁLVAR! WATCH YOUR BACK!
I SEE THEM!
WHATEVER YOU DO, STAY ON YOUR HORSE!
NUTS.
MARTÍN!
I'VE GOT HIM...YOU GET TO YUSUF!
I THOUGHT YOU WERE A NOBLE MAN, FAJAR! NOW YOU'VE GOT CHRISTIANS DOING YOUR DIRTY WORK?
IT ONLY GETS WORSE FOR YOU...WAIT UNTIL YOU SEE THE JEWS FIGHT!
CRACK!
I'LL END THIS NOW GENERAL!
ROWR!
TOSS!
CRASH!

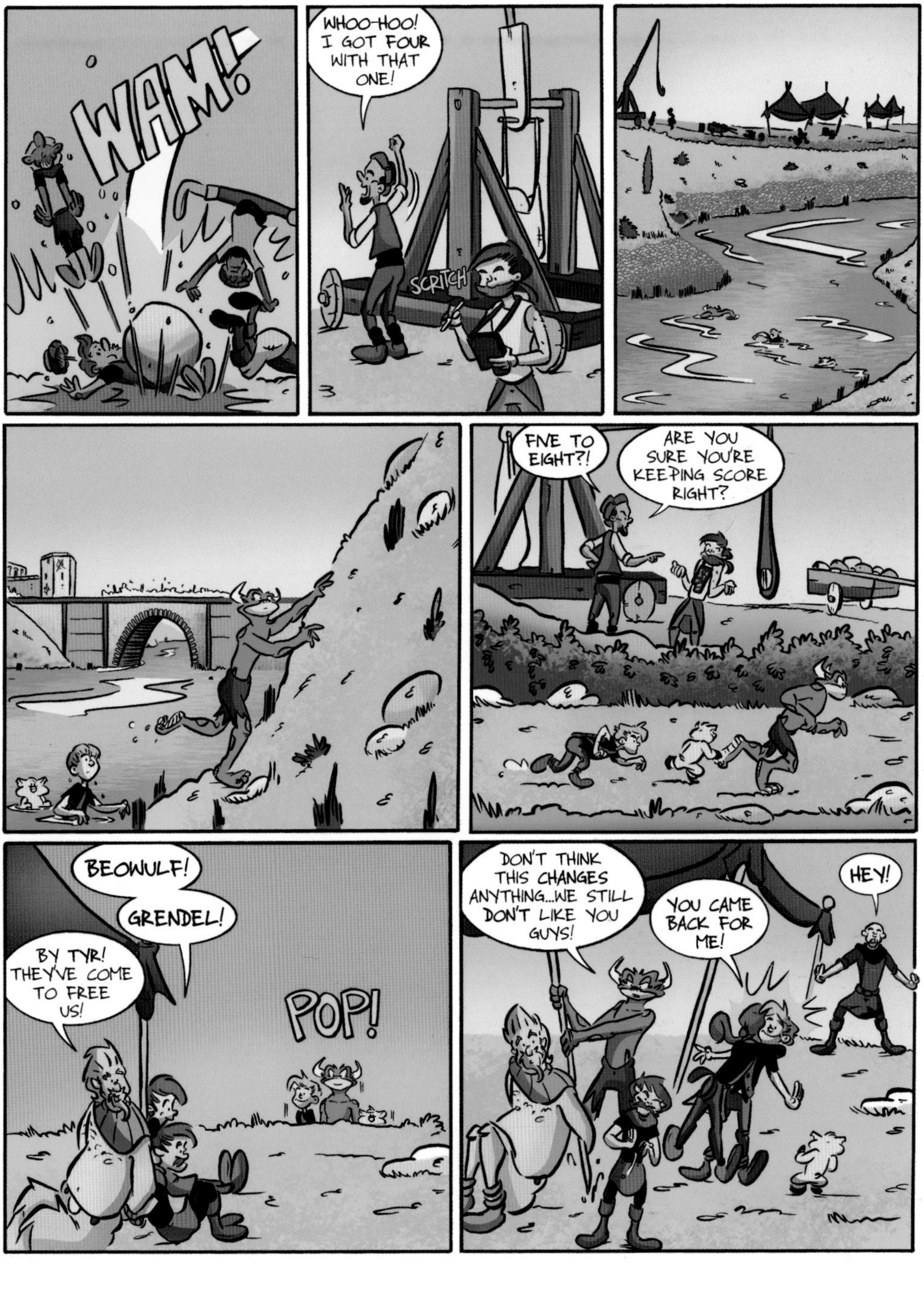
WAM!
WHOO-HOO! I GOT FOUR WITH THAT ONE!
SCRITCH
FIVE TO EIGHT?!
ARE YOU SURE YOU'RE KEEPING SCORE RIGHT?
BEOWULF!
GRENDEL!
BY TYR! THEY'VE COME TO FREE US!
POP!
DON'T THINK THIS CHANGES ANYTHING...WE STILL DON'T LIKE YOU GUYS!
YOU CAME BACK FOR ME!
HEY!

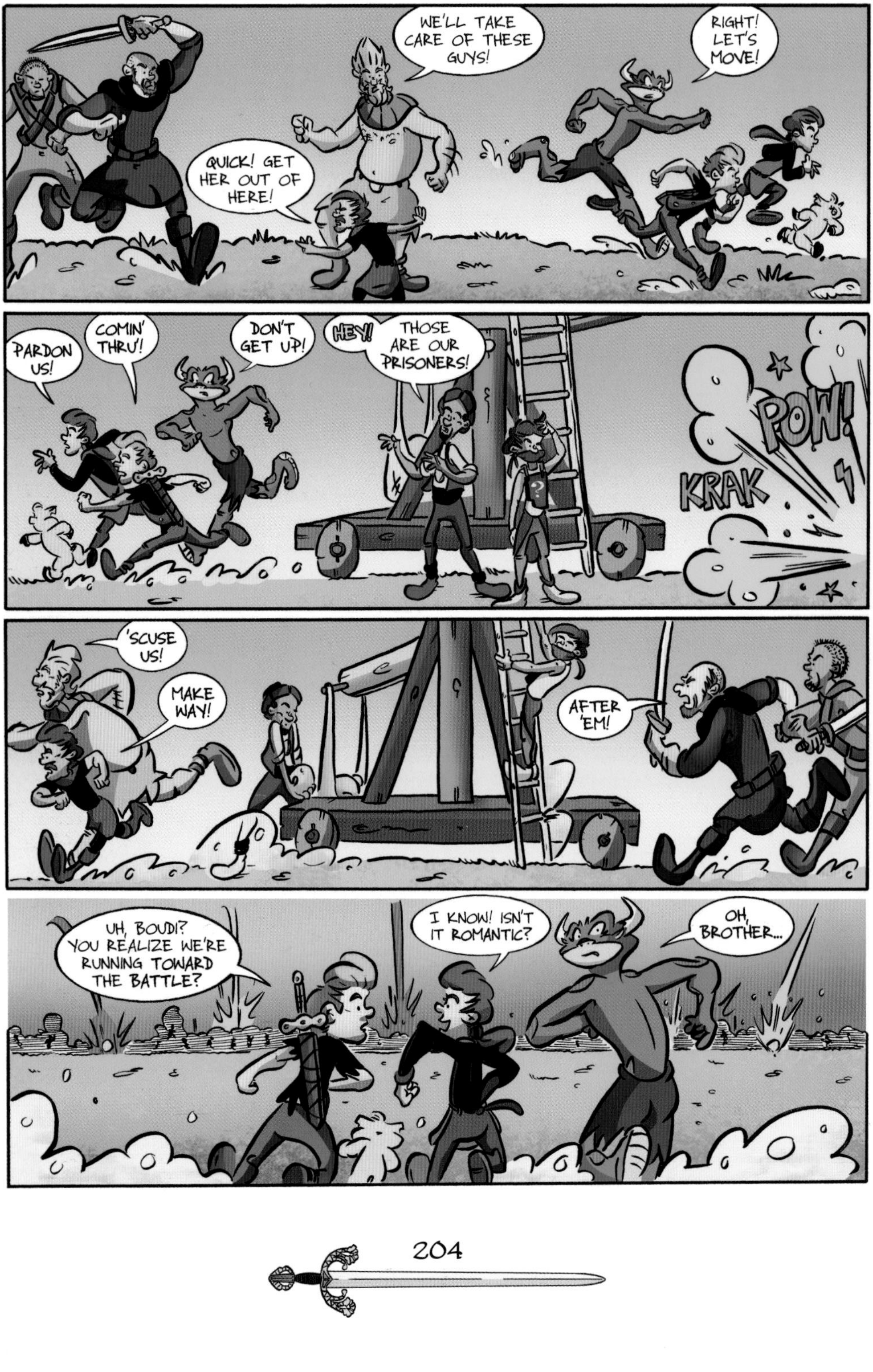
WE'LL TAKE CARE OF THESE GUYS!
RIGHT! LET'S MOVE!
QUICK! GET HER OUT OF HERE!
PARDON US!
COMIN' THRU'!
DON'T GET UP!
HEY!
THOSE ARE OUR PRISONERS!
POW!
KRAK
'SCUSE US!
MAKE WAY!
AFTER 'EM!
UH, BOUDI? YOU REALIZE WE'RE RUNNING TOWARD THE BATTLE?
I KNOW! ISN'T IT ROMANTIC?
OH, BROTHER...

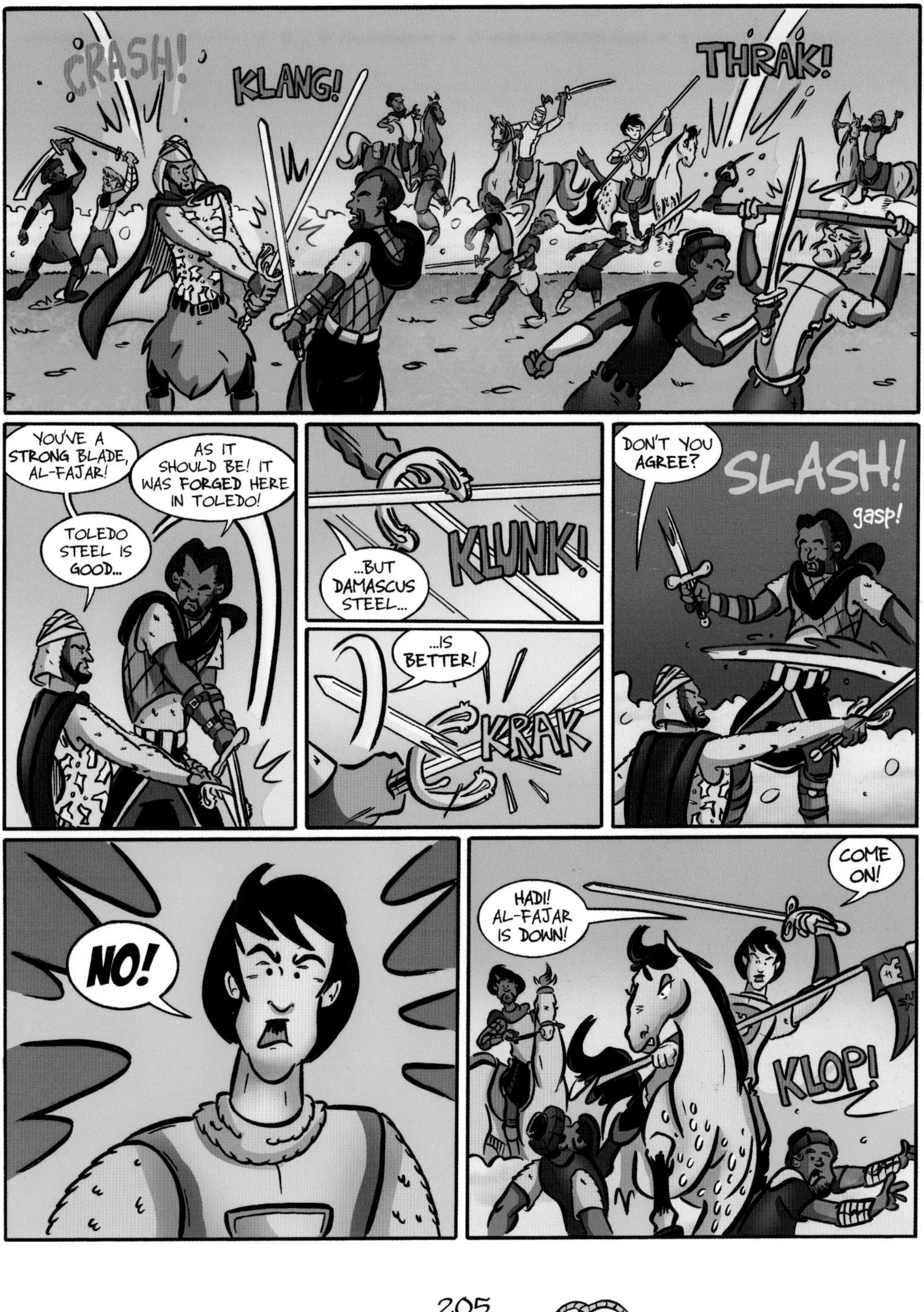
CRASH!
KLANG!
THRAK!
YOU'VE A STRONG BLADE, AL-FAJAR!
AS IT SHOULD BE! IT WAS FORGED HERE IN TOLEDO!
TOLEDO STEEL IS GOOD...
...BUT DAMASCUS STEEL...
KLUNK!
...IS BETTER!
KRAK
DON'T YOU AGREE?
SLASH!
gasp!
NO!
HADI! AL-FAJAR IS DOWN!
COME ON!
KLOP!

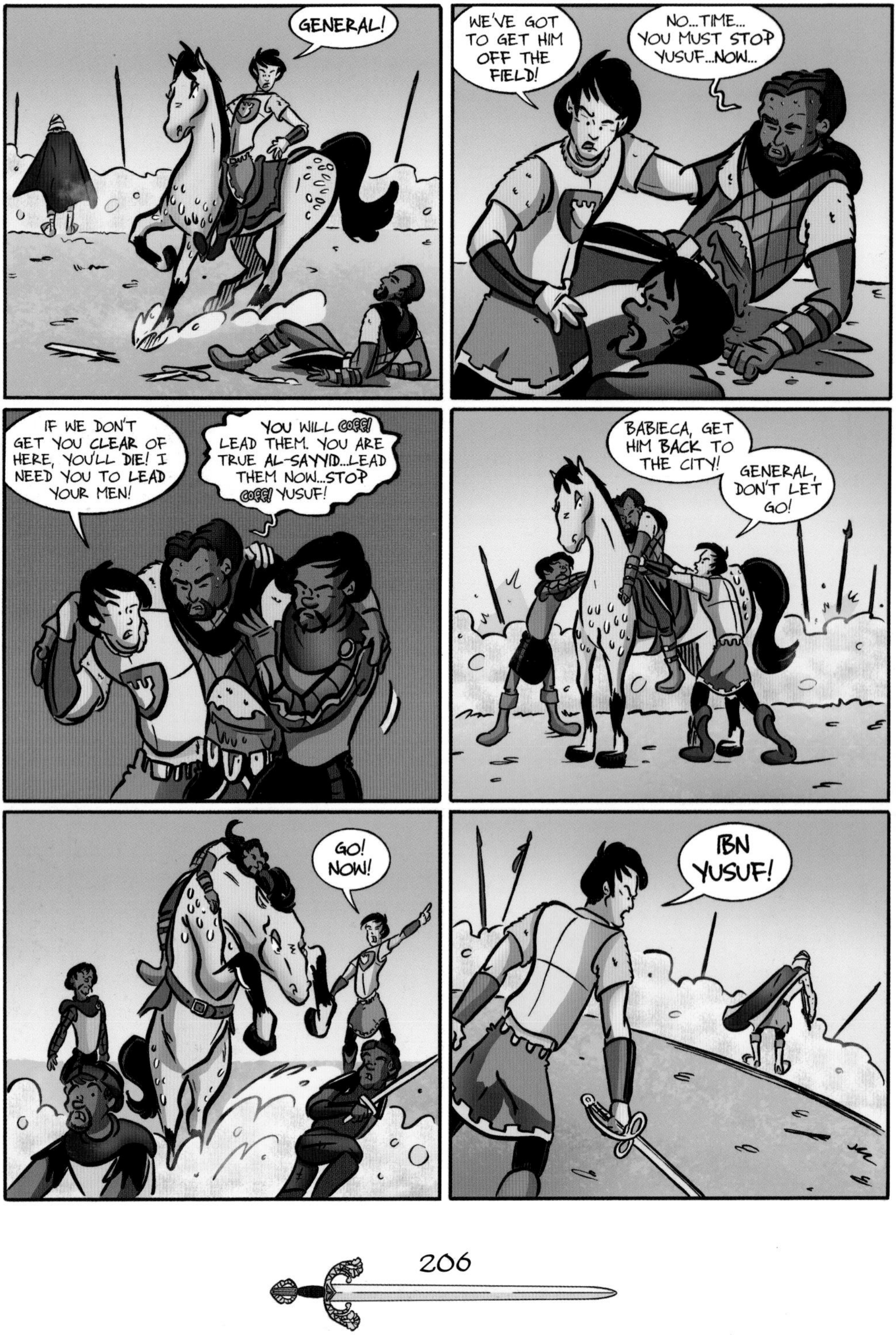
GENERAL!
WE'VE GOT TO GET HIM OFF THE FIELD!
NO...TIME... YOU MUST STOP YUSUF...NOW...
IF WE DON'T GET YOU CLEAR OF HERE, YOU'LL DIE! I NEED YOU TO LEAD YOUR MEN!
YOU WILL COFF! LEAD THEM. YOU ARE TRUE AL-SAYYID...LEAD THEM NOW...STOP COFF! YUSUF!
BABIECA, GET HIM BACK TO THE CITY!
GENERAL, DON'T LET GO!
GO! NOW!
IBN YUSUF!

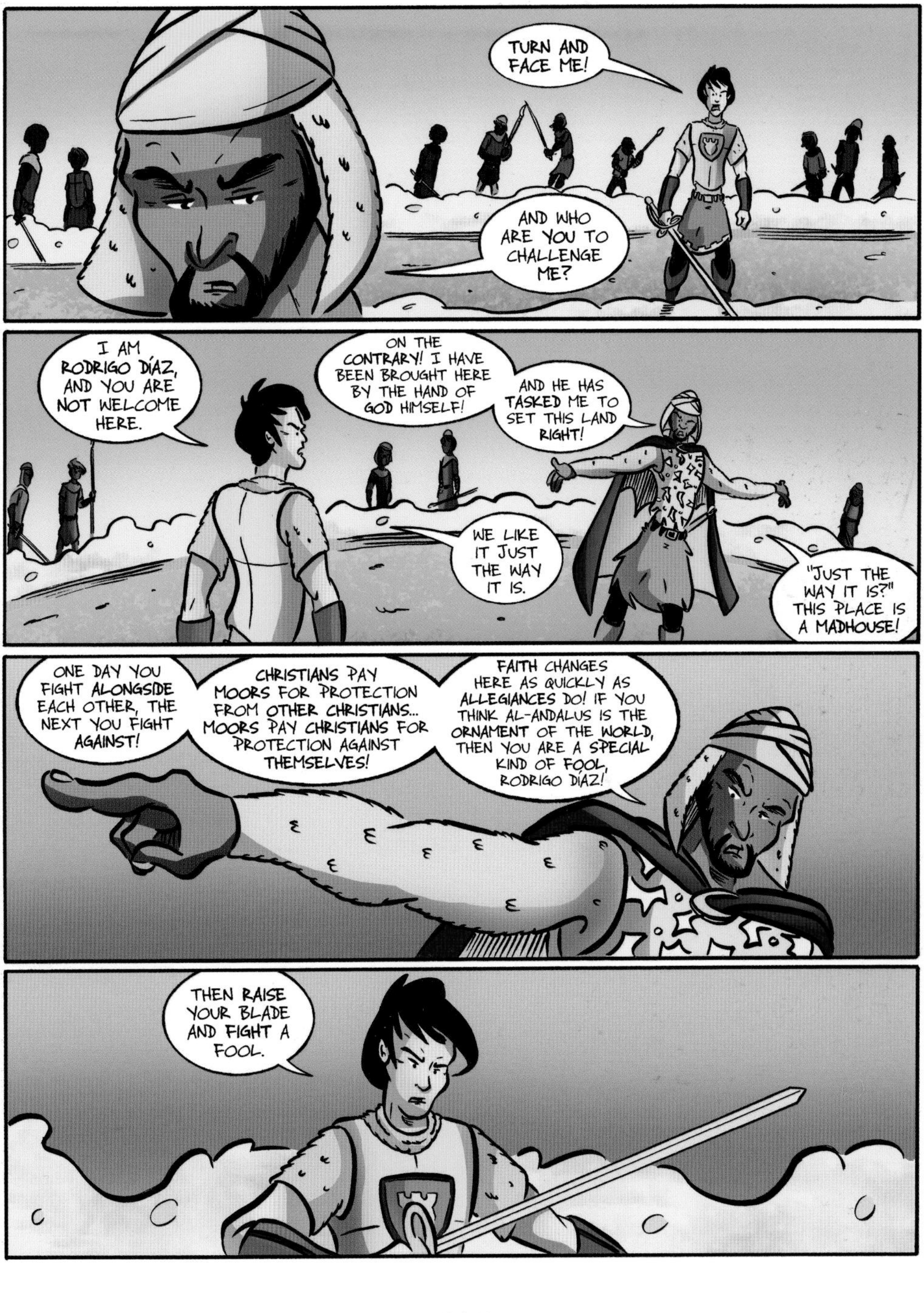
TURN AND FACE ME!
AND WHO ARE YOU TO CHALLENGE ME?
I AM RODRIGO DÍAZ, AND YOU ARE NOT WELCOME HERE.
ON THE CONTRARY! I HAVE BEEN BROUGHT HERE BY THE HAND OF GOD HIMSELF!
AND HE HAS TASKED ME TO SET THIS LAND RIGHT!
WE LIKE IT JUST THE WAY IT IS.
"JUST THE WAY IT IS?" THIS PLACE IS A MADHOUSE!
ONE DAY YOU FIGHT ALONGSIDE EACH OTHER, THE NEXT YOU FIGHT AGAINST!
CHRISTIANS PAY MOORS FOR PROTECTION FROM OTHER CHRISTIANS... MOORS PAY CHRISTIANS FOR PROTECTION AGAINST THEMSELVES!
FAITH CHANGES HERE AS QUICKLY AS ALLEGIANCES DO! IF YOU THINK AL-ANDALUS IS THE ORNAMENT OF THE WORLD, THEN YOU ARE A SPECIAL KIND OF FOOL, RODRIGO DÍAZ!
THEN RAISE YOUR BLADE AND FIGHT A FOOL.

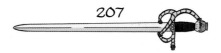

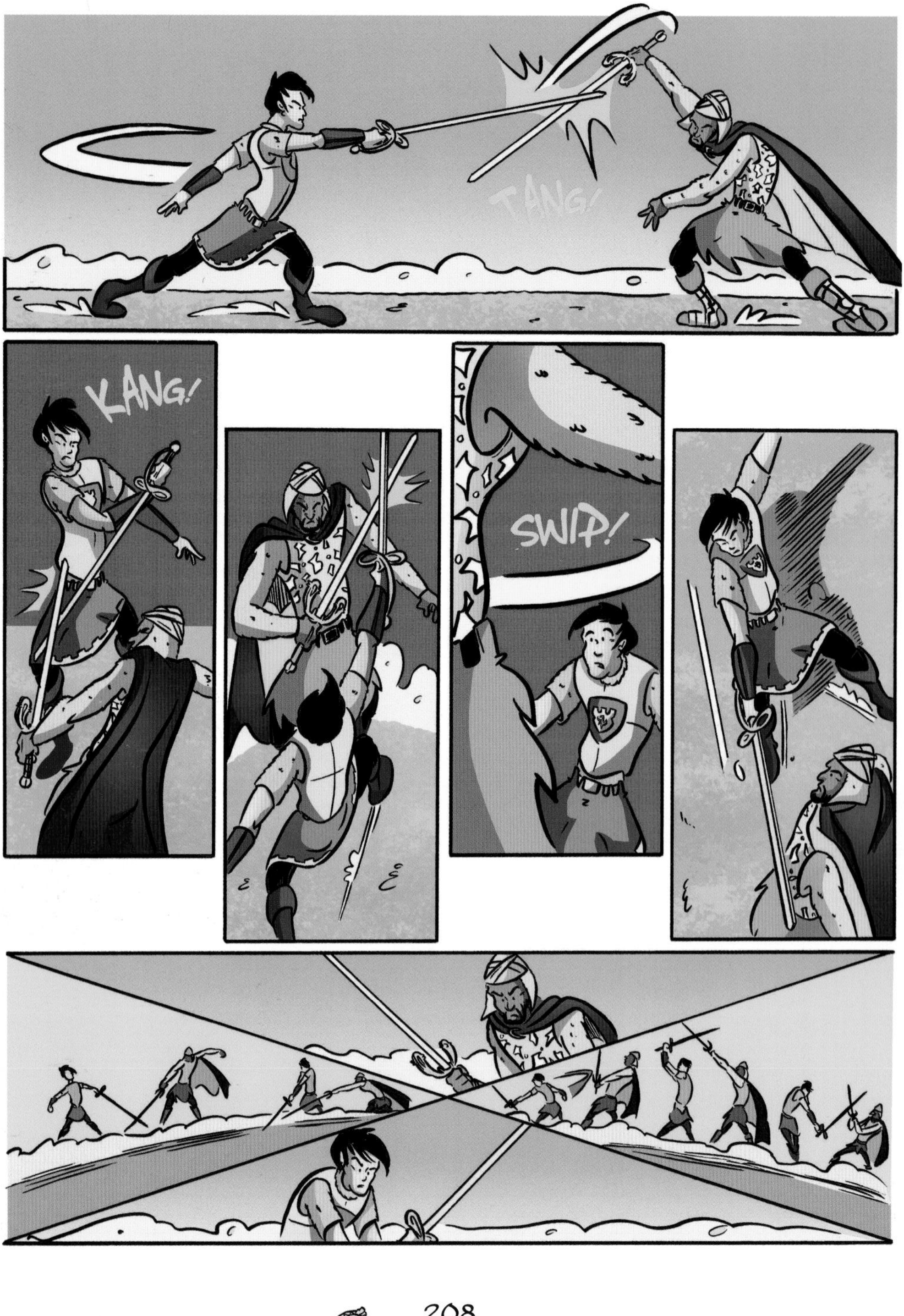
TANG!
KANG!
SWIP!

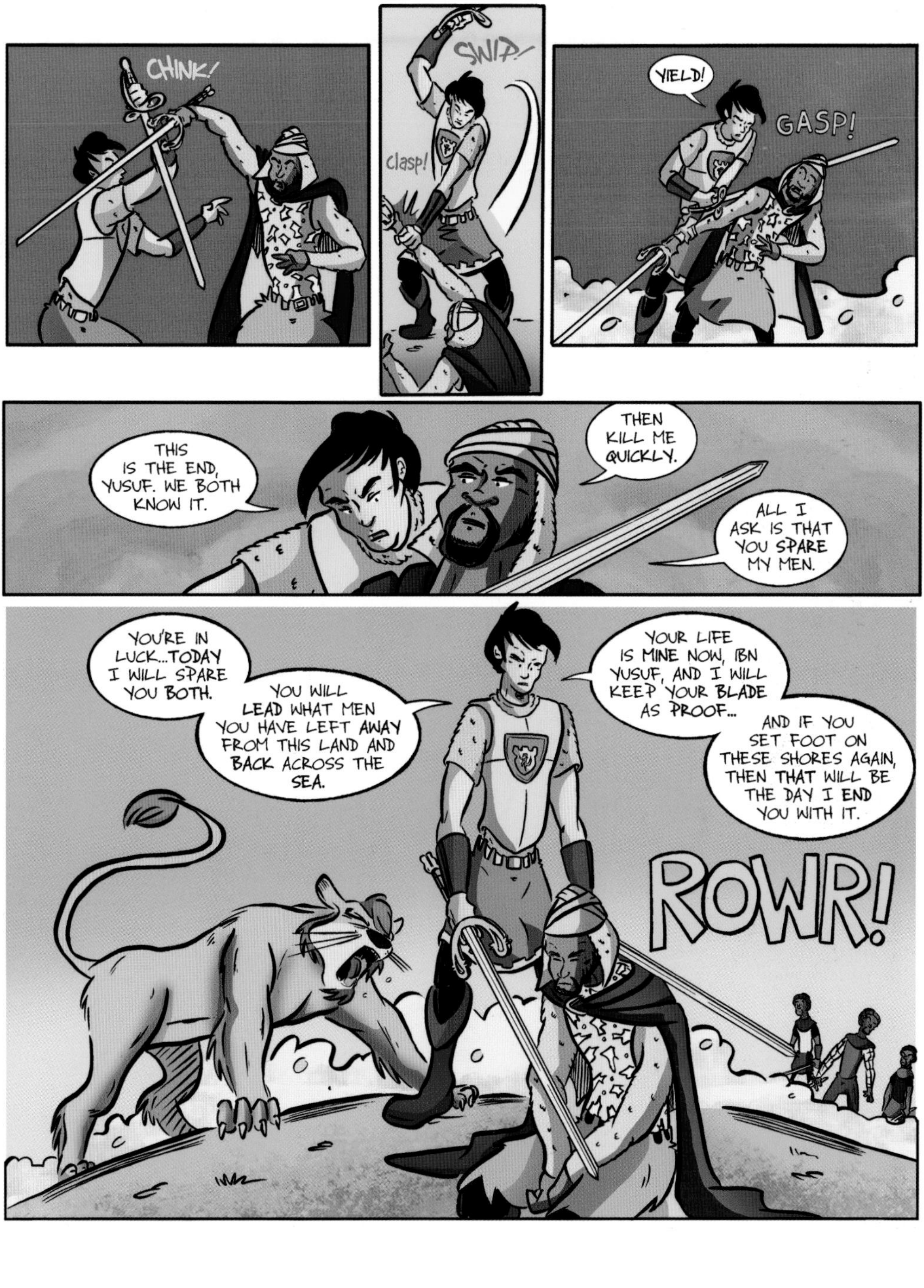
CHINK!
SWIP!
Clasp!
YIELD!
GASP!
THIS IS THE END, YUSUF. WE BOTH KNOW IT.
THEN KILL ME QUICKLY.
ALL I ASK IS THAT YOU SPARE MY MEN.
YOU'RE IN LUCK...TODAY I WILL SPARE YOU BOTH.
YOU WILL LEAD WHAT MEN YOU HAVE LEFT AWAY FROM THIS LAND AND BACK ACROSS THE SEA.
YOUR LIFE IS MINE NOW, IBN YUSUF, AND I WILL KEEP YOUR BLADE AS PROOF...
AND IF YOU SET FOOT ON THESE SHORES AGAIN, THEN THAT WILL BE THE DAY I END YOU WITH IT.
ROWR!

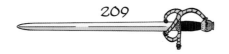

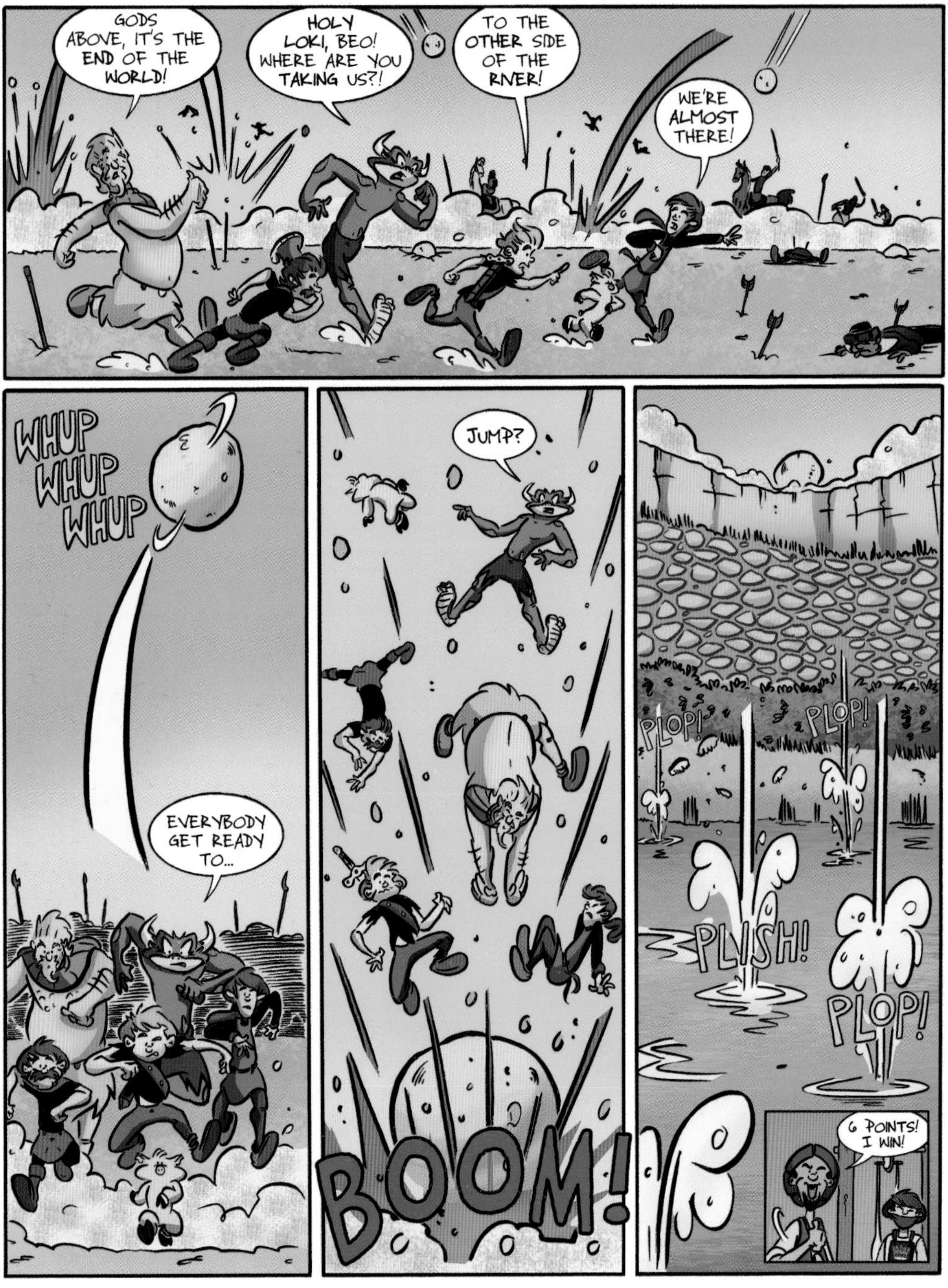
GODS ABOVE, IT'S THE END OF THE WORLD!
HOLY LOKI, BEO! WHERE ARE YOU TAKING US?!
TO THE OTHER SIDE OF THE RIVER!
WE'RE ALMOST THERE!
WHUP WHUP WHUP
EVERYBODY GET READY TO...
JUMP?
BOOM!
PLOP!
PLOP!
PLISH!
PLOP!
6 POINTS! I WIN!

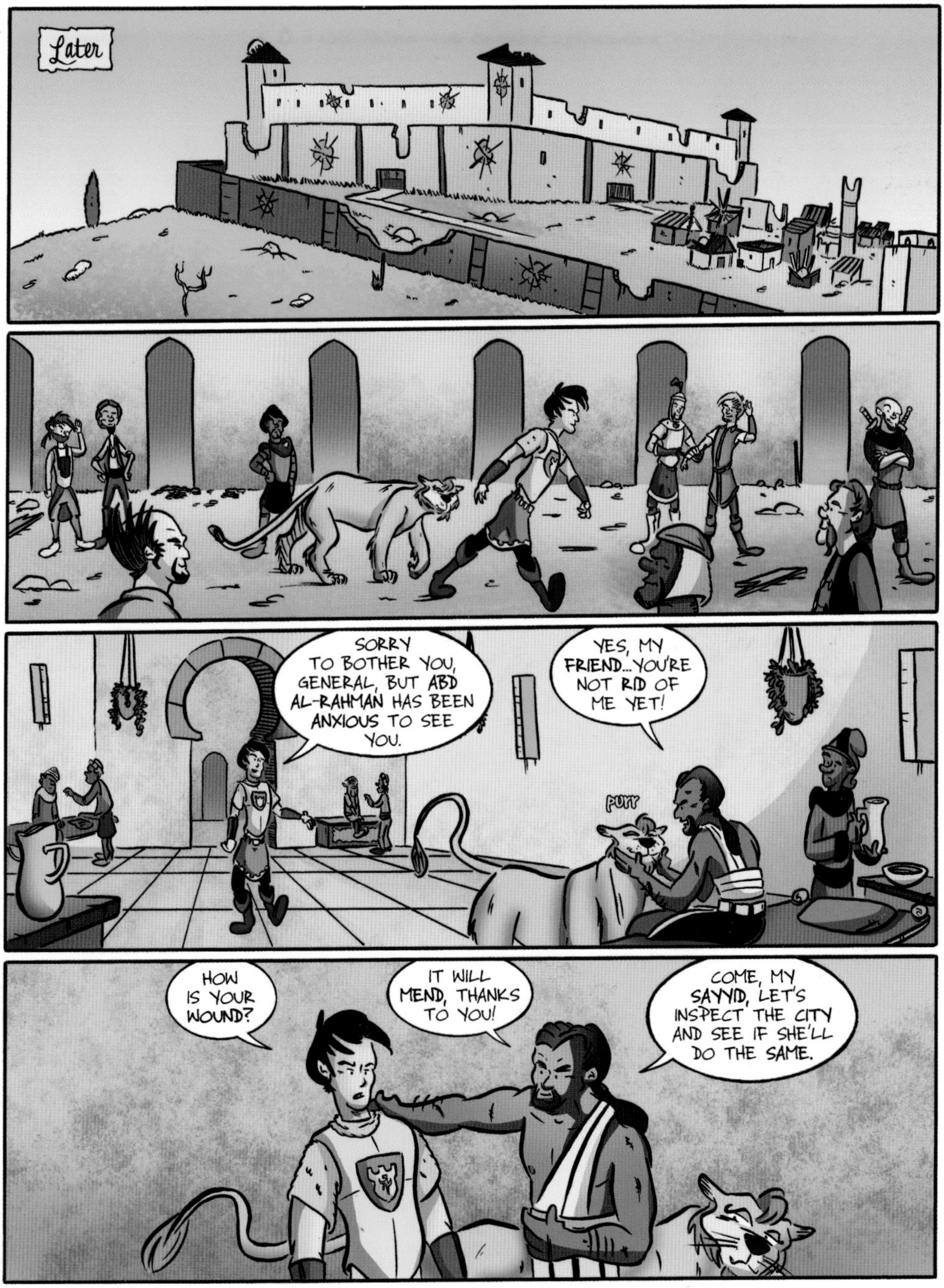
Later
SORRY TO BOTHER YOU, GENERAL, BUT ABD AL-RAHMAN HAS BEEN ANXIOUS TO SEE YOU.
YES, MY FRIEND... YOU'RE NOT RID OF ME YET!
purr
HOW IS YOUR WOUND?
IT WILL MEND, THANKS TO YOU!
COME, MY SAYYID, LET'S INSPECT THE CITY AND SEE IF SHE'LL DO THE SAME.

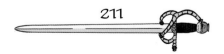

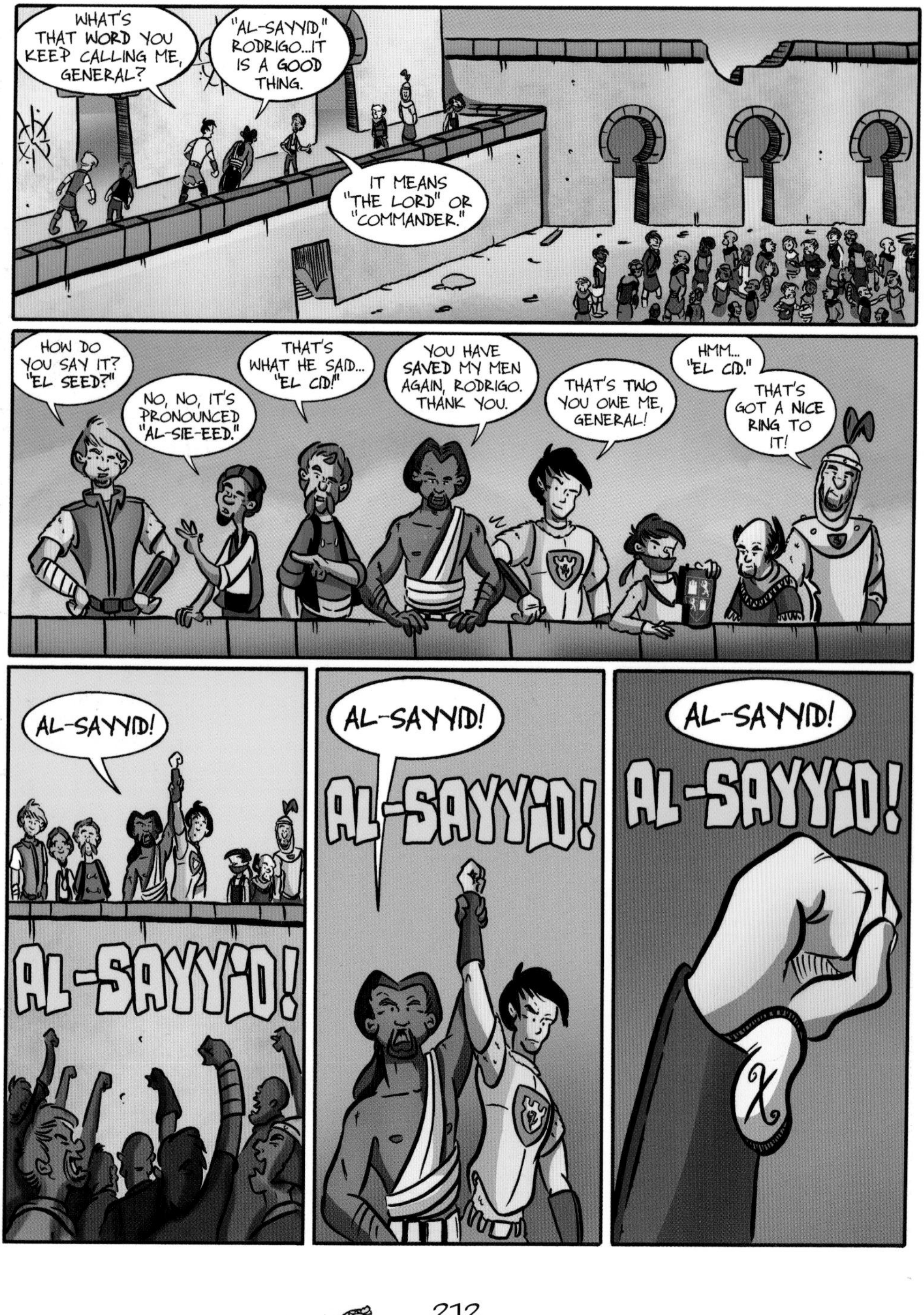
WHAT'S THAT WORD YOU KEEP CALLING ME, GENERAL?
"AL-SAYYID," RODRIGO...IT IS A GOOD THING.
IT MEANS "THE LORD" OR "COMMANDER."
HOW DO YOU SAY IT? "EL SEED?"
NO, NO, IT'S PRONOUNCED "AL-SIE-EED."
THAT'S WHAT HE SAID... "EL CID!"
YOU HAVE SAVED MY MEN AGAIN, RODRIGO. THANK YOU.
THAT'S TWO YOU OWE ME, GENERAL!
HMM... "EL CID."
THAT'S GOT A NICE RING TO IT!
AL-SAYYID!
AL-SAYYID!
AL-SAYYID!
AL-SAYYID!
AL-SAYYID!
AL-SAYYID!

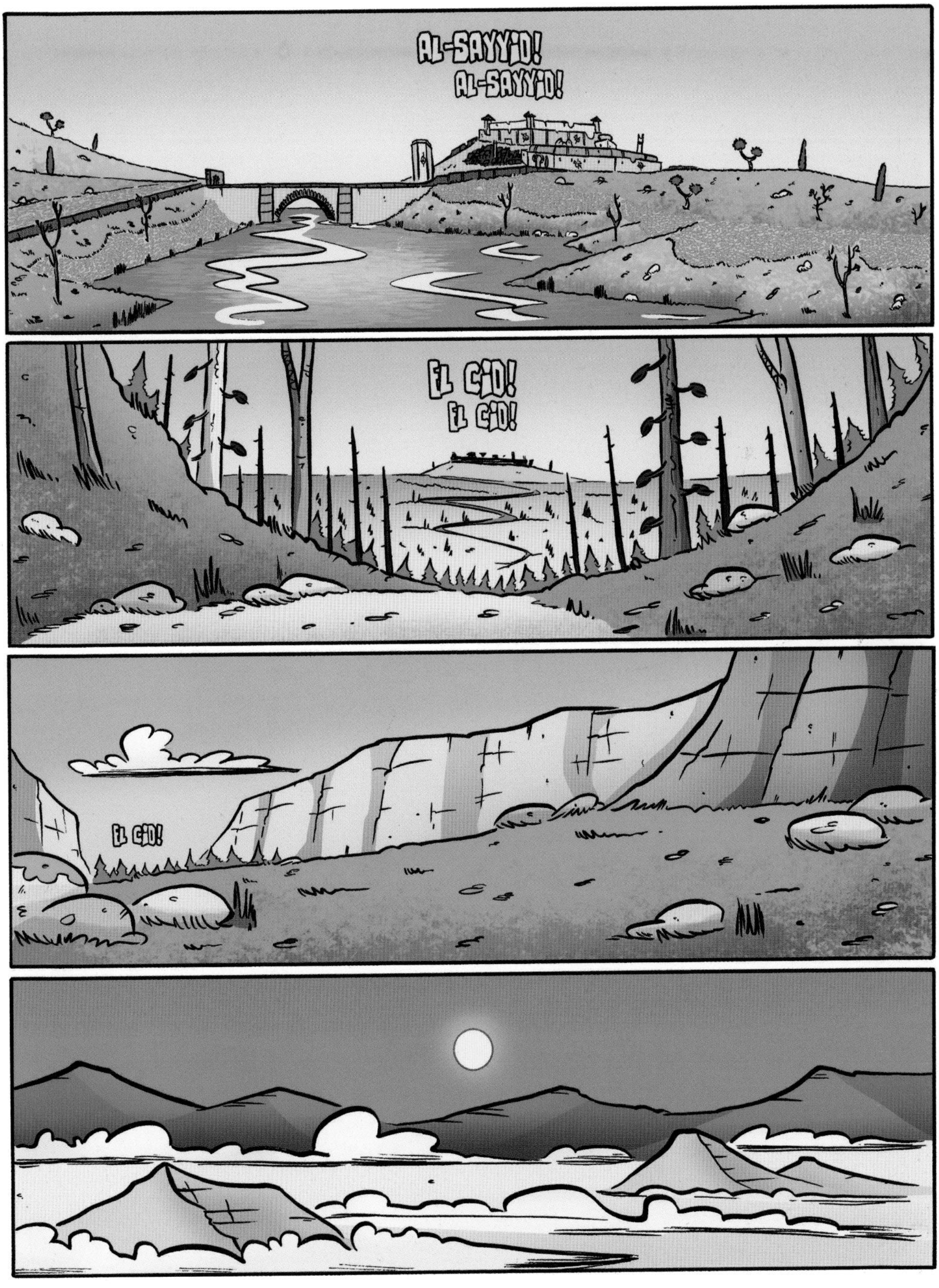
AL-SAYY'D!
AL-SAYY'D!
EL CID!
EL CID!
EL CID!

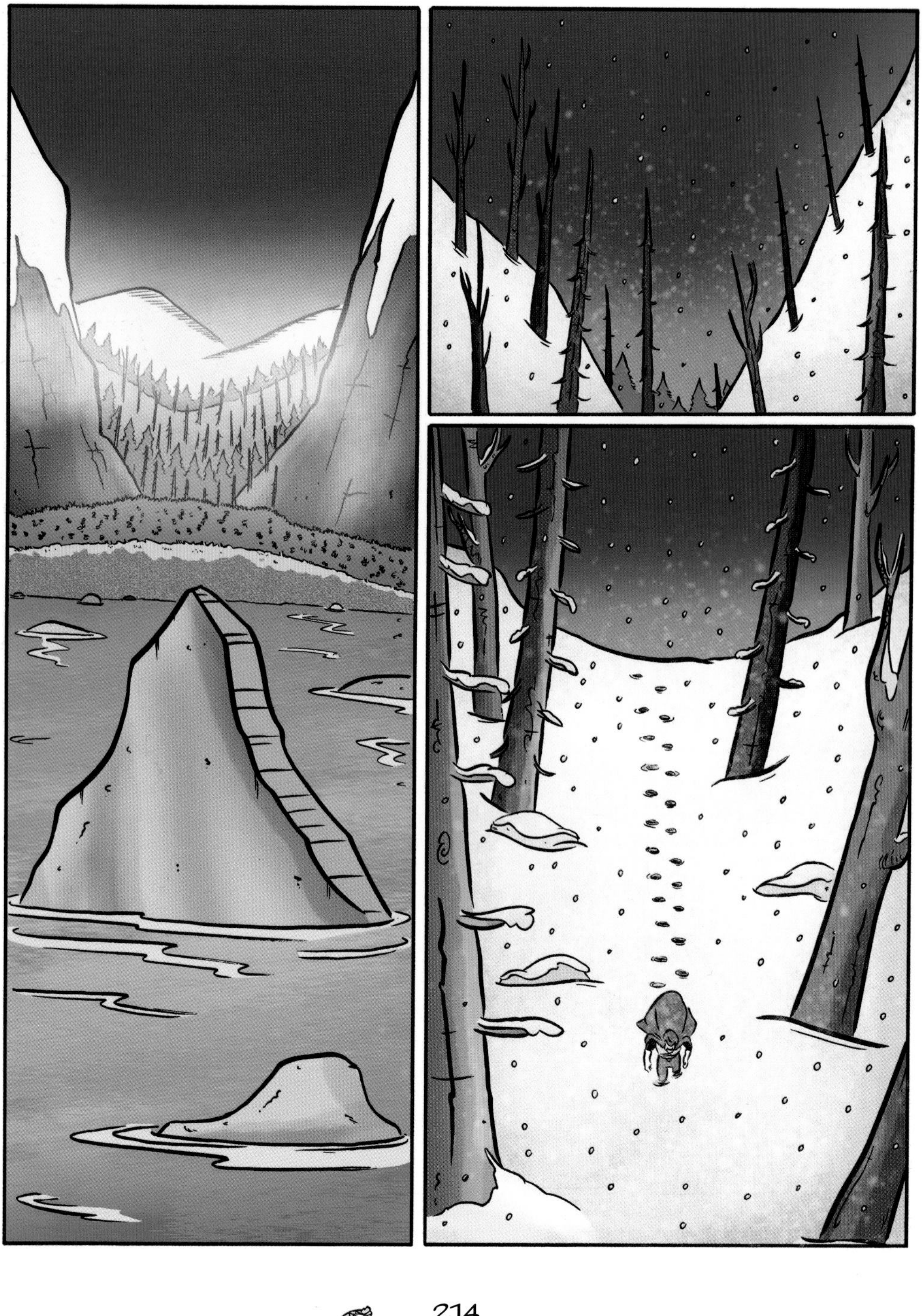

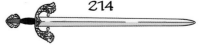

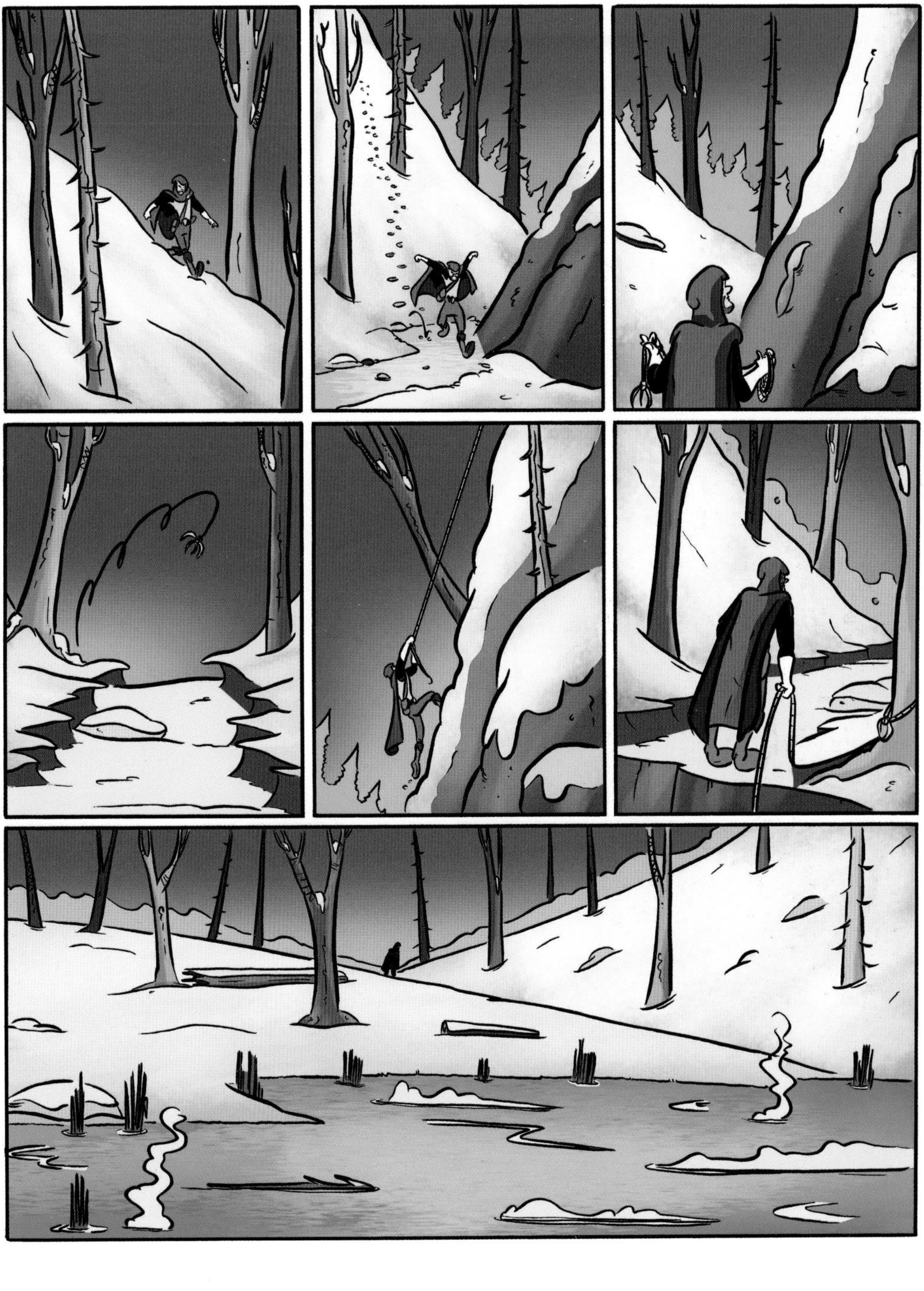

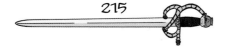

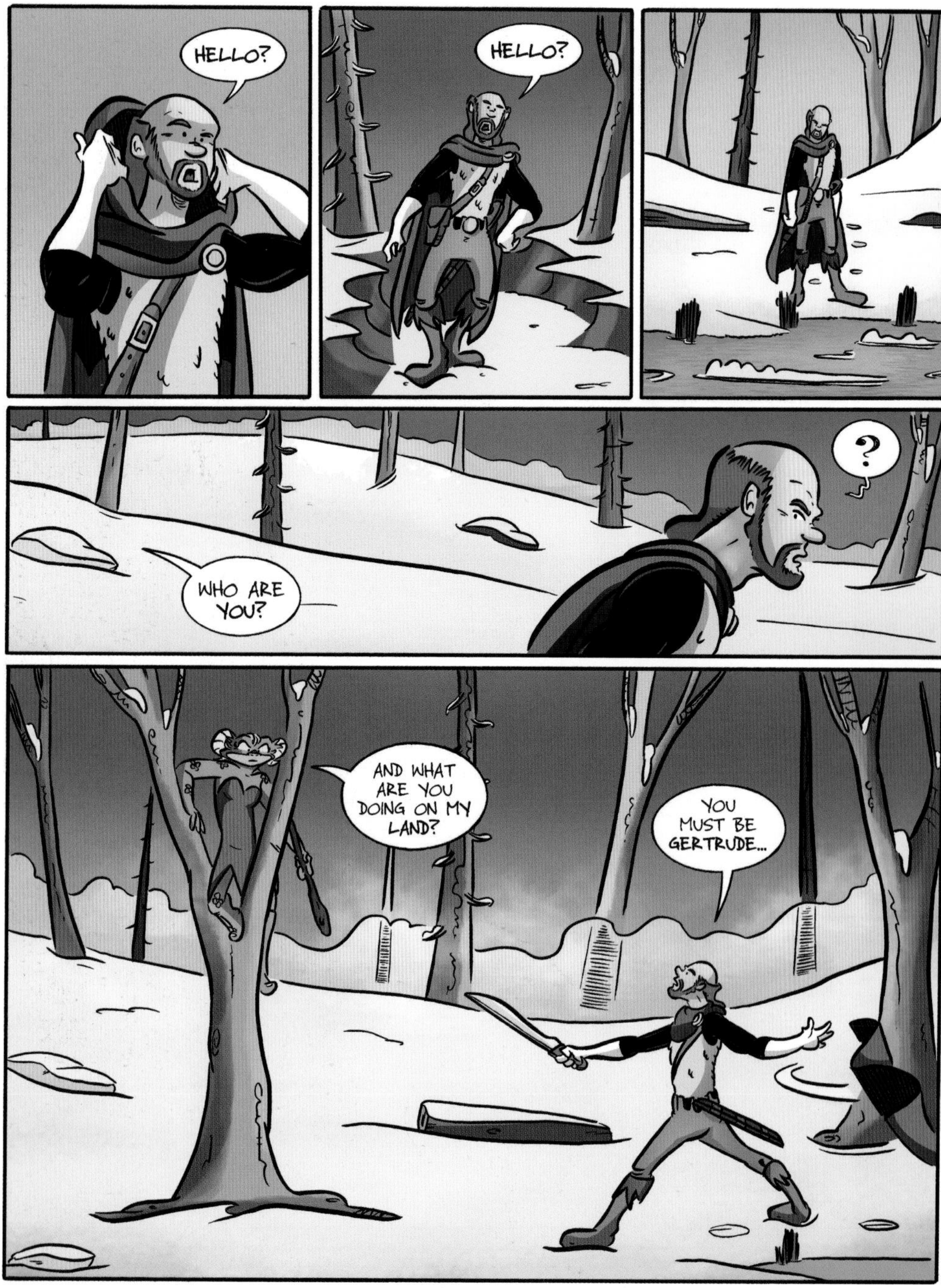
HELLO?
HELLO?
?
WHO ARE YOU?
AND WHAT ARE YOU DOING ON MY LAND?
YOU MUST BE GERTRUDE...

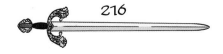

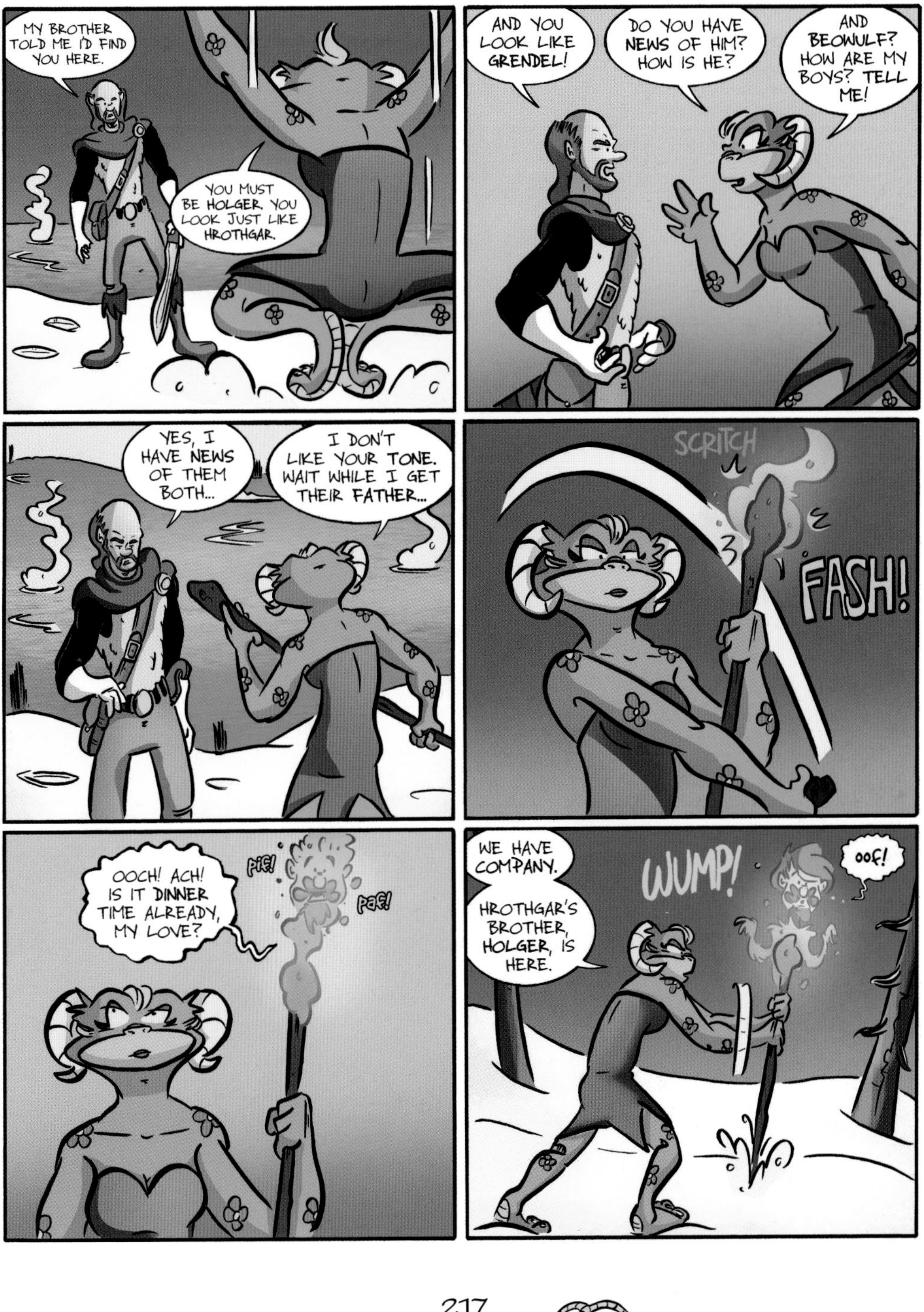
MY BROTHER TOLD ME I'D FIND YOU HERE.
YOU MUST BE HOLGER. YOU LOOK JUST LIKE HROTHGAR.
AND YOU LOOK LIKE GRENDEL!
DO YOU HAVE NEWS OF HIM? HOW IS HE?
AND BEOWULF? HOW ARE MY BOYS? TELL ME!
YES, I HAVE NEWS OF THEM BOTH...
I DON'T LIKE YOUR TONE. WAIT WHILE I GET THEIR FATHER...
SCRITCH
FASH!
OOCH! ACH! IS IT DINNER TIME ALREADY, MY LOVE?
pif!
paf!
WE HAVE COMPANY.
HROTHGAR'S BROTHER, HOLGER, IS HERE.
WUMP!
oof!

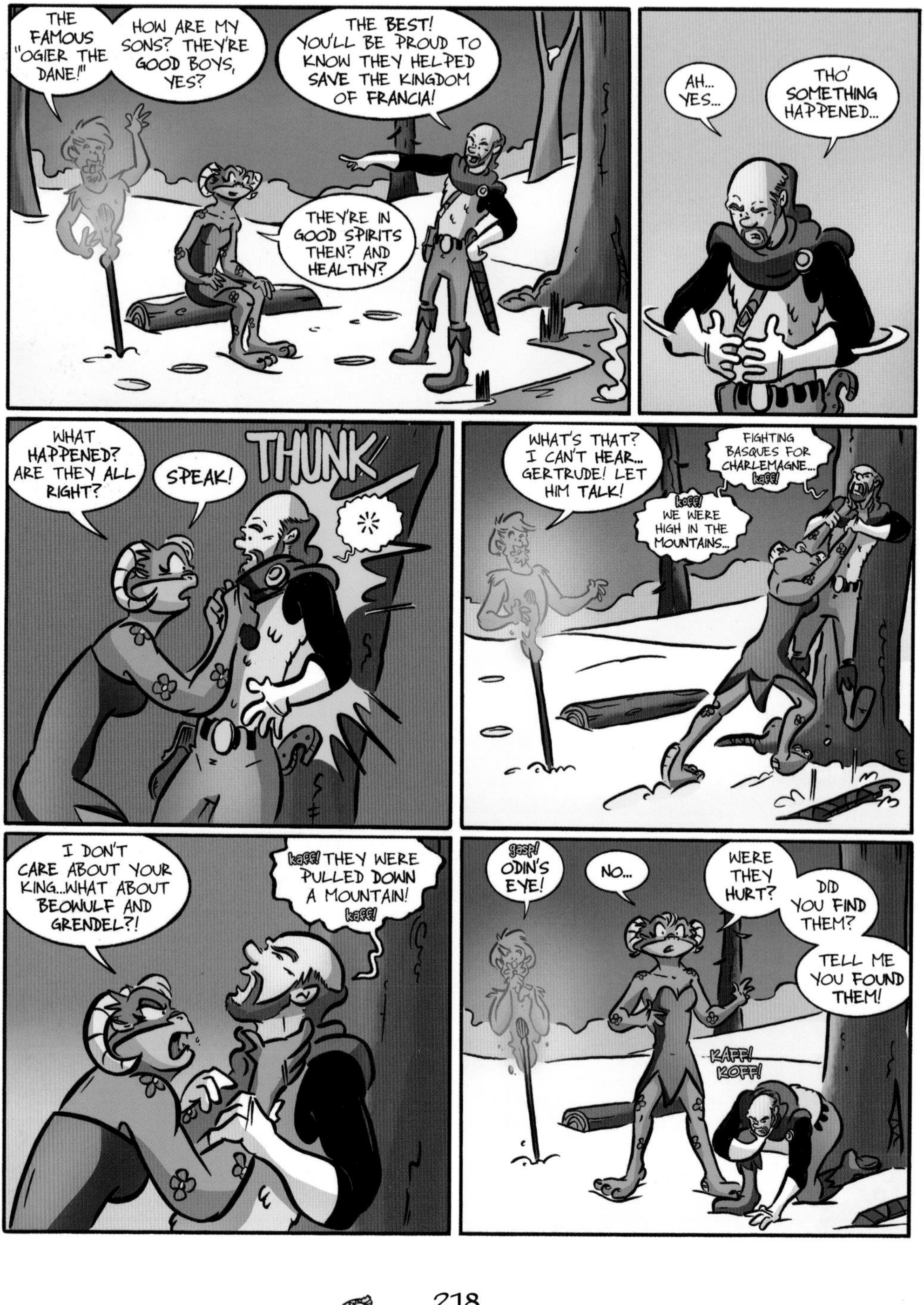
THE FAMOUS "OGIER THE DANE!"
HOW ARE MY SONS? THEY'RE GOOD BOYS, YES?
THE BEST! YOU'LL BE PROUD TO KNOW THEY HELPED SAVE THE KINGDOM OF FRANCIA!
THEY'RE IN GOOD SPIRITS THEN? AND HEALTHY?
AH... YES...
THO' SOMETHING HAPPENED...
WHAT HAPPENED? ARE THEY ALL RIGHT?
SPEAK!
THUNK
WHAT'S THAT? I CAN'T HEAR... GERTRUDE! LET HIM TALK!
FIGHTING BASQUES FOR CHARLEMAGNE... kaff!
koff! WE WERE HIGH IN THE MOUNTAINS...
I DON'T CARE ABOUT YOUR KING...WHAT ABOUT BEOWULF AND GRENDEL?!
kaff! THEY WERE PULLED DOWN A MOUNTAIN! kaff!
gasp! ODIN'S EYE!
NO...
WERE THEY HURT?
DID YOU FIND THEM?
TELL ME YOU FOUND THEM!
KAFF! KOFF!

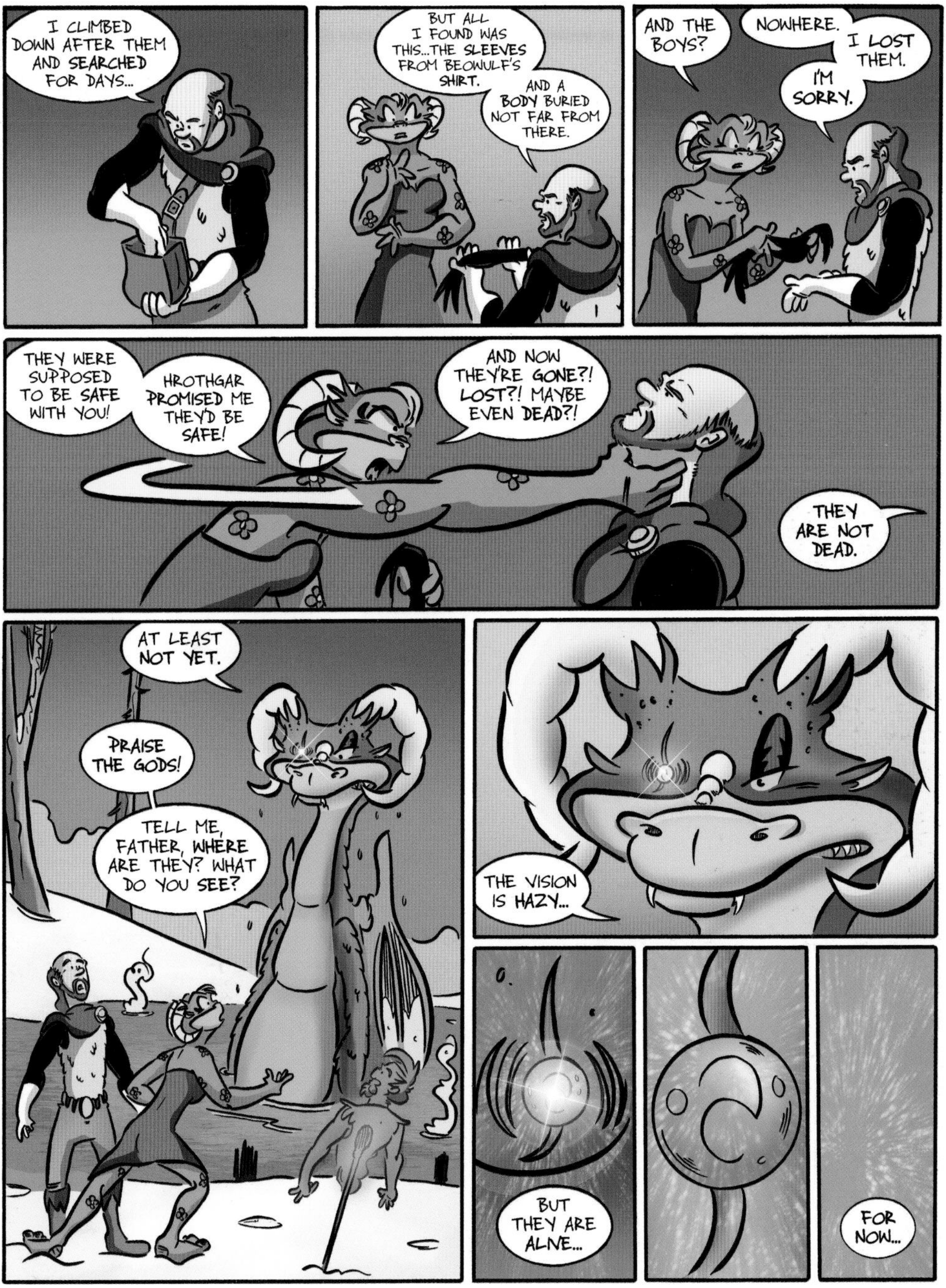
I CLIMBED DOWN AFTER THEM AND SEARCHED FOR DAYS...
BUT ALL I FOUND WAS THIS...THE SLEEVES FROM BEOWULF'S SHIRT.
AND A BODY BURIED NOT FAR FROM THERE.
AND THE BOYS?
NOWHERE.
I LOST THEM.
I'M SORRY.
THEY WERE SUPPOSED TO BE SAFE WITH YOU!
HROTHGAR PROMISED ME THEY'D BE SAFE!
AND NOW THEY'RE GONE?! LOST?! MAYBE EVEN DEAD?!
THEY ARE NOT DEAD.
AT LEAST NOT YET.
PRAISE THE GODS!
TELL ME, FATHER, WHERE ARE THEY? WHAT DO YOU SEE?
THE VISION IS HAZY...
BUT THEY ARE ALIVE...
FOR NOW...

"BUT BEOWULF AND GRENDEL ARE TOO FAR AWAY, BOTH IN BODY AND IN SPIRIT, FOR US TO REACH THEM..."

"THEY WILL BE AT THE MERCY OF OTHERS..."

"SOME WILL BE FRIENDS..."

"...AND SOME WILL BE ENEMIES..."

"THEIR FATES ARE BOUND TO EACH OTHER NOW..."

ROME

"MORE THAN THEY'VE EVER BEEN BEFORE..."

"AND IT WILL BE A HARD ROAD FOR THEM BOTH."

Fin

220

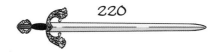

Mithras, God of the Midnight, here where the great bull dies,
Look on thy children in darkness. Oh take our sacrifice!
Many roads thou hast fashioned – all of them lead to the Light:
Mithras, also a soldier, teach us to die aright!

> – Rudyard Kipling
> "A Song to Mithras"
> from Puck of Pook's Hill, 1906

MORE TO EXPLORE!

spain circa 1067 a.d.

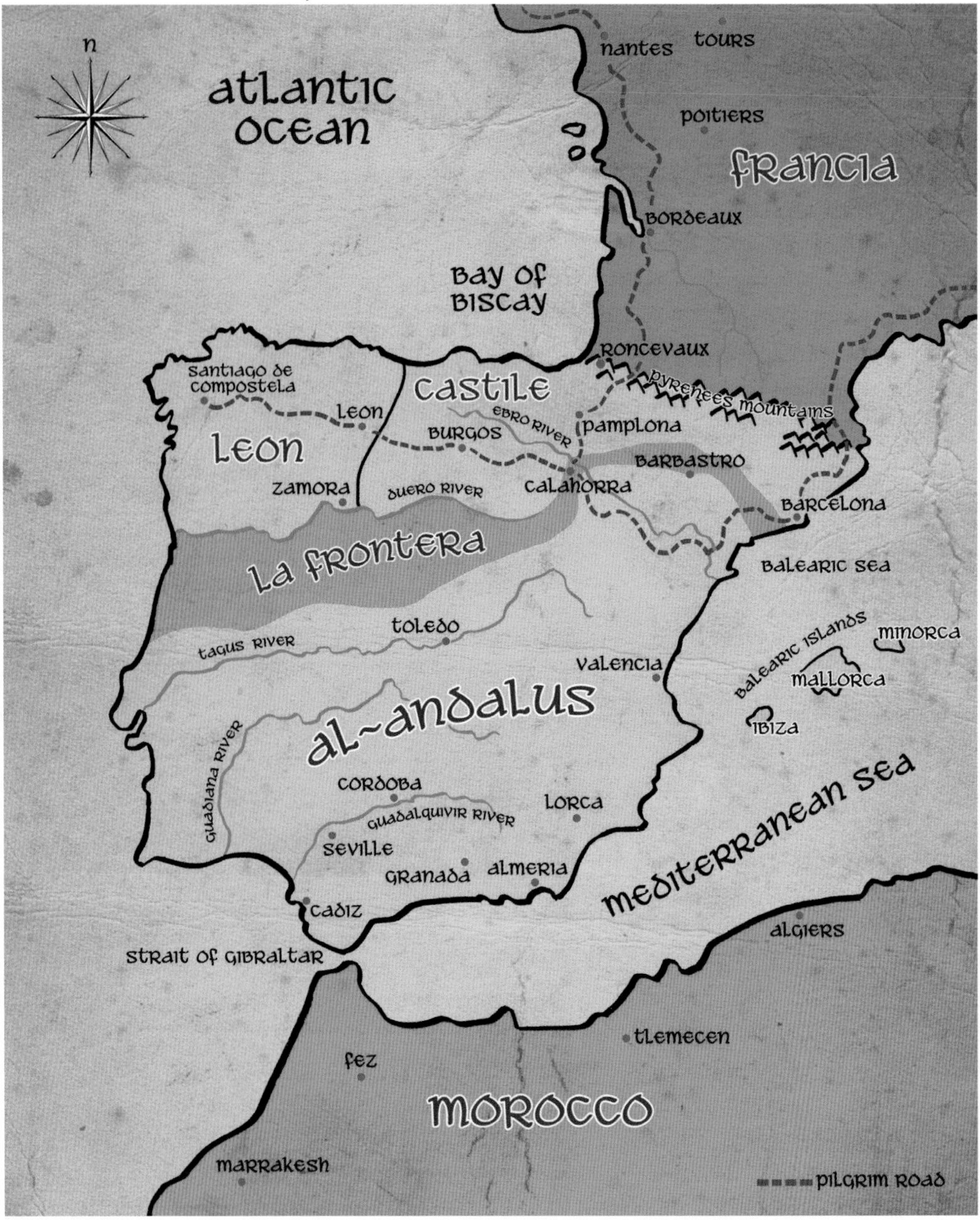
n
atlantic ocean
nantes
tours
poitiers
francia
bordeaux
bay of biscay
roncevaux
pyrenees mountains
santiago de compostela
leon
castile
ebro river
pamplona
burgos
leon
barbastro
zamora
duero river
calahorra
barcelona
la frontera
balearic sea
toledo
tagus river
minorca
balearic islands
valencia
mallorca
al-andalus
ibiza
guadiana river
mediterranean sea
cordoba
lorca
guadalquivir river
seville
granada
almeria
cadiz
algiers
strait of gibraltar
tlemecen
fez
morocco
marrakesh
pilgrim road

Book three in the *Kid Beowulf* series takes place around 1067 A.D. in the Iberian peninsula of Spain and Portugal. It is a land divided between Christian territories in the north comprised of the kingdoms of Castile and León and the Muslim kingdoms in the south called Al-Andalus. No one king rules either place; instead many of the Christian and Muslim territories fight amongst themselves in an attempt to consolidate power. Sometimes this led to Christian kings reaching out to Muslim mercenaries and vice versa to help each other's cause. Spain in the eleventh century is a very divided place.

key terms

Abd Al-Rahman (731–788) was a Muslim prince of the Umayyad dynasty who lost power to the rival Abbasid dynasty in 748. Exiled from his home in Damascus, he made his way to Al-Andalus in 755. After years of fighting, he became the emir of Córdoba and recreated the caliphate for his Umayyad family in Spain. During his reign, Córdoba was a place where all religions and ideas were welcome.

Al-Andalus (ahl-ahnda-loose) was the name given to Muslim-controlled Spain. At its peak during the eighth century, Muslims controlled most of Spain and Portugal. The empire contracted during centuries of war, and by 1492 the Christian rulers, King Ferdinand II and Queen Isabella, pushed the remaining Muslims out of Spain and finalized the centuries-long *Reconquista*. What remained of Al-Andalus was centered at the Emirate of Granada. Today, in modern-day Spain, the southern area known as "Andalusia" is derived from "Al-Andalus."

Almoravids (ahl-more-ah-vids) were a strong warrior tribe of fundamentalist Muslims based in North Africa and led by Ibn Yusuf. In 1086 Ibn Yusuf was invited by the taifa princes of Al-Andalus to defend their territories from the encroachment of the Christian king, Alfonso. In the epic poem *El Cantar de Mio Cid*, El Cid defeats Ibn Yusuf at Valencia and goes on to fight the Almoravids across Spain.

Castile and León were the most powerful kingdoms in Christian Spain. Originally ruled by King Ferdinand the Great, upon his death the kingdom was divided among his children: Castile went to his oldest son Sancho, León went to his youngest son Alfonso, and the town of Zamora went to his daughter Urraca.

Colada (coe-lah-da) and **Tizona** (tea-thone-ah) are the names of El Cid's twin swords. "Colada" describes the process of its forging; "acero colado" is alloyed steel without impurities. "Tizona" means "firebrand" and was won from Ibn Yusuf of Valencia. It is now on display at the Burgos Museum in Spain.

La Frontera was the name given to a large swath of land that cut east to west across Spain and divided the Christian and Muslim kingdoms. Ruled by bandits, castaways, and outlaws, La Frontera was the place where criminals went and exiles were forgotten.

Moors was a term to describe Muslims or Arabs during the medieval era. In the epic poem *El Cantar de Mio Cid*, the Moors rule Al-Andalus and were at war with the Christian Spaniards.

Taifa (tie-ee-fa) was an independent, Muslim-ruled principality. After the fall of the Caliphate of Córdoba in 1031, many smaller kingdoms, or "taifas," were formed across Al-Andalus.

Character Glossary

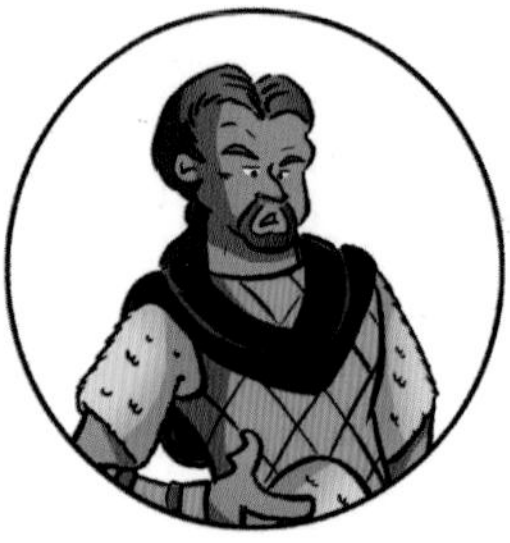

Ibn Al-Fajar (iben ahl-fahar) is the commander of an elite brigade of Moorish soldiers who help patrol and defend Al-Andalus. Fast on their horses, General Al-Fajar and his men are able to move from kingdom to kingdom to help whichever lord needs them. Al-Fajar has a pet lion named Abd Al-Rahman who helps him look out for his friends, his family, and his country.

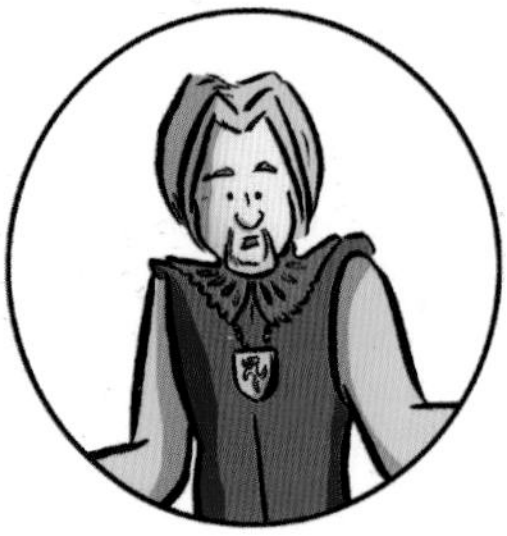

Alfonso (ahl-fon-soe) is the youngest son of King Ferdinand, twin brother to his sister Urraca, and younger brother to King Sancho. When Ferdinand died, he divided his kingdom among his children and gave Alfonso the largest and wealthiest territory, León. Ultimately, Alfonso believes that he and his twin sister could rule Spain quite well together, but his older brother Sancho stands in his way.

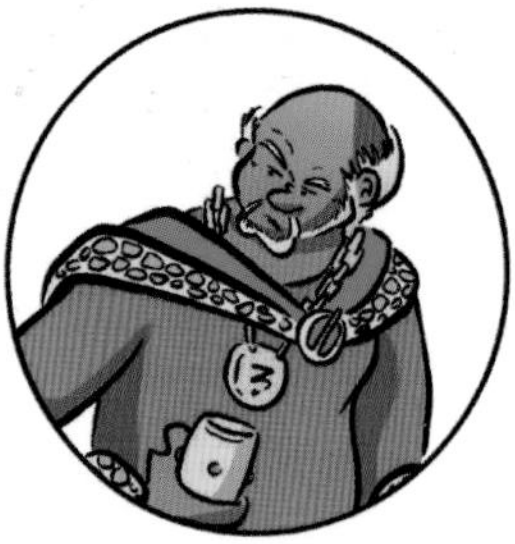

Al-Mamun (ahl mah-moon) is the longtime lord of Toledo, the taifa of Al-Andalus that most resembles the fabled days of Córdoba, where Moors, Jews, and Christians lived and worked together. Al-Mamun remembers those bygone days and is worried they may only live in memory, especially if the rest of the taifa lords have their way and wage an unnecessary war against the Christian kings in the north.

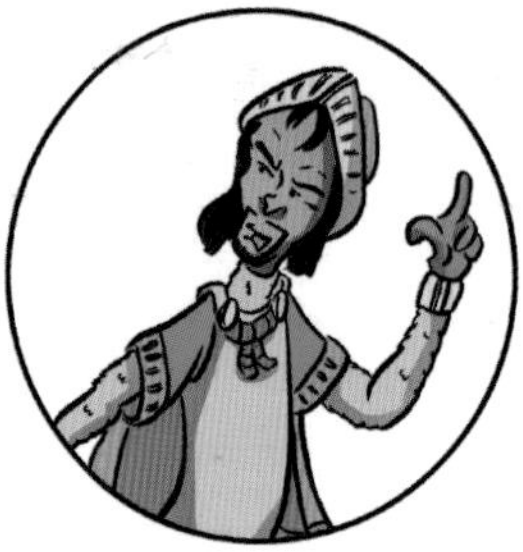

Al-Mutamid (ahl-mutah-meed) is the taifa lord of Seville, a kingdom in southern Al-Andalus. Although rich and powerful, Al-Mutamid has designs on expanding his lands and has convinced the rest of the lords in Al-Andalus that it is time they went to war with the Christian kingdoms in the north. So he invites the brutal warlord Ibn Yusuf and his Almoravids from Morocco to fight for them, not realizing that what he has brought is their destruction.

Babieca (bah-bee-ek-ah) is Rodrigo's horse and four-legged companion. Originally just a packhorse, Babieca took a shine to Rodrigo when he was a boy and decided to make him his own. "Babieca" means "dullard" in Spanish, but this horse is anything but that–he is so clever and well-trained, he can be ridden without a bridle!

Beowulf (bay-oh-wolf) and **Grendel** (gren-del) find themselves lost in Spain, far from the moral influence of their Uncle Holger and the Peers. Mistaken for gods in this strange land, the brothers are showered with adulation and gold which they can use to get back to Daneland. Now the brothers must decide whether lying and cheating are worth the price to get back home.

Boudi (boo-dee) is a nine-year-old girl far from her native home of Britannia. She travels with her Uncle Leo and Aunt Gemma, who are on their way to Italia, where they will partake in an ancient rite. Whether Boudi believes in her uncle's religion is up for debate, but she will do what she can to protect her family on the pilgrim road and the secret she carries with her.

Rodrigo Díaz (rod-ree-go dee-az) is a young man raised to believe in the Old World virtues of prudence, temperance, and justice, yet he lives in a place where those virtues have been forgotten, or worse, ignored. His ethics are constantly challenged, and whether he defends the powerless or helps the weak, Rodrigo trips into trouble. He tries to navigate a world where ideals are desperately needed but hard to find.

Don Diego (dawn dee-ay-go) had the sad fate to outlive his only son, and so it is only natural that he is overprotective of his grandson, Rodrigo. Diego taught him and many of Castile's finest knights the principles of knighthood, but he wonders if that ancient credo still means anything in the Spain his grandson has inherited.

Emer (ee-mer) and **Ermlaf** (irm-laff) are Heathobards who are out to get Beowulf and Grendel. At the end of the "Song of Roland," they found themselves on the losing side and were carted away to Spain with the Saracens. Desperate and broke, the duo took a dead-end job but are eager to get back to Daneland (by whatever means necessary). When they stumble upon a group of rich pilgrims, Emer starts a scheme to rob them blind and get back home.

Álvar Fáñez (ahl-var fanyez) is a high-ranking knight of León and part of King Alfonso's personal guard. Álvar embodies the best tenets of knighthood: He is truthful, steadfast, and honorable. Álvar is also a romantic and looks to serve those in need and in love.

Gormaz (gore-mahz) is Castile's and King Sancho's champion. Known for his prowess and severity on the battlefield, Count Gormaz will do what his king tells him to without question. A man ruled by practical thinking, he has little need for codes of chivalry or the silly people who adhere to them. Gormaz worries that his only daughter, Ximena, has fallen in love with such a man and that it will lead to her ruin.

Gemma and **Leo** are pilgrims and practitioners of an ancient religion called Mithraism. They lead their grandfather; their sacred cow, Luna; and their young niece, Boudi, across Europe and to Italia, where they hope to arrive in time for the annual Mithraic Mystery. When they stumble upon Beowulf and Grendel, they mistake them for their gods, Mithras and Tauro.

Samuel Hanagid (hah-nah-geed) is a Jewish poet, astronomer, and mathematician. He was part of the royal court at Córdoba when during a trip across La Frontera, he was separated from his caravan. He most assuredly would have died at the hands of bandits had Rodrigo Díaz not come to his aid. Forever in his debt, Samuel attaches himself to the young knight and his friends and proves to be an invaluable resource: on the field, with the books, and in the kitchen.

Martín (mar-teen) is a young knight of Castile and one of Rodrigo's best friends. He became a knight more out of fondness and friendship for Rodrigo than to uphold any particular ideals. Martín is cheerful and practical, and he is more concerned with filling his belly and saving his neck than following any idealistic crusade. Ultimately, he will follow his friends–always at their back and with a good quip at his side.

Ordoñez (or-dohn-nyez) is a young knight of Castile and Count Gormaz's right-hand man. On the field, Ordoñez is fierce, efficient, and ruthless; his only concern is getting the job done. He does what he is told and has no time for people who whine and squeal about "virtue" or "chivalry." He cannot stand Rodrigo Díaz.

Pedro is a young knight of Castile and one of Rodrigo's best friends. Pedro is mute but his voice is heard through the drawings he makes on his slate board. On the field, Pedro is a crafty swordsman, and his silent but deadly approach in battle makes him perfect for reconnaissance: No one likes, or is better at, sneaking around than Pedro the mute!

Sancho (sahn-choe) is the king of Castile, though as firstborn son of King Ferdinand, he believes he should rule all of Spain. Instead he has to share it with his siblings. Worse still, Sancho cannot keep his own territories in line: No one respects his authority, which makes him question whether he has any.

Urraca (oo-rahk-ah) is the daughter of the late King Ferdinand and sister to Sancho and Alfonso. She rules the kingdom of Zamora and has no desire to rule more than what she was given. She is shrewd, well-versed in the art of politics, and consistently underestimated by her siblings. For all her intellect, Urraca is a romantic at heart and does her best to counsel Ximena's rage-filled heart.

Ximena (she-mane-ah) is a beautiful and fiery woman of Castile. Her father, Count Gormaz, is the king's champion, and much to his dismay, Ximena has fallen in love with a young knight named Rodrigo, whom her father believes is far below her station. Ximena understands her father and Rodrigo are at opposite sides of an ideological war, and the last thing she wants to do is choose love over honor.

Ibn Yusuf (iben yoo-soof) is the leader of a powerful war tribe from Morroco called the Almoravids. He is a fierce fighter and an implacable proponent of extremist Muslim views and principles. He was invited by the taifa lords of Al-Andalus to help fight the Christian kings, but before Ibn Yusuf fights them, he must first deal with the decadent nation of Al-Andalus and set things right.

destreza ~ the art of spanish fencing

La Verdadera Destreza or "The True Art" was a fencing style developed in the fourteenth century by fencing master Don Jerónimo Sánchez de Carranza. The word *destreza* translates to "dexterity" or "skill." *Destreza* is not just a fencing form, but it is a way to look at the world: The movements are based on reason and geometry, its principles come from classical philosophy, and its morality emanates from a Renaissance humanist education. It was a tradition taught to young men and meant to instill good character and classical learning. The art of *destreza* was applied to both swordplay and to life.

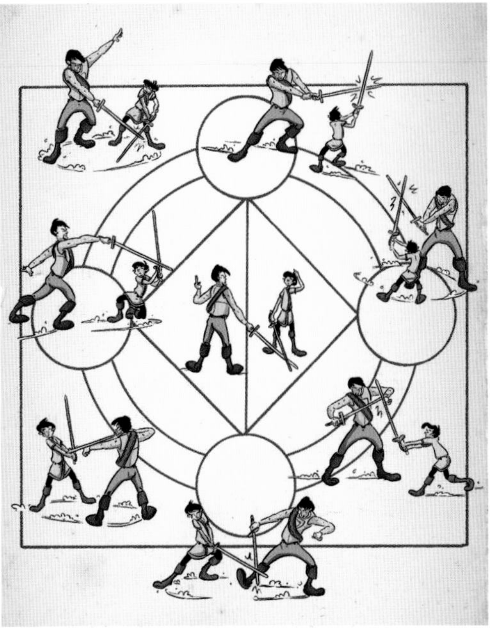

In *The Rise of El Cid*, Rodrigo Díaz is well-versed in the physical skills of *destreza,* but he wrestles internally with its principles as he tries to figure out what sort of person he wants to become. There are two moments in the book when the *destreza* fencing techniqes are put into practice. The *destreza* training map is used during a sequence in which twelve-year-old Rodrigo is being quizzed on swordplay and Spain's history by his father while both move clockwise around the map.

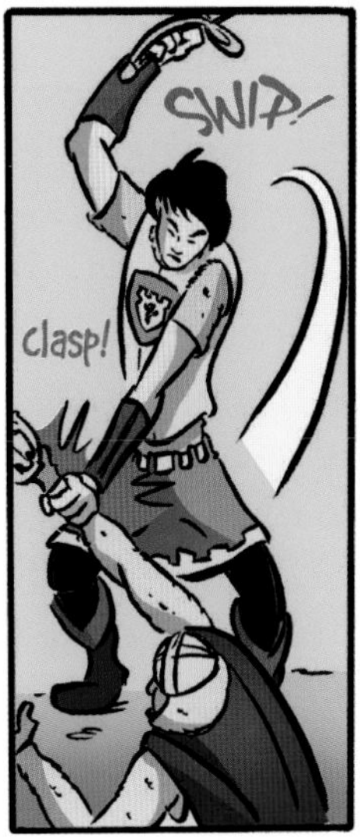
SNIP!
Clasp!

Years later, when Rodrigo confronts Ibn Yusuf, he uses a *destreza* grapple technique to disarm the powerful Muslim and save Toledo. It is in this moment when Rodrigo's moral quandary has also been allayed and he fully realizes the way of *destreza*.

Even though the events in *The Rise of El Cid* predate the fencing form of *destreza* by several centuries, I like to think that perhaps the art form took root with Spain's greatest epic hero, Rodrigo Díaz, who was a man of good character, broad learning, and fierce fencing.

*For more on Carranza and "*La Verdadera Destreza*" visit http://www.destreza.us online!*

el cantar de mio cid
origins of the epic poem

El Cantar de Mio Cid (*The Song of My Cid*) is a Spanish epic poem set in the eleventh century that concerns the exploits of Rodrigo Díaz de Vivar. Unlike Beowulf, who is imaginary, Rodrigo Díaz was a real person who made a huge historical impact. His story became the stuff of legend and its own epic poem.

The epic begins long after Rodrigo Díaz has won the name El Cid (derived from the Arabic word *Al-Sayyid* meaning "commander" or "lord"). With his army, he has won countless cities for King Alfonso of Spain, increasing the Christian territories of Castile and León. Despite this, enemies of El Cid claim he stole money from King Alfonso, and so the king exiles Rodrigo as punishment. El Cid departs Castile, leaving behind his wife and infant twin daughters. Now, far out in the Spanish frontier, and with an army to feed and manage, Rodrigo becomes a mercenary. He fights for whomever will pay for his blade, whether it is a Christian king or an Islamic emir. At the end of each conquest, Rodrigo pays his men and makes a point of sending tribute back to King Alfonso in Castile.

Eventually, Rodrigo yearns for a permanent place for himself, his family, and his men, and he sets his sights on the Moorish-controlled town of Valencia. After a long siege, El Cid claims the town for his own and calls for his family to join him.

Meanwhile in Castile, Alfonso is having troubles of his own as the Muslim-dominated area of Spain—called "Al-Andalus"—has invited a North African commander named Yusuf Ibn Tashfin and his fierce tribe of Almoravids to come and fight the Christians on their behalf. After a severe drubbing by Yusuf, Alfonso entreats Rodrigo to fight for Castile. His exile lifted, Rodrigo and his army beat Yusuf Ibn Tashfin back to Africa. Rodrigo Díaz regains his stature with Alfonso and even more fame.

The second half of the poem concerns the marriage of El Cid's grown daughters to a pair of noble princes, called the Infantes. Perceived to be good marriages for El Cid and his family, in truth the Infantes are cruel men who, shortly after the wedding, beat and abandon El Cid's daughters in the wilderness, taking their dowry for their own.

Ashamed and dishonored, Rodrigo calls upon King Alfonso to set things right. A trial is set, and the princes are quickly found guilty and must face off against two of El Cid's best knights, who will fight for his daughters' honor. El Cid bequeathes his two prized blades, Tizona and Colada, to these knights, Pedro Bermúdez and Martín Antolínez.

The Infantes are soundly defeated, and another marriage for El Cid's daughters is arranged, this time with two eligible princes who treat them with respect. Finally, Rodrigo Díaz de Vivar returns to his home in Valencia, which he defends until the end of his days with his wife, Ximena, and his horse, Babieca.

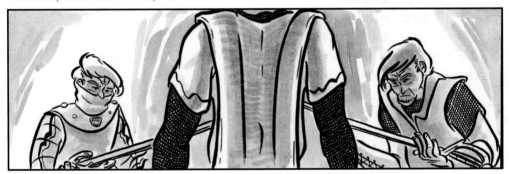

El Cantar de Mio Cid is a realistic epic poem: There are no monsters for El Cid to slay like in *Beowulf,* and it is not a polemic against "the pagan Saracens" depicted in the French epic *The Song of Roland.* The poem is about honor and justice and the transition of the medieval world from divine law (i.e., the will of God) to natural law (the laws of man).

The stark black-and-white portrayal of religion found in *The Song of Roland* has become, three centuries later, a murky shade of gray in *El Cantar de Mio Cid*; Rodrigo fights against and sometimes for the Moors and does the same with the Christians. Rodrigo Díaz is ruled by his own moral and ethical code.

El Cid is considered to be a hero of the *Reconquista*–a time period in Spain spanning approximately 780 years between 711 and 1492 when the Christians expelled the Muslims–but that is an oversimplification. The fact that Spain's national hero bears a name derived from the Arabic word *Al-Sayyid* is proof that Spain in the eleventh century was a very unique place, where heroes were respected on both sides of a religious divide.

the mystery of mithras

Book three in the *Kid Beowulf* series is the bridge book between the first trilogy and the next, which proved to have its own challenges: not only did I have to tell a self-contained story based on *El Cid*, but I also needed to find a way to move Beowulf and Grendel from Spain into Italy and make that move feel like a natural and inevitable segue.

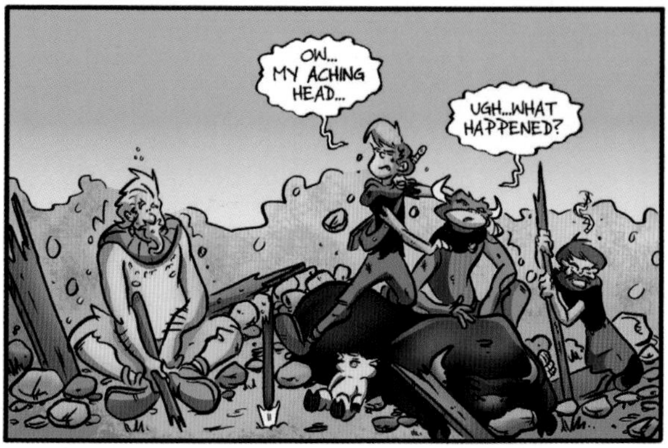
OW...
MY ACHING
HEAD...
UGH...WHAT
HAPPENED?

Above: After the chaotic running of the bulls, Beowulf and Grendel rise from the rubble and mimic the Mithraic bull-slaying scene.

Since the overarching theme between Beowulf and Grendel is the monster-slayer story, I wanted to drop that theme into this book in a real way and foreshadow the troubles the brothers will face down the road. During my research, I came across an ancient Roman religion called Mithraism, which centered around a boy god named Mithras who slays a bull. The boy and the bull caught my attention–they made for a nice parallel to Beowulf and Grendel.

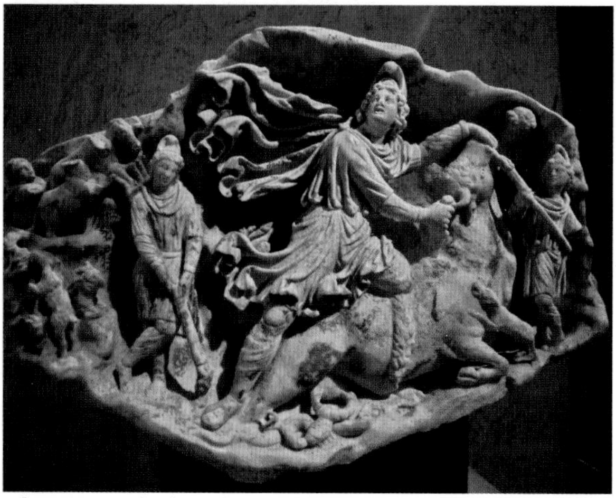

Above: A relief sculpture depicting Mithras slaying the bull. Reliefs like this were found across Europe.

Not much is known about the religion, and what is known has been derived from the art left behind. It was practiced across the Roman Empire between the first and fourth centuries. The center was in Rome, but it expanded as far as Britannia. There are several initiation rituals, many of them focused around the Zodiac. At the center of the religion was Mithras and the bull. Also worshipped was Sol (the sun) and Luna (the moon), and escorting Mithras were the torch bearers, Cautes and Cautophates. I built much of the mythology of Mithras and Tauro in this book from these elements and made it echo the future relationship between Beowulf and Grendel.

Boudica the Lost Princess

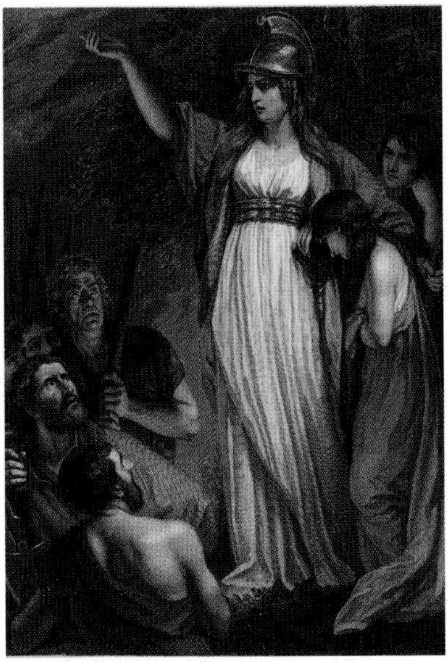

Above: *Boadicea Haranguing the Britons* by John Opie.

Boudica is a historical figure, and like Rodrigo Díaz, her story evolved into legend. She was queen of the British Iceni tribe in A.D. 60 and led an uprising against the occupying Roman forces. Her revolt was so effective it almost forced Emperor Nero to pull the Romans out of Britannia altogether.

The insurrection was eventually put down, and Boudica took her own life in order not to be captured. Not a great deal is known of her story beyond this, but she has become an important cultural symbol in Britain. When I came across her story, I knew she had to meet Beowulf (the alliteration alone was too good to pass up).

Boudica's historical dates lined up well with the Mithras storyline. So Boudica became Boudi, a nine-year-old girl who is fleeing the Romans from her homeland of Brittania under the protection of her eccentric aunt and uncle, Gemma and Leo.

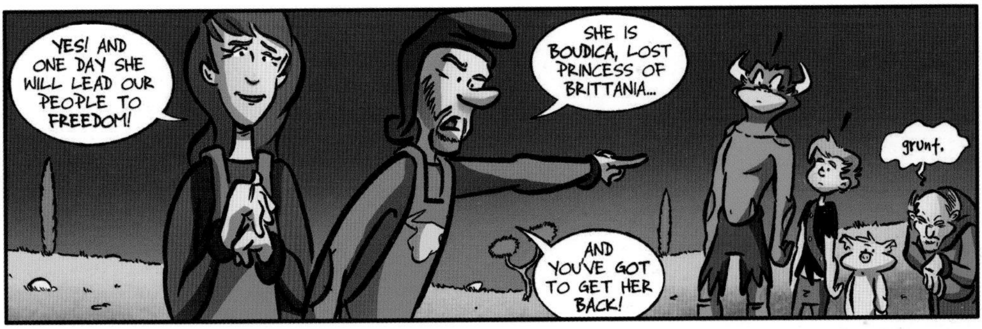
YES! AND ONE DAY SHE WILL LEAD OUR PEOPLE TO FREEDOM!
SHE IS BOUDICA, LOST PRINCESS OF BRITTANIA...
AND YOU'VE GOT TO GET HER BACK!
grunt.

I enjoyed pitting Boudi against Beowulf. She is the only one in her group who knows Beowulf and Grendel are not Mithras and Tauro, but her protests go unheeded. By the time the ruse is found out, Emer and Ermlaf have stolen the pilgrims' cow and their gold, and Boudi wants nothing more than to get revenge.

Beowulf and Grendel want to redeem themselves, but Boudi does not trust them. It forces Beowulf to go above and beyond to gain her trust and friendship. This makes their relationship fun to watch over the course of the book. Boudi is a character who will become an important part of the *Kid Beowulf* universe, and we will see her again.

fun facts

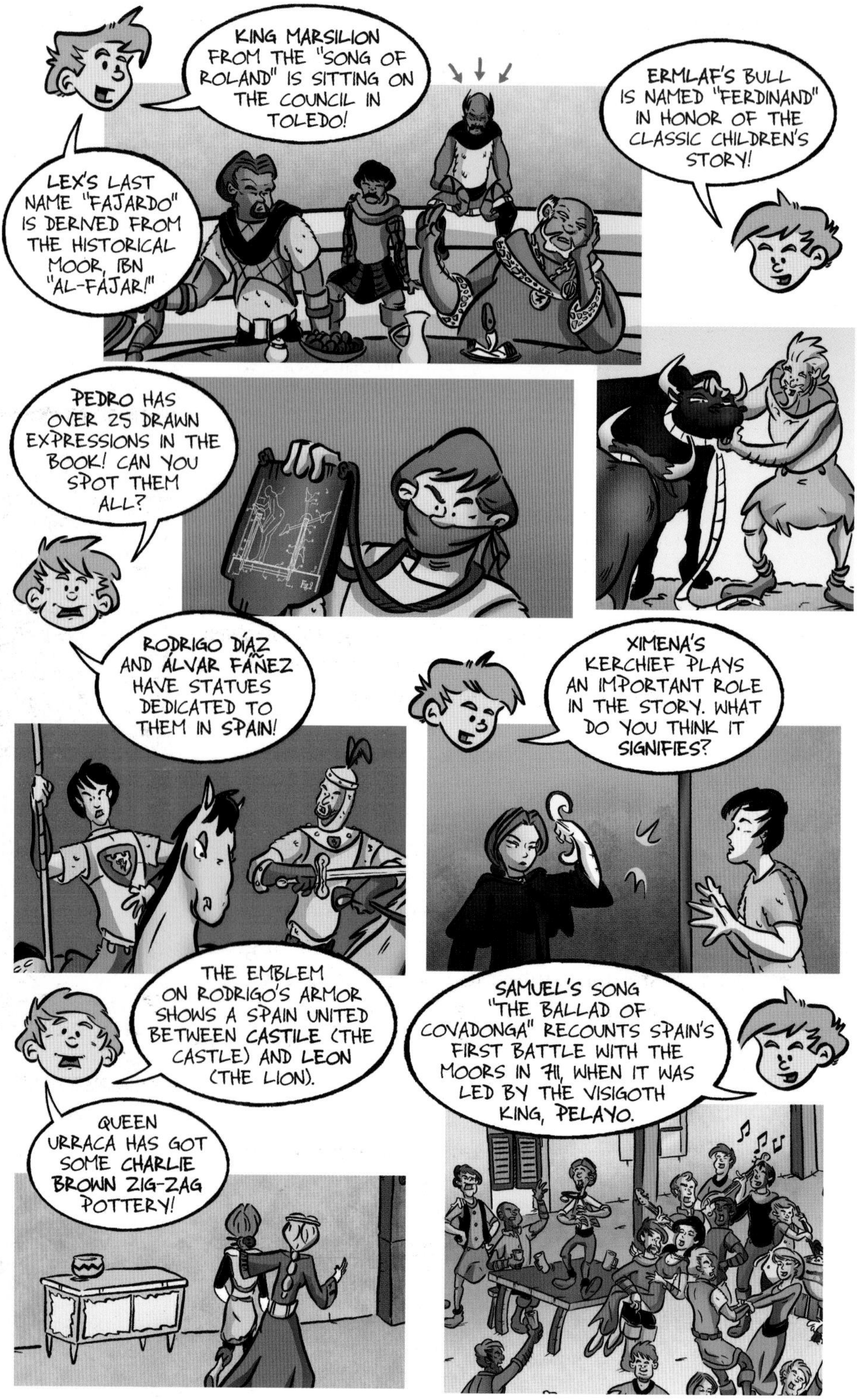
KING MARSILION FROM THE "SONG OF ROLAND" IS SITTING ON THE COUNCIL IN TOLEDO!
LEX'S LAST NAME "FAJARDO" IS DERIVED FROM THE HISTORICAL MOOR, IBN "AL-FAJAR!"
ERMLAF'S BULL IS NAMED "FERDINAND" IN HONOR OF THE CLASSIC CHILDREN'S STORY!
PEDRO HAS OVER 25 DRAWN EXPRESSIONS IN THE BOOK! CAN YOU SPOT THEM ALL?
RODRIGO DÍAZ AND ÁLVAR FÁÑEZ HAVE STATUES DEDICATED TO THEM IN SPAIN!
XIMENA'S KERCHIEF PLAYS AN IMPORTANT ROLE IN THE STORY. WHAT DO YOU THINK IT SIGNIFIES?
THE EMBLEM ON RODRIGO'S ARMOR SHOWS A SPAIN UNITED BETWEEN CASTILE (THE CASTLE) AND LEON (THE LION).
SAMUEL'S SONG "THE BALLAD OF COVADONGA" RECOUNTS SPAIN'S FIRST BATTLE WITH THE MOORS IN 711, WHEN IT WAS LED BY THE VISIGOTH KING, PELAYO.
QUEEN URRACA HAS GOT SOME CHARLIE BROWN ZIG-ZAG POTTERY!

Bibliography

The following books were used during the research and writing of this book. All come highly recommended!

NEW TRANSLATION
PENGUIN CLASSICS
The Song of the Cid

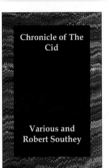

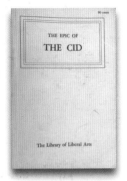

The epic poem comes in a variety of translations, and each one brings something new to the text. I read at least three different versions of *El Cantar de Mio Cid* (also called *The Song of the Cid),* including editions translated by Burton Raffel (Penguin) and J. Gerald Markley (Liberal Arts Press). The introductions for each edition are worth reading, too.

THE EPIC OF
THE CID
The Library of Liberal Arts

Chronicle of The Cid
Various and Robert Southey

Robert Southey's *Chronicle of The Cid* (Echo Library) is a good collection of stories surrounding El Cid's exploits outside the epic poem. French dramatist Corneille did his own version, *The Cid* (Penguin), written in 1637, which focuses on the romance between Rodrigo and Ximena.

PENGUIN CLASSICS
PIERRE CORNEILLE
The Cid / Cinna / The Theatrical Illusion

THE QUEST FOR EL CID
RICHARD FLETCHER

For historical reference, I turned to scholar and author Richard Fletcher and his two books, *The Quest for El Cid* (Oxford University Press), and *Moorish Spain* (University of California Press). *Quest* gives historical context to Rodrigo Díaz and portrays him outside his legendary status. *Moorish Spain* is a solid overview of Iberian Spain and its culture.

Moorish Spain
RICHARD FLETCHER

The Ornament of the World
HAROLD BLOOM
How Muslims, Jews, and Christians Created a Culture of Tolerance in Medieval Spain
MARÍA ROSA MENOCAL

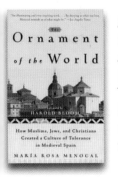

María Rosa Menocal's *Ornament of the World* (Little, Brown), is a terrific account and swift read of the Arab history and rise in Iberian Spain and the many cultures therein. The 1961 movie *El Cid,* starring Charlton Heston and Sophia Loren, is epic film-making at its finest and a good account of the legendary hero filmed entirely in Spain.

THE MIRIAM M COLLECTION
CHARLTON HESTON
SOPHIA LOREN
EL CID
"ONE OF THE GREATEST EPIC FILMS EVER MADE"
TWO-DISC DELUXE EDITION

about the author

Alexis E. Fajardo is a student of the classics–whether Daffy Duck or Damocles–and has created a unique blend of the two with *Kid Beowulf*. When he's not drawing comics, he works for them at the Charles M. Schulz Studio in Santa Rosa, California. Lex looks forward to moving into the Fajardo Castle in Spain once the wifi is hooked up.

photo by Cathy Barrett

Follow Lex on Twitter & Instagram *@lexkidb* – Discover more at *kidbeowulf.com*
Become a fan on *facebook.com/kidbeowulf*

kid beowulf will return

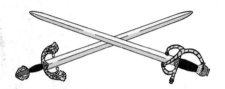

Andrews McMeel Publishing
a division of Andrews McMeel Universal
1130 Walnut Street, Kansas City, Missouri 64106

www.andrewsmcmeel.com

18 19 20 21 22 SDB 8 7 6 5 4 3 2 1

ISBN: 978-1-4494-9384-4

Library of Congress Control Number: 2018931991

Editor: Lucas Wetzel
Creative Director: Tim Lynch
Designer: Spencer Williams
Production Editor: Maureen Sullivan
Production Manager: Chuck Harper

Made by: Shenzhen Donnelley Printing Company Ltd.
Address and location of manufacturer: No. 47, Wuhe Nan Road, Bantian Ind. Zone, Shenzhen China, 518129
1st Printing - 5/14/18